An Angel from Auschwitz

H
Hereford Books

Copyright 2021

The right of the author to be identified as the Author of the Work has been asserted by them in accordance with the Copyright, Designs and Patents Act 1988. First published in Great Britain by Hereford Books.

All rights reserved. No part of this publication many be reproduced, stored in a retrieval system, or transmitted, in any form or by any means without the prior written permission of the author, nor be otherwise circulated in any form of binding or cover other than that in which it is published and without similar condition being imposed on the subsequent purchaser.

ISBN 9798795319513

In memory of Benjamin

PART ONE

1943

1

At six thirty in the morning of 14th January, 1943, by a ditch in a wood near the town of Tarnow in the east of Poland, Mordechai Levinson was supposed to have died. It was a simple matter, a bullet to the back of the head, like all the others. Four hundred and twenty seven yesterday, thirty six already this morning. Mordechai Levinson was supposed to be the thirty seventh. Thirty seven bullets, thirty seven Jews. One officer, SS Obersturmbannführer Fritz Stängl. It was an economical operation.

But Mordechai Levinson did not die that morning, for the simple reason that Captain Stängl's pistol ran out of bullets. It made a sharp click and the officer, irritated, turned to refill the magazine. That was when Motti Levinson stood up, completely naked, frozen and starving, and hit the German in the neck. He hit him so hard that he crumpled to the ground and lay there as if he were dead. Mordechai didn't know if he really was dead, and he didn't wait long enough to find out. He stopped only as long as it took to pick up the weapon and a box of ammunition.

In their queue, the queue for death, behind him stood Rabbi Gimpel and his three sons, all frozen, naked and starving, and they looked at him in fear, as if attacking the man who is going to kill you is a more fearful thing than a bullet in the back of the head. He wanted to tell them to run, remembered saying something, urgently but quietly lest the Ukrainian guards who were having a smoke behind the lorry nearby should hear, but they just stood there, unable to comprehend what was happening, like animals afraid to venture out of a cage with an open door. They stood there and waited for someone else to come along and shoot them. Motti wanted to scoop up the youngest boy in his arms and run off with him, but in that bizarre moment in time, when he had a chance, perhaps, to save a life, he respected the rabbi's decision, even though of course it wasn't a decision, it was an abdication, and they died because of it.

And anyway, you can't run with a child under your arm.

Motti did run. He ran quietly, naked, carrying the gun and the ammunition box. He didn't know what to do with them but he knew he had to have them. He needed clothes too, and he stopped when he realised this, and tried to get his breath back behind a dilapidated old hut. He had seen German officers loading pistols, and he tried to remember how they did it. He got the magazine out and fumbled badly with his frozen fingers and finally he had managed to put several rounds in and reload the magazine and then he cocked the weapon the way he had seen and luckily for him the safety catch was already off because Motti knew nothing about safety catches. It was lucky because he knew there was only one way to get something to wear, because his own clothes were in the ditch with the bodies and he wasn't going in there to get them back.

He heard four short bursts of automatic fire and he hesitated, because there are things a shtetl Jew does not comprehend, and although he comprehends death, if he lives at this time, he has only ever been at the receiving end of brutality and he cannot see himself in the other man's shoes. Nevertheless, even such a man can rise to the occasion, if his life depends on it. He is, after all, still a man, and even a shtetl Jew has the same genes as an SS killer.

He returned to the shooting ditch and there were the two Ukrainians, standing over the bodies of Rabbi Gimpel and his sons. Then, unaware of his presence, they knelt over Captain Stängl, and to do this they had to lay their rifles on the ground.

That gave Motti the chance to walk up, point Stängl's pistol at one, squeeze the trigger and then point it at the other who was only halfway to his feet and squeeze the trigger again. He was used to the noise but the recoil came as a shock, and when he came to his senses the ground was now littered with dead people.

He knew there would be more soldiers soon, and he wasted no

time. He couldn't wear their uniforms, but the shirts and boots would do, with a pair of trousers turned inside out. He put on both shirts for warmth, and then he changed his mind and took a greatcoat as well. He took both rifles and as much ammunition as he could stuff into the coat pockets. He searched the vehicle. It would have been good, he thought, if he could take it but he knew that would be too dangerous. Anyway, Motti couldn't drive.

He found some food and crammed this into the spaces left in his pockets and what wouldn't fit he pushed down inside the shirts. The last thing he did was to close the eyes of the rabbi and his sons, and quickly say the prayer for the dead. He wanted to throw the soldiers in the ditch, but he knew it would be wrong to defile the corpses of the Jews already there.

Then, and under all this weight, he lumbered into the forest. He ran as far as he could until he knew he would have to stop and eat. The soldier's German black bread stuck in his throat, and then he looked at the sausage and knew that it contained forbidden meat but he also knew that he had to eat it. He wanted to be sick as he forced it down and a pious Jew says a blessing before each type of food he eats but of course there is no blessing for pork so he said nothing. He cried while he ate, whether for the sin he was committing or the bodies he had left behind he didn't know. He hadn't cried for a long time, not since his wife and his own child died.

Then he was sick.

Motti Levinson was not a typical Polish shtetl Jew. The other boys in his cheder were all skinny and pale, and they wore glasses and as small as they were they tended to walk with a stoop. They were, in short, Jews.

Motti wasn't short or skinny, and he didn't wear glasses and he never stooped. He was, on the contrary, a big lad, healthy and straight. The rabbi looked at him and clicked his tongue as if to say are you sure you belong here. The women of the village gossiped sometimes that Motti's mother, Sarah, had conceived him by one of the Polish peasants who drank at the inn but the rabbi said they should be ashamed of themselves for spreading loshen hora, rumours, which was forbidden. Well, it might have been forbidden, but that didn't stop the rabbi's wife joining in and adding some petty items of her own. The rabbi's wife was not, to be honest, a good Jew and the rabbi sometimes wondered why he had married her, only of course he didn't know that when he had, because after all he only met her on the day of their wedding so how could he? It was, he often thought, some kind of punishment God had given him that he had to spend his life with a woman with such a cruel tongue.

Sarah Levinson had not consorted with a Polish peasant, because she was a good wife and true to her husband. She had, for reasons only God could know, produced a son who was not like the others. She worried about him, but she was also proud of him. As soon as he was old enough he helped his father in the inn they kept, collecting glasses and sweeping the floor. By the time he was twelve he could lift a barrel of beer onto the wagon his father used to make deliveries to the other villages round about. At his barmitzvah he impressed all the guests at the inn after the service by dancing with the rabbi on his shoulders, a prank the rabbi thought went too far but which his wife laughed heartily at.

The gossip grew worse when after more than a year since Motti's birth his mother failed to produce another child. She continued in this way for several more years, and people began to talk. They said her husband was impotent, and Motti's father must after all have been the peasant, Zielinski, who had been killed when a runaway horse had dragged him into the river and he had drowned. Motti grew up an only child, an unheard of thing in the shtetl where the women produced offspring every year like the peasants' livestock.

Motti studied in the village cheder with the rest of the boys, but in the morning before classes started he helped his mother, milking their only cow and collecting the eggs from the half-dozen hens who scratched a living on the bare earth at the back of the inn. Then he cut wood for the stove, and while he wielded the axe like a peasant the other boys came to wonder at such a thing and they made fun of him for being so Polish but secretly they envied him for his strength and vigour. It wasn't exactly Jewish but it was impressive.

Teaching in the cheder was in Yiddish, the language of the shtetl, but Motti grew up speaking a little Polish too, because his father's business had many Polish customers. The other boys in the cheder knew no Polish, and this set him even more apart from them. They were afraid of the peasants, not because the peasants did anything to them but because their parents taught them to be, and Motti, who in truth couldn't say much, just enough to get by in the trade, spoke their tongue and was somehow associated in the boys' minds and therefore in their parents' minds with the village Poles.

Nationality is in the eye of the beholder, and the boy who seemed a bit foreign, a bit Polish, to his comrades in the shtetl would, as a man, be classified as one hundred percent Jewish by the German invaders, because a broad back and bulging muscles didn't make you Aryan if your parents and their parents are Jewish, which Motti's were. But all of that was in the future.

Sarah loved her son despite his strange looks and the gossip, and his father loved him because he was strong and could help with the work, and also because Motti was a good student, and a man could be proud of a son who could not only lift the rabbi but who could argue with him over the finer points of the Talmud too. Reuben Levinson was a simple man. He didn't understand the Talmud but he was pleased that he had a son who did. He wasn't sure he even believed in God, but he was happy that his wife and son did, because their faith would ensure he too went to heaven.

Sarah loved her husband and respected him, which a wife should do, but sometimes she had doubts about Reuben's lack of education. Her parents had married her to him because his parents owned the inn and they knew she would never go hungry and that was enough, but since the birth of her son, and especially since he started at the little cheder, she had taken an interest in learning and often she borrowed Motti's books and read late into the night, after her work was finished, if a woman's work could ever said to be finished, but even so she found the time, and her husband sometimes complained that she should be in bed keeping him warm, not sitting up wasting candles on reading things that women should not concern themselves with. Reuben might have meant what he said, which would be fair enough, but on the other hand he might have been saying it out of jealousy, because having a wife who knows more than you do is not the normal way of things, and if he didn't want to study Talmud what right had she to do so?

Motti encouraged his mother though, and sometimes the two of them would sit under a flickering light and read late into the night and talk in whispers about things Reuben didn't understand and then he got angry and shouted at them, because after all a man is master in his own house and his wife and son should do as they are told.

Motti couldn't remember when his parents had died. They took his father first, and soldiers came and removed everything from the inn, all the casks of beer and the bottles of brandy so his mother had nothing to sell to the peasants, but in any case the peasants couldn't afford to drink at the inn now, even those who were left. The stronger ones had been taken away by the Germans, they said to work in factories in Germany, and the rest were trying to keep their little farms going as best they could, but from time to time the Germans and their Ukrainian auxiliaries came and took their produce and if a farmer complained they strung him up from a special gallows they erected for this purpose right outside the inn in the main village street as a warning to the others.

He thought at first that his father had been shipped to Germany with the Poles but then rumours came back to the shtetl that the Jewish men had been separated and taken to the forest and only the Polish men had been put on the trains. His father was in any case getting old now, and had a bad leg from years ago when a beer cask had rolled off the wagon and crushed it, so Motti didn't think the Germans would want him for their factories.

Motti had escaped the roundup. He took his wife and their son into the forest to hide, but they were both already sick with typhus, and with the lack of food and the terrible cold they couldn't live like that. They weren't as strong as him, and they just stopped trying. He begged them to survive, but they could not. His mother had stayed in the shtetl. Nothing would persuade her to run. She insisted that any day now her husband would return and she had to be there to cook for him when he did and she was there when the SS came for her. The one small blessing was that Motti was not there to see her shot, to see her nakedness and to see her fall head first into the ditch with the others. No, that, at least, he was spared.

That was all before, and now it was just a hazy memory. It might have been last week, or years ago. None of it made any sense to him, so he was unable to place it in the normal things of life. His mother, his father, his wife and son, they were all gone, just he was left, and he didn't know why. He felt it must be something to do with his strength, his ability but also his will to live, no matter what the circumstances. When there was no food he found it in the forest, things he had never eaten before, berries that made him sick but then he found other plants that didn't and he learned things a Jew had never had to learn before, not Talmud but life, life under impossible hardship, life you sometimes think cannot be worth living but still you go on, without knowing why.

They might never have caught him if he hadn't gone back to the village.

2

They left the village in a hurry. Everyone left, who could, in a hurry. The rumours had been coming for weeks and then Jews started appearing from other villages to the west, telling stories that no-one could believe, but they kept coming and they kept telling the same stories and the people of the shtetl talked among themselves about it, and some said it was impossible and others asked how many more stories did they need to hear.

Of course, the impossible can happen, because nothing is impossible. People only think something is impossible because it is outside their imagination. If that thing makes no sense to them that does not mean it cannot be. A man can imagine things he has already seen, and he can, if he has that kind of mind, imagine some things he has never seen, as long as those things are an extension of what has gone before.

But soldiers coming and simply lining people up and shooting them made no sense. Why would they do that? What had those people done? Well, they had done nothing, but what they had in common was inescapable.

The Jews of Poland understood their position very well, and had understood it for generations. No Jewish child grew up in Poland without knowing that he was different from the others, the people they called the Poles. Some argued that by teaching this difference to their children they were perpetuating the very difference they were afraid of, but in reality they didn't need to teach it because there were constant reminders. The Jews didn't make themselves different, they already were different, and this difference was perceived not primarily by them but by the Poles, especially the peasants, the uneducated. The shtetl Jews taught their children to read, admittedly in Hebrew and Yiddish, and admittedly mainly the boys, but most of the Polish boys in the villages and the fields could not read even in their own language. Being different is dangerous, but being cleverer, or shall we say being perceived as cleverer, has its own dangers. And the Polish peasants were poor as well as ignorant, and they were preyed upon by their overlords and by the Catholic Church, for both of whom hatred of the Jews was a very useful emotion, because if the peasants hated the Jews who killed their Saviour, they would forget to hate the people who were the real reason why they lived in poverty and ignorance, their overlords and the Church.

Those who stayed behind lived as long as it took to learn that the rumours were all true, and they experienced the horror for themselves, but they could tell no-one about the horror because there was nothing more, just the horror and then the death. Death came quickly, because a bullet in the back of the head is a very efficient way to die, but before the bullet came fear and cold and terror and for some, like eighteen-year old Rachel Abrams, who was seven months pregnant, a rifle butt in the belly that killed her unborn child and left her by the side of the road to bleed to death while her young husband stood and watched, his heart tearing itself apart with anger and shame that he could do nothing for her. His anger didn't last long, though, because an hour later he too was dead and if there is a heaven then he and Rachel were back together again but that's only if there is a heaven and if there is, well, one can only hope there is.

Motti was used to trouble with the Poles. There had been bad times, and good times when they left them alone, and even times when they seemed not to mind the Jews at all but there were not many of those. What Motti couldn't understand was who these invaders were and why they were doing this. He knew about Germany, at least he had heard of it, and he had heard there was a war. He didn't know why there was a war, or why the Germans had invaded Poland. He thought that if he had a choice in these things he wouldn't invade Poland, he would get out of it. What the Germans wanted it for was a mystery to him.

And now they were in his part of Poland, killing Jews. Fair enough they were killing Poles too, but only those they didn't like or who didn't do what they were ordered to do. The Jews, though, they just killed, even the women and the children. He simply couldn't understand what poor Jewish people could have done to upset these Germans so much, people they had never seen before. The Germans, he realised, were very angry people. And it wasn't just the Germans, because they brought with them Ukrainians from over the border to the south. Ukrainians in German uniforms, and if the Germans were cruel this was as nothing compared to the Ukrainians who seemed, as far as he could see, to have no humanity at all. They killed, it seemed, for pleasure. Human lives were as nothing to them. A Ukrainian could kill a child as if it were a farm animal, except that the Poles he knew did not enjoy killing their livestock. These men did. He called them men but really it was hard to believe they were. Perhaps, he thought, Ukraine was inhabited by some species other than human.

Motti had never hit a man before but he knew, somehow, what to do when Captain Stängl turned to reload his pistol. He had no thought of escape. Escape, as far as he had seen, was impossible. It was nothing more than the reaction any man would have when another man threatened his life. He remembered feeling humiliated when he had to take his clothes off, and of course cold too, terribly cold, and instead of this making him easy to kill, which was of course the idea, it stirred something in him that had lain dormant for two thousand years, an inheritance that made him no less a man than all the other men in the world, not a victim.

It would be true to say that the blow he dealt Stängl was a lucky one. For a man who had never raised his fist in anger before, it was a very lucky one. Motti was a big man, and with the luck that was his that day, and his physical strength, he took on his killer and won.

Now he found himself in the forest with the result of his action, freedom, and he wasn't sure what to do with it. The shtetl was a small community, where everyone helped everyone else. You didn't stand on your own, because that is not what a community is for. The shtetl had always survived because people worked together, but now the shtetl no longer existed. It could survive the day-to-day troubles but it had had no strength to resist the onslaught of recent days, an enemy which fell upon it without reason and without mercy, and it had been destroyed. Motti was, as far as he knew, the sole survivor.

His instinct made him seek out help, but who would help him? The Poles? He wanted to believe some of the peasants he knew, those at least who drank at the inn, would lend him succour, but his instinct told him he could not assume this. Well he could at least ask. He would wait in the forest until the whirlwind passed through the village and went on, as he knew it would, to another place to kill more people. Then he would come out of hiding and find out.

He stayed in the forest for five days, because he heard the sound of motor vehicles heading east and he knew that was the Germans, but he didn't know if it was all of the Germans and he was afraid to go back, but it was winter and he could find little to eat in the forest. He finished the soldier's food too quickly, but then he had been very, very hungry, but after that there was little to eat and he got hungry again and hunger can make a man make the wrong decisions.

So he crept back late at night. They had set fire to the inn but it had snowed and the fire had been unable to take hold. Part of the roof was gone, and all the windows were smashed, but still a man could find shelter there. Outside, three bodies swung from the gallows, and as the wind made them sway the ropes creaked all night and reminded him that they were there. Why had they been hanged, these people? Who could know that? Maybe they had done something to upset the Germans, like the Jews had, or maybe they hadn't done anything and the Germans just didn't like to leave the village with the gallows empty. And why, he wondered with all his powers, did no-one remove them?

It was, he thought, unlikely that anyone would look for him at the inn. It was, of course, unlikely that anyone was going to look for him at all, because they would surely all assume he was dead. From his hiding place he saw, the next morning, the village people going about their business, as if nothing had happened, but no Germans. One time, Woytek's dog came and sniffed through the rubble, but no-one took any notice of it. He heard Woytek call and the dog forgot whatever it was that had attracted his attention and bounded off.

He moved about more freely that night, with just the pistol for company. The rifles he hid in the kitchen of the inn, where no-one would look for them, but of course no-one was going to look for them anyway. The house lights had gone out, and he walked quietly down the main street, keeping close to the walls of the buildings, and it was clear to him as he went that the Germans had moved on and left none of their number behind. After all, why would they garrison a poor village like this? He wondered who he could call on for help, or at least a meal, and it dawned on him that there was no-one, that his own people were all gone, either dead or fled into the forest, that there were only the Poles left. Well, it would have to be them. He would go to Marek Zelikowski, the grain merchant who sold his father the barley to make the beer. Marek had dealt with his family for many years. He would not turn him away.

'Mordechai Levinson. I don't believe it. But I thought you were ... I mean I thought ..'

'No, Mr Zelikowski, I am not dead, and I am not a ghost. It would help me greatly if I could come in for a moment and get warm.'

'What? Yes, of course, of course, come in, come in.'

Marek ushered him in, but he looked around in the street to see if anyone had seen Motti come to his house. You couldn't be too careful. Motti wasn't being careful. He was tired, and he was cold but most of all he was hungry. He didn't know for sure he could trust this man and he kept one hand in his coat pocket on the handle of the German's pistol, although even he knew that if Marek gave trouble, and he had no idea what kind of trouble he could give, killing a Pole and a neighbour wouldn't be as easy as killing an SS officer.

'Good God, man, you look terrible. Maria, Maria, come here woman, look, it's young Levinson, returned from the dead.'

Marek's wife came in from the kitchen and gasped. She looked afraid, as if this Jew had come back to haunt her, as if she personally were responsible for what had happened in the village. Who can say where she got that idea from? Still, she couldn't help looking like she wished Motti wasn't there, and he noticed, but still, he thought, why should she care. Well he didn't need her to, he just needed to thaw out and eat something. Then he would be on his way. He didn't know where, but he knew he had to go.

She brought out food, and placed it on the table in front of him, a hot steaming dish, some kind of soup with dumplings and meat. Marek's wife knew that Mordechai Levinson could not eat pork but who was there to say she served it to him deliberately? The Zelikowskis were like everyone else in the village, hungry, and whatever was in the soup was likely all there was in the house.

Motti ate like the starving man he was, and the Zelikowskis watched him. He saw them watching but he had no way of knowing what was in their minds. Were they friends who were pleased to help him, or did they want him out of the house and out of their lives? Well, whatever they wanted, he would go as soon as he had eaten and warmed his body a little. But before he went there was something he wanted to know.

'Mr Zelikowski, tell me, I see there are three bodies hanging from the gallows. Why has no-one taken them down, and anyway why were they killed? What had they done?'

Marek hesitated. 'They had done nothing. The Germans were angry.'

'Yes, the Germans are always angry. They are angry people, but what especially about?'

'Two soldiers were killed, out by the ... the place ...'

Motti put his spoon down and looked him in the eye. 'I think, Mr Zelikowski, you are trying to say the ditch where the Jews of this village were taken and shot.'

Maria looked away, as if killing the Jews but not the Poles was somehow to do with her.

'They gathered everyone outside the inn and demanded to know who was responsible, for that and the theft of some weapons. No-one knew anything about it of course, so they said they would hang someone every hour until the culprit came forward, but no-one did because no-one here had done it.'

There was something in his voice that suggested he thought the three had died because Motti was somehow responsible, as if a Jew could kill soldiers.

'Well, they hanged one, and then a second, and then another, and it would have gone on but a motorcycle messenger drove up and reported something to the officer, and all the soldiers were driven away in lorries in a hurry, so no-one else was hanged, thank the Lord.'

'Yes, but why are they still there? '

'The last thing the Germans said before they left was that we must leave them there, that they would be coming back this way soon and if they were not there three more villagers would be selected to replace them.'

Motti had heard enough. He thanked the Zelikowskis profusely and made sure to tell them he was leaving the village and the area immediately, which was true. As he walked down the darkened street, he pondered on what Marek had told him. The Germans were coming back. Well, that might be true or it might not. They might have said it to frighten the villagers, but even so, it was not a risk he could take, especially now that Marek knew he was there. And Maria. Even if Marek could be trusted, his wife could not, he knew that. She was scared, and a scared person will do anything.

But there was another question, one that nagged at him as he settled down for his last night's sleep at the inn. Marek had said two soldiers were killed, but he said nothing about an SS officer. He surely would have done, which could only mean he hadn't died when Motti had hit him. He didn't know what that meant, but he was afraid it might mean something.

He woke very early the next morning, well before daylight, and before he left the inn he rummaged by the light of the moon though the debris for anything that could be helpful. There was a jar of boiled fish his mother had made in the summer and kept for the leaner winter days. He couldn't carry it, so he ate it all and as he ate he cried and his tears washed away the crumbs from his face. He cried for his mother and father, but also for himself. A man is only a grown-up child, and there are times when he wants his parents, and Motti knew something of the trials he was facing and that he would need all his strength for them, but just now, here at home, he wanted to be a child for one last time.

And then something miraculous happened. Among the broken furniture, in a drawer hanging halfway out of a chest, he found something he never expected to see again, his phylacteries. He had put them on every morning since his barmitzvah years ago and recited the prayers and every morning he had reaffirmed his Jewishness and now, under an open sky, he did it again, and he promised before God that he would do it every day of his life, whether that was long or short. His parents, his young wife and child, had died for being Jews. Well, he would be one now and for the rest of his days. That, they could not take from him.

Before he left though, there was one more thing he had to look for. The doorpost of the inn had been ripped from the wall when the soldiers burst in and it hung at an awkward angle, going nowhere, but Motti levered it away from the masonry to where he could reach it better. There, where his great-grandfather Szmul had nailed it more than seventy years ago, was the mezuzah, the sign on every Jewish doorpost that five generations of Levinsons had touched as they entered. He prised it off with a kitchen knife and placed it carefully in his shirt pocket. He didn't know where he was going, but if ever he had a home again it would be a Jewish home, with this mezuzah on the door post, in memory of the Levinson family.

Renewed in spirit and with this unwarranted belief that there could be a future, he gathered his few belongings, slung the two rifles over his shoulder, and crept out of the village of his birth for the last time. He wanted to look back, but something about Lot's wife came into his mind and he knew it might be just fancy but he took that to mean that forward was, from now on, the only way.

3

What Mordechai Levinson the shtetl Jew knew about the world outside the village where he had been born, married and spent all his life was extremely limited. He had been educated in Yiddish and knew the Torah and the Talmud as well as any man, he spoke a little Polish, mostly the words pertinent to the brewing and innkeeping trade, and he had some very small and very recent experience in the use of firearms.

He knew he couldn't trust the Poles, but he was in Poland. His normal constituency, the Jewish community, no longer existed, at least it didn't in that part of the General Government. He had no idea what happened more than a day's cart-ride from the village, but he knew about the war and the killing and whilst he didn't know why they were happening, to know they were happening was for now enough.

In fact if the Jews of Poland were suffering grievously, the rest of the people of that country weren't getting away lightly either. It is true that they were not subject to immediate extermination, and it is also true that many of them weren't too fussed that the Jews were. As far as the peasants were concerned, they had it coming to them. They were unclear why this was, but they were a deeply religious people, the poorer they were the more religious they were, and their priests told them not to pity the Jews. The Jews had killed Jesus, and that was why they had it coming to them. The priests didn't go too deeply into this belief because they didn't themselves know what it meant, but it was Church doctrine, and who were they to argue?

The peasants were afraid of the Jews and their own priests and the Germans, and they were also afraid of the forest. They went there in daylight to fetch firewood but it was a brave man who stayed there after dark. Once, many years ago, an old woman called Barbara Iwinska who they said had lost her mind went there and never came back. They said she was still there, ready to catch any children who ventured there after daylight hours. In truth, there was a crazy old woman called Barbara Iwinska and she had wandered off to the forest when her husband died and her son threw her out of the house, but she had died there and in any case that was a long time ago. No-one was ever going to find her body because it was taken by wolves.

The Germans hadn't gone into the forest either. The SS officer, Captain Stängl, had assumed there was no reason to go there because he knew that any fugitives would be afraid of it too, and in any case his own troops were mostly Ukrainian auxiliaries, and they were as superstitious as the Poles. No, if any Jews had escaped, Stängl knew they wouldn't survive long. The Jews, he knew, were not a self-sufficient people. They needed their synagogue and their petty trading and they would have no idea how to survive in the wild.

There were indeed no Jews in the forest now, but there were Poles. They lived there partly to escape the Germans and partly because it suited them, or some of them, because there was no law in the forest, and they weren't peasants and they weren't afraid. As well as the gangs who called them-selves fighters, there were the others, the real partisan groups, the Armia Krajowa, the army of the Government in Exile in London, operating under orders from there, the Armia Ludowa who were communists and took their orders from Moscow and for now fought the Germans but looked forward to the time when they would fight the Armia Krajowa, and then there was the NSZ, the so-called National Armed Forces, who killed anyone they could lay their hands on, Germans, communists or Jews, for reasons that were best known to themselves.

Motti had heard that there were fighters living in the forest but he had also heard the stories about the old woman, stories drunken peasants told at the inn when they had a belly full of beer and vodka, told to frighten young people like him, and he didn't know if they were true but he wasn't anxious to find out. Still, after the Germans, could there really be anything left to fear? There were wolves, he knew that from his short stay with his family, but now he was armed. He sat on a tree stump and took out the German's pistol. It was the very weapon that had killed his family and his friends and even touching it made his skin crawl but now, he knew, it might be all that stood between him and death. In a perverse reversal of roles, the gun might, with God's blessing, save him from the people who had brought it to Poland to kill him. So he didn't know, as he felt its weight in his hand, if this weapon was for good or for evil.

Well, for now there were more important matters to occupy his thoughts. He needed somewhere to sleep and even more than that he needed food and water. A Jew may have no understanding of the wild world outside the shtetl, but even so he knows these things.

The sun had started to come up now, but it was a weak sun, a winter sun, and it could not penetrate the gloom of the fir trees. It didn't even melt the snow on the boughs. Motti was cold, and he would have given the pistol in exchange for a warm fire. He decided it would be best to find a spot much further in before it would be safe to light one. As he walked he heard noises but he reasoned with himself that a forest has many inhabitants who make noises and that are perfectly harmless. Rabbits mostly, he thought, Well, if he saw a rabbit, he decided, he would shoot it. He had never eaten a rabbit so he wasn't sure if it was permitted, but the man who could tell him, the rabbi, was dead, so he felt sure, or fairly sure anyway, that God would forgive him for eating a forbidden animal out of ignorance.

As he walked, he felt the bulk of the mezuzah from the inn in his shirt pocket and felt comforted by it. He recited a passage from the Torah under his breath, and it reminded him of the days he spent sitting in the yeshiva, before he was married, studying with the other young men. In truth, he hadn't much liked it then, and he questioned his belief that studying was the right thing for a young man to do, because it didn't teach you how to get on in the world, it didn't even teach you how to run an inn or make ale and sell it to the peasants on the farms. He knew that studying was what young Jewish men did, and so he didn't resent it, because you have to do what has always been done, but sometimes he wished he could spend time on the farms with the peasants and learn what they knew about making food grow from the earth. It was a dream, he knew that. Jews could have a cow, a few chickens, but they were not farmers. In any case, who would sell them land?

Now, though, he wished he was back in the yeshiva, studying, in the world of the Jews, not here in the forest in a world he didn't understand, cold and hungry. He thought of his wife and their son too but when that happened he made himself think of something else, because he didn't know how to deal with those thoughts and so it was best not to let them find a space in his head, or a quiet moment to trouble him. Yes, if he could always think of something else when they came back to him, he would be alright. He made up his mind that when that happened he would recite an exposition from the Talmud, one that he and Rabbi Gimpel had argued about once. Rabbi Gimpel had called him a numbskull, but afterwards the others had come to him and clapped him on the back because he had been right and Rabbi Gimpel hadn't wanted to admit he was beaten by Mordechai Levinson, a big lump who should, he said, have been pulling a plough like a Polish ox instead of wasting his time in the yeshiva.

And while Motti was having these thoughts the sounds of the forest grew louder and as he walked they seemed to be following him. It was cold but he started to sweat and the shirt next to his skin, the shirt from the dead Ukrainian soldier, became clammy and stuck to him and that made him more conscious of the mezuzah and he tried to take comfort from it but he couldn't. The noises became louder still and his heart was pounding and his head started to spin and then ....

'Hey, you, stop, stop exactly where you are, and put your hands up in the air. Hey you, don't you understand simple Polish? '

No, Motti did not understand simple Polish, but he did understand several rifles pointing at him and instinctively he obeyed the order he didn't understand. He forgot instantly about wolves and old women. Rifles were enough to be afraid of. He knew very well what rifles could do, they could put a bullet through a man before he had time to speak or even think, and these men looked like it wouldn't bother them whether he spoke or died. In truth they were not interested in Mordechai Levinson. What they were interested in was the two rifles slung over his shoulder and his army greatcoat.

'Hey, are you a deserter? German? Ukrainian?'

Motti couldn't answer, because he didn't know what he was being asked, but the men were pointing at the rifles and he started to realise what they wanted. Well, they could have them. He was going to take them off his shoulder and throw them on the ground, but had he done that he would have died before they landed and it was fortunate that instead of doing that he said something to them, in Yiddish, but at least he spoke. He told them they could have the weapons. He called them guns, because he didn't know the Yiddish word for rifle, or even if there was one.

The men laughed. 'A zhid. A zhid in the forest with rifles. Well lads, this is something to be seen.' And they laughed more. Mordechai would have laughed too but he had the impression they were not inviting him to join in the fun. Anyway, he was still holding his arms up and they were getting tired.

'Well, zhid, I'm going to give you a choice. We can shoot you and take the weapons, or we can let you live and take the weapons. Personally, I'm in favour of killing you, but we need every bullet so I would have to order Jerzy here to slit your throat.'

Motti was tired and starving and he was scared. His head started to spin again and he remembered hearing the leader saying something and he wasn't sure if he understood it or not and then he thought he heard his wife calling him and he tried to answer her but then his head hit the ground and he remembered nothing more but he had a strange dream and when he woke up he wondered if it had been a dream or not, and then he wondered if he was dead, but he felt the cold forest floor beneath him and a pain in his head and when he moved he knew why he was so very cold, because his greatcoat had gone.

It was getting dark and snow was falling through the boughs of the trees and settling on his body. He knew he should get up but he didn't know if that was really what he wanted, or dying here would be better. He mumbled the prayers of the evening service he would have been saying in the synagogue now and then he felt for the mezuzah in his pocket. That, at least, they had not taken. Why would they?

He knew he would die if he didn't move, but he also knew he had no food and no way to light a fire, so as he lay there he debated the point of moving or living, and while he was having this argument with himself he thought he heard something. At first he thought maybe the bandits were back, and then he thought of wolves and he even thought of the old woman, Barbara Iwinska, but it was none of these. He heard men's voices now, whispered, in Polish, but something told him they were different men. There was something in their tone quite unlike the bandits, something that Motti instinctively felt he needn't be afraid of. And indeed several men came out from the trees, and they were armed with rifles too, but they did not point them at him and they did not threaten him. Instead, they picked him up, carefully, and moved off with him through the forest.

And then there was the thing he had been dreaming about, a fire. He remembered telling himself he would give up the pistol for a fire. Well he had lost everything, but the bargain he had made with God had, in some way, been kept. There was warmth from the flames and a blanket someone had put round his shoulders, he didn't notice who or when though, and there was hot soup, and sitting opposite him was a woman. She was dressed in men's clothes, but her hair, which had been tied back under her cap, was escaping in playful curls around her face and hiding her sex was impossible.

'You're Jewish, aren't you?'

It took Motti a moment to realise he understood what she was saying, and he understood because she was saying it in Yiddish. She smiled.

'It's alright, so am I. You're with friends here.'

'Jews?'

'No, just me, but even so friends. This is a company of the Armia Ludowa, under the command of the Red Army.'

Motti looked at her. He didn't know what the Red Army was.

'The Russians, the allies of Poland.'

This woman was being disingenuous when she called Russia an ally of Poland. The Soviets had carved up Poland with their ally, Germany, when it had suited them, and she knew all of this but she was a good communist and she quoted the party line.

'Here, Jews are Poles and we have nothing to fear. We are all fighting for freedom from the same enemy, the Germans.'

Motti thought about this. The idea that the Poles had the same enemy as the Jews was a new one to him, and that the Russians were friends was also new, and the idea that a woman, a Jewish woman, was somehow involved in fighting was too much to understand. The woman smiled, as if she was reading his thoughts, which in truth she was, because she too would have thought that at one time, had thought that.

'My name is Roza, Roza Weksler. Tell me yours.'
'Motti. I mean Mordechai, Levinson.'
'You're from that village back there? '
'Yes.'
'Are there any Jews left alive? '
'No.'
'Just you?'
'Yes.'
'How did you escape? '
'I killed a German, and two Ukrainians.'

Roza looked at him in disbelief. Fair enough, he was a big man, not like the shtetl Jews she had seen, but even so, a Jew who killed Germans? No, surely that was not possible. In the forests maybe, with the partisans, but was it possible this man had done it on his own?

Motti looked at her while she thought about this and he didn't know it was what she was thinking although he should have. It was an unlikely story, he realised. He wasn't completely sure he believed it himself, and yet it was only two days ago, and when he thought about it he could still feel the recoil from the pistol and he could still see the look on the faces of the dead men, and thinking that dead people all had the same look, Jews and goyim.

Then he realised the woman had gone, but a minute later she returned, with the leader of the group. She didn't introduce him, but she sat next to him and interpreted.

'So my friend, you are a Jew who kills the enemy. Tell, me, how did you do it?'
'I shot them.'

'What with?'

And Motti told them the story, the whole thing, going back to the beginning, when the Germans arrived and cordoned off the Jewish part of the village and within twenty-four hours the men had been taken off to dig a ditch and no-one knew why but then those men were shot and dumped into it, and then the women and the children, and then the people who had hidden and finally they found him. He spoke slowly because he needed to think at the same time, and Roza had no trouble interpreting what he was saying into Polish.

'So you killed Stängl with your bare hands then?'

'Stängl?'

'SS Obersturmbannführer Fritz Stängl, in command of Einsatzgruppe 2B.'

Motti didn't know what that meant, but he nodded. He supposed so.

'Except you didn't. Stängl is still alive. Yes, we know he is badly injured, a broken collar bone they say, and now we know how. Well, my friend, you did what many of us want to do, except if we had done it Captain Stängl would be dead now.'

Motti felt rebuked for not doing the job properly, but Roza smiled while she interpreted and he knew it was alright that he wasn't an efficient killer. The leader got up and left without saying anything more.

'He likes you.'

'He does?' Motti wasn't sure whether that mattered.

'Yes. He's impressed. You're not like the rest of the Jews, hiding in their synagogues, thinking God will save them and then dying without putting up a fight.'

Motti didn't like her saying this, but he knew it was true. He thought of Rabbi Gimpel standing there by the ditch with his sons, and he asked himself how Rabbi Gimpel and his boys would have fought Germans with guns. No, there was much this woman didn't understand, And yet she said she was Jewish. Well, she wasn't any kind of Jewish Motti recognised. She dressed like a man and she spoke like one too.

'I can see what you're thinking.'

'You can?'

'Yes, you're a village Jew and you're wondering what I am because I'm not like the women you have known, not like your mother or your sisters or your wife.'

'No, you're not.' He said that like an accusation, like she should be, but she didn't mind, she just laughed.

'No, I'm from Warsaw and I'm a communist and I come from a world you cannot imagine and maybe one day I'll tell you about it, but not now. It's late, you're tired, and tomorrow there is much to do. Sleep, my Jewish lion, the sleep of the just.'

4

Motti did sleep. He was woken from time to time by a dream and he lay there and saw the flickering in the trees from the camp fires and heard people talking quietly to each other, and some snoring too. These sounds and images informed his dreams when he fell asleep again, and when he finally woke in the morning he felt like he had been in the camp a long time, that he knew its people and its ways.

He put on his phylacteries and prayed and people gathered round to watch. Some thought it amusing and sniggered but then they wandered off like it wasn't that interesting after all. They were used to strange things. Motti continued as if they were not there in any case. Then he ambled round the camp as people went about their business, which was much like the business of people everywhere early in the morning, only these people had slept out of doors so it was not like anything Motti was used to. There was just one tent, and this he assumed belonged to the leader who had interviewed him yesterday, whose name he still did not know.

At that moment Roza herself came out of the tent. Motti would have found any reason why she had been in there if she hadn't been buttoning up her shirt.

'Ah, Comrade Levinson, you're an early riser. Yes, of course you are, you have, no doubt, already laid tefillin. I bet that caused a bit of a stir.'

'Yes, a bit.'

'But you carried on regardless.'

'That's right.' Motti couldn't tell if she thought that was a good thing or not. Roza's face, he was learning, showed nothing unless she wanted it to. She had an engaging smile and her eyes were constantly alight with some kind of energy he had never seen before in a woman. She was also, he saw now in daylight, rather handsome. Even dressed in men's clothes, she was unmistakably female, and she had none of the shyness or docility of the Jewish women he had known. He wondered if she was married to the leader, and then he remembered she had said there were no other Jews in the company, and he was confused about how this was possible if he interpreted her exit from the tent correctly.

Roza, for her part, yet again knew what this man was thinking, but she thought it was none of his business and declined to enlighten him.

'Come with me, and we'll eat. It's not much, and to be honest it's not very good, but we don't go hungry here. I'm afraid you are going to have to leave your dietary scruples behind while you are with us, unless you intend to starve.'

'No, I have already eaten pork.'

'Really? How? When? '

'I took some from the soldiers.'

'I'm more and more impressed with you, Levinson. You not only kill Germans but you eat their treif meat. I don't believe you're Jewish at all.'

Motti spluttered in self-defence, but Roza laughed and he knew she was teasing him.

'I like you, Levinson, so now you have two friends in this company. I think we will let you stay.'

Motti considered this. If these partisans were under the command of the Russians, then they were surely soldiers and he wondered how a woman could say, in that case, that they would let him stay with them. He thought about his own wife and he looked at Roza Weksler, and he could make no connection.

They sat round a fire and ate something Motti could not put a name too. Roza was right, it wasn't very good, but it was food and Motti would have eaten a pig right then without bothering to kill it. She watched him eat with amusement. He was a big man with a big appetite. They would need to feed him up for sure, but he could be useful to them. The Poles were strong enough, but they were, in her opinion, stupid. Here was an intelligent man with muscles. Yes, he could be very useful.

'Ah, Levinson, I see Comrade Weksler has taken care of you. How is breakfast? Not what you are used to eh? By the way, I am Comrade Belka, the commander here. In the Red Army I hold the rank of Major.'

Motti wondered why he told him this but thought nothing more of it. Roza knew though. Leszek Belka could see straight away what the dynamic was. A wandering Jew comes to the camp and is taken under the wing of the only Jewish woman, who happens to be his woman. It was nothing to do with fighting or politics, it was the age-old territorial threat that all men face at some time, another man who might threaten their supremacy. Motti could not, of course, threaten Belka's command of the company, but he could, he knew, take his woman from him, and Roza saw this in Leszek's eyes immediately. There wasn't much she missed.

Motti, of course, had no such thought. He wasn't even sure if Roza was this man's wife. It was a conundrum he was still trying to figure out, but what he wasn't doing was seeing the look in Leszek's eyes.

As for Roza, she was thinking that indeed Leszek could have something to worry about. Yes, Mordechai Levinson was a shtetl Jew, and that put him as far from her as Leszek the Pole was, but still, he was a Jew, and he was stirring something in her she had never felt before. Something in this man connected with a part of her she had not been conscious of in her life among the Poles. Roza was a city girl, educated, integrated, and Motti was everything but integrated, but sitting next to him Roza suddenly felt something she never thought she would feel. Jewish. Her parents had brought her up to be Polish and they had eaten forbidden food as if it didn't matter and spoken only Polish to each other and their daughters and gone to the synagogue only as long as it suited her father to meet his business contacts there but still, she had inherited something they had not given her but was in the air she breathed in Warsaw, along with the music lessons and her German teacher and all the things a shtetl Jew knew nothing about. Mordechai reminded her of home, which was crazy because nothing she remembered of home resembled Mordechai. Roza was confused.

She avoided Leszek's eyes, because she knew he knew. The stupid thing was, she didn't want Motti, nothing like that. No, it was nothing like that at all. Something quite different. She had felt it last night, this sudden connection, and it had been in her dreams and it was here now, not Mordechai the man but Mordechai the Jew. That was what Leszek saw in her face, and without understanding what it meant, because how could he, still it troubled him. This Levinson would have to go. A pity, because he looked strong, but Leszek the man was telling Comrade Major Belka the good communist to eliminate the threat.

'So Levinson, where are you on your way to?'

'I beg your pardon? '

'Well, where do you go now? As soon as you are fit and well, I mean. Home? '

'I have no home.'

Leszek knew that. No-one in the camp had a home. That was why they were there. This Jew was no different, in fact he of all of them had nowhere to go. Leszek knew there was nowhere that would be safe for Mordechai. The rest of them could go somewhere, anywhere, and blend in, even if it meant forced labour, but at least it would mean safety of a kind. As long as they had papers, or could buy forged ones, but a Jew could not do that. Leszek had seen what the Germans did to Jews, and as a communist he knew his duty was to protect all Poles, especially them.

'Well, we'll give you a few days. We can't feed useless mouths, so take those few days to make plans.'

'I don't want to be a useless mouth.'

Motti meant he didn't want to be idle, that he was willing to work, but some instinct told him not to push this idea. If he was fit, he could be banished from the protection of the camp. It wasn't much but it was a thousand times better than being in the forest on his own. And then there was Roza. Something about Roza made him feel safe.

'Well, keep your nose clean and don't get under anyone's feet. Meanwhile, if you're fit as you seem to be, you can work in the kitchen.'

Roza knew exactly what this meant. It was Leszek's way of emasculating him, giving him woman's work. Even Roza herself never worked in the kitchen. She felt sorry for Mordechai but she knew that Leszek's order would have to be obeyed. Motti, on the other hand, saw no problem. The kitchen, to him, was as good as anywhere, and if it meant he could stay he was happy. He smiled in the good-natured way he had and Roza felt it wasn't so bad and Leszek stalked off wondering what was wrong with the Jew that he didn't argue about it.

The kitchen comprised several trestle tables made from rough-sawn forest timber and a large fire that burned continuously, either for cooking or inbetween mealtimes for heating water. Motti found, though, that meal times were flexible. People came and went, he didn't know where, and when they returned to camp they were invariably hungry and expected something to eat.

The cook was a large woman, of indeterminate age, with long greasy hair and bony hands, called Krystyna. When Mordechai reported for duty she looked at him incredulously. That she was given a man to help her was bad enough, but she had seen his arrival at the camp and had thought it odd that a Jew was wandering in the forest to start with, because she had heard they were all dead or shut up in ghettos, but now here he was assigned to her. Krystyna had once been a maid to a Jewish family in Przemysl and now she had one as an assistant. The world had turned upside down. The funny thing was, he didn't look Jewish.

The food was a mixture of captured German rations, some rabbits that got shot as long as it was nowhere the enemy might hear, and what Krystyna called 'forest crops', which turned out to be anything that could be found that given enough cooking might be vaguely edible. There were also half a dozen hens kept in a wire enclosure. The eggs were for soldiers on special operations. She said special operations in a way that suggested she knew all about them but wasn't allowed to tell Mordechai. In any case, Motti's Polish was too limited to have much to talk about.

Motti amused Krystyna. She watched him as he worked, doing the most menial tasks, washing potatoes, skinning rabbits, scrubbing cooking pots, that kind of thing, and he seemed to her to be oblivious to what he was doing. Under his beard she could see his lips moving and thought he was mumbling silently to himself, but he wasn't, he was praying, for the souls of his family, because now he didn't have to think about surviving he could devote his mind to that important task. Washing potatoes wasn't work, it was merely an activity for his hands, and now Motti was back in the yeshiva, and inbetween prayers he debated with Rabbi Gimpel the points of Talmud they used to discuss and sometimes in these silent discourses he won a point and sometimes he lost and when he won a smile came over his face and Krystyna wondered what on earth he could be smiling about but how could she know and even if he had the Polish to tell her she still wouldn't have understood because Mordechai Levinson might have grown up fifty kilometres from her but they came from different worlds.

Roza passed by the kitchen and watched him and she knew what he was doing and she shook her head. This man was everything her parents had despised at home in Warsaw, the pious Jews who in turn despised her parents for being integrated and speaking Polish and educating their daughters. She had shared her parents' feeling. Of course she had. But she couldn't bring herself to despise Mordechai Levinson. He was unworldly, yes, but why did that matter? He hadn't integrated, but what good had integrating done her family? In the end, the Germans disintegrated them. Even the Poles who had offered to help them had in the end betrayed them. No, she would not despise this pious man whose suffering she could see with every movement of his lips.

'So, Rozinska, your Jewish compatriot fascinates you.' It was Leszek.

'Yes. Look at him.'

'What's he doing?'

'He's praying, and he is also probably doing what he used to do in the yeshiva, debating.'

'What's the yeshiva? '

'It's where pious Jews go to study.'

'You didn't.'

'I'm a woman.'

'I don't think the Party would approve of that attitude Comrade.'

She laughed. Leszek didn't often joke because there wasn't a lot to joke about in the life they led, but she liked to hear him say something, anything, lighthearted, especially about the Party. She sometimes thought he was a bit too serious about his communist masters. In front of the others Leszek treated Roza the same as any of the men. In the darkness of their tent, though, it was a different matter.

'He's a good worker, I'll give him that. He does everything he's ordered to, even by old Krystyna, and there aren't many men who would do that.'

'Mm. Maybe we could give him something more useful to do. Look at him, he's strong. He's wasted skinning rabbits. And he's clever.'

'You Jews, you're all clever, but not clever enough to live apparently.'

She hesitated. This was Leszek the Pole, not the party man, and something deep inside her hurt a little. In the end, Poles and Jews were different, and the Party couldn't make them the same, couldn't undo hundreds of years of hostility. Leszek was a good man but Roza never forgot what he was and what she was. What they had suited them both in this time and place but there would come a time, she knew, when it wouldn't, when something would flare up and it would all be over. If they lived long enough.

'Couldn't you take him with you, on an operation, see what he can do?'

'No, we don't know enough about him. He's not a Party man.'

'What do you think? He might be a traitor, working for the Germans?'

'Of course not, but I would have to get clearance from Kalinowski at HQ. Just because he's strong and clever and he hates Germans isn't everything.'

'It isn't? What else is there?'

He thought about that, and there was no answer, so he stomped off. Roza could be too clever sometimes. Clever women were a pain in the backside. Motti looked up from his work and his lips stopped moving. He smiled at Roza and she wanted to smile back but she just looked stern and he put his head down again. Just because she was

Jewish didn't make her the same as him. She was, as she had said, not like his mother or his wife. He didn't really know what she was, this woman who called herself a Jew but didn't look like one and certainly didn't behave like one.

5

The Armia Ludowa company was about a hundred strong, almost all men but with a few women, each of whom was paired up with a section leader. Rank, in the group, conferred certain rights, one of the most important of which was a woman. The benefit was mutual, because 'marriage' to a leader conferred status and therefore protection on the woman. Life in the forest was based on fairly primitive social principles.

'Operations' were carried out by those most capable of performing the tasks needed, regardless of gender. People with wounds or who were sick stayed in camp, the fit ones went out, either to fight or for some other task related to the welfare of the company, such as foraging for food or wood gathering. A guard was mounted twenty-four hours a day, in four-hour watches, at a defensive perimeter of a kilometre or so from the camp. Radio silence was maintained because the Germans listened with radio direction finders constantly. In any case, the company had only one set and no-one knew for sure if it worked. It was dropped by a Soviet plane months earlier, and it was to be used in an emergency only.

There was no shortage of weapons, mostly small arms but with one heavy machine gun and a medium mortar. The problem was ammunition. The machine gun was a great weapon, but it consumed ammunition at a prodigious rate, and more often than not they simply couldn't afford to take it on an operation. Anyway, it took two men to carry it. Leszek allocated it and the mortar for the defence of the camp, in case of attack. Any ammunition they used had to be replaced, and that meant an air drop, and that meant the danger of giving away their position to the enemy. The camp was moved every few months as a precaution, but the progress of the Germans through Mordechai's village was a worrying sign of increased activity in the area. Motti told him they threatened to return and Leszek pondered the possibility that it was no more than that, a threat, or they really were coming back and that might necessitate a move further away. The Germans' route east took them within two kilometres of the camp and that was a bit close for comfort.

Once every week a runner went to headquarters with Leszek's report and to bring back new orders, usually one of the younger, fitter ones. The orders were more often than not impossible to carry out. They were to attack a German column, or blow up a fuel dump or mine a road. Well, Leszek knew they didn't have the manpower or the training to do any of those things, and in any case without heavy weapons they simply couldn't match the enemy, let alone have a chance of overwhelming them. And how could they mine a road without mines? He sent a message to Kalinowski to this effect but all that came back was the Party expects. The Party could expect whatever it liked, but without mines that order was going the way of all the others.

Leszek himself decided what operations they could mount. They were always small scale, they always kept the risks to a minimum and they were, in truth, more to do with surviving in the forest than seriously taking on the enemy. Yes, he would have loved to mount full-scale attacks, but he would also have loved an armoured brigade with which to do it.

His company comprised an assortment of men of all ranks from the Polish army who had evaded capture and had decided to stay and fight rather than attempt the journey to England to join the Polish Free Forces. Some were experienced NCOs but many were raw recruits, given a uniform and a rifle in the last desperate days before the German and Soviet armies marched across the Polish borders.

Leszek himself was at the Staff College and had toyed with communism as far as he could without losing his commission. When the Molotov-Ribbentrop pact was signed, allying the Soviet Union with Germany and carving his country up between them, Leszek had a crisis of conscience. He felt sure Stalin knew what he was doing but even so, Poland was his country and it takes a great deal of understanding to accept the destruction of your homeland. Stalin and Hitler formally announced that Poland no longer existed. He left his wife and children at home in Krakow, Poland's ancient capital, threw away his uniform and went in search of the truth. Well, he never found that because it doesn't exist in the best of times and it certainly doesn't exist in war, but still, he joined up with one partisan band after another, each calling themselves the resistance and all of them doing nothing more than surviving, which in fairness was an achievement in itself in those dark days. Then in June 1941 Germany launched Operation Barbarossa, the invasion and annihilation of her erstwhile ally, Russia.

 Suddenly, it all made sense to Leszek. Stalin, the great strategist, has been playing for time, cosying up to Hitler while he prepared for the real battle, the struggle to the death between Communism and Nazism. Poland had been sacrificed for this greater purpose, but Poland would rise again from the ashes. Now, he was in command of a Communist force that was preparing to play its part in this battle. Survival, for now, was enough, in fact it was paramount. Colonel Kalinowski sent his orders which had little to do with the reality in the forest, and Major Belka sent back reports which had little to do with the orders, and both men knew it was enough, but then one day Kalinowski himself received an order and this order had to be obeyed. It was, his own superior officer informed him, of strategic importance.

 Supplies for the German armies attacking Leningrad had to pass through Poland. Stalin himself had ordered these supply routes to be attacked to relieve the pressure on the city that bore Lenin's name. The order was passed from Moscow to the headquarters of the Armia Ludowa in Bialystok and from there they were sent to Colonel Kalinowski at Brigade Headquarters and he called a staff meeting and a result of that meeting was that enemy troop movements through the forests were to be ambushed by, among others, the company commanded by Major Leszek Belka.

 When he read this order Major Belka sent a message back to say he would do his best to comply and Colonel Kalinowski said no, you will not do your best, you will carry out the order fully. He added some threats that Leszek, knowing Kalinowski, took seriously. The Colonel did, however, promise to send a detachment of reinforcements and with them a supply of rifle and heavy calibre ammunition. The order included an instruction to prepare the radio for use. This was the emergency it had been sent for, and the company should be prepared to break camp and move immediately after the operation.

It was well understood that one inevitable result of the operation would be a concentration of German troops in the area to stop partisan activity. It was, in fact, part of the plan. Any troops detained in Poland were not available in the Soviet Union. Stalin was still using Poland to draw the heat away from his own armies fighting for survival against the German onslaught. Leszek understood this. It was, he realised, one of the exigencies of war.

German troops fought well on the battlefield, on the plains where their tanks and highly mobile infantry and guns, with air cover, could move fast and overwhelm the enemy quickly. They were less well equipped, they themselves knew, for fighting in the forests of Poland. There, the partisans' inferiority in numbers and weaponry would be balanced by their experience in guerilla warfare.

Leszek knew, as did Kalinowski, that the experience of the partisans in guerilla fighting was to a large extent theoretical. They lived in the forest and it was therefore assumed they could fight in the forest, but in fact, certainly as far as Leszek's own company was concerned, they were under-trained and they had precious little battle experience. More men meant more food and time to train them and integrate them with his own men. Well, it might be a disaster, but they would, at least, die with weapons in their hands.

He told Roza about his worries. She was a good woman in many ways. Her body was always available and unlike his wife she genuinely seemed to enjoy him, and that did his ego a lot of good. And afterwards, they lay there and she stopped being his mistress and became his mother and he told her what troubled him. No-one in the company knew she did this because it would not do for their commander to be seen as weak, but Roza was a woman and she knew that men are weak. She was there to make him strong.

'It's a fool's errand, this operation, and I don't like it.'
'But the extra men, won't they make a difference? '
'Roza, the Wehrmacht have, to my knowledge, three divisions stationed permanently in this part of the country, with nothing to do but shoot Jews and string peasants up. Unless they've got fat and lazy by now they are going to be itching for a fight. We have a hundred fighters, two hundred soon, most of them not properly trained, and no heavy weapons. We might hold them up for a few days, maybe a week, but once they realise we're serious they are going to wipe us out.'

Roza held him close to her. He smelled bad, they all did. It was winter and people don't like washing in icy water in the open. But what she could also smell was fear, and she knew she was the only one who should know this.

'How long have we got, once the reinforcements get here?'

'I don't know. Kalinowski will send more detailed orders with them, but knowing him he will want to see some action pretty soon, two weeks at the most. It's going to be hard work.'

And he talked like this and she listened until his voice became calmer and quieter and when she heard him snore she knew it was her time to sleep. Leszek satisfied her needs in many ways, and he even let her mother him when he was like this. It was good. But not as good, she thought as she herself fell asleep, as having her own child. No, that was not possible, not with him or any other man. Her periods had stopped when the Germans walled off the ghetto in Warsaw and there had been plenty of times when she could have got pregnant but she never had and in a way she was happy about that because she knew that Leszek Belka was not a good father for her children and this was not a good time for them either. And in a way she sometimes thought a child would be good by any man at any time, because a child was her reason for living.

The ghetto. A year ago, it was. Almost half a million people pushed into a few streets and left to die of typhus and starvation and hopelessness, and with them her father, mother and sister. Many died, as they were supposed to do, but not fast enough because actually people, even people in conditions like those, retain their will to live, and the old and the children went faster but that left the strong and they survived in part because they were able to get outside the wall and smuggle food in, bought at inflated prices from the Poles or stolen. Roza stayed for six months, then without saying a word to her family she disappeared to the other side for ever. She looked as Polish as anyone else, and she spoke the language fluently. She even had some German, and with some jewellery her grandmother left her she bought the papers of a young woman who looked sufficiently like her who had died, God knew why or how, and with a change in hairstyle and without her glasses she passed for her, and Roza Weksler became Barbara Hausner, Polish mother, half-German father. That got her a job in a Wehrmacht officers' canteen where she ate well and stayed warm and tried to forget she was born Jewish.

The officer who raped her in the kitchen of the canteen one night wouldn't have done it if he had known she was Jewish. Sexual relations with a Jew were against the law. The last thing she did before she left the canteen for good was put rat poison in the food.

6

Roza said nothing when Leszek told her he had decided to send Mordechai Levinson with the section that would go out and meet the reinforcements at the rendezvous. They couldn't come direct to the camp, because no-one knew where it was, not even headquarters. It was a fundamental security precaution. The new men would be met the other side of the river and brought over a narrow footbridge the Germans never used.

Motti, said Leszek, would be useful. He was fit and strong and the new men were carrying a lot of supplies. They would welcome being relieved of some of that for the last few kilometres. He gave Motti the order himself, and it was an order, not a request. Motti understood that's how it was as long as he was with the company. He was free to leave whenever he chose, but as long as he stayed he was under Leszek's command. He wasn't going to leave. There was nowhere to go.

The rendezvous was scheduled for late the next evening. Both sides would hole up each side of the bridge until after nightfall to give any enemy a chance to show themselves and, if they didn't, to complete the journey under cover of darkness. That evening there was a clear sky and nearly a full moon. The men were glad because it made travel through the forest easier, but Leszek knew it also made them less secure. He liked darkness.

The men talked quietly among themselves for the first hour of the journey but Leszek ordered silence after that as they got nearer the RV. It didn't matter to Motti, because no-one was talking to him anyway. He picked up more Polish every day in the camp, but people treated him as if he was deaf and dumb.

Leszek was relieved when it clouded over towards midnight. It made everything darker but it also brought snow, and the men were getting cold waiting. At twelve exactly he signalled them to more forward over the bridge in single file, five men at a time, wait for thirty seconds, then another five. Once they were all over, he led them on for the last five hundred metres to where he knew the reinforcements were waiting in silence, watching them. He just hoped no-one else was doing the same thing, but so far it looked good. No-one who didn't need to knew where the RV was, so there should be no trouble.

It took Leszek several seconds to compute what he was looking at, and when he came to his senses he knew that what he was looking at in the moonlight and the falling snow was a massacre. A hundred men lay dead or dying in front of his eyes, and what he should have done was order his own men to spread out and take cover, because that's what his training had been, but training is one thing and doing it when you are faced with a scene like that is another.

But no-one attacked them. Whoever had done this was long gone. They had seen and heard nothing while they waited, so this had happened before they had arrived anywhere near. As his men tended to the wounded, this fact troubled him. The Germans, if they had done this, would have set up an ambush. It was obviously an RV, and even if they weren't sure they would have tortured one of the men until they were. So it wasn't them. That left only the NSZ, a renegade gang calling themselves the National Armed Forces. This was confirmed by the fact that all of the weapons and ammunition were missing. Even the men's greatcoats had been stripped from them, and their boots, and those who were not already dead were as good as, if not from bullet wounds then from hypothermia. This was a raid, possibly an opportunistic one, he didn't know, for supplies. What made him angry, bitterly angry, was that this was done by Poles, his own countrymen who were so greedy for fighting they would do this to their own, to men who were here to fight the common enemy, the Germans. Well, Leszek had two enemies now.

He gathered his men and explained what he believed had

happened. All except Motti, who couldn't understand, swore angrily. One of them tried to explain to Motti that this was not the Germans, it was Poles, and Motti found that impossible to comprehend.

Leszek asked them a question. He would not order them. It was their decision. They needed those weapons but especially they needed the ammunition. And they should punish the NSZ. It was, he said, a valid action under the conditions of war. This wasn't about communism, about politics, it was about Poland, and the NSZ, he told them, were murderers and enemies of the state. Did they want to follow him?

To a man, they said yes. They were cold and tired, but he told them they would have to set off immediately if they were to have a chance of catching up. They had lost a great deal of time waiting the other side of the bridge, and they didn't know how far their quarry had gone, but they knew they were heavily laden down, and that meant there was a chance of catching them. Then he turned to Motti. As best he could, he explained what was happening, and told Motti he was not a combatant and he didn't need to come with them. No-one would think the worse of him if he retraced his steps to the camp on his own. Motti thought about this. What Leszek said was right, this wasn't his fight. This was Pole against Pole, no Jews were involved, and Motti thought like a Jew, not a Pole. On the other hand, they had given him shelter and security. They had saved his life. No, he would go with them. He owed them that. Leszek looked grim, but for the second time in this war he felt a Jew could be a compatriot.

Motti couldn't fight because he didn't know how to. Alright, he had killed three people, well two if what Leszek said about Stängl was right, but that was luck. No, he couldn't fight. But he could do what he came to do, which was to carry the supplies back to the camp. If, that was, they caught up with these people, whoever they were, and if they overcame them. He didn't know what they would do with them if it came to a fight and they won, but he tried not to think about it.

They left one man behind to tend the wounded as best he could. Leszek thought very few would survive. They had been left for dead by the NSZ with good reason. Still, what could be done would be done.

The NSZ had left a fairly obvious trail. The snow had obliterated the tracks to an extent, but they were carrying heavy loads and it wasn't difficult to see which way they had gone. A man called Anton went ahead. He was their best tracker, and he moved so fast they had trouble keeping up with him. Leszek knew his men were tired, but he knew also that if they stopped to rest and eat they would never catch up, so there really was no choice but to push them. Levinson the Jew, he noted with some satisfaction, had no trouble keeping up.

It was getting light when Anton signalled them to stop and put his finger to his lips. They were close enough to be heard. The NSZ were making no effort to keep quiet. Why would they? It didn't occur to them they were being followed. Some of them were drinking as they walked and one or two were singing intermittent choruses of some popular song. From time to time they stopped while one of them put his load down and took a swig from a bottle. They were tired, drunk, and most importantly they had no idea they were about to be attacked. Leszek had just one decision. Should he give them a chance to give themselves up or simply kill them where they were?

He didn't like it but he knew what he had to do. These men were murderers in time of war. They had given no mercy to those people back there, good Poles and communists. They didn't deserve a chance. That was the moral argument, but there was a tactical one as well. Shooting a man is done easiest if he's not expecting it. They may be drunk but they were heavily armed and they were without moral scruple. No, this would be an execution, not a battle.

He placed his men in a line either side of the gang and they kept pace with them, the snow and fallen leaves muffling their footsteps. He waited for the right moment, and it came when the path went into a hollow, which put his men at a height advantage. When he gave the signal, they opened fire in a devastating volley from their automatic weapons. It wasn't militarily very elegant, but it was entirely effective. There were no survivors. Any wounded were shot cleanly through the head.

No-one was cheered by this victory. They were dog tired, and the sudden adrenaline rush left them exhausted afterwards. Leszek knew he would have to let them rest. He posted guards on the off chance that the gunfire had been heard by a passing German patrol but he knew that was unlikely. Then he let them sleep. They simply fell to the ground where they stood and within minutes there was silence, dead men and sleeping men indistinguishable even in the growing daylight. Leszek sat on a tree stump and lit a cigarette. This wasn't why he joined the Armia Ludowa, but he knew also that one day it would come to this, civil war, when the Germans were beaten, which he felt sure they would be.

Well, that was then and this was now. For now, he was commander of this company and they had a job to do. He would send a couple of men back to help with any wounded who could be brought back to camp, and after a hasty breakfast the rest of them would carry back the supplies they had liberated, plus any NSZ weapons they could carry. It was, he realised, quite a haul, but at a terrible price. Now they would have the weapons and ammunition to carry out the orders from HQ, but they would be perilously short of men.

Mordechai Levinson slept uneasily. It was cold, but he was used to that. He was troubled by what he had seen. The only killing he had witnessed until now was by the Germans and their Ukrainian auxiliaries. This was different, it was war, and he couldn't figure it out. Or was it so different? The men who pulled the triggers as they executed the wounded were just men pulling triggers, doing a job, like the Germans. And this business of Poles killing each other troubled him. In his mind, there was us and there was them, but here he wasn't sure who was on whose side, and if that wasn't clear then who was in the right, because surely someone had to be. He could comprehend war as a battle between right and wrong, but what was this? He wanted to ask someone, talk about it, but they were all asleep, and in any case he didn't speak enough Polish and on top of that he wouldn't have known how to ask even if he spoke their language.

There was another factor, too. The men sleeping around him were peasants, even though they were now in uniform, and they didn't think too much about these things. They farmed according to the dictates of the seasons and their masters, and now they fought in much the same way. Motti had been brought up, first in the cheder and then when he graduated to the yeshiva, to question everything, to see two sides, if not more, to every question, and to look for answers, to discuss, to argue, to think. He had killed, yes, but he had, ever since, been wracked by an internal argument about what that meant and how it related to the killing of his family.

He had got used to the Poles in the camp but they were soldiers. Here he saw what they existed for. Except that they hadn't killed any Germans. The only person here who he knew for sure had done that was himself, Mordechai Levinson. With that thought, and a brief prayer for the souls of his wife and son, his parents and his sister, he fell asleep too.

Leszek Belka watched him from where he sat, watched his lips twitching like a man saying a silent prayer. He thought and tried to imagine what it was like to be Mordechai Levinson but he couldn't. It made him think of Roza, a wonderful woman and a Jew, and he shook his head in incomprehension. It had been a long day and he felt suddenly the burden of his responsibility for these men. He was more tired than them but he would keep watch for now. For a brief moment he considered leaving them where they slept and simply walking away, where to he had no idea, somewhere far away, but he knew he wouldn't. He knew he loved them too much to do that, and having someone to love is a wonderful thing in such terrible times.

7

There was shock and disbelief in the camp when all the men had returned the next day. Roza, despite herself, said the Jewish prayer for the dead. She had to do something and it was all she had. Each person went their own way that day, and Leszek let them. You can push people only so far.

He was already planning though. He had received an Intelligence report that a major convoy of fuel tankers would be passing through his area of operation in a week's time. It was too obvious a target not to attack. For this reason it was going to have an extremely heavy guard, he knew, and he also knew therefore that not many of them would be coming back from such a mission. The Germans would have at least a battalion strung out the length of the convoy and they would be highly mobile and they would have heavy weapons. And, unless they were stupid, which he knew there were not, they would reconnoitre the route in advance to clear any mines and ambushes. Without the reinforcements, at company strength there was little Leszek could do but hit and run. Yes, they had the extra weapons, but a man can only fire one rifle before he runs or dies. They would take the mortar and the heavy machine gun, but because they had no transport there was no option but to place these in an ambush in advance, and cover them up as best they could.

He explained his strategy to his section leaders and they nodded in solemn agreement. It wasn't a good plan but it was the only plan.

Motti watched the lights in the tent and the shadows of the men inside as they held their conference. He wondered what they were saying, while he washed potatoes. Well, it was nothing to do with him.

But that evening, after everyone had eaten, Roza sat down next to him and explained it. There was no military reason, but she wanted to talk to someone, and she couldn't talk to Leszek because his head was full of plans and he had stopped being a person and was a commander. Roza needed to talk to a person.

'They're going to take you.'

'Me? What can I do? I'm not a soldier.'

'No, but they're going to need porters. There's a lot to carry. I hope you aren't offended.'

'No. If I can help, of course. What will I be carrying?'

'I'm not sure. Probably the heavy machine gun. Usually two men carry it, but we haven't got two men to spare. Do you think you can do it?'

'I don't know. How heavy is it?'

Roza took him to the gun emplacement.

'There. See how it feels.'

Motti got one of his big hands round the barrel and lifted. It was heavier than he had expected, but he tried not to show it.

'Yes, I think so. Are we going far?'

'It's about a day's march. When we get there you will leave this and wait behind the ambush. If there are any casualties you will act as a stretcher bearer.'

'And will there be casualties?'

'Of course. There always are, but this time ...'

'This time? '

'Well, a lot of casualties. And you won't be able to bring them back here.'

'Where then?'

'Anywhere, just as far away as you can get.'

'It's not a very good plan.'

'No, I know.'

They sat for a while and said nothing. Roza watched the snowflakes falling on Motti's beard and she was confused by the conflicting feeling that she wanted to protect him from all this and at the same time she wanted him to look after her. She couldn't understand it. Leszek had never made her feel protective. He was a man and she was a woman and in his mind, even as a communist partisan in these exceptional conditions, that was a simple relationship. To Roza, Motti represented the Jewish people. For all she knew he was the last one left alive in all of Poland, apart from herself, and she wanted to save him for posterity.

Motti was silent while she thought this. She could see from the look in his eyes that he was thinking. Probably, she reckoned, the same things that pious Jews had always thought about. She envied his ability to escape from the world she lived in.

But Mordechai Levinson wasn't thinking about those things.

'Roza?'

'Yes?'

'May I make a comment?'

'Of course? What?'

'I think it's a bad plan.'

'Yes, I agree with you. You said that already.'

'Uhuh. I have a better one.'

She looked at him. A better plan? What, military tactics from the lips of a shtetl Jew? 'Alright Levinson, tell me.'

'Well, you said there was no choice but to place the machine gun and the other thing, um ....'

'The mortar.'

'Yes, the mortar. You said the plan was to place them in an ambush and hope the Germans don't find them.'

'That's right.'

'No, that's wrong.'

'It is?'

'Yes. Hope is wrong. Wishful thinking, that's all it is. I don't know much about these things, but …'

'That's true.'

'No, but look, if you put them in place and the Germans find them they are going to know where the ambush is going to happen and they will be waiting to ambush you, I mean us, won't they?'

'Yes, but what choice do we have?'

'Well, put these weapons where you are not going to ambush the Germans.'

'What? Why would we do that?'

'Surely, when they find them they will concentrate their soldiers at that point. You will attack them elsewhere, while their guards are waiting for an ambush that isn't going to happen.'

Roza thought about this. Out of the mouths of babes and innocents. Where did this man get such an idea? She shook her head. It was brilliant.

'There's only one problem.'

'Yes? '

'Leszek won't agree to it.'

'Why not? '

She knew what the answer to that was, that Major Belka of the Armia Ludowa was never going to implement a plan proposed by a Jewish stray. She considered for a moment how she could tell Motti this, though.

'It would mean sacrificing the weapons. He won't do that.'

'Is there any chance that even if enough men survive the battle they will be able to escape with them?'

'Well, no. On the other hand, at least they will have been able to fire them. With your plan, they won't even be fired.'

Motti could see that was a problem, but he was not after all a military man and he couldn't answer that conundrum. At least if the commander would consider it.

'Well, leave it with me. I'll see if there might be some way. Meanwhile, keep these thoughts to yourself.'

Leszek never knew the idea came from Motti and it was, he realised straight away, a good one. He had only one adjustment to make to it. He asked for two volunteers to man the weapons on a suicide mission so they could at least get some use out of them and take out a number of Germans as well. Since the entire operation was a suicide mission anyway, which they all had realised by now, it wasn't hard to find two volunteers. They, at least, would be killing more of the enemy than anyone else.

The mood was sombre six days later when the raiding party prepared to leave camp. The men, who usually told crude jokes and sang popular Polish songs round the fires after the evening meal, were largely silent. There was a feeling that they weren't coming back, and strangely they now felt that this camp, with its one tent and its trestle table kitchen, was home, which of course for all of them it was, or the nearest they had had for a long time. Leszek told them they couldn't come back anyway, that they were under orders to set up camp elsewhere, but not many of the men believed that would be happening. The loss of the reinforcement detachment had hit them hard and now a feeling of hopelessness had got into them and he couldn't dispel it. Of course he couldn't. He felt it himself.

Motti felt it too, and for the first time he experienced a brotherly feeling for these people. He knew they didn't feel that way about him, but that didn't matter. For the first time in his life he could see how they suffered and whilst that didn't excuse their hatred of Jews just now he didn't, for reasons he couldn't understand, need to excuse it. He wished he could do more. Now, as the tension heightened, like them he experienced the desire for revenge, and he thought he had some understanding of what motivated the partisans. Each man had someone to avenge. Motti, though, had more than most.

Roza also had a need to avenge, but she wasn't going with them. Her job was to take command of the remnants, such as they were, the women, the sick and the lame, whose role was now to break camp and move to a designated rendezvous a week's march away. There were two handcarts, and Leszek made the painful decision to allocate one to the raiding party for ammunition and the other to Roza, without which he knew she and her people would never be able to move everything that far.

Ammunition is heavy. It's mostly lead, and the amount an army can carry largely determines what battles it is capable of fighting. A sub-machine gun can go through in one day's fighting more than a man can carry to get it into the field. Add to that grenades and bombs for the mortar, let alone the boxes of ammunition belts to feed the heavy machine gun, and one cart was the minimum they were going to get away with. The only consolation was that the machine gun and the mortar were likely to be overwhelmed in a matter of minutes, and therefore their need for ammunition was limited.

The men who had a woman said farewell to them as privately as they could and then, in an attempt to instil some military feeling into the column, Major Belka had the men stand to attention and give a salute. Roza returned the salute as Motti stood and looked in wonder.

As they marched off through the forest they heard the unmistakable sounds of the camp being dismantled. Roza was wasting no time. Each person was left with his or her own thoughts. It was, they knew for sure, the end of something, perhaps the end of everything, but it was what they had come for and suddenly every man and woman felt Polish. They were communists and they were taking their orders from the Red Army and ultimately from Moscow, Poland's one-time master, but for now they were patriots, and as each person steeled himself to the task ahead he gave himself over to thoughts of Marshal Pilsudski and Polish nationalism.

Except for Mordechai Levinson. Polish nationalism meant nothing to him. Motti carried the great weight of the machine gun over one shoulder, but with his spare hand he felt in his shirt pocket for the mezuzah he had taken from the doorpost of the inn in a previous life, and he said a prayer. It was said quietly, so no-one heard. Whether God heard it either only time would tell.

8

Roza Weksler's party comprised, apart from herself and Krystyna the cook, three women who helped around the camp but mostly kept their men satisfied at night, four men recovering from wounds sustained on operations, plus one who had broken his arm falling out of a tree when he had been playing a prank and had been severely reprimanded by Leszek for his foolishness, because no matter how it's done a broken arm is still a broken arm and a man with one is no use to anybody. And finally they had one man sick with something no-one knew what because no-one in the company had any medical expertise and neither did they have any medicines even if they had known what was wrong with him and therefore knew what to do for him. He vomited a lot and all they could do was give him water to prevent dehydration, but he was very weak and Roza was forced to let him ride on the handcart from time to time because the alternative would have been to leave him to die which she couldn't do. She knew what Leszek would have done. He would have shot the man, because a man left to die can be captured and interrogated by the Germans. Since she couldn't leave him and she couldn't kill him, taking him with them was the only other option. She might dress like a man but she wasn't one, and the difference between a man's world and a woman's world, even in the forest, even in the Communist Party, was as great as ever and, she supposed, always would be.

Women and men couldn't be the same, and for that, she also supposed, she was grateful.

Her father had brought her up to be independently-minded, to think for herself, in short not to be what her mother was, a Jewish wife and mother. Her parents wed in the usual way, not exactly an arranged marriage but a carefully orchestrated one all the same. He came from a wealthy family and so did she, but there the similarities ended. Her mother's family, the Lempels, were religious. In fact her grandfather Moise Lempel was the rabbi of the Great Synagogue in Warsaw. Everyone respected him and when his elder daughter Dora was old enough to be wed the family had high hopes of the right yeshiva graduate coming along, a boy of great erudition, even perhaps a rabbi himself. They sent word out not just in Warsaw but to all the great centres of Jewish learning throughout Poland and Lithuania and fathers brought their sons to the rabbi's house and some were alright and some weren't but none of them was good enough for Dora because she had fallen in love, with no help from anyone, except of course the boy in question was not a rabbi nor was he even a great scholar or even a not so great scholar. In fact he wasn't a scholar at all, and Rabbi Lempel said no, he would not do, but Dora was in love and what can you do when a girl is in love except either make her unhappy by forbidding her marriage to the object of her desire or allowing it and making her happy even if by doing so you are unhappy yourself, and in the end Rabbi Lempel weighed up his own happiness against his daughter's and did the right thing by her.

The man she married, David Weksler, was a scion of a great family even so, but a commercial one. The Weksler family had a multiplicity of business interests in Poland and Lithuania, from department stores to clothing factories, from breweries to tanneries. They even, and this was most unusual for a Jewish family in Poland, owned an explosives factory, supplying not just mining companies but the army itself. There were doubts expressed in the Army Department in Warsaw about a Jew owning a means of production vital to the country's defence but David's father, Isidor, had friends in high places. People owed him favours and one or two owed him money, and for the time being they protected him.

David, by the time of his marriage to Dora, was already in charge of many of the family businesses, but his greatest interest was explosives. He went with his father to meetings at the Army

Department and cultivated his own relations with people there and among serving officers, and while they all knew he was Jewish he was Isidor Weksler's son and he was obviously a Polish patriot and in any case he didn't, if you looked at him in a certain way, appear all that Jewish. He didn't attend the synagogue, which was a disappointment to his wife, but neither did he stop her attending and on the high holy days he went with her, but then all of Jewish Warsaw was at the Great Synagogue on those days, religious or not.

When Roza was born, and then her sister Irena, David was, his wife knew, disappointed not to have a son, and after Irena Dora had some complications and the doctors said there would be no more children and David had to bear his disappointment. Dora knew, even so, and she didn't object when he brought up his elder daughter, notwithstanding that she was the prettier of the two, the way he might have brought up a son. When she was thirteen he could not, of course, have her barmitzvah, but he put a case to his father-in-law for a special ceremony and at first the great rabbi demurred but David insisted and he also made a handsome donation to the synagogue and in the end Roza Weksler became the first Jewish girl in Poland to have a batmitzvah ceremony. It was, paradoxically, and certainly without him intending it to be, a small step towards the equality of women.

As she trudged through the forest with a heavy load on her back, in the snow, Roza wondered about this, about why her father, who became increasingly hostile to religion, not just Judaism, and in the end called it all superstition, put her through a deeply religious rite. Well, he was a conundrum, but then who wasn't? It was, she supposed, the last thing he could do that he would have done for a son, notwithstanding his personal beliefs because of course every Jewish boy, at that time and in that country, was barmitzvah regardless of his father's ideas, before she became a woman and left him. She wondered if she loved her father for what he did, making her an honorary man, or hated him, and decided she did neither. He was what he was.

She just hoped that now he was a prisoner with the rest in the Warsaw ghetto, that his strength would protect him and her mother, and her sister Irena. She would never forgive herself for abandoning them, but she thought her father would understand, that his teaching was the reason, that she could think for herself and the result was that she thought sitting there and dying of starvation was not the only way, that if one Weksler was going to live it would be her, that she would get out and survive and after the war she would marry and have children of her own and bring them up to know.

She couldn't help smiling to herself as she led this ragtag group of desperate people through the snow. What chance was there that any of that would happen? Well, for now, she was alive, and if you are alive anything is possible. And for some unknown reason just then she thought of Mordechai Levinson and she hoped he was alive. She felt bad about wanting him to live more than Leszek but she couldn't help herself. Leszek had a wife already and she knew that if they came out of this alive he would go back to her and forget Roza, and she accepted it. In which case, she thought, it was alright to worry more about Mordechai.

Anyway, it was unlikely that they were going to live long enough for any of it to matter.

The sick man, Andrzej, was her immediate worry. He could hardly walk, let alone carry anything. She let him ride on the cart more and more, but every time she did that she saw the looks the men gave her. If Andrzej rode, they had to pull and they resented it. They knew their commander would not do it like this but they were afraid to tell Roza to shoot him. Even Andrzej himself knew and he saw that look in his comrades' eyes and he knew what he had to do and after it got dark, before Roza gave the order to halt, while she was at the front of the column and couldn't see anyway, he slipped off the cart and fell to the ground and his friends left him there knowing they would have done the same thing themselves. When they finally did stop, they had gone another three kilometres and Andrzej had already died of exhaustion and the cold and only then did Roza ask where he was and everyone shrugged their shoulders and she looked at them and wanted to kill each one of them because they were men and they knew how to do this and she didn't and she cursed herself for being a woman and having a woman's heart and later that night, in her sleeping place under the cart, she wept silently and wished she were stronger and if she couldn't be stronger that she could be protected from all this by a man who was.

She prayed for Andrzej's soul. She wasn't at all sure that a Jew could pray for the soul of a goy, or if God would hear such a prayer, but in her grief she forgot what her father would have said, which was that she was thinking like a superstitious Jew and should cast aside such irrationality and be true to her beliefs. God could not hear her prayers because no such being existed. Roza's father had gone further. He had said that such beliefs were a sign of human frailty, because even considering the possibility of the existence of gods was ridiculous. He and her mother argued about that, but as he got older he believed it even more and whereas at first he had kept his thoughts to himself, as he aged he got more and more angry about it all and it became something that came between him and his wife. Roza and Irena had stayed out of the argument, and had gone to the synagogue every Saturday with their mother while her father stayed at home and pitied them.

The morning started even colder than yesterday had ended. They woke well before daylight and Roza looked at them and wondered if any of them were going to arrive alive, and indeed if there was any point, or if it wouldn't be better if she gave every man, and woman, leave to just walk away, go wherever their feet took them. But if she did that she herself would be alone, and she couldn't face the forest on her own. She needed them more than they needed her. She had woken with Warsaw in her mind and realised she had been dreaming of her family and just now she wanted to be back there with them, to share their horror instead of this one.

They brewed some of what had always passed for coffee in the camp, a concoction of roots that Krystyna ground up, and shared the last loaf of bread and half a sausage they had taken from a German soldier Leszek had killed a week before. Then they lifted their already weary bodies to their feet and moved off.

They walked in silence. Everyone had his or her own thoughts and no-one felt like talking. Roza let them rest regularly, but never for more than fifteen minutes. If they stopped too long they might not start again. She knew their morale was low. No-one believed in the operation so they couldn't see the point of setting up a new camp, and she sometimes wondered if they resented her for pushing them on. More than one thought of deserting, but it was fear of Leszek that stopped them, but even that wasn't all of it because like Roza they had a fear of being on their own. They might be going nowhere but they were at least going there together.

About midday they reach an obstacle. They had to cross a railway line, and they knew the Germans had patrols out all along the lines because of partisan activity, because of their own company and the others, the Armia Krajowa who also attacked the railways and even the NSZ who would do it if they thought there was something to gain, some booty to be had from a derailed train.

Roza let them rest longer this time because she knew the procedure. Leszek had taught her. You hide and wait, for a whole day if necessary, because the Germans knew how the partisans operated and sometimes they set up their own ambushes and waited and then everyone waited and the side that got tired of waiting first either left or got killed. She ordered silence but it was hardly necessary. Most of them simply slept but Roza set up the sniper rifle and with its telescopic sight surveyed both sides of the railway track as best she could. She couldn't see anything, but of course that didn't mean there wasn't anything to see. She detailed two men to do this every fifteen minutes and they did that for three hours and no-one saw anything and finally she decided they had to make a move.

And then a train came. It was travelling slowly and they had plenty of time to watch it as it pulled round a bend and headed towards them. They watched it in fascination, for no good reason, but they also watched for German activity. An approaching train was good reason for any ambush to break cover to give it maximum protection, but there was no ambush. The engine passed where they lay in hiding in a roar of noise and steam and they lay there stupefied, like some monster had entered their silent forest world. It was only a cattle train though, dozens of sealed wooden cars. They watched as the train rolled by, a seemingly endless line of trucks, all the same, and then at last it was gone, getting smaller and smaller until they could no longer see or hear it, leaving them to their accustomed silence.

Roza didn't know it but this line ran east from Warsaw to Treblinka, and the train was taking the first group of deportees from the ghetto to be gassed. David and Dora Weksler, along with their younger daughter, Irena, were in the fifth car from the front.

Roza watched though the rifle's sight as the last car disappeared into the distance, and then she scanned both sides of the track but there was no activity. There were no Germans, she knew that, and they could safely cross now.

9

The new site earmarked by Leszek for the camp looked unpromising when they first saw it. It was a map reference picked for tactical reasons, not comfort, and they despaired. It was too far from the nearest river. What must have looked close on a map turned out to be quite impractical because between the site and the river there was a steep slope and they couldn't see how it was going to be possible to carry enough water up for a company of a hundred people. The stream was crystal-clear and excellent for drinking, but just too far away.

In addition to that problem, although the trees gave good cover from aerial view they also prevented sunlight from filtering through, and Roza knew their people were going to need as much of it as they could get. Sunlight is food to the human body and given their terrible diet an essential nutrient. And anyway, even a weak winter sun made everyone feel better.

On top of those problems was a very practical one. A camp of that size needed good latrines, and the ground here consisted of a topsoil no more than half a metre deep before they hit rock.

No, it simply would not do, and Roza made a decision to move further upstream. If Leszek didn't like it, well, he could make his own decision but for now he wasn't here. They pushed on until they found a much better location. Tree cover was available but not oppressive. The rocks gave way to proper soil, and the river was down a gentle slope. Roza announced that she was satisfied with this new site and the others agreed. She hadn't asked their opinion but still it was good to have it. The company was a military unit and

Leszek did not run it as a democracy, and she saw no reason to change the status quo just because he wasn't here. He had delegated command to her and she would use the powers she had been given. It was fortunate that on this occasion at least her command of the small group was unchallenged.

It had been agreed that the company would disperse after the operation and take a week to follow different routes eventually leading back to this map reference. It was the minimum precaution they could take against the Germans following them back here, but it presumed one thing - that there was going to be anyone left to come back. Well, they couldn't know the answer to that, so they would have to wait and see. The day the camp was set up was to be the day of the operation, so they would have a week to wait, and it was going to be hard, they all knew that. The first day, they talked about the operation and its chance of success and the chance that some of the men would get back but after that there seemed to be nothing more to say. It was all guesswork, and after a while guessing seemed pointless, so they carried out their tasks quietly and in the evening they sat round the fire and talked about anything other than the operation or the men. They talked about home and family, of course, and then the women talked about men and the men talked about women, only by now they were sitting a little apart in same-sex groups, just like any normal community.

Roza didn't join in with the women's talk. She sat with Krystyna, the cook, who was too old for that kind of thing, and they talked about inconsequential things. Their backgrounds were too different for them to have a subject in common. They just knew that even though they were so different from each other they were even more different from the others. Krystyna called the women prostitutes, and in normal circumstances she might have been right but these weren't normal circumstances and what a woman did to survive in war wasn't the same as she did normally.

The men could be heard in the evening singing raucous songs and laughing uproariously at dirty jokes and once, after they had shared a bottle of vodka that had been liberated from the Germans, they started looking at the women in a way that Roza could see meant trouble and she stepped in to calm things down. The men resented it and the women weren't as grateful as she thought they would be. The next morning she heard some mutterings about her leadership, but as long as she had Leszek's authority they would obey. What they would do if he didn't come back was anyone's guess. Well, if that happened, they would surely split up anyway. She tried to decide how she would feel if he didn't, and she couldn't. Then she tried to decide how she would feel if Motti didn't come back and she knew. Motti Levinson, a shtetl Jew she wouldn't have looked at once. Now, he might be the only Jewish man she was ever going to find, and suddenly the connection between them mattered. Anyway, being in a partisan unit would change him, for the better she thought, rub a few hundred years of Talmudic study off him.

They waited a week and then they started to talk again about the company, about how long it would be and what they would do when they got back. The woman prepared dressings and whatever medicines they could muster, to deal with the wounded. Then they waited again. After three more days Roza sent two of the men out to scout for stragglers, wounded men who might not be able to make it in on their own, but they came back alone. Then it occurred to her that only Leszek himself and the three section leaders knew the location of the camp, and if those four were dead none of the others would find it. She worried about it but could do nothing except wait some more. Two weeks after they had moved, it started to look serious. The men were restless and she sent them out each day, two at a time, as much to give them something to do as with any hope that they were going to find anyone. And then they stopped going out and she didn't push it.

And then, in the middle of a late evening snow shower, Mordechai returned.

The men were sheltering under a tarpaulin playing a game of cards and they looked up, startled. One reached for his pistol, uncertain what was happening. The women had been watching the men and chatting but they stopped in mid-sentence. No-one knew what to say. Krystyna looked up from the table that now passed for the kitchen with a knife in one hand and a rabbit in the other. Roza was in the tent, deep in a book, but the sudden silence alerted her and her heart beat painfully as she came out, utterly ignorant of what to expect.

They looked at him in silence, unable to think what it meant, unwilling to break the spell, not wanting the news they were afraid he was bringing, and Motti stumbled forward and sat, silently, on an ammunition box out in the open. He looked at the people looking at him and for a moment seemed unsure who they were or why he was here, and then his eyes changed as he remembered.

He looked at Roza. 'They're all dead.'

'Comrade Levinson, what do you mean?'

It was of course clear enough what he meant. Roza didn't mean she didn't understand what he said, she meant she didn't understand why he said it.

'They all died. No-one came out.'

It was one of the men who answered. 'You did.'

'Yes.' He knew that, all too well. He had listened to them dying and then he had got out.

'Levinson, come, tell us everything. Krystyna, fetch him something hot. The man's starving, look at him, and you, bring some water. Now, start at the beginning.'

'Well, we put the machine gun and the mortar at the right point, and then the rest of us went up the road about half a kilometre I think and Major Belka gave the men their orders and they waited for the ambush. He told me to go with the stretcher further back, out of the way, to wait. I asked him for a gun but he said they couldn't spare one.'

Roza winced when she heard this. For any man to be in that situation unarmed was unthinkable, even a non-combatant. Why had Leszek done that?

'Go on Levinson. Could you see the ambush from where you were?'

'No. I went where he told me, the other side of a small hill, well hidden. He said to come out after the shooting stopped, when I was sure the Germans had gone.'

'And then what?'

'Well, we waited a long time and I wondered if perhaps it was a mistake, you know, about the convoy, and I wondered if I should go and ask someone but he said to wait and I didn't like to. After about four hours I heard engines.'

'The convoy.'

'Yes. I heard it stop, I suppose while some of the soldiers went ahead, like we said, I mean like you said they would, and that must have been when they discovered the machine gun because suddenly there was the most terrible noise, more than I have ever heard before, explosions. I think they must have got at least a couple of the fuel trucks, maybe more. Then there was a lot of shouting, in German and Polish but soon just the sound of the firing. It went on for a long time.'

'How long?'

'Oh, I don't know. Half an hour perhaps. Then it went quiet. I heard the Germans shouting to each other and a Polish voice, Major Belka I think but I wasn't sure. Anyway, he was shouting in Polish and I don't know what he was saying but then I heard a shot and it stopped.'

Roza interpreted this for the men and they looked at him intensely and each one was thinking their own thoughts about the significance of it. Roza didn't know what to ask next but one of the men spoke up.

'And then you ran away.'

'Yes.' Running away did not mean to Mordechai what it meant to the partisans. Running away was what you did.

'You didn't try to help?'

Now Roza found the right thing to say. 'Help? Help? You idiot, how could he help? What would you have done, without a weapon, against the German army? Come on, tell me, what would you have done?'

'Well I wouldn't have run away.'

'Yes you would. That's exactly what you would have done.'

The man stood up and whipped out his pistol.

'Yes, that's right, defend the Zhid. You're the same as him. What are you doing here? You don't belong with us. Go back where you came from.' And while he shouted this he cocked his weapon and pointed it at Roza's head.

Roza's weapon was in her tent, but she didn't need it. He wasn't watching Mordechai, but he should have been. Motti didn't understand what this man was saying but he understood a Polish gun pointed at the head of a Jew. He stood up quietly and, raising his fist for the second time in his life, he felled him with a single blow. He lay on the ground, like the German officer, and Motti didn't know, like that time, if he had killed him. There was silence. No-one knew what to do. Except Krystyna.

'You saw him. He threatened to shoot the lawfully appointed commander of this unit, and he had to be stopped. Now you two, see if anything can be done. If not, take him away and bury him. And you, Levinson, will answer to a military court if we ever get out of here.'

They were so unused to the cook talking like this they did as she said without question. Roza was shaking, from fear, from anger, who could say?

The man was indeed dead and they buried him, as good communists, without religious ceremony. It wasn't discussed. Anyway, there were much more important issues now. The company was in effect finished, they all knew that. They also knew that the Germans would be scouring the area for partisans and they had to move, fast.

Roza gave orders about packing up the camp and told everyone to get some sleep. They would be moving out before first light. Then she asked Motti to come to her tent. The men watched and she knew what they were thinking.

'Come in Levinson, come in. Have you eaten enough?'
'Yes, thank you.'
'Cold?'
'Yes, very, but it's alright.'
'Good man.'
'Well? You wanted to say something to me?'
'Yes. Um, look, I want you to help me with something.'
'Uhuh. What?'
'I want you to say kaddish with me.'
Motti thought about this. 'I'm not sure about saying a prayer for Christians.'
'They weren't Christians, they were communists.'
'Even so, they weren't Jewish.'

'Levinson, Mordechai, they were good men fighting for what they believed in and I want them to be remembered. I need to do this, can you understand that? Does it matter? God may not hear my prayer but I need to say it anyway. Can you understand that?'

Yes, he could. And so, by the light of a candle, in a tent in the middle of a forest somewhere in eastern Poland, two lost Jews recited the prayer for the dead in respect of a hundred men who, it is almost certainly true, would not have done the same for them.

And then Mordechai Levinson, Roza Weksler, and the cook known as Krystyna, slept in that tent in the forest while the frozen corpses of their comrades gathered a covering of snow, somewhere out there, unburied but prayed over.

And in the morning they woke and the first thing they noticed was the silence. The others were gone.

10

Roza told Krystyna they could go, anywhere they wanted, but they didn't want to go, not without her anyway. In any case, where could they go? Krystyna had no family. Her husband and her children and her grandchildren were gone, all of them, long ago. And Motti? No, there was nowhere for him. In a hostile world, the only Jew he knew was the closest thing to family he had.

Roza considered returning to Warsaw but only briefly. It was never a serious possibility. Knowing how bad things were before she left she could only imagine they would be much worse by now. What she didn't know was that the ghetto had already been emptied by the Germans and the train they had seen was the first bound for the gas chambers of Treblinka.

That left Brigade Headquarters. She was, at least nominally, in command of a Communist partisan company, one consisting of herself, an old cook and a Jewish refugee. She would report back to Kalinowski, the two disasters, the loss of the reinforcements and the failure of the mission, and also the defection of her group, because that's what it was, mutiny in time of war. No-one would be able to do anything about it, she knew, and anyway they would be far away before she got to Bialystok, if HQ was still there. There was no very good reason to go, but there was no reason to go anywhere else, either. It gave her a sense of purpose, something to aim for, and yes, it would be dangerous but just existing in Poland under German occupation was dangerous. She couldn't ask Krystyna and Mordechai to go with her, but on the other hand she hadn't, and they wanted to go. The three of them needed to be together, because being with someone in such times is a thousand times better than being on your own.

There was one thing in particular that worried her though, but she knew how sensitive he would be about it and she didn't know how to broach the subject. In the event, though, she didn't need to. Mordechai came to her and asked her to cut off his hair and beard.

'You can't walk half way across Poland with me looking like a Jew.'

'But you are a Jew.'

'That's no reason to look like one.'

'You won't mind? '

'Yes, I will mind, but I don't think God wants me to die for my beard. And if I die how can I protect you? '

'Oh, so you're going to protect me, are you?' Roza smiled at the idea.

'Uhuh. Who was it who saved your life yesterday? '

'I'm sorry, of course. It's just that ... that ...'

'You see me as a shtetl Jew and therefore one of those who allow themselves to be pushed around. Well, Comrade Weksler, I am a Jew, but I will not be pushed around, and if I can do anything about it nor will you.'

Roza was impressed with this speech. So was Krystyna. She put her hands on her hips. 'So, Levinson, you're going to single-handedly defeat the Wehrmacht and rescue your princess here. That's great. What about me?'

Roza translated the gist of this without the sarcasm, but Motti picked up on that anyway.

'Comrade cook, I consider it an honour to be your protector too.'

Roza told her what he said and Krystyna chuckled. Roza reminded them both that time was getting on though, and this was no laughing matter. She scanned the map while the other two packed up and collected any weapons that had been left, but there weren't many. All they had was Roza's pistol, the sniper rifle with two full magazines which thankfully had been in the tent last night, and an old revolver that Krystyna, to Motti's surprise, took out from under her skirts. It had, she said, six bullets in it, enough for five Germans and herself. Roza told her to put it away and not to be so foolish.

When everything was ready she sat Motti down on a crate and got out her scissors. It only took ten minutes, and then both women stood back and considered the result. Roza was shocked. Mordechai Levinson had shed one persona and taken on another. He was undeniably still Jewish, but she could no longer see him as what he was before. He wasn't that any longer, but neither was he like, say, Leszek. He was like the assimilated Jews of Warsaw, like, when she examined him closely, Szymon Alter, the man her mother had once wanted her to marry.

Krystyna was amused. 'So Levinson, this is what a Jew looks like under all that hair.'

'What do I look like? '

'A man, like any other. And not bad either. You know, if I were twenty years younger ....'

Roza interrupted her. 'Krystyna, if you were twenty years younger I believe the men would have taken you with them last night. Now cut it out and let's get moving. Mordechai, I'm afraid you are going to have to be our packhorse. The cart is no use now. We will take only what we can carry on our backs, and you have got the broadest back.'

They were heading north-east and had, by Roza's reckoning, perhaps two hundred and sixty kilometres to travel. If there were no detours necessary on the way to avoid the enemy. And if Brigade HQ was still there, something that worried and gnawed at her but she could do nothing about. They had the radio still, but she knew they couldn't use it. The Germans would pick up the signal and they would be as good as dead. She threw it in the river in frustration.

The mutineers had stupidly left most of the food in Krystyna's kitchen, probably on account of being drunk when they left, and Roza gave it priority, along with the weapons and ammunition, and whatever space they had left in their packs they pushed as much clothing into as they could. The snow had stopped and a weak winter sunshine filtered through the trees and made them all feel there was some hope. It was a meaningless sign, not a sign at all, but still, when you're desperate you clutch at such feeble straws.

They walked as fast as the slowest of them, which was the cook, and Roza worried they were going too slowly but she wasn't going to lose one member of a party of three, and in any case, she thought, what was the hurry? The war wasn't going to finish while they walked to Bialystok, and even if it did then so much the better. Their mission wasn't an important one. In fact, she realised, it wasn't a mission at all. It wasn't for the war, or Poland or the Communist Party, all of which they could do nothing for, it was for them, to give them all a reason to live.

She knew the other two depended on her leadership and as they walked she cast a glance at Mordechai and wondered why, why he let a woman do that, but then she thought why not. She was Roza Weksler, second in command to the leader of a partisan unit, at least in his eyes she was, because in reality she was the leader of precisely nothing. They could both go off without her and there was nothing she could do about it. She needed them as much as they needed her. No, Mordechai Levinson, the man who had killed two Ukrainian soldiers and then allowed himself to become a cook's assistant, was following her because she was leading him, but she had a feeling that he would soon enough take over her role if she needed him to.

She wanted to teach him how to fire the rifle but they didn't have the ammunition for him to practise so she left it. That was one thing they would all depend on her for. She knew she was a good shot. She had once killed a German officer from over a kilometre, on a windless day when the gods favoured her aim and a man had died because of her. That was the day Leszek Belka had first taken her into his tent. She became the company's official sniper and none of the men challenged her. It was one reason, apart from being the commander's woman, that they respected her enough to take her orders.

They left the tent behind. It was just too heavy and gave them no more protection from the elements than they could make with their own hands and their waterproof capes each night. It seemed natural that Roza and Motti would sleep close together to keep each other warm, and it seemed natural too that Krystyna would sleep a little apart from them out of respect for their privacy, even if she too would have liked someone to keep her warm. Nothing untoward happened of course because Motti would not have let it. He wasn't married to this woman and anyway he was still in mourning for his wife. It was also far too cold.

They rationed their food but Motti, they found, needed as much as the two women together. They could carry only a limited amount of water and Roza tried as best she could to ensure they camped each night near a river or spring. Some nights she managed and some she didn't and on those nights they rationed their water too. They all lost weight.

Roza realised that she was pushing them sometimes and had to remind herself that there was no point. When that happened, she took the sniper rifle and killed a couple of rabbits or, if she was lucky, a hare or game bird, and then they stopped for a day and rested and ate.

Every morning, Motti put on his phylacteries, much to the amusement of Krystyna. Roza wondered how he kept his faith after all that had happened, but even without his hair and his beard he was still a Jew, and would be, she knew, until the day he died. He couldn't shave because he had nothing to shave with, so from time to time Roza trimmed his beard and cut his hair to keep him looking as Polish as possible, and there were times when she thought he would pass muster but there were also times when she looked at him and thought if the Germans caught them he wouldn't have a chance.

Roza looked after him and Krystyna, and Motti looked after the women, and Krystyna, who was a lot older than the other two and felt the responsibility that comes with age, felt somehow that she was needed to look after them, which of course she wasn't but on the other hand you can never have too many people who care about you and indeed out there in the middle of winter in the middle of nowhere three people found themselves more cared for than any one of them had been in a long time.

They weren't, though, in the middle of nowhere, because from time to time they had to cross roads or railway tracks and each time Roza took them through the procedure and each time they crossed safely but it was only a matter of time before they would have to face the enemy. They could not remain invisible for ever.

It was especially cold the day it happened, and they were concentrating on trying to keep warm, not on what was going on around them or even where they were going. They almost tripped over the Tarmac before they realised they were standing in the middle of a road, and they looked at each other trying to understand it and then they panicked and Roza had them down in a ditch holding their breath. The days had become the same as each other, and the hours, and it was like they had been in a dream. None of them could remember what day it was, or even whether it mattered. Now, there was a road, and roads meant people and that inevitably meant Germans. They laid low and tried to get their breath back and after a few minutes Roza looked out and all she could see was the road covered in snow and the trees either side covered in snow and so it looked like there was nothing much to see but there was, because coming down the road was a motorcycle and sidecar. Poles didn't drive such things.

They stayed very low and the machine got closer and louder and then it was right there in front of them and then it wasn't because it was disappearing in the distance and the sound of the engine was getting fainter, and now they allowed themselves to breathe.

That was when they realised it was coming back. Why? Why had they turned round? What had they seen? Were they going to drive straight past in the other direction or were they coming to investigate something? The engine got louder and then, about a hundred metres away, it slowed to an idle and they could hear voices. Roza spoke good enough German but she couldn't hear what they were saying. Motti watched in awe as she positioned the rifle and uncapped the telescopic sight. There was just enough engine noise from the motor bike that the soldiers wouldn't her her cocking the weapon, she hoped, but in any case they were both wearing helmets which came down over their ears and balaclavas under that, so no, they wouldn't hear it, which was their problem. They came forward and held their own weapons at the ready, so they were suspicious of something, and that was enough for Roza. From that distance a sniper rifle, in the right hands, will hit any part of the body aimed at. The problem is getting the next round in the chamber and the weapon resighted before the second man comes to his senses and doesn't bother aiming but just sends a burst of automatic fire in your direction. Roza brought them both down before he even registered hearing the first shot.

Motti stood up and was ready to run over and check them out but she grabbed his sleeve.

'No, wait thirty seconds. Anyone near enough to have heard the shots will come and investigate. If not, we check them out, take their weapons, and get the hell out of here.'

They were a long thirty seconds.

'Right, Mordechai, come with me. Krystyna, cover us with the rifle, both ends of the road, remember.' The soldiers were dead. Motti was not so dehumanised that he couldn't feel some sorrow about it, and he told Roza that.

'Levinson, don't let me ever hear you say that again. Learn to hate your enemies or die.'

'But they're men.'

'No, they're not. Men don't do what they do. Now shut up and help me.'

Motti obeyed unquestioningly. They pushed the motorbike off the road and wedged it against a tree. It was heavier than either of them expected and it took several nerve-wracking minutes. Then, with yet more effort, they got one man in the sidecar and the other on the ground beside it. Roza found some matches on one of them, lit a rag and stuffed it into the petrol tank.

'It won't stand close inspection, but with any luck the bodies will be so badly burned they won't see the bullet holes. Anyway, it's the best we can do. Now, weapons, ammunition, food, in that order, and let's disappear.'

Motti obeyed again, and wondered why the partisans had needed Major Belka when they had Roza Weksler.

Their haul was two submachineguns, fully loaded with a spare magazine apiece, one bayonet, a pair of new leather boots that fitted Motti better than the ones he had, which was a relief to him, and a cheese sandwich. Those were the items of the most immediate value to them, but Roza found some-thing very much more important, if not to them then to Brigade Headquarters or even High Command. The man in the sidecar was carrying despatches. They couldn't hang around long enough for Roza to inspect them, but even so she knew immediately they were important. It was as if these two despatch riders had come to look for them so they could deliver this bonanza to them.

'Come on, let's get as far away as we can. If more soldiers come they are going to scour the area, just to make sure, especially if they spot the missing weapons.'

And they didn't stop until they had put two hours' march between them and the dead men, across the forest, at right-angles to the road. It wasn't exactly the way Roza had mapped out but that was of secondary importance now.

They finally halted and Krystyna and Motti made a small fire, enough to boil the kettle, while Roza took out the documents and tried to translate them. From the headings she could see, before she read their contents, that these were orders from at least a divisional headquarters, and they were signed by a General, von Scharping, but that meant nothing to her.

'What is it?'

'I don't know yet, Mordechai, give me time to understand it. And another candle would help.'

She sipped the tea Krystyna brought and read by candlelight and tried to work it out. It wasn't simply that she had trouble translating the German, it was also that she was having difficulty comprehending the meaning of what she was translating. Von Scharping was, from what she could see, the commandant of a Wehrmacht division stationed in Warsaw. The despatch seemed to be a list of casualties and replacements needed in the Warsaw area. This puzzled her, because as far as she knew there was no fighting in Warsaw or the surrounding area. The Wehrmacht had it tied down very tightly.

But the import of the despatch started to become clearer as she read. There had been a battle, one that had taken the Germans by surprise. It had happened when they moved in to destroy the remains of the Warsaw Ghetto. Von Scharping reported that he had lost a number of men and weapons but the orders had been carried out fully. The Warsaw Ghetto had, he reported triumphantly, been razed to the ground. There were no survivors.

11

Krystyna found Roza sitting staring into the darkness, the candlelight showing a blank look on her face, but more than blank. Something in it frightened her, and she fetched Mordechai.

She was gripping the documents tightly, so tightly they couldn't prise them away. In any case, neither of them would be able to read what they said, so they had no choice but to wait. They talked very quietly among themselves and ate the food Krystyna had cooked, but she didn't offer any to Roza. She knew there was no point. Whatever was on that paper, she knew, made food pointless. Krystyna had seen many bad things since this war started. Her son had been hanged in front of her, and in Roza's face she saw what she had been feeling ever since.

Motti too knew, had some idea what it must be. A German report, that much he knew, and looking at her he guessed something of what it was likely to be about.

They sat by the fire all night and Roza said nothing, just stared, and Motti came and put a blanket over her shoulders but she didn't stir. In the darkness once or twice he saw her lips move but couldn't tell if she was speaking and if so what she might be saying. Finally, he and Krystyna fell asleep more or less where they sat and it was pitch black when he felt a hand on his shoulder, and a mouth next to his ear, so close her breath was moist in the freezing air, and she spoke to him.

'They're dead, all of them. Mordechai, they're all dead. Wake up.'

He sat up as best he could and she sat in front of him, staring into his face.

'Do you understand? They're all dead.'

'Yes Roza, I understand. Come here.' And he put his arms round her and she buried her head in his coat and sobbed. She cried while he repeated the prayer for the dead, over and over. He didn't know how many had died but he knew if he said it until the day he died himself it would not be enough.

In the morning they woke together. Motti still had his arms round her and he didn't try to move, but she pushed him away.

'Levinson, get up, we have a new plan.'

'What? What are you talking about? What plan?'

'We're not going to Brigade HQ.'

'Why not?'

'We're going to find someone to show these to.'

'But why not your headquarters? Won't they do some-thing?'

'No, Mordechai, they will not. They take their orders from Moscow, and the fate of the Jews of Poland does not concern Moscow. You and I may be the only ones left, I don't know, but we are going to find someone to tell, someone who will care.'

'But who?'

'I don't know. OK, I don't know, but there has to be someone to tell, and I am going to find them. You can go your own way, or you can come with me, the choice is yours.'

'Do you really need to ask?'

She kissed him on the cheek.

'Hullo, what's this Comrades?'

'Ah Krystyna, Levinson and I have just made a decision. We're going to find the proper authorities to give this information to.'

'What information?'

Roza hesitated. 'The Warsaw Ghetto had, at one time, about half a million Jews living in it. The documents those despatch riders were carrying say that the Germans have killed them all.'

Krystyna looked puzzled. 'All of them? That's not possible. What about ... I mean what about ....?'

'Of course, them too. You think they spared them for me?'

'Oh my God.'

'I don't think, if you don't mind me saying this, that God comes into it.'

Krystyna, nevertheless, went down on her knees, made the sign of the cross, and started to pray. Roza looked at her and didn't know if she should feel pity or contempt. She let the old woman do whatever she had to do and meanwhile she and Motti packed up and put the fire out.

'Come on, we'll eat when we've covered some more ground.'

It was as if she wanted to put some distance between her and the place where she learned the terrible news. The others didn't complain. Despite their circumstances, no-one felt hungry just then. They walked in silence, each with their own thoughts. Whatever those thoughts were no-one had any clear idea where they were going now, not even Roza, and she was the one leading them wherever it was. The others put their faith in her and they would go where she went. There didn't seem a lot of point worrying about it. Motti wondered who she was going to find to tell, and what they would do. After all, if everyone in Warsaw was dead, what could anyone do? Krystyna tried to imagine what it felt like to be Jewish and failed. She had always found them slightly strange people, a bit foreign she always said, but at the same time she had always been a little in awe of them. Where she had worked before the war all the Jews were rich, or at least they seemed to be because they lived in big houses and employed people to do everything for them, but since then she had come into contact with the other Jews of Poland, the ones who were not rich, the ones who lived in the villages or ran smallholdings, those who made a living, just, and those who didn't, and she realised the ones she had known represented but a very small minority. Anyway, it was all academic now, because they were all gone, rich or poor.

She watched Roza and Mordechai from behind as they walked side by side and a part of her wished ... well, of course that was ridiculous. This was war, and who could think of such things right now? Krystyna didn't understand what war was and why men felt it necessary, but she knew what it wasn't. It wasn't quiet times, and it wasn't comfort and warmth, and it certainly wasn't people taking a lover. Maybe there would come a time, but on the other hand maybe there wouldn't. From Krystyna's perspective, the war looked like some vast thing that had rolled over Poland, squashing everyone and everything in its path, and she could no longer envisage a time that would be any different from how it was now. She could no longer remember the past, and she could not imagine a future. All there was was now.

Roza eventually let them stop and they lit a small fire, enough to cheer them a little and to boil a kettle. They sat warming their hands on steaming mugs of Krystyna's ersatz coffee while Roza pored over her maps.

'Where are we going?'

'Well, all I know is that we're not going north east any longer. The Germans are up there in strength, but then that's the same everywhere. To be honest, I don't know.'

'What about another partisan unit? Are they all Communist?'

'No, there's the Armia Krajowa. They take their orders from the government in exile, in London.'

'In London? Where's that?'

'Mordechai, do you really not know?'

'No. Why should I?'

Well, because people should know things. They should get an education and learn how the world works. And then die. Maybe he had a point.

'It's the capital of Great Britain, our allies.'

'Oh, so where are they fighting?'

'Well, not in Poland.'

'Why not?'

'I don't know. They don't consult me on these matters. The next time their Prime Minister calls I'll ask him.'

'You will?'

'Oh for God's sake Levinson. You can be extremely irritating at times. Did you learn nothing about anything in the village?'

'Yes, of course. I learned about the Torah and I studied Talmud and many other books. And of course about brewing beer.'

'Beer? Do they teach that in the yeshiva?'

'My parents kept an inn.'

'Oh. Well, anyway, the simple answer is I don't know where to head. If we go east there are Germans all the way to Leningrad, if we go north we fall off the edge of the land, if we go south we hit Czechoslovakia and that's more Germans and if we go west, well, that's just stupid because that's where the bastards have come from.'

Motti thought about this. None of it meant anything to him. He didn't know where Poland was.

'OK, look, let's analyse this in a different way.'

'Yes? Alright Mr Talmud scholar, you do that and let me know what you come up with.'

'Roza, do you want to talk to me about this or not?'

'OK, look, I'm sorry. Go on, dazzle me.'

'Well, you say north is the sea, but what's between us and it?'

'Germans.'

'Right, and east?'

'More Germans, and then Russians.'

'Right. And you say west is Germany itself.'

'You're getting the hang of this.'

'So since we can't stay here and we have to go somewhere, and none of those places is possible, that leaves south. What's south?'

'Czechoslovakia, which by the way is also German.'

'Right. And beyond that?'

'Austria, which is to all intents and purpose the same thing as Germany.'

'All right, and beyond that?'

'Oh come on, this is getting ridiculous. Have you any idea how far away these countries are? Just what distances we're talking about here?'

'No, none.'

'Well I'm telling you, by train it would take days and somehow I don't think we're going to be travelling that way, so on foot, avoiding German patrols and all towns and villages and foraging for food on the way, let me see, say a year.'

A year was something Motti could understand. It was a long time, but on the other hand if they spent a year travelling to safety, would it matter? After what they had all been through, what significance did time have?

'Alright, and what's beyond that last country?'

'Austria?'

'Yes.'

'Well, in the unlikely event that we got anywhere near that far, we would come to Switzerland.'

'Switzerland? Is that good or bad?'

'I don't know. It's a neutral country, so in theory it could be good, but I had a Swiss piano teacher and he was what they call Swiss-German and he said that Switzerland is like Germany only with more mountains. Anyway, I have no idea even if they would let us over the border, assuming of course that we got that far, which we won't.'

'Why wouldn't they let us?'

'Because, Levinson, the Swiss, from my understanding, are not the world's nicest, most compassionate people. From what I have heard they are sitting there behind their wall of neutrality waiting for all this to blow over, but they have no intention of helping anyone while it's all going on, other than themselves. Not unless you've got a lot of money anyway, and looking at me and you and Krystyna here I would say they are going to figure out pretty quickly that we're not rich industrialists. I'm sorry, but that's about it. We're in the middle of a war, right in the middle, and there isn't a door marked exit for people who don't want to take part. And in any case, you're forgetting one thing.'

'What's that?'

'You might be looking for an escape, but I'm not. I'm looking for someone to pass important information to.'

And having said that, she stopped and thought. He might, just might, have said something important.

'The Red Cross.'

'What's that?'

'Not what, who. It's a humanitarian organisation.'

'Can they stop the war?'

'Well, no, no-one can stop the war.'

'I can't believe that. Anyway, what do these people do that's humanitarian if they can't stop the war?'

'I don't know. I think they go around and make sure everyone's being humanitarian while they kill each other, something like that. Look, ignore that. I'm just being facetious because this is a pointless discussion. The Red Cross is based in Geneva.'

'Where's that?'

'Switzerland.'

'Oh.'

'Quite. I'm sorry, but you simply have no idea how impossible it would be to do any of the things you're suggesting. We're not going to Switzerland.'

Motti thought about that. 'Roza, you said they go around, and I know you weren't being serious, but really, can they travel to all these countries while the war is on?'

'Yes, I think so.'

'Well, in that case I think we have found your answer.'

'We have?'

'Yes. We don't go to them. They come to us.'

12

Mordechai, Roza thought, was a strange man. He was almost entirely ignorant of the wider world, and yet he was possessed sometimes of great insight. A man of his intelligence, she thought, given a proper education, not shut up in the self-imposed ghetto of the shtetl and the yeshiva, might do great things. Well, he might if it weren't for the war.

It sounded so easy. Find the Red Cross, tell them about the destruction of the Warsaw Ghetto, wait for someone to react. To Mordechai's simple mind it seemed entirely reasonable. To Roza, brought up in a world where anything can happen but mostly doesn't, it was a tantalising idea that would almost certainly come to nothing. It was also, though, the only idea on offer. She knew they would never make it to Switzerland. The distance was enormous, they were tired and hungry, half the German army was between them and their goal, and in any case it wasn't hard for her to imagine that in the extremely unlikely event that they got to the border the Swiss would simply turn them away. What were they going to do, knock and say excuse me we need to get to Geneva to see the Red Cross about something very important? No. On that basis alone, getting somewhere they had a practical chance of arriving, somewhere the Red Cross were likely to have a representative, was infinitely more sensible. The problem was, sensible is all relative. They might have more chance of finding a roving Red Cross representative than getting to Geneva, but that still came to almost no chance at all. She didn't know where to start. What country, what town? How would they recognise a representative if they met one?

Did they go around with big badges on, like umpires, making sure everyone was playing the game to the rules? No, it was tempting but it was still seemingly impossible. But how to tell Mordechai that? He was so full of belief, she didn't want to destroy that faith that she found so appealing in him, a faith she knew she would never have.

And anyway, what was this really about? Was it the Jews of Warsaw or was it her Jews, her own family? It was too late to save them, and she would mourn them until the day she died. She would never forget them, or her friends in the city, the other girls she had grown up with, and her cousins and her aunts and uncles, all, as far as she knew, gone now. No, whatever they could or could not do with this information, she would be the repository of their memory, and she would make sure someone else would carry on that task after her death, if at all possible.

But could they do more? Could they find this mythical Red Cross? The very idea of an organisation whose name was the emblem of a religion that had persecuted her own people for millennia struck her as paradoxical at the very least, if not offensive. Still, they were referred to as a humanitarian organisation, and they were reportedly able to send people into the occupied countries, so it was them or nothing.

And then she looked at Mordechai and Krystyna and she looked at the snow-covered forest and she knew they were just three small people whose first priority was to avoid being caught because that meant certain death, at least for her and him, and for the old woman too if she was caught with them.

Mordechai watched her as all this went on in her head and he had the sense to leave her to sort it out herself. He knew he knew nothing, that learning Torah and beer-making had in no way prepared him for what was coming, and he knew that without this woman he would have no chance to survive. He wasn't sure if he even wanted to survive. Some days he did and then suddenly it seemed pointless. Without his wife and his son, why would he want to? But now he had Roza to take care of. It was true, he needed her, with her understanding of the ways of the world, not to mention her skill with the sniper rifle, but he also knew she needed him, he wasn't sure why, but his instinct told him that he was after all a man and that still, in the insane upside down world where women wore trousers and killed Germans, counted for something, and he could see that when she looked at him, the way she listened to him when he spoke, with respect. Yes, strangely, despite her feelings about his yeshiva training, and he was in no doubt what she thought about that, she respected him as a person, and for that he was grateful.

This business about people from the Red Cross travelling around Europe sounded good when she said it to Mordechai but now she thought about it she wondered if it was fantasy. Why would the Germans let the Red Cross see what they were doing? And if they did, the Red Cross would surely know about the killing of half a million Warsaw Jews. No, none of it made sense. Well, if not the Red Cross, who?

That question was not to be answered for another four months. During that time, over the spring and early summer, they wandered aimlessly about eastern Poland. Roza consulted her maps every morning before they broke camp, but after a while Motti and Krystyna came to realise she wasn't leading them anywhere. She would say, when we get to so and so, or at such and such we'll do this or that, and they got to those places but nothing happened there and then they moved on, and on. Of course, they couldn't just walk into a town and ask questions, so they camped outside and Roza cut Motti's hair and beard which had a habit of growing and making him look more Jewish, and they dressed him like a Polish peasant, and sent him into town to look around. As they walked, Roza and Krystyna talked to him in Polish. In fact, Roza banned Yiddish altogether. She wanted Motti to think in Polish so he wouldn't get caught out in an unguarded moment. So when he went into a town he thought like a Pole, and very consciously put all thoughts about himself as a Jew from his mind. He didn't like it at first. His identity was of the greatest importance to him. But he knew they were right. As Mordechai Levinson he wouldn't last five minutes in a Polish inn.

What they couldn't do was to get Polish identity papers for him, so he had to avoid German patrols and checkpoints at all costs. Roza said she should go because she had Polish papers, but he wouldn't let her. He didn't know if he was more afraid for her or that she would run amok and kill someone, but that amounted to the same thing and she deferred to him the first time and he came back unscathed and the more he did it the less afraid she became.

Then one day he came back but he wasn't alone. Roza heard him approaching and as always she had one of the submachineguns cocked and ready. What confused her was not just that he had a strange man with him, but that they were talking to each other in Yiddish. As they approached, Roza challenged the stranger in German but he looked blankly at her. It was a test, but not a conclusive one. He looked anxious at two women pointing guns at him and speaking a language he heard a great deal but couldn't understand. It was hard to tell who was more scared, him or the women. Only Motti seemed unconcerned.

'Roza, Krystyna, it's alright. This is Tzvi, Tzvi Drobner.'

'How do you know?'

'How do I know? What kind of question is that? Because he told me.'

Well, Motti might be a bit stupid when it came to this kind of thing, but Roza could see the look she knew in his face in this man's also. Another yeshiva student. Whatever he was, he wasn't dangerous.

'Welcome Tzvi. My name is Roza Weksler, and this is Krystyna. She doesn't speak Yiddish.'

Roza stepped forward to shake this newcomer's hand, but he stood there, his own hands resolutely by his side.

'It's alright, I promise not to shoot you.'

Motti explained in Polish. 'Roza, Tzvi is very orthodox. He won't shake your hand.'

'Because I'm not orthodox?'

'No, because you're a woman.'

'What, is he afraid I'll be overcome by lust if I touch him?'

'No, he's afraid he might.'

Roza looked at him sceptically. 'No Mordechai, I don't think there's much danger of that. He looks half starved. I don't think he would have the strength.'

Krystyna sniggered. Tzvi looked blank. He could tell they were talking about him, and he could tell that they found him amusing, but other than that he was in the dark. Roza asked him to sit down and tell them about himself. While he did that Krystyna kept her weapon on her lap but it was so obvious he was one of them that she soon lost her fear. She couldn't understand a word he said so she wandered off to cook them all some food. She warmed to Tzvi when he removed from his greatcoat a loaf of rye bread and offered it to her.

Then he told them his story.

'I was in the square. By the way, this town is called Czyzew. There used to be a large Jewish community here, but the Germans took them to Warsaw. I don't know what happened to them after that.'

Roza wondered whether she should tell him but she decided not to interrupt.

'Well, I come into town sometimes, things I have to do for the group, and that was when I saw Mordechai here. I knew at once he was Jewish.'

Roza and Motti were both shocked at this information.

'How? We thought he looked like a Polish peasant.'

'He does, if he stands still and doesn't move his hands, but he was standing there, leaning against a wall, looking innocent enough, and he was stroking his side curls.'

'But I don't have any. Roza - I mean Comrade Weksler - cut them off for me.'

'Yes, I can see you don't have any. But that doesn't seem to stop you stroking them. It's a habit you have had all your life and you no longer need sidecurls in order to stroke them. You stood out a mile away.'

'Good God.'

'Well, no harm done. It was lucky I noticed and no-one else.'

'But I didn't see any soldiers in the town.'

'No, but they have spies and informers. Many people there will sell you to the Gestapo for a food parcel or a couple of bottles of vodka.'

Now that it was no longer important because Mordechai was safely back, Roza was more interested in what this man knew.

'Well, soldiers do come through the town from time to time, Germans and Lithuanians, and they're worse if that's possible. They haven't been here for a while but there are still the informers. I know who they are generally, but sometimes we get caught out. A month ago they got my friend Szmul. Still, we found out who the informers were and we paid them a visit.'

'A visit?'

'In this part of the country, my friend, that means we killed them. The locals know they will get a reward for informing on us but they also know the risk they run if they do that. It's the only thing they understand. It surprised them at first, Jews prepared to kill, but they seem to have got the hang of it now and we don't have too much trouble. That's not to say we walk around Czyzew freely but it certainly isn't as dangerous as it used to be. The townspeople turn a blind eye if they know what's good for them.'

Roza and Motti were trying to digest all of this but it was new to them and very strange.

'Tzvi, you keep talking about us and we. Who are you talking about?'

'I'm sorry, I should have told you, but it's not information I give without great care. We have, shall we say, a group.'

'A group? You mean partisans?'

'No no, not that. We have no weapons, well only a few we've come across by good fortune, but they are purely for self defence and thank God we have not yet had to use them, other than as I said, the occasional reprisal when we have had to kidnap an informer and take them into the forest. No, the group exists for one reason only, to survive. You see, it is entirely a Jewish group.'

Motti let out a whistling sound. 'You mean there is a group of survivors in the forest? Where? '

'Ah, that I can't tell you. It's not that I think you cannot be trusted, but it's a rule we have. You don't need to know, so you won't. Unless you decide to join us, of course.'

Roza ignored this idea for the moment.

'Tzvi, you said you have this group, I presume somewhere in the forest and you're right I don't need to know and I don't want to know. But what do you go into the town for?'

'Well, we sometimes risk buying food there, although we don't have money, except when we kill someone and then sometimes they have a little, or we have something of value to sell, and we buy food with that from someone we can trust. But mainly I go to the convent.'

'What?'

'The convent of St Agnes, in the middle of town. If we have a sick child, the nuns take them. That's what I was doing today. We have a child with a fever and we have no medicine. We have a doctor, in fact we even have a paediatrician who used to work at the children's hospital in Lublin, but without medicine there is little they can do. The child will have a better chance with the nuns.'

'And the nuns help you in this way?'

'Yes.'

But there was some hesitation in that yes, and Mordechai probed further.

'Well, they are happy to take a child from us. We know that it is not only to heal their body but their soul also.'

'What do you mean? Why does a child's soul need healing by Catholic nuns?'

'It's like this. Once the child is in the convent, the nuns can simply tell the authorities he is an orphan they found and took in. No-one asks any more questions than that. So the child stays there, and in time the nuns start praying with him and explaining how Jesus is the saviour and the Jews have got it completely wrong and must learn to love Christ and so on. The child is extremely vulnerable. We know we may never get him back once we give him to the convent. That is why we do it only in extreme need.'

'And their parents agree to this? '

'Mordechai, these children don't have parents. We have responsibility for them. We are their family now. And yes, it hurts, but in our hearts we believe it is better they should live in the convent than that they should die in the forest, and that one day, when this is all over, God willing, we will go and claim our children back in the name of their parents and their true faith.'

'But maybe they will want to stay there, in the convent. Maybe it will be too late to reclaim them.'

'Yes, maybe, we realise that. But tell me, what choice do we have? The nuns are good people.'

'I don't think so.'

'Yes Mordechai, they are. They have their beliefs and we have ours, and I don't blame them. And if one of these children survives, well, I trust in the decision we have made.'

'Do you truly believe that?'

'I try to.'

There was silence for a moment and at this point Krystyna interrupted with hot soup and rye bread. They all ate hungrily. Tzvi was the first to speak again.

'So, I think you have been considering what I said.'

'What's that?'

'Joining us. The more we are, the better our chance of survival as a group.'

'We would need to discuss that among ourselves. How can we contact you with our decision?'

'You can't. Mordechai, in two days' time, come into town again and stand where I found you today. Only don't tug on your sidelocks, remember. Tell me then. Meanwhile I will talk to the others, but I know they will agree. Except …'

'Except what?'

Tzvi glanced sideways at Krystyna. 'Well, it's a Jewish group. There is quite a lot of bad feeling there about the Poles. This lady would not be able to come with you. I'm sorry.'

The old woman had no idea what he was saying in Yiddish but she knew he was talking about her and since he was Jewish and so were Roza and Mordechai, she had a feeling about this. She could tell she was an outsider here, and without fully understanding why she began to be afraid. She needn't have been.

'Tzvi, if Krystyna can't come with, we're not going. In any case, I'm not going, because I have something I have to do. We're talking about Mordechai.'

'Me? If you're not going neither am I.'

'Don't be stupid Levinson. You're not attached to me. You don't owe me anything. Go if you want, go and survive.'

For the first time, Motti knew he didn't want to leave this woman. It was a feeling he had never had before, not even with his wife and he hadn't so far allowed himself to contemplate what it might mean, but even so, now she was talking about leaving him he knew that wasn't what he wanted.

'Roza, we have come this far together, all three of us.'

And here he smiled at Krystyna and without knowing what he was saying she felt better because she knew what he meant.

'Going with Tzvi is tempting of course, to be part of a Jewish family again, some kind of community, but you have to do this thing and, well, so do I. Let's see it through.'

'Excuse me Mordechai, would you mind me asking what this thing is that you and Roza have to do?'

'No I don't mind. We're looking for the Red Cross.'

When Motti said it like that, to a stranger, Roza knew it sounded ridiculous.

'The Red Cross? Why?'

'We have information we think they should be given. It may serve no purpose but even so, it's what we have decided to do.' Roza was grateful that he said it like that, we.

'I see. And where do you expect to find them?'

Motti shrugged his shoulders. 'We don't know.'

'I see. Well, if you have decided not to join our group, my friend, I may still, on this particular matter, be able to help you.'

13

Tzvi's group was affiliated to a Polish Zionist organisation, part of the Chovevei Zion, based in the Soviet Union. Their aim was to rescue Jews and keep them safe while they were trained in both agricultural and military skills, ready for the day when they would go to Palestine and build a Jewish home. No-one knew if that would ever be possible for these people, but it was their dream. The group had a static camp, deep in the forest, where they had cleared the trees and planted basic crops - potatoes mainly but also anything they could get seeds for that might take in the poor forest soil. They held classes, not just for the children but for the adults too, and they sang Hebrew songs round a campfire at night and kept alive the dream that they knew they might not live to see take shape. And they stood guard constantly, with the few weapons they had. They had no experience of battle, and in any case they couldn't even practise with their firearms because they couldn't spare the ammunition.

There were now more than a hundred and fifty souls in the camp, including a large number of children. In fact Tzvi sometimes thought it resembled a big kindergarten transplanted from a Jewish town into a Polish forest, with armed guards just to make it all the more unlikely.

When Tzvi had said he could put Roza in contact with the Red Cross he wasn't telling the whole truth, because he personally had never met anyone from the organisation, but he knew someone who had. The CZ, he knew, had connections, by a convoluted route though the American Joint Distribution Committee and their office in Geneva. The Joint was a large and very wealthy body with tentacles that spread throughout the world. Their money and their political power in Washington opened a lot of doors. It all seemed very unlikely here in the middle of Poland, but the link was there, and when he said he would help he meant it.

He thought Roza's obsession with the Red Cross was misplaced and futile but he could tell she wouldn't appreciate him saying that. He talked to Motti about it as they walked part-way back together and Motti said yes, well, you know how it is, she's got it into her head that it's how she apologises to her parents and her sister for not being there to die with them, and Tzvi nodded his head thoughtfully and understood. In any case, if either of them tried to stop her they knew it would be pointless. She would go on without Motti. She had already said that.

Tzvi had one last word of advice for him. 'Mordechai, I told you we wouldn't reveal the location of our camp to you.'

'Yes.'

'Well, think about it. You took me straight to yours.'

'Yes, but you're Jewish.'

Tzvi shook his head sadly. 'I wish I shared your faith in our brethren. Learn to trust no-one and you will live longer.'

'But surely …'

'No, learn to trust no-one. These are not normal times. I have seen Jews betray Jews to save their own lives. A futile effort, as it turns out, always, but still, people will do terrible things when they are put under impossible pressure. It's part of the Germans' tactics, to put people under pressure, remember that. Anyway, I hope you never have an occasion to learn about treachery but still, think about it, please.'

With that they shook hands warmly and agreed that they would meet in two days time for Tzvi to pass on news about his contacts.

Back at the camp Roza and Krystyna were arguing. Motti was shocked by this. It had never happened before, despite the terrible conditions they lived under. He let them exhaust themselves and Roza explained. The old woman wanted them to go to the Jewish camp. She would find somewhere in the first Polish village she came to and live out the war there. Roza explained that even if she was going to leave her to fend for herself, which she wasn't, in any case she had no intention of joining the group because she was going to find the Red Cross.

Motti had seen the woman's fear before, so she must have been thinking about this and come to the conclusion that it was time to make that sacrifice. It seemed that she had been trying to persuade Roza to do something that neither of them wanted her to do, so it had been a bit of a pointless argument. Still, it established or re-established loyalties.

Krystyna found food they didn't know they had and cooked what passed in that place for a feast. There was certainly nothing to celebrate so there could only be one other reason for her feeding them up. It was her own way of making the connection. Without food they were going nowhere, and without her, she knew, they wouldn't eat like this. Then, after the meal, Roza tried to persuade Mordechai to do something neither of them wanted him to do, to go to the camp on his own. It was another test. She spoke in Yiddish because this was strictly between them.

'You will be among your own people there. Think about that.'

'What? You're my own people, aren't you?'

'No, I'm not, I'm not a proper Jew, you know that.'

'No I don't. You think because you're not pious that you're not Jewish enough, but that means nothing.'

'Uhuh, but I don't think you would have said that before the war.'

'Well that was before the war and this is now and what's happened inbetween is the war. The Germans have changed the world for ever. They've changed what it means to be human. If we live, and that's a big if, we will never be able to see people the same way again. They've shown that humans can be less than human. They've destroyed my world, and yours, not only because they've murdered the people we loved but because they've shown it's possible to murder innocent people and get away with it. Those of us who survive, if we do, cannot go backwards from there. The Jewish life I led before was relevant to those times, but those times will never return. I have to think what's relevant to the future, and I take each person as I find them and what I find in you is, if you don't mind me being personal, a very fine woman, and a woman who is a daughter of Israel just as much as I am a son of Israel. You led a certain kind of life before because you were brought up that way, in a community that thought and behaved like that, and yes, that would have been quite alien to me, as if you were goyim, I admit that, but the new world we live in changes everything. To the Germans there is no difference between you, with your city ways and your Polishness, and me, the shtetl Jew. All they see is our Jewishness. Well, all I see is your Jewishness, and what I see I like.'

He stopped there. He thought he might have gone too far.

'And that's what you think, is it, Levinson?'

'Well, sort of.'

'In that case there's nothing more to say. How could there be? You've said quite enough already. So, you can go and meet your new friend and tell him we'll meet his contact then.'

'Right.'

'Right.'

That night they slept better than they had for a long time. It seemed like an end to their wanderings. That wasn't sensible, because how could it be? In fact it was more likely to be the beginning of more wanderings but still, now they seemed at least to have some purpose to their existence in the forest.

The next day the sun shone, weakly but at least it tried. The snow showed signs of melting and there was a little hope in the air. For the first time they had nowhere to go. Motti wasn't due to meet Tzvi until tomorrow, so they had a day of rest and, when Roza said this, they realised suddenly that it was indeed the Sabbath, at least for her and Motti if not for Krystyna, and Motti recited the morning service for the Sabbath. He was shocked to learn that there were bits he couldn't remember. Well, that was alright. It felt like the Sabbath at least, and in the afternoon he did what Jewish men do on Saturday afternoon, he slept. When he woke he wondered where he was because his sleep had taken him back to his previous life and finding himself in his new one made him sorry. None of this had gone away and the Sabbath itself was only a dream and his beloved wife and their son were a dream and they were gone for ever and he had to face the reality of the present but he didn't want to. He was minded to go back on his promise to Roza and go with Tzvi to the camp, to be part of a Jewish community again, but then he looked at her face and he knew he wasn't going to do that. They were hard times and such times require tough decisions. He hadn't been able to help his wife, to save her life, but he would save this woman's life if God granted him the strength to do so.

The evenings were drawing out now and before it got completely dark they went for a walk, which felt strange because walking was something they had all done more than enough of already, but this was different, this was a stroll through the trees, looking for the first time at it all not as something to be got through but for what it was, a thing of beauty, untouched by the war, and they said some foolish things about coming back afterwards, when the war was over and walking here together. Strangely, it never occurred to them to add a rider, to the effect that the Allies would have to win for that to happen. Perhaps in their minds the war wasn't something that was won or lost but something that was simply survived and had a natural end.

As they walked Roza slipped back into Yiddish. It felt more intimate. She told Motti about her home in Warsaw, about her mother and father, and her sister and all the aunts and uncles and cousins and Motti got completely confused as to who all these people were but even so she created in his head an image of a life that, as irreligious as it obviously was, was filled with Jewish family feeling. Roza came to see, as she talked, that all her father's attempts to bring up a secular family outside the traditions had been a failure. Roza knew she felt the connection every bit as much as Mordechai did. Now she knew that her rejection of her Jewishness meant nothing. Was it what the Germans had done that made her see it, or was it perhaps Motti? They had said she could not escape her background, and he showed her that she didn't want to, and in the end the result was the same.

As they walked the temperature fell and Roza instinctively clung to him in a way that forced him to put an arm round her and it felt very strange to him but it also felt good. He prayed that his wife would forgive him not only for doing it but for liking it.

She felt his apprehension. 'I'm sorry. Is this alright for two people who aren't married?'

'Comrade Weksler, it is my duty as a member of this partisan unit to protect its commander, and that is all I'm doing.'

'Excellent, Comrade. And since you are in the mood to obey orders, please hold me a little tighter.'

And early the next morning Motti set off for Czyzew. It was a two-hour walk, and Tzvi had warned him not to be late. He would wait in the square no more than five minutes to avoid attracting attention. Despite the need for speed, Motti didn't forget Roza's training. As he crossed each road, or even a dirt track that might be enough for a German patrol to use, he waited and watched, only moving when he was quite sure, at least as sure as it's possible to be and still be in a hurry. He carried the pistol in his coat pocket, but he wasn't convinced about using it again and in any case even if he didn't appreciate it Roza knew that one shtetl Jew with a pistol against a Wehrmacht patrol with automatic weapons wasn't much of a contest, in fact it wasn't a contest at all. The only way to survive the Germans, she told him, was not to meet them.

He got to town twenty minutes early and out of breath, and even Motti knew that an out-of-breath Jew hanging around the market square was likely to attract attention, so he sauntered as best he could trying to look innocent, which wasn't easy because sauntering wasn't something he had a lot of experience of in his previous life, and he had always in any case been innocent so it was difficult for him to avoid looking like someone who was trying not to look guilty and what was he guilty of anyway? Being Jewish? Only in this insane world could that be a crime, let alone a crime punishable by death without trial, let alone by a foreign government.

'You see those two gendarmes over there?' Motti swung round. It was Tzvi.

'Well they've been watching you for the past five minutes. Luckily, I've been watching them watching you, so even if you don't know you're in danger I do. Walk behind me and don't look back.'

Not looking back was something Motti was getting used to. Tzvi led him away from the square and they stood in a dark alley and waited in case the gendarmes had followed them. They hadn't.

'Just a bit curious, I expect, or bored. They've probably found someone more interesting to pick on already. Look, we can't talk here. Follow me again but don't look like you're following me. Think you can do that?'

'Yes.'

'Good, let's go.'

There was only one place Tzvi could safely take Motti in the town. The convent. Motti hesitated at the door. A nun in full sail stood in the doorway and beckoned him in but his feet wouldn't move. He was transfixed by fear.

'Look, Mordechai, either come in and do this properly, or stay out there and take your chances with the Polish police. It's time to decide, and by the way, this is Sister Teresa and she doesn't bite.'

Motti wanted to believe that but all his instincts told him otherwise. Behind the nun's head he could see a larger than life cross with a larger than life Jesus on it and he averted his eyes in case an evil spirit should find its way into his soul. He still couldn't walk through the door though, and in the end Tzvi laid a large hand on his coat and dragged him in. Sister Teresa smiled but said nothing. Another backward country Jew, she thought, and sighed to herself. This was none of her business.

She said nothing at all as she led them across a quadrangle and down a long cloister. Nuns looked at the small group and wondered and Motti could feel them watching but he was trying not to let them catch his eye. That way, he knew, they would be able to cast their spell on him.

They came finally to a large oak door. Sister Teresa knocked and waited, then they entered.

'Ah, our dear friend Mr Drobner.'

'Reverend Mother, this is Mordechai Levinson, the man I told you about.'

Motti shuffled his feet and looked at the carpet.

'I see, Well, Mr Levinson, welcome to the Convent of St Agnes. Let me introduce you. This gentleman is Herr Max Reiniger, of the International Red Cross in Geneva. I believe you have something you wish to say to him.'

14

An hour later Motti was walking with Tzvi through the forest and he was trying to understand what had happened. Max Reiniger had been very pleasant and had even offered Motti a cigar, which of course he refused. The Mother Superior had offered him tea, which he similarly refused. They were very friendly, but it wasn't a friendliness that Motti was used to, it was the friendliness of people who you knew were not your friends.

Tzvi translated from Yiddish into Polish and the Mother Superior translated from Polish into German, and Motti wondered who this man really was who only spoke the language of his enemies and whether what he said meant the same thing after it had been translated twice. He trusted Tzvi, of course, but who knew what the nun repeated?

Herr Reiniger had looked grave while all this went on and when it was told to him in his own language he looked even more grave and made all the correct noises and tutted, as if tutting is the kind of response you would expect to mass murder. Motti felt more and more uncomfortable, as if these people didn't want him to be there. It wasn't until after it was all over and Sister Teresa had shown them out of the door back onto the street that he realised that all the time he was talking the Swiss had not made any notes.

'You're disappointed, aren't you?'

'Well, yes, I suppose so. I don't really know what he thought.'

'Well look, he's Swiss German, the only kind of Swiss the Germans will give a pass to in the occupied countries, and even then he's only allowed to go where they take him and he's only allowed to see what they show him and when he gets back to Geneva he will write a report and someone else will read it and then, if my guess is correct, it will be filed. What you told him today is probably not news to him or his masters in Switzerland. The liquidation of the Warsaw Ghetto is an inconvenient fact, for sure, but this is war and the Swiss are not going to make a lot of noise about it, I'm afraid.'

'But isn't the Red Cross independent of the state?'

'Yes, I believe it's an independent body but they will do what is convenient for their government in the end. In our camp we have a man who used to be an international lawyer. I have discussed this with him and he says I am to tell you this. I'm sorry. What will you tell Roza?'

He meant how will you let her down gently.

'Well, she has been a woman with a mission up until now but without this, as pointless as you might say it was always likely to be, she has nothing. I really don't know how she will come to terms with it, what she will do with herself, where she will go.'

'And wherever it is, will you go with her?'

'Yes, I think so. We seem to be tied to each other.'

'Well, that is something at least.'

'It is?'

'Yes, two people coming together is always a reason to celebrate, even in these terrible times.'

Motti stopped and looked at him. 'No, I think you misunderstand. It's not like that.'

'Really? Are you sure?'

'Well, yes.'

'And Roza?'

'What about her?'

'Is she sure?'

Motti had to admit, if only to himself, that if he really considered that question he didn't know the answer. In another time and another place perhaps it would be different, but this was here and now and Roza was in mourning for her family and he was in mourning for his, only neither of them had been able to sit shiva for their loved ones and mourn properly, they had been thrown together and they were clinging to each other like bits of flotsam after a shipwreck and despite all of this God saw that they were a man and a woman and he did what he so often does in these situations because what happens between a man and a woman is the way the world continues, no matter what the interruptions and obstacles.

They walked on in silence for a while and then Tzvi put his hand on Motti's arm.

'Mordechai, stop for a moment.'

'Yes?'

'Look, let's stop here. Sit down, I want to talk to you.'

'Alright.'

They found a fallen branch to sit on and Motti waited.

'Look, I hear what you say about Roza, and I believe she is a women who could, if she has a task to occupy her, come through this reasonably whole.'

'Right.'

'No, I'll go further than that. I think she could achieve a great deal.'

'I see.'

'And you could help her. You could help each other.'

'You think so?'

'Yes.'

'But excuse me Tzvi, what are you talking about? Do you have something in mind?'

'I do.'

'Alright, tell me.'

'No, I want you to do something for me. I want you to persuade Roza to come to our camp. There is someone I want her to meet.'

'Who?'

'I'm sorry. I wish I could explain, but I can't.'

'Are you going to explain to Roza?'

'No.'

'You're just going to say come and meet someone but I'm not going to tell you what it's about?'

'Yes.'

'You don't give much away, do you?'

'No.'

'I see.'

'No, you don't. Mordechai, I wouldn't be doing this if it wasn't important. This business over the Red Cross, I knew it would come to nothing, but I did it because I want Roza, and you, to do something, something that will really matter, make a difference. I have talked to people in our group about you and they want to meet you. Put something to you that I'm not at liberty to discuss, not until you know the whole story. Look, you said it yourself, Roza has nowhere to go now. Well, we can give her somewhere, a reason to live, to stop all this pointless wandering.'

'I see. Is it going to be dangerous?'

'Yes. Are you telling me what you're doing now isn't dangerous? Anyway, what does it mean? You and I are alive because, depending on your religious perspective, we have been chosen for life, this far anyway. God could, if you don't mind me sounding flippant, change his mind about that. Well, here we are alive when so many are dead. What are we going to do, just say thank you and goodbye, or are we going to consider the possibility that there is a reason for being saved? Can you believe in that possibility?'

Motti considered the question. It wasn't one that had occurred to him so far, amidst all the destruction and death, but it was one that appealed to something in him.

'Alright, you know how to persuade me. But can you persuade Roza?'

'Not me, my friend, us. I need your help.'

'I'm not sure I can do that. It's not for me to push Roza one way or the other.'

'You care about her, don't you?'

'Mm, yes, I care about her, but perhaps caring excludes taking someone into more danger.'

'Mordechai, look around you. You are in the middle of a war of annihilation. You live from one day to the next. There is no more danger than this, believe me, but you have all this danger without the possibility of achieving anything. My proposition is that you accept the same level of risk but this time for a purpose, with the possibility of doing some good. That, I suspect, is what you and I can help your Roza to see.'

And so they walked back to the camp to do this thing, whatever it was. As soon as they approached they could see something was wrong. Roza had a submachine gun pointed at them as they expected but they also expected to see Krystyna with a weapon in her hand but instead she was sitting against a tree ignoring them. Roza put her weapon down.

'What's the matter, what is it?'

'It's Krystyna. There is a problem.'

'What?'

'Come and see.'

They went to the tree and saw the old woman was obviously in pain. Her left arm was cradled in her right and a rag was wrapped round her hand. Gently, Roza removed the cloth. What they saw was a badly swollen hand, discoloured and oozing pus from an open wound.

'What happened?'

'She cut herself preparing food.'

'Yes, but not like this.'

'No, it happened a week ago, apparently, and since then it became infected. She said nothing about it but it has obviously turned septic and what was an ordinary cut is now a major problem. She's in a lot of pain and she's frightened.'

The men could see that. Krystyna was visibly shaking and she avoided looking at them. What they didn't know was that in the partisan unit an injury like this, an incurable wound because they had no medicine, was a death sentence. She had kept it from them until now but that was no longer possible.

'Tzvi, can you help her at your camp?'

'I'm sorry, this is bad. We have no sulphonamide, which is the only thing that would help.'

'What about the convent? She's a Catholic.'

'Yes, but they only take children.'

'But surely, a woman in need?'

'No, they won't.'

Motti and Roza thought this was uncharitable. They didn't say so but Tzvi could tell what they were thinking and found himself in the strange position of having to defend the nuns.

'Look, if they took in everyone in the town who got hurt or sick they would be running a hospital, and they don't have the medical expertise or the medicines or surgical facilities. I can't do anything about it. That's how it is.'

He took them both to one side and spoke in Yiddish.

'Look, if something isn't done soon this is going to spread and she will die. Out here she has no chance. I've seen it before.'

'But what other option is there?'

Tzvi hesitated, but in the end he said it. 'Amputation.'

Roza looked at Motti and he looked at her and they both knew that was impossible, but of course the impossible can become possible depending on how desperate the situation is. They knew that too. They just didn't want to admit it.

It was way beyond any powers of imagination Motti might possess, but Roza had seen it before, with the partisans.

'Alright, say we do it, what is the chance she will survive?'

'Some. Without it, none. It's a stark choice, not a choice at all really. We must ask her.'

They did, and Krystyna's eyes opened widely when Roza said it but then there was a sense of relief, that it was a terrible thing they had to do but it was at least a possibility of life, and she realised suddenly that she wanted to live. She said yes.

There was no time to lose. Motti banked up the fire to get it as hot as possible and they put a knife in the base to sterilise it, the same knife that had caused the wound, because it was the sharpest one they had. Roza found a full bottle of vodka and before she made Krystyna drink from it she took a large draught herself, followed by both of the men. They boiled cloths in a pot over the fire while Krystyna drank and they waited for the alcohol to have its effect but it seemed the Polish cook could take her drink and she remained sober, so the other three took some more on the basis that if the patient wasn't going to be drunk they needed to be.

Motti did it. Then they took a cloth from the pot and soaked it in vodka and wrapped that round the stump of the finger in an attempt to prevent further infection, and then with nothing more to say, they each fell more or less where they were and slept from exhaustion. From time to time one of them woke and got up to check on the old woman. It was difficult to tell how she was other than alive because she was mumbling to herself, whether asleep or awake it was hard to say. If she was going to come through this it would be through her own toughness rather than anything they could do for her.

She did come through. It was touch and go for the next two days but on the third morning they woke to find her making breakfast. She looked pale, but then she always looked pale, which had as much to do with malnourishment as her operation. She had dressed the wound herself and tied it surprisingly neatly. Krystyna was going to be a hard one to kill.

Only now did Roza question why Tzvi was still with them, rather than returning to his own people. While they waited to see if Krystyna was going to survive he and Motti related the conversation with the Red Cross representative, Herr Reiniger. She listened silently and at the end she shrugged her shoulders and said nothing about it.

'Actually, I came to talk to you.'

'Yes? What about?'

Motti felt less sure about it now. Over the past two days he had put it out of his mind and hoped that Tzvi had done the same, but he hadn't. Tzvi had a job to do.

'I want to ask you to do something for me.'

'Well, you helped us to save Krystyna's life, so I owe you that.' She forgot to mention that he had also set up the meeting at the convent.

'Let's sit down. Mordechai too, and Krystyna, if you wouldn't mind.'

They obeyed him. Motti knew what for and was worried. Krystyna was curious. Roza wasn't. Whatever it was, she couldn't see that it would be of much concern to her.

'Well?'

'Well, I have a question.'

'Yes?'

'What are you going to do now? ' He spoke in Polish, and translated the few words Motti couldn't understand. In any case, Motti knew what he was saying.

'If you won't mind me saying this, Tzvi, I fail to see why you would want to know that.'

'No, of course you wouldn't. But I have a reason, a very good reason. Roza, I don't know how you feel now about what you might be able to do for the Jews of Poland. Probably you think there is nothing.'

'Yes, that about sums it up. I had an idea, a foolish one as it happens, and now I have none. It's not my job to do any-thing, other than survive this if I can.'

'Unless ... unless there is, after all, something you could do.'

'Like what?'

'I can't say.'

She stood up. 'Well, in that case it's been a short conversation.'

'No, no, Roza, please, sit down, hear me out. If I can't say it's because I'm not permitted to. You see there are people who know about you and they have asked me to ask you to work for them.'

'Me? What about Mordechai?'

'Yes, both of you.'

'And Krystyna?'

'Her too. She can go with you.'

'Go? Go where?'

'Well, first I need you to meet these people. They can tell you the things I can't. Please, you will have to trust me. I don't know because the fewer people who know such things the safer you will be. By the way, I forgot to mention, there is an element of risk involved.'

'How much?'

'Quite a lot.'

'Good, I'll come. Krystyna, Mordechai, get packed, we're moving.'

'Well, not so fast. I'm afraid Krystyna will not be able to come to the camp for the meeting. Security you see, I'm sorry.'

'OK. Krystyna, you will be alright for one night?'

'No.'

'What? Why not?'

'Rozinska, you do not fool me. I know you won't come back.'

Roza was shocked. It hadn't occurred to her that the old woman might not trust her. 'Krystyna, I promise, we will be coming back.'

'Roza, look, these are your people, and I think when you go there, to their camp, you will find yourself at home and you will forget about me.'

'No, that's not true. Please, listen to what I'm saying. I give you my promise we will return.'

'Your promise? What are promises worth now?'

That left little to say. They sat in silence and then Roza said the only thing that was left.

'Tzvi, I'm sorry. I won't leave Krystyna. If she can't come with us, I won't be going.'

He had nothing to reply to this. He knew his group would not accept anyone who wasn't Jewish. It was Motti who spoke. From his shirt pocket he removed a piece of rag, and this he unwrapped. From it he took the mezuzah.

'Krystyna, you have worked in Jewish houses. Do you know what this is?'

'Yes. You put them on the doorposts.'

'That's right. It's called a mezuzah. This one comes from the front door of my parents' home. I removed it from the burned wreckage after they were taken by the Germans. It is the only thing I have left in the world. When I removed it I made a promise to God that if I live I would fix it to the door-post of my own home once more. I think you can imagine how precious this is to me.'

The others all looked at it as if it were the most holy relic left in the world, which to him it was.

'Well, I want you to take it and look after it for me.'

'Me?'

'Yes. Take it, go on.'

She cradled it in her good hand and looked in awe.

'Now you know we are coming back.'

15

The journey to the Jewish camp was an awkward one. Motti and Roza wanted to ask questions, Tzvi wouldn't answer them. He tried to walk a little ahead of them, ostensibly to lead the way but in practice to avoid conversation. As they walked behind him they fell to talking among themselves but as always they were watchful because even here in the forest you never knew who was watching you. They weren't worried only about the Germans but the NSZ too because they knew now that they could be just as dangerous when it suited them. Even Motti carried a weapon, though Roza had little belief in his military prowess. Fair enough, he had killed two Ukrainians, but from his story he had the advantage over them. On the other hand, for a shtetl Jew that always had to be impressive.

Tzvi she couldn't make out. He had all the hallmarks of the pious Jew, except for the facial furniture which, like Mordechai, had had to go, but he was sharp. He told them a little of his story. He had of course studied in a yeshiva, a prestigious one in Vilna, but then his father had taken him into their timber business and he had learned how to deal with people, people in the outside world. He spoke Polish and Russian and he had an air of self-confidence. Whether that would go far if they were jumped she didn't know, but on the other hand if that happened how much of a fight were any of them going to put up, her included?

She had killed from a distance with her rifle, she didn't remember how many times, but she was conscious of her sex and with good reason she doubted her ability to take on an angry German trooper. She wanted to be out of this, to be normal again and get married and raise children and even perhaps keep a Jewish home, but she also wanted to kill, needed to kill. An eye for an eye. Well, Roza had a deep inherited belief in revenge, and it would take many dead Germans before she would be satisfied. She wondered too if she would ever be satisfied, or if she would have to go on killing until she herself was killed. Perhaps that was it, she needed to die. She was confused. Anyway, when the time came there was unlikely to be a choice. She would kill any Germans she could, and she would die when her time came, and when one ended and the other began was in God's hands. She smiled to herself when she thought that, about God, and wondered what her father would have said if he heard her. Well, he couldn't hear her now, and he was the reason why she was here. She knew that to think about God was, as he used to say, childish, but she watched Mordechai and she felt a tinge of jealousy that he had a relationship with this God that her father had scoffed at and she wondered who was better off with their beliefs, notwithstanding that Mordechai was alive and her father wasn't, which she knew had nothing to do with it but still, she couldn't help but notice the fact.

And she was moved by the way he gave his mezuzah to Krystyna. He didn't know they were going to come back because, yes, they intended to, but in this war intentions didn't always count for a lot. What if something happened and he didn't find his way back? Well, it was just a mezuzah for all that, and it wasn't the most important thing in the world which is, as everyone knows, life.

Motti was thinking about the mezuzah too. He knew it had been a grand gesture and now he regretted it. It was more important to him, he realised now, than whatever it was they were following Tzvi for, and he wondered why he had done it, and as a result of wondering he came to the conclusion that it was for Roza and then he wondered why Roza was so important and he couldn't decide if it was what she represented or who she was for herself. As they walked through the twilight chill he recited the evening service to himself and he searched for answers but found none.

He fingered the trigger of the machine gun they had given him and wondered how he had got here, walking with these people through a Polish forest, holding a weapon that meant only one possible thing, death, the antithesis of the Jewish ethos to preserve life. He wanted to throw it away and put himself in God's hands and then he thought about Rabbi Gimpel and his sons, praying for salvation by the side of a ditch full already of bodies and dying anyway but of course it wasn't salvation they had been praying for, not a physical salvation anyway but a moral one, that they would be accepted into heaven because they were going to die, Rabbi Gimpel knew that, even if his children were too young to understand just what it meant. And the children of Warsaw? Motti didn't know how many of them there had been, because he had never been there, never been to any city, but his imagination told him it was very many and a part of him wondered if the Germans killed the children as well, if that was really possible, but then he remembered the rabbi's sons and he knew that of course it was possible and it had happened. To kill like the Germans and the Ukrainians did, he knew now, you had to abandon any concept of people as human, and once you did that it wouldn't matter whether they were men or women or children or even babies.

The first sign that they were approaching the camp was when Tzvi signalled with his hand to an unseen person on the brow of a small hill and Roza realised that the security the Armia Ludowa employed was used here too, a circle of watchers placed far out from the camp, and she knew there would be an inner circle and that they would have some way to signal to each other in the event of an attack. It was the natural thing to do. She doubted that they had the firepower or the training that the AL had but at least these people would have some warning that they were about to die.

Twenty minutes later they were there, and the first thing Roza noticed, because for no good reason she had been expecting something resembling a partisan camp, was the children. There were young ones running around and playing, older ones involved in light work, even women carrying babies. As they worked their way through the tents of all shapes, colours and sizes, people stopped what they were doing and greeted them warmly, some in Polish, most in Yiddish, but some also in Hebrew and when they called shalom Roza and Motti self-consciously said shalom back and it sounded strange coming from their own lips but it also sounded good. Tzvi stopped by a fire and invited them to wait there and warm themselves. A girl of perhaps twelve brought them mugs of tea and chatted to them unselfconsciously and they answered her questions and it seemed so unreal, being with their own people again, that what came into Roza's mind was the prediction Krystyna had made and she knew the old woman had been right, that the pull would be a strong one, but she was also wrong because Roza's loyalty was unwavering, even in the face of all this.

To Motti the sound of people chattering in Yiddish brought joy and sadness and he looked at them as if his wife would walk out of the crowd carrying their son but he knew that was fantasy as much as he hoped for it but he remembered that he had buried them with his own hands and had said the prayer for the dead over their graves and they were now in heaven. He sat and wept and Roza came and put her arms round him and wept too and nothing was said between them but nothing needed to be.

'Mordechai, Roza, if you are alright, please come with me.'

Tzvi understood why they were affected like this. It had happened to him too when he arrived at the camp. It happened to everyone. You closed your heart to all emotions because there was no other way, but this brought it all back. It had taken him weeks to adjust to being with his own people again.

Rosa and Mordechai followed him to a large tent, the kind army commanders used in the field, only whose army this one had been stolen from was anybody's guess. It was gloomy inside and it took a few seconds for their eyes to adjust. Seated round a table were three people, who rose simultaneously and smiled simultaneously in genuine pleasure at meeting their guests. A fourth man sat in the corner and did not rise.

'Mordechai Levinson, Roza Weksler, please allow me to introduce our commander David Berman, this is Sonja Alter and this gentleman is Captain Michael Jacobs, from the American Joint Distribution Committee. Oh and that is Feliks Ziegielbojm.'

The others sat while David Berman spoke. 'Tzvi, Roza and I need no introduction. Roza, come here.'

They hugged long and hard and Roza cried audibly and no-one thought it strange although they wondered how these two people knew each other. David gave her time to compose herself.

'Roza was a student of mine at the art school in Warsaw, not, I might add, a very good one, but even so Roza I would not have recommended you give up drawing for this.' He pointed at the submachine gun in her hands.

'I daresay my story resembles your own, Mr Berman.'

'David, please, this is not the school and I am no longer a teacher.'

Roza wondered how a mild-mannered art teacher had metamorphosed into a resistance leader, but there would perhaps be an opportunity for explanations another time. What she knew for now was that whatever the reason for their visit, whatever David Berman had brought her here for, she would give it her wholehearted consideration. She sat next to Mordechai and waited for an explanation.

'Roza, Mordechai, I'm going to let Captain Jacobs here explain why we asked you to come and see us.'

Captain Jacobs was obviously Jewish but he was like no-one Motti had ever met. Even Roza struggled to equate him with the secular, cosmopolitan Jews she had known in the capital. He was, like everyone, in civilian clothes, but there was something military in his bearing, and also something, a kind of self-assurance that spoke of a very different culture, as far from eastern Europe as it was possible to be and still be Jewish.

He smiled at them both, but he smiled perhaps more at Roza than Motti. He spoke in Polish but his accent made it hard at least for Motti to follow.

'You people probably wonder why David here introduced me as Captain Jacobs. I hold that rank in the United States Army. My mother is Polish and my father is German. They got out from Berlin in 1933, as soon as Hitler came to power. They saw the signs in time, thank God. I was twenty two when we came to the US, and I already spoke Polish and German fluently of course, but now, naturally, my English is pretty good and so when I joined up I was approached pretty quickly by the Intelligence Corps for this work.'

He waited for them to overcome their surprise. 'I'm a serving officer in Army Intelligence, yes, but David said I'm with the Joint, and that's true too. The Army has become increasingly aware, through the Red Cross and other sources, of war crimes committed by the Germans and their allies, especially the Ukrainians and the Lithuanians. My assignment was originally to work with partisan units to attempt to learn more about the death camps.'

Motti and Roza blinked in unison and tried to absorb the idea of death camps. There was a lot they didn't know.

'Well, after my first report back it became apparent that the Allies can do very little at this time to prevent the killing, in fact I'm afraid there is nothing at all they can do, as much as we wish there were. There will come a time when those responsible will be called to account. We are going to win this war and the guilty will be made to pay for their crimes. My president himself has promised this, and so has Prime Minister Churchill.'

Roza's head was swimming. This man was some kind of angel. Motti followed some of what he said but even the bits he understood he didn't understand. This was coming from a world he knew nothing about. He saw, though, how Roza reacted, and he was glad.

'Captain Jacobs, I know I understand little of how these things work, but if you are in the Army how can you also be with this other organisation?'

'The Joint? Well, that involved some string-pulling in high places. You see, once I started reporting back to my superiors about the facts on the ground in Poland, people started asking questions about doing something to help. At the moment the Russians are carrying the major burden of the war, but the western Allies are preparing for something very big. I don't know myself what, or when it will happen, but it will be big, that much I know. All of this precludes any possibility of saving Jews now. The official Allied policy is to put a hundred percent of their effort into winning the war. That way there is at least a chance of saving some lives. Diverting resources to saving those lives now would have a negative impact on the overall war effort and it has been decided at the highest level that that is not going to happen.'

Roza almost spat her words at him. 'That's going to be too late. There isn't going to be anyone left to save.'

'Miss Weksler, please, I am a Captain, which as you may know is a lowly rank. I happen to feel the way you do. I am an American but many of my family didn't make it out. We don't know their fate but we can be just about certain that they are now dead. I promise you, I am on your side.'

He smiled to say he forgave her outburst, and she apologised.

'This brings me to my present mission, which involves you two people. I have heard a little about you from our friend Tzvi, the little you have told him, but there are some things I don't understand, which you might explain if you would be so kind.'

How could they refuse such politeness?

'Mr Levinson, I hear you killed four German soldiers.'

'Well, that's not quite true. There were only two of them, and I believe they were Ukrainian, not German. And an officer, who isn't dead apparently, through no fault of mine.'

'Well, that's still pretty good for a ... I mean ...'

'What you mean, sir, is for a shtetl Jew.'

'Well, with respect, it's not something I have come across before.'

'Well you have come across it now.'

'And do you think you could do it again? I mean kill, if you had to?'

Motti felt the weight of the weapon in his hands and asked himself the same question, the question he had been asking since he met the partisans.

'Yes, I believe so, if there was a good reason.'

'Isn't there always a good reason to kill Nazis?'

'Nazis?' Motti didn't know the term.

'I mean Germans.'

'Captain Jacobs, you might be right. I have done it before and yes, I suppose I could do it again. As to whether there is always a reason to kill, that is a matter I have yet to come to a decision on. In my religion ...'

'Excuse me, I think you forget ...'

Motti had forgotten. This man claimed to be Jewish but he was an American soldier and whatever that meant it meant he wasn't like Motti, not that kind of Jewish.

'Well let's say for now that yes, if you needed me to pull this trigger I could do it.'

'Thank you. And you, Miss Weksler, there is just one thing I am unclear on.'

'Yes Captain?'

'David, please. Well, I understand you were until recently a member of a partisan unit.'

'That is correct, a company of the Armia Ludowa.'

'Yes. They are a Communist force, are they not?'

'Yes. So?'

'Well, I'm sorry, but I have to ask. Would you consider yourself to be a Communist?'

'Why? What difference does it make? '

'To my superiors back in the United States, rather a lot, I'm afraid.'

In truth she had never even considered the question. She had joined the company by chance, and she had accepted its ethos without much thought, but if she did think about it, no, she had no commitment to that ethos. On the other hand, she felt a growing resentment that this man was asking her questions as if she had to prove something, and for what? Who had asked her to come to this place? Who wanted her to do something? On the other hand, although he looked at her grimly now, while he waited for her answer, he also had a look, something in his eyes, that said help me out here, say no.

'No. I'm not a Communist.'

'Good, then just one or two more questions, if you wouldn't mind? What was it you did with the partisans? Were you some kind of camp follower?'

'No, Captain Jacobs, I was not a camp follower as you call it, I was second in command.'

Before he could open his mouth in response to this Feliks Ziegielbojm in the corner spoke for the first time.

'You mean you were the commander's mistress.'

No-one was prepared for what happened next. Before anyone had a chance to realise it, Roza was on her feet. The submachine gun was cocked and she had this man's coat collar in one hand and the other hand held the weapon against his head. The cold hard metal pressed painfully into his skull and with her thumb she pointedly released the safety catch. People jumped to their feet but no-one moved from where they were.

'Look here, schmuck, it's several days since I killed anyone and normally I only kill Germans but in your case I am prepared to make an exception. While you have been living a nice quiet life in this holiday camp in the woods I have been fighting and watching my comrades die. I have, as you have probably noticed, taken extreme exception to that remark of yours, but I am prepared to overlook it, which gives you two choices. Either you apologise or I blow your brains out. Don't rush, because I'm not going anywhere. Think about it and let me know when you're ready.'

The sweat was pouring down his forehead and Roza was pretty sure he had wet himself. She was angry but she wasn't quite that far gone, and she prayed he would back down because she didn't know how to.

'I'm sorry.'

'What? I don't think everyone here heard you.'

'I'm sorry.'

'Well, you're stupid but you're intelligent enough, on this occasion, to stay alive. I advise you, though, to keep this little incident in your mind, should our paths cross again.'

She flicked the safety catch to on, and everyone in the tent breathed again. They sat down in relief. It was then that she noticed her old teacher, David Berman, had remained where he was in his seat. He didn't look worried. In fact he smiled.

'Michael, I believe we have found your woman.'

'Yes, David, I think you're right.' He smiled too and replaced his pistol in its holster. He hadn't realised he had removed it.

'Miss Weksler, I believe it is time to let you in on why we asked you and Mr Levinson to have this little chat. If you wouldn't mind, I should like to take you for a walk around the camp. Would you follow me please?'

16

The camp was the entire Jewish population of Poland in microcosm. Here a tailor sat on his workbench and sewed a pair of trousers, his hands in fingerless gloves in a vain attempt to fend off the cold. There a group of women baked bread and chatted to each other in Yiddish and laughed at some joke. A class of children was getting an outdoor lesson from a young man who had neither blackboard nor school books to help him, but seemed undaunted by that lack. There was even a yeshiva. Four youths in yarmulkas and side locks stood at makeshift desks and followed the reading of a rabbi, apparently oblivious either to the natural world around them or the danger of their situation.

David Berman smiled happily as each one, as he passed, looked up from what they were doing and said something in greeting or waved. Despite all that was happening in the wider world he was, they could see, a happy man, and these people were happy as a result. They all had a terrible tale to tell, Roza knew, like her and like Mordechai, but here they allowed themselves to be content with the present. They had no prospect of getting out of the forest, they knew nothing of the progress of the war or whether there was a chance of a life after it, but they had created this other world in which none of that mattered. Who could know what each man, woman and child thought as they lay down to sleep at night, when their past came back to haunt their sleep, but that was between them and their individual god.

'Well, what do you think of our shtetl? Everyone here is able to be whatever they want, whatever they were before ... before whatever has happened to them. I can see you are impressed. Mordechai, perhaps you would like to join the shiur Rabbi Horowitz is about to start?'

Motti thought about that and yes, it would have been easy, but no, it was wrong. He stopped and the others stopped with him. 'Mr Berman, yes, I am impressed by what you are doing here, but I don't think you brought us to the camp to show off or for me to join your 'yeshiva'. With respect, sir, I would be pleased to hear what your real reason was.'

'You are no fool, Mordechai, and I have no intention of wasting your time. It's the children.'

Roza and Motti looked around them. There were children in the ersatz school, and more ran around playing while yet others accompanied their surrogate mothers.

'You see, almost none of these children have parents. They have lost their mothers and these women have lost their children and somehow, when they come here, they adopt each other and make families, because that is what we all need, a family, and it works, in a way.'

'So?'

'I said in a way. It's time for me to tell you exactly why I asked you to come here. Please, come back to my tent and we can talk better.'

They sat down again, the same group, with the notable absence of Feliks Ziegielbojm. David Berman didn't speak, though, Captain Jacobs did.

'Mordechai, Roza, my mission with the American Joint Distribution Committee is very specific. It's to save as many Jewish children as I can. In this I have the full backing of the US government and my secondment to the Joint is indefinite, with the approval of the Secretary for War himself.

'My mission is, of necessity, a secret one, and is known only to the people in this tent, and a handful of Americans at Intelligence Headquarters and in the States. I might add that our British colleagues are not aware of it, and the reason for this will become apparent when I explain the mission to you in detail.

'This camp is one of a small number in highly secret locations in Poland. A surprising number of children have survived the Germans so far, largely through the sacrifice of parents who got them out before they themselves died. Many children, of course, didn't make it and one day I believe the truth about them will be known, but that makes our mission all the more important. Every child we save is a potential future for the Jews that the Nazis are seeking to obliterate. If we get just one child through, then despite all the deaths the Nazis will have lost, because they are not interested in killing Jews for the sake of killing, whatever it might look like to you. They have a different and very specific mission of their own, which is to bring the entire Jewish race to an end, at least here in Europe.'

He hesitated while he let this sink in. Roza's eyes had become glazed and Mordechai was staring down at the bare earth floor of the tent. Neither of them wanted to catch his eye.

'Well, my people have put a lot of planning into this and an escape route has been worked out, but it's only a plan and no-one has tried it yet. The destination of these children is Sweden. As you might know, Sweden is a neutral country. What you probably don't know is that when the Germans invaded Denmark the Danes put almost their entire Jewish population into boats and sent them over to Sweden. The Swedish government and people took them unquestioningly, an act almost unique since the beginning of the war almost anywhere in the world. The Swedes are waiting for our children. All we have to do is get them there.

'That's where you two come in. We have a fishing boat and crew available to take them across the Baltic Sea from the Polish coast. That in itself is full of risk but the bit before that is even harder. We want you to take them there.'

It was time to stop and give them a moment to digest this information. Someone came in with mugs of tea and freshly-baked bread, and they took these gratefully. They were hungry but they also wanted time to think about this. There was much that Motti, with his terribly narrow world view, simply hadn't understood, so it was up to Roza to ask the questions.

'Captain Jacobs …'

'Michael, please.'

'Alright, Michael, I have a lot of questions, but I suppose the obvious one is why us?'

'Why not you? No, seriously, how many Jewish partisans do you think there are in Poland? I'll tell you, almost none. There are a few serving with the Armia Ludowa but they are committed and the AL wouldn't accept us removing them. You've been with the AL, you're trained in the kind of fighting they do, you are, I'm told, an excellent shot, and I also happen to know, because I've seen it for myself, that you have the ability to kill. The same goes, in part, for you Mordechai. I can tell you that as an American I have been shocked at how few European Jews have that fighting spirit. And disappointed.'

'Captain Jacobs, Michael, that's very easy for you to say. You have come here from a rich and powerful country where Jews are fully accepted and integrated. I'm going to guess that you are American first, Jewish second. We have no nationality. You know perhaps little or nothing about the history of the Jews in Poland. There were about three and a half million of us before the war, a significant proportion of the population of the country as a whole, but at no time have we ever been accepted or integrated. My own family moved in high circles in Warsaw but they were fooling themselves. People accepted us because of our money but underneath that was the same hatred the village Pole felt for the shtetl Jew. It didn't take the Germans to instigate pogroms, you know. The Poles thought of that long ago. For many hundreds of years the Jews of Poland have tried to keep quiet and not be noticed. Now you want us to rise up and fight.'

'Roza, you might be surprised how much I know and understand. It might also surprise you to hear that the Jews of the Warsaw Ghetto did not give up without a fight. A few hundred of them fought the German Army to a standstill for several weeks very recently. You might not think that's much of an achievement but I do, because they fought heavy armour and trained troops with nothing more than small arms and home-made bombs and a massive amount of courage. Almost no-one survived, but a few did, and that's how we know about their heroism. They knew they couldn't win, but that didn't stop them fighting. I don't know that we will save these children, but I am here to ask you to give what your compatriots in Warsaw gave.'

Roza was silent for a minute, and Motti, who knew what she was thinking, kept his eyes on the ground.

'Michael, I think I should inform you about something. My entire family was in that ghetto.'

'Yes, actually, I know that. David has told me much of your history. I'm very sorry.'

'Do you think there is any chance any of them got out?'

'You tell me. Were they the sort who might fight?'

Roza thought about it. Her father, possibly, but he was middle-aged and, no, perhaps he hadn't. Perhaps he had simply stayed with his wife and daughter till the end, to support them in whatever way was left to him. She would never know.

'Alright, go on with your plan.'

'Well, we've been looking for a couple, like you two, who could accompany a small group of children to the coast. You can only take three or four, perhaps not even that many, given your ages. You're too young to have had a big family.'

'Not if we're orthodox Jews.'

'Yes, but that's the point. You will be travelling as Poles, not Jews. It's the only way. Jews are simply killed on the spot. For this reason you will be dressed in local clothes, Mordechai, your beard will have to go completely I'm afraid, and we will select those children who look the least Jewish. We want you to look like a family of Polish peasants on the move, refugees trying to escape the fighting. You will also, I'm afraid, be unarmed. If you are searched that would be an obvious giveaway. Your only defence will be your disguise. We want you to attract as little attention as possible.'

'What about Krystyna?'

'Krystyna?'

'The old woman we've brought with us.'

'Oh her. No problem. How old is she?'

'I don't know, why?'

'Old enough to be the children's grandmother?'

'Yes.'

'Then she will do very well. She can travel as your mother, or yours, Mordechai. Let us know, because we will need to make up identity papers. We have our own forgers here in the camp.'

'Alright, say all of that works, and we get, let's say three children to the coast, that's only three children. It's not a lot.'

Motti answered. 'It says in Gomorrah that he who saves one life, it is as if he saved the whole world. I would settle for three.' He was thinking of his one, and Rabbi Gimpel's two.

'Thank you Mordechai. Yes, it's an excellent way to look at things, but as it happens we're not setting this up for three children. You are the pathfinders. We need to know if it will work. We did think you could come back and take another three but we realised you couldn't keep doing that and maybe passing the same checkpoints with different children. You probably wouldn't be noticed but you might. It's too risky. No, once you get to the coast, you will travel with the children to Sweden. We will get a message back to say it went well and we will then send other 'families' on the same route. You will be doing a vital job, but a brief one.'

It hadn't occurred to either of them that this involved a one-way ticket for them out of the war. That would take some thinking about. Captain Jacobs had more, though.

'Sweden is not the ultimate destination for these children though. It's a refuge, for as long as the war lasts. Our planning is for after.'

'And what happens after?' Neither Roza nor Motti could imagine an after.

'They will be going to Palestine. That is why the British don't know about this operation. The British government is trying to keep Jews out of Palestine. It's a long story, but in brief it has to do with Arab oil. The Palestinian Jews already have an organisation in the British Mandate making plans to smuggle European Jews in as soon as this is all over.'

But he hadn't quite finished.

'Of course, you will be able to go to Palestine with the children. If you want.'

17

Motti and Roza had a lot to talk about on the way back to Krystyna. They had little doubt she would agree to come with them. After all, where else could she go? No, where they went, she would go too.

Motti had a question which he waited to ask until they had left the camp. 'Roza, tell me, that man in the tent. Were you really going to shoot him?'

'No, of course not.'

'I'm glad.'

'Well, I can understand that. Listen, there's something else I've been thinking about, something more important.'

'Yes?'

'Well, Captain Jacobs, do you remember he kept going on about my expertise with the sniper rifle, and how we're both capable of killing Germans?'

'Yes.'

'And do you also remember him saying that on this job we would be unarmed?'

'Yes.'

'And don't you think that's a bit odd?'

'Is it?'

'Come on, think about it. Why would our so-called military prowess matter if we're not going to be able to defend ourselves with firearms?'

Motti shrugged his shoulders. Much of the conversation had gone over his head. He must have missed that.

'Sorry, I don't know.'

'Does it bother you?'

'What, that we won't be armed, or that Captain Jacobs appears to have contradicted himself?'

'Actually, both. What is he expecting us to do if we come up against a German patrol? Make out that we're completely innocent but if they don't believe us overcome them with our bare hands and take their weapons?'

'I take it from the tone of that question that you expect the answer to be no.'

'Motti, didn't they teach you irony at the yeshiva?'

'No.'

'No, I thought not.'

The question niggled at Roza all the way back but she couldn't come up with an answer. They found Krystyna pointing the sniper rifle at them as they approached.

'Very good Krystyna, except that I happen to know you are a terrible shot, which is why we made you the cook. Now a submachine gun, that's a different matter. Point it in the general direction and squeeze the trigger, you're going to hit something or someone, but this thing, you couldn't hit a cow from a hundred metres. And by the way, despite what I just said, I'd feel better if you didn't point it at me because from this range perhaps even you couldn't miss.'

She gently eased the weapon out of the old woman's hands and put the safety catch on.

'There, we promised to come back, and here we are. Now give this man his mezuzah or I'll never hear the end of it.'

'So? Tell me, what was it all about?'

'Make us a cup of tea and then we'll tell you.'

'Why can't you tell me now? Is it so bad you want to put it off?'

'No, but when I say I want a cup of tea, that is exactly what I mean, not I don't want to talk about it yet. So, tea, or do I have to remind you I am still commander of this partisan company?'

Krystyna and Motti looked at each other, and then they looked around at the camp and its complete lack of anyone else, and they laughed, which is what she wanted them to do. Half an hour later they had drunk their tea and eaten some cold stew and Krystyna knew what was being suggested.

'Well? What do you think?'

'What do you think?'

'I asked first.'

'I think that if you go I'll go.'

'Krystyna, I appreciate the loyalty, honestly, but don't do this because of me. These children aren't your responsibility. They're Jewish for a start.'

'So? Roza, you have become fixated on the difference between you Jews and the rest of the world. Alright, I can see why, but give me credit for seeing you two as people rather than Jews. Can you do that?'

Roza shrugged her shoulders, looked at Motti and he shrugged his. It was an interesting idea, one they hadn't thought about.

'Roza, look, the point about these children is not that they are Jewish but that they are children. It's not how you see it. I wouldn't expect you to. But look at it through my eyes for once, if you can. I too have seen a lot of death since all this started, and here I am being given the opportunity to do something for some children, Polish children if you like, and the answer is yes. It would be yes even without you. And it's not only for them, it's for me too. I will be a grandmother again.'

Roza knew almost nothing about Krystyna. Now the old woman was telling her she had had grandchildren once. She had never told her her story. Roza's mistake was that she had never asked. She would rectify that mistake as soon as she could. Meanwhile, they had plans to make.

'Alright, we're all in agreement. We'll leave for their camp tomorrow.'

'Including me? Suddenly I can visit this Jewish camp?'

'Krystyna, the only reason was security. That is no longer an issue, because they have accepted we work as a team. In fact more than that, they want us to be a family, so you have a decision to make. Do you want to be my mother or Mordechai's?'

The next morning they packed up and moved out. The route to the Jewish camp meant skirting round Czyzew and with all their gear it took the best part of the day. They arrived at dusk, and those children who weren't already asleep ran up to greet them. It was like coming home. They greeted Krystyna too, possibly out of friendliness but possibly under instructions from David Berman, but did it matter which? They took her off to show her where she would be sleeping and they called her Bobba and Roza realised they weren't doing it for her but for themselves, because just as they didn't have parents they had lost their grandparents too. Not being Jewish wasn't an issue to them.

And so they settled down in this small community while plans were made and preparations completed. The hardest thing, they knew, was going to be choosing three children. They were going to be the lucky ones, but they were also going to be put in the way of great danger. Roza reasoned that the safety of the camp was a myth, one that could be destroyed at any time. They had been lucky for a long time, and no-one stays lucky for ever in a war. No, these children would be at risk, but they were at risk every day. In practice, their ability to fight off even a lightly-armed German patrol was very limited. She knew that and so did David Berman but no-one else seemed to and it was probably better that way. As far as Roza was concerned the more children they could at least give a chance the better. And Motti had his own thoughts to add to this. The fewer children, he said, who ended up at the convent being indoctrinated by the nuns, the better.

In the end they chose the three. The eldest was a boy of seven called Moise, big for his age, strong enough to walk long distances, with brown hair and eyes. Then they chose a girl of five named Dora. She wasn't especially strong but she had the advantage of strikingly Polish looks. David intimated privately to Roza that he thought she probably had just one Jewish parent. That of course, as far as the Germans were concerned, was one too many, so her life was at the same risk as all the others. Finally, they selected a baby boy with no name whom people called Adam, for the first man.

The safest way to choose new names for them was to let them choose them themselves. That way they were more likely to remember them if asked by strangers. Moise chose Masha and Dora had a doll she had brought all the way from Lublin called Barbara and so she and the doll changed names. The baby was easy. They simply continued to call him Adam, which could be Polish as much as Jewish.

Motti and Roza thought long and hard about a choice of names for themselves and in the end Motti remembered the couple who had helped him on his last day in the village, and so they became Marek and Maria Zelikowski.

While they were waiting for the camp's forger to make new documents for them Roza took some of the most likely candidates aside and gave them some training with the weapons. One young woman called Irena turned out to be especially proficient with the sniper rifle. Motti spent these days in the makeshift yeshiva, arguing with the rabbi and generally having a wonderful time. Krystyna got to know her new grandchildren and prepared as many feeds as they would be able to carry for the baby, and one of the several doctors in the camp examined her hand where the finger had been amputated and pronounced it a tolerably decent job and dressed it again.

David Berman and Captain Jacobs watched these preparations with some satisfaction but also with some trepidation, and then one evening, two days before they were to depart, Roza took the captain aside.

'So, Michael, what do you think?'

'I think you will be fine.'

'Really?'

'No, but I hope you will be fine and what I think doesn't matter.'

'But you're a serving army officer. Tell me truthfully, what are our chances?'

'Roza ...'

'Maria.'

He laughed. 'Maria then, look, I'm an Intelligence officer, not an infantryman.'

'So, apply some of your undoubted intelligence to this matter.'

'Well, I think you will be fine, I mean all of you. It's not you I'm worried about, it's the Germans. And not just them, but there are spies everywhere, Polish, Lithuanian, some even calling themselves partisans.'

'The NSZ.'

'Yes. You will be able to trust no-one. Your safest strategy is to avoid all human contact if possible, and limit those contacts you have to make to the shortest time you can. Avoid villages and small towns, because there you will be more noticeable. When you need food, either steal it from farms or go somewhere big and buy it.'

'With what?'

'Don't worry, I came prepared for that. You will have enough money. Not enough to arouse suspicion if you're searched but you won't starve either.'

They sat and talked for a long time and it got darker and colder and there was between them that tension, the one she had felt between her and Motti that time, but because she had felt it with Motti and he had put his arms round her to keep her warm she didn't allow the same to happen with this man. He was very nice, and it would have been easy, but she felt a commitment to Motti somehow. Instead, she asked the question that had been bothering her for several days.

'Michael, when we came that first time you said we would be unarmed on this operation.'

'That's right.'

'Well I can see the point. Polish peasants wouldn't be carrying German army weapons, or at least they shouldn't, and in any case we wouldn't last long against a German patrol, so I can see all of that.'

'So what's your question?'

'Well, you also said you chose us, in part at least, because of our proficiency with firearms. It doesn't make sense. Either you want us to be able to fight or you don't.'

'I see. You don't miss much.'

'No, not a lot.'

'I wish things were different and we could have you working in Intelligence. You would be good.'

'Don't change the subject please.'

'No no, I'm not. OK, let me explain. I hold a commission in the US Army, and they're happy enough for me to work for the Joint because there is a great feeling in the States about what is going on here in Europe and people want to do whatever they can, which God knows isn't much. But there is another agenda.'

'Yes?'

'Yes. When you get to Sweden you will be safe for the duration of the war. As long as the Germans don't invade.'

'Really? Is that likely?'

'No, very unlikely, but not impossible. Their neutrality won't count for much if they stop shipping iron and steel to Germany, but I don't think they'll do that. Anyway, that aside, you will be fine and I don't know how long it's going to take to destroy the Nazis, but I think we're talking about at least two or three more years.'

'I see.'

'And during that time you will have the choice of staying with your new family and being parents to them, or leaving. If you stay, the logical thing would be to travel with them to Palestine when it is finally over, because that is the agenda the Joint has established. Have you thought about that yet?'

'No. Well, Motti and I ... I mean Marek and I, have talked about it but to be honest the prospect of even getting to the coast is slight, let alone to Sweden, let alone to Palestine, and I personally find it hard to imagine that happening, so I don't see I need to think about it at this point.'

'That's fair enough.'

'Anyway, none of this answers my question.'

'Yes it does. We are under no illusion about life in Palestine. The Arabs side with the Germans. In fact we know that the Grand Mufti of Jerusalem is at this moment living as Hitler's guest in Berlin. German and British forces are battling it out in North Africa. If the Germans get to Egypt they will cross the Suez Canal and then nothing can stop them taking Palestine, where the Arabs will help them set up a death camp on much the same lines as here in Poland.'

Roza was finding all of this hard to take in, so he waited and let her have her own thoughts on it. He went on.

'Well, we don't, as it happens, think it will happen. The British are doing a great job and I for one am pretty sure the Germans will not only be stopped in North Africa but that it will be the first successful campaign of the war. Anyway, what I wanted to explain is that there is serious hostility to the Jewish community in Palestine. The Arabs hate them and to be honest the British haven't a great record either. I can foresee a time when the Jews in Palestine will have to fight the Arabs for their survival and possibly even the British. That has in fact already happened with the Arabs, despite the presence of the British Army and their police force in the territory. If a Jewish homeland is going to be built in Palestine, as I and many people think it must and will, they are going to need people who can fight. In short, Roza, Maria, the Jewish homeland wants you and Motti, not just these children. You have been chosen for that reason too.'

The next day they put their kit together and the things the children would need, and then David Berman took everything apart and searched for anything, the slightest clue, that they were Jewish. The only thing he found was the mezuzah.

'I'm sorry, but you will have to leave that here.'
'No.'
'But you must.'
'Well I won't. It was well hidden.'
'I found it.'
'Well I will hide it again, better, but it's coming with me.'
'Roza, talk to him, convince him.'
'No.'
'Oh God, not you too. Krystyna?'
'What, me? Why me? I'm not even Jewish, remember.'
'Alright, but you realise the risk involved?'

They did. Motti didn't like imposing that risk on the others even though they understood, but they were all in agreement about it so the matter stood there. There was, though, one other thing before they left. Motti had asked Roza, with great trepidation, the night before, and to his surprise she had agreed. They discussed it with David Berman and he agreed too. It made sense. They were to be married.

It wouldn't be a legal marriage from the State's point of view, but since the State of Poland technically no longer existed, they decided not to concern themselves with that. From an halachic point of view, since it was to be conducted by the camp rabbi, it was completely in order. David Berman himself gave up a gold tooth so that the camp's one-time jeweller could make a slim wedding ring for Roza. They rigged up a wedding canopy with pine branches and camouflage netting and Roza and Motti duly became Mr and Mrs Levinson, or, depending on how you looked at it, Mr and Mrs Zelikowski.

David gave the bride away, with his mouth shut, and they had no glass for the groom to break with his foot so they used a mirror someone had salvaged from an abandoned, burned out German truck. Then everyone fell to celebrating as best they could. They had no wine but that didn't stop them throwing themselves heart and soul into this crazy wedding in the forest.

And that night, for the first time since the ghetto, Roza started a period.

18

One of the men in the camp found a good place to hide the mezuzah. He undid the hub of the axle on the handcart they would be taking, wrapped the mezuzah in a large cloth to stop it moving about and making a noise, and pushed it into the space. With the hubcap back in place, it would simply never occur to anyone to look. They gathered round as he showed off his handiwork and admired the ingenuity of it. Then they loaded up the items a fleeing peasant family were likely to take with them on a journey like this, with a wooden box for the baby Adam and, for good measure, a little unnecessarily Motti thought but he didn't argue, someone made a simple wooden cross and attached it to the front of the cart with a nail. He would, he thought, remove that when they were well away from the camp.

They had almost three hundred kilometres to travel, and if they could average fifteen kilometres each day they should reach the coast within three weeks. They had, Captain Jacobs told them, until the last day of April. After that, the crew of the fishing boat would assume they hadn't made it. They couldn't afford to be seen waiting any longer than that, and in any case they had been paid to wait that long and no longer. Then they would need to head out to sea and catch fish. Roza asked what the plan was if they missed the boat through some unforeseen circumstance, of which she knew there were going to be many, and Michael Jacobs said there was no plan, after that they were on their own. The Joint could do a lot, but its reach in German-occupied Europe was limited.

He showed them a map and told them to memorise the route as

best they could. Motti and Krystyna had some difficulty with this because their geography of their country was pretty limited. Then he gave them each a crumpled piece of paper and asked them what they saw. In each case they said some notes, a letter they had never sent, something of that kind, and he said good, but now look on the back and what do you see and they said nothing, well, some meaningless lines and scribbles. Excellent he said, if that's all you can see, it's all anyone else will see. And then he took the three crumpled bits of paper and flattened them out with his hands and put them together. You had to know just how to do it and when you did what you saw was a rough representation of the printed map he had shown them. They were amazed. David Berman whistled in appreciation and slapped him on the back. With this, they reckoned, they would find their way.

The rabbi said a prayer as they stood ready to depart, and the last thing Motti did was hand his phylacteries to him for safekeeping. From now on, he was a Catholic Pole. It didn't guarantee him life, but being a Jew had guaranteed him death, so there was no choice. For Roza, it wasn't so hard to make the mental transition, but Motti, they both knew, was going to find it difficult to deny who he was. The children were young enough, even seven-year-old Moise, to forget the past. For a child it was all a long time ago. Moise didn't know what a seven-year-old Polish boy would feel like, but he had no good reason to believe it was much different from himself, and so he became Masha, and he and Barbara practised their new names and made a game of it.

And so Motti took hold of the handles of the cart, his new wife and mother-in-law by his side, and his ready-made family on board for the ride, and they left the safety of the camp. They knew it was an illusion, that safety, but even so for the few days of their stay it had felt good, and now they realised the extent of what they were setting out to do. Motti felt a gap where his phylacteries had been and Roza felt a gap where her rifle had been and Krystyna felt a gap where her finger used to be but if she felt anything else she kept it to herself. In any case, she had fallen in love with little Adam and she was happy.

By the end of the first day they had exhausted the promise of a picnic and looking for a stream to fill their water bottles and all the other ruses they could think of to encourage the children. Barbara wasn't a strong child, and from time to time she wanted to ride on the cart, which was fine because she added nothing to the weight Motti had to push, but then she would become fractious and insist on an adult carrying her, and what was nothing on the cart was a lot for Krystyna or Roza to carry in their arms. They were all glad to make camp that night, and the children fell asleep before they had finished their food, which in any case was only a light meal because the group hadn't had a lot to spare. They knew that after the first few days they were on their own, that they were going to have to find more supplies. Only Adam had enough to last the whole journey.

They made beds on the handcart for the children, and they thought that was a great adventure in itself. The adults did the best they could on the forest floor. Now that Roza and Motti were married, Krystyna slept a discreet distance from them. It was, after all, their honeymoon.

On the second day Roza woke to the sound of children playing, Krystyna preparing breakfast, and Motti praying. Krystyna had watched him in disbelief as he wound imaginary phylacteries round his arm before he recited the morning prayers and when Roza woke she watched as he took them off afterwards and wondered what he could possibly be thinking. Well, what he was thinking wasn't after all that hard to imagine. Each person creates their own world and Motti was in his.

On the fourth day they came to the outskirts of Ostroleka and they all knew they had to rest. The children had never done this before and what had begun as an adventure had turned into a hard slog. Barbara increasingly needed to ride or be carried, and when he saw that Masha decided he wanted the same treatment. Motti tried to reason with him but Krystyna reminded him that you can't reason with a tired seven-year-old, which in any case he was beginning to learn for himself. He had started by pushing the cart, and after a day of that he tried pulling it with the help of a rope he tied to the handles and put across his chest like a harness which was slightly better but then one of the women had to be sure to walk behind to keep an eye on the baby. To give him a break Roza pulled, but she just didn't have his size or strength and had to give up. Krystyna fared a bit better but in the end Motti decided it wasn't right to let an old woman be harnessed like a donkey.

So they stopped for a day. They knew it was a risk, because a day of rest would have to be made up somewhere on the journey, but they just ground to a halt and the decision was made by their bodies. Motti went into the town to buy some essential items of food, particularly for the children. He found the walk a great relief without the cart and surprised himself how fast he travelled.

It was his lucky day. The Germans were rounding men up for forced labour in Ostroleka and without doubt he would have been caught in the net, but because word had spread of the action, a farmer on the road into town had turned his donkey cart around and was heading for home when Motti met him. He had vegetables to sell, but more importantly fresh milk and cheese, some eggs and a brace of hares. He took more money from Motti than was reasonable but Motti didn't know what was reasonable and in any case he knew he was disobeying the rule about not buying conspicuously and the last thing he needed just now was to haggle over the price. The farmer went home a lot happier than he had been, and Motti was back sooner than expected with a sack full of food. When he told Roza how much he had paid she joked about sending men to do the shopping and told him that next time she would go and if a farmer argued about the price she would simply kill him and take all the food and his donkey cart for good measure. Motti thought she was joking but wasn't completely sure.

The next day they soon came to a farm and Motti crept in to investigate if there was anything worth stealing and there was, because what did he see leaning against the back of the barn but the very donkey cart from yesterday. One donkey cart looks much like any other of course, but this one still had sacks of potatoes and greens which the farmer hadn't sold, and when he got back to Roza with a sack over each shoulder she forgave him for his previous extravagance.

They ate well that week. Krystyna was in her element, with plenty of good food to cook, and the baby to coo over, and in good spirits they made better time. The children took their cue from the adults and everyone seemed to get into their stride and tiredness and sore feet were, for the moment, forgotten about. In the evenings they built a fire and sang songs and the children danced and Roza clung closely to Motti and the firelight reflected in Krystyna's ample cheeks and it really did seem that they were going to come through this.

The next day, which was the eleventh of their journey, they ran out of dirt track and came to a minor road. Roza scouted ahead and there was no track through the trees that way. There was no way they could pull the cart over the forest floor without some kind of path, so Motti went ahead on the road to see which direction it went in and half an hour later he came back and reported it veered off to the left so it was still following the general direction they needed to take. It was a difficult decision and yet not a decision at all. They looked like a normal peasant family on the move. If they came to a German patrol there was every chance they would simply be ignored. In any case, there was little choice. There wasn't time to retrace their steps and look for a better route.

It was a relief to wheel the cart on a metalled road surface. The big wheels ran smoothly and it required a lot less effort. Roza calculated that at that speed they would be able to cover twenty kilometres in a day, even with all the children taking a ride. They were in good spirits for two hours and sang Hebrew songs that the children taught them.

Who heard it first they argued about afterwards but could never agree. What they were hearing was engines, but there was nothing visible ahead so they looked behind and coming round the bend, at speed, was a German convoy. Roza cried out to the children and they threw themselves into the ditch at the side of the road. She followed them and Krystyna followed her, but Motti stood where he was, trying vainly to manoeuvre the cart to the side without letting it fall headlong into the ditch. And then the lorries were right on them and Motti and the cart were thrown off the road and he landed on top of Krystyna and the cart became stuck with one wheel on the road surface and one in the ditch with the handles sticking up into space. The convoy sped past, with somewhere important to get to which precluded any interest the soldiers might have in a family of vagabonds. As the lorries disappeared into the distance they climbed out of the ditch and brushed themselves off. No damage was done except for a sharp pain Motti felt in his left shoulder. It was the greatest good fortune that Krystyna had only minutes before taken Adam out of his box to carry him in her arms.

The cart appeared to be unharmed, but it was well and truly stuck in that position and as much as they pulled and pushed, with Motti's injured shoulder it didn't budge. That was when they heard singing. It was in a language they couldn't understand. It wasn't Polish, but neither was it German, but soon they saw the source of the voice and it was a soldier on a bicycle, peddling industriously towards them. Where he was heading on this road through the forest was anyone's guess, but he had his head down and seemed determined to get there wherever it was. Roza's first thought was that he was an easy shot but then she remembered she had nothing to shoot him with. It was disappointing.

There was no way to avoid him and whoever he was they reasoned that one soldier on a bike probably had better things to think about than killing stray Polish peasants. When he finally did look up and see them he applied the brakes hurriedly and looked earnestly at them through a pair of thick glasses. He had a rifle slung over his shoulder but it didn't seem to occur to him to use it.

He spoke to them in his strange language and they stood and shrugged their shoulders in the time-honoured way to say they didn't understand and they spoke to him in Polish, and he did the same only not in Polish. Despite the language barrier, though, it wasn't hard for him to see what had happened, and without further ado he unslung the rifle and put it on the ground with his bicycle, gesticulated to Motti what he wanted him to do, and between the two of them the cart came out of the ditch and settled nicely on the road.

They shook hands and, talking again about something which only he understood he went round to the front of the cart, bent down and kissed the cross nailed there. Then he picked up his rifle, mounted his machine, and, a little unsteadily at first, cycled off with a cheery wave of one hand. They stared after him in astonishment. Only Krystyna understood.

'Lithuanian. They're evil people, but they're ardent Catholics. You can thank God, any god you can think of, that we never removed that cross.'

Then it was Roza's turn. 'You know something? I can't believe I didn't just pick up his rifle and shoot him.'

'Why would you do that?'

Roza thought about it and shrugged her shoulders. 'I don't know. For the first time since this whole stupid war started, I'm actually glad I didn't.'

19

That night they went deep into the forest so they could light a fire without any danger of it being seen, and as they sat and ate Krystyna's food and drank tea they pondered on the day's events. The children were asleep, but Barbara coughed fitfully and each time she did she woke a little and called out for her mother.

During the night her coughing got much worse, and when Krystyna got up to check on her it was obvious she had a high temperature. The child was coming down with something serious but they didn't know what and they couldn't have done anything about it even if they had.

In the morning they could tell she had a high fever and they were worried. They had only a vague idea where they were, and even if they knew and even if there were a town they could go to and even if they could find a doctor, how could they risk that? No, there was no choice. They would have to move on and hope, or pray, or whatever each of them chose to do. They put her on the cart, as far away from Adam as possible, and either Krystyna or Roza walked alongside and mopped her brow and spoke to her or held her hand. It was slow going now, because Motti's shoulder was hurting and whichever way he tried, pushing or pulling, there was no way to ease the pain. Roza took his shirt off and sure enough a large bruise was starting to appear. She didn't think he had done any damage to the bones, but the muscles were wrenched and would take time to heal. They would take time even if he didn't have the cart to move, but how were they going to heal with that strain?

They stayed off the road now. They were feeling very vulnerable and no-one could face taking that kind of risk. The next convoy might stop and kill them just by way of entertainment.

And in the afternoon they came to a farm. They hadn't forgotten Captain Jacobs' injunction to avoid any place where they would be noticed and remembered, but they were tired, Motti was in pain and Barbara was getting worse. They had run out of food except for the potatoes, and they couldn't continue without protein inside their stomachs. Under the circumstances, they discussed it and decided to take a chance. Roza wished she had a weapon to resolve any argument that came up, but what she had instead was her husband, and for the first time she allowed herself to believe in his strength to see them through.

They needn't have worried. The farmer and his wife were elderly. Their sons, they said, had been taken away by the Germans for forced labour a year ago. No, there were no neighbours, just them, and visitors were welcome. Roza saw the woman glance at the cross on the front of the cart and again she knew it was protecting them in this place where Jews might not have been welcome.

They were fed well, round a large wooden kitchen table in front of a roaring fire, and the farmer's wife took Barbara and bathed her forehead, stripped her and bathed her fevered body with lukewarm water, and her temperature came down a little, but the coughing got no better.

They were invited to spend the night in the barn. There was plenty of hay. They would be warm and comfortable, and they accepted the offer gratefully. Masha played in the stacks of hay and he found a cat to play with too, and finally he tired himself out and fell asleep where he lay.

In the middle of the night they were woken by the sound of an engine and the squeal of brakes. There was banging and the sound of voices, German, they could hear from the barn, and they held their breath. If the soldiers didn't come near the barn they might be alright, but the soldiers did, in fact the barn door swung open and three men came in. They were drunk. The moonlight flooded the interior and the fugitives buried themselves in the hay, allowing just a small gap to watch what was happening. Krystyna covered Adam's box loosely with hay and prayed he wouldn't wake, while Roza held

Masha's hand and wished she had her submachine gun.

Then Barbara coughed, just a little, and the men were too drunk and too raucous to hear it, but Motti put a large hand over her face because he knew she would do it again. One cough always seemed to provoke another. She did, but he stifled the sound in his hand, and the more she coughed the harder he pressed, and the harder he pressed the more she coughed. The soldiers were fooling around and one undid his trousers and urinated into the hay only a few metres from them. Roza could smell it, mingled with their sweat and vodka, and she wanting to be sick, and all the while Motti pressed his hand against Barbara's face to muffle the sound of the uncontrollable coughing and then they heard a burst of gunfire somewhere outside, and the men stopped playing around and went out to join their friends and Motti released his hand a little but he didn't notice that Barbara wasn't coughing because he was too busy listening for what was happening outside.

Then there was a lot of shouting, orders by the sound of it, and men were running around and they heard the slamming of the doors on the lorry and the engine started up and revved for a moment and then it pulled away and drove off and then there was silence. It was broken only briefly by the forlorn braying of the farmer's donkey.

They waited and strained their ears but there was nothing. Roza thought the farmer might come and let them know they could come out but he didn't, and in the end they all moved at the same time, shook the hay off their clothes and crept to the open door. The moon shone brightly on the farmyard and they could see it was deserted. There was no sign of the lorry and there was no chance they had left anyone behind. Why would they?

Motti told them to wait in the barn but Roza came with him and together they crept into the farmhouse. In the kitchen were the bloody bodies of the farmer and his wife. In the end he had shielded her with his body but you can't stop bullets with flesh. Why? What had they done? The answer of course was nothing. There didn't have to be a reason for murder in this war.

They went back to the barn but what they saw in the moonlight was worse, much worse, because walking towards them was Krystyna, and she had Barbara in her arms, and the child was dead.

The old woman had tears streaming down her face as she held the body close to her breast and she said nothing, but Motti came up and silently he took the child from her and laid her down on the ground, and he knew he had done this, that he had held her too tight in his fear, his fear not just for himself but for all of them, and this child had died to save them.

Motti knew he would never be able to forgive himself for what he had done, and Roza saw this in his face and tried every argument she could muster to stop him blaming himself, but she couldn't do it. It wasn't only Barbara, she realised, but his wife and child, the family of his own that he hadn't been able to save, the people who were his responsibility but who had died anyway, and here he was, very much alive, while everyone around him died, and Roza sat him down and despite her own bereavement she held him close and let him cry while she remained dry eyed.

They buried Barbara and the farmer and his wife in the same grave. Krystyna prised the cross off the cart and put that in the soil, and Motti pulled a plank of wood from the barn and carved a crude star of David on it, and underneath he carved Dora. He didn't know her surname but he could at least lay her to rest under the Jewish name her parents, whoever they were, had given her five years ago. He said the prayer for the dead for all three of them and then Krystyna said a prayer of her own and that was it.

Roza told Motti over and over that he hadn't caused this, the Germans had. Masha asked what had happened to Barbara and they told her she had died and he just said oh and let it go. He had seen a lot of people die, and he was only seven, and Roza wondered if he would ever be a normal person after all this and of course the answer was no, how could he be? First, though, he would have to stay alive himself.

They searched through the house for anything that they could use. It felt like theft, especially from these good people, but Krystyna reminded them that you can't steal from dead people, and it was right to take if it helped them to complete their journey. The soldiers had smashed things up a bit but apart from any alcohol there might have been they didn't seem to have taken anything, because there was a well stocked larder, enough food to see them through to the coast for sure.

It was Krystyna who had the idea of taking the donkey. They harnessed it as best they could to the handcart and then they loaded up all the food plus some blankets and clean clothes and that was when they had the extraordinary idea of having a bath. Well, why not? They boiled up as much water as they could and first they bathed the baby and Masha, who protested, insisting, against the obvious evidence, that he didn't need a bath, and then Motti and Roza squeezed into the tub together and splashed about and Roza tried to take her husband's mind off the terrible thing that had happened and in part succeeded. Then they left Krystyna to enjoy a soak in quiet while they dressed in fresh clothes and searched for anything else they could use.

The sun was coming up over the trees now and it was time, they knew, to move. They said a last farewell to the new graves and put Adam and Masha on the cart and struck out with renewed vigour. The donkey made all the difference. It wasn't fast, but it was faster than Motti, and it seemed happy to pull this light load for them. Roza said they should choose a name for it but first they had to find out what sex it was and she did that and it was, seemingly, female, so they started suggesting names but they were all Jewish ones and Krystyna said no, she was a Polish donkey and she wouldn't understand Yiddish so they must give her a good Polish name and she chose Marika and they deferred to her.

They knew now that if nothing else went wrong they could get to the coast on time. Despite the sadness, they all felt inexplicably lighthearted as they set off down the path from the farm, and Masha sang them a Hebrew song he had learned in the camp and although they didn't know the words they caught the tune and hummed along with him.

They came in sight of the sea just one day behind schedule, but still with time to spare. It would take them another day or so to follow the River Leba down to the part of the coast where the fishermen should be waiting for them. Motti convinced himself that they wouldn't be there and this would all have been for nothing but he kept those thoughts to himself. They were depending on Captain Jacobs or his colleagues to have found the right people and he knew nothing about those people or come to that Captain Jacobs himself. He had watched him in the camp, especially the way he spoke to Roza and he knew now that he had been jealous, but now she was his wife and that was all in the past.

They lost sight of the sea again but they knew it was out there and they thought they could smell it but that might have been fanciful, especially since none of them had ever been near the sea and that meant they didn't know what it would smell like anyway. There was a feeling that they could relax a little now but Roza had enough experience of partisan life to know that that was when you died and she kept an even closer watch for the presence of Germans or come to that Poles. They had skirted to the south of Danzig but throughout the area there was increased German military activity and she warned Motti and Krystyna to be very watchful. Apart from a couple of sightings they spent the rest of the journey unmolested, though, and they spent the last night camped within sight of the small town of Leba and the sea beyond.

20

The next morning they released Marika from her harness, thanked her, and then Motti gave her a hearty slap on the rump upon which she whinnied, shook her head as if to say she didn't believe this, and finally cantered off to a life of freedom.

They carried their belongings the last few kilometres, and by midday they found themselves at the end of a path through some trees, where it came out directly onto the sand dunes. Roza and Motti put their pieces of the map together and Roza looked doubtful.

'It says there is supposed to be a spit of sand stretching out into the sea. I don't see it do you?'

'No. Maybe if we carry on up there?'

'No, I don't think so. We can see a hell of a distance from here. I think we'd spot it from here. Krystyna, what do you think?'

'I think I have never seen the sea before and I have no idea what a spit of sand looks like.'

'Well, come on, not like this anyway.'

'No, well, I'm sorry, I can't be of any use to you.'

They were terribly uncertain about the location but in the absence of any other ideas they stayed where they were in the hope that they would see the boat approaching from miles away and they would be able to signal to it where they were. But as they waited the tide started to go out and there it was, a spit of sand, gradually rising out of the water.

Masha played on the sand but they insisted he keep in the shadow of the trees. German boats patrolled this stretch of water. The sea, though, stretched before them to the horizon undisturbed by any sign of war. Danzig was only about fifty kilometres away but this beach was deserted. It was as if the fighting was happening on some other planet and here it was always going to be safe and Roza fantasised about setting up camp here and living out the rest of the war in peace but she knew it was a fantasy and she said nothing to the others but they were having similar thoughts themselves.

It was cold and misty but they couldn't light a fire, not even if they went back into the trees. It would be seen miles out to sea for sure. They had until night-time to wait for the fishing boat and it was going to be cold and miserable, which wouldn't have been too bad if they had absolute confidence that the boat was going to turn up but they didn't. They were worried about keeping hidden long enough, about keeping warm and fed while they waited, and about the boat coming, but what no-one talked about was the danger of crossing two hundred kilometres of the Baltic Sea in the face of the German Navy.

So they sat there and stared out at the waves and it came suddenly to Roza, something that hadn't occurred to Motti. She agonised over saying it and in the end she did so with great reluctance.

'Motti. I've just thought of something.'

'What?'

'When we left the cart, we forgot something.'

As soon as she said it he knew what it was.

'My mezuzah. No, I can't believe I was that stupid.'

'Well look, think of it as a good-luck charm. It got us here. Not all of us, sadly, but still. It's too late now.'

'No. No, actually, it's not.'

'Motti, no, it's not worth it.'

'Yes it is, it's important. Anyway, there's nothing for me to do here, I might as well.'

'But the risk ...'

'Risk? What about the risk all the way from Czyzew? We got this far didn't we? I can be there and back in a few hours.'

'Motti, no, please, don't go.'

He looked at her pleading face and he nearly gave in but he couldn't, not after all this. He had made a promise. He gave her a kiss on the cheek but she held him close to her as if she were never going to see him again. He made light of it. He didn't believe they could come all this way and have trouble now. No, he would be back soon and she would see he was right. In a few hours they would get on that boat with Krystyna and the children and sail away to a new life far from the horror. He wanted to say all that to her but he didn't, he just picked up his rucksack and went, back through the trees, retracing their steps. Krystyna watched him go.

'Where's he off to?'

'The idiot. He's gone to get the mezuzah. We forgot it. It's still in the handcart.'

Roza was crying now and watched him disappearing in the trees and Krystyna took her in her arms and held her like her husband should have been doing. She held her close to her as if she was never going to let go.

'You're right, he's an idiot. But don't worry, he'll be back. He has never let us down yet, has he?'

And they settled down to wait, for Motti, for the fishing boat, without being quite sure if either of them was going to come.

The boat came early, something to do with the tide, they explained. They stood out to sea and two of the crew rowed into the beach. Roza told them about Motti and how they would have to wait, not long, and they said they could wait for an hour, no longer, and Krystyna said that should be enough, he had been gone a while.

They waited for an hour and he hadn't come back, and the captain said that was it, come or not, we get paid either way. Roza stared through the trees, trying to make out any sound of footsteps. She told them to wait just ten minutes while she went up the path to see if he was coming. They waited ten minutes and then they took the baby's box and Masha and put them in the rowing boat. Krystyna got in, feeling disloyal, but she knew she had to. Roza came back and pleaded with them but she knew it was no good. Nothing she said was going to change it.

She hugged Krystyna and then they pushed the little boat out into the surf and took the weight of the oars. Roza watched them through her tears until she could stand it no longer and picking up her pack she headed back the way he had gone.

She walked fast but all the way she looked intently in both directions off the path in case he had fallen and was lying with perhaps a broken leg somewhere. He wasn't though, and eventually she came to where they had left the cart, hidden by some bushes. It was still there, undisturbed, and hoping she was wrong she carefully undid the hubcap the way she had seen it done three weeks ago, and it came away and inside the axle there it was. She drew out the cloth and unwrapped the mezuzah. Everything after that was a blur.

21

Motti walked as fast as he could and that was when he realised how tired he was after three weeks of this trek, but he wasted no time. It was getting dark and he tried to remember the way. When he came to a fork in the track he thought he was right but after ten minutes he convinced himself he was wrong and went back and took the other fork, which failed to alleviate his doubts.

It all looked so different in the dark and of course any path looks different going back the other way, and the landmarks he expected to see he didn't but he couldn't be sure if that was because he was on the wrong path or on the right one and seeing things differently. He started to run, with a sinking feeling in his stomach and he felt the fear he had felt in the forest when he left the village, and he stopped for a moment to rest against a tree and get his breath back, and that was when he heard it, just a crack of a twig. He looked down to see if it was his own boot that had done it, and it wasn't. He peered through the gloom but his eyes couldn't adjust to the failing light and he saw nothing except trees and more trees, but then he heard the unmistakable sound of the bolt on an automatic weapon, a sound he knew well.

They shouted to him but it was in German and he didn't know what they were shouting but even so he put his hands up in the air. He tried to stay calm but his breath just wouldn't steady. They came out of the gloom, soldiers, a lot of them, pointing rifles and submachine guns at him, and suddenly it seemed that everything that had happened in the past few months had been a dream, and here he was, back in reality, back where he had started.

An officer came out of the gloom, pointing a pistol at him and giving him an order which he couldn't understand and he just stood there, helpless, defenceless, at the mercy of an unmerciful god. The officer raised his weapon, that much he remembered, not to shoot him but to hit him, and then he lost consciousness.

He woke up on the floor of a hut. It was dark but he could see a crack of light under a door so he knew it was now daytime. His head hurt and he knew he had wet his trousers and that was surprisingly uncomfortable and he wanted to take his trousers off but of course that was ridiculous. Then he heard breathing and he realised he was not alone, and whoever it was opened the door from the inside and the sun streamed in but then it was blocked again by another figure and they dragged him out. The officer was there again, with the pistol in his hand again, and as Motti looked at his face he knew that he knew this man, because this was the officer, whose name he could not recall, he had hit such a long time ago. He averted his eyes to avoid recognition but it was a pointless gesture. Obersturmbannführer Stängl would never have recognised him, but it was of no importance. He issued an order and Motti's arms were pinned back and a rope was tied round his wrists. Then while someone held him from behind two soldiers came and undid the belt of his trousers and suddenly he was naked from the waist down. They laughed and joked, pointing at his nakedness, and then Stängl came up and placed the muzzle of the pistol in his groin and said something which the soldiers laughed about again but any chance of disguising his Jewishness was, he knew, long gone. The gun felt icy cold against his warm skin and now Mordechai Levinson knew there was no more road to travel, no more life to live, no more Roza to love. His lips moved automatically but in silent prayer.

Shema Yisroel Adonai Eloheinu Adonai Echad.

PART TWO

1944

1

Obersturmbannführer Fritz Stängl was angry. He was often angry, but on this occasion he was also drunk, although it would be true to say that these days that too was not unusual. Anger and alcohol are a dangerous mix. When applied to Lieutenant Colonel Stängl they were especially hazardous.

Barbara Hass wasn't afraid of him. Alright, she was a little afraid, because it was always safer to keep out of his way when he was in this mood. The problem was, he was in this mood more and more these days. Stängl's war wasn't going very well. It had started well enough, a commission in the Waffen SS, early promotion, and he managed to avoid a posting to anywhere dangerous for a long time. The biggest threat he had to face for the first four years was unarmed civilians, and even a man of Stängl's proclivities finds it easy to kill them. Lately, though, Germany had been experiencing what his commanding officer called temporary minor setbacks, only they kept happening and they were becoming less temporary and less minor and there were rumours that certain officers might be posted to rather more dangerous places and have to face rather more dangerous people, like Soviet soldiers with guns, a prospect that did not fill Fritz with good feelings.

He had fondly imagined that the little niche he had carved out for himself would last forever, well at least until the war was won by the Reich and he could go home and enjoy the adulation of a people grateful to its conquering heroes, not to mention the financial reward that comes with having an almost unlimited freedom to pillage any and all valuables that come your way, other than the really choice pieces which he sensibly sent back to headquarters as offerings to his masters, who had their own nests to feather and their own financial futures to plan for.

The Red Army, which Hitler had told them was defeated more than a year ago, was coming back at them out of nowhere. The German armies besieged Leningrad but the Russians simply refused to die, and before that the Communists had not only held the Wehrmacht at bay at Stalingrad but had pushed them back and taken tens of thousands of German prisoners. That, Fritz, considered, was more than a minor setback.

The Soviet Union, as far as he could see, was like a hydra. Every time they cut off one head another two sprang up in its place. From somewhere deep in the Russian interior came millions more men, and whole tank armies that weren't supposed to exist. How could a defeated nation produce tanks, better ones than they had, and more of them? No, someone, Fritz reckoned, wasn't telling the German people the whole truth about this war, and he was beginning to imagine things could turn bad for him personally.

And now he had been given this stupid order. He took another shot of schnapps and rubbed his neck. It hurt him sometimes, even now. He wished Rudi were here, instead of driving SS Gruppenführer von Stamitz around Poland. He worried about Rudi, and then, when he was drunk, he got angry with him instead but then when they met he felt bad about being angry but that didn't stop him sulking when he left again. Rudi's job as General von Stamitz's driver took him away for long periods and then Fritz drank more and shouted at his mistress.

Since the industrialisation of the killing, shooting Jews in the back of the head was out of fashion and Fritz had had to move with the times. He still enjoyed the occasional bit of sport when the opportunity arose but he had been reprimanded more than once for leaving bodies lying around when there were now the proper places for these things where everything was done with the greatest organisation and planning, where the bodies went in one end of the process and came out as fertiliser at the other. Yes, that was the genius of German industry, eliminating the Jewish enemy at the same time as wasting not a scrap of the material. Fritz had to agree with the idea, because it was brilliant, he knew that, but he just wished he didn't have to be a part of it. Nowadays, he felt, he was little more than a production manager, not a soldier at all. General von Stamitz had told him once that if he really objected there would be no problem re-assigning him, say to the Russian Front, and Fritz came to the conclusion that well, all in all, it could be worse. Rudi warned him about speaking out of turn in front of von Stamitz. The General, he said, liked to talk with his junior officers but he didn't like to be questioned by them. It gave him a fatherly feeling when they came to him with their problems, but it irritated him when they came with criticisms and complaints. Fritz, Rudi, said, should keep his complaints to himself.

No, there were times when Fritz looked around him, at his comfortable quarters well away from the smell of burning bodies, and at Barbara who was, he readily admitted, even to her, an excellent cook. Yes, the General himself had complimented him on his cook, and when he said that he winked because everyone knew that Barbara was more than that. It was no secret at all. Why should it be? She was even half German. Alright, the other half was Polish but the German half made her more than acceptable and on top of that she was a very good looking woman. Yes, Barbara Hass was admired by many of his fellow officers, and he enjoyed their jealousy. The General had even hinted once, when he had drunk more than his usual quantity of vodka, that Rudi might lend her to him, purely to cook for a birthday dinner he was planning for the Obergruppenführer of course, but as he was really very drunk when he suggested it Fritz wasn't surprised when he didn't remind him, or worse, order him to send her to Headquarters, when he was sober. Fritz felt strangely possessive of Barbara Hass. Alright, she didn't get on too well with Rudi but Fritz thought that was Rudi's problem, not hers. Fritz sometimes thought he would ditch Rudi, but then he knew he wouldn't, and the annoying thing was that Rudi knew that too, and given that he was only a sergeant Fritz did think that Rudi sometimes pushed his luck.

'Barbara, come here my little angel, come and keep me company. I don't want to be on my own this evening. Rub my back my angel. Look, I'll take off my tunic for you.'

She did as she was asked, and he groaned with pleasure. She was, he said to himself, a multi-talented woman. Yes, he was a lucky man. He tried to remember, as he sat there and enjoyed the massage, how he had found her but he couldn't. She seemed always to have been here and he found it increasingly difficult to remember a time before. But the war was like that. It went on and on and it was really quite boring sometimes and you thought nothing would ever change but it did, all on its own, nothing to do with you. But of course war is never anything to do with the individual soldier. You just get swept along on the tide and you go where they tell you to go and you hope you land on your feet, which he had. If it wasn't for the pain in his neck, and the stupid orders, he could even get to enjoy the war again, like before. Still, you can't have everything. There were many worse off than him, that was for sure. The strange thing was they kept giving him medals and promotions, as if he was some kind of hero. He was efficient, true, but even Fritz couldn't see himself as a hero. Still, he enjoyed the status his uniform and his medals and the death's head emblem on his cap gave him, and the fear he saw in people's faces. Yes, now he thought about it, he very much enjoyed their fear.

Sometimes he resented it that he couldn't see fear in Barbara's eyes when he looked deeply into them. No, what he thought he saw bordered on contempt, possibly nothing more than the contempt he knew all women felt for men, but even so it was as if she knew all his secrets and despised him for them. Rudi said she was dangerous, this woman, that she had a ruthless streak and she could destroy him if she wanted. Fritz laughed when he said that but deep down he shuddered. She could, it was true. He should get rid of her really, but Rudi would have to be the first to admit that without her things could be very much more difficult.

Fritz had considered trying to get Rudi transferred to him, to be his driver. Yes, that would be much better, but he knew that if he suggested that to the General, von Stamitz would give him that look, the superior one he used sometimes, and say very well my friend, I will swap Sergeant Schultz for that woman of yours. When Fritz thought about that he changed his mind. No, that wouldn't work at all. The woman was the only person who made it possible, the whole thing, Rudi. Of course, the General could do it anyway, but why tempt fate? Why even put the idea into his head? The General, Fritz thought, was excessively stupid, and he and Rudi laughed about this, when it was quite safe to do so because they were on their own, and Rudi did a wonderful imitation of him, with his Hitler moustache that everyone said was going too far, and even the General knew that because once the Führer himself had visited their unit and he had shaved it off the day before to avoid looking foolish.

Fritz thought about all of these things while Barbara rubbed his neck and his back, and on top of all that he thought about his mother, how she had done that for him, and about how proud she had been the first time he went home on leave in his lovely black uniform. Fritz was terribly proud of his uniform. He knew he was good looking, not just because he saw it every time he looked in the mirror but because his mother told him so, regularly. His father didn't say so. His father never said anything encouraging or warm or anything at all of the kind that Fritz thought a father should say. The last time he went home on leave his father had made some comment, he forgot now exactly what it was, but something uncomplimentary about not doing any real fighting, as if he didn't know that killing Jews was the highest service a man could render to the Fatherland, and Fritz, who had got so used to pulling out his pistol and shooting people he didn't like, momentarily had an urge to do just that, but of course he hadn't. He also had an urge to shoot General von Stamitz, almost every time he saw him in fact, but Rudi said that would be a bad idea and he had to agree it would. He contented himself with the hope that the General would get blown up one day out in his car. Fair enough, that meant that Rudi would die too but, well, every pleasure has a price.

And now the General had given him this ridiculous order, to drive round Poland collecting statistics, a job for a bureaucrat, not a soldier, and it would mean interminable hours in the car with that idiot driver of his, Corporal Riester, a man with not the hint of a sense of humour, who lectured him on National Socialist ideology while he drove, knowing that he had a captive audience, and who he knew suspected him of all sorts of things for which he could not only lose his rank in the SS but in all probability might even face a

Court Martial. Riester couldn't be sure about any of those things, and Rudi said don't worry about him, he just likes the idea of denouncing someone and getting a promotion as a result, and you will do as well as anyone else. Fritz decided that Rudi was probably right, and he determined that at the first opportunity, when they were in the middle of nowhere and they stopped the car for a toilet break, he would shoot Corporal Riester and make up some story about a partisan ambush which he heroically escaped from, killing seven enemy terrorists in the process. They would give him another medal. Come to think of it, Corporal Riester was unpopular with everyone because he lectured anyone who couldn't avoid him, so they would probably give him a medal if he told them the truth.

He told Rudi about this fantasy as well and Rudi said he was getting obsessed with shooting people and all this office work was unhealthy for a man with such a vigorous appetite. He suggested he should put in for a transfer to the Russian Front and Fritz laughed but Rudi didn't which made him wonder if it was supposed to be funny. Anyway, soon no-one would have to volunteer for the Russian Front because the Russian Front was rapidly coming to them.

2

Barbara Hass sat and waited for Fritz to fall asleep and she gently took off his boots and trousers and placed a blanket over him lest he should get cold in the night. Then she took his briefcase into the other room, opened it with the keys from his tunic pocket, and started to peruse the documents it contained. Some were routine and of no interest, others she would let her superiors decide on and memorised their contents the way she had been trained to do, a rough outline, committing numbers to memory especially. Then she checked to see if there was anything important enough for her to risk making a copy of, but today there wasn't, and she quietly closed the case, locked it again, and replaced it and the keys.

The first time she had done it she had, of course, been terribly nervous. She had missed several important documents in her haste and as a result an operation had gone badly wrong. But Fritz was a heavy sleeper, especially after a few drinks, and since he almost always had a few drinks before he fell asleep these days it had got easier to do and she had become less frightened, more matter of fact even, but what she never forgot was the importance of her work, or the people who were depending on the information she obtained by being the mistress of an SS Lieutenant Colonel with a position of responsibility for the transportation of Jews to the Auschwitz-Birkenau camp.

There was one piece of paper that interested her this evening though, among the routine stuff, an order not from General von Stamitz, his immediate superior, but from Berlin. He was to be assigned to a new task, it said, as liaison officer between the Reich

Security Main Office in Berlin and the German Railways for the whole of Poland. Fritz thought it was beneath him, a job unworthy of his rank and what he considered to be his special skills. Barbara thought even so that this could be useful for certain people to know, because a man with access to information about every railway movement throughout the country where all the largest death camps were was likely to be a very valuable source of information to anyone who might similarly have an interest in those railway movements, albeit for other reasons than their smooth operation.

She didn't need to take the risk of copying the order. It was simple, and she would deliver it as soon as the opportunity arose. It would be given by her handler, whom she would meet in the forest, to the partisan group operating in that area, who had agreed to pass information on to the Jewish Underground. It was a risk, because they could never be completely sure of the partisans, but it had so far been a risk worth taking. Since the news of Russian successes and German defeats had started to filter through, the Armia Ludowa were getting bolder. Orders came through more regularly from Moscow and they included offering assistance to the Jews, as long as it didn't compromise their own objectives.

Barbara knew that her position as Fritz's mistress was of the utmost importance to the Underground. She had no certain knowledge that her husband was dead, even if she knew in her heart that he must be, and she considered herself still a married woman. Her handler knew what a sacrifice this was and he never talked about it, and Barbara didn't disillusion him, never told him that what everyone knew for a fact, that she was Fritz's mistress, was not exactly what they took it to be, that it was a cover, because Fritz Stängl had no use for a mistress, since his sexual partner was General von Stamitz's driver, Sergeant Rudi Schultz.

Fritz needed Barbara because he was in no doubt what the penalty was for a homosexual relationship, let alone when it involved a senior SS officer. As long as she provided the myth that he was one of the lads, no-one queried his drinking bouts with the sergeant, even when the sergeant failed to return to his own quarters some nights. After all, serious drinking doesn't end until you fall over incapable. A man's ability to get seriously drunk was considered by many people, quite mistakenly as it happened, to be the hallmark of a real man.

Barbara slept in a small bedroom next to Fritz's, and at first the sound of what he and Rudi did next door made her nauseous but soon she decided that since Germans were all animals this was no more or less than the bestiality she came to expect from them.

She knew that Fritz was obsessed with being discovered, and that he depended completely on her to provide his cover, and she knew that it never entered his head that she agreed to act the role of mistress for anything other than the protection it gave her. Her spying activities were, for this reason, quite safe. She didn't kid herself that it would always be so. She knew that he was capricious and unpredictable, and that he was quite capable of withdrawing his protection, killing her even, if the idea got into his head. She knew that Rudi Schultz didn't like her, and although that naturally meant it was her duty to try at least to cultivate a better relationship with the driver, she had so far been unable to make herself do that. Fritz was evil, yes, but there was something worse in this man, something not entirely human.

Meanwhile Fritz got drunk and slept like a baby and she did the things his mother would have done for him. When she put his dinner on the table he had a look of eager anticipation in his face, like a little boy, and while she watched him eat with puerile happiness she tried to square this childishness of his with the ability to put a gun to the head of a man, or come to that a woman or even a child, and squeeze the trigger and watch their brain splatter in the wind. It was a problem she had always had, separating the Germans as people from the Germans as conquerors and killers. Under the shiny black uniform Fritz Stängl was a man like any other, his mother's son, so then what was the difference between him and a Jew? The Jew didn't hate the German so why did the German hate the Jew?

Barbara accepted the Germans as enemies, because knowing your enemy is a fundamental requirement for a partisan, but she could never quite understand why. They had mothers, like she had had. They had children like she had had so why were they not human like her? They appeared human in every way, but they behaved in a way that was outside the accepted range of human behaviour, because it was, she had learned at school, a fundamental that humans, like all animals, have survival as their absolute priority, and that human societies survive as a whole because of this imperative.

Where, then, had the Germans gone astray? At which point had they lost their humanity? It was, of course, an impossible question to answer, not only because Barbara was not a student of history and knew little or nothing about the Christian's hatred for the Jew, but because the entire picture was clouded by the fact that actually it wasn't just the Germans who hated the Jews, but to her certain knowledge the Poles did, and yet surely the Poles and the Germans were enemies. And then there were the Ukrainians and the Lithuanians. She knew from personal experience that both nationalities co-operated enthusiastically in murder. Well, all those people had mothers and their mothers must have loved them and nurtured them, but at which point did their mothers teach them to kill their fellow human beings?

She would have loved, right then, to wake Fritz and ask him why he hated Jews, enough to watch them be slaughtered. Did he even know himself, or would he simply mouth the National Socialist claptrap he read in his books? Did he have the intelligence to understand the ideology, and come to that did any of them? Or was it some kind of institutionalised madness and when every last Jew had been killed the entire German people would suddenly and permanently revert to being normal human beings?

She would have loved to know, but there was no-one to ask. She had asked the leader of the Underground once, but he had just shrugged his shoulders and said where do I begin, which was entirely unsatisfactory. He also said do these doubts make it hard for you to do your job and she stopped and thought about that and said no, because even if she didn't understand why the Germans were her enemies, there could be no doubt about the fact. They had killed everyone she loved. For that they themselves must die. An eye for an eye, a tooth for a tooth. Vengeance was once the Lord's work, but now it was hers.

And so it was that not the next day but the day after, because above all she had to take care, she went riding on the horse Fritz had so thoughtfully obtained for her at the cost of only one Polish life, and when she was in the woods well away from Bielsko and she could reasonably stop and tie the animal to a tree and sit for a few minutes' quiet reflection, she found, as expected, a man there to tell these things to, the things she had learned from Fritz's briefcase, and she made a point of telling him especially about the new order, and asked for instructions, because surely they would want her to do something about this, provide information to them about his new job.

The man she gave this information to accepted it without comment, and indulged momentarily in his fantasy of raping Barbara and one day, he told himself, he would do it. She was a German officer's whore, he knew, and if she could do it with the enemy she would hardly object to doing it with a Polish patriot. He would kill her afterward and no-one would ever know. She dressed like a man and she talked like one, but there was something about the very feminine curls that kept on escaping from her cap that he couldn't take his eyes off while she spoke. He didn't know that she carried a pistol Fritz had also thoughtfully provided her with because, he said, you couldn't be too careful, you never knew who you might meet in the forest, which was more true that he could have guessed, and the peasant-turned-freedom fighter didn't know that she would not hesitate to blow his brains out if he tried such a thing, because she could see the way he looked at those curls, but still he had his little dream.

On the ride back to town Barbara pondered the idea of killing the courier anyway, because it had been a long time and her anger had never subsided and yes, she did this work because that was what her handler ordered her to do but a part of her wished she was with a partisan unit killing Germans, where she could express her feelings from the barrel of a rifle. It was true that killing a partisan would be frowned upon but it was also true that he looked at her in a way that warranted such an action. Well, one day, she hoped, he would do what was in his mind to do and she would have a reason to do what was in her mind to do.

And meanwhile she rode back to the house she shared with Fritz Stängl. The German sentries waved her through without asking for her papers. She was well known at all the checkpoints. The sentries were afraid of Lieutenant-Colonel Stängl. They knew he had a violent temper and that he had beaten a private once who answered him back and they treated his mistress with a certain amount of respect because she was sure to report any slight to him. One man though dared to slap the rump of her horse. It unsettled the animal and it reared a little but she leaned forward and whispered some gentle endearments in Yiddish in its ear and this calmed it. It amused Barbara to do that.

Fritz was back and he was in a better mood today.

'Ah there you are, my little angel, been out riding I see. You know, sometimes I think you love that horse too much. In any case, it is dangerous out there. Perhaps I should send one of my men with you in future. Did you see anyone in the forest?'

'What? What do you mean?'

'There are partisans you know. They would kill you and take your horse without hesitation, if not to ride then to eat. They're not nice people, you know.'

She wondered if she was supposed to take this seriously. She also wondered if Fritz was as stupid as he sometimes appeared, or he was fishing. No-one trusted anyone these days, and why should he trust her? She had appeared six months ago and she had the correct papers and nothing had come back from the Gestapo to suggest there was anything wrong with her so he had asked her to move in and explained the terms of the arrangement and she had accepted, which of course she would because the Jewish Underground knew all about Lieutenant-Colonel Stängl and they guessed, correctly, that he would jump at the chance for the cover Barbara provided him with.

'Now my pet, I want you to prepare something especially tasty tonight. Tomorrow I have to go away for several days and I am going to miss your wonderful cooking. Look, I have brought some excellent wine. You must help me to drink it.'

'Isn't Rudi ... Sergeant Schultz coming?'

'No, the idiot has gone and got himself stuck in Breslau with the General. Never mind. We don't need him to enjoy ourselves, do we?'

No, they didn't. Barbara made sure Fritz's glass stayed topped up and he quickly became so drunk he didn't notice that she was only sipping hers, and she sat back and waited for him to become loquacious. He always did. His trip involved visiting other death camps in Poland, all subsidiary to his own at Auschwitz with its eight thousand a day capacity but nevertheless all instrumental in the war against the Jews.

'It's a bore but someone's got to do it you know. Those Wehrmacht people don't realise how stressful it is. Not for us the joy of the Front, facing the Russians. No, ours is the real work, yes, they think they're the only ones fulfilling the National Socialist dream but no, I tell you we're working hard too. And without the railways, well, what would happen, you tell me.'

'No, I have no idea. You tell me Fritz.'

'Nothing, that's what. Without the smooth running of the transport system it would all grind to a halt. We couldn't have that now, could we?'

'No, no, absolutely.'

'You do understand, my angel, don't you?'

'Completely. After all, why would they have given you that last medal?'

'The Iron Cross, First Class. Not everyone gets one, you know.'

He looked across at where his uniform tunic lay strewn over the back of a chair, the cross dangling from the chest with the other medals.

'You know, you're a very beautiful woman.'

'Am I?'

'Yes. Don't think I haven't noticed. Not as beautiful as my mother, but she's my mother, you know.'

'Yes, I know.'

'My father doesn't deserve her. He's a swine. Have I ever told you that?'

'Yes.'

'Well he is.'

Fritz was lapsing into his regional dialect and she was finding him difficult to follow. She needn't have worried though, He wasn't saying anything important. Nothing of value to the Underground was likely to come out this evening. He was getting maudlin, and he was no use to her. She just wanted him to fall asleep so she could be done with him. The sooner he did that the sooner the morning would come and he would go away and she could have a well-earned holiday. If he thought people didn't appreciate how hard this was for him, what would he think if he knew what she had to go through?

They all thought she was a tough woman, the people back at Headquarters, but the strain of it, every day having to listen to this monster, hoping she didn't lose control, hoping she didn't talk in Yiddish in her sleep, hoping she didn't simply go mad, it was trying, very trying. To quote Fritz, someone had to do it. She just wished sometimes it didn't have to be her. Every night, before she fell asleep, she whispered in Yiddish goodnight to her son, and hoped that someone was teaching him the language of his own people. He was at least out of all of this, out of the war, safe in Sweden. Whatever happened to her, he would survive.

3

Back then Barbara Hass was Roza Levinson, also known as Maria Zelikowska, nee Weksler.

She put Krystyna in the boat and turned back, back to the war, to look for her husband, Motti, whom she had married only three weeks before.

The cart was there, where they had left it, and she obeyed the rules she had learned with the partisans, the Armia Ludowa, and watched and waited but it wasn't a trap. Wherever Motti had gone, wherever they had taken him, it wasn't here. The mezuzah was still in its hiding place and as it slid out into her hand she knew he hadn't been here for sure.

She held it, this ridiculous reason to die, and she cried, for him, for her, for them all. She had never been so alone in her life. First there was her family and then there were the partisans and finally there was Motti but now there was no-one. No-one was going to tell her what to do, take her by the hand, now she was completely on her own. She tried to think like a partisan but she couldn't, she could only think like a woman lost in the forest.

The boat had gone, so Sweden was no longer an option. She could simply strike out and get lost in the war like everyone else, but that was lonely and right now she wanted to belong with someone. If not Motti, then was there any other choice? No, the more she sat and thought about it the clearer it became. It had taken them three weeks to push and pull the cart with three children, two if you took into account the one who died on the way, but now she was on her own she felt sure she could cover the distance in two. If, that was, she didn't meet any Germans on the way.

On that long lonely trek she convinced herself this wasn't only about self-preservation but about reporting back too. She had been given a job to do, and she had lost one of the children in her care and she had lost her husband as well, but if there was a reason to live now it was to let the Jewish Underground know that the route to the Baltic coast was viable, and that more children could get to Sweden and safety. Yes, they would need to know that.

And she did make it back, and she did give her report, and they asked about Motti but she shrugged her shoulders and said she didn't know, couldn't be sure, and they said well he's a strong man, he might simply have got lost but that didn't mean he wouldn't find help somewhere. He was a survivor, they said. It was all possible of course, and she tried to believe it but it was very hard.

Then she had done the obvious thing and volunteered to take another group, all the way to Sweden this time, and they found another man who could pass for her husband and three more children and she took her new family back along the route that was now familiar and they faced many dangers on the way but none of them proved fatal and they reached the lonely beach and waited, and as before the rowing boat came through the surf and took them to the fishing boat and that delivered them safely to a beach near Karlskrona where they were met and looked after and a week later Roza found herself reunited with Krystyna, and the boy, Masha, now called Moise again and the baby Adam. They were living on a farm with a Lutheran family who had never met a Jew before but seemed not in the least put out by these strange people in their home or the Catholic Krystyna and who welcomed Roza as if she were the children's long-lost mother. She had difficulty understanding the depth of the Carlssons' feelings for strangers and she and Krystyna worked hard on the farm to repay their kindness and even seven-year-old Moise helped Mr Carlsson in the fields because it was summer now and there was much to do and the Carlssons' two boys were serving in the army, training in case the war visited Sweden as well.

And in the winter that followed, Roza gave birth to Motti's son. She named him, inevitably, for his father.

Four weeks later they had a visitor at the Carlssons' farm in the form of Captain Michael Jacobs of US Army Intelligence. He was still working for two masters and it was hard to say if there was any difference between the two when he asked her to work for him because he had a difficult assignment and he needed her because he had no-one else who could do it. She spoke Polish and reasonable German, she had proved her courage beyond any reasonable doubt, and he had a feeling she would want to stay in the fight. What he didn't know until he arrived in Sweden was that she was now a mother. He cooed over the baby and said sorry, it was a mistake, he couldn't ask her now.

And she said don't be stupid, it's not your choice, it's mine. He knew what was in her mind, the possibility that Mordechai might still be alive and her living out the rest of war in the safety of Sweden gave him no chance of being found. He wanted to say that's wrong, frankly he's almost certainly dead but even if he isn't Poland is a big country and the Germans occupy it still, remember, and the chance of you finding him, even if he is alive, is exactly nil. He didn't say that, though.

He asked Krystyna to make her see sense and Krystyna said I can't do that but look, the solution is in your hands, just refuse to take her, and Captain Jacobs knew she was right, he had the power to stop this, but he didn't, he said alright. Krystyna thought she would never forgive him for that. Captain Jacobs would have to live with her opprobrium. He had a war to fight.

Lieutenant-Colonel Fritz Stängl had come to the attention of the Underground and they had passed on information about him to the American Joint Distribution Committee, who shared Captain Jacobs with the Army. When he gave this name to Roza she remembered it. He was the SS officer, she said, who had once tried to kill Motti and who had in turn been felled, almost killed, by him. So, if he was alive and could help the Underground, yes, she was interested. In a way only she could fathom, it brought her closer to her husband. She had a ridiculous notion that getting close to Stängl might miraculously lead her to Motti. Once she knew the mission involved Stängl, she wouldn't take no for an answer, even if Captain Jacobs had been saying no, which he wasn't. Krystyna shook her head in disgust and walked out of the room. She was already a surrogate grandmother to Moise and Adam. Well, now she would bring up baby Mordechai when his mother didn't come back.

It was late by the time they had finished arguing back and forth and Captain Jacobs accepted Mrs Carlsson's offer of hospitality. He and Roza wrapped up in coats and sat on the stack of logs at the back of the farmhouse.

'Michael?'

'Yes?'

'Do you remember when we did this once before? It seems like years ago, in Poland, we sat and talked.'

'Yes, I've never forgotten. You know I fell in love with you then.'

'You men, you're hopeless. Can't you be serious for a minute?'

'No.'

'Well it's just as well then that half the world's population is female.'

'Anyway, who says I wasn't being serious?'

'Bless you Michael. You're a lovely man. And one day a lovely woman, a lovely American woman, is going to fall for your charm and make you happy.'

'I could take you there you know, and the baby, help you to bring him up.'

'Do you know, I believe you're serious about that.'

'OK, I'm serious. We men, you know, we can be serious when we need to be. So, how about it?'

She put her hand on the sleeve of his coat in a friendly gesture, a friendly but negative one.

'It's tempting, but no. You know why.'

'Yes, and I think you're wrong but I have enough respect for you to not say so.'

'I see. Is that how you Americans show your respect? By insulting someone and then saying you didn't? Anyway, never mind all this, there's something else I want to ask you.'

'Yes?'

'This Stängl. I mean ... if I get a chance to interrogate him?'

'You won't.'

'I might.'

'Oh yes? You're going to be in the middle of Nazi-occupied Poland, on your own, and you're going to say, hey Fritz, look, I wonder if you wouldn't mind giving me some information.'

'No, well, I might say it but not like that, more likely with a gun to his head.'

'No, whatever you do, don't do that.'

'Why? He's a German. Why can't I kill him if I get the chance?'

'First of all because you won't get the chance, at least not and come out alive, and secondly Stängl is worth far more to us alive than dead. Look, I know he's an SS officer and I know as well as you do, if not better, what he's almost certainly guilty of, and there will be a time for retribution but that time is not now. If I think you are going to go around shooting Nazis I'm not sending you. Apart from anything else you will certainly get yourself killed if you try it and I'm being serious when I say this but if there is anyone I don't want to get killed it's you.'

'I see. But you don't mind sending me into the lion's den.'

He looked grave. 'Yes, of course I mind. If there was any way, any better way, you wouldn't be going, but I'm an officer and I have a duty and I'm trying to do it the best way I can.'

'A duty to whom?'

'To my country and my people too, by which I mean the Jewish people. Look, the only way we are going to save any Jews, I mean a lot, and trust me there are still a lot who can be saved, is by ending this war, and the only way it's going to end is with the destruction of the Nazi war machine, the destruction of the German people's will to fight. You have no idea, I imagine, just what a vast effort is going into that. The invasion of France was a feat never attempted before in the history of warfare. The Soviets are tearing up whole German armies as we speak. Between the USA and the Soviet Union the industrial and military forces the Nazis are faced with are now utterly impossible to defeat. It's only a matter of time. I wish we could do it all faster but we can't. Meanwhile people like you and I can do what little that can be done to save a few more. The Nazi killing machine is in full swing right now, and anything we can do, if not to stop it then at least to slow it down, we have to do. Your man, Stängl, holds one of the keys. That's how important this operation is, and that's why I'm asking you to do something that I would do myself if I could but I can't.'

'I see.'

'So promise me, no killing, Stängl or anyone else. Go in, do your job, and get out when we decide to lift you. OK?'

'Yes Sir.'

'Oh, and one more thing.'

'Uhuh?'

'I hope you find him.'

'Who?'

'You know who.'

And so Roza held her infant son close to her and said a prayer and shed a tear, and then she held Krystyna close and asked her forgiveness for doing what she had to do and they both cried but they both knew it had to be like this. The last thing she did was to give Krystyna for safekeeping the precious mezuzah that had probably cost Motti his life.

And then she took the dangerous passage across the Baltic Sea again, in the same fishing boat, and landed once more on the same beach and just then she would have given anything to turn back but she couldn't and she didn't.

4

That was more than six months ago, and in that time she had allowed herself to be 'found' by her target, and she had become indispensable to him in a way she could not have predicted owing to the Rudi Schultz situation, and she had sent back a wealth of information that had surprised Captain Jacobs. He hadn't intended to kept her in place for so long, but the information kept coming and there was never a time when it would have been good to get her out.

Back in Army Intelligence headquarters there was a great deal of debate about the specific value of the information. No-one was prepared to draw up plans for attacks on trains carrying Jews from the ghettos to the camps. There was no-one on the ground with that kind of resource. The partisans attacked trains, but trains whose destruction had value to the Allies, trains carrying men or arms, not trains carrying Jews. Lieutenant-Colonel Stängl's responsibility was restricted in any case to the lines leading east to Auschwitz. Six trains rolled in every day carrying two thousand people each time, and they had all this knowledge about it but no-one was planning to do anything about it. Calls had been made, Jacobs knew, for the Allies to bomb the tracks, but all such requests had been turned down as 'impractical'. In any case, the Red Army was within striking distance of some of the camps. It was only a matter of time before they were liberated. Of course, the Germans could kill a lot of people before that happened.

But now there were the new orders, Stängl's new job. If he had control of the entire Polish railway network, that suggested that carrying Jews to their death was receiving a higher priority in German High Command than carrying vital war supplies. That was hardly credible, given that the Russians were pressing the German armies very hard and were about to break out from the Ukraine and the Baltic states and overrun the whole of Poland. Hitler was seemingly sacrificing his armies to ensure that even if the war against the Allies were lost the war against the Jews would be won. If the Allied commanders had read Mein Kampf, they would have known he would do that.

It also meant that Captain Jacobs might be able, now, to convince people that those tracks were worth attacking. A railway line that couldn't be used for transporting troops or materiel also couldn't be used for transporting Jews to their death. That was how he saw it. How he put it in his reports, though, was that railway lines that were controlled by the killing programme could be attacked as part of the general war effort, and in particular could prevent the Germans bringing reinforcements up for their hard-pressed Eastern Front. The Polish railway system suddenly looked more important, whichever side you were on, and that made Lieutenant-Colonel Fritz Stängl a hot property.

Roza would stay.

In any case, she didn't ask to be pulled out. If she had, well, there would have been no choice, but as long as she didn't Captain Jacobs felt justified in not suggesting it.

Fritz never got far on his tour of camps. He set off with his driver and a bodyguard from Bielsko, but when they stopped at the checkpoint on the edge of Lodz he was handed a message. It was an order to go straight to Warsaw, to ignore all other orders or signals, and to report in person to SS Obergruppenführer Bergmann, commander of all the SS in the General Government of Poland.

He told his driver to plan the new route. Corporal Riester noted the grim look on his face and kept his mouth shut. The guard, sitting next to Riester, hadn't spoken so far and none of this concerned him. He went where they told him. Sitting in this nice comfortable car was a lot better than getting shot at by Russians.

What they found in Warsaw was the beginnings of panic. Soldiers were running around, officers were shouting at them and lorries were careering about the city. Fritz hadn't realised how close the Reds were until he saw the look of fear in the eyes of German soldiers in Warsaw. SS General Bergmann had that look too, and this confirmed Fritz's deepest fears.

'Colonel Stängl, thank you for coming so promptly.'

Fritz wondered is this was sarcasm. An order from SS Headquarters was normally answered promptly.

'Lieutenant-Colonel, General. You said Colonel.'

'Yes I did. Here is the order for your field promotion.'

'Promotion? What have I done ....? '

'Nothing yet. This is in recognition of what you are about to do. Sit down, Stängl. Now, tell me, how much do you know about Operation Reinhard?'

'A little. It closed last year sometime, didn't it? '

'That's right. October. The three camps at Treblinka, Sobibor and Belzec are now farms. You would never know they had been there.'

'How many ... I mean ...'

'Oh, something over one and a half million, give or take. You lose count, you know.'

Fritz didn't think the SS ever lost count of dead Jews. His own record of deliveries to Auschwitz were meticulous. He could have quoted the number to the General there and then, down to the nearest fifty. Bergmann, he suspected, was being disingenuous.

'Well, we have a job for you in connection with those facilities.'

'But if they no longer exist ...'

'The camps have gone but there are, shall we say, certain items pertaining to the, er, victims, that the Reich has an interest in.'

'Which items would they be, sir?'

'Well, there are many, you know, junk mostly, hair, shoes, that sort of thing, all very useful but frankly of limited interest at this stage of the game.'

Fritz hadn't realised it was a game.

'I don't think you've brought me here to discuss the hair of dead Jews, have you Sir? '

'No. I brought you here because I need someone I can trust. I mean the Reich needs someone like you, Stängl, with a proven record of efficiency and reliability.'

'To do what, exactly, sir?'

'To make sure that some very valuable property of the Reich is delivered safely.'

'I see. May I know the destination of this property?'

'Yes, Switzerland. And before you have to ask, yes, I am talking about gold. Gold that the Reichsbank urgently needs to pay foreign companies for shipments of weapons. That gold is now the only way Germany can pay for foreign currency. It would not be an exaggeration to say that the success of your mission will seriously prejudice the course of the rest of the war. Now down to details. The gold I'm talking about is in its unprocessed form, and it's being held securely here in Warsaw. In addition to that there is a large amount from the camp at Kulmhof to the north which needs to be collected, and then there is of course the hoard at Auschwitz itself.'

'Auschwitz? I was not aware ....'

'No, well, it has, until now, been none of your business. There are officers charged specifically with the collection of gold there, and there is a special storage area for it.'

'I was not aware of that.'

'No, no-one is who doesn't need to know. Well, now you are one of those people. You are to drive back to Auschwitz immediately, where you will collect their gold, and from there you will come back to Warsaw and add ours, then you will proceed to Kulmhof to collect the last of it. From Kulmhof you will take the gold to the Degussa smelting plant in Hamburg, where it will be melted down and turned into bars with the stamp of the Reichsbank. The Swiss insist. They are, it seems, a little fussy, which is a novelty for them, but they have an eye on the future and at this stage I don't think they are putting their money on Germany. From Prussia you will escort the gold to the Swiss border, where you will be met by agents of the Union Bank, who will be expecting it.'

Fritz sat back in his chair and allowed this to sink in. He avoided the General's eye, because the General, he thought, was avoiding his.

'And, if you don't mind me asking, Sir, will you be issuing me with written orders for this? I mean, I wouldn't like to get stopped by the Gestapo with a lot of gold and no apparent reason to have it in my possession.'

'Excellent, excellent, a man after my own heart. I knew I had chosen the right person for the job. You think of everything, and I personally don't blame you for your caution. Naturally, I shall be issuing the order myself, so everything will be, as our friends say, completely kosher. Anything else you would like to know?'

'Yes, one or two things. When? '

'Tomorrow. A lorry will be here to meet you for the trip to Auschwitz in the morning at 0730 hours.'

'A lorry? Well I think that helps to answer my next question. How much gold are we talking about?'

'To be precise, at the present count four thousand one hundred and twenty five kilos.'

Fritz gave an involuntary gasp. Bergmann noticed it.

'Yes, it's a lot. Enough to purchase a new airforce.'

'Really?'

'Well, a figure of speech. Between you and me there would be little point building a lot of planes right now. We don't have the trained pilots to fly them and in any case now that the Reds have overrun the Romanian oil fields we couldn't find the fuel for them to take off. No, I don't actually know what will be done with this money but I feel sure the Führer will have a plan. As we speak, a major counter-offensive is being prepared. The Russians think they have us on the run but I assure you they don't. We have some surprises for them yet. We are going to win this war and we are going to realise the true destiny of the German people.'

Bergmann was getting a little over-excited. Fritz thought he sounded like his driver, Corporal Riester, except that Riester, being just a corporal, didn't have the power that this man had and wasn't therefore as dangerous, to Germany if not the Soviet Union. Fritz had seen these maniacs before, throwing away good men's lives for their own personal belief in the glory of the Reich. The only lives they never risked were their own. He had a bad feeling about this whole business. It was a feeling that he was acting as errand boy for some personal scam of the General's. He had a horrible feeling that the gold and the General were going to disappear over the Swiss border never to be seen again. He didn't care a lot about that because it wasn't his gold and General Bergmann could go where he liked at far as he was concerned. What he cared about was taking the blame if it got out, and get out it most certainly would. Stealing over four tonnes of gold was a good trick, but it wasn't something you could do without anyone noticing. Of course, he could be getting over-excited himself. It was a perfectly feasible story. Alright, it was odd, but these weren't normal times.

Fritz had the written order in his briefcase early the next morning, signed personally by SS General Bergmann. The lorry was waiting for him and in the back sat six soldiers, one of whom was an NCO. He had them out of the vehicle to inspect them, not because he was interested in whether they had shaved that morning or polished their boots, but because he wanted to see what calibre of men they were. For a start they were Lithuanians. That was alright, except that the sergeant was the only one who spoke German. He instructed him to tell his men that they were to guard this lorry with their lives and the Sergeant saluted him and said something to the men that could have been guard this lorry with your lives or it could have been this bloke thinks we're here to protect his backside but look here, men, I say at the first opportunity we shoot him in the back, take the lorry and scarper.

Fritz was finding it hard to trust anyone these days. He had seen the panic that reigned in the city, and he suspected General Bergmann wasn't the only one getting ready to cut and run if things got really unpleasant vis-a-vis the Russians. He knew enough history to know that the Lithuanians owed no loyalty to Germany. They were only fighting because they hated the Poles who had at one time been their masters.

It occurred to Fritz to wonder why the General had given him Lithuanians, who were surely less likely to be loyal than a squad of SS men, but it only confirmed that he would prefer German soldiers not to know what was going on. He didn't suppose that they were going to be moving bags conspicuously marked gold, property of the Reichsbank. No, the General, he was sure, had arranged for the 'goods' to be packed as clothing or ammunition or something equally uninteresting. The same applied to the reason for sending all that gold guarded by only six soldiers, plus Fritz and his driver and bodyguard. It wasn't a security detail for a shipment worth so much, and the General had explained his reasoning, which was that a large guard would attract more attention from the partisans. No, this was to look like a routine Wehrmacht delivery of something hardly worth stealing. With that thought, Fritz realised his previous idea about marking the gold as ammunition was also a bad idea. No, it would be something a lot less interesting that that, something a gang of partisans wouldn't want. He couldn't think what it might be that the partisans wouldn't consider worth stealing, but still, he was sure the General had. All Fritz wanted was to get the shipment to the Swiss border and off his hands. It briefly occurred to him to steal it for himself but he knew it was a fantasy. No, it took a lot of organisation to get away with something like that, the kind of organisation and contacts an SS General had at his disposal. Assuming, that was, that this was a scam and not simply what he had been told it was.

The sun was already high in the sky, and the day promised to be hot. Fritz had Corporal Riester put the hood down on the car. He would at least enjoy the ride in the back. Now he was a full Colonel he felt entitled to enjoy the salutes that junior officers threw him when they spotted the flag on the front of the Mercedes as it drove slowly through the crowded streets of Warsaw. The soldiers in the back of the lorry might be plotting his murder, but for now the air was pleasant and he had no thoughts to trouble him. He sat back and thought of Rudi.

In fact Rudi was dead. Fritz's dream of General von Stamitz's car being blown up had come true. They had driven over a mine placed by partisans of the Armia Krajowa on the road between Lublin and Krakow and their car had erupted into a fireball. The General and Rudi were at that very moment being burned into charred corpses in the blazing vehicle. Fritz, of course, could not know that.

5

Barbara was enjoying her holiday. The last time she met the courier she got news of the war and it was good. The news she got from Fritz was all propaganda. She couldn't tell if he believed it, but she didn't, and for all she knew the courier's news could be propaganda too but she didn't think so. He had recently lost the surly look he had always had, and he was even quite excitable. The Red Army, he told her, was advancing across the border. They had taken the Ukraine and Lithuania and now they were poised to liberate Poland. From what Barbara knew about the Soviet Union, she would not have used the word liberate but she knew what he meant and she didn't want to disappoint him. Poland had been a sovereign state only from end of the last war to the beginning of this one, then split between Germany and the USSR and now the Russians were about to 'liberate' it. Well, that kind of liberation Poland could do without. On the other hand, could any master be worse than Germany?

For Barbara it was an academic question. She had no intention of staying in Poland after the war. Poland had no memories she wanted to carry into her future. She was going back to Sweden and from there she was going to take her baby son and live in Palestine. She thought she might also take Krystyna but she wasn't at all sure Krystyna would want to come. What would Palestine mean to her? Well, maybe baby Mordechai would be reason enough.

These thoughts made her think too that perhaps she had done enough, that she should get out of this. Captain Jacobs had said she could end it any time she liked. She only had to send a message and they would arrange for her disappearance from Bielsko. If the Allies really were winning the war was there anything else she could usefully tell them? The Germans, surely, would have better things to concern themselves with than killing the last few Jews. It was a very reasonable idea but it was also wrong. Barbara, though, could not know that.

It was hot these days, and she had nothing to do while Fritz was away but sunbathe in the garden of the little house he had requisitioned. It was, she knew, actually someone else's house, perhaps even a Jewish family had lived there, but whoever it had belonged to they were long gone. This war, people moved around, those who didn't die anyway, and who could say what anyone owned any more? Most people didn't even own their own lives any longer.

She wondered who lived in her family home in Warsaw now, probably some senior German officer. She found herself hoping they would look after it and she had to remind herself that it didn't matter, that no-one was going back there. She knew she hadn't had time to mourn for them and she knew that probably she never would, that in war death is so commonplace you can't observe the normal rituals of mourning because, well, you would never have time for any-thing else. War cheapens death to the point where no-one any longer takes much notice of it.

She felt guilty about it but what she felt especially guilty about was that she missed Motti more than her parents or her sister. She couldn't understand why this was, why she could see his face simply by closing her eyes, but no matter how hard she tried she had difficulty conjuring her mother's face out of the past. She tried to remember whose crazy idea it was for her and Motti to get married. It had seemed perfectly natural at the time. He was, she knew very well, someone her father would never have approved of, her father who deep down despised the religious Jews for what he called their superstition and backward ways. He had brought her up to believe what he believed but in the end she had followed her heart and married a man for one reason only, and she could hardly believe she was saying it, but yes, she loved him. She wondered if she would have loved him if he had come to her house, with his long black coat and side locks, before the war. Her father wouldn't even have let him through the door. No, perhaps she wouldn't have loved him, so perhaps that love came from somewhere else. Perhaps it took the war and all the dying for her to love Mordechai Levinson. Well, she could only ponder. One day, perhaps, when she and the blessed child of that crazy marriage lived in the Jewish homeland, perhaps she would try to explain to her son what she herself had so much trouble understanding. Yes, perhaps he would help her to know.

She would dress him like a Palestinian, like the photographs she had seen in a Zionist newspaper, in khaki shorts and a shirt wide open at the neck, and he would grow up free and strong and the Mediterranean sun would turn his skin brown and he would become a farmer and make the desert bloom. She hoped he would never have to take up arms to defend his people, but from what Captain Jacobs had told her she realised that was a hope unlikely to be fulfilled. Palestine, he had said, was going to need strong men and women to defend the Jewish national home. Defend it from whom, though? He had told her about the Arabs but she hadn't really understood why the Jews were going to have to fight them, in Palestine of all places. When was the fighting going to end? How many more people had to die? She closed her eyes and let the strong Polish sun warm her through, the same sun that warmed the Jews in Palestine, and she imagined that if she opened her eyes again she would be there, in the desert that miraculously produced food for the hardworking, bare-armed Jews who cultivated it, and that there were Jewish children running around and laughing and singing the Hebrew songs the child had taught them on that first journey to freedom. She tried to remember his name but it wouldn't come. She remembered the name of the girl who had died, though, because she had taken it for herself for this operation. She had done that quite deliberately, to perpetuate the name of the little girl she had never actually known, whose parents had given her up and died themselves, leaving a woman called Roza to care for her but she couldn't, she couldn't save her, as much as she wanted to. Well, out of all that had come her own son, another Mordechai Levinson, her offering for Palestine.

She was woken first by a shadow that came between her and the sun and then by a voice. It took her a moment to think why someone was speaking to her in German and then she remembered where she was and she wanted it not to be true but it was.

'Excuse me Miss, but I have been ordered to give you a message.' She shielded her eyes from the late afternoon rays that came over his head and shone through his blond hair. She thought at first it looked like a halo but then she remembered who he was, Private Müller, the young soldier who came with messages sometimes for Fritz. This time it was a message for her. Her skirt had slipped and she was showing a lot of leg. Private Müller looked embarrassed, and she wondered how old he was but she left it where it was because to move it would have shown that she was embarrassed too.

'Excuse me Miss, a message from the colonel.'

'The colonel?'

He looked puzzled. 'Colonel Stängl, Miss.'

Yes, of course, how could she forget so quickly? 'Ah, that Colonel, of course.' She smiled to explain it was all a joke, this confusion. She couldn't tell him he had dragged her back from the desert where SS Colonels didn't exist.

'Yes Miss. He called to say that he is coming straight back to Bielsko. A change of orders apparently, and will be here for dinner tonight.'

'I see. Well, thank you …'

'Müller, Miss.'

'Yes, thank you Müller.'

So, the holiday was over. A shame. Her dreams would have to be put on hold for a while.

As she was thinking that, Fritz was in the Mercedes, enjoying the sunshine, with the steady grinding noise of the lorry behind him, and he was being lulled into sleep. His eyes were closing against the fierceness of the sun's rays and he felt disinclined to bother with opening them. He was beginning to wonder if they should stop and put the hood back on the car to shield them from the heat. Riester, he could see, wiped the sweat from the back of his neck from time to time with a handkerchief. Fritz adjusted his peaked cap to provide a little protection for his eyes. That was when he heard another sound, a sound he could not quite make out at first, but then he recognised it, a plane. It was too far off and he tried, for no good reason, to decide if it was a Messerschmidt or a Stuka. A fighter, for sure, he could hear the pitch of the engine, and it got louder now and that was when he saw it, no more than a speck on the horizon. The sun was behind it and he blinked and each time he did that he got a brief view of the black speck becoming larger and larger. It was following the road, probably as an aid to navigation, he thought. Then he noticed that instead of flying a steady course it was losing height. A moment of fantasy had him imagining it in trouble and the pilot bailing out and the plane crashing on them, but it was only a fantasy after all.

Then it was closer, close enough that when the wings dipped a little and the sun no longer blinded him he saw the markings, and he tried to figure out why on a Luftwaffe fighter where there should be a swastika there was instead a red star, and in the split second it took him to realise that something was terribly wrong the pilot opened fire.

Heavy calibre rounds slammed into the road surface and bit large chunks out of it. A single round hit the side of the car and killed the bodyguard instantly and his body flew backwards propelled by the violent impact and the rest of the burst hit the lorry immediately behind them, killing the driver and two of the Lithuanians in the back. One man was thrown out over the tailgate but the rest of them died when the lorry careered off the road, crashed into a ditch and burst into flames. Private Riester instinctively swung the wheel of the car and turned the vehicle a hundred and eighty degrees. That enabled a large fragment of burning tarpaulin from the lorry to catch him full in the face and he caught fire and then he was blinded by the heat and then he died. Fritz tried to pull the heavy canvas off him but it was impossible. His hands got burned and then he was helpless and anyway it was heavy and his old shoulder injury drained the strength from his left arm and he had no choice but to give up. In any case, he could see it was too late. He jumped out of the car and finding a little muddy water in the bottom of the ditch he plunged his hands into it and that brought a little relief.

The man who had been thrown out of the lorry wasn't badly hurt. He had a broken arm and multiple cuts and scratches, but he was going to live. No-one else in the convoy was. Fritz surveyed the scene of devastation and what he felt was anger, anger that a stupid

Russian pilot had had the audacity to fly into his war and shoot at him. Well, there it was. The priority now, he knew, was to get himself and the surviving soldier back to Warsaw for medical aid. The soldier was unable to drive because of his broken arm, so Fritz had no choice. The engine of the car started first time and he lifted the bonnet to check if any vital parts had been hit but they hadn't. He pulled Riester and the bodyguard out and left them by the side of the road with the others, and then he wrapped strips of cloth round his hands, soaked them in the muddy water, and turned the car northwards.

'Excuse me Miss.'

'Ah Müller, again. What is it now?'

'Well Miss, another message.'

'Yes?'

'Yes Miss. Colonel Stängl has gone back to Warsaw, Miss. His car was hit in an air raid. He's been hurt. Not badly, but they say he will be in hospital for a while.'

'Oh, I see. Er, did they give any indication of how long?'

'No Miss, but I got the impression it would be some time.'

'I see. Well, thank you Müller. Thank you very much.'

6

It was time to go. The war was moving faster now, and with Fritz injured who knew what would happen, where he would be posted afterwards? Without his protection she was in an impossible position. Anyway, he was the reason for her mission. Without him, she had no job to do.

The next day she rode out and met the courier at the appointed time. She gave him a message for Captain Jacobs to the effect that there was nothing more for her to do and he should arrange to have her pulled out. She would keep the rendezvous as normal a week later, and expect the courier to have orders to take her with him. She didn't want to wait for a formal acknowledgement of her request. She was suddenly in a hurry to get away from all this and go back to her son. She wasn't convinced that she had done much good anyway, and now it all seemed pointless. Her enthusiasm for hitting back at the enemy had waned and she was tired. She had found working undercover stressful and sometimes she woke in the morning and couldn't figure out who she was. Well, it was time to be herself again, or at least whatever remained of herself.

A week later she packed the maximum she could reasonably carry if anyone stopped and searched her. She was going out for a long ride and would need enough food for the day and spare clothing in case the weather changed, but that was all. There wasn't much else in the house of hers anyway. She looked round before she finally closed the door and wondered why she even thought of it as home.

She took a longer route than normal as an extra precaution, and was slightly late for the rendezvous. The courier, she knew, would wait half an hour and no more. She wasn't that late. But as she walked the horse along the path she knew so well she could tell there was something wrong. He always whistled when he heard the horse's hooves, but today there was silence. And then she had to pull the horse up sharply because from the trees stepped two German soldiers. They pointed their rifles at her and ordered her down. There was no sign of the courier but suddenly she saw him, lying face down by the side of the path and there was a dark red stain spreading from his chest and soaking into the earth. Her heart was beating fast and she hoped when she opened her mouth that she wouldn't give herself away. She tried to think about Fritz, tried to make herself feel German. One of the soldiers spoke to her in broken Polish and she replied to him in fluent German, which was a good start.

'Show me your papers. What are you doing here?'

'Well, Corporal, I should think that is fairly obvious.'

'Don't get smart with me. I asked you a question. Who are you?'

'Well, as you will see from my papers, I am Barbara Hass. As you will also see, I am under the protection of SS Lieutenant-Colonel Fritz Stängl. I think you know what that means.'

'Yes, we know what that means alright. Well, so much for who you are, but why are you here?'

'No particular reason. The Colonel is away on important business for the Fatherland and I am amusing myself in the forest and exercising my animal here. He gets restless if he doesn't get a good long ride.'

'But why here?'

'Why not here? I understood it was perfectly safe to ride through these woods, but I see I was mistaken. Who is that man?'

The soldier didn't like being asked questions, but he felt it prudent to be polite at least.

'We caught a partisan. He's dead.'

'So I see. Did you manage to question him before you shot him? I mean, surely, catching a partisan for interrogation would be a feather in your cap. A promotion even, if I had a word in the right ears.'

The soldier thought about this and she could see him working out if he could lie, but he realised the danger of making up intelligence he hadn't actually obtained.

'No, he pulled a gun on us and we had to kill him. Shame.'

'Yes, a shame. Well, very well done even so Corporal ... Corporal ...?'

'Schuster, Miss.'

'Very good, Corporal Schuster. I shall be sure to mention your name. Well done.'

'Thank you Miss. And you be careful now. There could be more of them out here. If I were you I'd go straight back to town. Can't be too careful, you know.'

And with that he gave her a salute, and then seeing how it was going his friend did the same, and she mounted her horse and rode off. She knew, now, that the courier hadn't given anything away. But she also knew that any chance of escape was, for the time being, blocked to her. With a heavy heart, she rode slowly back to Bielsko.

By the time she arrived back at the house, she had made up her mind what she had to do. It would take more preparation but there was no time to lose, because she wanted to be away before Fritz got back and Private Müller saying he would be in hospital for a while didn't actually mean anything. A while could be a year but it could also be a week. She had no idea how serious his injuries were and she also had no-one she could ask. It was while she was trying to clear her head and put some practical ideas into some sort of plan of action that she received a visit from an SS Sturmbannführer.

'Miss Hass?'

'Yes. How can I help you Major?'

'Major Gerhardt Ebert. May I come in?'

It was politely asked, but it wasn't a question.

'Well, I am here acting on information that you were seen riding your horse in the woods nearby.'

She tried desperately to read his mind but the only way there was through his eyes, and she didn't want to look into them, because they could be a trap.

'Yes, that's correct. What about it? Have I done something wrong?'

'Oh no, not at all, please put your mind at rest there.'

She heard his assurance and decided to ignore it.

'So?'

'Ah yes, well you see, I am here concerning your safety.'

'I see. Am I at risk?'

'Well, as you discovered today, there are partisans in the area, surprisingly close. They are of course stupid to come here but I expect they have their reasons.'

Barbara pulled out the pistol Fritz had given her and thought she saw a flicker of concern in Major Ebert's eyes now. It amused her.

'As you see, Major, I am armed and ready.'

'Yes, but with respect I suggest your chances against a gang of terrorists would, I'm afraid, be somewhat limited, even with that, which by the way I suggest you put away.'

She put the weapon down on the table beside her, where he could still see it. She had no intention of using it, not on him, not just now, but she liked to think that he thought she might. She had no doubt that this man had shot many women in his time, but she doubted very much if any of them had ever fired back.

'So, notwithstanding your obvious bravery I am afraid I must ask you not to leave the town until further notice.'

'Oh. Is that an order?'

He smiled to reassure her that it was a suggestion which they both understood to be an order. He shrugged his shoulders as if to say what can I do, I have my own orders, and he made the correct polite noises a man would make to the mistress of his commanding officer, and left.

She had little doubt that this was a formality, that if she actually tried to ride out of town she would be detained with rather less politeness. It would be very easy to shoot her and tell Fritz when he returned that they found her body out in the woods, killed by the partisans for her horse. Would he doubt them? Would he even care? Her status, and therefore her safety, depending entirely on Fritz Stängl, and he wasn't there and for all she knew he might not be coming back.

So, her holiday, it seemed, had started again. Only now she sat in the garden and sunbathed and racked her brains for a way out of this. The net was closing round her. The courier gone, a ban on riding, it was getting hard to see how she was ever going to leave.

And she didn't. She sat in the garden and pretended none of this was happening, that the greatest extermination of innocent people in the history of mankind wasn't taking place just fifty kilometres away while she sunbathed because she was powerless to do anything else. She went every day to the stables and groomed her horse but she could do no more than walk it round the cobbled streets of the town to ensure the minimum amount of exercise, as if amidst the mountains of dead a horse mattered.

She did that until three weeks later Fritz came back. His hands had light bandages on them but the damage would heal. If he lived long enough. He had recently learned about Rudi, and he wasn't sure how he felt. Lost, but in a way relieved. He wondered if he still needed Barbara but there would, he knew, be other men, so he did.

She asked him to rescind the order about riding, for the horse's sake she said, and he promised to look into the matter. He suggested they ride together, which would be safer, and she couldn't, for the sake of form, object to that, but in any case she was well aware that he didn't mean it, that there wasn't going to be time. Nevertheless, she agreed readily, because it might create a precedent, and that was just what happened. They were due to go out together just a week later but he called to say he had been detained at the office as it were, and would she mind going without him. He called the local commandant and told him it was authorised. He wondered if he did that in the secret hope that the partisans would kill her and save him the trouble, but he wasn't sure.

So she went riding, and because she hadn't been prepared she didn't use the opportunity to make her escape. Still, what she did once she would able to do again.

It didn't work out like that though. Fritz's hands were getting better and he informed her he would be going off soon to complete the operation he had attempted before. He didn't say any more, because he didn't need to, because that night he got more drunk than usual and she had plenty of time to take his briefcase and keys and look through his orders. That was when she knew that everything had changed, not just for him or even for her, but for a lot of people.

She memorised as much as she thought she was going to be able to recall, but she took the precaution of drawing a sketch map to replicate the one in the case, his exact route not only from Auschwitz to Warsaw and Kulmhof, and then on to Germany, but more importantly his second journey down the length of Germany to Switzerland. The orders from General Bergmann were very detailed, and they left Barbara in no doubt that now any thought that her mission was completed was quite wrong. This was what she had been sent to him for, even if no-one had known it. Now, she could do something that was going to make it all worthwhile. Now, the Jewish Underground were going to steal four tonnes of gold.

Then, after she had replaced the briefcase and keys, she carefully tore the map into three pieces, like Captain Jacobs had done once. Alright, there weren't three people to carry a piece of the jigsaw, and she would have to do that herself, but she would hide them as best she could, and she would take the chance. This was important enough to take that chance and many more.

7

A few days later Fritz left Bielsko. He said goodbye to Barbara and looked like he believed he would not be seeing her again. She knew that for a fact. He drove in convoy this time, with a motorcycle in front, then his car, then a lorry with twelve SS soldiers now, and bringing up the rear was another motorcycle and sidecar. They would of course have no chance against an opportunistic Red Air Force pilot with a grudge but they should have enough firepower to see off anything but an extremely determined partisan band.

Which left Barbara free to carry out her own plan. She complained bitterly to anyone who cared to listen about being alone, and then she went to the stable and complained to the stable boy about not being able to exercise the horse properly and how the way things were going the animal would probably be captured by the Reds and used to feed their troops, and the stable boy took badly to that bit of news and saddled up the horse and said go on, ride, I won't tell anyone. It was a nice gesture but a bit pointless because she could hardly ride a chestnut mare through the streets without being noticed. Strangely, though, that was exactly what did happen. She packed a bag for a day's riding and walked the horse over the cobbled streets for the last time expecting at any moment to be stopped by a sentry but it didn't happen, and she mounted up and rode off out of town and the sentry on the little wooden bridge over the river saluted her and she gave him a grin and a mock salute back and free of the paved roads for the last time she put the horse into a canter and said goodbye to Bielsko and Colonel Fritz Stängl. For now.

She took the road north-west out of town and rode into the woods, where she immediately turned east and kept going in a straight line. She had a good idea of where she was heading because the courier had let it slip more than once that his base was near a village called Nowy Korczyn and although she didn't know where Nowy Korczyn might be she had heard him talk about crossing the River Nida close to where it branched from the River Wisla. That gave her enough clues to orientate herself based on the maps she had seen in Fritz's briefcase. From Nowy Korczyn the Armia Krajowa partisans would be able to lead her to the Jewish Underground.

She estimated that she would be able to cover up to a hundred kilometres a day on horseback, providing she could find feed and water for the animal, which was unlikely to be a problem. On that basis she was going to need two days or so to reach the AK camp, and she had enough food for herself to see her through that far so the only real worry she had was avoiding German patrols. She had Fritz's pass that instructed all German sentries to let her through, but the further she rode from Bielsko the harder it was going to be to explain where she was going so she decided on the second day that she wouldn't use it but would make up some other story. It would of course be better if she didn't meet any Germans and therefore didn't need another story. She knew that the horse made her a lot more conspicuous but she also knew that without it the journey was going to take very much longer so she decided she would ride for now at least. Besides, she enjoyed the company. The mare whinnied from time to time and Barbara answered her in Yiddish, freely now, and the animal didn't know what she was saying of course, no matter what language she spoke, but even so it seemed to like the sound of her voice.

She met no patrols that first day and she rode until it got dark, so by the time she went to sleep that night under the shade of an elm tree she reckoned she had covered more than half the distance.

The morning dawned bright and it was obviously going to be another hot day. She would be staying under the cover of the forest for most of the time though so keeping cool wasn't going to be too much of a problem, and after a light breakfast she mounted up with the thought that by the evening she should be in the company of Poles who were fighting the Germans and that she reckoned was going to feel good, like the old days, and as she rode she thought of Leszek Belka and all the others who had died that terrible day at the hands not of the Germans but of the Poles of the NSZ. The confusion of this war never stopped. You never knew who to hate and who you might have to kill, or be killed by. All the teaching her father had given her about being Polish first and Jewish second or even not at all as far as he was concerned had come in the end to be worthless. It was made painfully clear by the Germans that you were Jewish first and last, and not only the Germans but the Lithuanians, the Ukrainians and not a few of the Poles themselves. The Polish government, he told her, had already enacted anti-Jewish legislation before the war, in the hope that they might stave off an attack by Germany, that Hitler might see Poland as an ally, not a country to be overrun. But toadying to Hitler had done Poland no good, and they had died alongside the Jews, though not of course in anything like the same numbers.

Barbara Hass thought about these things as she rode and as she thought about them she became Roza Levinson again. She stopped and searched in her saddlebag and there it was, the ring that had been fashioned for her at the camp, and she slipped it on her finger again and it felt good, and in a daze she let the horse carry her through the trees while she thought of Motti and tears ran down her face. She tried to imagine him living in the forest on his own, scavenging for food, waiting for the war to end, putting on his imaginary phylacteries every morning and turning to Jerusalem to pray. And then she imagined him dead and she knew that of the two the latter was the probable truth.

And later that day she came to a river. She couldn't know if it was the right river but having little choice in the matter she turned south and followed it. After another two hours she could hear rushing water and knew she had come to the confluence of the Nida and the Wisla, and there, exactly where it should be, was the wooden bridge. Then she obeyed her partisan training, dismounted and led the horse into the tree cover and waited. She was impatient but impatience, she knew, gets you killed, so she curbed her anxiety to get among friends.

She watched the bridge with the pistol in her hand and wished it was her old sniper rifle but it wasn't and it would have to do. She had no illusion about her ability to take on heavily-armed German soldiers, but she would take at least one with her when she died and whatever happened they would not take her alive.

So she waited and watched and listened and after an hour the light started to fade and she considered it was safe to cross. The horse's hooves made a lot more noise on the bridge than she was happy with but still, no-one seemed to be listening and in a minute they were safely over and she made a dash for the tree cover on the other side. Again, she stopped and listened, because if anyone had followed her she was sure to hear them, even though she could no longer see the bridge itself. And what she heard was the unmistakable sound of a rifle bolt, in fact not one but two, and she tried to calm her breathing so she could detect where the sound had come from but it had come and gone and now, somewhere out there in the darkening woods, were two men with weapons who knew she was there. They had seen her cross and lain in wait for her and the only chance she had was to move quietly in the dark.

Carefully, she tied her horse to a tree and slipped away. They might even be after the horse and not her. Either way, she didn't think they were Germans. Germans, in her experience, came full tilt at you firing as they went, not this cat and mouse business. No, these were partisans. The question was, whose side were they on? If they were AK men, she wanted to make herself known to them but given that they weren't expecting her would they shoot first and ask questions later? She could come out with her hands up but then if they were NSZ they would almost certainly simply shoot her where she stood because the NSZ, in her experience, didn't take prisoners and whilst they were nominally Polish patriots she had seen what that meant a long time ago.

In the end she had no choice to make. A Polish voice came from the darkness somewhere and she knew that whoever they were she was now at their mercy.

'Put your weapon down on the ground and face this way.'

Face this way? Which way? She put the pistol down and stood up again, trying to locate the voice.

'Now, move forward and keep moving, with your hands up.'

She did exactly that and came out of the trees by the bridge again. In front of her was a man pointing a rifle at her head and now, behind her, was another. She turned to face this one.

'Papers. Give me your papers.'

She reached into her jacket slowly and pulled out her ID. It was of course German, in the name of Barbara Hass. Would she get a chance to explain? In the event, she didn't need to. They didn't look at the document. Perhaps, she considered the possibility, they were simple peasants really and they couldn't read. Well, certainly they wouldn't be able to read German. Or perhaps she was lucky and it was just too dark for them to bother. Whatever the reason, they took her and her horse with them and twenty minutes later she was at the camp she had all along been looking for.

The two men swaggered into camp to show how clever they had been to catch this woman, and not just a woman but a horse too, which was always of great use to the group, and she came face to face with a large man who not just by his size or even by the crossed bandoliers displayed ostentatiously on his barrel chest but by the look of contempt on his face she knew immediately to be their leader.

'My name is Roza Levinson. I am with the Underground and I have forged papers in the name of Barbara Hass because I have been working undercover in Bielsko.'

This information caused no change in the look. He came close to her and glared into her eyes. Then he slapped her face. She reeled back and felt the blood trickle from her lower lip.

'Yes, I know who you are, bitch. You are the woman who betrayed Stanislaw Piwnik.'

Stanislaw Piwnik? She racked her brains to think who he was talking about and who she might conceivably have accidentally betrayed.

'Either you are good at deception or you have dismissed a Polish patriot as unimportant to your Jewish cause.'

Roza was tired and frightened and she tried not to but she started to cry. These people were supposed to be friends, and she didn't think she could stand any more of this madness.

'My name is Roza ...'

'Yes, yes, I heard you the first time. You are the woman we promised to help and then when our courier came to get your information for your own people, not for the Armia Krajowa, you betrayed him to the Germans.'

Now she knew who Stanislaw Piwnik was. He had of course never given her his name.

'But wait a minute. I had nothing to do with that.'

'Well, we'll let a field court decide on that in the morning, and I promise you I shall be the judge, jury and executioner, so don't expect any mercy.'

He waved his hand dismissively. 'Meanwhile, take her to my tent. If she's going to die tomorrow, I might as well enjoy her tonight.'

And they dragged her off to one side of the camp. Set slightly away from the other tents was a larger affair that obviously served as headquarters and sleeping accommodation for this man. And whichever women he took a fancy to. Two men roughly threw her inside and made it clear that they were standing guard outside. She heard them talking and laughing. She couldn't make out what they were saying but there was little doubt it was about her and what their chief was going to do to her.

There was a great deal of drinking that night and with the drinking came singing and raucous laughter and then came the chief, much the worse for vodka, with a lantern in his hand and an evil look in his eye. He had lost none of his anger.

'So, you look like a man with those clothes, but let's see what you look like without them. Take them off.'

He stood there, swaying, too drunk even to undress her, so she obliged him. She took everything off and stood there in the lamplight naked and he whistled.

'Very nice, yes very nice. Come here, my angel, and let me feel you.'

'No, you come here. Come on.'

She slid onto the bed and looked him intently in the eye. There could be no doubt what he was to do. He undid his belt and stepped towards her at the same time. For a sober man that's a difficult move but for a man in his condition, in the semi-dark, it's nearly impossible. He stumbled and was on his knees in front of her, wondering how he got there. He never saw her slide her hand under the pillow, never saw the knife, and felt nothing as she ran it across his throat. As he fell on to the bed he tried to speak but with a gaping slash in his neck he could make no sound. She dressed quickly, picked up his rifle and ammunition and left him there to die.

With the same bloody knife she cut a slit in the canvas at the back of the tent. It was facing away from the camp so she slid out and peered round the corner. The camp was full of sleeping men who lay where they had fallen in a drunken stupor. By the fire sat one man, awake, but only just. She pulled herself erect and walked over to him as if that was a normal thing to do, and as he looked up at her standing there she plunged the knife down with all her strength into the back of his neck and he fell forward into the flames.

The horse whinnied a little as she untied its harness. They hadn't even removed her saddlebag, so there was nothing for her to do but tie the rifle securely, drape the bandolier over its rump and walk the beast out of camp. She knew about partisan camps and she knew where they would have placed their sentries, and so she took a different path and was unchallenged. After a full twenty minutes she mounted up and rode off. It would be several hours before they woke up and found the carnage, and by that time she wanted to be a long way away.

8

As Roza rode through the trees she shook uncontrollably. She had killed men before, but never like that. It had always been at the end of a rifle, hundreds of metres away. Never before had she seen a man's face as he knew he was going to die. Usually they died without knowing it. This was different, and she knew that now she was tainted with the same guilt they carried. She reasoned that she was right to do it, that they were murderers, even the AK, that they were going to kill her and she had told Motti once you have to know who your enemy is and you have to have no mercy toward him because he has none for you. That was the world that men had made and even if she was a woman those were the rules she had to abide by. Kill or be killed.

She knew, though, that behind that fateful stabbing of the man who was not threatening her was hatred and anger, not for him particularly but for everything, and she realised she had become a slave to her hatred, that her anger would never be expunged, that she had been impossibly brutalised by the men who made this war and killed everyone she loved. Well, not everyone, because now there was her son. But would she ever be capable of being a normal mother? Would she ever be able to leave this brutality behind her and rejoin the human race? Only time would tell.

And right now time was not a luxury she had. She must put these thoughts behind her and find the Jewish Underground, make contact with Captain Jacobs if at all possible, because the stakes were very high. She was painfully aware of Colonel Stängl's schedule, and that meant that even if she found the Underground they would have to put the operation together very quickly, perhaps more quickly than was possible, but still, she had to try. By her reckoning if she didn't get to them within the next two days it would be impossible. If she did get to them in time, it might still be impossible, but that was not her worry. She had to find them.

Partisan headquarters tended to move as the need arose, but that was last year when it had been part of her life with the Armia Ludowa. Now it was different. The Russians were advancing across Poland and their proxy army, the AL, was becoming much more active as the Soviets were able to supply them more readily with arms. She knew all of this from Stängl's briefcase. She had read the reports and she was as well informed as Allied Intelligence, in her part of the country at any rate.

The Jews were last based somewhere between Przemysl and the San River but that was an area that a whole battalion of men might search for a month and not find them. She knew that because the Germans had tried exactly that, and failed, so what chance did she have? She couldn't answer that. She could only ride in that direction and hope for some kind of miracle. She knew that Motti, in this situation, would have prayed for one, but she couldn't make herself do that, pray to a god she always knew had been a fantasy for weak-minded superstitious people. That was what her father had taught her and as much as she would have liked to overcome her upbringing, she found it impossible, so instead she prayed to no-one in particular, not because she thought her prayer might be heard by anyone except her but that was good enough. It comforted her to pray, and she didn't think her father would have minded that.

So she turned her horse south-east and sang one of the Hebrew songs she had learned on that first journey in another place and another time, and she sang in memory of those people but mostly she sang to raise her spirits and at first she sang quietly but soon she lost her fear and the words rang out and this part of a Polish forest echoed with the sounds of a language from far off to remind the trees that the Jews of Poland might be dead but here was one of their number who was very much alive and meant to stay that way. She defied the trees to tell anyone she was there, and all that day and all the same night they kept her secret.

She slept so deeply that in the morning she took a minute to figure out where she was and why, and she knew that today she had to find her people, so she wasted no time. She ate a little and gave the horse a good drink because she was going to ask it to keep going for as long as it took to reach her goal. Then she mounted up yet again and with last night's dreams still occupying her mind, set off.

They made good time all morning and as the sun reached its zenith she allowed them both a rest to eat and drink but afterwards she worried that it might have been a mistake because as the sun moved inexorably towards the horizon it seemed that she would ride for ever and never arrive.

That was when she met Taras. She had speeded the horse up a little in the hope that she might still arrive before nightfall and so she wasn't paying as much attention as she should have been and he literally ran under the animal's hooves. The mare reared in fright and Roza would have fallen off but the boy grabbed the reins and calmed her down and stroked her neck and whispered in her ear something Roza could not make out and in any case it was a language she didn't know. She sat in the saddle not knowing how to react, not knowing who this young person was and if he was a threat. She wanted to believe a boy this age, what was he, eleven, twelve, could not be an enemy but everyone could be your enemy, and no-one was a friend until they proved it.

Still, why was he calming her horse if he intended her harm? He spoke to her in his strange language, looking up at her, shielding his eyes from the late afternoon sun that struck through the forest canopy. He was in rags, forest dirty, but she was used to that by now, and he looked at her in the way she looked at him, wanting to believe the other was a friend, but ready to run if they were wrong, but how, he thought, could a woman on a horse, on her own a long way from the Germans, want to hurt him?

'Armia Ludowa?'

He understood that, because he shook his head.

'Armia Krajowa?'

He shook his head again.

'NSZ?'

He looked blankly at that, which she took to be a good sign.

'Polish?'

At that question he shrugged his shoulders. He didn't know if he was Polish, and Roza could relate to that. He was an outsider living among Poles. He wasn't Jewish though, which left only one possibility.

'Roma?'

At this his face broke into a big, innocent smile, and he started talking quickly in that strange tongue of his, of which she understood not a word, but it was clear to her that this boy was lost and having found her he had done what any child would do in more normal times, he was asking her for help. She held out her hand to see if he would trust her and he thought about it for a moment and then he decided that he did. He took it and she lifted him up on to the saddle behind her. He was light, and she knew he was hungry, the kind of hunger that's not normal or healthy in a child but that comes from living wild. Still, she reasoned, he couldn't be living that wild. He looked lost, but if he really was living entirely on his own he couldn't be, because to be lost you have to belong somewhere. No, this child had people somewhere, people who right now were probably looking for him.

Now he was on the horse he seemed to regain his confidence and he chattered away oblivious to the fact they she didn't know what he was saying but pointing too, and she trusted him to have some good idea why. It didn't occur to her that she couldn't afford the time to take him to his people.

In the event the boy wasn't far from home at all. In half an hour they saw smoke through the trees and he jabbered excitedly and she knew this was it. She rode into a small camp, incredibly dirty and disorganised, with filthy children running around completely naked, the adults in rags, and as she rode on they stopped and looked sullenly at her but then they saw the boy sitting behind her and they came to life and a woman grabbed him and pulled him down off the horse roughly, shouting angrily at him. It could only, she thought with a wry smile, be his mother.

Roza could have ridden on but she didn't. She dismounted and stood there with the reins in her hand and a number of people came and looked at her and talked in that strange language that meant nothing to her and finally they moved aside to create a gap and through the parting came a man, as dirty as the rest but with an air of authority and he was carrying a rifle, a German one, she could see, and she could only guess how he came to be in possession of it. He didn't point it at her but he didn't need to. Anyway, he could see what had happened and he spoke to her again, and this time in German and to be on the safe side she pretended not to understand him and she replied in Polish and that was the language they settled on.

'My name is Roza Levinson. I'm looking for the Jewish Underground. Have you seen them?'

'Roza Levinson, you are welcome. You found the boy, and for that we are grateful. We know nothing of the Jewish Underground, although we have heard of it. Are you armed?'

She considered the question and looked around her. He was, and so might some of the others be. If she lied, she had a feeling they would know and she knew it was better to tell the truth. In any case, even in the dark they might have spotted the rifle tied to the saddle of her horse. She took the pistol from her jacket pocket, held it by the barrel and offered it to him as a show of faith. He took it from her and felt its weight, as if that was how he measured its worth, and smiled. It was German, like his rifle, and as this woman was plainly not in the German army she could only have got it in much the same way as he got his rifle and he looked at her anew and with more respect. He turned the weapon round and offered it to her as a sign of his own good faith, and she took it gratefully.

Having settled that, in no time at all Roza found herself seated round a fire with a plate of hot food in her hand and behind her her horse was being attended to by the boy and she felt strangely at home. People came and sat next to her and talked but they didn't seem much bothered by the fact they they spoke in Romany and she spoke in Polish, which most of them had only a smattering of.

It was plain that these people were going to be no help to her as far as finding the Underground was concerned, but she felt a strong disinclination to refuse their hospitality, and she made up her mind that one night in the company of people who called themselves friends could be forgiven, that she still had another day and that would be enough.

As she fell asleep by the fire she listened lazily to the strange chatter of these people as they themselves prepared for sleep, and she wondered about them. All this time, since the start of the war, she had thought only of her own survival and that of her family and her people, as if this was a war between the Germans and the Jews, but she was reminded that it wasn't true, that the Roma were equally persecuted, that they were out here in the forest, in an environment that they were far more accustomed to than were the Jews, and they were living out the war and waiting for better times. After, if there was an after, they would carry on living here in the woods, because that was the life they had always lived, she knew that much about them, but no longer would they fear the flash raids by German troops hell bent on murdering them.

She slept peacefully, waking from time to time and feeling the warmth of the fire in the cool summer night and hearing the Gypsies murmuring to each other, and when she woke it was already daylight and the camp was bustling around her prone body. She was offered breakfast and took it gratefully. It was hard to say what it was, but these days food was food and if it filled your stomach that was all that was required, and anyway, looking at the squalor of these people she preferred not to know about their cooking arrangements.

Taras had fed her horse and groomed it thoroughly. There were, she could see now in the daylight, a number of horses tethered together in the camp, and she guessed that this was one thing the Roma really knew about and she could see they cared for their horses, it had to be said somewhat better than themselves.

They didn't have much food but even so they insisted she take a parcel of provisions for the day's ride and the man who was their chief said that if, as she said, the Underground were to be found by the San River, she was a little off course, and directed her further south. If she continued the way she was going, he said, she would eventually miss the river and was more likely to cross a route the retreating Germans were using. She knew then that finding the boy had been a gift from God, that not only was she now rested and fed but that without these people she would never have found the Underground and might well have ended up caught by the Germans.

She motioned to Taras to come to her and she put her arms round him with a motherly hug and he flushed and the people laughed. Then she mounted her horse again and rode out of the camp. It felt like leaving the safety of home and she wished she didn't have to go, but she knew she did.

Today had to be the day when she found the Underground, or it would all be for nothing.

9

Now Roza rode with a lighter heart, as if the Gypsies had the power to remove the evil spell that was hanging over her. She knew of course it was fantasy, but when you spend as long as she had talking only to yourself and a horse that doesn't understand either Yiddish or Polish you start to think strange things.

She made good speed all morning and it was all the better for knowing she had narrowly missed going the wrong way. She came to a stream and there she allowed herself another break to eat some of the Roma food as the sun came up high overhead and she felt it wise to let the horse have a rest and a drink. Half an hour later she set off again, and soon crossed a number of paths through the trees and shortly after that she could see the woods were coming to an end.

Then she came to a road.

It was a wide road, and all her instincts told her to follow the procedure she had always used, the one that had kept her safe every time, at every crossing of a road or railway track. The instinct was too strong to ignore, and she tied the horse and lay in wait to watch and listen. Now, she had not only a German pistol, but a rifle as well. She stripped and reassembled it to make sure it was clean and oiled and it was. The partisans might have been a drunken rabble but they hadn't neglected their weapons. She loaded a full magazine of twenty rounds, cocked it, and lay in wait. It was agonising, because every minute that passed was another minute lost, but she just told herself over and over again that it was right, that Leszek would have said do it no matter what, and it was while she was thinking this that it happened, a convoy of German lorries appeared in the distance to her left. She tried to count them. At least three, maybe four, it was hard to see. In any case, she had no option but to let them pass. She didn't have a company of partisans to attack them, just one rifle, so as much as she would have liked to hit them there was absolutely no choice. They came closer now, and then they were rushing past her and there were four of them and in the back of each she could see there were men, tired men, defeated, holding their rifles but instead of the aggression she was used to in Germans there was only hopelessness. These men, she knew, had escaped from the Russians and they were fleeing, and it gladdened her heart to see it.

They rushed past now and she trained her rifle on a man in the back of the last one and wondered if she squeezed the trigger anyone would hear the shot or they would just keep driving, and then the strangest thing happened because she did hear a shot. She looked down at her weapon to see if she had fired it, as if that might be possible without knowing she had, but she hadn't. The safety catch was on. And now there were more shots, small arms, and now mortar fire, and the lorries were careering off the road, and one of them exploded in flames and men were throwing themselves out and burning.

The gunfire was everywhere now and it was coming from the trees either side of the road about five hundred metres to her right and she realised that all the time she had been lying there in watch a partisan unit had been doing the same, within spitting distance, and now they had ambushed a German convoy right under her nose.

She slipped the safety catch off on the rifle and waited, and sure enough one of the German soldiers came running in her direction. She could see the terror on his face and then she killed him. He continued in his forward rush on the road for another two metres or so and fell onto his back and was still. Then there was another and she took him out and then another, and they kept running towards her in their panic to escape the ambush and unbeknown to them an enemy just as implacable was right there in front of them and they were running into her rifle sight. It was only an ordinary assault rifle, without a telescopic sight, but it was enough. There were twelve men and twelve shots. None missed. One man, she thought, for each of the twelve tribes of Israel.

And then, as suddenly as it had started, it stopped. There was an eerie quiet, and in the silence now men came out from the forest and surveyed their handiwork. From time to time they came upon a wounded German and executed him. Roza watched them. She watched their leader point in her direction and she could hear them talking but she couldn't hear what they were saying but it didn't sound like Polish and she couldn't figure it out, because neither was it Russian so what was it? They were talking, obviously then, about the dead men all facing the same way and arguing about how that was possible, because they were out of range of the ambush, and the three of them started walking towards the bodies and as they came closer she realised what language they were speaking. It was Yiddish!

And their leader was Captain Michael Jacobs.

He dropped his rifle in amazement as this crazy woman rushed out and threw herself at him, jabbering incoherently in Yiddish and Polish and at last he grabbed her arms and held her from him to see who this person was and it was Roza, impossibly it was Roza, and then he grinned like a maniac and held her close again and said her name over and over and she cried and cried into his jacket and he continued to hold her and the other two men watched in amazement and shook their heads but they grinned too because this was all very strange, and on top of that they were elated by the battle they had just won and for a minute or two everyone was insane with emotion of one kind or another.

And then, because a reunion in the middle of the road in German-occupied territory was a bad idea, they ran to the lorries, where the company had already loaded up the bodies, and leapt into the cabs. Then Roza said wait a minute and she climbed down and ran back to her hiding place. She removed the saddle bag, and then she slipped the harness and saddle off and slapped the mare on the rump, setting her free. As she saw her beautiful chestnut tail disappear into the trees Roza silently wished her a long and happy life. She would have thought about when she had done that to a donkey once, but she didn't have time.

And then the whole convoy was on the move. The ambush had taken no more than ten minutes, with no loss of life. And by some miracle no-one could understand, it had brought Roza back to them.

Michael drove and listened to her explaining it all but she talked so fast he couldn't follow it and so he let her do that and he drove and let it flow over him because there would be time to do this properly, to debrief in the proper military fashion, but that time was not now.

It took them over two hours to reach their camp and Roza finally fell asleep, despite the grinding of the engine and the bumpiness of the unmetalled road they were driving on. Michael Jacobs carefully lifted her out then and put her to bed. She didn't wake but she mumbled something in her sleep which he was unable to decipher and he wondered what she had been through, what he had put her through, and he thanked God for delivering her back to him safely.

She woke before dawn and got up in a daze. There were men's voices, speaking in Yiddish, and then she heard Michael's American accent and she smiled and remembered and went to say hullo.

'Ah, the sleeper awakes. Feeling better?'

'Yes thanks. And thank you for finding me.'

'Not at all. A pleasure. And by the way, thank you for dealing with twelve enemy soldiers.'

'Was it that many?'

'Modest, huh? I know, you ran out of ammunition.'

'No, I ran out of targets. Listen, Michael, I need to tell you something.'

'Yes, I expect there's lots to say.'

'No, you don't understand. I was looking for you. I have important information.'

'I expect so.'

'No, listen, I mean really important.'

He could see she was serious, and so could the others, and they gave her the respect that was her due and listened. She told them the story of the gold and gave Michael the three parts of the map and explained it all to him in detail and he made careful notes. He looked very serious and said something she didn't understand. He asked the others if they should tell her.

'Michael, tell me what?'

'Roza, it's about the gold. We now know where it has come from.'

'But I know where it's come from. Jewish victims they've murdered. There must be gold jewellery and glasses, wedding rings, coins, that sort of thing.'

'Yes, that too.'

'What do you mean that too? Michael, what is it? Tell me, please.'

'Look, Roza, this is not something you need to know.'

'Not something I need to know? What the hell are you talking about?' She was shouting now. 'Look here, I've killed men, you know that yourself, but there's a lot more than that. I've sat there with the devil and cooked his meals and listened to his drunken orgies while my people were being killed and I did it because you asked me to and I never complained. Well now it's your turn. If you know something, tell me.'

'Alright. Come with me.'

He took her out into the gloom of pre-dawn and they crossed the camp and came to a tent. A strange noise was coming from within.

'Follow me Roza, and learn the truth for yourself.'

In the tent a lamp was lit, and she saw a cot with the wizened form of a man on it. Next to him sat a woman, holding his hand and speaking soothing, mothering words. She looked up at them as they entered.

'Alright, here it is. We don't know his name, because we don't think even he remembers it any longer, but bit by bit we've coaxed his story out of him. A few months ago he escaped from a death march after the Nazis closed down the extermination camp at Sobibor, east of Lublin. He was found wandering along the road, incoherent, like this, and we've been looking after him since then. He was part of what the Nazis call a sonderkommando. It's a group of men who aren't killed in the camps. The Germans use them to drag the bodies out of the gas chambers and burn them. But before they do that they have another job. They remove all jewellery, gold rings, glasses and so on, but then they have to take a pair of pliers and wrench out any gold teeth. The victims' mouths are conveniently wide open because their last act in life is to gasp for air and their muscles go into a spasm. Roza, some of that gold Stängl is carrying comes from the gold teeth of dead Jews. We don't know how much and in any case does it matter but I'm afraid it is probably quite a lot.'

Roza said nothing, but she bent down and let her tears fall on this man's parched skin. Then she walked out of the tent and Michael followed her.

'My father had a gold tooth. It could be in that consignment.'

'I'm afraid it almost certainly is. From your information we would say Stängl is delivering perhaps all the gold the Nazis have ever extracted from their victims in the past year. What do you want to do?'

'I want to come with you.'

'What do you mean?'

'Michael, either you go after that gold or I'll go on my own.'

10

Fritz Stängl sat in the back of his car and nursed his hands. They still hurt, even with the cream the medical officer had given him. He wasn't in a good mood, and he didn't like this operation any more than before. He was still sorry about Rudi's death. He thought he wouldn't care but he did, only in truth he was more sorry for himself than for Rudi. Still, it meant when he got back, what with another posting almost certain, he would get rid of Barbara. She was a good cook but she was beginning to annoy him. There was something about her he couldn't put his finger on, but he was starting to realise he really didn't like her. Rudi had always said it was because she knew too much about him. Yes, perhaps that was all it was, she was dangerous because she knew about Rudi.

Summer was getting past its best. He wondered if while the gold was being melted down in Hamburg he could take a couple of days to go and see his parents, by which he meant his mother. Late summer was a good time on the coast. He would do some fishing perhaps, if he could find his old rod. Maybe she would come with him and they would take a picnic and talk about the old times. He wanted to tell her to get away, further west, because people were starting to talk, secretly of course because such talk was tantamount to treason, about the Russians conquering not just the whole of Poland but the fatherland itself. No-one he had spoken to was in any doubt that Stalin wouldn't stop at the old border. No, Germany had attacked Russia and now Russia would, if it became possible, take its revenge.

He hadn't personally had much contact with Russians but he didn't like the rumours he heard, that the Red Army included non-ethnic Soviet subject races who didn't even speak the language and whose officers had virtually no control over them. Barbarians, that's what they were. The Führer had been only right in trying to destroy them and bring civilisation to the East. Yes, sometimes Fritz thought he would have made a good Nazi. He didn't need that lousy driver of his, Corporal Riester, to lecture him. This man was much better. Kept his opinions to himself. That's what you want in a driver, he thought, someone who drives and keeps his mouth shut.

Still, it was a bit odd, now he thought about it, the way General Bergmann had assigned this new man. Not, Fritz realised now, the kind of thing a General would bother himself with, a minor personnel matter. Fritz looked at his neck from behind, as if that was going to tell him anything, and wondered if in fact he had been duped, if this new man was a plant, given to him to spy on him. Yes, of course, if this whole exercise was some kind of scam, naturally Bergmann would want to keep an eye on him. What better? Perhaps he even arranged for that Red Air Force pilot to shoot them up? No, perhaps not. His imagination was running away with him. Still, this new man, what was his name? Schiller? Yes that was it, Schiller. An odd name, a famous name, too famous for a driver. On the other hand, if they were going to make up a name would they make up such an obviously fake one? On the other hand, why would they make up a name at all? Why not just use his real name? By now, Fritz had made up his mind, anyway, that his driver was spying on him. And that could only be because Bergmann had set this whole thing up for his own benefit. Yes, the more he thought about it the more Fritz realised he was being used to provide for the General's retirement.

In that, as it happened, he was quite wrong. General Bergmann wasn't feathering his own nest. Not with four tonnes of gold, because that's a lot of money for one person. No, General Bergmann was putting aside the funds that would be needed to start a Fourth Reich in the event of catastrophe. Had Fritz known that he would have shrugged his shoulders and said they're all crazy, but he didn't. That was something he would never be privy to. The men who had hatched this plan knew who they wanted, and Colonel Fritz Stängl wasn't one of them. He was ruthless, which was good, but he was a homosexual, which unofficially they were well aware of. Bergmann had seen his file long ago, and had decided it would be useful if ever he needed to put some pressure on him, but for now he was a useful pawn in the very dangerous game they were playing. Hitler, naturally, knew nothing of this plan, because he would have called any plan that assumed the end of his thousand-year Reich a treasonous one.

So Fritz was only partly right about Sergeant Schiller, and he decided there and then that he would be extremely careful what he said to him, or indeed in front of him. He got as far as guessing that in fact this whole operation was probably under Schiller's control rather than his, and he was there to provide the rank that would be expected for such an important mission. He wondered if he cared about that and decided he didn't.

When the convoy arrived in Warsaw they drove straight to Bergmann's headquarters. The city was in turmoil. There was little doubt that despite the official propaganda they were expecting the Red Army to break through and were getting ready to abandon the capital. The General was calm though.

'Ah Colonel Stängl, on time, very efficient, good, good, do come in. Sit down, please. Cigar?'

'No thank you General. I don't smoke.'

'Aha, the Führer would be proud of you. He hates smoking, you know. Not so proud of me, I'm afraid. It is my only weakness.'

The General was being disingenuous. He had a number of weaknesses, but none of them concerned Fritz so he didn't enlighten him.

'So, you have the consignment from Auschwitz-Birkenau?'

'Yes Sir, as ordered.'

Bergmann already knew this because Schiller had reported to him first by telephone as soon as Fritz had given him his orders and left him in charge. He knew that, and Fritz guessed it, but he didn't know that Fritz might know it and of course he went through the ritual.

'In fact the lorry is already loading up the, er, goods, in the city here.'

'Oh, I see. Well, shouldn't you perhaps be supervising?'

'Oh no, Sergeant Schiller is also very efficient. He has my full confidence.'

'Well, if you say so. So when do you leave?'

'It's getting late now. We won't start out until the morning.'

'Oh. Don't you think it would be better to make a start now?'

'No, the roads are too dangerous after dark. The partisans, whom you and I both know don't exist, operate mostly at night. There's no point taking that risk.'

'I see. Yes, very wise, I'm sure. We don't want you to take any chances with such a precious and important cargo. The Fatherland is depending on you, you know.'

Even so, he rather hoped that Fritz would get out of Warsaw as quickly as possible. He wasn't convinced about this officer's reliability, but he had been overruled. Well, if it was going to go wrong he would prefer it to go wrong somewhere else.

And first thing in the morning Fritz checked in the back of the lorry and there it was, sacks and boxes, old ammunition boxes, and any containers found to be serviceable, they were all stacked up at one end of the vehicle and between the seats. On either side sat a row of six SS men, stiffly to attention for the Colonel's inspection. Honour done, he patted the snout of the heavy machine gun set up by the tailboard and lowered the canvas canopy. Now, they relaxed for the journey, which they all knew was going to be very boring. As the lorry started up and moved slowly out of the yard they laid their weapons on the floor, removed their caps and passed the tobacco round. It was alright for the Colonel, he would be travelling in a car with comfortable seats. He had no idea what it was like to sit on a wooden bench and be thrown around in a lorry all day. They didn't suppose, they said among themselves, that he even cared. In that, naturally, they were completely correct. Next stop Kulmhof.

Fritz calculated they had about two hundred and fifty kilometres to go, and, barring any mishaps, they should be there by lunchtime.

The first mishap occurred an hour later as they sped through one of the endless tedious grey villages along the River Vistula. There was a bang and suddenly everyone woke from their stupor and grabbed their weapons. The normal procedure was to keep going and drive straight through any ambush, except this wasn't an ambush, it was a burst tyre on the lorry, so they couldn't. The convoy halted in the main village street and Fritz ordered the men out and on the ground taking defensive positions, which they did very efficiently and they waited for any attack, only there wasn't one, in fact there wasn't anything, no people, no donkey carts, no movement of any kind or sign of life. It was like a ghost town, and it made Fritz nervous, as if partisans could arrange a burst tyre at just the right point for their ambush, but then of course they could because they could lay metal spikes on the road surface.

He went over the road to look for any evidence of this and found none. In any case, if they had done that the motorcycle, or at least the car, which were both ahead of the lorry, would have been affected. No, this was just a burst tyre. It happens in the best regulated of armies.

The men tried to jack up the lorry but it was too heavily laden. There was more than three tonnes of gold on board and they had no choice but to unload it to lighten the vehicle to the point where the men could even get the wheel off the ground. It took an hour, and by the time they had finished the men were puffing and sweating and they were also swearing under their breath. Fritz had them take turns unloading and guarding, but as much as they watched still nothing moved. He became so worried he had a squad of three men patrol the village and ten minutes later they heard shots and stopped what they were doing. Fritz halted the unloading and had every man stand to with his weapon at the ready, but the squad returned, three of them, and when he asked what had happened, who had fired, they said they had. They had found the villagers in the church, hiding, and when they interrogated them they said nothing so they shot a few and they still said nothing, not the dead ones obviously but the others too, they just wailed and cried and in the end it was obvious there was nothing to be learned so they left them to it.

It took another hour to change the wheel and then nearly two more to reload, because humping the gold up onto the lorry was obviously a slower process than throwing it off. Fritz told the men to eat from their rations while they drove. They had lost a great deal of time and even if this village was peaceful they had no intention of hanging around while the troops refreshed themselves. For the men, it could have been worse. They at least had a few bottles of beer they had found in one of the houses.

The next mishap took place on the outskirts of Kulmhof. They came to a checkpoint and the convoy slowed down and came to a halt and Fritz waved his identification at the sentry in a desultory fashion expecting the barrier to be raised only it wasn't. Two soldiers stood smartly to attention but no-one did anything.

'Corporal, what is the meaning of this? Open the barrier at once. We are on urgent business.'

'I'm sorry Sir, it will take a few minutes. We're just telephoning now to check your documents.'

Fritz was tired and hot, he wanted to get into town and he didn't want to wait.

'What are you talking about? Read my orders for yourself. Why do you need confirmation?'

'I'm sorry Sir. Orders. We have been told to be extra vigilant.'

Fritz got our of the car and pulled himself up to his full height, which unfortunately still didn't match the corporal's. He adjusted the cap on his head to emphasise the death's head insignia in the hope of intimidating this soldier, which it did, but not enough.

'Look at us, Corporal, and ask yourself it we look like partisans in disguise.'

The soldier didn't want to do that but a colonel had given him an order. He looked. No, they didn't look like partisans. On the other hand, partisans didn't always look like partisans either. He had been told that, although he had never actually seen one for himself.

'Well?'

'No Sir.'

'Then let us through, now.'

The corporal weighed up in his mind the chance that this colonel was going to get nasty against the certain knowledge that if he disobeyed a direct order from his own sergeant he would certainty get put on a charge and, biting his lip, he held his ground. Fortunately for him, the telephone rang, and he went into the hut to answer it. Fritz watched him through the window, nodding his head, then shaking it, them apparently saying uhuh, uhuh, I see, and putting the receiver down.

'Well?'

'Well Sir, it seems they have no record of your orders. I have been instructed to hold you here Sir until they check with Warsaw. If you would like to come inside Sir, and wait in the shade.'

'No, Corporal, I would not like to come inside. And what the hell are you talking about anyway? Can't you read? My orders are very specific, and they require you to let me through.'

It took another hour. In that time, unbeknown to Fritz or any of his troops or the sentries, orders had been telephoned through from Berlin to Warsaw and General Bergmann had been placed under arrest. That would have been the end of the operation except that more telephone calls were made and someone somewhere decided that if the General had set up this whole operation so well they might as well go ahead with it. There seemed, in any case, little point in diverting so much gold when it was clearly on its way safely to the smelter and thence to a secure bank account in Switzerland, as far away from the Russians as it was possible to place it. After hasty consultations in high places, it was decided to allow the operation to go ahead.

Fritz was not privy to any of these decisions and had no idea he was no longer working for General Bergmann, who in any case was tried by a court-martial the next day and shot. All he knew was that the corporal signalled for the barrier to be raised, gave him a very smart salute by way of apology and, considerably delayed, they finally rolled into Kulmhof, known to the Poles as Chelmno, the site of the most westerly death camp in Poland.

11

Asher Spiegel showed his passport to the immigration official in his first-class compartment on the Berlin-Zurich Express.

'Good afternoon, Mr Weber, and how long do you expect to be in Switzerland?'

Asher Spiegel took back his passport in the name of Paul Weber and replied courteously. 'Oh, a week, no more, some banking business, you know.'

'Yes, of course, well everything is in order. Good day, Mr Weber, and I hope you have a pleasant and successful trip.'

He nodded in a perfunctory way to the other occupants of the compartment and slid the door closed behind him. They had received the minimum of courtesy as required by the situation, but the official knew who they were, that they had acquired the right to enter his country because of their money, that they were fleeing from Germany with at least some of their wealth intact, and they knew he knew this and they were unable to look him in the eye. The man had the air of one who had been used to commanding respect before, and his wife too, in her fur coat, a ridiculous thing on such a warm day. They had a right to be where they were, but they were fleeing all the same. That right had been bought, at great expense, like everything these days, because every-thing was for sale if you had the price, and these two were lucky, they did, but even so there was no disguising what they were. Jewish.

Paul hoped too that his trip would be successful, but pleasure was not on his agenda. Now that he was officially Paul Weber, place of birth Kaiserslautern, rather than Asher Spiegel son of the late Rabbi

Spiegel of Berlin, he had just one interest in this trip, and he had only two days to complete his task, not a week.

His passport had cost a lot of money. This whole trip was costing a lot of money, but for the American Joint Distribution Committee, which was funding it, the stakes were high, over four tonnes of stolen gold. Stolen by the Germans and about to be stolen back by the Jews. Gold that had literally been wrenched from the murdered, that would, if all went well, bring about a new life for thousands of refugees from the terror when they landed in Palestine and had a rifle put in their hands with which to defend their new homeland.

Paul knew just how critical his job was, but he was confident. The son of a banking family, his grandfather had trained him to take the place on the Board his father would have taken if he hadn't instead dropped out of the money business and gone into religion in a big way. His grandfather had shaken his head when his son told him of his decision. Well, one rabbi they could cope with, as long as no-one else in the family got any fancy ideas about God instead of learning the Spiegel tradition of making money.

That had been before 1933, before the Nazis had come to power. The family had moved as much as they could abroad, to the United States, to South America, to Britain, but his grandfather had said it will blow over, we will stay and see this through, you will see, the Nazis will disappear as suddenly as they appeared, but for the first time in his life he was wrong, and when the axe fell it was too late for them because they went in the cattle cars like all the others, rich or poor. Even at that late moment his grandfather had tried to buy the family's way out of Germany, when he realised it was too late to simply emigrate after the doors were slammed shut, but the officer who took the money disappeared and still the trains took them, and they were turned, like the others, into so much smoke and ash.

Paul would do this one last thing, he would do it well, and he would make his grandfather proud of him. He settled back in his comfortable seat and watched the Swiss countryside pass his compartment window like a moving picture, like a holiday brochure for this strange country that behaved as if over every one of its borders there wasn't a war raging.

He hated the Swiss. He had disliked them when he was on the

Board of Bank Spiegel and he had to do business with them, and that dislike had turned to real hatred when they sat behind their iron neutrality and watched their former business partners taken away and disposed of. Making money was one thing, there was nothing wrong with it, even his father the rabbi had said so, but the Swiss did it with no sense of connection to the rest of the world, as if the rest of the world was there for their profit. They had no souls. The passport officer had no soul, Paul saw that in his face. Welcome to Switzerland. Yes, as long as you're not a penniless refugee in which case you can go away and burn for all we care. Welcome to Switzerland only if you're a German banker on the business of the Reich.

Well, this week he was just that, and he was welcome in this place. He would be welcome too in Zurich, that he knew for certain, because in Zurich he was seeing the head of Bank Dreifuss, who was not only Jewish but who had been clandestinely conducting banking business for the American Joint Distribution Committee since the beginning of the war. Dreifuss was protected by the much-vaunted Swiss banking laws which guaranteed total anonymity, secrecy even the federal government could not break, and that secrecy had been put to good use when it came to protecting Jewish interests. Now, the Joint had one last favour to ask of Maurice Dreifuss, but it was a big one. If the secrecy was ever broken it would mean not only the opprobrium of the Swiss Banking Association but quite possibly a jail sentence.

Maurice Dreifuss was going to do what the other Swiss Banks had been doing for years, quite openly, when they laundered money, stolen money, for the Reichsbank, and turned it into convenient foreign exchange so that Germany could pay Swiss and other companies in neutral countries for the armaments they so badly needed.

Of course, Bank Dreifuss would not be doing this openly, but what is sauce for the goose is not necessarily sauce for the gander, and a Jewish bank laundering gold for a Jewish organisation would most certainly be frowned upon, even if it could be proved that that gold had been stolen by Switzerland's friends and favourite customers.

Setting up the necessary account with Bank Dreifuss was only a part of the whole operation, of course, Paul knew that. The people who had to liberate the gold from the Germans were doing the hard part, the dangerous bit. But still, if he didn't get this right they would be driving round Europe with a lorry load of gold trying to find somewhere to hide it. The critical part of Paul's work would be the apparent legality of the account, because when the lorry arrived at the Swiss border it was going to be hard to explain the gold to the immigration and customs officials unless everything was absolutely in order in Zurich. The Swiss would want to see the arrangements made completely correctly, according to their banking laws. Any deviation from those laws would not only land him in trouble but jeopardise the whole operation. They wouldn't care about the provenance of the gold, but they would want to know that no-one was playing fast and loose with them.

That was going to be tricky, though, because the gold was going to be in ingots marked Deutsches Reichsbank, and why a Jewish bank would be accepting what everyone knew was stolen gold from the Germans would certainly take some explaining. That was why Paul needed Bank Baer.

Hans Baer was the wild card in the pack as far as the Swiss Banking Association was concerned. Even by their standards he had sailed close to the wind in the course of this war. Hans Baer had inherited his father's taste for the exciting side of banking, and a number of dictators of certain countries depended on his discretion which went just that bit further than the Swiss norm. Bank Baer would, in short, do anything for anyone if the price was right. Hans Baer didn't care if they were Jewish, because Jewish money was as good as anyone else's. Nevertheless, he was well aware of the predicament the Jews were in, as was everyone, and when he received an urgent call only two days earlier from Maurice Dreifuss to arrange a most secret meeting, his interest was already pricked. The cut that Bank Baer would earn from this deal was attractive, so attractive that he could only say yes. It hurt the Joint to have to pay such an extortionate rate, but they were pragmatists. They knew that was going to be the price. Pay it or get out of the game.

The train was held at the frontier station for a while, and the couple opposite were getting restless. Paul leaned out of the window to see what the delay was and there they were, a family, mother, father and four children, herded out of a third-class compartment onto the platform. Jews who had hoped to get across without being noticed, an impossibility if they had only known. Paul knew what was going to happen to them. They were going back to Germany and almost certain death, because they didn't have the money to get away with it and Switzerland was not a home for poor refugees. He desperately wanted to do something and the frustration tore at his heart, because of course there was nothing he could do except carry out his mission successfully. That would mean saving countless lives, not the family on the platform because they were doomed and beyond anyone's help. The border police of course could have saved their lives easily enough, but they had no desire to do that. They were following their orders, accept the rich ones and throw the rest back to the wolves. That's life, except of course it isn't life, it's death. As the engine took the weight of the train, Paul's compartment came alongside this pathetic group. The mother was crying into her husband's shoulder and just at that moment the man happened to glance up and what Paul thought he saw was a look of pleading, as if a stranger in a train could possibly help him, but in a flash it turned into loathing, hatred for someone who had what he couldn't give his family. If there was only some way Paul could let him know, not that his family could live but that someone was doing something, that other Jews would live. But of course he could do no such thing. He sat down with a tear in his eye and as he took out a handkerchief to wipe it away the man opposite looked at him with a question in his face, a question he couldn't ask. Had he recognised Paul for what he was, Asher Spiegel, a Jew like him? Well, he wasn't Asher, he was Paul, and if his travelling companion saw something he thought he recognised that was up to him. Paul flicked his newspaper in a way that brooked no conversation, and studiously read the latest Nazi propaganda.

The Express pulled into Zurich on time. It was a cliché, Paul, thought, that everything in this country ran on time, but even so it was true. And there to meet him on the platform was the smiling face of his old friend.

'Paul. How good to see you again. A pleasant journey, I hope?'

'Yes, yes, thank you Maurice. One or two delays in Germany but nothing we couldn't make up.'

'Yes, it's easy for us Swiss to forget there is a war going on over there.'

So, Maurice was after all, as well as being Jewish, Swiss. An interesting mixture.

'Come along, I've got the car here, give me your bag.'

Paul followed him out of the station and there was the limousine, where Maurice's chauffeur held the door for them and took Paul's luggage.

'Well, now they know you're here.'

Paul looked out of the window as they drove away from the station. 'What do you mean?'

'The Swiss security service. They keep an eye on me. And sometimes German agents.'

'But why? I don't understand. Do they suspect something?'

'Of course they do. They always suspect something. Suspecting is what they're paid to do.'

'But in that case do they know something?'

'Ah now, that's different. No, they know nothing. As far as they are concerned you are an old banking friend. The immigration people will have called the police once they saw your passport on the train, because all foreign visitors are reported, that's all. You only become interesting because of your contact with me.'

'But in that case surely you should not have met me at the station.'

'What? And have no-one to welcome you to our beautiful city? Nonsense.'

'Maurice, I'm not sure you're taking this as seriously as you might.'

Maurice put his hand on his friend's sleeve.

'Paul, I assure you I am taking it very seriously indeed. The Swiss security services are very jumpy just now. Switzerland knows where quite a lot of the skeletons from this war are buried, and every visitor to the country is of interest to the police. We are surrounded by countries involved in the war.

'No-one comes here on holiday. Everyone who comes here has a reason that is likely to be connected to the war. Your papers say you are a banker. Well, Switzerland has an especial interest in people of our kind. No, wherever you went, they would follow you. Well, we have saved them the trouble of following the two of us separately. You see, I am saving my country some money. I should get a commendation, yes?'

And they drove through Zurich with an unmarked car on their tail and when Maurice's car pulled up outside Paul's hotel it did the same.

'You see, they are not very good secret policemen, are they? They make no effort to hide the fact that they are following us.'

And with that Maurice waved to them and they scowled back at him. Up in Paul's room Maurice explained his tactics.

'In my experience, policemen expect anyone who's doing something wrong to behave furtively. If we tried to hide you, they would become suspicious. This way, we show we have nothing to hide. Hopefully, they will lose interest and leave us alone.'

'I hope you're right.'

'I am, you will see. In any case, we will get them used to following my car, so that when you slip off to meet Hans Baer they won't know that you're not with me.'

'I see. My friend, I apologise for doubting you. Come on, let's eat. I hope there's better food here than in Germany.'

There was. Switzerland lacked for very little. Zurich was booming, and the restaurants were busy with diners. Paul shook his head. He had been undercover in Germany for a long time and hadn't eaten this well in months. He could tell that neutrality, especially the Swiss brand, was highly profitable.

They talked about nothing of any significance because they had to assume any conversation held in public was being heard by someone and reported to someone else. They talked about Maurice's wife and children and about Paul's family, who of course did not actually exist, but even so it was fun to make up news about fictitious people, and then they went back to the hotel for coffee and at some point in the very pleasant evening Maurice informed Paul that the meeting was arranged for one o'clock the next day.

At ten to one the next afternoon Maurice left Paul's hotel in the chauffeur-driven car but the man with him wasn't Paul Weber, it was a man called Pieter who had been drinking coffee in the restaurant of the hotel just before, met up with Maurice in the lobby like an old friend, and walked out with him and got into his car. Hans looked quite uncannily like Paul Weber.

Ten minutes later, when Hans Baer walked into the lobby of the hotel, there was no-one to notice, because they were following Maurice Dreifuss's car. No-one noticed either when he took the lift up to the third floor and knocked on the door of room 316. And so it was that that day the arrangements were made for documentation to accompany the gold across the border from Germany in the name of the Reichsbank. It would then be deposited in the vaults of Bank Baer in Zurich within hours and would simply disappear from prying eyes. It would then take a little while but within weeks from that date funds in Swiss francs would be transferred, minus of course the necessary fees and commissions, into Bank Dreifuss down the road, to the account of The Swiss-Levant Trading Company a.g., which interestingly enough was an entirely new enterprise that had yet to start trading.

That evening Paul sent a telegram to New York to the effect that Uncle Adolf was doing better than expected and he would be returning home the next morning. Twenty-four hours later that information was relayed to Captain Michael Jacobs via US Military Intelligence, without anyone at the latter knowing what it meant, and the operation was on.

12

Fritz Stängl's convoy left Kulmhof early the next morning, having loaded up the last of the gold overnight. Fritz had never seen the Kulmhof camp, and the commandant there was pleased to show him around. The gas chambers and the crematoria were quite different from Auschwitz-Birkenau, but then Auschwitz-Birkenau was unique, a triumph of planning and engineering. Fritz thought that there had never before been anything like it and that there never would be again, in which he was correct.

The Kulmhof complex was a lot smaller, but from a professional point of view Fritz found it quite enlightening. He particularly liked the speed with which the Jews were moved from the trains to the gas chambers. That was something he had always had difficulty with at Auschwitz. Yes, the commandant, SS Obersturmbannfuhrer Ernst Grabner, had got it down to a fine art. Get them off the train and running as if their life depended on it, down the barbed-wire corridor that led to the gas chambers. It was interesting to see the look on their faces as they ran, the determination in their eyes not to be left behind. He shook his head and pondered the question he had never been able to answer in all his time doing this work - did they really believe what they were told, that they were going to have a shower? Really, how stupid was that? Couldn't they see the chimney belching the smoke of their friends and their families? What was wrong with these people that they were so easy to fool? Fritz congratulated Grabner on the efficiency of his operation and the latter glowed with pride because a compliment from an officer from Auschwitz-Birkenau, which he himself could only aspire to, was a compliment indeed. Fritz promised to mention him in his report. There wasn't going to be a report of course because that wasn't what he was there for but he just got a bit carried away.

Autumn seemed to have started that morning, and they had to drive more slowly than Fritz would have liked because of the fog. The fog in fact reminded him that they were closer to the sea now, and as they drove he decided that, yes, he would take the time to go up to the coast and do some fishing. He even thought he would make a special effort to be friendly to his father. Now that he was a full Colonel, his father surely would have to accord him some respect. He himself had not achieved that rank during his own service in the first war.

He left his convoy in Hamburg, with orders to Sergeant Schiller that the men were confined to barracks and that the gold was to have an armed guard of at least four men at any one time, round the clock. It was in a high-security area anyway, this being a mint, but he was taking no chances. Fair enough, they were in Germany now so there was no risk from partisans, but even in Germany people, unscrupulous, unpatriotic people, had been known to steal the property of the State.

Sergeant Schiller asked Fritz if he didn't think he should be there himself and he said no, he had complete faith in the sergeant and if any of the gold went missing he personally would shoot him. The sergeant smiled at this as if he was supposed to take it as a joke but after Fritz left he wasn't so sure that it was. Still, he had his orders, from higher up than this Colonel, and that funnily enough had also included a threat of shooting if he got it wrong. Well, he thought, they can't shoot you twice, and anyway, he had no intention of letting anything happen. He himself would sleep only when the gold was under the highest level of security in the works itself and he would threaten the staff there with shooting if any of it went missing. He didn't think, though, that the staff of a mint would try such a thing, surely

Fritz drove himself to his home. It was only a couple of hours drive and he put his gloves on to protect his hands and they still hurt but there was no possibility of taking Schiller with him and he didn't want to order any of the other soldiers to do it because it would have looked like he was demanding to be chauffeur driven, and he knew what they would think of that, since he had to face the fact that this was a holiday, not official business. He wondered if Schiller would report the trip back to his masters and decided he probably would and then he decided he no longer cared. As long as the gold got delivered safely he didn't imagine anyone was going to worry too much about a Colonel taking a spot of unauthorised leave. With the armies in the west falling back to Belgium and the armies in the east hard-pressed by the Russians, no-one was worrying too much about the formalities these days.

As he drove northwards he tried to feel the familiarity of it all but it just wasn't there. Had it changed or had he? It didn't feel like a homecoming. Perhaps he had seen too much, yes, perhaps he had changed irrevocably and this was no longer home. Perhaps, even, he should turn the car round and forget about it, but he didn't do that and he knew he wouldn't. He wasn't sure why he was determined to go home but he realised now that he really was. Was it his mother or his father he especially wanted to see?

All along the coast road there were anti-aircraft batteries and heavy gun emplacements, and he knew that Germany itself, the Fatherland, was at war. It had waged war abroad and now that war was coming home to the people them-selves. Would they have the stomach for the fight? Would his parents? His father was full of bluster about the old days but really, he was just an old soldier who liked to talk, they always do, and he wondered if he would be like that one day, going on about the good old days. Well, that would depend a lot, he could see, on whether he survived.

He had felt safe here in Germany but the gun batteries unnerved him a little. Germany was on the defensive, and that was something that wasn't supposed to happen. They had been supposed to stand astride Europe like a Colossus with Hitler at their head, but here they were scanning the Baltic Sea and the sky for an invasion and Hitler was making ever more bizarre strategic decisions. He had taken over the day-to-day running of the war from the Generals and really, what was he, a corporal. It was madness.

Fritz had heard about secret weapons being developed that would win the war once and for all, but where were they, and how long were they supposed to wait for them? The Soviets now had more men on the Front than Germany did, and the Americans and the British were pouring more and more men and materiel into France. Now he was home, it all suddenly seemed rather fragile. He had an image of disaster, the kind of disaster that you weren't allowed to discuss with anyone because it could get you arrested, and he thought about his mother and wondered if there was any way she could escape, if there was anything he could do to get her out. They lived too close to Hamburg and Bremen and the way things were going this area was going to be swarming with enemy troops before long, and those guns he passed weren't going to stop them. Already the US and British airforces were mounting day and night bombing raids more or less at will over German cities, and that wasn't supposed to happen. The more he thought about it, the more depressed he became, and now the fog closing in round the car enveloped him in an unbreakable mood of pessimism. He began to wonder if he couldn't smuggle his mother and the gold to Switzerland but he knew that was pie in the sky. No, whatever, happened, he would have to see this operation through. Then he would plan the future.

Out at sea he heard a ship's foghorn and it sounded like the dying agony of some great sea creature and he began to dread going home. He tried to throw off the mood that had settled on him, and as he turned the car at last into the driveway of his parents' house he put on a smile and when he pulled up at the front door he did so with a certain élan that said look, I'm home.

His mother came out to greet him and first she threw her arms round him and then she held him from her so she could see how handsome he looked in his uniform and then she hugged him again.

'Hullo Mutti, is father not here?'

'Yes my dear, he's in the house, in his study I think. Greta will let him know you've arrived.'

Fritz rather thought his father knew he had arrived. The sound of the car on the gravel was enough to alert his mother, and she would surely have called him to come down. The old bastard had declined. Well, he could sit in his study and sulk.

'Come in dear, come in. There's a fire in the kitchen, we live there most of the time now to save fuel. And Greta has managed to find some rye flour and baked your favourite cake. And I've saved an egg for you.'

It dawned on him that the food he got as an SS officer was a lot better than the families back home were able to buy, even wealthy ones like his. He regretted not bringing some supplies with him, but how could he have known?

Even at this time of the year the fog had chilled him and the kitchen fire was welcome. Greta curtsied and looked embarrassed when he stood there in the full glory of his SS uniform and surveyed how dowdy the place looked. Clothes were hanging by the fire to dry and that gave it a squalid farmhouse air. It wasn't how he remembered it, and his determination to appear cheerful wavered. His mother was scanning his face to see what he thought and she saw he was disappointed.

'Now come along dear, sit down and we'll have coffee.'

He noticed that she poured coffee for him from a separate pot but said nothing. It was plain that whatever she was drinking, it was some kind of ersatz coffee, and she had saved the real stuff for her son.

'Greta, be a dear and take a cup up to Herr Stängl's study, would you?'

Fritz heard the tone and was surprised. So, it had come to this, that she spoke to the maid in such a familiar way. The war, it seemed, had brought them down to the level of the servants. And was his father not coming down? His mother seemed to read his thoughts.

'Your papa is very busy just now, dear. I don't like to disturb him.'

'Busy? Busy with what? What is a man his age so busy with that he can't come and say hullo to his son who is home on leave from serving the Fatherland? '

His voice was rising and he knew it.

'Shhh dear, now don't shout, you know it upsets me.'

No, it wasn't herself she was thinking of, it was her husband. He felt like shouting louder and letting the old fool hear his anger, but his mother came and put an arm round his shoulder to restrain him. He smelled the old familiar soap smell he had forgotten and he wanted to stay there with her and his anger subsided.

They drank their coffee and Fritz ate the cake and tried to look like he was enjoying it but it wasn't like it used to be, nothing was. He smiled and complimented Greta and she beamed in gratitude for him not noticing its defects and then she surprised him further by coming and sitting down at the end of the table and pouring herself a cup. His mother saw the look he gave her and explained, they were all one family now, no us and them. Like the Army, she thought. Fritz didn't disabuse her. The Army, thank God, still put people in their proper place.

'You'll be doing some fishing I expect, while you're here, dear?'

'Yes Mutti, if I can find my old rod.'

'Oh, I thought of that. It's up in your room. I found it in the attic.'

He was pleased she had thought of it, but as he sat there there was really only one thing on his mind, and that was his father sitting up there in his study knowing he was here and refusing to come down and greet him. They had argued for so many years now that no-one could remember why they had started, but this was too much.

'Greta has taken your bag up to your room. Why don't you go up and get changed? And you can say hullo to Papa while you're there.'

So that was it. She couldn't bring herself to say go up to him but still, while he was there, it was a reasonable suggestion. Well, no, it wasn't. If the old man wouldn't come down Fritz sure as hell wasn't going crawling to him.

But she looked at him in that way she had that said do this for me, not him, and he was unable to resist.

Both she and Greta watched anxiously as he got out of his chair and walked to the kitchen door, like a man who was trying to put off what he had to do. They followed his heavy footsteps up the oak staircase and looked at each other in sympathy, and they waited. Fritz went to his own room first and there was his bag where Greta had left it and his fishing rod leaned against the washbasin in its canvas bag and all his old things from his childhood, preserved by his mother, but they seemed foolish now, things he had collected from the seashore the way boys do, silly things, and he felt ashamed of them. This was a million miles from the world he had come to know first in the Army and then the SS. He tried to picture his office at

Auschwitz-Birkenau but he couldn't, couldn't make the connection between that world and this, and the more he tried the more irritated it made him.

And that was the mood he was in when he knocked on the door of his father's study. They heard that, downstairs, and they heard him go in and the door click shut, and they waited.

It didn't take long. They heard, even through the heavy oak door of the study, the sound of shouting, first one man's and then the other's and they looked at each other wondering what to do and Frau Stängl signalled with her eyes that they should stay out of it but then there was an inexplicable sound, a kind of bang and something like the scraping of furniture on the floor and that was too much. Frau Stängl leapt up and ran up the stairs and Greta was right behind her. She flung open the door and it was clear immediately what had happened. There had been a scuffle and now Fritz stood over the prostrate form of his father who was half on the sofa and half on the floor. He had obviously hit the old man. His father's hand was to his face and a little blood seeped between his fingers. Fritz's face was highly flushed and the anger he had been holding back but which had then exploded uncontrollably was slowly subsiding. He turned and looked at the women standing in the doorway, but said nothing. Then, slowly, he let go of his father's collar and let him slump to the floor, turned on his heel and, pushing past Greta roughly, stormed off to his room.

He broke the fishing rod in two. Then he grabbed his bag and went downstairs. He didn't say goodbye to his mother. He was never going to see her again, and maybe if he had known that he would have, but he didn't.

He remembered little, later, of the drive through the night to Hamburg. He remembered seeing American bombers flying overhead and then the explosions coming from the city and the docks and still he drove towards the mayhem, perhaps in the hope that that would be his end because that was how he felt, but by the time he arrived in the centre of the city there were fires and fire engines and the usual chaos of a bombing raid but it was over and he was in one piece. So was the Degussa works, and he drove straight there, because he knew they would be working through the night on his gold and he didn't, in any case, as tired as he was, feel like going to bed.

As he walked into the office he was greeted by a man in civilian clothes.

'Ah, Colonel Stängl, I presume. We have been looking for you.'
'You have? And who are you?'
'Fischer, Gestapo. Colonel Stängl, you are under arrest.'

13

They were all there, sitting in a circle in the big command tent. Captain Michael Jacobs, Roza Levinson, Dovid Lempel the armourer who used to be a dentist in Lublin, Meyer Edelman the navigator who used to be a taxi driver in Warsaw, Daniel Foxman the explosives expert who used to be an anaesthetist in a big teaching hospital, Moise Halberstam who used to be a violinist and still was but because of his dexterity had become a passable forger, and finally Jakub Alter, who used to be a gangster in Krakow and now was the group's most ruthless killer.

Between them, in two days they had put together an operation that in a real army would have taken weeks or months but more likely would never have been attempted at all.

'Right people, you all know Roza by now, and you know she was second in command of an Armia Ludowa company and is, I promise you, the best shot I have ever known. For these reasons, and more, and not only because she brought us this operation, she will be my second in command. Any questions about that?'

Michael waited while they digested the idea of accepting orders from a woman. Roza looked around the tent to see if anyone was going to say something about it, and they all met her searching gaze as her eyes sought out their souls. She wanted to know that every man here was going to give her their absolute loyalty, and she found no-one wanting. They all knew about the gold by now, and they knew that what they were doing had to be done. It was the ultimate act of resistance. They couldn't take on the Wehrmacht, but they could do this.

Well, that was what they believed, at least that was what they said to each other, but of course they were all aware that their chance of success was limited, and their chance of coming back alive was equally limited, but no-one talked about that. If they died doing this they would have died well, and no man here had an overwhelming desire to live.

Michael continued with the briefing. 'Now each of you has done his bit but I want to bring you all together to understand the operation that Roza and I have worked out. You all know, I hope, the way I work. If you don't like any aspect of it, say so. If you have a better way, I want to hear it.'

They listened to his New York-accented Yiddish. To most of them, America was the goldene medina, the golden land where men were taller and unafraid and being Jewish was not something that made you a victim. They would have liked him for being American, a member of the United States forces that was fighting the Germans, but in their eyes a man who could do that and be Jewish at the same time commanded huge respect. They would have followed him anywhere. They were about to. They were about to go to Germany.

'Now, we have here a map that Roza managed to get out showing the exact route of the convoy, and we know the number of vehicles and the number of men they will have, so we can plan pretty accurately the resources we will need. Ideally I would like a three to one superiority in numbers but that isn't possible. We don't have the personnel for it, and in any case moving that number of people over a large distance adds to the complications.

'They will have one lorry, one car and two motorcycles. It's a small convoy for such a valuable load but my guess is that they don't want to attract attention to themselves with a bigger guard. There will be a squad of twelve SS soldiers in the lorry, plus the driver of the car and another soldier there, and two motorcycles carrying three men, so that's seventeen in all, plus Stängl of course, makes eighteen. There will be thirty five of us. Each of you will be assigned a small group of your own, and each group will tackle specific enemy targets. Now we can't be sure yet where the ambush is going to take place so it isn't possible to plan it in detail at this stage. The idea just now is to find the right place, put together a plan on the spot and hope we don't miss anything. The big question is whether we take them on the road or stationary. I favour the former but Roza feels our chances are better if we wait for them to stop. Look, they both have advantages and dis-advantages, and I'm not going to say one way is better than the other. All I can say for now is that we will see which opportunity presents itself in the light of the circumstances.

'So for now all we can do is plot a route that will enable us to intercept them somewhere where there is the least chance of interference from other military units that might be in the area. I know you all feel that going into Germany itself is risky but actually I believe you are wrong. The German armies are fighting for their lives in Poland and France right now. My Intelligence reports suggest that the forces left in Germany itself are limited largely to the Volkssturm, local people formed into a sort of home guard. You could take them on with one hand behind your back.'

He allowed them to laugh at this idea. It relieved some of the tension.

'We have the transport and the uniforms, thanks to our very recent successful ambush. Some of the uniforms have holes in them but they've been patched as best we can. Next time we need German uniforms aim for the head so you don't damage the material.'

They laughed again. It was going well. So far.

'There's no shortage of weapons but ammunition is limited, so this is going to be tight. I wish I could have let your men have more for practice shoots but I can't. Dovid, are there any weaknesses there?'

'No, well, as you say, apart from the limitations on target practice. I've been able to rig up a reasonable telescopic sight for Roza, so if it turns out to be a static ambush she should be able to pick off a few with very limited ammunition usage. I believe there's no such thing as a wasted bullet with this lady.'

He bowed courteously and she smiled. It was slightly flirtatious but too obvious to bother her. Dovid was like that. He had the bedside manner of a dentist and was pleasant to everyone. She hoped he would be unpleasant to the Germans when the time came.

'OK, now I've been asked what happens if we hit a German checkpoint. Well I can tell you we will. We have IDs from the troops we killed, which isn't enough for all of us, but I'm hoping we won't need need one for every man in the back of each lorry, just the drivers, and we'll pick IDs with the closest match and hope for the best. They will also need to be fluent German speakers. If we have any trouble, we will open fire, and I'm telling you now so you can make it clear to your men, we cannot afford to leave anyone alive to call through a distress message. Is that clear?'

He looked at each of them in turn and they nodded their agreement or just shrugged their shoulders.

'Good. Make sure your men understand the situation. We've got written orders to travel to Cologne from a fictitious General, courtesy of Moise here. It will stand up to scrutiny but not, of course, a phone call to verify it, so this again points to the necessity of speed. Either the sentries pass us through immediately or we open up and move on with no witnesses. Any questions?'

No questions but a comment from Daniel Foxman.

'It's not a great plan is it, I mean hope for the best and shoot our way through if it goes wrong?'

'No, you're right, it's not a great plan, but in the absence of a better one it will have to do. I don't think I have to remind you of the importance of this operation, and if we had another couple of weeks and a battalion of trained troops I daresay we could to it a hell of a lot better, but since we don't this is how we're going to do it. And don't forget, we will have surprise on our side. That deep into Germany it will never occur to Stängl that he might be ambushed. They will be off their guard. I cannot emphasise enough how important surprise is in an operation like this. That's why I favour a hit on the move, but I completely accept that that may not be possible or even desirable in any situation that presents itself. So, any other questions? Or comments even?'

Daniel had another question. 'How much fuel have we got? Will it get us all the way there?'

'Good question Daniel. No, it won't. We're going to have to tank up on the way.'

'Oh, I see. How? Pull into a garage and ask them to fill it up?'

'Yes. More or less, except it will be done under duress and then Jakub here will make sure, again, that there are no witnesses. I myself will get out as soon as we arrive and look for telephone wires, which I will cut while the Germans are occupied with the arrival of a convoy. Anything else?'

There wasn't. Everyone knew it was full of holes. They were going into unreconnoitred territory on a wing and a prayer. On the other hand, they were all excited about having a go, and Michael knew that.

'OK, we leave at 0600 tomorrow. That's six o'clock in the morning to you non-army types. So get the last-minute preparations done now. Don't leave anything until the morning. Go to sleep with a clear conscience, get up at five, have a good breakfast, and pray.'

They went over it time and again and when there was nothing left they could possibly check everyone gathered round the fire and drank hot soup and talked about anything but the operation. Michael and Roza walked through the trees to get some privacy.

'OK Michael, tell me, what do you think, really?'

'I think it's the best we can do in the limited time with limited resources.'

'Yes, but that's what I mean. Is it going to work?'

'The truth?'

'Please.'

'I have no idea. I've been part of operations in the past, from an Intelligence perspective, that have taken weeks to prepare and still gone wrong because one thing you learn in the military is that if something can go wrong it will. Here, we're dealing with a large number of factors that we have simply no knowledge of. All we've got is the plan you brought from Stängl. We don't, to be honest, even know if that's still the plan. The US Army regularly changes operational plans before they go ahead and I don't suppose the Germans are any different.'

'Oh God, I hadn't thought of that. What if it's all a complete waste of time?'

'Well it might be, but then again it might not be, and as an Intelligence man I have to weight up the likelihood against the risks and that's what I've done, and that's why we're going.'

'But tell me honestly, if this was your own army, you know, the Americans, would you be doing it?'

'Honestly? No. But Roza, you know partisan groups work very differently from armies. The risks are much greater, which is always accepted. When I said at the briefing that I wanted a three-to-one tactical superiority, I meant it. That's the military standard. But I can't run this like a US Army operation and I'm not trying to. These people are all volunteers and they know the risks.'

'They don't know that the plans might have changed. You didn't say that before.'

'No, well, I didn't think there was any point. Do you?'

Roza thought about that and shrugged her shoulders. 'No, you're right, you're always right.'

He smiled at that idea and knew it wasn't true but if it gave her more confidence to believe that then he owed it to her to let her carry on believing it.

'Roza, now I want to ask you a question.'

'OK.'

'Are you still thinking that Mordechai is out there somewhere alive?'

'Do you?'

'I don't come into it.'

'Alright. Yes, I think he might be.'

'And you think Stängl might know something?'

'No, well, yes, maybe.'

'And has this operation got something to do with that situation? I mean, I know you would want it to go ahead any-way but would you still be coming yourself if it weren't for the chance perhaps to meet Stängl?'

'Maybe not, I don't know. Does it really matter?'

'Well it might. You might be hoping to talk to him but he might be dead before you get a chance. We're not going to put him on trial, you know, we're just going to shoot him, if we get the chance, that is.'

'Yes, but if we get the chance, and we don't have to kill him straight away, there might be a chance of talking to him.'

'There might. OK, if it's possible, you can. I won't say any more.'

'Thank you.'

He didn't think for a moment that Mordechai was still alive, but what was the point of saying that to Roza?

'Michael?'

'Uhuh.'

She stopped now and leaned against a tree.

'I want you to do something for me.'

'Anything. What is it?'

'Don't say anything until you hear what I'm going to ask. You might want to say no, and I won't blame you.'

'OK, that's reasonable. I promise to consider it seriously. Now, tell me.'

'If I don't come through this I want you to look after the baby. Get to Sweden and, you know, help Krystyna, make whatever arrangements you can for his upbringing. Take him to America, even, and adopt him when you find that nice Jewish American girl to marry.'

'Aren't you assuming something here?'

'What's that?'

'That you don't come through and I do.'

'OK, well, you might not either, but I mean if you do, will you do that for me?'

He put his hands on her shoulders and she let him pull her towards him. He held her, that was all, and for a moment neither of them spoke.

'Yes, I believe I can make that promise. Young Mordechai will be safe if I have anything to do with it.'

'And Krystyna?'

He laughed. 'Oh, her as well? What, don't tell me you want me to marry the old woman?'

'No, don't be silly, you know what I mean. She's looked after Mordechai all this time. I want to think she will be alright, you know, after the war.'

'Yes, alright, I'll do whatever I can. Now, can we stop talking about this because I'm going to make you another promise, which is that if I have anything to do with it you will be going to Sweden yourself after this.'

She gave him a brief kiss on the cheek. 'Michael, you're very sweet. I wish I had met you a long time ago, before life went horribly wrong.'

'It's not too late you know. You could come to the States with me, afterwards, and I'll adopt Mordechai. I'll even adopt Krystyna if that's what it takes.'

Then she looked him in the eye and said something he hadn't expected.

'You know Captain Jacobs, one day I might just hold you to that.'

14

'If you wouldn't mind, Colonel, giving me your weapon, I have a car waiting outside.'

Stängl was so utterly bemused he didn't know what to do. His instinct was to obey the order, but it was an order so completely preposterous that he was having trouble understanding it. Why on Earth would he be under arrest? And for what? Well, that was a good place to start.

'I'm sorry, I don't understand. What am I being arrested for?'

Sergeant Schiller stood behind Fischer, and avoided Stängl's eye. So, was he involved in this? Was this part of the plan, to take over the gold from him and have him quietly disposed of? Well, if it was there was nothing he could do. It was the two of them against him. Neither of them had a weapon drawn and he was being told to draw his, so there was a chance, a small one, that he could take them both before they could react. He looked Schiller in the eye as he undid the clasp on his holster, to see if he was steeling himself to jump him, but no, he seemed quite calm, as if the idea hadn't occurred to him. It was this lack of fight in him that was Stängl's undoing. He just couldn't kill the man in cold blood, and Schiller too. He knew he should, but he didn't.

Instead, he released the magazine and handed that and the pistol over. Schiller took one in each hand and smiled, the kind of smile a man has who has won and knew all along that he was going to win. And then the smile froze on his face, as if he was unable to change the expression that was now fixed there, and he said nothing but a strange sound came from his throat and a small trickle of blood crept out of his mouth and ran down his chin. The pistol and magazine slid from his hands and landed with a clatter on the desk that woke Stängl from his stupor, and then the Gestapo man simply fell forward and landed face down across the desk. In his back was a bayonet, Sergeant Schiller's bayonet.

'I advise you to pick up your weapon again Sir. You may need it.'

Stängl was almost lost for words.

'But ... but Sergeant. Do you know what you've done?'

'Yes Sir, I've killed an agent of the Gestapo. And it's not Sergeant, Sir.'

'What? What are you talking about?'

'It's Lieutenant, Sir, SS Lieutenant Schiller. The Sergeant's rank is a cover.'

'A cover?' Stängl was pushing Fischer's body aside and recovering his weapon.

'It was felt that you were more likely to have a sergeant in a convoy of this size, so that's what I became. I am under orders to accompany you to make sure that whatever happens the gold is delivered safely. My orders are that there are people who might try to steal it from us, and I am authorised to use all force necessary to prevent that.'

'Felt? Felt by whom?'

'By the people in high places who want to make sure that whatever happens in the war the gold is available for those of us who are left to fight again.'

'What? You mean this is not some kind of scam? General Bergmann isn't, well, stealing it?'

'General Bergmann?' Schiller laughed. Alright, I'll tell you the truth. Yes, he thought he was, but really he was stealing it for us.'

'Us? Schiller, who is us?'

'A group of officers who are preparing a redoubt from which we will fight the enemy and continue the Führer's work, no matter what. Of course, I am only a very junior officer, but I am proud to be playing my part.'

'But does the Führer know about this? I mean, has he ordered the operation?'

'I can't say, Sir. That's way above my head. I'm just following orders. Anyway, let's see if this man really was a Gestapo agent.'

He turned the body over and it slid off the desk onto the floor. From an inside pocket he fetched a leather wallet and yes, he really was who he said he was.

'I don't know what this means, if he's genuine and the Gestapo are trying to take over the consignment, or he's working on his own, I just don't know. Anyway, if you wouldn't mind, I believe it's time we were leaving. We should lock the office door behind us. That will give us a head start.'

He went to the window and looked down at the road.

'He was right, he has got a car. One man in it as far as I can see from here. We need to get down to the lorry without going out of the front door. Do you know if that's possible?'

'Yes, of course, I'll lead the way.'

They found the lorry ready loaded with the gold, and another one standing empty and on the spur of the moment Stängl decided to take that as well. He had the sudden notion of using it as a minesweeper ahead of the lorry carrying the gold. It took Schiller no more than ten minutes to gather up all the men and get the convoy ready to move. In five more minutes they had driven out of the large garage doors in the basement of the Degussa building and up onto a side road, and as they turned left on the main road Stängl looked to his right and there was the Gestapo car, facing the other way. The second man wasn't in it, so he guessed he had got worried about the time his boss was taking and had gone inside to investigate. They drove off unseen into the night.

The streets were dark because of the blackout and they sped through the city unchallenged. It had started to rain and Stängl knew that in the rain sentries are more likely to wave vehicles through a checkpoint because it's human nature. No-one likes getting wet. Over the noise of the engines they heard the air-raid siren and then a few minutes later the crump of the first bombs of the night falling on Hamburg. Leaving the city felt like the best thing they could be doing, and the soldiers in the back of the lorry held on tightly as their driver picked up speed and left the outskirts of the city behind them. Stängl looked round and saw the flames and hoped the bombs would hit Degussa and obliterate the evidence. At the very least, it occurred to him that it was Schiller's bayonet in Fischer's back, not his own, and that made him feel a lot better.

He wanted to ask Schiller a lot of questions but it wasn't possible over the noise of the car's engine and in any case there was the other soldier in the front. He was suddenly exhausted and that reminded him that he hadn't slept in a long time and despite the lurching of the car he nodded off. He didn't even know which way they were heading but Schiller seemed to know everything and for once he was happy to leave him in charge. As he drifted off he wasn't thinking about what had just happened back in Hamburg, he was thinking about his father.

They drove through the night with a stop in the early hours of the morning for a change of drivers and then as the sun came up Stängl stopped the convoy to allow everyone to stretch their legs and brew up. The German soldier, he knew, could be asked to do most things as long as you let him have a regular brew and a smoke. They didn't want exercise. Most of them simply lay on the grass to get some sleep without the constant movement of the vehicles, and so did he. Schiller woke him with a cup of coffee.

'Morning, Sir, brew up?'

'Thank you Lieutenant.'

'Sergeant Sir, if you don't mind.'

'No, quite. Well, where are we?'

'Just past Nuremberg. We're making good time, and we're ahead of schedule now. We could be at the border by nightfall.'

'But that's no good. Our orders are to be there the day after tomorrow. Any earlier and they won't be expecting us.'

'Well in that case, we can afford to take it more slowly and find somewhere tonight where everyone can get some real sleep. Shall I let the men have longer here, Sir?'

Stängl was wondering if this was a request or an order.

'No, it's a bit exposed here. Let's move off as soon as they've had breakfast. We can look for a suitable place to hole up later, but I'd like to get as far south as possible while the going is good.'

Except the going didn't stay good because while the men were lounging about on the grass, eating and smoking and generally behaving in a fairly unmilitary way, a staff car pulled up. Schiller called the men to attention and Stängl buttoned up his tunic and put his cap on. The Oberfuhrer stepping out of the car wasn't an SS officer but even so he outranked him. Stängl threw him a smart Heil Hitler and the Brigadier General, noting Stängl's SS insignia, returned the formality.

'Good morning Colonel. Enjoying your breakfast?'

'Yes, thank you Sir.'

'I see. And where are you off to?'

'South, Sir.'

'Yes, I imagine you are. But where exactly? You see, I am in command of the Volkssturm for this area and I have not been informed of an SS convoy passing through my jurisdiction.'

'No, well, I have my orders, Sir, so may I respectfully suggest you contact my superior officer for confirmation?'

'Possibly. And who is your superior officer?'

'General Bergmann, Sir, in Warsaw.'

Schiller tried to catch his eye, without success. He would have preferred not to mention Bergmann's name but it was too late now.

'Warsaw, eh? That's a long way from here. I find it hard to imagine what the SS from Warsaw are doing in my area, especially, if I might say so, without informing me. I have my orders too, you know, and I am supposed to know who is travelling through my part of Germany. May I see your orders?'

Stängl threw out his chest and tried to look taller than he was.

'No, Sir, I'm sorry, but we are on a secret operation and I am under strict instructions not to divulge information to any-one.'

The Brigadier-General went red in the face. He would have shown his temper but Stängl was only just his junior and he was an SS officer and on top of that he was making a perfectly reasonable claim. He desperately wanted to show this officer who was in charge, but he was afraid it wasn't him, and in any case he could hardly force the issue. He could, though, make life a little uncomfortable for him.

'Well, Colonel, as you say, you have your instructions. In that case, as I have a little time to spare, I shall have my car turned round and I shall personally accompany you as far as Munich, where my responsibility ends. Have your men get ready to leave immediately.'

It felt good to be able to give this man an order, even if it wasn't a very big one, and watch his squad jump to it. Fair enough, he would be late for his meeting, but the order had been given now and he couldn't back down.

As Stängl climbed into his car he whispered to Schiller. 'Just promise me one thing Sergeant.'

'Yes Sir?'

'Please resist the temptation to shoot him. That I would have difficulty explaining.'

'No Sir, I don't think that's likely to be necessary.'

The General's car went a bit too fast for them and Schiller picked up speed to keep up with him but Stängl looked round and he could see the lorry with the gold was having difficulty with this. It was carrying a lot of weight. He instructed Schiller to slow down. If the General wanted to keep an eye on them, well then he would have to slow down to their speed.

They arrived in Munich a couple of hours later and while they waited for their papers to be checked Stängl got out and thanked the General profusely for his assistance in a matter of great importance to the Fatherland. The General had by now forgotten what he had done or why he had done it and returned Stängl's salute with due pomp. It wasn't often that a retired first war officer got the chance these days to perform an important task and this was something to boast about when he finally got to his meeting in Nuremberg. It would be only reasonable to embellish the story a little and, anyway, who would know?

The convoy still had plenty of time to drive south and find a suitable overnight camp, and Stängl allowed them to drive more sedately now and enjoy the Bavarian scenery. They stopped for lunch at a roadside inn and he allowed his men one beer each in turns, while half of them stayed with the gold in the lorry at all times. He couldn't imagine what danger there might be in this peaceful village, but he wouldn't feel entirely safe until they had crossed the border and he had discharged the gold and with it his responsibility.

Meanwhile he was stuck with four tonnes of gold and nowhere to go for two days. Without the lorries he would simply have had himself a little holiday, but this was no time for such frivolous thoughts. He had to protect the gold, and he had to keep the men's minds concentrated on the job. He decided to camp tonight, then drive towards the border in the morning, and camp again. That way, the men would always have something to do and they would be more likely to remain alert. It was a completely reasonable decision. It was, though, a decision that was going to put the convoy on a fatal collision course with a group of angry Jews.

15

The plan went wrong before it started. During the night, Daniel Foxman developed serious pains in his abdomen and his cries woke the others. They didn't know what was the matter. Daniel was the closest they had to a doctor, and he was the one who was ill. He managed, though, inbetween bouts of pain to get out his diagnosis. Appendicitis.

They stood around in the lamplight and wondered what that meant. Well obviously it meant he was in a bad way, but did it also mean he wouldn't be able to come with them, or that he might get better if they delayed? They could only delay for a maximum of one day, and would that be enough? They couldn't go without him. Actually they could, but they had no-one else who understood explosives and while they might not need to blow anything up they might, and going without him was going to further compromise an already difficult operation.

Michael waited for the pain to subside and asked Daniel what the prognosis was. Not good, apparently. Without surgery, he would get progressively worse and there was a serious chance of it developing into peritonitis and if that happened he would die. Surgery simply wasn't an option though, because the last time one of their number had needed an operation he and Dovid Lempel the dentist had done it but he could hardly operate on himself. Anyway, the patient had died, which was hardly surprising in the conditions

they had to operate under. Daniel knew he was probably going to die. Michael asked if there was any way he could get through the mission, and he said possibly, they had a small supply of morphine, and he could administer that to himself. It might be enough to see him through.

Michael called an emergency meeting of the leaders and put it to them. Abandon the operation, or take a chance with Daniel? No-one liked it, they could see the pain he was in, but they said they should carry on, if he was prepared to do it, and he said he was. He gave himself the first dose of morphine and half an hour later he fell into a fitful sleep and everyone calmed down, and now they felt a bit better about him they tried to get a little more sleep themselves.

They didn't leave camp until seven, an hour later than planned, but they were all tired and it was better to be late than not go at all. Daniel lay on a cot they made up in the back of one of the lorries and Roza, as the only woman, instinctively took it upon herself to nurse him. There wasn't actually much she could do but her calm presence seemed to help, and she sponged his face with tepid water to try and keep his temperature down. He gave himself another dose of morphine before they moved off and so for much of the journey he slept. He had already prepared explosive devices in case they were needed. The problem would come when it came to setting them, because he was still the only one who could do that. Several people had watched Daniel as he played with the components in camp but no-one had any confidence in being able to actually set one of his devices off. They could only hope that either he would be able to do it himself, or in the event they wouldn't be needed. Roza was worried about something else, something unconnected with the operation, and that was Daniel himself. Her pre-occupation was with keeping him as comfortable as possible, and what they were going to do if he got worse. No, not if, when, because he had assured them he would.

Meyer Edelman the navigator had plotted a route as best he could based on the maps they had found in the German lorries, with the addition of any information they were able to gather from the various members of the group who of course had themselves lived throughout Poland. No-one had come from Germany, but they would worry about that if and when they got that far. They discussed navigating by the stars but apart from knowing it should be possible no-one was actually sure how to do it so that idea was held in abeyance. At the very least they knew they were heading west and simply by observing the sun they could work that out. The problem then was that they needed to avoid the major roads which the larger German military traffic would use and where the checkpoints were more likely to be. Michael put Meyer under pressure to find the shortest possible route to save time, but at the same time he wanted to use quieter roads, so it wasn't easy. Still, Meyer knew that being a commander wasn't easy and he accepted the challenge Michael gave him without complaint.

It had been a sombre parting as the convoy left the camp. Those left behind wondered if they would ever see their friends again, and those in the lorries wondered the same.

After only two hours they passed their first German motorcycle courier and Michael waved to him without knowing if that was normal between soldiers on the road. It seemed natural to him. The courier didn't wave back but that Michael thought that might be difficult when you're riding a motorbike. He had never ridden one, so he didn't know. Anyway, it hardly seemed likely that a wave would give them away, but he decided that next time he would only wave in response to a friendly gesture.

They saw no more traffic until later that afternoon when they passed a German staff car with two pompous-looking officers in the back. Roza craned her neck to see how they reacted but they just went on talking among themselves, apparently about something too important to concern themselves with two very normal-looking army lorries. That made them all feel a lot better, to know that they could blend in and not be noticed, that no-one was going to take one look at them and know they were Jews.

It got dark about eight o'clock but Michael pushed them on for another two hours, then he pulled them off the main road onto a track and they wound their way round a small hill which afforded some protection and then on into some scrub that was just tall enough for them to hide the vehicles in. Everyone was relieved to get out and stretch their legs. It was hard riding for the passengers and arm-breaking work for the drivers, and to start with they just walked around trying to get some feeling back in their legs.

Lighting fires would have been too dangerous, even this far off the road, so they had to make do with cold food. Roza tried to get

Daniel to eat something but at any given time he was either doped up by the morphine or in too much pain to be hungry. She said come on you've got to eat and he said why and she said I don't know and he gave her a weak smile. He knew she was trying to help him, and he also knew it wasn't only about the operation, that she cared. Well, in his experience, that was a woman thing and only to be expected, even in the brutal environment they were in. They were on a mission to kill people, not least Roza would be involved in that, but she hadn't lost her humanity and she could still love a fellow human being and want to help him. Had he known she needed to hear him say that he would have done so but he didn't.

Michael established a lookout post on the hill, which gave a good view for about ten kilometres in each direction. He put two men on it, to keep each other awake, and gave them a torch with which to flash a warning if they spotted any road traffic.

He was worried about the timing of this operation. They were taking a lot for granted - that Stängl's orders hadn't been changed, that he hadn't himself decided to alter the route because even a slight alteration would mean they were simply going to miss them, that the German convoy hadn't moved forward or back by even one day. The more he thought about it the less sensible the whole thing looked. He would never have put together an operation like this in the US Army, so why was he doing it now? Well, there was an obvious answer to that question. Because first they had no choice because they were working with the best intelligence they had, imperfect though it was, and second because the stakes were so high. Even a small chance of success was worth trying for. He wanted to talk to Roza about his doubts but he knew that she felt responsible for it all because she was the one who brought them the information in the first place and it was she who was the motivating force behind the operation. If it went terribly wrong she would blame herself, so what she didn't need right now was to hear about his doubts. He worried that to Roza this was as much about a chance to interrogate Colonel Stängl as it was about the gold, that she was still obsessed with finding Mordechai, and if not finding him them finding out what had happened to him. Michael was in little doubt about what had happened. He had been in this war a long time and the disappearance of someone more often than not simply meant they were dead. In the armed forces it could also mean they were captive and one day they might surface from a prisoner of war camp, but Mordechai Levinson wasn't a POW, of that Michael could be absolutely certain.

He fell asleep with these thoughts in his head and in the middle of the night he was woken, as instructed, to carry out an inspection of the lookout post. It was cold, autumnal, and he wanted to be in bed asleep, preferably in New York. He climbed up the hill and gave the password, Mount Carmel, and found the two lookouts tired and chilled but in good spirits. He looked out across the rolling hills and realised that if he trained his binoculars westward he was probably looking at Germany, the land of the bitterest enemy the Jewish people had faced in their thousands of years of existence, and the home his own parents had once known. The moon cast a little light through the clouds and as he looked he thought it seemed much like anywhere else. He couldn't bring himself to see the land itself as an enemy, and the inevitable consequence of that idea was to wonder if there would come a day when this country would be inhabited by a people whose first instinct was not conquest and the subjugation and slaughter of their fellow men.

He left his two men and promised to send up their relief immediately. Back in camp he found it hard to get back to sleep. He wandered around the sleeping bodies, poked his nose into the lorries and found more men asleep in them, and Roza stretched out on the bench seat in one of the cabs. He gazed at her face for a while bathed in moonlight and let his thoughts wonder. Her long curly hair fell into her eyes and in her sleep she flicked it away. He wanted to lean into the cab and do that for her, pin it back so it wouldn't disturb her, but he didn't allow himself that luxury. Then for something to do he broke off a piece of black bread and chewed on it as he sat on the tailboard of a lorry and tried to make good use of the time by planning tomorrow. When he woke, stretched out on the tailboard, it was already tomorrow and the sun was starting to warm up the autumn morning a little. People were milling about quietly, shaking the sleep out of their heads, lost for something to do in the absence of a fire and hot coffee.

Michael woke Roza and together they checked on Daniel. He was deeply asleep and for a moment they looked at each other questioningly, but he was still alive. It was the morphine. He had given himself a larger dose during the night and it had at last knocked him out. He came round groggily and smiled at them as if to say don't worry about me, for which they were grateful.

There was nothing to hang about for. As soon as the two men on lookout reported back, they loaded up and set off.

The fuel had lasted well, supplemented by the jerry cans they had loaded, but tanking up was going to be the next worry. The more Michael thought about pulling into a German Army depot and asking for gas the less he liked it. It had sounded just about possible two days ago but now it sounded ridiculous. They had forged orders that would entitle them to fuel but even so, none of them knew the procedures and the chance of any of them looking like they were used to it was slim. He talked to Meyer Edelman about it but Meyer just shrugged his shoulders. He could find a depot from the maps he had, but that was all. What happened when they got there was up to Michael. Sorry.

It was Jakub Alter who came up with a solution. Well, it was an idea at least. Whether it was going to be a solution they would have to wait and see. Jakub was a thief by profession, and his motto was never buy what you can steal. And how do you steal fuel from a fuel depot? You don't. You wait for a tanker to leave, you follow it, and you steal that, well, not the tanker, but some of its contents.

It was an excellent idea, but would they have time? Michael was well aware that their schedule was tight, that even if Stängl's itinerary didn't change, blowing the whole operation out of the water, it was going to be tight, but this was likely to wreck it entirely. On the other hand, what choice did they have?

They found the depot within an hour, and then they quickly put the plan into operation. One lorry was hidden half a kilometre away from the ambush, and the other was stopped on the roadside with its bonnet up. A worried-looking driver tinkered with the engine. In truth, he had no idea what he was looking at, but he wiped his hands on an oily rag from time to time to make it look like he did, and half an hour later what should come along but a fuel tanker, heavily laden by the look of it, and they heard the squeal of brakes as it ground to a stop.

Five minutes later the two-man crew were dead and dumped inside the tanker. Roza got one from two hundred metres and other fell to Michael's knife. Hoses were rigged up to both lorries. It took a while for the fuel to siphon into the tanks, but there was no possibility of leaving until they were full. They could only pray that no other tankers were due along this stretch of road until they had finished. They could also set an ambush in each direction, which they did, but this day their prayers were answered and they weren't needed.

Before they left, Daniel climbed off his cot and rigged up a small explosive device that would blow the tanker up when the ignition was started. It was a small contribution, but a satisfying one. No-one would ever expect a partisan attack this far into Germany and in any case there would be no evidence after thousands of litres of fuel had gone up. It would be reported as an accident.

They made good speed after that and Michael began to feel they were back on course. They passed a number of Army vehicles on the road but no-one stopped them. Why should they? They all gained confidence with every kilometre of German territory they crossed, almost as if nothing could stop them now. Well, they knew there was a lot that could stop them of course. The operation was, every man among them knew, hanging by a thread. It felt good just now, because they had got away with so much and the sun was shining, but even if they found the convoy it was only the start of the operation really, because then they had to overpower the German soldiers and then they had to drive the gold to Switzerland and then they had to hope that the arrangements for crossing the border had been made because actually no-one knew that for sure because there hadn't been time to verify it before they left.

They skirted well to the south of Munich and followed the signs for Ravensburg. They needed just one more day of driving and then they would at least, with God's help, be meeting Colonel Fritz Stängl and four tonnes of stolen gold.

16

Setting the booby trap in the German fuel tanker had been done at a price for Daniel. He took increasing doses of morphine and Roza feared for him. Michael worried about his ability to do his job, if they needed him to, and after all they had already needed him to and it seemed likely that his skill with explosives was going to be important. The more he thought about it the more Michael came to believe that Roza was right, they had a better chance of success in a static attack than an ambush. Ambushing vehicles travelling at speed was always risky. You only got one chance because if they got away you had a chase on your hands and what might just work in a Polish forest had almost no chance of working on a German highway. They could try to carry out an ambush on a quiet road but now they were in Germany and Michael could see how long and straight the roads were he realised that Stängl would almost certainly stick to them, thus depriving them of a nice quiet place to attack.

Michael knew from long experience in Intelligence that no matter how much information you think you have before an operation you never have enough, that there are always surprises. The Overlord landings in Normandy had been preceded by the biggest Intelligence effort ever carried out in the history of warfare, and still there were surprises, still there were things they didn't know that they would have benefited from knowing. It occurred to Michael that this operation was probably the first Allied invasion of Germany and Eisenhower and Montgomery new nothing about it and never would. Nothing would be written about it when the history of this war came to be recorded, if only because they were unlikely to come out alive to tell anyone and even if they did survive they still couldn't tell anyone. He veered between optimism and pessimism about the whole thing on an hourly basis and as they drove he found that the people around him had less and less to say about it.

Given his growing realisation that they simply couldn't plan a mobile attack without more knowledge of the terrain and Stängl's movements, their only chance, he admitted to himself, was to find the enemy, stalk him, and kill him. That meant, inevitably, a night-time raid, and it also almost certainly meant the need for Daniel's skills. Roza had to keep him alive long enough.

There was almost nothing Roza could do about Daniel other than stay with him and fuss over him as if the back of the lorry were a hospital ward and she were a trained nurse, both of which were patently untrue. The vehicle jolted constantly, and she felt the pain this visibly caused him and sometimes she saw a look of hopelessness come over his face and she thought that if she and the others weren't there in the lorry with him he would simply throw himself over the tailgate and die on the road. Other times his expression changed to one of determination. She didn't know where that came from, but when she saw it she squeezed his hand and smiled to encourage him. She prayed for this nightmare journey to end, for him, but for her too, because she didn't know how much longer she could give him the support he was depending on. When they stopped and the lorry was still, he showed her how to inject the morphine so that she could do it if he couldn't. She wondered, if he got that bad, how the hell he was going to get out of the lorry and set explosive charges, but she didn't ask. Perhaps he would find the strength for that. He would have to.

They all needed to stop and take a breather and get their leg muscles working again but Michael didn't let them. They had to push on because if they were late it was all a waste of time. He knew they were tired and he knew that tired men were less effective in combat but what choice did he have? He was in command and that required some hard decisions. Even when Roza pleaded with him for a longer break on one occasion, for Daniel, his face took on that steely expression he had when he did something he didn't want to do and he said no, we're moving off now, and she saw what it cost him to say that and she said nothing more.

These people, Michael knew all too well, were not trained soldiers. They were just ordinary men whose lives had been turned upside down and who now found themselves pretending they could carry out a military operation against a trained and ruthless enemy. They had only one advantage, apart from the obvious one of surprise, and that was their anger. Every man knew about the gold because he had made sure they knew. He had wanted them to want to do this, and they did, all of them. Everyone had lost people, more often than not their entire family, and as repugnant as they found the idea of handling the gold they all felt that it was even worse that the Germans had it.

For Michael, who knew so much more than they did, the stakes were very much higher. The gold in the Germans' hands gave them the money to buy armaments that could prolong the war. Depriving them of that was in itself an essential war aim. But of course money they didn't possess meant it could be used by the Jews, if they could get it to Palestine. Getting people there was hard, because people are very visible and the British could stop them landing on the beaches, but money was very different indeed. It existed on paper. It could be moved around the world without the British Army ever seeing it. It could travel from Switzerland to Palestine, and from there to any country that would sell arms to the Jews, and no-one could stop it. And Michael knew that after this war, which was going to end for sure within the coming year, Europe was going to be awash with weapons that were suddenly surplus to requirements and looking for buyers. With this gold they would able to buy enough perhaps to ensure the survival of the remnant in Palestine. When he thought about the implication of what he was doing he felt overwhelmed by it, by a responsibility he felt quite unequal to. Well, there was no-one else.

There hadn't been time to contact the Jewish Agency for Palestine about this operation, but by now, as they drove, he knew that his colleagues in the Joint in the States would have informed them, and so there were a lot of people right now who were hoping and praying for their success. He felt the burden of their expectations but he also felt supported by their prayers.

That night he pulled them into a wood by the side of the road and yet again he had to forbid the lighting of fires. He checked on Daniel and was disappointed by what he saw. Had he seen Daniel when he wasn't trying to impress, that would have been even worse. Roza took him to one side.

'Look, Michael, don't be fooled. He's worse than he looks. I know, I've been holding his hand all day.'

'And?'

'Well, what are you going to do about him?'

'OK, Roza, you tell me, what would you do?'

His tone gave away the stress he was under. With anyone else he would have hidden it but with Roza he didn't want to.

'I don't know. I'm not a commander.'

'Come on, you've been the deputy commander of a partisan company. Don't tell me you didn't have to make this kind of decision.'

'Leszek always made the hard choices. I backed him up but he would have done it without me, regardless of what I thought. He liked to have a woman to talk to at night, to explain why he did what he did, but even if he asked my opinion he had already made his decision. I think you've already made yours, haven't you?'

'Yes, we go on, with Daniel, and when it comes to it tomorrow night he either can or he can't help us. If he can't, well then we will have to do it without him. That's it really. Pretty well what you would expect, huh?'

It was.

'Now let's get something to eat, then let the other commanders know I want to have a briefing with them in an hour, followed by a general briefing for everyone.'

'Yes Sir.'

He took that to be a joke, which it was.

An hour later the commanders met in the lorry where Daniel lay. With the flap down and tied tightly, it enabled them to light a couple of lanterns.

'OK people, it's on for tomorrow. Well, when I say it's on of course I have no real idea if that's true. All I can say is that if we can find them it's on, so of course we might drive all the way to Berlin and not find them in which case we'll just give Hitler our regards and push off.'

No-one laughed. It could have been the way he said it or it could have been because it was too late for humour. Roza held Daniel's hand.

'Well, I have finally come down in favour of Plan B, which you will remember was Roza's suggestion of a static attack. That means we've got to find them, follow them, wait for them to stop and then go in. Naturally, we will have to draw up a plan of action for the actual attack, but you will appreciate that it's impossible to do that before we see where they stop. They might make it easy for us or they might not. One thing is for sure, they won't be expecting us. They will certainly take precautions but I don't expect those to be insuperable. We outnumber them, and we will be taking them by surprise. On the other hand, if we don't get it right first time they will undoubtedly have the advantage over us.'

He looked at them and saw what they really were, a taxi driver, a violinist, a dentist and a gangster. And an anaesthetist with appendicitis. And what was he? Not, for sure, an infantry commander. Roza had more field experience than any of them. He continued before they saw the doubt in his face.

'A static attack will almost certainly mean an explosion, Daniel. Is there any way of blowing a lorry up and killing its occupants without damaging the gold?'

'But what makes you think there will be men on the lorry?'

'Because Stängl isn't going to leave four tonnes of the stuff without having a very close guard on it. Well?'

'Well, it takes a lot less to kill men than to melt gold, for sure, but to be honest it's all going to be guesswork. I might underdo it, I might overdo it.'

'Err on the latter. As long as the explosion kills a few guards, I'll be happy. If we have to wait for the remains of the lorry to cool down before we can pull the gold out, well we'll wait.'

'But couldn't we just shoot them all?'

'We could try, but although we outnumber them they will certainly outgun us. I want to even things up a bit right from the beginning. Well, we will just have to see how things are placed at the time. Now, for the harder bit.'

Moise Halberstam asked the question they all had in their minds.

'You mean there's something harder than killing a lot of SS soldiers?'

'Yes, my friend, finding them. Now look here. This is the road we expect them to be on. They will be driving south, so we have to be driving north. We will start as close to the frontier as possible to avoid any chance of missing them, so we'll join the road, let me see, uhuh, here. We need to be at that point no later than midday tomorrow. Then all we have to do is drive until we see them. What happens once we do is that we keep going, as if we're not interested in them, make sure they don't have a security tail, then turn round and follow them. The clever part is going to be watching them without them knowing we're watching them. It's not as bad as it sounds, because most convoys don't look behind them, so we'll keep them just in sight all the time. They're due to cross the border first thing the next morning, so my guess is that they will camp within a few miles of it and be up early and ready to go, except of course they won't because we'll be paying them a visit first. So that's Plan B folks, and the rest we'll make up as we go along, by which I mean that once they have made camp somewhere we will reconnoitre and decide how to hit them. Easy, huh? Any questions?'

It all seemed so unlikely that no-one could think of anything sensible to ask. Jakub asked the only reasonable question under the circumstances.

'Is it going to work? '

'Is it going to work? How the hell should I know? I'm an Intelligence officer, not a miracle worker. If I'm right in all my assumptions, and Stängl hasn't changed any of his plans, and the Almighty for once takes pity on the Jews, yes, it will work. Any more than that I can't say. Now, let's talk to the men.'

He gave them much the same information and when he asked for questions funnily enough someone asked the same question and he gave the same answer and began to feel like a fraud, like he was leading them to their deaths and these people had put all their trust in him. Why? Because he was in command? Because he was American and they had some unwavering belief that that meant more than it did, that if all else failed the US Cavalry would come charging in? Or simply because they would have put their faith in God but in the light of the events of recent years there probably wasn't a single man there who felt much like doing that? Nevertheless, a few of them gathered to recite the evening service, not because they thought it was likely to do a lot of good but for the comfort it brought, the memories of another time and place, to remind them that here they were with friends.

Without a camp fire to sit round, no-one felt like talking and one by one they lay down, in the lorries or on the open ground, and slept. Michael, like most commanders the night before an operation, couldn't do that, and neither could Roza, and there was some comfort for both of them in one of their late-night talks.

'Don't, whatever you do, ask me if it's going to work, please.'

'No, don't worry, we got your message.'

'So, tell me, what do you think? Do you think it's going to work?'

'Michael, if you don't know, how can I?'

'I didn't ask you what you know. I asked you what you think. What does your heart tell you?'

'It tells me I want it to work, that it has to work.'

'Well, Roza Levinson, that will do for me. If we all want it enough, we will surely do our best tomorrow.'

'And if our best isn't good enough?'

'I think you know the answer to that.'

They sat on a fallen tree trunk and were silent. A bat flew in circles overhead and made them look up. It was a crystal-clear night and there were more stars in the sky than they had ever thought existed. It was a magical show, and they were content to sit there and watch it. They turned to look at the moon.

'It will be full tomorrow night.'

'Is that good or bad?'

'Well, it means we'll be able to see them, which is good, but they'll be able to see us, which is bad.'

'I see. Simple really.'

'On the other hand, once the fireworks go off, the moon is going to be neither here nor there. Look, I wish there was some better way of doing it but I'm afraid there's going to be a hell of a firefight, and that worries me. If there is any possibility of setting you up in a sniper position away from the centre of the action, where you can use the rifle, that will be a great help.'

'You mean where I'm less likely to get shot?'

'That too, but look, really, you can do an invaluable job. Once people start shooting what generally happens in these things is that everyone just points their weapon and fires off a lot of rounds. It's not the way to win any battle, but people get scared, even experienced soldiers. These men, well, they're not, with respect, soldiers at all. They've had no proper training and I really don't know what they will do in a battle. I want you sitting watching the fight from the outside, as it were, where you can pick your targets and make every round count.'

'It makes sense.'

'Good.'

'And if I do that and in the end you are all killed, what do I do?'

'You're asking me?'

'Yes.'

'Well don't.'

'Well in that case don't get killed. Promise?'

'Promise.'

17

It was a fine night but in the morning a little light rain set in. The men grumbled as they went about their morning routine, the ablutions and the coffee making. Stängl had them parade for inspection, which surprised them a bit, but that was what he wanted, to keep them on their toes. They were almost there but almost wasn't there and he had had a disturbing dream that night. He couldn't, of course, tell the men that.

It occurred to him, strangely only now, that if he was to bring his men back he would need the second lorry. He wondered why General Bergmann hadn't thought of that, and hoped it wasn't an ominous sign that they weren't supposed to be going back. The order was to hand the entire lorry over, with its contents, to a driver who would have the correct paperwork signed by Bergmann himself and, as an extra precaution, the password, Eva Braun. Someone's idea of a joke, he presumed. He imagined the new driver would be someone from the Gestapo, whom he knew operated in Switzerland.

He worried now that he had no orders about the men. He himself was to report back to Auschwitz-Birkenau, so he reckoned it would be alright to give them an order to return to Warsaw. If that was wrong, well it was too bad. If they had any sense, they would turn the lorry west and keep going until they got to Spain, but he didn't actually suggest that to them.

His next worry was whether the little business back in Hamburg was going to have repercussions. Unless a lucky American bomb had hit the mint there was going to be a dead Gestapo officer on the floor and that was the kind of thing people took badly. He was on record as having used that office and he was the senior officer. He had a feeling that telling a court-martial about a man called Sergeant Schiller who was really Lieutenant Schiller and he was working for a clandestine organisation and had actually killed the agent himself was going to be disbelieved, and now he wondered if Schiller himself had thought about this and that explained why he was so relaxed about it, because he knew that Stängl was going to take whatever grief was coming.

And as for the story about the gold being hidden away for a secret project to rearm in the event of defeat, how credible was that? Hitler himself didn't know about it, Schiller said, but how could there be anything in this war that Hitler didn't know about? On the contrary, the rumour was that you couldn't move these days without him putting his oar in. And anyway, why would they be planning another round without him? Did they think he would surrender to the Allies? Surely not.

That was when a much scarier answer came into his head. It was another attempt on the Führer's life. The recent one, in July, had been a fiasco, and a lot of officers had been rounded up and despatched as a result. Hitler was almost certainly by this time getting paranoid about assassination attempts, so how likely was a coup to succeed now? On the other hand, if there was a coup brewing, why had he been roped in? A full Colonel to do a job like this seemed a bit excessive, notwithstanding the value of the consignment. Were they planning to bring him into their plot? Were they planning to dispose of him once the job was done?

And then for some reason he couldn't fathom an even more bizarre idea came to him. Perhaps there was no gold. Perhaps this whole thing was a decoy. After all, he himself hadn't actually seen any gold. No, actually that wasn't true. He had seen it at Auschwitz-Birkenau, or at least some of it, and he had seen it at Kulmhof, and then he tried to remember if he had seen it in Warsaw and he couldn't recall but it didn't matter because one way or another he knew there was a lot of gold on that lorry when they arrived in Hamburg.

What he didn't know was whether there was any gold on it now. They had left in a hurry. Now he thought about it, he was a bit surprised that not only was all the smelting completed in that time but it was all nicely loaded up and ready. And then that Gestapo agent just happened to be there when he returned, earlier than he or anyone else had expected, and Schiller killed the man and gave him some cock-and-bull story about orders to protect the gold, and then they ran for it. The more he thought about it the more it looked to him like he was driving a lot of empty boxes around Germany and Schiller was using him as some kind of decoy. Somewhere there was a lorry load of gold but the more he thought about it the more he convinced himself that it wasn't his lorry.

He wanted to check, but how could he do that without alerting Schiller? Come to think of it, what about the other men? He hadn't selected them, they had simply been assigned to him. Perhaps they were all part of this plot, perhaps he was the only one who was being fooled here. If that was true, there was no chance of him opening those boxes and seeing for himself, not with all those men about. And anyway the boxes were sealed. If he broke through a seal they would know when the lorry was delivered in Switzerland. On the other hand, by then it would probably be too late for it to matter. He just could not figure out what the hell was going on. Anyway, if it was true, and he wondered if he was just getting carried away by it all but if it was true, then what he did with the men after delivering the lorry was academic. What was more significant was what they were planning to do with him.

Well, gold or no gold, it didn't concern him. The only issue now was how to get away, on his own, immediately afterwards. He started to work up a number of possible plans for that in his mind, all of which involved driving the car west. He could get across France, almost certainly, and then he would be in Spain and free. He considered driving back north and getting his mother and taking her to Spain with him but realised that was not going to be possible. No, if he was going to run, it would be alone. He wished momentarily he had Rudi with him, but Rudi was dead.

Whatever happened in the next twenty-four hours he would have to get the lorry to the frontier, and whatever they needed him for they needed him to do that so he was safe until then. He gave his orders and they moved off. The motorcyclists at each end of the convoy, who before he had found reassuring, now looked to him like they were guarding him, not the gold, and he became depressed as they drove. The rain cleared up again and it turned into a pleasant, sunny day, but the sun didn't lift his spirits. He was reminded of his premonitory thoughts on the coast when he had seen the guns waiting for an invasion, and the bombers over Hamburg, and he wondered if this was all going to go bad sooner rather than later.

If there were people doing their own thing, really hatching plots without the Führer's approval, then Germany was going down the tubes. No-one had ever thought the western Allies would be able to land in France, let alone break out of their beachheads, but they had, and no-one thought the Russians had anything left to fight with but they did, and now he didn't see this war as such a good thing after all. The only good he could see that had come out of it was the success they had had with the Jews. They had taken on the German people's most deadly enemy and beaten them. However much longer the war went on, he felt sure at least that the battle against the Jews was going to be won. Most of Europe was now, thanks to dedicated officers like him, almost Jew-free. Yes, that was an achievement they couldn't take away from him. If Germany lost the war, well the Jews had certainly lost it too and one day the rest of the world would thank the Reich for what had been achieved. The Jews had threatened civilisation and they had been exterminated, like vermin, and no-one could bring them back. He just hoped the Wehrmacht could hold the Allies at bay long enough for the SS to complete the job once and for all. That made him feel a bit better and he sat back and decided to enjoy the drive. He watched Schiller's neck from behind, and wondered what it would be like to put a bullet through it. He hadn't shot anyone for a long time. Yes, it would, he reckoned, feel good. Alright, the man was a German, not a Jew, but he had set himself up against Stängl and when that happens you have to look after yourself. Yes, he looked at the neck and decided that come tomorrow it would give him great pleasure to shoot Sergeant Schiller or Lieutenant Schiller or whatever his name really was.

He stopped the convoy at another pretty village and the innkeeper brought them out mugs of beer and plates of black bread and sausage. From the flurry of activity it was obvious he hadn't had any customers for a while and he laughed and joked with the men and asked impertinent questions about what they were doing on this road and Stängl started to suspect him and that was when he realised this had gone too far, this whole conspiracy thing, and he had to stop suspecting everyone. The innkeeper's wife came out and kept the party going and plied the men with more food and drink and Stängl called a halt eventually and paid the bill from his own pocket.

Then he ordered the men to board the vehicles and as they were about to move off a voice call out. Where's Schultz?

Schultz? Stängl wasn't aware of the man but then why should he be? He told Schiller to find out if they were missing a man and he came back and reported yes, there was a man called Private Schultz and no-one had seen him for a while. He was known as a bit of a tearaway and had only the month before been confined to barracks for some misdemeanour. Stängl tutted in irritation and ordered the men off the lorry to go and search for this Schultz. They found him in a nearby barn with the innkeeper's daughter, and Stängl was so annoyed he had Schiller tie his hands and throw him in the back of the lorry to face disciplinary action when they got back. If they got back, except of course he didn't say that. Well, if this lot were going to have a go at him tomorrow, at least there was one less of them who could do anything. It was a small victory, but it was a start.

He gave the innkeeper a large tip by way of apology for the discourtesy one of his soldiers had displayed, and finally they moved off to look for a suitable place to camp. They drove most of the afternoon before they found the right place. Nothing unusual happened in those hours. They passed one army convoy going the other way and Stängl had a strange moment when he imagined he recognised one of the soldiers in the cab of a lorry but of course he had seen many men in his years of service and perhaps he had come across this one somewhere but it hardly mattered. Even so, there was something about the face that preyed on his thoughts on and off for the rest of the day but finally, what with the arrangements to be made for their final night, and with other things to worry about like was he involved in some deadly conspiracy or wasn't he, he managed to forget about it.

18

They hit the road they were looking for almost by accident. They came to a crossroads where they weren't expecting one but then their maps were hardly helpful because they comprised Roza's sketch and a printed map of completely the wrong scale. The signpost pointed north for Regensburg and that, by Meyer's calculation, was the road Stängl was going to be driving southwards on, towards them. They had a brief conference and decided it was the right road and if it wasn't there wasn't time to drive on in the hope of finding a more likely one.

So they turned the convoy north. Roza now rode in the cab with Michael so she could spot Stängl. She was the only person in the group who had ever seen him, so her identification was essential. They hoped for good weather and as the day wore on the drizzle stopped and there was bright sunshine. This would help enormously, because Stängl was likely to drive with the top down on his car, making it much easier to see him. They were likely to close at about a hundred and fifty kilometres an hour, so she would get no more than a few seconds. She could use the binoculars from a distance but it wouldn't do to be seen peering through them when they got close.

Straight stretches of road were good, because of course they could see a long way ahead, but each time they came to a bend the stress level went up and they hoped their target wouldn't come the other way too fast for them to identify. After the first hour they were tense but after the second they were like limp rags. It took another two and a half hours by which time it was getting late in the afternoon before they saw the first vehicle. Through the binoculars

Roza thought she could see a lorry but it wasn't possible to see from a distance if there was a staff car in front of it. Anyway, could they be sure the car would drive in front of the lorry? Probably.

It wasn't them. Three lorries but no car or motorcycles. They relaxed a little and Michael said well it's good practice for the real thing and hardly had he said that when the real thing appeared. Roza could clearly see a lead motorcycle and yes, there was a car, and yes the top was open. She could see the lorry behind that of course and she asked Michael to slow down, not enough to arouse suspicion but enough to give her a vital extra second as the two convoys closed.

It seemed to take ages before they got close, and suddenly it was upon them. Roza tried not to appear to be searching but she couldn't help it. She leaned out of the window a little, straight into his eyes. She flushed and looked away but her body had gone stiff and Michael knew immediately she had seen him. What he had seen, though, was a second lorry. They had been expecting one. Did that mean more troops?

They drove on for another kilometre, well past the next bend, and then they pulled up to confer.

'There are two trucks.'

'What? I didn't see.'

'No, you were watching Stängl, but there were two.'

'You're sure?'

'About two trucks? Hard to miss.'

'What does it mean?'

'Well, I can only guess, but the most likely answer is more guards. We could be facing a numbers problem. We don't know which one the gold is in, or even if it's spread over the two vehicles.'

'So what do we do?'

'Exactly what we were going to do. Come on, we can't stand here discussing it. We have to catch up with them.'

And so they turned the lorries round and raced after their quarry. It took another twenty minutes but then Roza saw through the binoculars the tail-end lorry and another motorcyclist behind that. Michael pulled back a little so that most of the time they were out of sight. He knew where this road headed because they had driven along it themselves earlier, and he knew there were no significant turnings. On his map there was a straight line to the border, and they knew that Stängl couldn't approach it until the morning, so they also knew he had to find somewhere to wait that night. They could afford to hold back and they were certain to see if he stopped.

After an hour they came round a bend and Michael braked sharply and hoped that Meyer driving the lorry behind was able to do the same, because about six hundred metres ahead there was the convoy, turning slowly onto a forest track. Stängl must have halted while he sent one of the outriders ahead to reconnoitre, and he had reported back that there was a suitable place to camp.

They watched and waited as the last vehicle disappeared through the trees. There was little likelihood of the track having another way out, so whatever happened Michael could see that Stängl had bottled himself up. That was good, as far as it went, except of course that the Germans had over-whelming firepower and could surely blast their way out of any trap. He considered laying an ambush at the junction of the road and the track but these considerations outweighed the attractiveness of the idea. And what would happen in the admittedly unlikely but not impossible event that as they were springing the trap more Germans would come along the road? No, they were going to have to go in after them.

He pulled the two lorries into the trees well before Stängl's turnoff. If the German had any sense he would already have posted a man at that point. As it happened he hadn't because it didn't occur to him they could possibly have a tail, but Michael didn't know that. He was feeling extremely cautious.

He sent two men ahead to reconnoitre and they were back forty minutes later with a general layout of the Germans' camp. They had driven about half a kilometre into the forest and come to a clearing with some kind of woodsman's hut. The lorries were parked next to each other with the car and motorcycles to one side. The Germans were busying them-selves establishing a base and the two scouts had come away at that point to avoid the slightest chance of being seen.

So now Michael had a rough idea of where they were, what their disposition was and the surrounding terrain. He called a meeting of his leaders and asked them for ideas. The conversation went on for twenty minutes without getting far because they didn't actually know enough yet. As an Intelligence officer Michael knew he had to have more information. He asked for a volunteer to do a deep reconnaissance. Daniel, lying on his cot but feeling a bit better, put up his hand and they laughed. In the end, after both Dovid Lempel and Jakub Alter volunteered he chose the latter. Jakub was probably the best man they had for undercover work. He was used to hiding, first from the police in his former capacity as a gangster in Krakow and then as a smuggler of black market goods from which he turned a tidy profit but which in fairness kept quite a few Warsaw Jews alive. Until they died. Dovid volunteered out of a sense of duty, Michael could see that and anyway he knew the man. For a dentist he made a fair partisan fighter but he wasn't up to this. He sent Jakub, but Roza warned him first that Stängl would already have put sentries out and to be extremely careful.

They put out their own sentries because it would be foolish to get jumped at this point, and they waited, quietly. There was nothing they could do and they were all dog tired and they lay about in the back of the lorries which now at least weren't throwing them about like they had for the last two days, and they dozed. Daniel took advantage of his renewed energy and prepared some explosives. It seemed likely, now that they knew there were two lorries, that he he would be asked to blow one of them up, and since they had the same type of lorry themselves, courtesy of the Wehrmacht, he was able to plan the job in considerable detail. He showed one of the men in his section, Szmul Halberstam, what he was doing in the hope that if he became incapacitated Szmul would have at least some chance of completing the job. Szmul was by trade a tailor and good with his hands. He was also a patient type, which a tailor would be, and patience is definitely a virtue when handling explosives.

Michael briefed Jakub on the information he especially needed - the precise disposition of each vehicle both in relation to the other vehicles but also in relation to the woodman's hut and the treeline, where the men settled themselves, because soldiers are social creatures and they like to sit and talk while they smoke and drink coffee, where Stängl was, and most importantly where he posted the sentries and how long a watch they took.

Michael knew the recce was going to take at least two hours. To ease the tension he had each man clean his weapon and present it for inspection. It instilled some discipline and stopped them talking among themselves about what might go wrong. Michael knew well enough what might go wrong but it wasn't healthy for the men to worry about it. In any case, he found a number of dirty rifles and he gently reprimanded the owners. Think like soldiers, he told them, to which they replied they didn't know how soldiers thought because they were teachers and innkeepers and shoe-makers, and he shrugged his shoulders because they had a good point, only he wished he hadn't reminded them. What he wished for more than anything else right now was a company from the US 101st Airborne Division, plus perhaps a mortar platoon for good measure.

He avoided Roza because this was no time for the kind of conversation they tended to have. He wanted to remain focussed. If the men couldn't think like soldiers, he at least could. Roza in any case was busy. She cleaned her rifle very carefully because she had been with the partisans long enough to know that a jammed weapon gave you a good chance of dying in the next ten seconds. She had seen it. The rifle was a Belgian FN .303 with a ten-round magazine. If she killed five Germans with it, which she knew she could if she found the right sniper position that gave her good line of sight and the light was good enough, if, if, then she would be happy. After the rifle she cleaned her pistol and reloaded the magazine, in the hope that she wouldn't have to use it because a woman with a pistol against a German soldier with a carbine was going to have the odds stacked against her. Well, if nothing else she would use it on herself. One thing she was sure about today was that she was not going to be taken alive by Colonel Fritz Stängl. Finally, she stuffed her pockets with spare ammunition in the unlikely event that once a firefight started she was going to have time to reload.

When everyone had had a chance to rest and the final weapons check was complete, Michael ordered them all to eat. Some said they weren't hungry, which he knew was nerves, but even as an Intelligence officer he had enough experience to know that battle takes a massive amount of energy, it sucks the strength from a man and leaves him helpless for the next challenge. Eating wasn't an option, it was an order, and they obeyed. He also instructed each man to carry a full water bottle, because there would be a certain amount of waiting to do and that's when a mouth gets dry and he wishes he had a drink with him. Michael couldn't fight this battle for them, but he could give them this much help. He was depending on Daniel and Roza to kill a lot of Germans and improve the odds, and he looked straight into Roza's eyes at one point as he did his inspections and he saw what she was thinking. Whatever else happened, if the tailors and the cobblers failed the test, she wasn't going to let him down.

They waited and worried about Jakub but at least there had been no shots but still they worried and finally, at almost eleven o'clock, he came back. He was smiling. He had enjoyed it.

'Right, give me a piece of paper and a pencil and I'll draw everything I can remember.'

He did that and they gathered round.

'This is roughly the shape of the clearing, there's the hut, it's bigger than I expected, the lorries are right here, about four metres apart I think, and the car and the motorbikes are over there.'

'What about the disposition of the men?'

'Well, there are a lot of soldiers walking around. They don't seem to have a lot to do. Some of them seem to have settled in the hut, that's where Stängl is, and quite a lot are using one of the lorries, this one.'

'Not that one?'

'No.'

Michael pondered this information. 'OK, that's the one with the gold. Everyone agree on that'

They did. It made sense.

'Daniel, four metres. Is that enough to blow this one without damaging the other?'

Daniel thought about it and did a quick calculation in his head. 'Yes and no. I can blow this one but there will be some damage, at least to the canvas covering. At that distance though it won't touch the gold, not even the boxes.'

'And will you be able to get from the trees to the lorries without being seen? Don't forget you'll be carrying all your stuff as well.'

Daniel thought about this and they waited for his answer. How could he know that?'

'Yes, I think so. No more morphine before though. Better to be in pain than sleepy.'

'Good. Now Jakub, tell me about the sentries.'

'Right. That's what took me so long. I saw all this from a tree which gives an excellent view right into the whole place. It's about a hundred metres from the hut. Roza, it's got to be the place for you with the sniper rifle. You could sit for hours where I was and be really comfortable.'

'Thanks, Jakub, but I'm not looking to be really comfortable. Will I be able to see the door of the hut from there?'

'Easily.'

'In that case it will do.'

'Anyway, I stayed there for a long time in the branches and I watched the rotation of the sentries. They've got six, in a circle, placed I would say about four or five hundred metres out.'

'You would say?'

'Well, I timed the relief going out and the old ones coming back and, unless they stopped to talk that's my estimation based on how long it took them.'

'Good work Jakub.' Michael was impressed. They all were and there was a general murmur of approval. Jakub was pleased.

'By the way, there's one more thing.'

'Uhuh?'

'In the back of the lorry with the gold, they've got a heavy machine gun.'

'I see. Now you tell us. Manned?'

'I couldn't really see in the darkness and in any case a gunner would have been under the canvas. Sorry.'

'It makes a big difference but still, at least we know of the possibility. Look, give me a few minutes to figure this out. I can't think with you all waiting for some magical plan. Leave me alone for a while.'

It took just five minutes, and he called them back.

'OK, here it is. Jakub, you've done well. Now I want you to do more, and it has to be you because you've been there and you're familiar with the layout now, but also because you're the most lethal man we've got.'

Jakub smiled at that. He took it as a compliment.

'I want you to take one man with you, choose him yourself, and I want you to locate each sentry and kill him, quietly.'

'Captain Jacobs, with respect, yes I have a certain facility with a knife, but I don't know about creeping up on six men just like that without raising the alarm.'

'You won't have to.' Michael rummaged in his kitbag and brought out a pistol. With a silencer. Jakub's eyes opened wide with greed.

'I take it you know how to use this?'

'Oh yes.'

'Think you can do it now?'

'Oh yes.'

'Good. How long would you say it will take for all six?'

'Let me see. About forty or fifty minutes.'

'And they change the guards every two hours?'

'Yes.'

'OK, so you move immediately after a change. Then as soon as you get back to my command post and we know all six sentries are dead, that's when we move.'

19

Jakub ate some cold food before he left. He took Szmul Halberstam with him because the latter had wanted to volunteer before and it was good to let him do this. He wasn't much of a fighter but he could be Jakub's eyes and ears. He was of a slightly nervous disposition and that is actually an asset when you don't want anyone to see you, like an antelope with its nose twitching, scenting danger.

The rest of them did what they had done before, they waited. After twenty minutes Michael got them on their feet and gave them an order that made them smile. He told them to relieve themselves. You will want to soon enough once the shooting starts, he said, so better now while you can, then you'll be comfortable. Roza smiled and wondered what kind of field commander this man would have made. A Jewish one.

Then he moved them into position. Every man knew what he was to do, what signals to wait for, and most importantly he knew that the others were depending on him. He wanted to tell them to remain calm but he knew that's the worst thing you can do, and then he stood still, they all did, while a few of them said a prayer. Even those who wouldn't have thought to do that were glad of it, not excluding Roza. She thought of Motti, and she knew he would have been doing that too, and she knew as much as anything she was doing this for him, and at that moment, although she could barely remember what he looked like, she loved him. That love had taken her this far and with God's help it would take her back to their son and a new life.

Half an hour later Jakub and Szmul were at the rendezvous with

Michael, job done, six Germans dead. Roza had already left and by now was up in her tree. She parted a few branches and found the right one to use as a rest for the rifle. There was already a round in the chamber, to avoid the sound of the bolt. After the first shot that wouldn't matter. The moon was shining brightly down on the German camp and in addition to that they had lit a fire outside the hut and there were sundry lamps hanging in the trees and from the lorries. She could see at least a dozen men at any one time. They moved around a lot but she was pleased to see that a number of them, at least four, she thought, climbed into one of the lorries and from the sound she could just make out they were playing a game of cards. The sounds brought a few more of their friends to watch the fun and she realised that if Daniel could blow the lorry up that was going to dispose of at least eight of them, which with Jakub's six would be almost all of them. It could, she thought, be that easy. She saw the lorry next to it, with the snout of the machine gun sticking out, but it didn't look like anyone was on it. Why would there be?

Then she saw Stängl and her blood froze. He wandered out of the hut, gave someone an order, turned a little in her direction, and it all came back, the months she spent with him, the times she had wanted to kill him. She lined up the sight on the iron cross on his chest and her finger took the first pressure of the trigger. It would be so easy. But of course it would also wreck the entire operation, and in any case she didn't want to kill him yet. She wanted to talk to him first and then kill him. She prayed that he wouldn't die in the battle. He was, she knew, a coward. She didn't think he was going to be leading his men from the front.

All she could do now was wait. Daniel, she knew for sure, had the hardest job. He had to creep out of the trees, get between the lorries without being seen and set the explosive devices and get out. Then he would have to run the detonator wire back to the trees and set it all off before anyone else could do anything. They were all waiting for that signal to open fire. Roza knew more about Daniel than any of them. She knew he was stubborn, but she also knew that he could collapse in pain at any time. He was certainly the weak link in Michael's plan, because unless they could get the men in the lorry in one hit they were going to have a major fight on their hands, one they were ill-prepared for.

She watched the treeline anxiously, and after a while she thought she saw a little movement. Looking through the telescopic sight she could just make out a twitch in the lower branches of a bush and she knew Daniel was on his way. It was agony for her, so what must it be like for him? She counted the seconds off, tried to imagine how far he had got, when he was in position, now he would be sliding under the lorry, dragging his heavy bag behind him. He had rehearsed it on their own lorry and she had watched, so she knew what was going on, she knew he had to get to the propshaft in order to pack the explosives against the underside of the vehicle. It had taken him ten minutes to complete the operation in practice, but that was then and this was now, for real, and she imagined his fingers slipping and fumbling in the dark. He said he could do it with his eyes closed and that was just what he was having to do, because the moonlight was of no help to him under there.

Come on Daniel, come on Daniel. She muttered it in Polish and Yiddish and then she tried to say it in Hebrew and found she couldn't. When they got to Palestine, her and little Mordechai, she would learn Hebrew properly. He would learn it at school and he would teach her.

Now it was long enough. He should be ready to make the dangerous journey back to the safety of the trees and run the wire. She looked through her sight again and there it was, the reason he wasn't doing that. While she hadn't been looking a German soldier had wandered behind the lorry and lit a cigarette, cutting off Daniel's line of retreat. He would have to wait, except that now another soldier joined the first one, and they started to chat about something. Roza could only vaguely see them in the shadows but she could tell this was going to take time. Time they didn't have. All the men would be in position, waiting, and the new sentries would be setting out soon to relieve the old ones. Time was something they just didn't have. Daniel knew that.

That was why he set the explosion off from where he was, under the lorry. There was a blinding flash and Roza nearly fell out of the tree, a loud crump rushed past her and echoed in the forest, and when she looked again there it was, the lorry on fire, one man still alive, jumping out with flames arcing from his back. She took aim but decided not to waste a round. He would die in his own time.

Men came rushing out of the hut and she cut them down one at a time, three of them. Aim, fire, release the bolt and take aim again. It felt good and she tried not to think of Daniel's body under the burning lorry. Rounds poured into the hut from the trees and she smiled. Her Jews were firing for all they were worth, after all the instructions firing at nothing, hitting no-one but probably scaring the hell out of anyone left alive in there. There was a lull, and it was long enough for a German to dash out of the hut and throw himself onto the tailboard of the second lorry. He swung the machine gun round, cocked it, and it spat a hail of lead indiscriminately into the trees. Her friends were going to die if this went on and she knew there was only one person who could stop it. She couldn't see the gunner under the canvas but following the barrel of the weapon she had a good idea where he was. After the first shot the gun stopped, but then it started again. She had hit her target but he was still able to fire. She looked at the canvas awning and let her mind's eye see the man behind it and she fired again, and this time the gun stopped for good.

Then she watched the figure of Michael Jacobs run out from the trees to the lorry and he too jumped up and took control of the machine gun. He fired a short burst at the hut and wood splinters flew in all directions as the heavy-calibre weapon took off part of the front wall.

The gun stopped and silence reigned. Smoke curled up from the fire still burning on the lorry and the canvas awning of the other vehicle burned away too, as Daniel had predicted. But no-one fired.

Their men started to come forward from the trees but Michael shouted at them to get back, to wait. They did that, but no-one came out from the hut, and then he called to them and they came forward, gingerly, waiting for his orders. He told Dovid Lempel to take over the machine gun and he jumped down to look for Daniel's body. There was nothing to see and he stood up and leaned against the other vehicle and covered his eyes. Somewhere in the dark someone was chanting the prayer for the dead.

There was one more thing to do before they checked the gold.

They had to find Stängl, either him or what was left of him, but they had to know. Michael led them into the hut. There were only two rooms, and the front one had more or less been demolished by the gun. There were two bodies on the floor there, but no officer. Michael fired a short burst from his submachine gun through the doorway and waited and then kicked the door open. There, with a pistol in his hand, was the very much alive person of Fritz Stängl. He took aim at Michael as he walked in, but he didn't fire. His hand was shaking and he pointed the weapon first at one man then another, but he didn't fire. Michael took the pistol from him and hit him full in the face with it and blood spurted from his nose.

There was a crude wooden table in the middle of the room, and two chairs. Two of his men came and sat Stängl down, holding his arms firmly behind him. And then Roza walked in.

He didn't see her at first but then she came round to the front of the table, out of the shadows, and the moon shone through the window full onto her face. He looked at her in disbelief, shaking his head, trying to work it out but it just wouldn't be worked out.

'Barbara.'

'No, Roza, Roza Levinson, with the Jewish Underground Army. Barbara Hass was the woman who took your briefcase every night and learned all your filthy secrets, and passed information about your orders to people who were very interested in them. Colonel Stängl, it is my pleasure to inform you that your men are all dead and you are our prisoner.'

'But don't be ridiculous. What are you talking about?'

Roza took out a bayonet and laid it on the table. 'What I am talking about, Colonel, is that we have just stolen four tonnes of gold which is going to be used to arm more and more Jews, those you and your people could not reach in Palestine, and we are going to rise from the ashes to haunt you and your people for ever.'

She had rehearsed what she was going to say if ever this happened, but this wasn't it. Stängl struggled but he was held fast. He looked at the bayonet, whether in the forlorn hope of killing her or himself she couldn't say.

'You may think of this as a war-crimes trial in the field. Except that I am going to be the judge, the jury and the executioner. Yes, that's right, you are going to die. I want you to think about that. Your victims had time to think about it, didn't they, before you shot them in the back of the neck.'

He winced and listened for the cocking of a weapon, to feel the cold steel against his skin, but it didn't happen.

'Oh no, it's not that easy. First I want to ask you a question. No, two questions.'

Suddenly, she realised there was something else she had a burning desire to know, that there would probably never be another chance to ask, of him or any other German.

'Why?'

'Why? Why what?'

'Why do you and your kind hate us?'

It was a frighteningly simple question. The other men in the room pricked up their ears. They hadn't expected the question, but they all wanted to know the answer as much as she did.

Stängl wasn't sure of the answer himself. Hating Jews was just something he had always done. Well, not always. He couldn't remember when he first found out he hated them, but the National Socialists had helped him to realise it and he had never looked back.

'Well ...'

'Yes? Were waiting.'

'Look, it's not that simple.'

'Not that simple? No, I don't suppose it is. Warsaw, Lublin, Krakow, Lodz, I could go on. A lot of people, Stängl, and there has to be a reason doesn't there? I would like you to think hard and give me some kind of answer.'

'Will you let me go if I tell you?'

'No.'

'Then why should I tell you?'

He had a point. This wasn't the time. It was the only time, but still it wasn't the time. The question would never be answered. Perhaps there was no answer, not one that a sane human being could make sense of or articulate.

'Alright, question number two. What happened to Mordechai Levinson?'

'Who?'

'Let me refresh your memory about Mordechai, Colonel.'

She leaned over the table and placed one hand on his right shoulder. He winced. She pressed, harder and harder, and he flinched in pain.

'That Mordechai Levinson. My husband.'

He looked at her and knew everything now. He slumped in the chair in defeat and she sat down too, and she waited. Michael Jacobs coughed, but she didn't hear him. There was no-one else in this room but her and Stängl, and she waited.

And then, in a sudden fit of arrogance, Stängl stood up and broke free from the men who were holding his arms. He made no attempt to go for the knife but planted his hands heavily on the table next to it. Even so Michael put his gun against his head, in case.

'So, that was your husband.'

A ghastly kind of smile appeared on his lips, and the blood from his nose trickled over them.

'Yes, we caught him near the coast that time. I knew who he was immediately. The man who did this to me. So, that was your husband was it? Well, Barbara, or whoever you really are, my angel from Bielsko, I will tell you what happened to your man. I took his trousers down to check he was Jewish, and then the opportunity just sort of presented itself when I saw the evidence and I took my pistol and sent him back to his god, that's what happened to him.'

And before anyone, Stängl, Michael or anyone else, had time to realise what she was doing, she picked up the bayonet, lifted it up in the air and with all her strength she brought it down through the back of his hand and pinned it to the table. She heard the bones breaking as the steel sliced through them and embedded itself in the wood. Stängl screamed in pain, pain he had never imagined was possible, and tears rolled down his cheeks. His other hand came up and tried to reach for her but Michael grabbed his wrist and it took all his strength but he got it down on the table. Calmly, Roza walked round, took the SS dagger from his belt and, bringing that up in the air like before, plunged it down through his other hand. His screams could be heard in the forest. The trees heard them but the trees were no use to him.

'Scream, Colonel, scream all you like. No-one will hear you. We're all Jews, and to be honest we don't care how long it takes you to die. We are going now, with your gold, no, with our gold, and you are staying here.'

Stängl was slumped on the floor now with his hands pinned to the table and he raged like a wounded bull one minute and cried pitifully the next.

'Cry, cry, Stängl, cry for your mother, the mother who bore your warped brain in her womb. May she die in agony too for doing it. Die for Mordechai, my Motti, die for my mother and father, my sister, and all the others. There is no death that repays you for what you have done. You called me your angel. Well, know this. I am the angel of death.'

And then they walked out of the hut and left him to his agony. His cries followed them but they weren't interested now. A group of men had gathered round the entrance, curious to know what was going on in there. Roza said nothing but walked out into the moonlight. It shone brightly on her and you could at that moment have believed it, that she really was an angel.

And then the shot rang out, just one. It came from the roof of the hut. Dovid reacted immediately. He swung the barrel of the big machine gun up and opened fire. Heavy calibre rounds tore the top of the roof away and a man, the one they had missed, the one who had climbed up there and waited for the right moment, was cut into two and slid heavily down the roof to the ground.

And Roza Levinson, now on her knees, a bullet through her spine, her lifeblood seeping from her belly, slowly fell forwards onto the earth, her curly hair bursting out from under her hat for the very last time, and died.

20

No-one should die before their time, but this was war, no, it was something much more than war, and all over the world people were dying before their time.

A man puts on a uniform and takes up a gun and he goes out to kill his enemy before his enemy can kill him. It makes no sense, and yet it is, it seems, the destiny of man to revert to his most basic instinct, when all the civilisation he has learned through the generations suddenly counts for nothing.

Mordechai Levinson knew nothing of war, but war found him, and his family, and to the day he died he had no idea why. Roza understood his death better than he could have, because she was a woman but in her short life she had learned the ways of war. She knew it made no sense, that there was a fundamental flaw for civilisation in the concept of self-destruction, but as intelligent as she was she never understood the impulse men felt, and it was surely men, not women, to create this havoc.

In this war she didn't understand Roza had killed men, she hadn't know how many, and she hadn't known why, except that she was obeying the instinct to survive. Her parents had gone to their deaths obeying an imperative to die, alongside who knew how many thousands or millions, sucked into the insatiable industrial machinery whose sole purpose appeared to be the destruction of humanity. Someone, somewhere, had decided that blood must be spilled, oceans of blood, to satisfy some insane reversal of normality.

The German people and their allies had taken a decision to go to war with the civilised world. Mordechai knew nothing about the

Germans but Roza knew more. She understood a little of their history, knew there had been a war before this one, equally destructive perhaps, that had failed to quench their thirst for blood. In her more reflective moments Roza had looked upon this madness as a second great flood representing God's desire to punish the pathetic humans he had created, but that was only in her more reflective moments, and that was especially after Motti, because Motti had woken some connection with her Judaism that her upbringing had tried but failed to remove from her psyche.

She knew the Jews were not the only victims of this war, but she had some instinctive understanding that for the Germans the destruction of the Jews was a reason for all of this, that if Frenchmen or Belgians died, well, that was what happened in war, but killing Jews was what drove them on, even when they had to die themselves for it.

As much as Roza thought sometimes that she hated the Germans, in truth she didn't. They were the enemy, and she had killed them when she could, but she didn't hate them any more than she would have hated a rabid dog before she shot it. And if she hadn't hated them why had they hated her? What had she died for? What had Motti died for?

Well, there was no reason, except that it happened. Roza had been brought up to think of her Jewish heritage as incidental, but if Motti had taught her anything it was that one's Jewish heritage is not incidental. It hadn't taken the Germans to teach her that, it had taken Motti, strange, outdated, impractical Motti, the right man at the right time, sent, who knew, by God?

And now there was their child, a new Mordechai Levinson to take the place of the lost one. Motti had been sent to Roza and Roza had brought his son into the world, and who could know what the child would do with his gift of life. For now, he was safe, and God alone knew what he would bring to the world. What was certain, though few would have hazarded to guess it among the carnage, was that this child, among others perhaps, would give the world a future.

The gold, and this boy, were Roza's gift to the future, and if there are angels in heaven they would surely take her into their midst, and from there she would watch over Mordechai Levinson, and his people, Israel.

PART THREE

1945

1

Krystyna Celinska stood on the dock with her three grandchildren, two cardboard suitcases, a package of food from Sweden, and a mezuzah wrapped in an old rag. They weren't her real grandchildren. Moise and Adam must have had parents once, somewhere, but they were lost in the fog of the war and Krystyna was all they had now.

Mordechai had once had a mother and a father too, and Krystyna knew what had happened to them, and Mordechai was as close to her as if he were her son. They were gone too, Krystyna's own, with all the other millions the war had taken, and the three little ones were all she had now, and it would have been hard to say who needed whom more, except what was easy to tell was that they had, in the year and a half they had spent in Sweden, become some kind of family, all unrelated to each other but clinging to each other like bits of flotsam after a shipwreck.

Captain Jacobs had come, in the end, after the war was over or so they said, and found her on the farm and told her that Roza was gone and how it came to pass and she had cried in his arms and carried on crying until it was exhausted, and there had been no more tears since that day. Captain Jacobs had cried too, and in all the years that were left to him on this hard hard Earth he never forgot Roza Levinson, but his is another story and it happened in another place in another time.

Krystina had thought long and hard, when he came and found her, about the future. There hadn't been a future to think about for so long that she no longer knew what it meant, to plan tomorrow, not just tomorrow but the day after and the day after that in the knowledge that those days would surely follow one after the other because that was the way God had made it before and where he had been in the terrible years she didn't know but even so now the world went on the way it did before. Now, to say tomorrow was possible, and you knew that all other things being equal it would come about, if not the way you planned it because that was the way of life and always had been, but still it would come because after the war you knew, if you knew nothing else, that there would be tomorrows, many of them, if not for you then for those you loved, and Krystyna Celinska loved the three little ones she now called her own.

It was for them, for their tomorrows, that she had said a sad farewell to the good people who took her in with the children and gave them a home without asking for anything in return and who, it would be fair to say, had come to love them too. It was strange, she sometimes thought, to find so much love in a time of hatred. She didn't understand it but there it was. She had gone to the little Lutheran church with the Ragnarssons every Sunday and even though she was a Catholic the tiny congregation had taken her and the children to their hearts and loved them, her a Catholic and the children all Jews, and none of it mattered to these good people because all they seemed to see was people, people in need, and she tried very hard but she could never fathom why these people had such a capacity for human love when the Germans, and the Lithuanians and the Ukrainians, and for all she knew many others too, found it so utterly impossible.

She had wanted to help Moise to know that he was Jewish and to understand what that meant, but what did she know herself? She had once worked in Jewish homes in Warsaw but that was too long ago. Anyway, she had been a servant. It had all been a mystery then, the strange things her employers did, and it had not occurred to her that she might learn so she could instruct this lost boy one day.

Some people came to the farm once, from a Jewish welfare organisation, and they gave the Ragnarssons money they hadn't asked for for food for the children and they asked Krystyna if she would let the children go with them to the city, to live with Jewish families, and Krystyna had looked at the Ragnarssons and they had looked at her and between them they knew that even if it all looked wrong it felt right there and that they couldn't send the children away, so they hadn't. She would never know if they had made the right decision, if it was nothing more than selfishness because her need for these little ones was so great she had kept them when she should have let them go and she had asked the pastor of the little church what he thought but what could he say? He knew the Ragnarssons of course and he saw how good this new family had been for them and, yes, call it selfishness again, but he had told Krystyna to follow her heart, which is easy to say, but when your heart is so full of love for someone else's children is that really helpful?

She decided the future for these children would, if it was possible, be constructed from the past. They could stay in Sweden and pretend there was no past but that would give them no foundation for their lives and surely one day, as adults, they would want to know where they had come from and why they were there and then she would have done them a disservice. She had said that to Captain Jacobs and he had listened to the idea but he hadn't commented. He had his own thoughts, he couldn't tell Krystyna what to do and in any case even if the war was over it wasn't really over for him because wars don't just stop, they leave behind them a trail of destruction that has to be tidied up and Captain Jacobs was one of the people who was charged with doing that, so he couldn't make the decision about the children. His thought was that they should go to Palestine, but this was not the time for that and he had no way to make it happen. He had promised Roza, and he would do everything in his power to keep that promise but for now Mordechai, her son, was in good hands. Michael would know where Krystyna went, and he would smooth her path wherever he could though he didn't say that to her, but he couldn't go with her.

Since the past was in Poland, that was where the future had to start and that was where she took them. As she stood there and felt the firm ground under her feet again after the crossing from Sweden to Gdansk, she looked around her for some sign that she had come home but it wasn't there. This country had been under the jackboot for so long it was no longer a country at all. Around her she heard Russian, which shocked and frightened her, she who had served in the communist Armia Ludowa. She couldn't understand what they were doing here. If the war was over and the Allies had won, that surely meant that Poland was now free again. Perhaps these people were here to help Poland.

A large banner over the entrance to the harbour carried a picture of someone she recognised, Joseph Vissarionovich Stalin, and it had large writing which she couldn't read but even so she had an idea that Gdansk, for some reason, was occupied by the Red Army. There were soldiers everywhere, and Russian sailors too and in this crowd of strangers there were some speaking Russian and some speaking Polish but the two didn't seem to be speaking to each other.

There was bustle bordering on chaos. What there wasn't was anyone, a single person, to meet her. She knew this was Poland but she couldn't feel it, and her instinct was to get to Warsaw. Warsaw was the capital, Gdansk was some alien place. In Warsaw there might be people who knew these children, perhaps even families. She had heard that all the Jews were dead. Well, not all because she had three of them. Perhaps if she went there she would find some trace, some-one the Germans had missed who would know them. It was a crazy idea, but these were crazy times. Everywhere she looked, on the ship, in the port, on these streets, were countless people all displaced by the war and looking for someone or somewhere to belong to. The pervading feeling was one of homelessness and the desire to feel something different, as if now that the Germans were beaten people deserved at least some measure of recognition for their suffering and some help to start again. Krystyna herself had come from Warsaw and so had Roza. It was the only possible place to start.

She had no idea how to get there, though. There were people everywhere but no-one to ask, even where the station was. No-one stopped to ask if they could help her and she felt if she stood there for ever no-one would notice. The children were restless. Moise complained he was hungry and she sat him on one of the suitcases and gave him some of the food she had brought from Sweden. She had no Polish money, and in any case she didn't even know if there was such a thing as Polish money. There wasn't in the war. Baby Adam started to cry and among all the adult noise and bustle the sound seemed to wake Krystyna from her stupor, but more importantly it attracted the attention of a woman in the crowd in uniform. She had a clipboard in her hand as if she was looking for statistics to collect and these people might be one. She looked officious but kindly, and she spoke to Krystyna in bad Polish.

'Hullo my dear. Are you lost?'

Krystyna looked at her as if she didn't understand. She hadn't spoken Polish for almost two years, not to an adult anyway. Then it started to come back, and she tried to figure out the answer to the question, if she was lost or not. She wasn't sure.

'I'm sorry, I don't know.'

The woman in the uniform laughed, but kindly. 'You don't know if you're lost? Goodness. Well, why don't you and the children come over here, out of all this bustle, and we'll see if there is anything I can do for you.'

Krystyna obeyed her. It wasn't an order, just an offer of help.

'I'm sorry, I haven't introduced myself, most remiss of me. I'm from the International Red Cross in Warsaw.'

Krystyna looked puzzled. The Red Cross rang a bell in her head, and she tried to remember why. Something to do with Roza, but what? But this woman said Warsaw, and that was good news.

'I'm trying to get to Warsaw myself. Can you tell me where the station is, please?'

'I can do better than that my dear, I can put you on one of the buses we're running. Look, give me the baby and I'll take you there.'

And she did. On the way she explained that her name was Julia, that she was from England and her husband was in the Polish Army and that she worked for the Red Cross whose job it was to try and find missing people and get those who had a home back there, especially the children. It was, she said, a massive task, and Krystyna didn't doubt it, but there were people like her all over the country doing this work and if in future she needed any help she should ask a Red Cross staff member, that was their job. Krystyna found it a strange notion that there were now people in Poland whose job it was to help. The last time she had been here it was quite the opposite. She had so many questions she didn't know where to start. Julia had her own questions, though.

'Now these three, are they your grandchildren?'

'Yes. Well sort of.'

Sort of didn't faze Julia. There was a lot of that in Poland these days. Nothing was simple.

'And what are their names?' She looked directly at Moise. 'And who are you, young man?'

She smiled, like people do with children.

'Moise, Moise Grynberg, Miss.'

Julia stopped. 'Oh, I see.' She turned to Krystyna. 'Is this little boy, um, Jewish?'

'Yes, of course, and this is Adam and this one is Mordechai Levinson.'

Julia seemed unsure what to do with this information.

'And you my dear, are you?'

'Am I what?'

Julia showed for the first time a slight sign of impatience. 'Jewish, my dear, are you Jewish?'

This was an interesting question. A year ago if you answered yes to that question you died. It wasn't a question you answered just like that, Krystyna knew that, and here was this woman, in uniform, asking her. It was too late, though, because in her innocence she had told her the children were, and if Krystyna had got everything wrong and had answered that question without thinking, stupidly, then she had already condemned the children to death. Julia lost her impatience and saw the confusion in this old woman's face and she knew she had to take this slowly.

'Look my dear, I know what you have been through.'

'No, you don't.'

'I am here to help you. The Germans have gone, and there is not the slightest danger any longer. Look around you, there are soldiers with guns but they are friends, they have liberated Poland and this is now a free country. No-one is going to hurt you, I promise, or the children.'

'No, I'm Catholic. My name is Krystyna Celinska.'

Julia asked her to spell that and wrote it down on her clipboard and looked happy that she had gathered some information.

'Well Krystyna, I am very pleased I found you, all of you. Now let's go and find that bus.'

2

Krystyna had been unprepared for the devastation. Sweden had somehow smothered her memories but now they came flooding back, as if Sweden were nothing more than a dream. The bus stopped regularly, for road blocks while Russian soldiers came on board and checked their papers. Krystyna and the children had Red Cross papers now, temporary documentation that gave them refugee status.

A man on the next seat to her explained that the soldiers were looking for Germans, especially SS.

'But why would they be here, on this bus?' She whispered and looked around her furtively. She noticed a young man two rows behind her. He saw her look and averted her eyes. Well, she was used to that.

'They arrest all SS people and take them away. They hide in with the refugees, a lot of them have Red Cross papers. They're easy to get.'

Yes, she knew that from Julia, who had been keen to give them to her, as if she had some kind of quota to fill.

'And what do with they do with them, the Germans?'

'Well, they take them away and they shoot them somewhere.'

Krystyna involuntarily turned and looked at the young man, and he looked away, as before, but a Red Army soldier saw her look and followed her eyes and they lead him to the young man. There was some shouting and the man struggled but they got hold of him and dragged him off the bus. Krystyna was in turmoil. That was because of her. If he really was ex-SS, well, then he deserved whatever he got, but she had little doubt about the judicial procedure involved. She had a feeling that if they didn't like his answers they would shoot him anyway. Either he spoke German or Polish and if it was the former it could be a death sentence. She knew nothing about SS tattoos under the arm, so she didn't know that the Russians had a foolproof method for detecting their prey, as the SS had once had for detecting Jewish males. All she knew was that if he turned out to be German he was probably going to die. He looked very young, too young to be guilty of anything. On the other hand, if he was hiding, what was he hiding from? Maybe he was just trying to get home. It was all very confusing, not least because she tried to figure out what she was feeling about that young man and couldn't. Her instinct as a mother told her to pity him but her instinct as a Pole, and as a former partisan, told her not to, that one death more or less was neither here nor there. She realised that now Poland was at peace it was going to take some time to adjust to the normal way of thinking.

What helped was having three children to take care of. It had been easy in Sweden, where no-one had been threatening them, but suddenly Poland seemed like a place where there was still danger. Captain Jacobs had warned her it would be like this, that life in Poland could never again be the way it was before the Germans came. If Krystyna had been Jewish she could have told him something, that Poland was no bed of roses before the Germans, that there might once have been three million Jews here but that they had never been accepted as part of Poland. Well, could she expect anything else now? She had to remind herself that she wasn't Jewish. She realised she had come to think like the children's grandmother, with all that implied racially, and sometimes she forgot she was a Catholic. It hadn't been hard on Sundays because she had gone to the church with the Ragnarssons and even if it wasn't like a proper Catholic church it was at least Christian. Now, though, she felt unsure about what she was. That Red Cross woman, Julia, had her down as Jewish, she could tell. Plenty of Jews denied it, and still did probably out of habit, and Julia, she reckoned, simply assumed that was what she was doing when she claimed to be Catholic, as if that was some kind of protection. Yes, it was going to take a long time to stop thinking like that, like everyone could be dangerous, even women who claimed to be there to help you.

The two little ones were tired and fell asleep with the motion of the bus. The passengers were strangely silent. They just looked out of the windows as if talking was forbidden and Krystyna reminded herself that just as Julia had thought she knew what she had been through she herself should not make the same mistake about these people, that she had escaped from Poland and seen the rest of the war out in peace but they had lived through it and were, she could see it in their eyes, deeply traumatised. They didn't chatter, the way people normally do at the start of a journey, they just looked out. There were no families, just individual people who were used to keeping their own counsel and did so now. What they were thinking she couldn't tell.

Moise's voice was the only one to be heard on the bus. He asked Krystyna repeatedly where they were and he sat on her lap and pointed out of the window and asked her to tell him about the things he saw, but she couldn't do that because she didn't know what she was seeing, except that this was clearly a land of devastation. What the Germans hadn't destroyed when they moved in they had destroyed when they moved out. Buildings on either side of the road were often just piles of rubble. People picked through the wasteland of bricks and stones looking for something, what she didn't know, but whatever it was the pickings were thin. The destruction was total. And in any case, others had been there before them, looking, and they themselves had probably found little or nothing, and surely others would come after them, because now this was a land of scavengers, where hunger reigned and the smallest item to be found could either be eaten or worn or sold, something that at one time no-one would have thought of any value now could mean the difference between life and death.

Red Army trucks drove by constantly, and the bus frequently had to stop to let a convoy pass. The Russians had precedence, always, and Krystyna wondered if they were liberators or conquerors. Well, whichever they were they weren't here to hurt her children, that much she knew. And what she hoped was that when they got to Warsaw there would be a nice Red Cross lady to hold out her hand to them and make it a bit easier, another Julia with her uniform and her clipboard.

At Torun the bus stopped yet again and yet again soldiers came on board to inspect everyone's papers but this time they found no-one to shoot. That didn't mean they could move off again though, because this time an officer came on board and he had an argument with the driver. Krystyna couldn't make out what they were arguing about from where she was sitting but the driver waved his hands about in the general direction of his passengers as if to say what can I do, I'm just a driver, talk to them, but the officer didn't do that, he just stood there with a black look on his face. The passengers were trying not to catch his eye, as if they had some instinctive understanding that they were not popular with the Red Army. What you had to do to be popular with the Red Army was anyone's guess but Krystyna looked around at her fellow-passengers and they didn't look to her like a liberated people. Still, that might not be the Russians' fault. No-one was ready to celebrate after more than five years of terror.

She wanted to say to this officer I served with the Communists, have some respect, but of course that would have been silly. What she didn't know was that on Stalin's orders the Red Army had stood outside Warsaw while the Armia Ludowa wasted its blood on a pointless revolt, that he wanted the partisan army destroyed as a prelude to Soviet control of Poland. Former membership of the Armia Ludowa wasn't something just then that you boasted about if you knew what was good for you.

She was beginning to think that the best thing she could do for the children was to keep her mouth shut and her eyes averted. The little ones slept fitfully, what with all the stops, and they cried from time to time and the other passengers looked at her as if she should stop them, as if she wouldn't if she could. The Russian looked at her because the passengers were looking at her because of the crying babies and he came up and looked down at them. Then he reached out a gloved hand and stroked Mordechai's face and said something in Russian and Krystyna looked into his eyes when he wasn't watching her and she thought she saw a wistful look and she knew that this man had children somewhere back home and that he missed them. Or maybe they had been killed and he missed them. That she couldn't know. She asked him in Polish and he couldn't understand her but he seemed to respond to the tone of her voice because he did a strange thing, he gave her a salute, and with that he walked back down the aisle and off the bus. What it was all about she had no idea, but the passengers looked at her more favourably now, as if the Red Army had given her its seal of approval, and the bus was waved on and a few people started to talk to each other now, about what had happened and how peculiar it all was and whatever was going to happen and what strange times these are we are living in and so on. They looked at her but they still didn't speak to her, and she put her arm round Moise and he sucked his thumb and buried his face in her side and she felt grateful for the way he needed her. She sighed and looked out of the window as they moved off and out of the city. The world, she thought, was full of lost people.

She looked down at the children and wondered if she had made the right decision, bringing them back here. What was there here for them? They probably had no families, or at least none she would ever find, and all around them was poverty and degradation. In Sweden there had been fresh air and good food and decent Christian people and a life free of worry, and she had taken them away from it all. She must have been crazy. Well, it was done now, there was no turning back. She would get to Warsaw and look for someone who might be related, that was a start. Julia had told her that the bus would take them to the Red Cross offices and there she could register the children and they would start to look for their families, so she wouldn't be doing this on her own. Except that while she knew Mordechai's surname, and his mother's maiden name, she had precious little information about Moise or Adam. She realised the chance of finding who they belonged to was nil, so why was she taking them? Well, she wasn't really, because what she was doing was taking Mordechai and they just happened to be with her as well. There was no reason why she shouldn't leave them at the Displaced Person's centre in Warsaw like Julia said she could, and concentrate all her efforts on Mordechai. The other boys were not her responsibility. Somewhere in Warsaw there would be people who would adopt them, people who had lost their own children and would be only too happy to have someone else's.

The bus rumbled on and the day grew dim and it was nightfall before they came into the capital. As she peered through the windows she tried to make out something she recognised of the city but it was like she had never been there. She had imagined that a city whose inhabitants had been devastated could somehow remain the same, as if how could there not always be a Warsaw like the one she used to know. People come and go but cities surely are there for ever because they are built of things harder than human flesh but it seemed that the invading German army had taken the city as if it was a living thing and they had squeezed the life out of it, as they had with the people themselves. She had been used to fighting with the Armia Ludowa but she knew nothing about the power of heavy artillery and aerial bombardment.

The Red Army had fought its way into the city a building at a time, and what was left standing by the Germans was systematically razed by the Russians. Krystyna knew nothing of the Warsaw ghetto uprising which happened after she and Roza left to join the partisans, or the revolt by the non-Jewish Poles somewhat later, both of which gave the Germans cause to demolish large parts of the city. As the bus pulled in to a small square she realised she had made a terrible mistake coming back. There was nothing here. No-one would be able to help her, because there was no-one. The city, even at this late hour, was alive with people, but they were Russians and they were refugees who were going somewhere and only passing through, or perhaps like her they had come back to the city they used to know to find what they could but like her they would realise the impossibility of it, that there was no-one and nothing to be found.

The passengers woke up and rubbed their eyes, looking out of the window as if they imagined they had arrived home and their friends would be waiting to collect them, and then they would wake up properly and realise it had been a dream, and this wasn't the end of the journey but the start of one. They tumbled out of the bus and in the absence of anywhere else to go allowed themselves to be shepherded into the DP centre by staff in uniform carrying clipboards, more Julias. The bus driver stayed in his seat and when the last person was off he drove away without a goodbye to any of them. He didn't think about them, but then they didn't think about him. They didn't know that he had a son the other side of the city, waiting in what was left of their apartment, with a broken leg and unable to help himself and waiting for his father to come home with some food and maybe a bottle of beer if it had been a good trip and he had been able to buy some on the black market while he was away. No, the passengers didn't think about him. Some of them thought about the young man the Russians had dragged off the bus but most of them didn't think about him either, they thought about somewhere warm to lie down and sleep and perhaps some hot food first.

In these wishes they were in luck, because both were provided by the Red Cross, and Krystyna had enough to think about with three children. Mordechai had a soiled nappy and was crying miserably and a kindly woman took them to a quieter room where Krystyna could change him. They didn't have nappies for babies but this lady found a length of curtain material that could be cut into pieces and she told Krystyna where she could wash out the dirty one and hang it up over a small stove to dry. Those pieces of curtain material were going to become part of the little boy's wardrobe for a while to come.

They went to sleep in a large hall full of people like them, people moaning in their sleep or from delirium perhaps. There were one or two drunks, God knew where they found vodka in this place, but the woman in charge of the place shooed them out. It was like the dormitory of a public school, not that Krystyna or indeed probably any of the other people had had such an experience, but the people who ran it had, British matrons shipped in by the Red Cross to inject their own brand of self-sufficiency in the mess.

Krystyna kept the children close to her, as if someone might steal them, and tried to sleep, all of them on one army bed. Somewhere in this large room a man was crying, but no-one in that place wanted to know about a crying man. Out in the corridor lights were on and she heard the sound of shoes on the hard wooden floor and voices in a language she couldn't understand and never, in the whole war, had she felt so alone, so in need of her own parents, as she did now.

3

The morning light was harsh and unforgiving and the people in the room looked embarrassed as they got out of bed among strangers and gathered their things together. There was food in another hall down the corridor, some Polish, some Russian army rations, whatever the Red Cross people could scrounge. Refugees were already queuing there when Krystyna and the boys arrived. It was obvious that they were used to the routine of this place and they stood there with metal plates held out waiting their turn, some in silence, some, having made friends already, chatting quietly. A few of the men smoked together in one corner and looked like they disdained to join a queue with the women, but no-one bothered them and they bothered no-one.

Krystyna found there were more children in some of the other rooms and there was an area of the dining hall just for them with special food and tables and chairs someone, she thought, must have found in a bombed-out school, and then she looked around and realised that this building was itself a school. She sat with the children and fed Adam and Mordechai and as she looked around something troubled her, a sense that she had seen this place before, a long time ago, a very long time ago, and when they had all finished eating she picked up Mordechai, and Moise held Adam's hand and they wandered round the place, Krystyna trying to discover why it looked familiar, why she might have been here before, and then, as she entered one room and saw a row of benches and a blackboard at one end she sat down on one of the benches and she knew, she had been here before. It was half a century ago, but there was no mistaking it. This was her old school. She sat on a bench and tried to figure it all out, what had happened between then and now but found she was unable to make a connection between the little girl she had been then and who she was now, none at all. That world had vanished, and this place couldn't bring it back.

If she had expected that anyone at the DP centre was going to help her find Mordechai's family she was mistaken. The staff there were responsible for housing and feeding people but that was as far as it went. Half-way through the morning a Red Army officer came in and with a couple of soldiers went among the refugees asking for papers and Krystyna watched the people's faces as they did this and she could see what they thought, that the centre was some kind of sanctuary but it was one that this officer could destroy at will, that if he chose to he could simply haul them out into the street and no-one would ever hear of them again. The Red Cross staff made no effort to impede this process and it was clear that they were here in Warsaw on sufferance and that the Soviets could close this place down if they decided they didn't want it here.

Krystyna tried to remember where this school was, how to situate it in the city, but it was too long ago, her family had moved more than once, then she had gone to work in a factory outside the city and after that she had got married and had children and as she tried to retrace her steps through time she found she kept going down blind alleys and there were just so many gaps in her memory that she got nowhere.

One staff member of the DP centre was especially helpful and Krystyna said she was a wonderful English woman but this woman, whose name was Margaret, said, no, she was not English, she was Scottish, but Krystyna didn't understand what that meant. Margaret just smiled and tried to think how to explain it but couldn't and anyway it hardly mattered. Krystyna's comprehension of the world outside Poland was almost non-existent. She knew there were other countries out there besides Sweden, and even that experience was restricted to the village where she spent eighteen months, but she had never been to any of them and neither did she have any expectation of ever doing so. Poland was the beginning and end of her world.

Margaret spoke a little Polish but what she lacked in her ability to communicate verbally she made up for by smiling at everyone. Krystyna tried to understand how or why anyone would smile in this place but she couldn't figure that one out either, until one of the residents explained it to her.

Margaret, he said, smiled because unlike them she could go home. Krystyna wondered why she didn't then but was too polite to ask her that. Margaret found the special things the babies needed and moved the little family into the dormitory where the other families slept. It was noisier there at night but it was a good noise, of children playing, even children crying, but that was a lot better than men crying.

Moise made friends with a little boy about his own age called Marek, although it was hard to tell how old children were when they were malnourished. The children in this dormitory weren't Jewish because almost the only Jewish children the Red Cross found were orphans and they were sent to an orphanage elsewhere in Warsaw. Moise was used to non-Jewish people by now and played with Marek entirely oblivious to any difference between them.

Then a couple of days later the children were all given baths, and the boys were bathed three at a time in the same tub and Marek noticed the difference between him and Moise then and he told his parents what he had seen and after that his parents said Marek shouldn't play with the Zhid. Marek couldn't understand what that meant or why they forbade him to play with his new friend but even so he went around saying that Christian boys can't play with Zhids and soon all the children were saying it and Moise came back to Krystyna with tears in his eyes and asked her why. She held him close to her and tears ran down her cheeks too and wet his hair and she didn't know how to answer his question. One day he would understand, he would learn about his heritage, but not now, please, she said, not now.

So they kept themselves to themselves and Krystyna tried to amuse the children but soon she knew she would have to go and do what she had come for. She had already made some enquiries about the orphanage for Jewish children and Margaret said that in a day or two, when she had time, she would take her over to the other side of the city to see it. Krystyna was in no hurry for that. She knew she had to do it but there was no hurry even so.

Roza had once given Krystyna her parents' address in Warsaw, at 35 Jagiello Street, and she had remembered it all this time. Jagiello Street wasn't in the ghetto, it was her real address, the apartment they lived in before the Germans came. That would be a start. There might be someone there who knew if anyone had survived. They might not, but still, what else was there? She would have liked to ask Margaret to look after the children because the atmosphere now in the centre was less friendly but she realised that was unreasonable. The woman had plenty of people to look after and it was unlikely she would have time to babysit, or even be allowed to. There was no choice but to take them all with her.

So the next morning, immediately after breakfast, she carried Mordechai in her arms and Moise held Adam's hand and they walked out into the street. Krystyna clutched a piece of paper on which she had written the directions Margaret gave her. She said she didn't know if the building or even the street was still there and shrugged her shoulders when Krystyna said they would go anyway. It took them almost two hours on foot. From time to time Adam wanted to be carried too and so Krystyna picked him up and gave Mordechai to Moise to carry but Moise was only nine himself and it was slow going.

Jagiello Street was still there and amazingly number 35 was too, in fact most of the buildings were not only still standing but many were inhabited. As they stood outside, a policeman walked past and made a mental note about them but moved on. A woman in a first-floor apartment looked through some dirty lace curtains at them and said something they couldn't hear to someone they couldn't see in the flat. Krystyna rang one of the bells but without knowing if it was working she rang another one and then she rang them all. She let Moise play with them, but no-one answered, so either the building was full of people who didn't want visitors or the electricity was off. As it was a cloudy day she looked up at the windows because someone would have a light on but no light showed so either no-one wanted to see their way around or the electricity really was off, and she decided it was the latter.

Which just left banging on the door, which she did. Krystyna was not a small woman and she had peasant cook's hands but even so she got no reply. She knew someone at least was in but no-one answered her knocks. She stood back in the street and looked up and the woman who had been looking down at her had gone, probably skulking where she couldn't be seen. She banged again, with the same result, and then the policeman came back.

'What's the matter Granny, locked out?'

'No Sir, I don't live here.'

'I see. Then who are you after?'

'No-one. Well, someone to ask about this little boy.'

'Mm, what about him?'

'I'm looking for his family. He's an orphan, you see, but this is where his mother lived, with her parents, before the war, and I'm looking for any relatives who might still be alive.'

The policeman shook his head as if he thought that was unlikely. 'What's his name?'

'Levinson, Sir.'

'Levinson, you say?'

He looked closely at Mordechai now, as if he was suddenly more interesting. While he did that Krystyna glanced up at the first-floor window and there she was again, the woman, curious now there was a police officer involved. The officer saw where Krystyna was looking and he did the same and the woman behind the window could hardly escape now because he had her fixed in his gaze and he motioned to her with his hand to come down and open the door. They waited in silence and with it taking rather a long time Krystyna began to wonder if she would come and if she didn't if the policeman would do something to make her come but she didn't know what that might be and in any case if he would do it at all.

But in the end they heard a key turn in the lock and the door opened and there she was, and behind her a man dressed just in trousers and a vest. They looked like they were afraid of the policeman but put on a defiant face to hide the fact.

'Yes, what do you want?' The woman addressed Krystyna, as if she were the one who had told her to come down. Perhaps she didn't want to antagonise the policeman, but he answered anyway.

'This woman says she's looking for someone.'

'Really? Well, I don't know anything about that.'

'No, well, why would you? I haven't told you who she's looking for yet. Come on Granny, tell her what you told me.'

And Krystyna did that and the woman shook her head all the time as if she couldn't wait for her to finish before denying any knowledge, that whatever the question was the answer was no. And it was, no.

'No what? You don't know this little boy's family?'

'No, I don't know anything.'

The man in trousers and vest stood behind her but didn't say anything. He looked like he didn't want his wife, if that was who she was, to get involved and wanted her to come away. But still, if a policeman asks you questions what choice do you have?

The officer didn't know what to do. He knew there wasn't much he could do and in truth he didn't want to get involved either, but he had the honour of his uniform to uphold. He had only recently returned to duty since the end of the occupation and, although no-one else standing on the pavement knew this, he felt the shame of the Polish defeat in 1939 because he had run away when the Germans came and hid his uniform because there was a rumour going round the force that the Germans shot police officers on sight, which was as it happens true. He didn't like the woman from the flat and he certainly didn't like her husband who was too quiet by half, but it wasn't his job to like or dislike people, just to uphold the law. On the other hand no-one here was breaking the law, and in any case since the Russian occupiers had taken over from the German occupiers what was or wasn't the law was at the moment not exactly clear. He began to regret coming back to these people. It was only nosiness, that and boredom, that made him do it. Anyway, these children were clearly Jewish, even if the old woman wasn't, although you could never be sure, and for heaven's sake if they were what chance was there of their parents being alive? They were lucky to be alive themselves. He started to look for a way to get rid of these people.

'Now look here, Granny, these children are Jewish, aren't they?'

'Yes Sir, they are. Why do you ask?'

'Well, because there's a Jewish orphanage you know for kids like them. I can show you where it is.'

'I know where it is, but this is where this one's mother used to live and that's why I've brought him here.'

And then the woman from the flat gave the game away. 'Well they're all dead. The apartment was empty. We were told they'd gone away and we could have it.'

She looked at the policemen with pleading in her eyes. Everything would have been alright if this stupid woman hadn't come round poking her nose where it didn't belong.

'Anyway, there's no proof, is there? He could be anyone. She could be making it up. She's got no proof.'

The officer realised that although this person had almost certainly stolen the flat she was right in that there was no proof that a small child had any claim to it on the say-so of an old woman who wasn't even his grandmother. He shook his head. He didn't want to get involved in this.

'Now look here, Granny, she's right. How do I know that anything you say is true? If this kid ever did have parents here, well they're long gone now for sure. Everything's changed, see, and you can't just come back here claiming things just because you say they belong to him.'

Krystyna had never said she was claiming anything. It had never occurred to her that Mordechai might have inherited the title to the apartment or its contents. It occurred to her now that there would have been a number of valuables when this woman moved in, but of course she would have sold them long ago and in any case she had no idea what they might have been. All she wanted was to find any living relatives, anyone who might care about Mordechai, but it was clear there was no such person here. The officer was probably right, they were all dead long ago.

And without another word she took Moise's hand and, shifting Mordechai from one hip to the other, she walked off down the road. Moise looked back over his shoulder, and there was the officer scratching his head and the woman and her husband looking triumphant, but he said nothing to Krystyna. He didn't know what any of it meant.

4

Margaret listened to Krystyna's story sympathetically. She had taken a liking to this 'family.' A Polish woman who had suffered so much herself, had lost her own family, was devoting herself to three children for whom she had no real responsibility. Not many people in this country, she had found since she had arrived, would do such a thing, and no-one, in her experience, was interested in Jewish orphans.

She couldn't blame people, she knew that, for being single-minded in looking after their own interests. Everyone in this country had suffered. Margaret had spent the war in Scotland as a teacher. What she knew about Europe was from the papers and newsreels, but what she saw when she volunteered to work for the Red Cross and come to Poland had completely thrown her. Here were things she had no mechanism for comprehending. Nothing in her life had prepared her for the things she saw and heard. It was outside the realm of normal human behaviour, at least it was if you had lived a sheltered life in Scotland. She looked at the stoical faces around her, not least Krystyna's, and she felt humbled by these people, and embarrassed that she had not been through it herself. Two of her colleagues who came out from Britain with her had already resigned, unable to cope with the daily exposure to so much suffering, but that only made her more determined that if she had done nothing while these people went through it, she would be here for them now.

As Krystyna told her about the apartment and the woman who she was convinced was living there in what was not her property, she shook her head. It was, she already knew, a common thing. When the

Jews were evicted from their homes it produced a vacuum, and people had been sucked into the places they had vacated. It wasn't hard to understand. And if someone came back, after all this time, and demanded what was rightfully theirs, it also wasn't hard to understand that the new owner considered it was too late, that what they had taken as the spoils of war could reasonably be kept. What Margaret had also seen, in the few months since she arrived, was that the sympathy the Poles felt for the Jewish victims of German brutality was strictly limited. She couldn't understand such lack of compassion, and she tried not to let it affect her work with ordinary Poles, but it troubled her deeply. Her Presbyterian upbringing had been completely devoid of religious prejudice. In fairness, she had never met a Jew until recently, but who could fail to be moved to pity by the terrible stories that were coming out? No matter how much the Christian Poles had suffered, why were so many of them incapable of feeling anything for the Jews who had lived among them? The only possible answer, to Margaret's simple way of thinking, was that they had felt no compassion for them before the Germans had arrived, that in some respects the Poles and the Germans were not that dissimilar, that had Poland fought on the German side ... well, she tried not to think what would have happened then.

'So Krystyna, what are you going to do now?'

'I don't know, What do you think?'

'Well, I think before you can do anything for Mordechai you have to do something for Moise and Adam.'

'You mean the orphanage?'

'Yes.'

She watched the struggle the old woman went through, and she watched her lose. Krystyna knew she was right, and any delay just made it harder. She had looked after these children all that time in Sweden and she was all they had, but how could she deny them the things the orphanage could give them? She herself could give them nothing, and she was only agonising over that fact without getting anywhere.

'Alright. When?'

'This afternoon?'

'That soon? What about tomorrow?'

Margaret knew what she was doing and she let her. Another day wasn't going to make any difference.

'Alright. You'll have them ready first thing in the morning? I'll be free immediately after breakfast.'

'Uhuh.'

'And what will you tell them?'

Krystyna shrugged her shoulders. What could she tell them? That the one person they thought they could trust was going to dump them? How do you do that?

'I could say we're just going to look at a place for them to stay while I sort Mordechai out.'

'You mean you'll imply you'll be coming back?'

'Well, yes.'

'But you won't, and if you lie to them it will only be worse, not for you but certainly for them, and also for the person who has to pick up the pieces. Adam is still young but Moise will see it as a betrayal and he'll never forgive you.'

Margaret had never had children, but you didn't need to be a parent to know that. Krystyna knew it herself, of course, but she needed Margaret to say it all the same, to remind her she was doing this badly. She wished she could find a better way for Krystyna but she couldn't. It was a tough world, and these two boys were going to have one more hard knock. In time, they would get over it, especially Adam. He was only two, he would forget. Some kindly people would adopt him one day and he would forget all this. She didn't necessarily believe any of that but even so she hoped it would be true, that when she was safely back in Scotland all this mess would somehow be worked out.

And so early the next morning, as soon as the children had eaten, the two women set off on foot across the city, each one carrying an infant, and Moise trotted happily along beside them, looking into every doorway they passed, full of curiosity.

'So, have you told them?'

'Sort of.'

'Krystyna, what does sort of mean? I think I know what it means but you tell me.'

'Well, I've told them we're going to see a special place for children, where they might live for a while.'

'Might?'

'Well come on, that's right, isn't it? I'm not making any commitment beyond seeing it for myself. How can I? It might not be suitable. I think you owe me that, that I have to judge for myself. And them too, especially Moise. If he likes it and wants to stay, well, it's his decision.'

'I see, so you've left it to him to decide, at the age of nine?'

No, she hadn't. She was making this up as she went along, but Margaret decided not to challenge her any further. This was clearly painful and it wasn't for her to make it worse. They talked about nothing important for the hour or more it took to walk there, and all that time Moise ran up to them breathlessly to tell them what he had seen and once a dog followed them and he wanted to catch it and take it to the new place with them but the women said no and he did what all children do, he made a fuss at first and then he forgot about the dog when it ran off and something more interesting caught his attention.

They arrived at the orphanage suddenly. They turned a corner and there it was, more or less a ruin in a bombed-out block. Krystyna stood back and looked at it in disbelief.

'This can't be it. It doesn't even look habitable.'

'Well I assure you it is it. It's not as bad as it looks once you get inside.'

Krystyna doubted that. Still, what had she expected? Warsaw was a bomb-site, and this was no different from anywhere else. Moise trotted in innocently before them. He didn't notice the dilapidation. He was used to it.

'Krystyna, let me introduce you. This is the director here, Mrs Halberstam.'

Mrs Halberstam was not like Margaret. Margaret carried with her, everywhere she went, an aura of the world she had come from, a safe world where people didn't live in fear. This woman had seen it all. It was written on her face. It was impossible to tell how old she was. The lines could have been there for years, or they could have been war-lines. The amazing thing was, though, that when she smiled the lines seemed to disappear, her eyes lit up, and she became, for that moment, a different person.

'Ah, Mrs Celinska, I've been expecting you. And these are your charges. Young man, what is your name?'

'Moise, Miss, Moise Grynberg.'

'I see, and these two little ones, Moise?'

'That one's Mordechai, Miss, he's one and a half, and this one is Adam, he's two.'

'Excellent. Are they your brothers?'

'No Miss. I haven't got any brothers now.'

Moise had been happy to answer her questions until now but his face clouded over and he clammed up. His thumb went into his mouth and with the other hand he held tightly to Krystyna's coat. She put a protective arm round him and while she watched Margaret wondered how this was ever going to be possible. All of Moise's suffering was visible in that moment.

Nevertheless, Mrs Halberstam took them on a tour of the place and, yes, it was dark and shabby, and at one point the ceiling had come down and they had to walk round a pile of rubble, but as they progressed children's voices got louder and louder and by the time they reached the doors of the play hall Moise was there in front of them, his sadness forgotten, and no sooner had they walked through than he was off. Moise, it seemed, was not going to be a problem.

The problem wasn't even Adam. He allowed himself to be led by the hand by a nurse to find some children his own age. Margaret looked at Krystyna and they both knew this had to be done. They called Moise back and Krystyna asked him.

'Well Moise, what do you think? Would you like to live here?'

'With you Bobba?'

'Well, no. I have to go, you see, to find Motti's family.'

Moise looked doubtful. He wanted, at that moment, to go and join in a game the children had just started. The sound of it all made him feel good, but he couldn't reconcile that with losing Krystyna. She saw it all in his face.

'Look, Moise, what if you stay here tonight and I'll come by tomorrow and see if you like it. I can come every day if you would like, and well, we'll see if it works out. But I won't be leaving the city for a while. I might not leave at all. So it's just a holiday, yes?'

That sounded better. He said yes. She picked Adam up and he said yes, he would do what Moise did. She held him close and his arms round her neck felt warm and damp, but she had such difficulty putting him down again. Moise led him off to introduce him to his new friends, and that meant at least that neither of them saw the tears trickling down her face. She picked Mordechai up and buried her face in his warm and familiar smell, and Margaret took her arm and led her out into the street.

The problem was Mordechai. He had a tendency to hold on to Moise, and without him he fretted. As they walked back to the DP centre he insisted on being carried all the way, and he pulled at Krystyna's coat collar the way he always did when he was upset instead of crying. He rarely cried. They got him back and offered him a drink of milk but he refused, and when supper-time came he wouldn't eat so Krystyna had no choice but to put him to bed hungry. She lay down with him and he pulled at her clothes constantly and she silently begged him to stop but of course he couldn't hear her and even if he had been able to he wouldn't have been able to stop. He finally fell asleep but it was a hard night, for them both.

And in the morning, as early as was decent, she took him back to the orphanage to see Adam and Moise. They were happy enough, and relieved that she had come so soon to see them, and when she asked them the question they agreed, readily, and that was it. By lunchtime they were back at the DP centre, all of them.

Margaret stood in the doorway, with her hands on her hips. 'Well my dears, that was a short holiday. So, what now?'

Krystyna looked sheepish, but she soon regained her determination. 'It looks like we're a family. I think we will do this, whatever it is, together.'

Margaret picked Adam up and held him wistfully. Yes, it was a good decision. A hard one, but what decisions weren't in these times? She would be going home at the end of the year, and all this would be a story she would tell her fiends over dinner parties in Edinburgh, but Krystyna, and the other people here, would have to live with the decisions they made now, and only they could make them. She didn't know what these four people would be facing but she was fairly sure it was going to be hard. The chance of finding any of Mordechai's family alive was almost none. She knew that, and she suspected Krystyna knew it. And if not that, then what? What do you do with three children who aren't your own family, in a country devastated by war, where the only hope of a roof over your head and a meal in your stomach is the goodwill of international charities? Well, as long as she was here in Warsaw she herself would do what she could. Other than that all she could do was pray for them.

5

So Krystyna, Mordechai, Adam and Moise settled down in the DP centre. They had nowhere else to go, and until she could think of how to search for Mordechai's family Krystyna was stuck and since she had no idea how to do that it was a never-ending circle with nowhere to go.

She wasn't one to be idle, not that you can be idle with three children to look after, but in time they settled into the routine of the place and the children made friends outside their little 'family' and so one day Margaret came to Krystyna and said she was spending a lot of time with nothing to do, it was only a suggestion, but would she like to work in the kitchen? There was no wage, but neither was there any charge for staying there and Krystyna, she felt, would be happier if she were contributing. Margaret heard from Moise what a great cook she was, and they were short-handed in the kitchen, so it made sense, didn't it? The food supplies at the centre were erratic and the cooks they had had little experience of making do with spasmodic deliveries and odd ingredients. Krystyna was used to that, Margaret knew, from her time with the partisans. Perhaps she could show them how to feed all these people? Yes, she could.

She loved it. As long as the children were content, she was, and she was happier than she would have thought possible with her arms in a huge mixing bowl of dough made from a bit of wheat flour and some rye and one or two other things that no-one had ever made bread from before. She couldn't make it taste good but she could make it taste edible which no-one else had been able to do, even old Jakub Lau who had once been a baker in a small town near Bialystok.

In those days he made white bread and even rye bread, but especially he made challah for the sabbath and at Passover he made matzo but now he was old and arthritic and his sight was exceedingly poor and he couldn't bake bread for all these people with such inferior ingredients.

Krystyna showed him how and although he had once been a master baker he was happy to follow her lead and be her assistant. They worked side by side and in time he told her his story. He had followed his father into the bakery and every night he worked at the bread-making until it came out of the oven and then his father let him take a warm loaf for his breakfast and run along to the yeshiva to study. In the evening he came home to his parents, ate supper, and went back to the bakery. It was hard work but he didn't complain and when he was seventeen the matchmaker came to his father and six months later he was married to Dora, the daughter of the cantor in the synagogue. Her father had no money for a dowry but Jakub's father didn't mind because she was a strong girl and she would be able to help in the bakery and in due course, with God's blessing, she would bear him many healthy grandchildren.

That didn't happen the way he hoped, because Dora got pregnant quickly enough, as was right, but she miscarried and the family grieved but they said well she was young and healthy and she would do better next time, only next time the same thing happened. Jakub had a little money saved up from what his father gave him and he took Dora to see a doctor. The doctor charged him a lot but could tell him nothing except go home and pray that God would grant them more good fortune next time. Jakub had already prayed to God and he thought it was a bit odd to pay a doctor for the same advice but still he prayed some more and lo and behold Dora produced a healthy baby girl, and they named her Rochel. Jakub's prayers, though, seemed to have exhausted God, because not only did his wife not produce any more healthy babies but she didn't even get pregnant. She fretted terribly about it, of course. Who wouldn't? One child was not was what expected in a community where the women went on producing until they dropped.

Rochel therefore was the recipient of all their love and she grew up a happy, confident child until the age of ten when a band of travelling Ukrainians came and camped just outside the village, and drank and danced and sang their foreign songs, and one evening two of the men from the band caught her as she was walking home from the synagogue and raped her. She nearly died but the doctor came and stitched her up and told them to watch over her and pray, which of course they did, and she didn't die but neither did she ever recover. From that day on she might as well have been dead because they could do nothing with her or for her. She became a non-person and as such she neither spoke to them nor heard what they said. Jakub prayed and prayed but his prayers were to no avail and all he could do then was weep, which he did unceasingly. His wife tended the child who never grew into a woman and she and Jakub became distant with each other as if each blamed the other if not for it happening then for not being able to help their daughter now.

Jakub worked in the bakery and when he could he studied in the yeshiva, which was his only solace, and in due course his father died a peaceful death and he took over the business but his heart wasn't in it. He and his wife and daughter lived from day to day but they didn't really live at all, and the only way they were ever going to change was by dying.

That didn't happen, though, until the day the German army marched into Bialystok, and then they came to his little town, and one evening Jakub went straight from the yeshiva to the bakery and found that two German soldiers had broken in and when he walked in they pointed a rifle at him and told him that from this day he would bake only for the army. When he asked them about baking for his normal customers they replied that there would be no more customers, and they were as good as their word, because Jakub's customers were all Jewish, and within a few days they were all dead, including Dora and Rochel.

Every night a soldier stood guard while Jakub baked and he mixed the dough with his tears but he wasn't allowed to stop. The soldiers in the town had to be fed, and if Jakub wouldn't bake for them they would simply shoot him and find someone who would. He often wished they would do that but he had a perverse desire to live which overcame his natural desire to die and so every night he baked and wept. Many times he held a knife in his hand and thought if he did it quickly enough he could cut his wrists before he changed his mind but he never did. He felt ashamed of his weakness, but even so he had to live with it.

He baked until the Russians came, well almost until then because having come this far he knew his German masters would kill him before he could be rescued by the Red Army. They never did that, though, because he had been saving some rat poison for this very occasion and he baked that into the bread and when the Russians arrived there was an entire garrison of dead Germans to welcome them.

Now Jakub was a broken man but he was alive, and he worked, as best he could, and he was at least among his own people and all week he saved a little of the white flour and on Friday he baked enough challah so that everyone would have at least some for the sabbath. When he wasn't baking he sat on his cot and prayed. There was nothing now to pray for but even so the act of prayer gave him some comfort.

At first he was doubtful about Krystyna. He could see at once that she wasn't Jewish but on the first day in the kitchen all three boys came in to see what she was doing and each day they came to her and took the biscuits she baked specially for them and Jakub was confused about three Jewish boys with a Catholic grandmother, but in time he accepted the idea, somewhere in his muddled brain, and so he took to talking with her and that was when she learned his terrible story.

She also learned from him that before the war he had had a teacher in the yeshiva who had moved to Warsaw, and one morning, after the bread was baked, he told her he wanted to find this man. Krystyna tried to tell him there was no point, that he was certainly dead, but Jakub wouldn't listen. He didn't go that day but the next morning he told her again he was going and she saw the strange look in his eyes and realised that whatever he was thinking about she couldn't stop him, so she said she would come with him. It would be good for her and the children, a small adventure. In any case, it could do no harm, and she would be there to console him when his mission inevitably ended in failure.

She dressed the boys quickly for fear that Jakub would go without them. She already feared for him and even if she was a woman she had been with the partisans and she knew how to protect herself, and him if necessary. Anyway, his sight was so weak now that she was afraid even if he found where he was going he would probably get lost on the way back.

He led them through parts of Warsaw she wasn't familiar with. When she worked for Jewish families before the war they had apartments in the better parts as fitted their wealth and status, but Jakub led them through back ways and small lanes into the part of the city that had once been inhabited by the Jewish artisan class and the tinkers and beggars. The war damage here was as great as anywhere and everywhere they looked were bombed-out buildings and walls with jagged edges going nowhere seared by flame, whether German flame or Polish or Russian she didn't know. She carried Mordechai on her back in a sling and Adam in her arms. They were heavy but she was used to it by now and found they balanced each other out as she walked. Moise, as usual, ran ahead and wanted to look everywhere and she told him not to but he did it anyway. She would have felt better if he stayed by her side.

Jakub walked faster than her, despite his age. He seemed to feel some sense of urgency about this mission, which worried her all the more since it only meant his dis-appointment was going to be the greater when it came to nothing.

She worried too when she noticed they had walked in a circle. Derelict buildings look much the same but there was a small church in which a stained-glass window had somehow managed to stay intact despite the destruction of almost all the surrounding stone work and she looked at it and realised she had especially noticed it before, almost an hour ago. They were lost, she knew that, but she didn't have the heart to tell him. She was on the verge of calling out to him to stop, though, that they were getting nowhere and should turn back, when Moise ran back to her in fear. She looked down at him and then she looked up and what she had thought was a deserted little road wasn't deserted at all. Standing there, barring her way, were three men. They had Jakub by the arms.

'So, what have we got here? A Zhid, I see. Well Zhid, how did you escape, huh? You should be dead, old man, not wandering around here. This is our place, and we don't like Zhids in our place, do we boys?'

The other two agreed with him.

'No, we don't. So, got anything interesting, have you?'

Krystyna watched in horror as they searched him. They found nothing of course because what did he have? They were intent on him and neither Krystyna nor the boys seemed to interest them. Moise clung to her coat and whimpered quietly.

They found nothing on Jakub and this annoyed them. That was when they hit him, first not too roughly but when he didn't react, as if an old man could react to such an assault, it provoked them and that was when they started to beat him seriously.

It took Krystyna a moment to realise what was happening, and once she did that she got angry, very angry, and she did something that came as a surprise, to the men but to her too. She reached inside her coat pocket and drew out a pistol, the one she had brought from Sweden and before that from Poland, the one she had carried with the partisans. She knew how to use it. Shifting Adam's weight to her left arm, with some difficulty she cocked the weapon. The sound stopped the men in their tracks.

'Alright, leave him alone. If you don't, I will shoot.'

'Oho, the little old lady's got a gun, has she? Now you be careful with that, Grandma, because someone could get hurt.'

'Yes, you.'

'No, I don't think so, Grandma.'

And, as one, all three of them drew guns themselves.

'You see, I told you. Now look what you've done. You've gone and made me angry.'

And, saying nothing more, he suddenly jerked Jakub's head down, jabbed the barrel of the pistol into his neck, and squeezed the trigger. The noise, in this narrow lane, was deafening. The force of the explosion sent the old man sprawling across the road as if there was some life left in him, but there wasn't of course, and he lay quite dead on the road.

The others pointed their weapons at Krystyna, unsure what to do. She herself held her pistol pointed at the ringleader but she asked herself what she was doing. She had three children with her and she was suddenly in some kind of battle. Jakub was dead, there was nothing she could do for him. The men hesitated. Killing an old woman wasn't too hard, but they weren't sure about the children. It was a stalemate.

'Look Zhid, look what you've done.'

'I'm not a Zhid, I'm a Catholic.'

'A Catholic, huh, well, that's different, you should have said. And what about the brats?'

She hoped from that distance their Jewishness would not be too obvious.

'They're my grandchildren.'

'Right. Well, in that case Grandma, you can go, and the kids. Run along, go on, before I change my mind.'

She turned, the pistol still cocked in her hand, and slowly walked away. If they made a move, if she heard anything, she would turn quickly and fire, die fighting, save the children if she could, but all she heard was laughter, and they were still laughing when she turned the corner and leaned against a wall and tried to get her breath back. The little ones were alright, but Moise had seen it all and he was still whimpering in fear. Down the road she spotted a Russian military lorry coming her way. She briefly considered flagging it down and reporting the murder, but she was holding a gun and behind her was a body, and on balance she decided it would serve no useful purpose and quite probably get her into trouble, so she put the weapon back in her pocket and the lorry rumbled past.

It was late when they finally arrived back at the DP centre. Margaret was just going off duty, but Krystyna took her to one side and told her what had happened. She was shocked, and Krystyna could see this was all new to her, this killing business, and she wondered how she would cope. Margaret was stronger than she looked though.

'Well, can you cope in the kitchen without him?'

'Yes, until you find a replacement, for him and for me.'

'For you?'

'Yes. This is no place for Jews. We're leaving.'

6

Roza talked often about Palestine. It was where she wanted to take Mordechai. Krystyna had no idea where it was but she got a fixed idea now that it was where she was going, not just with Motti but with all three boys. Poland was no good for Jews, so Palestine sounded as good as anywhere, and as the days went by she thought about it more and more until she reached the point where she could not have been dissuaded from trying to get there, not that there was anyone who was going to try.

She asked Margaret where Palestine was and Margaret just clicked her tongue in that way she had that was supposed to suggest doubt, and did, and tried to explain, but since Krystyna knew nothing of the geography of Europe, let alone the Middle East, it was impossible. All she could say was that it was a long way, a very long way, but even that meant little to Krystyna because a long way is entirely relative.

Krystyna left it for a day or so but then she asked again and Margaret remembered that upstairs in the school, in a room they didn't use, there was a map of the world pinned to the wall. Krystyna went up there with Moise while Motti and Adam slept after lunch. It was full of dust and cobwebs, and some pigeons had flown in through the broken windows and built nests. There it was though, the map, and she pulled a desk across so Moise could stand on it and look with her, and they searched for Palestine.

It took a long time. Krystyna had never realised there were so many countries in the world. Having located Palestine she had to find Poland, because her schooling had never extended as far as knowing where her own country was. If this room had existed when she had been a pupil here, she didn't remember it. With a finger she drew a line in the dust between the two but she could get no sense of the scale. Then she told Moise to jump down off the desk and help her find some other map, one that might be more useful than one of the world, on a more appropriate scale. They rummaged around and raised a lot of dirt and frightened off the pigeons who up until now had cooed undisturbed but finally decided to fly off out of the windows. It took a while but it was Moise who found it, in a cupboard with a pile of dusty old papers. It was an atlas.

Downstairs again, they wiped the dust off and carefully opened it. Moise had no idea what it was or why it was important but he sensed Krystyna's feelings and he got excited. For some reason she didn't understand it was printed in Germany, and the names of some of the towns like Breslau and Stettin were in German. Gdansk was called Danzig. Still, that didn't matter. It would do for her purpose, which was to plot a route south. The problem was, she knew now where Poland was, and she also knew where Palestine was, but she had no way of knowing either how to get from one to the other or whether she could even enter Palestine. On the map it showed as a British mandated territory, but that meant little to her, other than the obvious point that it was ruled in some way by Britain. Well, that country was an ally of Poland, had apparently gone to war to save Poland from the Germans, so she couldn't see that taking Polish children to Palestine was going to be a problem.

She had money, because Captain Jacobs had given her a supply of US dollars, but she didn't know what transportation systems were running, what restrictions there were on internal travel in Poland or crossing international borders, of which she could see from the map there were a number, and how one got from mainland Europe to Palestine, whether there as a land route or it was better, or even possible, to take a sea crossing. Added to that she knew it was all very well having Palestine as her goal, but what would she do when she got there? Who might there be to help her and the children? Would they arrive and then simply starve?

Krystyna's enthusiasm for this project waned as she added up the list of unknowns. Moise got tired of this game and wandered off to look for a better one, but she closed the book with a sigh and sat back, staring at the ceiling with its crumbling plaster and flaking paint, and wondered if it was all just a dream and they would be stuck here for ever.

'Not much of a place, is it?'

It was in Polish, but she didn't recognise the accent. She stood up and turned. He was a young man, perhaps thirty or so, obviously Jewish, and yet not, somehow, like the Jews she had always known, not even like the refugees in this place, like he belonged to the group, but was also an outsider. All this she saw at first glance, but of course his accent helped.

'Excuse me?'

He chose not to answer the question.

'I'm Avrom, Avrom Benzimra, but everyone calls me Avi.'

'Everyone? Who is everyone, Mr Benzimra?'

'Avi, please.'

'Alright, Avi, who are these people who call you that?'

'The Jewish community in Poland.'

'Really? I'm not aware there is one any more.'

'No, well, you're right. I mean those who are left.'

'Alright, I'm Krystyna Celinska.'

'Yes Krystyna, I know who you are.'

'You do?'

'Yes, and I know why you are here, for the boys, and yes, before you say it, I know you're not Jewish too.'

'Well Avi, and how do you come to know these things?'

'It's my job.'

'Ah, you have a job. Not many people here have one of those. And I have a feeling you are now going to tell me what that job involves.'

'That's right.'

He smiled. They had said that she was smart in her own way, Krystyna Celinska, and he saw it straight away.

'Shall we sit down? Over there perhaps, where it's quiet.'

Krystyna had been with the partisans. She knew what it meant when someone wanted to talk to you in a quiet place, that they had things to say for your ears only. She was already beginning to get a feeling for what kind of man this Avi Benzimra might be. He had a nice face, but also a face that gave nothing away. A gentle voice, but one that brooked no opposition. This man was not going to waste her time. This was not, she could see, a chance meeting.

'You've been watching me, haven't you? Now I think I've seen you round here before.'

He laughed. 'Well, perhaps I'm not as good at being invisible as I should be. Yes, I've been watching you, and the boys.'

'For how long?'

'A few days. I came with you when you went to the orphanage, and came with you again when you went back for Moise and Adam, and I may say that I was pleased you did.'

'Oh? Why was that?'

'I'll come to that in due course, if I may. I also came with you when you went out with Jakub Lau. A bad business.'

'You saw it?'

'Yes, I saw it.'

'So why did you do nothing? Why didn't you help him?'

She was angry now. She hadn't got over it yet and she wanted someone to be angry with and here was this person who apparently had watched and done nothing to save the old man.

'Krystyna, please believe me, I would have if I could. I was unarmed though, unlike you, I might add. It was all too quick. I was as shocked as you when they shot him, just like that, and I was very much afraid they were going to shoot you too, and the children, but I was powerless to prevent it. On the other hand, I can tell you that those three men have already been traced, and they have been tried and executed for Jakub's murder.'

She was stunned. 'Executed? By who? The authorities can have known nothing about it. The Russians? The Polish police? Who?'

'Neither of those. Never mind by who. Trust me, they were punished. Anyone who takes a Jewish life will be punished now.'

He said that with a strange look in his eyes, and his mouth was set hard. He spoke quietly, but every word seemed to reverberate in her head. She had never heard anyone speak like this. But then she remembered she had. It was Roza, yes, Roza had this way of speaking sometimes, with that gleam of quiet hatred in her eyes. It was when she spoke like that that Krystyna accepted she would never know what it was like to be Jewish, that these strange people carried something in their hearts she would never touch. She looked at this man and started to know why he was here.

'So Avi, I think you have something to say to me, about the boys.'

'Yes, I do. Let me explain. I work for an organisation called Bricha.'

'I've never heard of it.'

'No, you wouldn't. It's Hebrew. It means escape, like the flight from Egypt when the Israelites fled their persecutors to go to the promised land. In this case that means the British mandate of Palestine.'

He stopped to let her absorb this information. It seemed to her that simply by finding the atlas she had found someone who might be able to make it possible, and she wondered who was making this happen. She had once been a practising Catholic but her faith had long since disappeared. He saw the puzzlement in her face and smiled again. When he didn't have that hard look on his face, Avi Benzimra smiled a lot.

'You're wondering how I know, aren't you? About getting Mordechai to Palestine.'

He said Mordechai. She noticed that, not Moise or Adam, but specifically Motti.

'OK, I'll tell you. You know, I believe, a man called Michael Jacobs.'

'Captain Jacobs?'

'Well, he's not a captain now. He left the US Army. He works for us now, in Bricha.'

'Where is he?' She looked around the room as if he might suddenly appear.

'Oh, he's around, somewhere. And he's looking after you.'

'He is?'

'Well he sent me, didn't he?'

Krystyna stopped and considered that. Had he really? Why would this man lie? She was too used to people lying. It was time to change.

'OK, Avi, so how can you help us?'

'Well, let me ask you a question first. What help do you think you need?'

She told him. There were all the problems she had been enumerating to herself and more, because the more she thought about it the more impossible it all sounded. He listened with a neutral look on his face, and it was clear he was taking her seriously. When she finished, he smiled again.

'So, is that all? Yes, I think we can help you, if you can help yourself.'

'What does that mean?'

'It means that between here and Palestine there are, as you have so clearly explained, a number of obstacles. There are also, I'm afraid, obstacles you haven't thought of, which I could tell you about if I wanted to depress you, which I don't, so I won't. We have operatives along all of the routes across Europe, and at any point you can count on them for assistance, but at the end of the day it is you who have to make the journey, with a child and two infants. Ideally, you would do it in a group with others, because travelling on your own is always harder, but I'm afraid our policy is always to recommend the smallest group possible, to avoid attracting attention, either from the authorities or any unwelcome parties like the one you bumped into recently. We could of course send a lot of people in a large group with an armed escort, but, well, I imagine you can think for yourself what problems that might cause with the Allied occupation forces. So my question is this - could you, with some help from us of course, make a journey of that length with the boys?'

Krystyna considered that question. It would be easy to say yes and bluff her way through this, and it would be easy to say no and walk away from the whole thing, but in the end she gave the only answer she could sensibly give.

'I don't know.'

It was the right answer, the only one Avi considered reasonable. He wasn't going to back her if she didn't understand the formidable obstacles she faced, but on the other hand what he really didn't want was for her to give up. Avi wanted everyone in his charge to make it, but this boy Mordechai Levinson was special. Michael Jacobs had made a promise, he knew that, and after this war there was no room for sentimentality but if you couldn't allow yourself to dream there would be nothing left. He would, if humanly possible, ensure the child got to Eretz Israel, the land of his forefathers. Every survivor who escaped from this accursed place was one more person to fulfil the dream, but Avi knew something of the sacrifice this child's mother had made for the Jewish people, for the future of the Jewish nation, and he made the promise himself, that he would get Mordechai to Palestine.

7

Krystyna's port of embarkation for Palestine was to be Trieste. There, she would be met by a Haganah operative and the rest would be out of her hands. All ships to the mandate were run by Haganah, the nascent army of the hoped-for Jewish state in Palestine. It was therefore a military operation.

From Warsaw to Trieste was a journey that could take anything from a few days to a few months to never. People had tried it, not just from Warsaw but from all of Poland and other countries too, and not arrived. No-one would ever know what happened to them. Poland itself was effectively occupied by the Red Army and movements were restricted, not least because the Russians were still looking for German war criminals, so the first obstacle was to get out of Communist-controlled areas into a country controlled by either American, French or British forces. Between Eastern and Western Europe stood the impenetrable obstacle of Switzerland, so the favoured route was south-west, through Germany and into France, and from there doubling back across the Alps and across Italy. It was further but safer.

The preferred method of travel was by rail. Where trains were running, it was faster than by road, and a lot safer. The railway stations were thronged with refugees and the Allied military police didn't bother anyone without good reason. An old woman with children was less likely than most to be stopped and questioned.

Krystyna listened to all this and had only one question. 'Why? Why would the military police even be interested in where anyone is going?'

'Good question. By and large they're not. But like the Russians they are keen to winkle out wanted Nazis. Also, the western Allies have a agreement with the Soviet Union that Russians found in their areas of occupation will be repatriated. Most of them, as you might imagine, don't want to go back. A lot of them were prisoners and in Stalin's eyes that is tantamount to treason. We have reason to believe the Red Army POWs sent back are shot. The rumour has got around and a lot of them are desperately trying to get as far away from Russia as they can. Then you've got the others, the ones who willingly or unwillingly changed sides and fought for the Germans. Returning, for them, is an automatic death sentence.'

'Look, that I can understand. And agree with.'

'Well, yes, there I'm with you, but what it means is there's a hell of a lot of people moving west across Poland and you've got to move with them and not get caught in the net. As I said, with the children that shouldn't be a problem. What you do have to be careful of is the very people I've been talking about. They might be scared for their own lives, but a lot of them still have a lust for Jewish blood. Whatever you do, do not let the boys out of your sight, ever, and do not let anyone know they are Jewish unless you are absolutely certain who you are talking to. Got that?'

'Yes.'

'Good. Now, there's another problem. You're heading for Trieste, not Palestine.'

'But …'

'No, listen. Immigration for Jews is illegal. The British are very keen to stop Jewish survivors from reaching the Palestinian coast, and they have agents everywhere. They know what we're doing, and they are trying their hardest to stem the tide. You are going to Trieste, a Catholic woman with her three Catholic grandchildren, to find their family who you have reason to believe escaped from Poland to Yugoslavia. I can show you on the map later where that is. With that story, it's fairly unlikely that any British MP will question you further. We will have to cut the boys' hair short. It's all we can do to make them look less Jewish. We will give Moise a new identity and you must impress upon him that he has to play this new part. Can he do that, do you think?'

'Oh yes. He's done it before. He thinks it's a game.'

'Good. It will take a little while but we will be providing you with new identity papers and cash. You'll have maps and instructions and with a bit of luck you'll make it. Oh, and by the way …'

'Yes?'

'That pistol you carry in your pocket. Can you use it?'

'What do you think?'

'I would say you can.'

'Then you would be right.'

'Well, keep it well hidden, but keep it handy. I hope you never have to use it, but it could be all that stands between you and disaster. To be honest your greatest weapon is up here.' He tapped his head. 'Think before you do anything, think before you speak to anyone, say nothing you don't absolutely need to, trust no-one, always assume the worst of people. I'm sorry if that sounds a bit desperate but remember this advice and you may survive. You know, you might think I'm being sentimental but I want to say something else. I think what you are doing is fantastic. I think it is what we Jews call a mitzvah, which is a good thing but it's also a Jewish thing, so that inevitably leads me to a question. Why? Why are you doing this?'

Krystyna didn't answer immediately. She wanted to be sure she knew why herself before she tried to explain it to Avi. She grew up, like most Poles, in the Catholic Church, and the Church was no friend of the Jews. So was she trying to make amends? No, it wasn't that. No, she knew what it was alright, but could she admit it? Yes, she could.

'I'm not doing this for the Jews, or even to be honest for these three boys, well, I admit I am doing it partly for Mordechai and for his mother, but no, that's not the complete answer or the whole reason. If I'm honest I'm doing it for me. You see, I lost my children in the war, and their children too. I don't know why I stayed alive but I did, and now I'm on my own and these boys are all the family I've got. You could say I've adopted them but it might be more truthful to say they've adopted me. I'm an adopted grandmother. I don't honestly know what I would do without them. That's why I couldn't leave Moise and Adam in the orphanage. They might have been happy but I wasn't. Was that selfish? I hope not, but anyway that's how it is. Does that answer your question?'

Avi looked into her face as she spoke. He had known Christians, many of them, some good and some bad, and he had no illusions about this woman, but he also knew she had a pure heart and that she had told him the truth. These boys could have no better protector than a woman who needed them. She would fight for them, he could see that, and if they had any chance of getting to Palestine it would be with her.

He made her promise to tell no-one what she planned to do, including Margaret. Margaret was a good woman but she was British, and Krystyna had to start her education, the bit about telling no-one anything they didn't need to know, with her. He said the documents would take at least a week, and in that time she should carry on baking bread for the refugees and the children should play with their friends and everything should look normal. When the time came, to avoid having to answer awkward questions they would simply disappear.

Avi took that week, while they waited for the forged papers to arrive, to talk Krystyna through every stage of the journey, how to use public transport in the countries they would be passing through, the best way to exchange currency without getting fleeced by the many people who were taking advantage of refugees, and more. He used the old German school atlas to give her a geography lesson so she would have a better sense of direction, and he gave her the names of the Bricha agents in each town so she could ask for help on the way. She would not, he assured her, be doing this on her own. She said no, she had Moise and he chuckled. Moise was a clever child but he was still a child. Children had grown up fast recently, if they survived at all, but one day, if he got to Palestine, Moise would perhaps have a chance to be a child again before it was too late. Avi warned Krystyna not to expect too much of him. He had seen these children who survived. It was easy to think from their confident manner that they faced the world with equanimity but they had seen too much and lost too much and one day children like Moise would have to face their past and some of them, perhaps many of them, were going to pay the price for it all. Krystyna didn't actually need him to tell her this. She had seen it in Moise's eyes when he fell asleep, when his guard dropped and he became, for that fleeting moment, a little boy again, a look of such frightening vulnerability that she feared for him and stayed by his side while he slept to protect him from the evil spirits that might take advantage of his helplessness.

They chose Margaret's day off for the departure. Because the Scotswoman had more or less adopted Krystyna and the boys, it meant that the other staff largely ignored them, and that meant that no-one was going to miss them. Anyway, people came and went. There was no obligation, other than Krystyna's job in the kitchen, but they would just have to find a replacement. Moise asked her if he could say goodbye to some of the other boys and she wanted to say yes but instead she said no. She couldn't see why secrecy was so important, because after all the war was over and surely all of that was over too, the fear they all used to have, but Avi had told her a bit about the Russian liberators who some called occupiers and between them and the British it was, he said, better that no-one knew for a while that they had gone. What he didn't tell her was that the Red Army had orders to arrest anyone who had served in the Communist Underground, the Armia Ludowa. All he said was don't talk about the past to anyone, that now she had no past, like a lot of others milling about Europe getting in the way of the occupation forces, looking for somewhere to go and trying not to attract too much attention.

So early one morning Krystyna and the boys stood on the steps of her old school and one-time home with two cardboard suitcases containing the few clothes they possessed, a tattered school atlas, as much food as she could steal from the kitchen and several lengths of curtain material to be used as nappies. The first stop was the railway station. Some trains, Avi said, were running, and all anyone could do was go there and wait. Russian troops and Polish police were checking everyone's ID when they bought a ticket but with so many people trying to get on trains it was only a perfunctory check and in any case they were looking primarily for men of a certain age, not grandmothers.

Krystyna was still called Krystyna, and Adam was still Adam, but Moise reverted to Masha again and Mordechai, who of course had not been born when they fled Poland last time, became Marek because it was a name Moise would find easy to remember.

Summer had long since passed into autumn and a stiff wind brought a fine drizzle to the streets. People scurried about and the soldiers standing around on the pavements turned up the collars of their greatcoats. It was a perfect day for not being noticed, and the little family made their way past the bombed-out buildings of Warsaw to the central station.

The chaos there was unbelievable. Everyone, it seemed, wanted to leave the city but there were no trains and the majority of the people looked like they had been camping there for weeks. Wherever there was room people had marked out sleeping spaces for themselves and if they were families they left one member to guard the space and their belongings while they went repeatedly to the ticket office to check on trains. Children ran around the concourse as if the station were some enormous playground, getting under people's feet and making them swear. The atmosphere was one of bad temper. People were frustrated and tired. They were tired of the waiting but of course they were already tired of the war before the waiting.

The queues for tickets snaked round the concourse and out of the entrance into the street, and it didn't look to Krystyna like there was much point in joining them, not if there were no trains. In any case, even if a train did come in there would surely be more passengers already with tickets, or ahead of her in the queue than could possibly get on it.

She looked for a space to set up camp and it took a while but eventually she spotted a family gathering up their belongings and getting ready to leave the station. They had had enough of waiting. A young woman saw what was happening and hovered near but it was more space than one person could use and she conceded that Krystyna and the boys should have it and she moved off to look for somewhere else to settle. Ten minutes later, she was back.

'Look, Granny, can't you move up and make just a small space? I've been sleeping outside but it's raining now. Please.'

Krystyna shrugged her shoulders. How could she say no? It wasn't her bit of floor.

'OK. Marek, move up and let the lady sit down.'

It took Moise a second to think that meant him and he did as he was told. The young woman plumped herself down beside him.

'What a good boy. And what's your name?'

Krystyna looked anxiously but she had no time to answer for him.

'Marek, Miss, Marek Celinski.'

'Well how do you do Marek. My name is Kazimiera. Can I shake your hand?'

She held out her hand so Marek had no choice but to take it. She was a friendly woman anyway. She wanted to talk, and Krystyna watched carefully to see how Marek responded, but he knew his part. In any case, he had few answers to her casual questions so rather than let the conversation flag she kept up a stream of information about herself, none of which of course was of interest to a nine year old boy. In the end he fell asleep and Kazimiera tried talking to Krystyna but found her uncommunicative so she gave up and just sat and watched the world go by with no more than the occasional comment about this man or that woman, people who didn't interest Krystyna in the slightest. She thought if this woman was going to talk so much she might in the end get exasperated and move on, despite the paucity of space, but it was while she was thinking this that a sudden noise filled the station and it took a second to figure out what it was but it was what everyone was there for, the sound of a train pulling in to one of the platforms. A great cloud of steam shot up and, finding its way to the sky blocked by the enormous tarpaulins that stretched across what was once the glass roof of the station, billowed down again and filled the concourse with its welcome soot and smell.

The mass of people on the floor stood up as one and started moving towards the ticket office, but there was really no point. The queues were already longer than the train could possibly accommodate but it didn't stop anyone. They poured out of the station to find the end of the queues and suddenly it all went quiet. Krystyna and the boys stayed where they were. Mordechai started crying and the sound of it echoed in the emptiness. And then, appearing from nowhere, was Avi Benzimra.

'Here are your tickets.'

'Excuse me?'

'Krystyna, don't waste time. In a short while a thousand desperate people are going to be looking for space on that train. Take these and go, now. And good luck.'

He turned and left her, stupefied, holding the tickets in her hand. And then she did what he said and boarded the train.

8

The train stood on the platform for three hours. First all the seats were filled, then the corridors, and then when it looked like no-one else could possibly get on they kept coming. The longer it stood there, the more people kept getting on. Krystyna thought surely the railway authorities would have some of them taken off, for the sake of safety, but there were no railway authorities.

All the windows were open, despite the chill autumnal air, just to give everyone a chance to breathe. The boys had all shared a seat to start with but as more and more people pushed into the compartment even that became an unaffordable luxury and she was obliged to take them all onto her lap. If this carried on, she thought, it would be impossible for any of them to get any sleep. Krystyna had an ample lap, but a nine-year old boy took most of that, which left little room for two infants. Fortunately, she had a window seat, so Masha sat on her while Adam sat on him and Mordechai squashed between the three of them and the window. Their cases were in the luggage rack above but passengers kept pushing more bags up there and Krystyna despaired of how she would get to anything, especially nappies for Mordechai. The pistol was in her inside coat pocket and it dug into her ribs and she regretted not putting it in one of the cases. It seemed ridiculous now to have such a thing with her but she couldn't get to the cases to put it in there and in any case she could hardly do that in front of the other passengers.

And when she thought this was impossible to stand any longer, let alone for a night and a day, and she would just get them all off and find some other way to travel, the engine belched a great cloud of steam and, taking the weight of the train, pulled slowly out of the station. Krystyna didn't know if she was relieved about it or scared. There were no lights in the compartment and once they left the illumination of the platform and pulled out into the evening it went quite dark. Some light came in from parts of the city as the train threaded its way through but not enough to see the faces around her. The boys were tense, she could tell. They didn't like the crowded compartment, and neither did she. It felt like she would suffocate, despite the open window right by her head. Then, bizarrely, despite the lack of lighting, the heating came on and within minutes people were gasping for air and trying to find enough space to undo their outer garments, and then they started to stand up to take their jackets and coats off but they had to put them somewhere once they had done that and the situation just got more chaotic. Men and women held their hats in their hands and their coats on their laps and everyone quickly became irritable. Someone even made a comment about children taking up room but Krystyna couldn't see how they could take any less space than they did.

Then Masha said he needed to go to the toilet. Krystyna could hardly move, so the thought of getting up and taking him, and then trying to get back into the compartment again afterwards, filled her with dread. Anyway, there were the two little ones. She could neither take them with her through the packed corridor nor could she leave them on their own. If there had been some kindly woman in the compartment who might look after them she would have been tempted, but there wasn't. There was no choice but to send him on his own. She whispered to him what to do but he just jumped down and pushed his way out of the compartment. He had no fear. She had enough for both of them.

She took the opportunity of his temporary absence to stand up and reach for some food from one of the suitcases. First she stood on the toe of the man next to her and he grumbled about people being careless, then she opened the wrong case, which anyway she couldn't see into because it was above her head and fetching it down was quite out of the question so she was having to search blind. In the end, she found what she was looking for and sat down again to wait for Masha. They would eat their supper when he got back. Ten minutes later there was no sign of him and she started to get anxious. After another five minutes she was panicking. She tried to reason with herself. A child can't come to much harm on a train full of people. Then she thought of the things that might have happened. He might have leaned out of a window and fallen out. No, he was too short for that. He might have got into a fight. No, how could anyone get into a fight in this crush? Perhaps he was locked in the toilet and couldn't get out? She would have to go and search for him. She decided to give him five more minutes before resorting to such drastic action, and as she was about to stand up after all he came in through the open door.

'Moise ... Masha, where have you been?'

One of the passengers, a man sitting opposite, looked at her, wondering why this old woman couldn't remember the name of her own grandson. Masha climbed up onto her lap.

'Grandma, she's here, on the train.'

'What? Who's here?'

'The woman from the station.'

'Masha, what are you talking about, which woman?'

'You remember, the strange woman who came and sat with us, she's down in the next carriage, sitting in the corridor.'

'But Masha, that's not possible. She wasn't even in the ticket queue. How could she have got on the train in front of so many people?'

Of course Masha couldn't answer that question. She sat and pondered it. Avi had filled her with such anxiety about secrecy, secrecy she didn't really believe was necessary because after all the war was over wasn't it, that now she suspected anyone and anything that was out of the ordinary. She was, she knew, getting jumpy. There could be a perfectly reasonable explanation why the woman was on the train ahead of other people. She could have a friend working for the railway. She could have bribed someone. She could be working for the British. Avi had warned her about the British but surely they had better things to do than follow Jews halfway across Europe on the off-chance that they might be heading for Palestine. And why shouldn't Jews go to Palestine anyway? Avi never explained that to her satisfaction. Something about keeping the Arabs happy but Krystyna didn't know who the Arabs were or why they had to be kept happy so she had some doubts about the whole thing. As far as she was concerned, there was no reason why, once they got to Trieste, they shouldn't simply book a passage to Haifa.

Of course the British were doing exactly what she thought they wouldn't be doing, not because any single Jew on a train travelling across Europe might become an illegal immigrant but because if they caught one they might be able to break into the Bricha organisation and prevent the large-scale infiltration of Palestine that was so vexing them. Krystyna knew nothing about any of that, though.

The train rumbled on slowly and the passengers rocked gently with the movement in the semi-darkness and Krystyna took advantage of what little light there was to feed the boys. Helping Adam and Marek with the little solid food they ate was hard work in such cramped conditions, and with Masha on her knee it was unthinkable that she would eat anything herself. She wished the other passengers would be less unkind, that someone would see the difficulty she was in and would help, offer to hold one of the babies perhaps, or look after Masha, but no, no-one wanted to help, no-one was in that kind of mood, because they were thinking of themselves and their own discomfort.

When he had finished his food Masha whispered something in her ear. He had, on his way to the toilet, met a boy of about his own age in a compartment just along the same carriage. Could he go and talk to him? At any other time it would have been a reasonable request and she wanted to say yes but she knew it was wiser to say no and she also knew he wouldn't complain, because in all the time she had looked after him he had never done that, had always accepted what he couldn't have or do. In the end though she said yes. It would be good for him and it would also be good for her, give her a chance to concentrate on Adam and Marek, but also maybe to have something to eat. She made him promise to be back in half an hour. She also made him promise that if he met the woman from the station he was not to talk to her. And finally she reminded him, but this she whispered in his ear, that his name was Masha.

The passengers had nothing to do, since it was too dark to read a newspaper or a book, but stare out of the window or, since they were now in open country and there were almost no lights visible, at each other. The only illumination now was the moon and sometimes it cast a beam of light across the compartment and sometimes they were plunged into complete darkness as it passed behind a cloud. Krystyna looked at her fellow-passengers when she could and what she saw was the usual mix of people she had got used to since she arrived back in Poland, refugees escaping from somewhere or something, some past they wanted to forget, going somewhere they hoped would be better but was likely to turn out to be no better at all, or even worse. The train was heading for Berlin and she wondered why so many Poles wanted to get to Berlin but then she remembered what Avi had said about the Russians, that there were rumours about them which made a lot of people simply pack up and head west, even to the country that had brought such catastrophe to Poland. Times change, and the enemy changes with it. Germany was no longer an enemy, but the Soviet Union might be, and anyway most people had nothing to lose, nothing to leave behind. There was a young man sitting in the opposite corner and she thought he had probably been in the army, and then it occurred to her he might even be a German and that at the border a soldier might get on the train and drag him off, like the bus from Gdansk to Warsaw. She tried to look at him to see his face, to see if he was German or Polish, and even when the moon shone fully on him it was impossible to tell, because after all what was the difference?

Adam slept but Marek was fretful. He was teething and he sucked on her hand and dribbled and from time to time he bit her and even with his bony gums and the few teeth he had it hurt. In the darkness she imagined it was her own son Wojtislaw, all those years ago, and no-one could see but it made her cry and that made her love this child more but it also made her resent him and she was ashamed of herself for such a feeling against a helpless infant who was blameless in all this mess. She had time, now, to contemplate the undertaking she had made, and the stupidity of it. None of these children was hers or her responsibility. Alright, perhaps Marek was, because she had promised Captain Jacobs and he had promised Roza but still, that was in wartime and people say things in wartime that they don't necessarily mean. On the other hand, she had told Avi the truth, that these boys were all she had now and if for no other reason than a selfish one, to give her a reason for living, she would see this through. She had no idea what she herself would do when they got to Palestine, if they ever did get there, but that was a long way off and it seemed pointless worrying about it now.

The young man opposite had fallen asleep now and she thought in the moonlight that he looked a little like her Wojtislaw, but that could have been her imagination. Whoever he was, he was someone's son, and she wondered if he still had a mother, and if she was waiting for him to come home, or if he was on his way, right now, here on his train, to a new life and he was never going to see her again. Every person in this compartment had a story to tell. Even in peacetime everyone has a story to tell but now especially so. She didn't know how many people there were on the train, hundreds, thousands maybe, but each one of them had seen things, done things, that would have been better not seen and not done, and if they were anything like her they were hoping to put those things behind them.

She realised that Marek had stopped biting her and fallen asleep and she allowed herself to close her eyes. She wouldn't sleep, not yet, not until Masha was safely back with her. She would just rest her eyes for a little while.

She was vaguely aware, at some point, of a boy pushing his way onto her knee, of shifting the other two around to make room for him. It could have been Masha or it might have been any other boy, some child who wanted the comfort of a grandmother's lap and in her half sleep she decided not to worry about it. In the morning it would all sort itself out.

A session with our Derby hypnotherapist The train rumbled on through the Polish countryside. From time to time they passed through some station but it didn't stop. Once, they woke when it came to a halt and took on water, but people just mumbled to themselves and shifted their weight a little trying to get comfortable again, and soon they were asleep. The people in the corridor slept as best they could but every time someone tried to get to one of the toilets they grumbled and shifted themselves unwillingly and so the night passed with lights and noise and moaning and snoring and the movement of the train and the clack of the wheels on the track and a thousand people passed another night of their lives going from one place to another, from one life to another, and dreamt of better times tomorrow.

9

The train was re-routed during the next day to Potsdam and when it pulled into the station a man in uniform, it could have been any kind of uniform, came along the platform shouting that they should stay on the train and it would be returning to Berlin very soon. Very soon turned out to be optimistic, because an hour later it was still there, and a number of passengers decided to get off because Potsdam was close enough to Berlin for them. That eased the pressure in Krystyna's compartment, because the young man who could have been German got off and so did a woman with so much luggage that when she went the compartment suddenly seemed half-empty.

Everyone was exhausted from the previous night, and the boys spread themselves out onto a vacant seat and slept, and that gave Krystyna a chance to get some more sleep too. She wanted to go along to the toilet to wash but the last time she went the bowl was overflowing and it was so insanitary as to make any kind of ablutions pointless.

They slept in Potsdam station for the rest of the day and it was already dark when suddenly the whistle blew, causing those passengers who had got out onto the platform to stretch their legs or to go in search of hot coffee to rush back in case it went without them. In fact one of the passengers in Krystyna's compartment didn't return and a man by the opposite window started eyeing their luggage as if to say they won't be needing that any longer so I might as well have it myself. He glanced down at Krystyna and saw her looking at him and he knew she knew he intended to steal it but he was only very slightly embarrassed by this knowledge and determined to get it before she did, on the basis that some-one stuck in Potsdam was never going to recover it and it only made sense to put it to good use. These were not ordinary times and you took what you could find. She looked at him and saw the hunger in his eyes and decided that what he did was none of her business. She wasn't so desperate that she was prepared to take advantage of someone's lost baggage. Not yet, anyway.

As the train finally pulled into Berlin the only thing Krystyna could think of was to get the children off. They had done well, but they were at the end of their patience. She needed to give the younger two some exercise and she also needed to find some hot food, not least for herself. On the station, a number of vendors had set up selling ersatz coffee, sausages which they claimed were pork but had that distinctive smell of horse, and soup which they ladled from large cauldrons set on braziers which attracted people as much for their warmth as for the soup itself, which many passengers had no money to pay for. The station was crowded with soldiers, Russian mostly, but here there were Americans too, as well as British and some French. The noise was what they noticed most, the cacophony of languages and dialects, the shouting of the vendors and the laughter of the soldiers, a child crying somewhere and some kind of announcement over the loudspeaker system which no-one could hear over the hubbub but just made people shout all the more to make themselves heard.

There were washrooms on the station but they were no better than those on the train. Nevertheless, the children had to be washed and Mordechai was desperate for clean nappies. He was at that awkward age for toddlers when he could go without, providing he could get to a toilet in time, but that was hardly possible under the circumstances and Krystyna just kept him in a nappy and saved toilet training for a different place and time, when the normalities of life might have a better chance.

The problem with washing the bits of curtain material that served this purpose was that they then had to be dried. She dragged the boys round the station looking for somewhere they could camp for the night that had some heat for this purpose. Masha said they should hang them on the locomotive of one of the trains and

Krystyna said that would be fine until the train moved off with their nappies flapping about gaily as it steamed through Germany. They laughed at that, despite the tiredness, and for a moment it made them feel a little better. And then, just as she was getting desperate for a solution to their problem, an answer appeared in the form of a woman, about her own age, who came up and spoke to her in German, which of course meant nothing to Krystyna.

She smiled though, a big toothless grin, and that works in most languages, and she nodded at the boys and the nappies and said something which Krystyna took to mean follow me because she turned and disappeared through a door with a sign on it that might have meant no entry for passengers but still this woman seemed to be expecting them to follow so they did. Inside the door was a short dark corridor and at the end of that they went through another door and they could just see her back as she disappeared down another dimly-lit passage and finally she stopped and they were in some kind of boiler room. She smiled again and spread her arms as if to say this is all mine, and you are welcome to share it with me. It was gloriously warm. Hot pipes ran in every direction and in no time Masha had helped her to spread the nappies out and almost immediately they started to give off steam as they dried from the intense heat.

The woman signalled them to sit down, and they found a couple of old chairs with the stuffing oozing out and there was even a large steel mesh frame that the woman spread some sacking in and Adam and Marek were put in there to play. For the first time since Warsaw Krystyna relaxed. This woman was German, but she was a woman, and she was about the same age so probably she was a grandmother herself and she talked to Krystyna and Masha with enthusiasm despite the fact they they couldn't understand a word she said, but her hospitality was welcome and Krystyna guessed that they too were welcome into her secret world, far from the crowd on the concourse that seemed miles away now, so silent was this place. Its quiet was broken only by a faint hissing of steam somewhere, and from time to time the old woman shuffled off in her slippers to adjust some valve or push a switch and then she came back smiling all the more as if she was pleased that someone was here to see how well she ran her little kingdom.

The old woman pointed at herself and said Inge and then she pointed at Krystyna with a quizzical look on her face and Krystyna gave her name and the boys, their non-Jewish names because even here she knew they had to keep up the pretence. This woman was kindly, but she was still German.

She had a kettle on the boil and in no time they were sitting round a rickety wooden table eating and drinking. Krystyna didn't know what it was and suspected it might be some of the horsemeat sausage the station vendors were hawking, but it was hot and filling. She had eaten far worse in the forest. After their meal the woman spread out some cloths on the floor and it was apparent that, for her visitors anyway, it was bedtime. There was no natural light in this place so it was impossible to gauge what time it was but after their night on the train any place that was quiet and dark was welcome and they all fell asleep quickly. Adam and Marek, tired of playing in their cage, simply lay down together and slept, and the old woman came and covered them with a blanket and sat down in her chair and enjoyed the silent company of these sleeping foreigners. She had no idea where they had come from but for now she was happy to share her world with them. It was almost certain that until very recently they were the enemies of Germany, but even if she would never have dared to express the thought during the war, enemies of Germany didn't concern her. What concerned her was keeping her boilers going. In the war there had been many days without coal but she had come to work anyway and then suddenly a train had pulled in with a spare load and now she had a good stack of it piled up at one end of the boiler room and it was hard work stoking the boilers without the boy but he had gone off somewhere and there was no-one but her to do it.

Krystyna was vaguely aware of one of the babies crying in the night but she was too tired to do anything about it. In any case, he soon stopped so she slept on untroubled. When she woke, it wasn't because of any sunlight but for the simple, rather novel, reason than that she had slept enough and was refreshed. Her first thought was to see to Adam and Marek but the old woman was there, as if she never went home, or perhaps she did but anyway not that night, not with guests to look after, and she had already changed Marek's nappy and the two small ones were sitting on her lap eating a crust of bread. She looked happy, but more importantly so did they.

Masha was nowhere to be seen and she panicked for a moment but Inge could see what she was upset about and said no, no, don't worry, Masha is here, only one word of which did Krystyna understand and that was Masha, and Inge pointed to where he was, and where he was was exploring the boiler room, fascinated by the dials and switches and the seemingly endless maze of pipes and wires. He had, apparently, already had breakfast. Inge, like any German at that time, had little enough food, but what she had she was happy to share, or at least to swap in return for their company.

They spent the whole day there, washing and drying clothes, just enjoying this place which was for this brief moment in time their home, with this strange woman who wanted them to be there. Krystyna offered her money in return for food but she wouldn't take it, so instead she went out into the city and bought food and brought it back for them all to share. There wasn't much on sale in the streets and what there was was very expensive, but they had, for now at least, a plentiful supply of cash. She even bought a pair of second-hand shoes from a pathetic woman who was standing by the roadside with a small table on which were displayed perhaps the last few worldly goods she possessed. These people, who Krystyna had hated for so long during the war, turned out to be a pitiful sight when you got close to them. They were hungry and cold, just like Poles or anyone else. What they were not was superior to the rest of humanity.

On the streets of the city military vehicles were every-where, and everywhere German civilians stopped and let them pass. The difference between this and the German occupation of Warsaw was that the Russian soldiers weren't killing people. Actually, Krystyna had not been privy to a lot of the killing that went on when the Red Army arrived but that part of the occupation of Berlin was now over and what Germans were left in this place had a lot to be grateful for, that the army that occupied their capital didn't treat them the way they had been treated by the Wehrmacht and the SS.

In some of the faces she observed she saw contempt and barely-disguised anger that a race they considered inferior to themselves was in possession of their capital but on most faces what she saw was a sad resignation to the facts, and had she stopped and asked the people what they felt what they would, most of them, have answered was that they felt relief, just relief that the titanic struggle was over, that they could lick their wounds and hope the the future was going to be better than the past. These people, who had cheered when their leaders told them they were going to conquer the world, had had a rude awakening to the realities of losing a war they had started.

Krystyna didn't know what to think. She had hated them for so long she didn't know how to feel anything else, but as she watched them in their own capital city she believed that some other feeling might, in time, be possible.

Inge was inordinately grateful for the shoes. She cried as she put them on in place of her slippers. They were a touch too big but she stuffed some newspaper in and they were fine. She beamed at Krystyna and gave her a hug. Krystyna was shocked that such a small act of kindness could produce such a reaction, but then a pair of second-hand shoes to a woman with none is not really such a small act.

In the course of the day Inge showed her a worn photograph of a young man in uniform. She repeated the name, Hans, with obvious pride, entirely oblivious to how a Polish woman whose family had been killed by the German army might feel about that. They were just two old women mourning their dead and despite herself Krystyna said, yes, a very nice young man, because it felt right. Only two years ago she had been with a partisan band killing such nice young men. Maybe one of the soldiers in her unit had killed Inge's son.

From Inge's boiler room Krystyna explored the station. It was partly bombed out but there was enough left that some kind of service was running. There was of course no timetable. Trains just came and went. She learned that many of the lines out of the city had been destroyed so whatever trains did run had to share what lines were usable and often had to make detours to get to their destination. In any case, the military had absolute priority over all available capacity, and sometimes even passengers who had already boarded a train were unceremoniously turfed off when the army needed it.

The next city on Krystyna's itinerary was Frankfurt, in the south west of Germany. She consulted the old school atlas to see where it was and then she asked at the ticket office about trains. The clerk was tired of people asking about trains that weren't running. Sometimes he told them the truth, that he didn't know when the next one would be, and sometimes he told them a lie just to get rid of them. Since he didn't speak Polish and Krystyna didn't speak German he just shrugged, as if to say I don't know what you're talking about, as if Frankfurt in a Polish accent meant nothing to him.

The next time, Inge came with her and she shouted abuse at the clerk and he was obviously a little afraid of her and gave her the information they wanted. A train would be leaving for Frankfurt the next morning, at seven thirty sharp. Inge sneered when he said sharp, as if to say don't be stupid, we all know it will leave when it's ready, and that might be at seven thirty but it might not.

Nevertheless, at seven fifteen the next morning, she said goodbye to Krystyna with tears running down her face, and hugged each of the children as if they were her own family. Krystyna was herself caught up in the emotion of the moment. The boiler room had, in the short space of two days, become home, and even taking the boys and their luggage out onto the concourse seemed like they were leaving somewhere they had been unexpectedly happy and secure. The boys were ready. They were more than ready, and talked excitedly about the adventure, but Krystyna knew it wasn't going to be an adventure. She envied Inge for her security, for her warm dark home where no-one bothered her. She said a lot of things to the old woman, silly things really which fortunately Inge couldn't understand, and then they left her standing at the door with a dirty handkerchief at her eyes.

In the morning the train couldn't leave at seven thirty for the simple reason that there was no train. There was a rumour of a train coming in, expected about eight, but it was only a rumour, and those abounded during the course of the coming hours. The excitement and emotion of the early morning evaporated, and Moise became surly and said he wanted to go back to the boiler room to play, but Krystyna thought better of renewing their friendship with Inge and then having to break it again. That had been a good interlude in their journey, but now it was over.

So they did what they had done at the station in Warsaw. They found a spot to camp and got settled in. Masha asked how long they would have to wait and Krystyna could only tell him the truth, that she didn't know. She felt pretty dispirited herself so she was in no mood to placate him, and as the hours ticked by and she had nothing more she could tell him he took to wandering off and at first she admonished him but eventually she just let him go. He always came back and it was easier than trying to keep him entertained. He said there was a boy somewhere and they played together, but she didn't think to ask who or where, as long as he came back.

And then he didn't. Not for more than an hour, and then she started to worry. Half an hour later he still hadn't returned, and she went and asked at the ticket office if anyone had handed in a lost boy but the surly clerk just shrugged his shoulders as if to say what do you think I can do about it. No, he knew nothing, and there was no-one to whom a lost child might in any case be handed to, and what was more the station was packed with people and probably a lot of children were lost but would get found again. In other words, go away and leave me alone because really I don't care. She hadn't expected him to actually. She just needed to do something. Then she worried because Masha might have come back to their spot on the floor and found them missing, so she rushed back, but no, there was no sign of him. And then a familiar face appeared.

It was the strange woman from the station in Warsaw, the woman Masha said he had seen on the train, and about whom she had completely forgotten. And she was leading Masha by the hand.

'Hullo again. I'm Kazimiera. Remember me? Look who I found.'

'Oh, thank God for that. Masha, where have you been? I've been looking everywhere for you.'

'Playing with some boys. I told you.'

'Well you didn't tell me you were going to be all morning and worry me half to death. Now come here and eat some-thing. You must be starving.'

She pulled him down next to her and pushed a chunk of bread into his hand. Kazimiera stood watching enviously.

'Well, you look hungry too. Look, I'm really very grateful to you. Why don't you sit down and share this with us?'

'I am. Thank you. I haven't eaten for a while. No money, you see.'

'So how are you going to buy a train ticket?'

'I'm not. I'm just going to hang around here until I get picked up by some nice American soldier.'

'I see.'

'I expect you do, but what would you do in my situation?'

Krystyna could think of a number of things, none of which included that, but she just ate and said nothing. Kazimiera, on close examination, wasn't as young as she first appeared, and she wondered if American soldiers were attracted to war-worn Polish women. Krystyna didn't know what to say. Looking at Kazimiera she reckoned her earlier fear was unfounded. It didn't seem likely that she was any kind of threat to her or the children. She was just a woman trying to survive. How she got on the train to Berlin was now a bit easier to understand. There was, if you looked for it, an explanation for everything.

They spent most of that day camped there on the floor, with hundreds of other people, while countless more moved around them as if all this was quite normal. Kazimiera eyed up passing soldiers, especially the officers, on the grounds presumably that officers had more money, but although they looked they didn't stop and talk. Sitting with a grandmother and three children couldn't have helped, Krystyna thought, but for some reason the younger woman preferred to sit with them than be on her own. Krystyna shared any food she bought with her and for now perhaps that and the company were enough. She tended to the little ones when Krystyna was busy with Masha and she was grateful for that. Adam especially seemed to like her and she taught him to say her name which he did with a laugh and every time he got it right she rewarded him with a kiss, which made him laugh again. Krystyna watched this game and thought Kazimiera should have children of her own. Perhaps she had. A lot of women had, but didn't have them now. Yes, perhaps that was it, maybe she had lost her family. She could have asked but she didn't. It was none of her business.

From time to time people got up and rushed to a platform when a train pulled in but there was none going to Frankfurt. They gave all sorts of names, none of which Krystyna recognised, and it occurred to her that some other place might do, might take them a step closer to where they were going, but Avi had said Frankfurt and at least there she knew the name of the local Bricha agent and that meant a lot. No, she wouldn't go to some strange city where she would know nobody at all. Adam got restless and wanted to walk. He was at the age when she had to keep a constant eye on him, when he knew his legs worked and he wanted to try them out. Looking after two toddlers would be a full-time job for anyone but for a woman of her age, on a crowded station concourse, it was started to wear her out. Masha took him for short walks, but only as far as Krystyna could see them both.

She went out to find them some more food and left Kazimiera in charge of all three boys and when she got back they were fine, so later that evening, when Masha asked for permission to go and find his friends again, she let him, as long as he was no more than an hour, and if a train came in he was to rush back in case it was theirs. The two women chatted. Krystyna was finding Kazimiera a little easier to talk to now, and in any case it was good to have some adult company. Kazimiera still told her nothing about her past, and she still didn't ask. Someone who wants you to know these things will tell you without needing to be asked.

Marek was teething and biting on her hand, and then Adam wanted to go for a walk, and one woman can't do both of those things, so Kazimiera said sure, don't worry, you take Adam and I'll let this one bite me for a change. Adam took her for a long walk, right round the concourse. And when they got back Kazimiera and Marek were gone.

10

Their bags were still there, but there was no Marek, Mordechai. Strangely, though, Masha was there. He had come back but was puzzled to find them all absent, and he was relieved to see Krystyna, but he saw also the panic in her face. The people continued to mill about as if nothing had happened, but they were a blur, all she could see was the two cardboard suitcases and the other bags, as if that was somehow normal, and she had to shake her head to realise that no, it wasn't normal, there was a child missing. She looked around with fear in her eyes and such was the expression on her face that some of the passers-by commented to each other that she was perhaps deranged. Well, there were many people like that these days.

But she knew she wasn't deranged, that something terrible had happened, and that she had to snap out of this dream, no, nightmare, and do something. She picked Adam up in her arms abruptly and that made him cry but she didn't hear him, and she ran, just ran around in circles with Masha following her more and more distressed, looking desperately for what wasn't there, trying to figure it out and knowing now that this woman, Kazimiera, or whatever she was really called, had planned this, had got close to them so she could steal her grandson.

She dashed here and there for a few minutes before she realised that it was pointless, that she was wasting time, so she decided to ask for help, not from the people on the concourse because she instinctively knew there would be no help from them, that they concerned themselves with no one but themselves. No, there had to be a policeman somewhere. There were a lot of soldiers, and they had so many different uniforms on she couldn't be sure what that meant. She tried to remember if she had seen a policeman here in Berlin, what uniform the German police wore, but she couldn't.

And then, she didn't know where he came from but someone caught her arm and stopped her.

'Whoa, what's the matter Grandmother, what is it?'

'What? Who are you?'

'Sergeant Krasov, Military Police. Now, Grandmother, stop for a moment. Who are you?'

In response to her, he spoke Polish, but with a heavy Russian accent.

'Me? Krystyna Celinska.'

'Celinska? Polak?'

'Yes. Look, Sergeant, my grandson, he's gone.'

'What do you mean? You've lost him? Here on the station?'

'No, I mean yes, here, but I haven't lost him, he's been stolen. By a woman.'

'Whoa there, look, I think you had better come with me.'

'No no, I can't do that, I have to find Marek'

'No no, come with me. I promise, we will get some help and find your grandson.'

And there being little else to do, she followed him. He took her to an office where he saluted an officer and explained in Russian the little he knew about the case. Krystyna looked around desperately, as if this was all a waste of time or perhaps as if she was going to find Marek here in this place. The officer addressed her.

'So madam, Mrs Celinska, I'm Lieutenant Yusufov of the Military Police. You say a woman has stolen your grandson?'

'Yes, yes, just now, her name is Kazimiera, well that's what she said.'

'And do you know her family name?'

'No, she never told me.'

'And your grandson, what is his name?'

'Marek Celinski, he's my son's son.'

'I see. And may I see your papers please, and his?'

She handed them to him impatiently. This was wasting time, but she felt so helpless that she simply did what she was asked because there seemed to be nothing else she could do. Someone, at least, was taking some kind of responsibility. In any case Lieutenant Yusufov wasted no time. He glanced at the documents and handed them back.

'OK, now do you have any idea where she might have taken your grandchild?'

'No, how could I? She came from Warsaw, like us. She said she was just going to hang around the station.'

'Oh yes, why was that?'

'Well, she had no money, that's what she said anyway. She said she was going to find herself a nice Russian officer to take care of her.'

The Lieutenant blushed. He was very young.

'I think either she was mistaken in any notion that an officer of the Red Army would do such a thing, madam, or else she was lying to you. In any case, this is not helping. I shall have my men search the station first of all, but I'm afraid it is very unlikely she is still here. The city, as I am sure you realise, is in chaos. We can look, but once she has left the station she could be anywhere. There are very many lost people. I sympathise but I am afraid it doesn't look good.'

He shrugged his shoulders and immediately he regretted saying that. It was true but it was also terribly harsh. He had seen so much destruction since he arrived in Berlin, and mostly he didn't trouble himself with it. The Germans, who could care about them? But this situation was different.

Anyway, he was as good as his word and in no time a squad of his men were searching the station for a woman and child who might answer to the description Krystyna gave. She fretted and wanted to go and search too but he persuaded her not to. She would be more useful giving him information here.

Half an hour later Sergeant Krasov returned and she knew immediately that they had failed. He did, though, have one bit of information. He conversed with the Lieutenant in Russian and she could understand nothing, but Yusufov listened intently and then he gave an order and the Sergeant saluted and went out again.

'Mrs Celinska, they have, as I was afraid they would, had no success. However, it seems there is a man on the station, a corporal in the Red Army, who remembers talking to a woman who might very well be the one we are looking for. I have sent Sergeant Krasov to fetch him here immediately.'

Krystyna didn't know whether to let herself be hopeful or not. It seemed such a small thing, a man who might have spoken with her, but still, she allowed herself to believe that it might help. What else was there?

In a few minutes the sergeant returned, and with him was a soldier in his early thirties, very good looking Krystyna thought, and yes she could imagine Kazimiera might have tried it on with him. He saluted the officer smartly and she saw he was anxious about this, that he thought he might be in trouble. Lieutenant Yusufov put him at his ease and asked him a lot of questions. He nodded as he listened to the answers. Krystyna had no idea what was being said but from the expression on Yusufov's face she felt certain this was useful information. He smiled a little, and then finally he dismissed the man and turned to her.

'It seems we are in luck. This man says a woman who is almost certainly the one we are looking for spoke to him at length earlier, about an hour or so ago. He thought nothing of it, just an attractive woman after, well, what you said, he knew that, but he was under orders to move soon and nothing happened. Anyway, that was that, but it seems he saw her again, only ten minutes ago, here on the station. At first he wasn't sure it was her, because she had a small child with her.'

Krystyna's heart jumped so hard she felt the pain in her chest. This must be them, surely.

'It seems she was heading back to Warsaw. At least, she was on the platform waiting for the Warsaw train. It was just pulling in. I think we must go and investigate this train immediately. Please follow me.'

She didn't need to be told twice. He issued orders and several soldiers followed too. The little group headed for the platform, where they could see a train, the only one. As they approached they heard doors slamming and a whistle blew. By the time they reached the back of the train, the locomotive belched out a cloud of steam and started to pull away from the platform. Krystyna panicked. It looked like there was nothing they could do. She turned to Lieutenant Yusufov and he too seemed helpless. Sergeant Krasov, though, had different ideas.

On the end of the platform stood a motorcycle and sidecar. He leapt on this and started the engine. Revving hard, he put it into gear and roared off down the platform. Passengers scattered to either side in fear of their lives but he didn't slow down. He headed straight for the far end of the platform at full speed and overtook the locomotive with twenty metres to spare. Waving violently with one hand, he finally managed to attract the attention of the driver and in a squeal of brakes and a great shuddering and clanking of metal on metal, the train came to an abrupt halt. The motorcycle with the brave sergeant disappeared off the end of the platform but a minute later he walked back up from the tracks with a broad grin on his face, rubbing his shoulder, in pain but happy.

There weren't many passengers on the train. Few people were travelling east these days. It took only a couple of minutes to find Kazimiera and Marek.

Kazimiera looked surprised, which was expected, but not surprised for the reason they expected. She held Marek closely to her and looked puzzled. Lieutenant Yusufov put his arms out to take the child but she seemed not to understand why he was doing that.

'Give me the child please, madam. You are under arrest.'

'Why? I don't understand. What have I done? Why do you want my son?'

'Your son?'

She looked at him blankly but avoided Krystyna altogether.

'I'm sorry, what is this about? We're going home. To Warsaw.'

'Not yet, you're not. What is your name please?'

'Kazimiera Lapinska, and this is my son Andrzej. Why, will you please tell me what is going on?'

'Mrs Lapinska, there seems to be some confusion here. I must ask you to come with me.'

She seemed reluctant to do that but there really was no choice in the matter. As they all walked down the platform back to the office the guard blew on his whistle and the train moved off again without her.

In the office once more, the Lieutenant asked for more chairs and sat both Krystyna and Kazimiera down. Kazimiera sat Marek on her lap facing her and played with him. Adam sat on Krystyna's lap and and Masha stood by her side with a puzzled look on his face. He couldn't understand any of this. Neither could Lieutenant Yusufov, but it was his problem now and it wasn't one he could walk away from.

'Right, one more time please, Mrs Lapinska, you say this boy is your son?'

'Yes Lieutenant, of course.'

'Now, Mrs Celinska, you say he is your grandson?'

'No, I don't say, he is. I don't know what game this woman is playing.'

'Yes, well, leave that to me. So, Mrs Celinska, may I see his papers again please?'

Krystyna took them out again and handed them over. There wasn't much he could do. It was just an identity card without a photograph. Infants didn't have photos on their ID.

'And now, Mrs Lapinska. Do you have any identity for this child?'

'Of course I do. Just a minute, here, look.'

'I see. Andrzej Lapinski.'

He put both cards on the desk and his head in his hands. How was it possible that two people both claimed this child and both appeared to have proof? Of course, an identity card proved nothing, but still, why would either of them be lying? In desperation he turned to Masha.

'Young man, now look at me, and I want you to tell me the truth. You see this baby. Is he your brother?' Masha was taken by surprise. An army officer had never spoken to him before and it made him afraid. On the other hand he remembered what Krystyna had told him, that their lives could depend on what he said to people, about his identity. He looked Lieutenant Yusufov in the eye and answered.

'Yes sir. That's Marek, my brother.'

Krystyna beamed and Kazimiera scowled. Lieutenant Yusufov sighed. He wanted to believe that was proof, but of course it wasn't. The boy could easily be saying what his grandmother wanted him to say. His own instinct told him that the old woman was telling the truth. If not, why would she have come to them for help in the first place? On the other hand, the other had the child, and taking him away from her was a big responsibility, bigger than he was prepared to accept. This would normally be a matter for the civilian authorities but there were none in Berlin. The Red Army was the only authority, and in this station he was its representative.

Then Kazimiera spoke, not to him but to the baby.

'Now, Andrzej, listen to Mummy. Remember the game we always play? I say my name and what do you do?'

She looked at the Lieutenant. 'Now, I'm going to show you how he reacts to me. I tell you now, so you know what to expect, that he will laugh. I can make him laugh. It's our little joke. Watch.'

'OK Andrzej, ready? Kazimiera. Kazimiera.'

And as she knew he would Marek laughed. He giggled happily. He was unable to see Krystyna but even if he had been able to it would have made no difference. He was used to the two women being together now. He just giggled.

'There! There, you see? I told you he would do that. Now you tell me, how did I know if he's not my child?'

It was odd, certainly, and Yusufov sighed. He knew it would be meaningless in a court of law, but still, it seemed very odd. This child gave all the appearance of being this woman's son. On the other hand. On the other hand. There were too many hands in this altogether. He was a soldier, not a judge. Why was he in this terrible position anyway? He could refuse to deal with the matter and refer it to his commanding officer, but he knew what his reaction would be, that if he couldn't deal with the ridiculous matter of a lost child he was hardly ready for a more senior command. No, it would reflect badly on him if he had to refer this upwards. Better perhaps to get it wrong than blot his copybook. He was minded to come down in favour of the younger woman. He didn't like it, but then he didn't like any of it. No, it was time to do something.

Then he noticed that Masha was pulling at Krystyna's sleeve. She tried to ignore him but he insisted, so she bent down and he whispered something in her ear. Her face lit up with understanding and she stood up and spoke. 'Lieutenant, I have the answer. We should ask Inge.'

'Inge? Who is she?'

'She's the old woman who works in the boiler room, here on the station. The door is on the other side, over to the right. It's just a small door, but if you go in there and down a passage you come to the boiler room. That's where Inge works. She knows us. She will vouch for Marek.'

Yusufov didn't understand how or why this should be so, but she seemed so certain he considered it was worth trying. He ordered the sergeant to go and fetch Inge. They sat quietly while they waited. No-one wanted to say anything. Krystyna felt happy now. Marek gurgled on Kazimiera's knee, but he would soon be back where he belonged. The sergeant returned quickly, but instead of Inge he had with him an old man. He said something in Russian to Lieutenant Yusufov and a soldier went out and nothing happened until he came back with another soldier, one apparently who spoke German. They conferred with the old man the sergeant had brought and the old man explained something Krystyna couldn't understand but he shrugged his shoulders a lot and it didn't sound good. Then Lieutenant Yusufov dismissed him and turned to Krystyna.

'Mrs Celinska, this man says that he has taken over from the woman called Inge. She has, it seems, now gone on leave. I have ascertained that she left this morning on the train for Bremen, where her sister lives, but I am afraid that is a long way away and it really would not be possible now to trace her. I am sorry.'

Krystyna considered this information for a moment and they waited to hear what she would say.

'Alright, Kazimiera, I will concede.'

Kazimiera and Yusufov both looked shocked.

'If you can answer one question to my satisfaction, you may take him. Lieutenant, if she gives the right answer I will give him up. Is that acceptable to you?'

'Well, I don't know what question you are going to ask, but yes, alright.' Secretly he was pleased. 'Let's just get this over with.'

'Now, Kazimiera, my question is this. Well, it's two questions, really. First, are you a practising Catholic?'

'What? Yes, I am. What of it?'

'And so you have brought this child up in the Faith, I expect?'

'Yes, of course I have.'

'Now, my real question is this. Where did you have him baptised?'

'And if I answer correctly you will let go of him?'
'Yes.'
'But how will you know if I'm telling the truth?'
'I will know.'
'Alright.' She stopped and thought. The safest answer was Saint John's. 'Saint John's Cathedral, in Warsaw.'
'I see. Lieutenant, I am going to ask a small favour of you.'
'Yes?'
'I would like to speak with you in private. Just you, me, and the baby.'

It seemed like a reasonable request. Kazimiera looked doubtful. She feared a trick. Nevertheless, he ordered every-one out of the office, even the children. Masha carried Adam out. He didn't want this woman anywhere near him.

Once they were alone, Krystyna said nothing. Silently, she unfastened the pin in Marek's nappy. Then, carefully rolling it back, she exposed him to the Lieutenant's gaze. It would have been enough, during the war, to get the baby killed. Now, it served to save him.

'Lieutenant, no Polish Catholic baby is circumcised.'
'But I don't understand. What does it mean?'
'This child is Jewish. He is a survivor. I knew his mother and father. They were both killed by the Germans. His mother was Roza Levinson and she was second in command of a Communist partisan company for most of the war. I have promised to take this child, and the other two, who are also orphans, to a safe place. We are on our way there now. I hope that this information will go no further than these four walls, but it was necessary to tell you.'

Yusufov stood there and wondered. He had seen many strange things, even in his short life, but this was something new.

'But that woman. Why did she claim he was hers?'
'I'm not sure, but I think she lost a child, her own son. I think she saw Marek, whose real name, for your information only, is Mordechai, and something in her head snapped. I don't blame her. I feel sorry for her. Will you report her for this?'

'No. Who to? We'll put her on the next train to Warsaw and forget about her.'

'That would be good. Thank you.'

'Well, Mrs Celinska, I have learned something today. Take your grandchildren, and I hope you find the promised land.'

11

The promised land? Why had Lieutenant Yusufov said that? Anyway, Palestine seemed as far off as it ever was.

All Krystyna could do now was get them all safely on a train for Frankfurt. After that, the next stage would be to cross the border into France. Then, once they were out of this hated country, she would feel they were getting somewhere. She knew nothing about France, but she knew it was occupied during the war, like Poland, and she knew it would be better than Germany.

Frankfurt. Well, the obvious answer was to find a train going there, so she took the boys back to the ticket office, with their two cardboard suitcases and sundry bags, and enquired. There was, apparently, a train expected to depart from Frankfurt that very afternoon, at three o'clock. It was now almost twelve. Not long to wait. She told Masha the good news and he jumped with excitement, even if he had no idea where Frankfurt was or why they were going there. She told Adam and Marek too and naturally got no response from them but still, she just wanted them all to know.

At half past two they were standing on the appointed platform and ten minutes later, to the surprise and delight of the crowd of people waiting there, a train pulled in. There was a rush for seats and Krystyna was at a disadvantage with the babies and the luggage so they didn't get one this time. Still, they found an unoccupied corner in the baggage car, and Masha arranged their belongings to effect the semblance of a private compartment for them. The floor of the car was just planks of wood, but they had enough coats they could put down to make it a little more comfortable. The scheduled journey time was only seven hours. If that turned out to be true, it wouldn't be too bad.

It seemed like a miracle to them and their fellow passengers when the train pulled out of the station only fifteen minutes later than scheduled. It boded well for the journey. It picked up speed nicely and they settled down as best they could. Krystyna fed the children and ate a little herself. She wanted to save some food in case the trip took longer than expected, which in the way of things it would almost certainly do. She didn't want to get caught on a train stuck in a siding with three hungry children. Masha might understand but the other two wouldn't.

It was about an hour later that some of the other passengers in the baggage car began to talk about what they could see out of the windows. It didn't look right. Someone said they were coming back into Berlin and another passenger said don't be stupid, that's not possible. It was not only possible but it was true. Twenty minutes later they came alongside the same platform they had left earlier that afternoon. There was general incomprehension, mixed with a great deal of disappointment. Krystyna was unsure if it was wise to follow the other passengers, who were piling off the train onto the platform. Perhaps they should stay where they were? Perhaps the train would be leaving again?

But that was not to be. An official came down the platform and announced that the train was cancelled. A rumour went round that an unexploded bomb had been found by the side of the track and the Army was going to blow it up to make it safe, or perhaps to defuse it, the rumour wasn't specific about that. It was confirmed when Krystyna arrived back on the concourse. The track was closed for the foreseeable future. There would be no trains to Frankfurt for at least two days.

People were already settling down on the floor of the concourse for the night, some with resignation, some with anger, and arguments broke out and even small fights which everyone else tried to ignore. There was no choice for Krystyna but to go out on the streets again and look for food for them, and there was no choice either about taking the children, all of them, and their luggage, with her.

It was as they spilled out into the street that they saw it. A motorcycle and sidecar pulled up by the pavement. The driver dismounted, took out from the sidecar a large placard and held it in front of him. It said, simply, South. It said it in several languages. South? Why was this man giving people this information? She stopped and took out the old atlas and looked for Frankfurt, and then she looked for Berlin, and there was no doubt about it, they themselves wanted to go south. Was it possible? There was only one way to find out.

'Excuse me, Sir, do you speak Polish?'

'What, what is that you say?'

'Do you speak Polish?'

'A little, why?'

'I want to ask you - what does that mean, South?'

'It means, Madam, that I am travelling south and looking for fare-paying passengers.'

'I see. So, when you say south, do you mean south Berlin or south Germany?'

'Huh? South Germany. I'm going to Munich.'

'Wait a minute.' She looked at the atlas again. Yes, it was possible. To get there he might well pass through Frankfurt. 'And, excuse me, but how many people can you take, I mean in that thing?'

She pointed at the sidecar, it has to be said, with a certain amount of disdain. He ignored the comment but answered the question.

'One. And one on the back, behind me.'

'OK, we'll come.'

He looked at the children.

'I see you and three children. That makes four.'

'No, three children make one, plus me, that makes two. As I said, we'll come.'

He looked at this woman who showed no fear. He liked her already. It wasn't what he expected, and he might wait for someone else, but there was something about her. Yes, it might work.

'Have you ever ridden on the back of a motorcycle before?'

'Yes.'

He could tell that she lied with a certain amount of aplomb. He was smiling now. 'Well, let's see if we can fit the children in. Come on.'

Masha didn't have to be invited. He jumped in and told Krystyna to pass both of the boys to him. The sidecar had a canvas covering and quite a lot of legroom, so with a certain amount of planning both of the little ones could be accommodated by his legs. The suitcases were strapped onto the back, precariously balanced on top of the existing load, and then finally Krystyna climbed onto the pillion. She got off again.

'So, what's the price?'

'How much have you got?'

'I asked first. I'm not giving you everything I've got. And if you're thinking of taking us out into the country and robbing me I warn you now that would be a grave mistake on your part.'

'Alright, let's say you buy all the fuel, and believe me at black market prices that's not going to be cheap, and food as well. Have you got dollars, American money?'

'A little.'

'Good. Let's say ten dollars for each of you at the end of the journey. And by each of you I do mean all four of you, not three children counting as one adult, OK?'

She had no idea what ten dollars were worth. All she knew was that she had the hundred she had been supplied with in Sweden. Spending forty of them to get to Frankfurt seemed reasonable.

'OK. My name is Krystyna Celinska. These are my grandchildren, Masha, Adam and, down there, Marek.'

'Alright Krystyna Celinska, and where are you going?'

'Frankfurt. Are you going there?'

'I could.'

'Well then, let's go.'

She climbed on again and put her arms gingerly round his waist. He took each one in a gloved hand and wrapped himself tightly with them and smiled to himself. This was crazy, he knew it but still, the old woman would keep his back warm. He stood on the starter and the engine roared into life. Krystyna looked at Masha and the bump in the canvas that was one of the boys and suspected this was a big mistake but before she could say so the combination moved off sharply into the road and she felt her stomach sink to her knees and her grip on this man tightened instinctively. Well, she thought, if they crashed at least he would be in front to protect her. She wanted to ask him some questions. She realised she hadn't even got his name, that she was trusting a complete stranger with herself and her charges, but she also realised that that was in the nature of the present times. In any case, the noise of the engine was too great to shout over so she just clung on and gave herself over to the journey. She felt the pistol sticking into her side as she pressed against the driver and as uncomfortable as it was she felt reassured by the pain of it.

It was already late when they left and after an hour the man slowed down and then came to a stop. They had left Berlin behind and this was some kind of dormitory town. The buildings here were as badly damaged as those in the capital, but where they found themselves was by a public park and apart from a large bomb crater and some uprooted trees, in the moonlight it had the look of a place you could camp for a night. The nearby houses had no lights, probably because there was no electricity, and the deserted street added to the effect of a ghost town.

'Alright, we're going to stay here tonight. Everybody out.'

Masha's legs were stiff and he ran around the park to get them moving. Krystyna warned him not to go out of sight but she knew it was pointless even to say it. A minute later he was gone. Adam and Marek had slept, despite the noise and the vibration, and now they wanted to walk around themselves. It took all her time and energy to look after them, and so their companion was left to set up camp on his own. Camp consisted of a tarpaulin which he spread from the motorbike with two branches from a fallen tree to make a minimal kind of shelter, and that was it. He unloaded a bedroll for himself, and then called Masha.

'Now, young man, do you think you could find us some wood for a fire from those trees?'

'Yes Sir.'

'Nothing too big, just little ones, understand?'

'Yes.' He looked at Krystyna to check it was alright with her. Well, it would give him some much-needed exercise and keep him out of mischief. In half an hour they had a good fire going and water on the boil. It was a cool evening but the rain held off. All they needed now was some food, and it was decided that the man should take some of Krystyna's money and go in search of provisions to buy. He offered to take Masha with him, and the boy pleaded to be allowed to go, but Krystyna hesitated. No, not yet, not until she knew this man better. She didn't even know his name.

'Gottlieb Fischer.'

'German?'

'Yes, well Sudeten German actually.'

'Sudeten? What does that mean?'

'It means I'm from Czechoslovakia, but a part called the Sudetenland, in the north. My family are ethnic German but we consider ourselves Czech. At least we did until the Nazis decided that the Sudetenland was really part of Germany. Do you not know about these things?'

'No. How would I know? I'm just an old cook from Warsaw. It's not my business to understand politics.'

'Hm. Well, when the Germans annexed the Sudetenland in '38 and made it part of Germany, I became a German myself. The next year I was conscripted into their army.'

'So you fought on their side?' Krystyna was seriously beginning to think that this journey might be a mistake.

'Yes, well, no, not fought. You see, I'm a doctor. I served as a medical officer. I was posted to Lublin first, and then Warsaw. I was lucky not to get sent to the Russian Front. Anyway, I spent most of the war in Poland and that's how I came to learn your language.'

'I see.'

'That's good. I'm not a soldier, you know. I've never killed anyone in my life. My job is to save lives.'

'Alright, I believe you. Well, you might as well know that I have.'

'Have what?'

'Killed people. I served in the Communist Underground, the Armia Ludowa, as a cook but believe me I also carried a gun and I have killed Germans. How do you feel about that?'

He shrugged his shoulders. He didn't know how he felt about it. He couldn't easily imagine this elderly woman killing German soldiers, but on the other hand she had a hard glint in her eye, so yes, she was telling the truth. Anyway, why would she make it up? To frighten him?

'So, that's what I could feel in my back, a gun in your pocket.'

'I'm sorry, did it bother you?'

'Well, I suppose it should bother me that you might use it, but it bothered me more that it stuck in my back, so if you don't mind, tomorrow, perhaps you could carry it in some other place?'

'Sure. Now, since we have made the proper introductions, you may take my grandson and find some food before we all starve.'

She liked this man, and she had liked Inge in Berlin. It worried her that it was possible to like Germans because like a lot of people she had decided that for the rest of her life she would hate them. When he and Masha went off it gave her time to consider this dilemma. Did it mean that there were good ones and bad ones, or was it something else? Had Gottlieb and Inge cheered when Germany was winning the war and creating all that destruction? Were they good Germans now because their country was defeated, or had they always been decent people? Would she ever know the answer to that? Anyway, there were bad people in Poland too, so the Germans didn't have a monopoly on evil. She had seen that only too recently.

Had she been right in letting him take Masha off with him or was she forgetting herself? Well, she had his motorcycle and all his things so he was obviously coming back. She smiled and moved the pistol to another pocket. Perhaps she should pack it away, or even throw it away. How likely was it now that she would ever have need of it? She hoped she wouldn't, that the war really was over once and for all. Surely, once they got over the French border, it would be different? People would not be able to scare her there. That was what she hoped, anyway.

12

In the early morning, when she woke, Krystyna could see the sky, and for a moment she imagined she was back in Poland, in the forest, and when she looked around and saw she was in a park in Germany she wasn't quite sure how she had got there.

There were immediate needs to attend to. The boys were hungry, and Marek needed clean nappies. They all could do with some clean clothes and come to that a bath. Gottlieb informed her that last night he and Masha had found an empty house in the town.

'Well why didn't you say so last night? We could have slept there.'

'But just because it's empty doesn't mean it doesn't belong to someone. It doesn't give us the right to use it, does it?'

She looked at this man and wondered how he had survived the war with that attitude, and then she remembered he hadn't had to survive the war because he had been in the Wehrmacht.

'Actually, yes it does. An empty house is an empty house, so why did we sleep in this park? Come on, show me where it is.'

'They loaded up the motorcycle and Krystyna and the boys walked alongside, across the park and down two or three streets. Some people were about now and stared after them but they didn't care. When they came to the house, a few people had followed them as if daring them to go in, but still they didn't care, at least Krystyna didn't. There was a small front garden and a gate which still hung from one hinge. Gottlieb closed this as best he could and then once they were all in the house Krystyna closed the door firmly behind them and had Masha draw all the curtains. There weren't any windows but it gave them a measure of privacy.

There was water and a bath, and there was a fireplace and furniture, so Gottlieb and Masha broke up the latter and put it to burn in the former and Krystyna found a large iron pot in which to heat water over the fire once it got going. It wasn't perfect but it meant each of the boys got a bath. Masha insisted he didn't need one and that Krystyna could take his place, but that argument didn't last long. They heated water constantly and in the end both Krystyna and Gottlieb got a bathful of luke-warm water too. Then she washed as many clothes as weren't actually on people's backs and hung them up over doors and anywhere else she could think of to dry.

They stayed there all that day and another night and decided that by the time they left the following morning they would at least be refreshed and clean and have full stomachs. In the evening, after the children were asleep, Gottlieb made a cup of tea for Krystyna and himself and they settled into a pair of old armchairs and sipped and talked.

'So, tell me about yourself Gottlieb, tell me about this Sudetenland of yours.'

'What can I tell you? My family come from a town called Trutnov, very near the Sudeten Mountains. On the other side of these mountains is Poland. My father was a doctor and I helped him in his practice and when I was old enough I naturally went to the medical school in Prague. Medicine was all I ever wanted to do, only when I qualified I became a surgeon and worked in the local hospital. Then I got married to Petra and we had two daughters and we were very happy, and then the war came and changed it all.'

'I see. Do you know what happened to them, if they are still there?'

'Well, until almost the end I received letters, but since the Russians came that stopped and to be honest no, I don't know, but I trust in God that they are safe and well.'

'I expect you are eager to get back to them. I'm sorry if we have slowed you down.'

'No, don't worry, it's been six years. Another day or two will make no difference. Anyway, I like your boys, your grandsons, except of course they're not your grandsons, are they?'

'Is it obvious?'

'That they are Jewish? Yes, to me. I saw a lot of Jews in Poland. I had never seen one in Czechoslovakia, not in my whole life, not that I was aware of anyway, but in Poland there were so many of them. Of course, they were in the ghettos and I had nothing to do with that but still, I saw some. I had a Jewish assistant for a while, an excellent doctor from the hospital in Warsaw.'

'What happened to him?'

'He wasn't allowed to treat the men, because the law forbade a Jewish doctor to treat Aryans, but I kept him as long as I could, sterilising instruments, making bandages, that sort of thing.'

'And?'

'And then they took him. I tried to stop them, said I couldn't manage without him, but it made no difference. I'm sorry.'

'Why are you apologising to me?'

He hung his head, as if he felt genuine shame for what his people had done. 'I couldn't save him.'

'No-one could save them. Not against the evil forces that were determined to destroy them. You're not responsible for one man. You tried, and he lived longer than he would have done without you.'

'Maybe, but what for? If you're going to die, how does it help to live another six months or even a year? What for?'

'Do you want me to answer that question?'

He looked into her hard but kindly eyes and wondered how much suffering she had seen.

'No. Now, it's your turn. Why are you taking three Jewish children to Frankfurt?'

Avi Benzimra had warned her to tell people only what they needed to know. Gottlieb didn't need to know, but she needed to tell him, needed to tell someone, anyone she could trust, just for the sake of sharing it, and she told him, about Roza and Mordechai and Palestine. He listened intently and then he asked her the only question he could think of.

'Why? Why are you doing it?'

It was a simple question, but it had no simple answer. She had tried to understand it herself but given up. All she knew was that she was driven, that these three boys were like her own, that she needed them as much as they needed her, and that she owed it to Roza who had once been her friend and now she was responsible at least for her son. No-one had made her do this but on the other hand no-one could stop her. She would see it through.

'And when you get to Palestine, and you hand the boys over to someone Jewish to care for them, what will you do then? You will be in the right place for them but the wrong place for you. Will you stay there?'

'I can't say because I just don't know. I haven't thought about it too much. I suppose I just haven't believed we are actually going to get there. All I know about Palestine is where to find it on a map. I live from day to day, survive, take care of them, get them a little bit closer each day. It's enough, isn't it?'

'Yes, I would say it is.'

The next day, the same people who watched them come watched them go, but they said nothing and backed away when Gottlieb started the motorcycle with a lot of noise and exhaust smoke and stood there in a small group as they watched it disappear down the road, one or two of them shaking their heads as if to say well I never.

It had felt good to take a break but now if felt good to be on the road again. Adam and Marek chatted away to each other in the well of the sidecar, and Masha spread his arms wide like wings and Gottlieb smiled. They were good children, he thought. It made him anxious, though, to get home to see his own family. He didn't know what he would find when he got back, but even so he had to get back.

Gottlieb and Krystyna both started that day with a sense of urgency to their journey, so he drove the motorcycle faster than yesterday and she didn't object. They had to stop frequently, for the children, but they never stopped for long. Food was purchased on the road whenever they came to a village where some farmer was selling produce and on one occasion they stopped and let Masha crawl into a hen house and steal some eggs. They could have paid for them but somehow stealing them felt better.

Whenever they passed a settlement people stopped and stared at them, a man in goggles riding a motorbike with a granny on the back and a boy in the sidecar waving to them. Masha made a point of waving to people. When they came to a town they always seemed to find someone who was selling petrol from cans by the roadside and they haggled because the prices were ridiculous but even if they had to pay a lot for it at least it was never in short supply.

The next night they camped in a barn. The farmer gave them permission and sold them milk and freshly-baked bread. Masha passed the evening chasing mice and even Adam tried to join in the fun. In the morning the farmer let them watch while he milked the cows and Krystyna knew they should be going but she also knew this was good for them, all of them. They had loved being on the farm in Sweden, and this reminded them of those good times, times when normal things happened. The farmer's wife put together a basket of food for them to take with them and Krystyna thanked her but she also paid her well. It had been like another holiday.

Back on the road, they got back into their routine, drive hard, stop regularly, get back on the road again. Krystyna was finding it tough going sitting on the back holding on for dear life all the time, trying to keep an eye on the boys as well, and looked forward to their brief breaks. In the middle of the afternoon when they drove past a small lake and Gottlieb stopped and suggested a swim, she readily consented.

The water was cold but they all had a dip. She undressed the babies completely. It didn't matter now that Gottlieb knew they were Jewish. They had nothing to hide. They took one each and let them splash about in the water while Masha paddled. He had never swum before but the shore was shallow and he couldn't get into much trouble. After their swim Gottlieb and Masha gathered firewood and they boiled a kettle to make some coffee. The babies were wrapped up again and the adults were sipping the hot coffee when they noticed Masha was missing. There was a stand of trees nearby and Gottlieb searched there and they both called and then Krystyna turned her head abruptly when she thought she heard his voice and she was just in time to see a splash in the water, about fifty metres out.

'Oh my God, Masha, it's him, for God's sake, Gottlieb, it's him out there.'

Gottlieb scanned the water but he couldn't see anything.

'It is, it is, oh God, I can't swim, please, do something.'

But he didn't need telling. He was not dressed yet and before she had finished speaking he was in the water striking out for where she had pointed to. He was a powerful swimmer and it took him just a few seconds to reach the spot. She watched in fear as she saw him take a deep breath and dive. She prayed fervently while she waited and there he was, in answer to her prayer, with the boy in his arms. He put Masha down on the grass and immediately started resuscitation.

Masha's face looked white but in seconds it turned to red and he coughed and then Gottlieb turned him over and he brought up a lungful of water. Krystyna stood there wringing her hands and praying but when Gottlieb sat Masha up and pronounced him well she sank to her knees beside him and proceeded to dry him off and scold him at the same time. It was while she doing this and Gottlieb was drying himself off that they noticed a car had stopped beside their motor cycle. They stood up as the driver got out and closed the door. They looked at him in disbelief, as if they couldn't credit his existence, but he was real enough. Gottlieb knew instantly what type of man he was. Prussian officer class.

'Hullo there, I saw there was some trouble so I stopped.'

He stood there towering over them, his legs astride, and it brought everything back to Krystyna, the Germans, the war, as if it had never gone away. This man had a way of looking threatening just by his presence. Not understanding German, she let Gottlieb speak.

'Thank you, but we are alright. The boy had a small swimming accident, that is all, but he is fine now.'

The man came over and inspected Masha, as if he didn't believe what Gottlieb told him. Masha was naked. The man peered more closely, as if he had seen something which disturbed him. He had.

'This boy is a Jew!'

'That is correct. I am Major Gottlieb Fischer, formerly a medical officer with the Wehrmacht. I am assisting this lady and her grandchildren.'

'Grandchildren? You mean they are all Jews?'

Gottlieb pulled himself up to his maximum height, which wasn't very impressive when he was dressed, but in his underwear he was no match for this officer, who towered above him, in size and in rank, but mostly in arrogance.

'Well, Major, you surprise me. Assisting Jews. You could have been shot for that in the war. I must insist that you stop, at once.'

Gottlieb was shocked out of his timorousness. Now, he was angry. 'What? Who are you to tell me to do anything?'

'I, Major, am SS Colonel Erich von Eisenach. If you disobey a direct order I shall be forced to take action against you.'

'What are you talking about? The war is over, you silly old fool. You're not in the SS now. There is no SS. Are you mad, going around telling people just like that what you used to be. The Allies would arrest you immediately.'

It was, apparently, the wrong thing to say because it was correct. The Colonel's face went bright red, and in his anger he did something from force of habit, he pulled a pistol from his pocket and pointed it directly at Gottlieb's head. Everyone froze, even Masha. He had seen this sort of thing before.

'Major, I am giving you an order. If you disobey, I shall be forced to shoot you before I shoot these Jewish brats. I will give you five seconds to decide.'

He only got as far as three. He was so enraged that he failed to hear the sound of Krystyna's pistol as she cocked it. The first bullet went straight through his heart and out the other side, and the second one, albeit superfluous as he was already mortally wounded, through his belly as the impact sent him flying backwards. Masha screamed but Krystyna didn't hear him. All of her attention was focused on killing this man. She had failed to do what was right in Warsaw and Jakub Lau had died in front of her eyes. Well, never again.

13

They dragged the body into the ditch by the side of the road. Krystyna made Masha look after the little ones to give him something to do that would take his mind off what he had just seen. It couldn't really do that, of course. How does a nine-year old boy put from his mind that his grandmother has just killed a man? Still, in the war children saw things that were infinitely worse than that.

That left them with the car to dispose of. Gottlieb eyed it greedily.

'It's a lot more comfortable than the motorbike.'

'Yes, but it's not ours.'

'Krystyna, the house wasn't ours but you said it was alright for us to borrow it. Well, forgive me for mentioning this but you have just killed the owner of this vehicle and between you and me I don't suppose he really was the owner anyway. It's a German staff car. We'll take it as war reparations.'

'Reparations? What does that mean?'

'It means we Germans started the war and you Poles get to take anything you want by way of repayment.'

'But how can Germany ever pay for what it has done?'

'Well, and I speak as a German, it can't. But it can show willing, can't it? Anyway, why are we having this discussion? What are we going to do - leave it here for someone to steal?'

'Well, no.'

'Right, as the only representative of the late German Reich in this area I hereby and officially assign these goods to you Krystyna ... Krystyna ...'

'Celinska.'

'Thank you. Alright, now it's officially your car. Congratulations. Can you drive?'

'No.'

'Well I will be your chauffeur. We just need to get rid of the motorcycle. I know, we'll push it into the ditch on top of the body and then it will look like a road accident.'

'Oh, you mean he drove off the road and then shot himself. Twice.'

She was shaking, and Gottlieb realised this was no laughing matter. He had seen many men die but he had never actually killed one himself. This old woman had just had an experience he never had, and it was time to respect that. He wondered if he should put his arm round her but he didn't.

'Look, Krystyna, before we go any further, I want to thank you.'

'Thank me? What for?'

'Well, you just saved my life.'

'Yes, I suppose, but if I hadn't put you in this position I wouldn't have needed to.'

'Alright, that's true, but think about something else. That man was a homicidal maniac. God alone knows how many people he killed in the war. You have done the world a big favour. He might well have got away with his crimes, but now he's paid the price, thanks to you.'

'Well I can accept that. Yes, that sounds good to me. OK, we'll take the car. Let's move our things.'

They opened the boot of the Mercedes and it was crammed full so they threw everything out. First there were several uniforms with a variety of medals and they threw these into the ditch with the motorbike and the body. There were several suitcases which gave up a variety of useful items and some good food, not to mention several bottles of French brandy.

Gottlieb went through the man's wallet and found not only his SS papers but a document which puzzled him. He unfolded it and tried to make sense of it. He himself was a Catholic, so he recognised the insignia of the Papal See on the letter, but the first part was in Latin, and what little he learned in church as a child was no use to him now. The next paragraph, though, was in German, and he read it and shook his head in disbelief. Krystyna was curious.

'What is it? What does all this mean?'

'Well, believe it or not, it's some kind of laissez-passer, from the Vatican.'

'A what?'

'Like a passport. It means that anyone presented with this is to help the carrier wherever he wants to go. Across borders, anywhere. And because the Vatican was neutral in the war, the Allies will respect it. This is how he was going to avoid being arrested.'

'But I don't understand. Why has he got it? Did he steal it?'

'No, look, it's got his name on it. No, hold on, this isn't his name. What did he call himself?'

'Er, von Eisenach, I think.'

'Well this is in the name of Eisen. It's got his photograph, though, No, it's definitely his.'

'Not forged?'

'No reason why it would be. No, for some reason I don't understand, the Vatican was helping this man to escape justice for war crimes.'

Krystyna herself was a Catholic. It just wasn't possible to understand it. Gottlieb was going to throw it away but she stopped him. She didn't know why, but it might be interesting to take it. You never know who might find that information useful. She was thinking like a partisan again.

They continued to empty the boot, and when there was nothing left to dispose of, for no reason he was able to remember afterwards, Gottlieb lifted the carpet where the spare wheel was kept, except that it wasn't, because in the space where it should have been was an old brown cloth, and under the cloth was a hoard of silver bullion.

They stood there in shock and looked at it. Masha came and looked at it.

'What is it?'

'It's silver, Masha.'

'Silver? What's that?'

'Well, it's like money, only better.'

Then she heard a muffled call. Gottlieb was in the back of the car. He had pulled out the back seat.

'Hey, I think you should come and look at this.'

They were Reichsmarks, he said, high denomination notes. Hard to say how much, but perhaps half a million marks, even more.

'Our friend was on the run for his life, and since he doesn't have one of those any more he won't be needing his pension either.'

'You mean it's ours?'

'Krystyna, look around you. Do you see anyone else claiming it?'

'But it might be stolen.'

'Wrong, it is stolen, of course it is. But who from? Well, that's an unanswerable question. We have just found a solution that doesn't have a problem. Come on, let's get our things loaded up from the bike.'

'Just a moment.'

'What now?'

'I've been thinking.'

'And?'

'Look, how far are we from Frankfurt now?'

'Oh, about a couple of hours' drive I think. Why?'

'Well, look, the deal was to take us to Frankfurt, right? But we're nearly there. What happens then?'

'Well, I turn left for Munich and you carry on and head for France.'

'But how?'

'I don't know. What was the plan?'

'There wasn't one. I've always assumed we would go by train but …'

'Yes? But what?'

'Now there's the motorbike.'

Gottlieb stood up straight and put his hands on his hips. He wasn't quite sure if Krystyna meant what it sounded like she meant.

'Do you mean …?'

'Yes.'

'Good God. You can't be serious.'

'Why not? OK, it sounds crazy, but tell me anything that doesn't sound crazy. I'm taking three children to Palestine and now it seems we're rich as well. So, why shouldn't we take the motorbike?'

'But come on, you've never ridden one before.'

'I've just ridden all this way from Berlin, haven't I?'

'No, that's different. Look, you've never driven a car, have you?'

'No. But I've been in one.'

'Quite. Now you appreciate the difference between riding on the back of this thing and actually driving it.'

'You could teach me.'

'Oh yes? How long have you got?'

'An hour?'

Gottlieb fell against the bonnet of the car laughing. He laughed so much it made the children cry. Krystyna couldn't see why it was funny.

'What is it, is it because I'm a woman, or because I'm old?'

'Yes.'

'What do you mean, which one?'

'Both. Grandmothers don't ride motorbikes.'

'Grandmothers don't normally shoot SS officers either but somehow I think you are going to have to get used to a new way of looking at things, young man. Now, are you going to teach me or shall I teach myself?'

'Do I have a choice?' He was still laughing.

'Yes. I've still got sixteen rounds left in this thing.'

That sobered him. 'OK, you've made your point. Right, now put these goggles on and let's see what you look like.'

She did, and now it was Masha's turn to laugh. She snorted at him and looked at herself in the car's wing mirror.

'Hm, no worse than you. Now show me how to drive this thing.'

An hour later she was riding up and down the road with the same confidence with which she wielded a gun. Gottlieb considered she was probably going to be a danger to other road users, but if they stayed out of her way there was a chance no-one was going to get killed.

Masha had thought the motorbike was great fun at first but now he wanted to go in the car. Krystyna explained that that wasn't possible, that Gottlieb wasn't going to France and so they had to say goodbye to him. She realised that in a very short space of time they had made friends. Masha helped him to transfer half of the banknotes into the motorcycle. Krystyna had already insisted that it would be enough, that he could take the silver, all of it, because he would know how to sell it. Because of that Gottlieb then insisted that she take two Reichsmarks for each one he kept, and she agreed that was fair. It was when they got her two thirds of the money out from under the seat that they found what was hidden even further down. It was a small leather bag, and when Gottlieb lifted it it felt heavy. They put it on the bonnet of the car and opened it. What they had seen so far had not prepared them for what they saw now. Masha peered into the bag, curiously.

'What are they? Bits of glass?'

Gottlieb put his hand on Masha's shoulder. 'No, my boy, they're not glass. They're diamonds.'

'Diamonds? What are they?'

'Well better than money, and better than silver. I have no idea what they are worth, but I can tell you it's a fortune. Our late friend was going to live very comfortably on this lot in some safe place, courtesy of the Vatican and God knows how many poor devils who contributed to his savings scheme. The more I see, the more I'm happy your grandmother shot him.'

'I didn't like that.'

'No, well, I'm glad you didn't. I hope it's something you never have to witness again. But she's a brave woman you know, and we should be glad to have her on our side.'

'She's not really my grandmother, you know. I never had one of my own, and so I adopted her.'

Gottlieb put his arm round the boy's shoulder. Of course he had once had a grandmother, probably two of them, but if he couldn't remember them, well, that was no bad thing. Krystyna was all the grandmother a boy could want.

He closed the bag again and handed it to Krystyna.

'What, all of them?'

'I've got the silver, you've got three boys and a long way to go. Diamonds are as good as ready money, better. Just don't sell them too cheaply. Use them wisely and they will take you anywhere you want to go. Oh, and one more thing.'

'What?'

'Promise me you won't shoot anyone else. Not unless it's absolutely necessary.'

'Oh, in that case I can promise.'

She also promised Masha that, at least when she was a bit more proficient on it, she would let him ride behind her sometimes. For now, though, he was to stay in the sidecar and look after Marek and Adam.

She took out the German atlas and laid it out on the bonnet of the car and asked Gottlieb to direct her westward for France. He laughed again. This crazy woman was really travelling halfway across Europe with nothing more than an old school atlas.

'OK, now look, we're about here, and that's Frankfurt. I've heard the Americans have their headquarters there so you will be quite safe. West of that my guess is you will find the French on this side of the border, and after that you will cross into France.'

'Will they let us?'

He shrugged his shoulders. 'Your guess is as good as mine, but I don't see why not. The Wehrmacht tore down the border and I would be surprised if the French have got as far as putting it back in place, especially if they have forces in Germany. No reason to, I would say, but I hope I'm right. Anyway, it's not like before the war. There are millions of refugees, and I don't suppose many of them have anything as helpful as a passport, so I think you just go where you want. Anyway, once you are in France, you need to head south, and then east. You're heading for Trieste, right?'

'Yes.' She pointed at something on the map. 'What's this?'

'That, I'm afraid, is the Alps. Mountains. And by the time you get there there is going to be snow. So find whatever warm clothing you can as you go, because the cold in the Alps is not like the cold of Poland. And that's about all the useful advice I can give you, I'm afraid. I'm not actually taking the Frankfurt road now. I'm hoping there will be another road that turns west up here, so it's goodbye at this point. You just keep going down this road and you should come into the city. I don't think you will have any trouble with the Americans, as long as you don't take that gun out, anyway. Oh, and one last thing about the money. It's only going to help you in Germany, so if you get a chance in the French occupation zone, try to exchange if for francs.'

'What are they?'

He shook his head. How she had got this far was a mystery. Still, she had.

'It's what the French money is called. You should find someone to change it, but don't change all of it with one person. If they see how much you have got they will either rob you or report you to the occupation authorities, so change it in smaller chunks. It will take a while, but it's worth doing.'

Krystyna was amazed at how much Gottlieb knew. She was, she realised, an uneducated woman. The boys were ready, so she mounted the motorbike and started the engine. Before she put the goggles on, Gottlieb put his arms round her.

'I will remember you, strange Polish woman. I hope you get to the promised land.'

She revved up and slowly the machine moved off. Masha turned and waved to him. It was, she remembered, the second time someone had said that to her recently.

14

Gottlieb shook his head as she drove off, and prayed for her success, for her, and for the boys. He liked them. Jews. He couldn't understand what all the fuss had been about right from the beginning. The National Socialists hated them and suddenly everyone hated them, if they were Nazis or not, even people, like him, who had had little or nothing to do with them. It was like some collective madness. Why? It was a question he would never be able to answer. Still, they had brought him good luck. Now, for some reason that was equally impossible to understand, he was a rich man. It was then that he remembered that Krystyna had forgotten to pay him the ten dollars per person they had agreed on. He chuckled as he got into the Mercedes and turned the key. He just hoped she didn't remember later. It would be just like her, he thought, to turn round and chase after him.

She didn't though. She was concentrating too hard on riding the motorcycle. She came to think after a couple of kilometres that her enthusiasm for motorbikes might have been misplaced. The machine seemed to have a mind of its own. It wanted to go left, or right, for no reason she could detect, when all she wanted to do was go straight ahead, and then when they came to a sharp bend and she pulled on the handlebars, it suddenly decided it didn't want to turn after all. It was, she considered, because it was a German motorcycle. A Polish motorcycle would have better manners.

Her arms ached after the first hour, and Krystyna was not a slightly-built woman. She remembered that Gottlieb had laughed at the idea of a woman riding such a machine at all, and now she knew why.

Still, she rested often, for her and for the boys too, especially the little ones. They had enjoyed the sidecar at first and thought it was an adventure to make a home in it but children tire of the same game for hours on end and it was necessary to let them stretch their legs regularly.

Even so, they made good progress. The next day Krystyna knew they were either in French occupied Germany or perhaps even in France itself, because they were flagged down at a checkpoint that had a tricolor flag flying and she got the atlas out, which being a school book fortuitously had the flag of each country printed on the appropriate page. The soldiers manning the post looked at her in incredulity. When Adam and Marek climbed out of the sidecar they were lost for words. They gathered round the machine and peered inside the sidecar to see if she had any more children in there, like Old Mother Hubbard. Had they lifted the cloth in the footwell they would have found a large stash of Reichsmarks and a bag of diamonds, but they had no reason to search. An old woman and three children could not possibly have anything to hide.

The soldiers chattered away to her but she couldn't make out a word of course, and they gave food and drinks to the boys. They were used to refugees. All refugees were hungry and thirsty. It was only to be expected. Krystyna could have bought half of France but they didn't know that. What they did do that was most welcome was to take the motorbike over to a bowser of fuel and fill the tank. Krystyna didn't know what fuel it needed, and Gottlieb had forgotten to tell her, but these men seemed to know. This was, it seemed, not so much a checkpoint after all but a French army refuelling point. She took out a ten Reichsmark note and proffered it in payment but they say no, no, they couldn't take money from her. They shouldn't have given her French Army fuel at all, but it seemed to them the decent thing to do.

She wanted to know where they were so she showed the soldiers the atlas and made a gesture that is recognised the world over which they understood to mean they should show her. They looked at the map and frowned. A sergeant came over and looked, and he frowned too. The map was, of course, on a hopelessly small scale. It took him a moment to realise that what he was looking at was the whole of Germany. The French border was about twenty kilometres further. He showed her twenty with his fingers and then he pointed west and she understood.

Then she and the children took their places again and she started the motor with a roar. Last of all she pulled the goggles over her face and the soldiers stood back in amazement. Then they started shouting at her to stop and she got the gist of that so she just stood there and finally one of the men returned with a camera and took a picture. In years to come he would sit in a bar somewhere in France and someone would buy him a drink for him to tell the story.

Finally, they saluted her and wished her bon voyage. They said they hoped she would find France alright. She didn't know they were saying that of course. If she had, she might have wondered if for them France was the promised land.

An hour later, although she didn't know it because there was no sign to tell her, she crossed out of Germany and into France. They passed a sign for Strasbourg and she stopped to check which country that was. It sounded German to her but it turned out, from the atlas, to be French. She let all the children get off and they held hands and sang in Hebrew and Polish and danced around in a circle. Adam and Marek didn't know why they were dancing but even so they caught the spirit of the moment.

That evening they pulled into Mulhouse and found a pension for the night. They all had hot baths and the landlady helped her to wash the clothes and nappies and hang them to dry, and fed them steaming plates of something none of them had eaten before but whatever it was it tasted wonderful. Krystyna and the landlady could not exchange one word with each other but they were both grandmothers and they put the children to bed and settled down in front of a fire with mugs of coffee and a bottle of brandy and for Krystyna it felt good and without knowing anything of the other woman's story she could tell that they had something in common, something they could not communicate but which nonetheless they were able to share for that brief evening in the dimly-lit parlour.

In the morning there was a moment of awkwardness when Krystyna realised she had no French currency with which to pay the bill. She was wealthy beyond imagination but she could hardly pay a French landlady with Reichsmarks, let alone diamonds, but in the end she found that Dollars were very readily accepted and when the time came for them to leave they were seen off with a big smile and a lot of incomprehensible good wishes, the gist of which were abundantly clear though.

It occurred to Krystyna that before she went any further it would be necessary to find a way to exchange some of the German currency into French, but where? Where would she even find someone she could speak Polish to, so she could ask? It was while she was sitting on the motorcycle by the kerb that the answer appeared, in the form of a soldier, waving to her. Krystyna was not used to being waved at by soldiers and was inclined to ignore him, but this wasn't wartime, and the soldier was smiling, as if he knew her, which was of course impossible, except that it was true, because he ran up to her and all soldiers looked alike to her but to him there was only one grandmother on a motorbike so he knew who she was immediately. He got his camera out and now she knew who he was. He had driven all the way from the French Army post behind her. He had an errand in Mulhouse, he had to report to the barracks, but she looked lost and he wanted to help.

She took a wad of Reichsmarks out of her pocket and at first he thought she wanted to give them to him, like before for the petrol but no, she made a sign that he managed to interpret enough to get his wallet out and with the aid of a hundred franc note of his she managed to convey the idea that she wanted to exchange one for the other. He took her to a bank. It was as easy as that. If only she had known the word for bank in French.

Now that she did know, she spent two hours driving round Mulhouse changing as much as she dared at any one time. Once or twice the cashier looked at her suspiciously and she realised she was tendering rather more than a grandmother should rightly be in possession of, especially a foreign grandmother, and especially Reichsmarks, which not unnaturally the banks all treated with a certain amount of suspicion. Still, they were legal tender in Germany and there was no reason, just after the recent war, to suspect that they might be counterfeit. There were many counterfeit British pounds and American dollars in circulation because the Germans had forged large quantities in the last stages of the war in an effort to destabilise the British and US currencies, but no-one had been forging German currency.

Krystyna was now in possession of enough French francs for any conceivable eventuality. She didn't know what they were worth, but when she checked the price of a hotel room, and compared that with what she had stuffed in every pocket of her coat, she began to get the measure of her wealth. How much the diamonds were worth was a complete unknown, but as it was, according to Gottlieb, a very large amount, she took the precaution of carrying the leather bag with her everywhere they went. The sidecar of the motorbike was hardly a safe hiding place, and even if she had come by them by a stroke of unsought good fortune, she saw no reason to share them with anyone else. These stones were going to be needed.

It was getting late and Krystyna decided to stay the night in the town. She considered going back to the hotel she had just checked out but money or no money she knew it was out of her class, and that three children might not be welcome, so she found another place, run down enough that they wouldn't be noticed but not so scruffy that they would be uncomfortable. The motorbike was uncomfortable enough and she reckoned they were owed a decent place to spend the night. When she paid the proprietor so readily he looked at her as if he was wondering if he could have raised the price but now it was too late, and gave her a key.

They were hardly settled in the room when there was a knock on the door. The children stopped running around. They had learned suspicion well, and they clung to her skirt as she cautiously opened the door. She wished she still had her coat on. Her gun was in the pocket.

'Hullo. Mrs Celinska?' He spoke in Polish, but with a strange accent she remembered from somewhere.

'No, sorry, wrong room.'

'Good.'

'Good? Why?'

'You have learned well. Don't trust anyone, even a man who claims to be from Bricha.'

'From Bricha?' She looked puzzled. She was puzzled, completely. How was that possible? She didn't have to ask the question, because it was written on her face. The man laughed.

'And this, unless I'm mistaken, is Masha, otherwise known...' and here he looked furtively but not seriously up and down the hallway, 'as Moise, and you will have to forgive me because I wasn't told which was which, these are Adam and Marek, or should I say Mordechai?' Hullo children. My name is Dov.'

'Dov? Dov who? And who told you, all of this I mean?'

'The answer to the first question is just Dov, if you don't mind, and the answer to the second is an old friend of yours in Warsaw, Avi Benzimra.'

'In that case, just Dov, you had better come in.'

He sat down and the children lost a little of their shyness. He had a big smiling face and they found him hard to resist. He was the kind of man who was used to putting people at their ease, adults and children. Within five minutes Mordechai had climbed onto his lap.

'So, just Dov, how did you find us?'

'Well, to be honest Mrs Celinska, a woman your age with three children on a motorbike isn't that hard to find, but the truth is we watch the banks. You walked into seven in all today, exchanging Reichsmarks. Each bank would have no reason to be interested, but we were. Where, not that it's really my business, did you get the German money?'

'A retired SS Colonel donated it. Just before he died.'

'Really?'

'Yes.'

'I see. Avi told me you were ....'

'Uhuh, that I'm what?'

'An interesting woman. Anyway, down to business. Actually, there might not be any business, because to be honest my primary job is to give you enough cash to see you through the next stage of your journey, but it looks like that is unnecessary.'

'Oh yes. I think you can say we are well supplied with cash.'

'I see. Er, just out of curiosity, how much did your obliging Colonel leave you in his will?'

'A lot.'

'I see. Enough to get you to Palestine?'

'Well, I don't know how much that is going to cost, but I think, yes, enough for that.'

'Well, excellent. We need to save all we can. All I need to do, then, is help you plan the travel arrangements between here and Trieste.'

'That would be good.'

She got out the old German school atlas and Dov's reaction was the same as every other person who had seen it, incredulity.

'You mean you have come all the way from Warsaw with this?'

'Yes, why not?'

He couldn't answer that so he didn't try. He opened it at the page that showed western France, and then he turned the page and found northern Italy.

'OK, now look at this. You are here, Mulhouse, and there's Trieste. You have only one more border to cross, from France into Italy, but come here for a moment.'

She followed him to the window, and the children followed her. She picked Adam up in her arms. Dov pointed into the distance.

'You see over there?'

'Yes, but what am I looking at?'

'Those are the Jura mountains in those clouds. And beyond those are the Alps. Between here and Trieste there are no trains running. Italy, don't forget, was on the Axis side in the war and things are, well, pretty chaotic right now.'

'I didn't know that, I mean about Italy.'

He looked at her as if that wasn't possible, but he reminded himself she was a cook from Poland. Why would she know?

'Well it's true. My second job, once I've dealt with the money side of things, is to find transport for you. Believe me, there are people trying that trip on foot, but I don't think you would make it. It would take weeks for a healthy young adult, but for you, with these three, no, it's not possible. To be honest your best bet is the motorbike. Think you can ride it all that way?'

She looked at Moise. She knew he was tired. He had to keep the other two happy while she rode the bike. It was a strain on him. She wouldn't do it if he said no, even if it meant waiting here for trains to start running again. Walking, obviously, was out. Moise thought about it and he climbed up on a chair and looked at of the window at the mountains, and then he thought again.

'If you can do it, so can I.'

That was all she needed to hear. He had grown up a lot since Sweden. Krystyna looked at Dov and closed the atlas.

'We'll do it.'

'Good. Well, I assume you're not in a rush to leave just tonight, so what do you say we go and find something to eat?'

15

The restaurants of Mulhouse were serving an interesting mixture of local French food and US Army rations, but Dov, Krystyna, Masha, Adam and Marek sat round a table and ate as if it was going to be their last meal. The wine was, strangely, German, but they drank it anyway. Dov wanted to give Masha a glass but Krystyna thought that was a bad idea.

'But we do it in Palestine. All the children learn to drink wine.'
'Palestine? You live there?'
'Yes. Where did you think?'
'I didn't think. I've never met anyone from Palestine before.'
'Yes you have. Avi.'
'Avi's Palestinian?'
'Uhuh, of course, we all are. Didn't you know?'
'No.'
'Oh yes, we all served in the British Army to fight the Germans. Some of us went off to join Haganah and a few of us are in Bricha.'

Krystyna looked completely perplexed. None of this meant anything to her. Dov asked her if she wanted him to explain and Masha said yes, which she was going to say anyway, so he did.

'Well, first the British. Palestine has been occupied by Great Britain since the first war, when they took over from the Turks, who ruled it before. The League of Nations, which was an international organisation, gave Britain a mandate to govern the territory, but before that a British politician called Arthur Balfour wrote a letter that officially promised to help establish a Jewish homeland there. Am I going too fast?'

'Yes, but don't slow down.'

'OK. In 1922 Britain split a big chunk of the territory off, about two thirds of it, and created a separate state for the Palestinian Arabs, called Transjordan, which means the other side of the river Jordan.'

'I've heard of that, from the Bible.'

'Right, well now Palestine is a lot smaller, but even so a viable Jewish state could still be established there. Since the beginning of the century, local Arabs sold their land to the Jews and more and more Jewish farms and settlements sprang up. It was a thriving community and it brought a certain amount of prosperity to the territory, for the Arabs too. But then the Arabs decided there were too many Jews and even though it wasn't their territory, it was British, they decided to try and stop Jewish settlement. There has been violence ever since. All Jewish settlements out of the cities have to have permanent armed guards. That's the job of Haganah. It's the Jewish self-defence force.'

'But if Palestine is governed by Britain, I mean, shouldn't they protect the Jews?'

'Theoretically, yes, and to an extent they do, but British policy is to appease the Arabs.'

'Why?'

'Because although the Palestinian Arabs are not true Arabs they are Moslems, and the rest of the Arab world is also Moslem and other Arab countries have oil, which the British war machine can't run without. The British need the Arabs but they don't need the Jews.'

The boys had all fallen asleep.

'But you said the Jews from Palestine served in their army.'

'Yes, that true, and what's worse the Arab Palestinians supported the German side, but that counts for nothing now we have helped them to win the war. Arab oil trumps everything.'

'Even loyalty to the people who fought with the British?'

'Do you really want me to answer that question?'

'No need, you just have.'

'So, to finish the story, there are a lot of us now who have British Army training, which to be honest was part of the reason we joined up in the first place, not just to save Palestine from the Germans.'

'What? The Germans were going to invade Palestine?'

'Yes. There are about four hundred thousand Jews living there. The Arabs were planning death camps to help the Germans kill them all if they ever took it from the British.'

Krystyna had a hard time taking that one in.

'This is all new to you, isn't it?'

'Completely.'

'I suppose it would be. Well, now there are a lot of us trained and ready to defend ourselves, and when a Jewish homeland is created we will form an army, a proper Jewish army under Jewish command, and then no-one will ever murder Jews again.'

'Do you believe that?' She looked into his eyes and she could see again it was a superfluous question. He believed it. She hoped he was right, not least for these precious three boys she was taking there. Krystyna had never thought about politics in her life but Dov's story prompted a question that needed to be answered.

'Dov, who really owns Palestine?'

He sat back in his chair and looked at her and the sleeping children. It wasn't an easy question and it certainly wasn't one he could give a simple answer to.

'Well, where do I begin? It's one of those places that has never really been what you might call a sovereign country. The name Palestine was used by the Romans but the Turks, who were the rulers for the longest, didn't use the name. To them it was just part of Syria. Different rulers have come and gone over two thousand years and different peoples have settled different parts of it. The Jews have always been there but only in small numbers. Of course, originally, it was the Jewish homeland, but that was in biblical times and even the most ardent Zionist would have to admit that's a tenuous claim on the land. Some religious Jews say that God gave us the land and we must return there, but I don't think like that. God is not part of my Zionism. Anyway, the British took over in 1917 and they decided to resurrect the old Roman name, Palestine, which makes us and the Arabs there Palestinians, but to be honest no-one actually uses the name. I don't think this is really helping, is it?'

'Yes and no, but carry on, if there's more.'

'Not a lot. The Transjordanians want the land for themselves, and I suppose the Arabs who live there would be happy enough to live under Transjordanian rule. I mean, they never complained about Turkish or British rule.'

'But don't the Arabs want the land for themselves? I mean, to have their own country there?'

Dov shrugged his shoulders. 'If they do, I've never heard anyone talk about it. It's not something, I think, that has ever occurred to them.'

'So what happens to them if a Jewish state comes about?'

'Well, I guess they will live there. Why not? It can't be any worse than living under the British. A lot better, probably. I don't know of any Jews living there who wouldn't want them to stay. They're part of the landscape.'

It was as far as they could go. This was all hypothetical to Krystyna. She had never met an Arab, had never been to Palestine, found the whole thing beyond her imagination. The more Dov told her, the more perplexed she became. If she ever got there, well, that would be the time to try and understand it.

They woke Masha up and each of them carried a little one back to the hotel, where Dov said goodbye.

'You won't see me again. Look, you're doing really well. Of all the people I have helped along this route to Palestine so far, if anyone can make it you will. Most of them are half-dead already but you have tremendous strength, and this young man I can see is a great help.'

He shook Masha's hand solemnly, as if to say he trusted him to be a lot older than he was.

'Well, goodbye Masha, Moise. When you get to the end of your journey you will have your Hebrew name back and you will use it with pride. Meanwhile, look after Krystyna and the little ones, won't you?'

'Yes, Sir, I'll do my best.'

'Good man.'

He saluted him, and then he shook Krystyna's hand too. 'When you get to Milan, you should look for an agent called Shimon. On the other hand, just drive around on your motorbike and he will find you.'

They laughed and said a final goodbye. Krystyna carried both toddlers up to bed and when they were settled she came to say goodnight to Masha. He wasn't ready for sleep now. He wanted to talk.

'Grandma, he was nice, wasn't he?'

'Who, Dov? Yes, he is a good man.'

'But nice too?'

'Yes, nice too.'

'When we get to Palestine I think I'm going to like it, I mean if the people are like him and Avi.'

'I hope so my sweet, I do hope so.'

'Grandma?'

'Yes?'

He hesitated, and she let him take his time. She didn't know what he was going to say, but she knew he was a deep thinker. Masha didn't say a lot but when he did it was usually important.

'Do you think, I mean when we get to Palestine, it will matter that you're not really my grandma?'

'Oh no, I don't think that at all. A lot of people, I mean, well, you know there are many people who don't have their own grandparents now, because of the war you know, and well, as far as I'm concerned you are really my grandson.'

'But I can't be, can I?'

'Why is that?'

'Well, because you're not Jewish.'

That was a tough one. For years being Jewish was something you regretted, now the world was different and they were going to a place where you didn't have to apologise for it. Now, well if they got there anyway, she was going to be the different one. She hadn't had time to think about it, but Masha had made her. Well, not right now, anyway.

'No Masha, I'm not, but we're all God's people and somehow I think if it's alright with God it will be alright with the people in Palestine.'

He thought about that and while he was thinking she could tell it wasn't a very good answer.

'But the Germans are God's people too, aren't they? But it's not alright with them, is it?'

If she didn't get this right she knew there would be more. And she couldn't get it right. She just clammed up and found no answer. The Germans were supposedly Christians and they had murdered her Catholic husband and her children and their children, just lined them up and shot them for being in the wrong place at the wrong time. The Germans weren't Christians. How could they be? They weren't even human. How could she answer him?

'Grandma, why did they kill my Mummy and Daddy?'

In the half light of the bedroom she could see tears streaming down his face. He was, after all, a child, and the question he had never been able to ask now demanded an answer, but she didn't know herself so what could she say to him? In any case, she too was crying and was quite unable to speak. She held him close to her breast and hugged him and hoped that would be some kind of answer, that whatever hate he had experienced in his short terrible life, now there was love and always would be. So they sat there and cried together for the families they had lost for ever, and now they belonged, truly belonged, to each other, and Krystyna knew that whatever happened in the promised land, she would not leave these boys and they would not leave her.

She woke in the morning sprawled across Masha's bed. Adam and Marek were already up and playing. They had, apparently, been fed. Masha had seen to it. He was their big brother again now. Now, it was another day, and at the end of it they would a bit closer to Palestine.

Winter was fast approaching and the morning was cold, but at least it was sunny. As she mounted the motorcycle, Krystyna looked up at the mountains in the distance and shuddered. Just looking at them made her feel cold. The sidecar was well protected, and as they climbed higher she would be able to add more layers to protect the occupants from the wind. She was well supplied with clothes and if this had been Poland she wouldn't have worried but here she didn't know what to expect. She found a black-market fuel seller and tanked up completely. They would call in at Annecy and tank up again and buy food before they headed into the mountains. After that they would just have to keep going. The plan was to stay in Annecy overnight and make a very early start the next morning. That would give them the best chance of arriving in Italy while it was still reasonably light. She didn't want to get caught on the mountains after nightfall. The temperature would surely drop even further then, and with poor visibility the chance of an accident was greater. Anyway, a stop in Annecy would give them a chance to chicken out. It looked like about two hundred and fifty kilometres from Annecy to Milan but once they were in the St Bernard Pass there would be no turning back.

They kept up a good pace all morning. The sun glinted off the Jura Mountains on their left and she knew that some-where beyond them was Switzerland where they couldn't go. From time to time the road took them closer to the mountains and then Masha became excited. He wanted to see them, to get out and climb, but of course appearances are deceptive. They were still a long way off and in any case this was not a holiday and on top of that he was nine years old and nine-year-old boys don't climb mountains. So he had to be content to look. She told him that they would be turning into the mountains the next day and he would be able to see much more then because they would actually be driving right across them, and that got him more excited. He told Adam and Marek, in their safe space by his feet, all about it.

They reached Annecy late that afternoon and as soon as they had settled into a small hotel Krystyna took them off shopping. She found a sheepskin coat for herself and for the sidecar she bought fleeces to tuck in for insulation round the boys. It made it all a bit cramped, what with the diamonds and the banknotes and the boys, but there was no choice. The sidecar had a small luggage compartment at the back and their bags were already stuffed into there and what wouldn't go in was tied on top. For Masha she found a thick knitted balaclava and then she came across a motorcycle shop where she left the bike to be serviced. When they went back two hours later it was in tip-top condition, and she made Masha happy when she purchased a pair of goggles for him. He walked around the town in the balaclava and goggles attracting a lot of attention but she wasn't worried about that. There was no-one here who could hurt them. It was surely not reasonable that the British would have agents in a place like this. Dov had said to watch out for them in Milan, but not here.

The hotel room had a large radiator that was piping hot so she took the opportunity to do some washing and let it dry overnight. Marek was getting better without a nappy but there were still accidents and that meant washing. They all had hot baths too and it felt luxurious in sight of the snow-topped mountains to be so warm. Krystyna remembered her promise to herself that she could chicken out here and she gave it serious consideration, but actually there was already no turning back because how could they go all the way back to Poland? They could stay here, of course. They had enough money but what was a pleasant interlude was hardly a place to stay for the rest of their lives. Anyway, she had made the promise, and only Palestine would do, and that was somewhere on the other side of those mountains. She fell asleep on crisp white sheets, with the bag of diamonds beside her, and dreamt about her parents. She hadn't thought about them for a long time. She wished her father could be with her. He would take charge, he always had. He was a big man, strong as an ox, a woodsman in his time. The mountains would hold no fears for him. Well, she was her father's daughter, and they would hold no fears for her, either. In twenty four hours they would be across and safely on the other side, in Italy.

She woke to bright sunshine streaming through the windows and she felt good. Somehow she knew that this was going to be alright. She had no fear. She, who had lived for three years with the partisans in the forest, had killed to save a good man, had brought these three orphans this far, could cross a mountain range on a motorbike. She didn't know if there was a patron saint of such specific matters in the Catholic pantheon, so she said the Paternoster and hoped it would do.

16

God must have been listening to Krystyna Celinska that day, either that or he was guarding, for some reason best known to himself, three Jewish boys out of all the millions, but nothing stopped them.

It helped that a British military convoy was crossing ahead of them. As they climbed, snow started to fall, but the British had come prepared and they were preceded by a snow plough and by the time that and a dozen army lorries had driven over the road the surface was clear. The last lorry was full of soldiers and they leaned out and jeered but then Krystyna came up closer and they could see beneath the goggles and the thick furry hat was a woman, an old woman to boot, and they cheered, and it seemed that a camera was standard equipment for soldiers here because they too wanted to take photographs. Masha waved to them and they waved back and they took his picture too. They had nothing to fear from the British here.

There would be no stopping on this part of the journey, nowhere for the little ones to get out and play, so Masha had to keep them amused as best he could. As it got colder he found that harder to do because now he was so wrapped up in clothing he could hardly move. Adam wanted to peep up above the rim of the sidecar and when he saw the mountains he forgot the cold and he must have said something to Marek because he too put his head up and they chattered away to each other happily for a while. As the day progressed the sun rose higher and higher and it became strangely warm and so Krystyna stopped so they could all take one layer of clothing off. She gave the boys ten minutes to play in the snow by the roadside while the British lorries disappeared in the distance. Ten minutes was as much as she dared give them. After that time and no more she knew she could catch up with the lorries. They travelled quite slowly and it had been easy to keep up with them. The road dipped here and she could see the convoy as it dropped into a small valley several kilometres away.

She quickly put Adam and Marek back in the sidecar before the snow had a chance to penetrate their clothing and soak them in freezing water. Masha objected but she pointed to the convoy in the distance and pleaded and he gave in. There was a moment of panic as the wheels of the motorbike skidded on the road surface when she started up but this was all new to her, she had never been on such a contraption until only a few days ago, let alone taken one over a mountain range. It settled down though and she knew they couldn't afford to lose the protection of the lorries because the road would freeze over and become dangerous very quickly.

After the valley the road climbed inexorably and the temperature dropped suddenly as the sun disappeared behind a bank of dense grey clouds. Although the lorries were only just ahead now she knew she would have to stop again for them to put on the extra layer of clothing they had only recently taken off. She hadn't realised how suddenly the weather could change here. The convoy was travelling more slowly now, the four-tonners grinding up the slope with difficulty, so it was easy for the motorcycle combination to stay right behind. On the peak, the snow came down much more heavily, and for a little while she could see no vehicles in front of her and neither could she hear them over the sound of the motorbike's engine but then suddenly the road started to dip again and the snow stopped and there was the sun, and there were the lorries. They could see the road sloping away before them for at least five kilometres. This, Krystyna knew, must be Italy. They were over the worst. The British Army drivers must have felt the same relief she did because they picked up speed to what she considered the point of recklessness. Still, if she lost them now it wouldn't matter. Nothing could go wrong now.

It didn't for her, but it did for them. She came round a bend at speed and had to learn in one short lesson how to do an emergency stop, because there in front of them was a lorry at a nasty angle across the road with its bonnet crushed against the rock wall. Men were jumping out of the back and someone tried to prise open the door on the driver's side which was stoved in where it had hit an outcrop of rock. Steam was hissing from the radiator.

The rest of the convoy had continued on its journey. That seemed odd to Krystyna. Why hadn't they stopped to help? Well, perhaps they hadn't seen. Perhaps the lorry before just carried on round the bend ahead and this one hadn't been missed yet. They would be back. Meanwhile, the road was blocked. With a rock cliff on either side and the lorry more or less straight across, there was nowhere for her to pass.

There was a lot of shouting and general mayhem but no-one, just at this moment, seemed to be in charge of these men. There was obviously at least one serious casualty, the driver, but she couldn't see the co-driver from where she sat. What she could see was that no-one here seemed to have any idea what to do, and that gave her no option but to instruct Masha to watch the boys while she went forward to help.

'Excuse me Madam, but this is a military vehicle. Please stand clear.'

From the expression on Krystyna's face it was obvious she didn't know what the soldier was saying, so he tried Italian.

'Excusi Madama but no passa hero, comprendi?'

He was disappointed that this produced no better comprehension, but he was even more unhappy when this old woman simply pushed him out of the way and barged ahead. He shouted after her but to no avail. Before anyone could stop her she was standing on the running board of the lorry. She felt the man's pulse. It was weak, but then she saw why. The steering column was broken and a long shaft of metal had impaled his abdomen. She had seen many war wounds. She knew that this man was going to die if he didn't get medical treatment very soon.

Then a corporal appeared and instructed two of his men to take the wounded driver one at each shoulder and Krystyna saw with horror what he intended to do.

'No! No!' She screamed at him to stop. She shouted in Polish because it was the only language she had and he understood not a word but she made the meaning clear with her gestures. If they pulled him free, and the shaft was through an artery, he would bleed to death and die right there and then. The only chance he had was to leave him where he was. She needed something to pad the wound with and by signals tried to find out if the lorry carried a first aid kit. The corporal understood that. The first-aid kit was under the driver's seat. There was no possibility of getting it.

Somehow she managed to get one of the soldiers to find a clean cloth and she stuffed this around the wound. At all costs the bleeding had to be suppressed. She knew that from the partisans. A man who is bleeding is a man who is dying.

Krystyna could see they had already radioed for help, so all she had to do was keep him alive long enough for it to arrive. She felt his skin, it was cold. He was going into shock. She had some hard decisions to make. If they left him here, he would die of that before help came, but the only way to move him was to cut the steering column away. It would have to be that, but how? She tried to make the corporal understand cutting and he did. What she didn't know was that they were a detachment of Royal Engineers. In the back of the lorry they had not only saws but an oxyacetylene torch. The corporal checked there was no danger of a fuel leak, and then he got to work himself. Two men steadied the patient and in twenty minutes the steering column came away. Meanwhile he had instructed his men to take anything they could find on the vehicle to start a fire. They broke up the packing cases from the equipment they were carrying and used that. They scoured the mountain for firewood too but there were few trees at this height. Nevertheless, they got a blaze going and by the time the patient was lifted out of the vehicle they were able to lay him by the fire to get some warmth. It also meant they could get to the first-aid kit under the seat and within minutes he had had a first shot of morphine. The fire made everyone feel better. Masha brought Adam and Marek over to join the group by the flames and the men made a space for them. By this time a queue of traffic had backed up and more and more people came and stood by the heat, and those who could brought some fuel for the fire.

It took three hours for the medical team to arrive, by which time it was completely dark. It must have been a strange sight that greeted them. They brought with them a heavy-lift truck and that soon had the lorry moved to the side of the road, so now there was nothing to stop the traffic moving off again, including Krystyna, but now it was dark and she was tired. The corporal saw it on her face.

'Never mind love. I tell you what. Let's get this machine of yours on the lorry. We'll take you all down in that.'

She didn't know what he was saying, but when the men pulled down ramps from the back of the vehicle, and one started up the motorbike she panicked at first but then realised what they were doing.

Two hours later they were at a British Army barracks in Italy. They slept the rest of the night there and were treated to a bumper breakfast when they woke.

As the boys ate hungrily, soldiers came up to their table and thanked them. The words meant nothing but the meaning was clear. Then an officer came to talk to her. He spoke no Polish but he went away and five minutes later he was back with an interpreter.

'My name is Major Hughes. I've heard all about what happened last night. You will be pleased to know, I expect, that Private Matthews is going to make it. I've come to add my personal thanks, and the official thanks of the British Army, for the work you did last night. Without you he would have died. Where did you learn your first-aid?'

'In the Communist Partisans in Poland, Major, the Armia Ludowa. You know of it?'

'Yes, I've heard of it. Communists, eh?'

'Well, yes, but don't worry, it's just a name.' Bricha had warned her the British and Americans had a dim view of the Communists.

'I see. So, Mrs ..., I'm sorry, I don't know your name.'

'Celinska. Krystyna Celinska. And this is Masha, Adam and Marek, my grandchildren.'

'I see. And their parents?'

'The war, Major.'

'Oh, I see. Well, and where, may I ask, are you going with them?'

'To Trieste. We have family there, if they are still there.'

'Trieste? Now look, I don't know if you are aware, but the war might be over with the Germans but there is still fighting in that region. The Communists, I mean the Yugoslavs are having a spot of civil war over Trieste. It might not be all that safe. Perhaps you should reconsider.'

'Thank you for your advice, Major, and for the excellent breakfast, but I think it is a chance we will take. We are non-combatants. We will come to no harm.'

Major Hughes knew that was wildly optimistic, and so, as it happened, did Krystyna. She had taken this information on board, but she didn't want a British Army officer to know that.

'Well Mrs Celinska, I admire your courage, I'll say that. I will also issue you with an Army pass that will help you get through British controlled areas. It's not a lot but it might help. Wait here will you while I get that organised?'

'Yes, of course, and thank you.'

As it turned out, it took a long time and they stayed the whole day. She washed all their clothes in the army laundry and by the time they were dry it was too late to leave so they were made welcome for a second night. In the evening, while the children played on the sergeants' mess, she visited Private Matthews in the hospital. He was conscious, just, and he wanted to thank her too.

It felt strange. Bricha had warned her about the British. She knew that what they were going to attempt, to land in Palestine, was something the British would stop if they knew, but here they were guests of their army, receiving their gratitude. It made her chuckle.

It was a short drive from the British base to Milan, no more than three hours, Major Hughes reckoned, depending on traffic and the weather. She should show the pass at any army checkpoint, it would speed things up. She thanked him and loaded the children up into the sidecar. Masha wore an army beret on his head with great pride, and saluted the major as they set off. It had been another good interlude, and somehow the terror of the mountains had been overcome with the help of fate. She prayed, as she changed up through the gears and left the base behind her, that fate would stay on their side. It had, so far, been a hard journey and a tiring one, for all of them, but they had stayed safe, they were all well and, thanks to their friends in the British Army, they had a full tank of petrol and plenty of food. Next stop Milan, then Trieste, and then a ship for Palestine. It was all starting to seem possible.

17

It came to a shuddering halt about five kilometres short of Milan. Krystyna became aware of Masha prodding her in the side. At first she took no notice. He was prone to that sort of thing. But he became more insistent and finally she looked down and he gesticulated at the engine of the motorcycle. There were sparks coming from it. She pulled over abruptly and stopped on the grass verge and shouted at him to get out of the sidecar and help her with Adam and Marek. By now, there was smoke coming from somewhere under the seat and she didn't know if the fuel tank might explode but she kept the boys as far away as possible. There wasn't much traffic, and what there was just drove by without a second glance at what was going on. She took a chance and emptied the tail compartment of their baggage and then she took another risk and got some of the money out of the sidecar but then the machine burst into flames and she beat a hasty retreat.

There was nothing they could do but watch it burn. The sidecar appeared to be made of wood because it ignited readily and burned steadily. One or two drivers sounded their horns at the spectacle for no readily discernible reason, but no-one stopped to render assistance. They just stood there and stared in disbelief that this was happening. Adam started to cry, and Krystyna knew how he felt. She picked him up but it was as much to hide her own anguish as to relieve his. She didn't know if she felt the loss of the money more keenly or the motorbike. One was their passage to the promised land and the other was their transport to Trieste, and now neither of them existed. In a flash of time, everything had changed. What was alright before was now suddenly hopeless. She was left standing by the side of an Italian road with three children and no means of getting them anywhere. The flames finally ran out of combustible material to consume and subsided to a glow, and while they did that she counted out the money. It was in French francs, and there were tens of thousands of them, but she didn't know what that meant, if it was enough, and enough for what anyway?

She waited for the carcass of the machine to cool down, not just to sift through it for anything that might have survived, but to delay setting off on foot, the only viable option now. It didn't take long to search the remains, because there weren't many. And what she found was the leather bag. It was charred, and it was still hot and as she tried to pick it up it fell apart in her hands, but what fell out was diamonds, hundreds of them catching the weak winter sunlight. She scooped them up in her hands, still warm from the fire, but otherwise, as far as she could tell, quite unharmed. It takes more, apparently, than a short fire, to damage diamonds. Well, they had no transport, but they were still very wealthy. They would get to Milan and there they would use some of the diamonds to secure their onward transportation. She explained it to Masha and he told the little ones, who of course didn't understand and were still in shock from the fire. All they could see was that the nice sidecar that had been their home for the past few days no longer existed. The fire had temporarily warmed them, but now they were in danger from the growing cold. Krystyna opened the suitcases and found more clothes to wrap them in. She would carry one at a time, and Masha would have to carry at least one suitcase while the other toddler walked. It would be slow, but it was possible. She stuffed the diamonds loose into her coat pockets, and what banknotes were left went into the bags in the space now made by the clothes the boys were wearing.

Krystyna explained to the boys what they had to do, and pointed towards the city they could just see in the distance and promised them a slap-up meal when they arrived. Vehicles rumbled past without stopping and the backdraught of the lorries only served to make her feel more miserable about this. The diamonds meant a lot, but that was later, when they could be turned into food and warmth and transport. Out here, in the cold, they had no value. She found carrying one child as much as she could manage. It was a real struggle to carry a case as well, and on top of that she had to make sure that the other child was holding firmly onto the hem of her coat. They stayed as far as possible off the road itself for safety, but that meant walking through long grass and over rough ground and that made it even slower. She considered walking on the road because that would greatly increase the chance of someone stopping and picking them up, but with Adam and Marek it was just too dangerous. Army lorries thundered past and from ground level it was pretty scary, even for an adult. She considered waving the letter Major Hughes had given her but who was going even to look at it from the cab of a lorry? Anyway, she felt quite sure the Army's policy excluded giving lifts to refugees.

So they walked, and they got slower and slower. In despair, she sat the boys down in the grass. This was hopeless. The little ones couldn't help it. They just weren't ready for a walk like this, and she couldn't carry them both and the bags and Masha, bless, him, was trying but he was nine. One suitcase was a struggle for him. No, they would have to wait there while she tried to flag down a lift.

The problem was that no-one seemed to want to give a lift to an old refugee woman. The drivers had seen it all before, hundreds of times. If you stopped for one there would be more. She saw them looking the other way, in their nice warm vehicles, avoided her eye, pretending they hadn't seen her. And then she heard a different sound, not an engine at all, a sound she remembered from somewhere, a long time ago, the sound of a horse and cart. She knew immediately the best chance she had was with the boys, so she rushed back and dragged them to the side of the road. The cart was still a little way off. It moved really quite slowly. It looked empty, but the horse was old and thin and the driver wasn't going to ask any more than this of the poor beast. The traffic swerved round and horns were sounded angrily but the old man with the reins took no notice and neither did the horse. They looked like this was all quite normal. And as he approached the old man didn't avoid Krystyna's eye. On the contrary, he looked at her with interest and the expression on his face said he was interested to know what this old woman was doing with three children by the roadside.

As the cart pulled up the horse just stopped, as if it knew its master's wishes without any instruction. The old man said something but it was of course quite meaningless to Krystyna, but even so the obvious thing was to say something to him and he didn't know what she was saying either but after a mutually unintelligible conversation she and the boys and the bags were loaded up on the cart, and the horse, satisfied that they were all safely on board, moved off into the traffic. There was hay in the back of the cart and the boys were safe and warm in that. Krystyna sat next to the driver and all the way to Milan they kept up a pointless conversation over the noise of the traffic. They drove steadily through the outskirts of the city and then, by the side of a run-down house in a small dimly-lit street, the horse, unbidden by its master, came to a stop. This, it seemed, was home.

That was verified when the old man climbed down from the seat and went inside. Krystyna and the boys just stayed where they were, not knowing for sure if this was the end of the ride or what it was. Was that it, no goodbye? Or maybe he had said goodbye in Italian but she hadn't understood. On the other hand, it's pretty obvious when someone is saying goodbye, whether you know their language or not, and none of that had happened. It was as if the horse was in charge here. Then she noticed the old man hadn't even tied the animal up. It just stood there as if where else was it going to go? If this was its home, there was nowhere else.

Now a light appeared at the door and the old man came out again. He said something but there was no way of knowing if he was addressing them or the horse, but he took some hay from the back of the cart and put it down in a pile on the road for the animal. He looked at Krystyna and the boys as if he dimly remembered them and raised his hat to her. It might have meant hullo or goodbye, or it might have meant nothing, and then he disappeared inside again. Krystyna looked at Masha and he looked at her and they both shrugged their shoulders and laughed. Then they gathered up their belongings, each took a child by the hand, and went in search of a hotel.

Fifteen minutes later, which was as long as they could walk with two toddlers and all this baggage, they found a place. It was badly lit and not very welcoming, but it was obviously a hotel and it would do. The receptionist looked at this little group of people with deep suspicion and demanded payment in advance for the room. When Krystyna tendered US dollars his doubts were assuaged. You could never tell these days, there were a lot of strange people about. If she had known what he was saying Krystyna would have agreed with him. She had just had a ride with one of them.

The next priority was food for them all. Krystyna took the precaution of opening up the lining of her coat a little and sewing small pockets all around the hem to keep the diamonds, without them rattling and advertising their presence. The loose change, as it were, she kept in her pocket. Then they went out into the city and searched for a restaurant.

It had been a long day. First, Adam fell asleep over his food and then Marek did. Masha's eyes looked heavy and Krystyna knew how he felt. She had enough dollars left to pay for the meal and was grateful that they seemed to be a universal currency in Europe at this time. Tomorrow she would go to a bank and change the francs that they had salvaged. She would also need to start thinking about the diamonds. They were valuable, but she had no idea how valuable. She should, she supposed find a jeweller to give her a valuation but she remembered Avi's advice, even though he hadn't been talking about diamonds. She would need to show only one or two stones at a time.

The next morning she got rid of her francs at a bank and was given instead a large quantity of Italian banknotes in what seemed like impossibly high denominations and had no idea what they were worth. She went back to the hotel first to check their tariff, and that gave her some idea of the value of the lira, which it turned out was not a lot. The next decision was what to do about the children. She was reluctant to take them with her to a jeweller and Masha could see she was troubled by the decision and he volunteered to stay behind in the hotel and take care of the little ones. She promised to be no more than an hour. If she hadn't found someone in that time she would come back regardless. She told him to lock the door an let no-one in.

Milan was as full of foreign soldiers as each town they had been through so far. Here they seemed to be Italian and British mostly, as far as she could tell. She had Major Hughes' letter with her, just in case it might get her out of trouble. She didn't know what kind of trouble she could get into but she had learned so far that it came in many shapes and sizes and you could never have too much help when it happened.

She found in the centre of the city there were a number of jewellers and she walked past several trying to get a feel for the most respectable. Finally, she picked one with a large brass plate by the door and gold writing on the window and what looked to her like some very expensive items on display. As soon as she walked through the door she knew it was a mistake. Her coat, which she hadn't thought about before now, suddenly felt extremely shabby. Milan was shabby. It was trying to recover from the war. But this place looked like there had been no war, like it expected only people in fur coats to walk through the door, and she was met by an assistant in a black frock coat who looked over his glasses at her as if to inspect a piece of rubbish blown in by the wind.

She asked if anyone there spoke Polish and it was clear from his manner that no-one did and even if they did they didn't want to talk to her and she fled. She realised what she must look like, a refugee from eastern Europe begging. The diamonds didn't make her feel rich, because that man had seen her for what she really was. She couldn't explain to him because she couldn't speak his language. No, she would have to find a shop that was rather less grand, one where they would understand a diamond or two even if they didn't understand Polish.

She found it down a side street. It was, she guessed, a pawnbroker as well, and as she went in a man looked up from a desk at her. He had a jeweller's eyeglass and was examining a piece in his hand for a customer. He said something contemptuous and handed it back. The customer sounded angry but the jeweller just shrugged his shoulders dismissively and turned to her as if to say the interview was over and the customer brushed past her and stormed out. She didn't think this boded well, but still, she was here now.

Now, he looked her up and down as if to say she could not

possibly have anything that might interest him and she had served her purpose but now she could leave. She sat down, though, and he looked up in surprise. She asked him if he spoke Polish and unsurprisingly he looked at her blankly. She could tell he wanted her to go. Slowly, she put her hand on her pocket and withdrew one medium-sized stone. She held it out in her fingertips and the lights of the shop brought it to life. She didn't take her eyes off his, though, and what his eyes showed was greed. Yes, she had come to the right place.

Instead of reaching out for the stone he picked up the telephone and said something briefly into it. Then he held out his hand. While he was looking at it through his eyeglass the door opened and a small man walked in as if he was expected. Krystyna didn't turn round to look at him because she didn't want to turn her back on the jeweller. She watched him instead in a mirror on the wall behind his head, and he came and sat down. The two men spoke a few words and then the small man introduced himself. It wasn't Italian he spoke, but whatever it was she understood it no better than if it had been. So he tried another language and that was no good so she spoke to him and there was a look of recognition in his eyes and he switched to Polish.

'Good, I speak a little Polish, if you speak slowly please. I am Gheorghe Mihailescu, from Romania, I speak many languages.'

'I see. Well, Mr Mihailescu, would you please tell this gentleman …'

'Signor Amaduzzi.'

'Well, please tell Signor Amaduzzi I wish to sell this diamond. How much will he give me for it?'

There followed a translation and Amaduzzi nodded his head in understanding.

'Signora, Signor Amaduzzi asks, where did you get this diamond from?'

'Tell him I haven't come here to tell him my life story, just to sell a diamond.'

'Madam, please …'

'Tell him it was a gift.'

'A gift?'

'Yes, that's right.'

'I see. One moment please.'

The jeweller looked at the stone again, then he put it on a small pair of scales on his desk and they waited while he took a reading.

'Signor Amaduzzi says this stone is over three carats. It is, he says, a big gift.'

'Yes, well, that's none of his business is it?'

The Romanian repeated this and Amaduzzi chuckled. He was weighing up not only the diamond but this woman too.

'Signora, Signor Amaduzzi says he can give you a hundred and fifty thousand lire for this stone.'

Krystyna looked not at Amaduzzi but at Mihailescu instead. The little man looked uneasy. His face told her she was being taken for a ride.

'Please tell Signor Amaduzzi that I will not sell at that price. Tell him I would like the diamond back, that I will find a jeweller who will pay the proper price.'

Now, she looked at the jeweller. She wanted to see his reaction. He was watching the Romanian so he didn't know she was watching him, and his face showed greed again, and fear that he might lose this stone. He had already assessed the amount of profit he would make if he stitched up this stupid Polish woman, and he didn't like the idea of losing it. He offered two hundred thousand.

'Tell Signor Amaduzzi three hundred thousand, no less.'

She worked on the reasonable assumption that he had offered a maximum of half its value. She watched Amaduzzi again as he heard this demand and saw his brow crease in anger. His bluff was being called and he didn't like it.

Mihailescu spoke to her and as she moved to watch him she noticed Amaduzzi turning the stone over in his podgy fingers. Now, he tossed it from one hand to the other, as if he was weighing up its real worth to him, and as Mihailescu spoke she became aware that he did this over and over and when she turned back to him the stone was no longer there.

She looked at him in alarm. 'Signor Mihailescu, please inform Signor Amaduzzi that I would like my diamond back. Now, if you please.'

She waited. Mihailescu spoke to her again, but now he showed a great deal of nervousness.

'Signora, Signor Amaduzzi asks, what diamond you are talking of please?'

'What? The diamond I gave him, the one we have been discussing.'

She watched as Mihailescu translated this anxiously, and Amaduzzi answered calmly and shook his head as if to apologise for some misunderstanding.

'Signora, there is no diamond. Signor Amaduzzi asks what you mean please.'

Krystyna was angry, not only with the jeweller but with herself for being so easy to dupe.

'Tell him I will go and fetch a policeman, and that I will insist that you are a witness to this theft.'

Amaduzzi chuckled now while he gave Mihailescu his answer. He had her on the run.

'Signor Amaduzzi says please, he is a respected business-man here in Milan, The police know him. You are a vagrant from Poland. They will believe him, not you. I am sorry Signora.'

She could see this was true, he was sorry. He hadn't expected this turn of events. She breathed heavily while she considered her options. There weren't many.

'Signor Mihailescu, please tell Signor Amaduzzi that it is not quite how he thinks. You see, I have a friend, and my friend will be angry and hurt him if he does not return my property. Please tell him that.'

He did, and the jeweller laughed and looked around the little shop as if to say oh yes, and where is this friend of yours?

'Signora, he knows you have no friend. He says you must leave now. Please, it would be best.'

Krystyna stood up, slowly and deliberately. Mihailescu started to look relieved. The expression on his face changed, though, when she pulled out the pistol, cocked it, and pointed it at the jeweller's head.

'Signor Mihailescu, please introduce Signor Amaduzzi to my friend. If he has any doubt that I will kill him, please inform him that the man who gave me the diamond was an SS officer and he died by this gun, so he should be in no doubt that this is his last moment on Earth if the answer is no.'

She waited while the Romanian translated all of this as best he could. Amaduzzi shouted at her and angrily slammed the stone down on the desk.

'Signora, Signor Amaduzzi says please take your diamond and go.'

'No.'

'No?'

'No. I came here to sell it. I want the money, not the stone.'

'Signora, he says alright, he will pay you three hundred thousand lire, but please go.'

'No.'

'No?'

'No. The price has now gone up. I want four hundred thousand. It is the penalty for his sin.'

'His sin?'

'Yes, please translate that.'

He did. Amaduzzi's eyes became vicious now. She would have been afraid of him now, if she hadn't been pointing a gun at his head. Slowly, as if he hated every movement, he reached into a drawer. The tension increased on her trigger finger. She was ready for him. But what he produced was not a weapon, it was a wad of notes. He counted the money out and slammed that down next to the diamond. With her free hand she scooped it up and stuffed it into her pocket, except for one note which she gave to the Romanian.

'Signor Mihailescu, this it to say thank you for your services. Now tell your friend that I am going, and he should remain seated where he is until I am out of that door. Good day to you.'

She didn't breathe until the door closed behind her. She had the money. She had succeeded. It felt good. Actually, it felt very good.

18

She took the boys out and bought them all ice creams, and for herself she bought a coat, not a very good coat because there were no very good coats for sale, but even so a lot better than the one she travelled in from Warsaw.

Over the next two days she visited every jeweller she could find in the city and at each one she got more confident and obtained a better price for a single stone. Many of the jewellers shops had Jewish names over them and these ones were closed down. She presumed their owners had been murdered.

Now, she had a good supply of Italian money, and she needed to find a way to get to Trieste. She enquired at the railway station but that was a forlorn hope. No, there were no trains, she was told, none at all. There might be a train next week, to Rome, but Rome was no use to her. She began to get impatient. She took the boys out into the city but it wasn't a very interesting place, especially for children, and that soon palled. She bought them coats as well and that made them happy, but even the excitement of new coats wore off after a while. That was when she saw what she was looking for. She took them back to the hotel and collected their belongings and checked out. The receptionist said he was sorry to see them go. Well, that might or might not have been true.

Then she took the boys back and found the taxi rank she was looking for. The driver got out and loaded their bags into the boot and held the door open for the signora and the bambini. Then, when they were seated, he said something which she took to be where do you want to go, and she said Trieste. He swivelled round in his seat and repeated it in a way that clearly meant was she serious. She said it again, Trieste. He said no, which she understood, and she replied yes, which he didn't, so he got out and opened the boot and started to remove the cases onto the pavement.

Krystyna got out and put her hand on his arm and he stopped what he was doing for now. Then from her coat she took a wad of banknotes and started to count them out. He watched without interest, but she kept counting and suddenly he found himself paying attention. When she stopped she still had some uncounted notes and he looked at those. She took one more and put it in her other hand, the one that contained his fare. He smiled and said yes, and that she understood. Then she split the money in two and put half into his hand. Waving the other half in his face she said Trieste, several times, and he was in no doubt that he would get that when they arrived. Well, he could live with that. The idea of taking these people only as far as Verona and chucking them out there had briefly occurred to him, but not as a serious option. Now, he surely would have to take them all the way.

They set off with high hopes and Krystyna and the boys sat back to enjoy the ride. For the first time since leaving Warsaw, she had no responsibility for the journey. Now, she could let someone else take care of everything. He was courteous to her and the boys, and stopped from time to time for a toilet break for the children. She wished she could talk to him but she couldn't. She hadn't been able to have a proper conversation with anyone in her own language for a long time. She chatted to Masha, but a nine-year old boy doesn't have the same interests as a sixty-seven year-old woman. Nonetheless, she enjoyed the drive. It was so different from her home country. She was familiar with the Polish country-side, and the capital, and more lately the forests, but none of it was anything like this. She had had no notion that such places existed as she had seen on this journey. Being with the partisans during the war had opened her eyes to another world, but this was different again. Now she could relax she had time to think, and what she thought was about Palestine, what it was going to be like. She had heard about the desert but she couldn't imagine it. All she knew was that it was going to be hot, and after the winter in Europe that sounded not unattractive. Until now there had been no future, because the present had fully occupied her thoughts, coping with day-to-day existence, but now the future was something she had to face. For the boys, she could imagine, it would be good, in a new country with good opportunities, but for her? What was Palestine to her? She was only going for the boys, for Marek especially. What she was afraid of, she now realised, was that once they got there they might be taken over by the authorities, because after all they were really orphans and she wasn't actually their grandmother, and she would be left on her own. Well, when they got there she would ask them what they wanted to do, and if they wanted to stay with her she had enough money to set up home for all four of them. She wouldn't ask them now. In any case, Adam and Marek were too young even to understand. It would come down to Masha. What he decided would perhaps decide the future for all of them.

They got as far as Padua. There, on the far side of the town, they hit a roadblock set up by the army. She wasn't sure which army it was but even so a roadblock is a roadblock. Some of the soldiers at least must have been Italian, because the driver got out and spoke with them. He came back and spread his hands out in a gesture that could only mean sorry, we can't go any further.

Krystyna got out of the car. She had to know what the problem was, if it was temporary, and they could wait a while before proceeding, or this was something worse. None of the soldiers spoke Polish. They seemed to be a mixture of Italians and British. She got out the letter from Major Hughes and showed it to them and they just shrugged their shoulders as if it was all very well saying she should be allowed past but they had their orders and letter or no letter no-one was passing.

She got angry and started shouting at them and at first they ignored her temper but in the end one of them got on the field telephone and called someone and asked her to wait, showed her half an hour on his watch, and she understood. She didn't know what might happen in half an hour but she had seen him calling so she assumed that after that time someone would come who could deal with this.

They did, in the form of a British Army sergeant. Unfortunately, he didn't speak Polish either. He was the unit interpreter, but that meant he spoke English, Italian and German, but not Polish. However, he came over to the car and tried his best. He looked at the driver, and then he looked at Krystyna, and then he looked at the boys, and then he spoke to Masha. He spoke in a language that meant nothing to her but sounded like she had heard it before if only she could remember where.

It was Yiddish.

He asked Masha if he could translate for him, and the boy said he would try.

'OK, my name is Sergeant Barry Silver. I'm from London, and I'm serving with the British Army, in the Gloucestershire Regiment.'

Masha stumbled over a lot of this, but Krystyna got the gist of it.

'You are going to have to trust me, and to help you I am going to show that I trust you, by telling you something very secret.'

He paused, not only to let Masha translate, but for Krystyna to see how serious this was.

'I know these boys are Jews, and I know where you are going, all right? How do I know? Because as well as being with the British, I am also in Bricha. Do you know what that means?'

Krystyna nodded. She looked at this man intensely. She had to trust him, she knew that. She let him continue.

'Good. Now I have to tell you something. Trieste is closed. There is fighting going on between the Communists and the Yugoslav nationalists. I can't explain it, but there are no ships going into the port or out again. The port is closed, so there is no chance of you getting where you want to go by boat from there.'

He glanced furtively at the driver, as if by saying the word Palestine he might give the game away, but the driver wasn't interested in this meaningless conversation. He was staring idly out of the window.

'Now, have you by any chance got a map with you?'

Krystyna said yes and got out the school atlas and opened it at the page for Italy. Sergeant Silver was surprised, like everyone else, but drew it closer and tried to find Padua.

'Now, look here. This is where you are now, Padua, and there is Trieste, where you were going. My advice to you is to turn west, back the way you have come, I'm afraid, and head for Genoa. From there you should be able to find a boat to take you to Marseille. It's in France, over here, see?'

Krystyna nodded. They had come from France, she said.

'Well, I'm sorry, but now you're going back. The good news is that Bricha is running a ship from Marseille to, you know, the other place ....', he stopped and did a quick mental calculation, 'on the fourteenth. That gives you, let me see, eleven days. It's enough, if you get a boat from Genoa in time. We have a man there, I'll give you his address. He should be able to help you. Do you understand all of this?'

'Yes, and thank you Sergeant Silver. I'm sorry it has turned out like this, when we thought were almost there, but worse things happened in the war, and we will push on, we will go to France, to Marseille.'

He gave her back the letter. 'It says here that you saved a man's life, a soldier.'

'Does it? I don't know what it says.'

'No, well. You know, in my religion we have a saying, he who saves one life, it is as if he saved the world. It is my hope that you will be blessed on this journey. Goodbye to you.'

He shook her hand, and then he shook Masha's hand and thanked him for his help and he looked at the beret, the one from the Royal Engineers, which was too big but the boy wore it with pride, and he smiled. He had seen many strange things, and he would say a prayer for these people, that they would reach the promised land.

Then he spoke with Giovanni, the driver, and what he said was that these people were going back where they came from and the driver shrugged his shoulders. Well, it was better than going all the way to Trieste. He would get back that night to his home and his family. He liked these people and he was sorry they hadn't made it, but he would at least make certain they got back to Milan safely. Sergeant Silver said they weren't going to Milan, they were going to Genoa. Giovanni's eyes opened wide. Genoa! This was getting crazier. Well Milan first and then if they had enough money he would see. He slammed the door shut as if to remind everyone whose car this was, and accelerated away back the way he had come.

They arrived back in Milan late in the evening. Giovanni's wife came out to greet him home and shout at him for making her worried about him, but then she saw the children in the car and some kind of argument ensued between husband and wife and the end result was that she came out to Krystyna and said she must bring the children in. It was late, and they must stay the night. Krystyna didn't understand this, but the woman opened the back door and took the children out and Krystyna had no choice but to follow her into the house. An hour later, when they had all eaten together around the kitchen table, she understood that they were to stay. She hugged Giovanni's wife and said thank you in Polish.

By the morning she had managed to wash some clothes for the children and nappies for Marek and they had dried overnight over the big fire in the kitchen and after they were all loaded up into the taxi Krystyna gave the rest of the money, and more, to the driver and she wanted to give some to his wife too but the woman would not accept it. Well, when they got to Genoa she would give him some more and she knew he would take it.

It took all day to drive to Genoa. There were numerous roadblocks and each one took time to get through and by the time they arrived it was already dark and Krystyna worried about Giovanni. He didn't look worried, though, she paid him well and he looked pleased, and he insisted on shaking hands with Masha and kissing the little ones before he drove off into the night. Sitting in the back of a car all day had been tiring. The priority was to find somewhere to stay again, and food for them all, and in the morning she would look for the address Sergeant Silver had given her.

As they walked through the town they could smell the sea and that evoked ideas of their onward journey to Palestine. It had been a big backward step coming here but somehow, being near the sea, it seemed just the opposite. With any luck they would now have done with overland journeys. No, Genoa felt good. Masha became excited, and when they found a small restaurant on the waterfront he insisted they stop there and eat supper overlooking the harbour.

They slept deeply that night to the sound of the occasional ship's horn as a constant reminder of why they were here. To Krystyna it seemed more than ever that they would make it to Palestine. They had met good people on their journey, and some bad ones, but there had, she realised as she thought back, been more good ones. As she started to doze off she pondered this, and said a prayer for all the people who had helped, and then she said one for the boys, and for their parents, and she was going to say one for her own children and grandchildren but she fell asleep.

19

She found Vittorio in a bicycle shop on the other side of the harbour from their pensione. She didn't know if he was the proprietor, or the owner let him use it as a branch office of Bricha, but he seemed to know who she was, or more specifically he knew about Mordechai Levinson and spoke about him in a hushed tone. Was that because of his mother or because of the fact of them having come this far from Warsaw? Either way, he was able to help. There was a coastal steamer due to leave for Marseille the next day. He knew the captain and would make the arrangements for her, only she would need money, and he could let her have a little if necessary. There was no need, she had money.

They spent that day on holiday, another of their little interludes, when everything that could be done had been done so they had nothing to do now but enjoy themselves. It was milder here. The early winter sun still had some warmth in it and they sat on the harbour wall and enjoyed the feeling on their backs. Krystyna held one child in each arm. She didn't want to lose them into the sea. Masha she had to trust to be sensible. Anyway, after nearly drowning not so long ago he was in no hurry to go into water again.

They ate lunch at a little outdoor cafe. Postwar Italy couldn't provide a very rich menu but they had come from postwar Poland and didn't expect much. They ate fish, even the little ones, and Krystyna drank wine and it really felt like a holiday. She felt all the better because of what they had achieved, that this day was deserved, by all of them. Adam and Marek had done so well, as if they knew that they had to help her with this and not add to her burden.

They went by the bicycle shop as the sun went down and Vittorio was able to confirm that the arrangements had been made. The boat sailed at six-thirty. They would need to be on board by six. No problem.

And indeed, as if to say this was all going to succeed, there was no problem. By six forty-five the boat was steaming out between the harbour walls into the Mediterranean Sea. The captain advised her that the trip was likely to take until some time the following morning unless they were boarded for inspection by the British navy, which had many ships patrolling the area. Krystyna asked what they were looking for but since they were mainly using sign language to communicate at all he was unable to say. She wondered if it was refugees, like them, but on second thoughts, looking at the captain and this old boat, she reckoned it was more likely to be contraband. In fact Captain Matteoli's business was arms smuggling, goods that started in the dumps of captured German weapons and ended, after a circuitous route to evade British and Italian forces, in the hands of Yugoslav guerillas. The return trip to France was usually with an empty hold so these paying passengers made a nice extra bit of profit for him.

The trip gave Krystyna a chance to tackle the ever-present problem of laundry again, and when she persuaded the engineer to allow her to hang nappies on the hot pipes in the engine room he made her promise, as best he could with no Polish, not to tell the captain.

The wind was surprisingly strong out at sea but they managed to shelter in the lee of the superstructure most of the time and enjoy what little sun there was. The food they were served was good, even if it was fish again, which Adam complained about, and Krystyna shared a bottle of rough red wine with the captain and the engineer over lunch and again at dinner.

Unsurprisingly, they all slept especially well that night. The rocking of the boat and the constant thrum of the engine seemed no bar to falling off for any of them, and in Krystyna's case the wine helped as well. The captain wanted to give Masha some but she had prevailed. He asked how old the boy was and when she held nine fingers up he laughed and said something to the effect that his son was only eight and could already outdrink any woman. Looking at Matteoli, Krystyna was inclined to believe him.

It must have been a fast crossing, because they had hardly finished their breakfast the next morning when the captain came to tell them to get their bags ready. Krystyna went out on deck and there it was, the French coast. It was just a line on the horizon but it gradually grew bigger and an hour later they were within sight of the harbour at Marseille. Captain Matteoli came to see her and tried to give her some important information without the benefit of actual words. The best she could make of it was that the French police had a large contingent in the harbour and he, for reasons of his own, did not want to dock. He would pull alongside the ship that his passengers were looking for. It had been in harbour since yesterday, he was informed on the radio, and they would board from his boat without touching French soil. Well, she could see no problem with that. Until she saw the ship, anyway. The Levantine Trader towered above the little coastal steamer, or it seemed like it to her standing on the deck of the smaller boat. The crew of the Levantine Trader threw down a rope ladder and a man climbed down to talk to her. And miraculously he spoke Polish. His name, he said, was Dan, and he knew who she was. They had been expecting her. He said they would pull the little ones up in a sling but she and Moise would have to climb up. She was shocked when she heard him say Moise and realised that it meant they had made it, they were safe now, and the boys could use their real names. The relief of that almost, but not quite, overcame the anxiety she felt about the rope ladder. She didn't know if she was more afraid for Moise or herself. Well, she had fought with the partisans, this was a small thing, but Moise was a little boy and she was terrified for him. He wasn't though, and he was halfway up before she had time to realise he was on it at all. She didn't know whether to watch in case he fell and she had the slightest chance of catching him, or she should just close her eyes and pray. But he was up and over the rail of the Levantine Trader before she had time to decide and she found herself breathing again to make up for lost time. Then Adam and Mordechai went up in a sling one at a time, which just left her. Someone shouted come on Grandma and that was enough to rile her and she went up in double-quick time just to spite them. A sailor hoisted their luggage up by rope, and there they were, on board the vessel that was going to take them to the promised land.

Dan was there on deck to meet her and he said well done which she found a little patronising but when she thought about it it wasn't really. Not many women her age would climb up the side of a ship. On the other hand, not many women her age would do a lot of the things she had done.

'Dan, where is Masha, I mean Moise?'

'Oh him, don't worry, he's off exploring the ship.'

'What, already? He shouldn't have done that. It might not be safe.'

Dan looked her squarely in the eye. 'Mrs Celinska, look around you. With only two exceptions, everyone on this ship is Jewish. Moise is home.'

'Home? I see. Two you say. I assume you count me, so who is the other one who's not Jewish?'

'The captain, Johansson. He's Norwegian American. I don't know if he has a religion, apart from the sea. Come on, bring the little ones and I'll introduce you.'

'Me? Why would the captain want to meet me?'

'Because it's you we've been waiting for. Well, not just you. The boys, especially Mordechai.'

'Really? What, do these people think he is the messiah or something?'

He laughed. 'Don't suggest such a thing. These people, as you call them, have been to hell and back. They're very vulnerable. Tell them the messiah is on board and half of them will believe you. No, you may not realise it but the story of Roza Levinson and the Nazi gold has spread around Palestine and beyond. She has become something of a legend, and now we have her son on the ship. People are talking about him and, well, if not the messiah he is, shall we say, seen by many as a good omen. We were due to sail earlier but when we got a message from Genoa that you were coming we decided to wait. Anyway, come on, I'll take you to the bridge. Here, let me take Mordechai. Which one is he?'

Krystyna handed him over, and as she did so she felt a strong sense that these people had now taken possession of him, that they had already adopted him as their mascot and she felt a pang of something indefinable but to do with loss. Dan, though, saw the look.

'Don't worry, no-one is taking him from you. You have come a long way together, and if we can do anything it is to ensure that you stay together. I promise you that.'

They walked along the deck to some steep steps leading to the bridge.

'You? And who exactly are you with, Dan? Bricha, I suppose.'

'No, not exactly.'

'Then exactly who?'

He smiled. 'I can see already what you're made of. I know now how you came this far. No, I'm in Haganah, I'm a soldier. Do you know what Haganah is?'

'Yes, someone told me about it. The army of Palestine.'

'Well, not quite. The army of Palestine at the moment is the British Army, because they occupy the country. When we have our own homeland there, then yes, we will be its defence force. Now, mind your step here. OK? Good, nearly there.'

He knocked respectfully on the entrance door to the bridge and a loud voice ushered him in. He wasn't given time to make the introductions.

'Aha, so here you are, the amazing Krystyna Celinska who brought three more saved children to us. Wonderful, wonderful, and they told me you were a grandmother but surely there has been some mistake? You are much too young.'

Dan translated this with a wry smile, including the compliment, and Krystyna blushed. It was silly, but it was a long time since anyone had bothered to say such a thing to her. Captain Johansson stood at over two metres and he was almost as broad as he was long. His presence filled the bridge with both his physical size and his personality. On his head was a battered nautical cap with a large amount of gold braid on the brim, but he wore it at such a jaunty angle a shock of Viking hair escaped from it on all sides. He had an enormous smile which showed the teeth he still had and those that were missing. The captain had been in one or two fights in his life, but teeth were the only part of him that came off badly.

Dan, by comparison, she now saw was small and Jewish-looking, a product of the ghetto and the yeshiva, but for all that he also had a strong colour to his face, the result of two years working on a farm in Palestine, and he had a hard look too, a look she remembered from the partisans, men who knew how to laugh and sing but who carried memories that gave them that edge, that hardness they never lost. Dan and the captain came from different worlds, but they were the men fate had put in charge of this ship and these saved souls. In those seconds, Krystyna weighed them both up and found them satisfactory. They were men she could deal with.

The interview with Captain Johansson was over almost before it started, and she was ushered down the steps again to the deck. There, they were quickly surrounded by people who wanted to see the baby Mordechai. He was passed from one woman to another amid a babble of chattering in a dozen languages and to her relief Adam was taken up too. These women mostly just wanted to hold a baby, and she wondered if they had lost what she had lost and knew that of course they had. There were children on deck too, running around laughing and screaming, and she was quite unable to guess who belonged to whom. It was a community of one family. Dan said there were over seven hundred people on board, and from the noise she could believe it.

What she could not avoid noticing was the obvious poverty. Whatever had been possible to steal from them had been stolen. Their clothes were like hers, worn and shabby. They had bad skin and teeth and all the other symptoms of malnutrition and everywhere she looked were people with a limp or some other defect. These were not whole people, they were badly damaged. But still, they had come this far, like she had, and they were going home, and because of that they smiled and laughed with each other. It was both sad to see and a joy at the same time.

Dan watched her watching them with amusement. 'Yes, interesting, isn't it? What people they are. Now let me introduce you to two very special women. Krystyna, this is Sarah and Rachel. They're both Polish, from Lublin, and I have asked them to help you look after the boys on the voyage.'

Krystyna shook their hands. Sarah was a healthy-looking girl of perhaps seventeen, thin, like most of them, but she radiated energy even so. Rachel, on the other hand, did not. It was impossible to judge how old she was. She was shy, and looked down at her feet and Krystyna saw across one cheek an ugly scar which was perhaps the reason for the shyness. She deliberately selected Mordechai to give her but the girl refused. She said nothing but shook her head vigorously, and put her arms out to take Adam. It was as if she didn't consider herself good enough to take charge of this golden child she had heard so much about. Sarah explained.

'Please excuse my sister, Madam Celinska, she does not speak. I speak for her. She will be happy to look after Adam for you, but not Mordechai.'

'Yes of course my dear.' She wanted to ask why but knew it would only add to Rachel's embarrassment, so she handed both children over and as she put Adam into Rachel's arms she saw an unmistakable look in her eyes, the look you see in a mother's face and Adam made this girl happy, or as happy as it was possible to be, and Krystyna knew that Rachel and Adam were going to get on very well. He put his arms round her neck and clung to her and everyone laughed, Rachel included. It was the finest thing he could have done.

For the rest of that day she saw the boys only fleetingly. It took a while to let go of them and feel safe but Rachel and Sarah brought the little ones to her regularly, on Dan's instructions, and from time to time she spotted Moise running around the deck with a gang of boys about his own age, and once or twice he caught her eye and smiled or he called to her and he knew he was still hers. Now, she could relax.

The living conditions on the ship could only be described as squalid. She was used to living in hard conditions but this was something else. There were simply too many people on board for it to be sanitary. Everywhere she went there was the same smell, of dirty people and overflowing toilets. She quickly found the galley and there it wasn't much better. She had fed men in the forest with primitive facilities but here, even if it was a properly-equipped galley, it was old and it was far too small to cope. People rushed around chaotically carrying pans of steaming soup. Soup was the mainstay in the forest and clearly it was the same here. Soup you could put anything into, food people might baulk at eating otherwise.

For want of anything else to do, she rolled her sleeves up and got stuck in. No-one seemed to be in charge and since Nature abhors a vacuum Krystyna gradually began to assert her authority. Those who spoke Polish were quickly assigned tasks as her assistants and those who didn't became the assistants' assistants. Everyone seemed to know who she was and perhaps it was for that reason that they accepted her orders, or perhaps it was simply that it was good that someone knew what they were doing.

The food supplies were monotonous but there seemed to be enough of them at least. There were all the ingredients for bread but no-one had made any because no-one knew how to. Soup was alright as far as it went but she knew that the people would appreciate fresh bread and she set about picking the most likely bakers among the volunteers and teaching them the art of bread making. The galley and its ovens had been built for a cargo ship with a crew of perhaps twenty or so. Now, they had to cater for seven hundred, and that meant working round the clock. What Krystyna needed to know, first of all, was how long the voyage was going to take. She asked for someone to go and see Captain Johansson but there were no volunteers. He had, apparently, a reputation and they were all afraid of him. Well, she could do that herself.

He said he didn't know, three days, perhaps, four, even more, if the engines didn't pack up. He also didn't know when they would be sailing because the port authorities were making some kind of fuss about them. Dan was on the dockside right now trying to sort it out. She should wait until he got back.

She sat in a corner of the bridge to keep out of the way and while she sat she looked. She didn't know much about ships, in fact she knew nothing, but she could see for herself that this one had seen better days. The metalwork was rusty and what paint was left was trying hard to become detached. Even the chair the captain sat on had a broken leg tied up with electrical wire. He saw where her eyes went and laughed. He spoke to her through one of the bridge crew.

'I know what you're thinking. You think my old girl isn't going to make it across the Mediterranean. Well, let me tell you something Mrs Celinska. You could be right. I bought this old tub in the States for this run and it was the best I could get for the money. How we got her across the Atlantic I won't try to explain but I can tell you it took a lot of seamanship and not a little prayer. Are you a Christian, Mrs Celinska?'

'Yes Sir.'

'Well, good, because we're going to need all the prayers we can muster on this trip.'

'What about them?' Her arms swept across the ship to mean the passengers. 'Jewish people are good at praying, you know.'

'Yes, but they're all busy praying for their Messiah to come. They seem to think Captain Johansson is a miracle worker and so God can concentrate on other things.'

Just then Dan knocked and entered the bridge. He smiled gravely at Krystyna and reported to the captain.

'They won't let us leave. It seems the British have got wind of where we're going. They've asked the French authorities to hold us here. We can't leave port and we can't disembark the passengers. They mean to starve us out.'

Captain Johansson turned to Krystyna and his face was now deadly serious. Dan translated for him.

'Mrs Celinska, I don't know whose side God is on today, but I think you had better start praying, don't you?'

20

They say that every problem has a solution. What they could add is that given enough money that solution can usually be found.

The British had the ability to put pressure on the French, but on the ground, or to be more precise on the dockside at Marseille, the French government was a long way away. There were people here, people who could let a ship sail without authority if there was enough money to bribe them.

Captain Johansson, Dan and one or two of the others debated the problem but they knew the answer all along, except it wasn't the right answer because what money the captain had brought from the well-wishers of America had been spent getting the Levantine Trader this far. Marine fuel was expensive and in any case mostly had to be bought on the black market, and then there was food for seven hundred passengers. No, he couldn't put together anything like the sort of amount it would take.

The bridge went quiet while they absorbed this information. They knew that the British were serious, and they knew they had enough food on board for only a few days. More importantly, the water tanks might not even last out that long, just for drinking and cooking, let alone washing. For once the captain was silent. He just didn't have an answer.

Krystyna took advantage of the silence to remind them that she was still here. She asked Dan to interpret.

'Can you please tell me how much we would need, to bribe these officials?'

The captain listened to Dan and then raised his eyebrows.

'Without meaning to be insulting my dear lady, unless you happen to have shall we say about two thousand dollars in your pocket ....'

Krystyna stood up and put her hand in her pocket. It looked like a joke, and no-one was in the mood for jokes.

'These are each worth something more than three hundred thousand Italian lire. How many would you need?'

Three hours later, having taken on extra water in jerry cans that now lined the decks, the Levantine Trader steamed out of the harbour mouth. Krystyna swore all on the bridge to secrecy. It would not do for people to know she was walking around the ship with a king's ransom in diamonds in her pocket.

Since she was going to be working in the kitchen, she was persuaded that Captain Johansson should lock the coat with its precious cargo in the safe in his cabin. As the ship ploughed into the Mediterranean, she got to work baking bread for the multitude. It was simply impossible to bake enough for everyone, but there was at least enough for everyone to get a taste. The soup was passable, but the bread was something that the people on the Levantine Trader trader would tell their families about in years to come. They might have exaggerated its wonderful flavour, and the texture as it melted in your mouth, but it was after all the first fresh bread most of them had tasted for years.

Krystyna insisted that all three of her grandchildren were brought together at mealtimes so they would eat together, and afterwards the tables were moved and suddenly there were musicians, a couple of violins, an accordion, a clarinet and the ship itself provided a tuneless old upright piano but someone managed to squeeze a recognisable melody out of it. And there was singing and dancing. They sang in Polish and Russian, in German and Italian, in Yiddish and Ladino, but when they sang in Hebrew the dancers stopped and listened as if the very words were manna from heaven, as if they somehow connected them with the promised land that in a few days they would at last see and touch. Krystyna saw the yearning in their eyes and it made her feel something she was unable to understand. It might have been just plain homesickness for Poland but here on this ship heading out across the sea, with this people who had taken her into their hearts, with Adam and Mordechai on her knees, it felt, even for her, like a yearning for Palestine.

The only chance the ship had of reaching Palestine undetected by the British navy was to sail a zigzag course and confound their calculations of her progress, especially at night. In the day, if one of their spotter planes happened to locate her, then that night they would change course again. Ultimately, though, the coast of Palestine was limited in length, and if the Haganah units waiting for them to land were to have a chance of helping such a large number of weary refugees onto the shore, they were further restricted to a small number of beaches. The answer to Krystyna's question about how long she had to make the food last was that there was no answer. As long as necessary. Well, she was used to that. In the war she had fed the men without ever knowing when there would be fresh supplies.

For the first two days there was no sign of a warship or a plane but early the next morning they heard the drone of aircraft engines. It came down low to inspect them and there was no doubt it was British. It was low enough for everyone to see the roundels on the wings. There was a groan of disappointment. The people knew well enough what it meant. What it meant for now was an extra day's sailing to try and confuse the navy. It was a risk they would have to take, that the water might run out before they got there, but what choice did they have? Before now, Haganah ships had sailed straight into British hands. Dan knew what it would mean for the passengers if that happened, but he kept the information to himself.

That evening he and Krystyna took a stroll round the deck as had become their custom, him smoking a cigarette and exchanging personal history with her.

'Dan, I want to ask you something.'

'Anything.'

'What is the chance of us getting through?'

'Well, anything except that. OK, the short answer is I don't know. Some ships succeed, some don't. If we're caught, there's just about nothing we can do.'

'But I still don't understand why they are so desperate to stop these poor people going to Palestine. I mean, surely, it's not a lot to ask, is it?'

He stopped and leaned against the railing to consider this

question. No, it wasn't a lot, she was right, but.

'Look, if you are a politician in London, these people don't matter. They are just not part of the calculation. The Arabs have to be appeased at all costs, and if a shipload of Jews have to be turned back, well, they've got a whole navy to do that job.'

'But, I mean after what has happened. Do they have no heart, these people in London?'

'I'm sorry, but the answer is no. That's why they're politicians. In any case, the British have never liked us. They admire us and to be honest I think they are little afraid of us, but they don't like us. British society is founded on Christianity and you're not going to like this because I know you are a Catholic but it was the Church that taught them to hate the Jews.'

Krystyna stood by his side and looked out across the sea. She thought back to her childhood, when her father had enforced church attendance and the priest had drummed into them that the Jews killed Jesus and were condemned for ever for their crime. At the time she had given it no thought, just swallowed the story whole, but now she had to think about it, examine it, consider whether it was a reasonable statement. Her time with the Communists had given her a healthy disrespect for religion. She remembered then a Jewish family in her town who had come to the church to be baptised. The priest had stood them before the congregation and announced that by accepting the Lord as their saviour they were now absolved of the sin of their people. Her mother had dragged her out of the church. She called it all rubbish. She was like Roza's father. Maybe that was why she and Roza had got on so well despite their other differences.

She nodded in acknowledgement of the truth he spoke. Well, whatever the Jews' crimes, the Germans had made them pay beyond the Church's wildest dreams.

'Anyway, you still haven't answered my question. Look, I know you can't say if we will get through, but there's another question. What will happen if we don't?'

It was the question he was hoping she wouldn't ask. He didn't want to lie to her.

'In the past they have tried sending ships back to their port of departure, usually in France, but the French aren't keen on that. It gives them a problem they can do without. If we get caught and sent back to Marseille, well, they might not let us disembark the people and that would be terrible.'

'I can imagine. But surely, the ship could go anywhere.'

'Yes, but anywhere we go the British can persuade the government not to accept us.'

'So, then what? Don't we become a problem for the British? They have to do something with us, don't they?'

'Well, yes.'

He went no further. The ship ploughed on and all around them people chatted and laughed and children played but Krystyna was aware only of the man beside her and what he was going to say next.

'Well? What then? What if we become their responsibility? What will they do with us?'

She waited while she held on to the rail and watched the swell of the sea as it rushed past them. She would not speak until he had.

'Alright, I'll tell you, but you must promise to keep this to yourself.'

'Alright'

'They will send everyone to a camp.'

'A camp? What, like a prison camp? They will put these Jews in a prison camp?'

'Yes.'

'I see. Where?'

'In Germany.'

21

Krystyna kept herself busy in the kitchen to stop herself thinking about what Dan had said, and with that many people to feed in that little galley there was never a moment to spare. The boys came and visited her at intervals during the day and they ate together too and so she knew that whatever happened they still needed her as much as she needed them.

But after three days she could tell that Dan was becoming more tense. He spent a lot of time in conference with Captain Johansson and the other Haganah people. On the rarer occasions now when he could talk with her she tried to get him to share his worries, but he wasn't the sharing type. Anyway, he didn't want to worry her with the truth because the truth was that they had received radio communication that the British were increasing their strength in the eastern Mediterranean. Landing a shipload of people on a Palestinian beach was never easy but now their navy had just raised the stakes.

On the last evening Dan came and found her and took her for a stroll round the deck. Maybe he had reached the point where he did need to share, where the stress was becoming too much for one man. He talked with his comrades, but Krystyna was like his mother. It was different with her.

Now, anyway, she knew what the plan was at least. They were within thirty miles of the coast. They had slowed down, which she had noticed, and would stop soon and wait for darkness. If there were no spotter planes they would head full speed for the coast and beach the ship at one of two predetermined points. A Haganah company would be standing by on both shores to receive them. Once they beached they would have very little time. The Haganah teams would each take a small group and rush them away into hiding. A lot would depend on how fast the unloading could be achieved. That was likely to be a problem, because old people and children couldn't just be got off a ship this size quickly. And all of this depended on them being able to beach the ship without being spotted in the first place.

Krystyna listened, and the more she heard the more she thought it was a crazy plan. She wondered how Haganah had ever managed to land any people at all under those conditions, but still, Dan said they had. They surely must have, otherwise this was simply suicidal.

He also said that she and the boys would be in the first group to disembark. She understood why and didn't argue. They had become some kind of symbol of hope for the passengers and seeing them land safely in the promised land would mean a lot, help them to believe that they could do it too.

An hour later the ship came to a halt. The engines stopped, and Captain Johansson issued an order that all lights were to be extinguished. The Levant Trader was to become invisible. The British had radar, but that would only help them if they were using it in this sector. Otherwise, in the dark, they were blind. Krystyna didn't know anything about radar but she had a bad feeling that the captain was understating its importance.

She was proved right. The ship was silent, other than the occasional snoring sleeper and crying baby. Most were asleep but many weren't, and they heard it first, the unmistakable sound of a ship's engines. People clambered out onto the deck and peered into the darkness and there it was, a pinprick of light that grew bigger and bigger until they could see in the light of the moon the shape of a warship silhouetted against the sky. As it approached, searchlights were turned on and the passengers shielded their eyes from the onslaught of the beams. They must have presented a sorry sight to the sailors, like a family woken from their beds in the middle of the night by a housefire.

Silence was pointless now, and in any case there was from all parts of the ship the sound of crying. The word quickly went round that this was the British navy, that they had been found out, and as the meaning of this sank in the crying became louder and more forlorn. Then, before they knew it, the warship was lying off their starboard side, its searchlights seeking out their darkest secrets. People stood on the deck in bare feet, wrapping their coats round them as if this could protect them from the importunate gaze of the sailors.

Then an amplified voice boomed out across the water.

'Motor Vessel Levant Trader. This is HMS Argyll of the Royal Navy. You are under arrest. We are coming alongside. Prepare to be boarded. Any attempt to resist will be met with force. Do you understand?'

There wasn't much to misunderstand. The captain grabbed his megaphone and gave his answer though.

'Argyll, this is a United States-registered vessel. We are in international waters. Should you attempt to board we will consider it an act of piracy under international law and invoke the right to repel you with force. Please be advised we have armed men on board.'

Krystyna turned to Dan. 'Is that right? Do we?'

'Well, it's a small exaggeration. There are twenty Haganah people with small arms. Against that ship it doesn't amount to anything.'

They waited for the Argyll to respond. Krystyna considered the pistol in her baggage and then she looked at this warship and laughed at the notion.

'Levant Trader, this is Commander Forsythe. I repeat, we will board and you must give way for inspection. We are advised that you are carrying illegal immigrants and intend to land them on the Palestine coast. To avoid bloodshed you are strongly advised to lay down your arms. A contingent of Royal Marines will board you and are under orders to return lethal fire. We do not want civilians to get hurt, but we will defend ourselves. Do you understand?'

'Argyll, this is Captain Johansson of the United States Navy. I repeat, your action is illegal. We are in international waters. Please stand off and allow us free passage.'

This caused a hiatus in the conversation. Krystyna wanted to know if it was true, the bit about the American navy.

'Well, it's true that he holds that rank, but to be honest he's retired. I don't think he can claim to be under Navy orders and get away with it.'

'And is this ship registered in America? What does that mean?'

'Yes, that bit's true. Under international law the British have no jurisdiction, and they know that. The problem is they treat the whole of the Mediterranean as their backyard. They consider anyone in it is under their jurisdiction.'

'But they can't get away with that, can they?'

'In theory, no. In practice, yes, they always do. You see, there's no-one to challenge them.'

'But the Americans?'

'The Americans are a bit tired of the British. Now the war is over they act as if they are a Great Power and want all their old colonies back. The Americans don't agree with them. As far as they are concerned if the British want to strut around as if they own the place they just think it's slightly humorous.'

'But they won't do anything?'

'Not unless US interests are directly challenged, no.'

Commander Forsythe seemed to have got over his surprise. 'Captain Johansson. I have received further orders from Haifa. They tell me you are not on the Navy List. Nice try, but now I really must ask you to prepare to be boarded.'

Five minutes later a launch cut across the water from the Argyll. There was still a scrambling net down the side of the Levant Trader and too late the captain realised it was impractical to pull it up. The Marines were already alongside. The Argyll shone a searchlight beam in a sweep along the deck of the ship and what it revealed was twenty men with rifles and submachine guns, and they were all pointing downwards. The Marines commander considered for a moment what to do about this. Without covering fire from the Argyll he could not board, and he knew that Commander Forsythe would not order his crew to fire on a ship with hundreds of civilians on board. There was only one decision he could make. The launch turned round and headed back to the warship. The Jews had won round one. It was a small victory but it gave them heart.

There was nothing they could do now but wait. The odds were stacked against them but for now at least they were free. The Navy would have to make the next move, and Johansson guessed that

Commander Forsythe would wait for orders from Haifa, possibly even London. What Haganah wanted, he was well aware, if they couldn't land their people in Palestine, was an international incident. It was second prize, but a valuable weapon in their campaign for a homeland. He had seen it before. The sympathies of the world, in the light of what had been discovered in Germany and Poland, especially Poland, by the liberating armies, were well and truly with the Jews. Seven hundred survivors of Nazi atrocity dragged off to a British prison camp was worth a lot and they would pay that price if they had to. In any case, they would probably have no choice. He had taken this job at first because it gave him command of a ship again. He found the Jews hard people to deal with. They looked through you as if they were seeking the truth about whose side you were on. It was difficult at first, but now he was used to them and he admired their courage in the face of hopeless odds, like this situation. They wanted one thing and one thing only, to go somewhere they could call home after the slaughter. He didn't know if they were going to get what he heard them call Eretz Israel but from what he had seen so far he thought they might just do it. And if there was anything he could do to make that happen he was going to try.

Commander Forsythe appeared to be in no hurry to trigger an international incident. As far as he was concerned, he would be happy to just sink this old tub and have done with it. It was a disgrace. He could smell it from his bridge and wrinkled his nose in disgust. He had asked for a Far East command after the German defeat, to go and finish the Japanese as well, but they had given him this posting instead. It was a lousy job but he was a career naval officer and orders were orders. Well, he would make no decisions here. He would let someone else carry the can. His ship could stand here for the next year if need be. The Jews were going nowhere.

It became obvious to everyone that there was a stand-off, and gradually people went back to their bunks to try and get some more sleep. The Haganah people kept a watch on that side but most of them stood down and got some rest too. They would need it.

As dawn broke over the Mediterranean, the passengers woke to two new sights. To the east, over the superstructure of HMS Argyll, was a faint line on the horizon that they knew to be Palestine. It was for almost everyone the first sighting they had ever had of Eretz Israel, and there was dancing and singing despite the threatening bulk of the British warship that stood like a bulldog barring their way.

And to the west was another ship approaching at full speed. Within half an hour a second warship stood alongside the Levant Trader, this time on her port side. As if one warship wasn't enough they were now well and truly trapped.

'Captain Johansson, good morning. I hope you slept well. You will notice the presence of our colleagues on HMS Arran on your port side. I am in receipt of specific orders this morning not to let you proceed. We will not board you but neither may you start your engines. If you attempt to do so I am authorised to fire on your ship with my main armament.'

As if to emphasise the point, the barrels of the Argyll's four inch guns levelled and pointed at the bridge of the Levant Trader. It was a bluff but it was an effective one. There seemed no point in replying to this message. What could the captain say? He called a conference with the Haganah people, and asked Krystyna to join them. The biggest issue now was going to be feeding these people.

'Well gentlemen, and lady, sorry, I don't think I need to elaborate on the situation. Landing in Palestine is now not possible, I am sure you realise that. I am only your captain, so it's up to you to let me know what you want me to do. Dan?'

'It's a limited choice, isn't it? We could try going back to Marseille but first of all I don't think the French will let us dock and secondly what would we do with seven hundred people even if they did? The only other option is to let the British arrest them all. I don't like it but no-one is giving me an option I do like.'

'Well, is that it then? We give in?'

'No, not quite like that. We will extract as much value from the situation as possible. We're not alone. The people in Palestine know we are here. We will sit here for as long as we possibly can. So, Krystyna, it's over to you. How long can you feed them for?'

She thought about it. She didn't want to be overly pessimistic, but on the other hand she owed it to them to be realistic.

'Well, as far as the food goes, another week possibly, but food isn't the problem, it's water. There is already only enough for drinking and to make soup with but no-one on this ship has washed since they came on board and the toilet situation is becoming a serious health hazard. There are babies with serious skin conditions now from lack of water to wash them with, including my own grandchildren. These are not really my areas but since my kitchen needs water you need to tell me how much I can have from what we've got left. Either way, it's nothing like a week. Three days, at the most, even if we ration drinking water. By Sunday we need to be in port taking on fresh supplies, or begging that warship for help.'

It wasn't what they wanted to hear, but they knew it anyway.

And so they went about their business in the shadow of two British destroyers and from the deck they saw the sailors going about their business too, and always there were men on the warships with binoculars watching them, as if they might be doing something remotely interesting.

All that day the Jews carried on as if this was normal, and by the evening when it got dark the British turned on the searchlights again to remind them they were here and there was no possibility of them going away, and that began to get on people's nerves. The next morning they went through the same ritual and that day was Friday and Krystyna called her cooks together and announced they were going to make challah for the sabbath. It was a crazy notion but it did at least focus people's minds, and word spread that the strange Polish cook was making challah and that meant it was the sabbath and suddenly people remembered who they were and forgot what was happening either side of their ship, and prepared to do what they had done for thousands of years, to bring in the sabbath. The Germans hadn't been able to stop them, and neither would the British.

As dusk descended over the ship the British searchlights came on again and what the sailors saw now left them open-mouthed. White cloths had been laid over every available surface and the ship was aglow with candles. Women everywhere said the sabbath blessing over their small group, adults and children, and every single Jew on that ship, religious or not, broke a piece of Krystyna's challah and recited the blessing. Captain Johansson watched from his bridge and tears ran down his face. He would never understand these people, but surely to God their luck must turn some day.

Then they sang, sad, nostalgic songs full of yearning, and the children of Israel wept and called for the land that was so near and yet so far. They had lived through the worst barbarity imaginable, had starved and watched those around them swept up unto death but never, in all the years of pain, had they wept like this. The sailors on the two destroyers stood in absolute silence and watched in awe. No man who witnessed that sight ever forgot it. The searchlights went out one by one, perhaps in response to an order but more likely simply because each sailor felt it, the need to leave these people in peace, just for this one night.

And finally they took themselves to bed. They knew it was over, that this was as close as they were going to get, perhaps ever. They had, though, as far as they were concerned, brought the sabbath in in Eretz Israel, and no matter what became of them no-one would ever take that away from them.

It started in the middle of the night. The lights came on again and then those who were still asleep were woken by the shots. They rushed out on deck and saw what had been done. Each storage drum of water had been shot through and the precious fluid gurgled out onto the deck and ran over the side into the sea. They stood and looked in disbelief. Now they knew, it was surely over.

As the sun came up on that last day, though, Dan and his Haganah comrades had other ideas. The people could take another day. He needed them to do that. The megaphone on the Argyll opened up.

'Captain Johansson, this is Commander Forsythe. The game is up. You have no water left. Don't let your people die of thirst. We can supply you with water on the condition that you allow us to board.'

'This is Captain Johansson. I remind you, Commander, that you are committing an act of piracy. You have no right.'

'For heaven's sake, man, be reasonable. You have women and children there. They can't last another day. Give in. We know you have Haganah people on board. Tell them to consult their superiors and get permission.'

Johansson left it for ten minutes, and it had the appearance of having held a conference, but in point of fact there was no conference to hold. They had their plan and they were sticking to it.

'Commander Forsythe. At the risk of boring you, I remind you we are in international waters. We will resist any attempt to board with force. Stand away and let us pass.'

'Oh for God's sake man, stop this nonsense. It's gone on too long. They're only bloody Jews ....'

He knew as soon as he said it that he had gone too far, but it couldn't be unsaid. There was silence for a while.

'Commander Forsythe, I should advise you that we are in permanent contact with Haganah headquarters in Palestine. Your intemperate outburst has been transmitted to them and is as I speak being forwarded to every news agency and radio station in Europe and the United States of America. I can now inform you that my government plans to call your ambassador in Washington in to explain this action. Until I receive further instructions there will be no change in this situation.'

Commander Forsythe was by now beyond caring. He issued an order and a minute later a heavy machine gun opened fire. There was a great deal of hysterical screaming on the Levant Trader, but in fact no one was hurt. The target wasn't the passengers. They watched in dismay as a hail of lead brought down the radio antenna strung the length of the ship above their heads. They knew now that they were incommunicado. Any public relations benefit of carrying on was lost for ever. It is an axiom of warfare that the only battle that matters is the final one, and they had just lost that.

An hour later British Royal Marines boarded the ship, bringing water and medicines with them. By midday the Levant Trader had got up steam and was turning in a wide arc, flanked by the Argyll and the Arran, and heading west, away from Palestine. The passengers looked forlornly over the stern, trying to keep that thin line of coast in their sight for as long as they could. And then it was gone.

PART FOUR

1946

1

Switzerland didn't look any different after the war than it had during the war. It was still fat and prosperous and self-satisfied. Fair enough, profits might be down since Germany's defeat, but the past few years had been good and there were still profits to be made even now, in the normal way of business of course, but a lot of money had flowed into Swiss banks for those years and it was still sloshing around earning interest. Some of it had no known owner now, on account of the depositors having been murdered by the German government and its armies, and some of it had an owner in that the people who had murdered the owners and stolen their wealth were still, many of them, in circulation and one day, inevitably, they would be back looking for the loot. Well, the money belonging to the murderers would be available whenever they needed it. The money belonging to their victims might be a lot harder to obtain. Should anyone come knocking on the banks' doors claiming to be the inheritors of these funds, Swiss bankers would know what to do.

Asher Spiegel stepped off the train in Zurich and it looked to him like nothing had changed. The world beyond Switzerland's borders had altered beyond recognition, but this city hadn't. Late summer flowers bloomed in the hanging baskets and the window boxes and unlike the drabness that haunted postwar Germany this city was alive with colour. It seemed to Asher that even the people themselves resembled bright summer flowers in their gay holiday clothes. He had chosen a bad day to do banking business in Zurich, but a good day to see the Swiss at play. Somewhere he heard a street band playing and all around him were the voices of people in high spirits.

Well, he would take a holiday himself. Business would wait another day. What Asher had come to Zurich for wasn't going to go away. It was sitting in the vaults of Bank Baer, and with interest payable, even after the bank's exorbitant charges, it was worth at least five million dollars. He would meet his old friend Maurice Dreifuss and talk about world events and ponder over the future, now that there was a future, which there hadn't been the last time they met. Perhaps a sightseeing trip in one of the horse-drawn carriages, and dinner at an open-air restaurant, or perhaps Maurice's wife would invite him to their home out of town. Yes, that would be good.

It was starting to come back to him, the feeling of being a banker instead of a fugitive. It would be good, he mused, to pretend the past thirteen years hadn't happened. His father had said in '33 that the Nazi thing was a temporary craze, it would go away, they shouldn't worry about it too much, the people of Germany were more sensible than that, but he had been proved wrong. The people of Germany had suffered from some kind of collective madness which didn't go away. It could be cured only by the most drastic surgery, the destruction of their state and the evil genius who had woken the sleeping devil in them. Asher's father had paid the ultimate price too for his error. He should have got out. Five words Asher repeated to himself every day of his life.

Well, he had his life, and he would rebuild his father's bank, but for now there was another mission, and it involved five million dollars-worth of Swiss francs. The money itself wasn't that much, would quickly get swallowed up, though with his consummate skill as a banker and more lately as a blackmailer it would soon be doubled and doubled again and then it would amount to a sum that could do some real good. No, this money had a past and he owed it to the people from whom it was extracted at the point of death to recover it for the survivors.

He knew the story of Roza Levinson, everyone did now, and he knew also about her child, the son she named after her husband, Mordechai, the boy who was locked in a British prison camp on the island of Cyprus for the sin of being Jewish. He shook his head as he walked down the Zurich street and bit his lip. The boy, treated as the Nazis would have treated him, but this time by the people who had fought the Nazis. Asher tried to understand it but it was impossible. In the war a first rule of survival was to know who your enemies were. Well, the British were supposed to be friends but they had taken the Jews by surprise. The Jews would be allowed to lick their wounds just as long as they did it quietly where they couldn't be seen, but no, they had to go making a fuss about Palestine, and that the British would not tolerate, not if it upset their Arab friends.

Friends and enemies. It was, these days, hard to know who was who.

With the Swiss at least you knew where you were. They were on the side of the money. It didn't matter to them who had it. Alright, they had an instinctive Germanic dislike for Jews, but now that their friends to the north had been defeated they were a bit more amenable. Asher could cross the border under his own passport now. There was no danger that a zealous frontier guard would turn him over to his enemies. Now, a German banker with a Jewish name could walk down a Zurich street unafraid because he belonged to that exclusive club, he was a banker in a country of banks, a banker first and a Jew second.

Even so, he still needed Maurice Dreifuss, and Maurice Dreifuss still needed Hans Baer. Maurice was accepted by the Swiss Bankers Association as one of them and if that was all that mattered Hans Baer could be dispensed with, but Hans Baer was their key to unlocking the secrets of another pot of gold. Unwittingly, by his greed in 1944 when he laundered Roza's gold, he had opened himself to blackmail. He was sitting on a huge pile of loot, cash, bonds, insurance policies, even fine art stored in his bank's cavernous vaults. His German friends were busy right now extricating themselves from the occupation armies, but they would be back, he knew that, and their stash would be waiting for them. Unless, that was, Asher and Maurice could get it first. That they were coming for him, he didn't know.

He would have to be persuaded to let them have it of course, and right now, on this sunny afternoon, Asher had no idea how that was going to be achieved. He had had some success with a couple of small German banks, had persuaded them that it was in their interest to release some of their loot in preference to being tried for war crimes by the Americans. It wasn't his fault that after they opened their vaults the Americans had somehow been tipped off anyway. His department was recovering stolen money, not punishing the thieves.

Having checked into his hotel he enjoyed the rest of the day at leisure and that was followed by an excellent night's sleep. He awoke refreshed in the morning, enjoyed a hearty breakfast, and knew that in less than twenty-four hours he had slipped back into his old ways. Now, he really felt like a banker. He wandered out of the hotel and down the road to get at least a little exercise in the sunshine before his meeting. He hadn't gone far though when he was stopped by the smell of fresh coffee and allowed himself to be tempted by it. He sat down at an open-air cafe and wrapped his coat around him. It was already June but a fresh Alpine breeze was a reminder that spring could still bite. He ordered a black coffee and apfel strudel. It had been his favourite before the war and after the years of deprivation he found he couldn't get enough of it. He laughed at his self-indulgence so soon after breakfast and then he laughed again at the fact that a simple thing like that could be called such. He wasn't expected at Bank Dreifuss until eleven and he remembered exactly where it was, how long it would take him to walk there from the cafe.

Zurich is a small city, in more ways than one. It amused him that his presence had already been noted, that even now the Swiss police liked to know who was who. Perhaps it was a wartime habit they had yet to break. It occurred to him they might trace his last visit under a false passport and get him on that but no, that was the past, and hardly worth the effort, even for them. Things happened then, in the war, everyone knew that, and after all they would assume that somewhere along the line a Swiss bank had made a profit from his visit, so that was alright. If they knew what he was about to do, that would be different. Yes, taking someone else's money out of a Swiss bank was likely to be something they would frown upon. On the other hand, someone else's money was a moot point. Possession is nine tenths of the law, and very shortly Asher was going to be in possession of it.

He was surprised when a man sat down at the table, without even the usual courtesy of asking for permission to share. His heart raced, the old fear, that this must be the police, and he had to remind himself that he had nothing to fear from the police, that he had committed no crime in Switzerland. Yet.

'Mr Spiegel?'

Asher looked surprised, and it wasn't feigned.

'I beg your pardon?'

'Do I have the pleasure of addressing Asher Spiegel?'

'No, I'm sorry, there must be some mistake.'

The man looked into his eyes, and he knew there was no mistake. He was cool and Asher was flustered, so he had the advantage. He took his wallet out from his suit pocket and removed a business card. It claimed he was Marcus Rosen, of the Swiss-Levant Trading Company. By way of credentials he casually pulled his sleeve up a little, in a way no passer-by would notice, but there it was, a tattooed number. He had been in a camp.

'I'm sorry to do this to you, but I have been given your description and this seemed better than meeting at the bank.'

'Bank?'

'Dreifuss.'

'You know a lot about me and my business, Mr, er, Rosen. I know a certain amount about you, yes, but I am afraid I am unaware of why you are here.'

'I want you to do something for me.'

'Oh yes? What might that be?'

'Introduce me to your friend Maurice.'

'Oh yes? Assuming I have a friend called Maurice, would you care to explain to me why I would do such a thing for a complete stranger?'

'Yes, because Michael Jacobs wants you to.'

That was different.

'Mr Rosen, perhaps we should take a walk. It might be more private.'

He paid his bill and left the last mouthful of strudel on his plate with regret.

'So, Mr Rosen …'

'Marcus, please.'

'Alright Marcus, so Michael Jacobs sent you.'

'That's right.'

'Why?'

'Well, once you have extracted from Hans Baer what you came to Zurich for, I have some questions to ask him.'

'What kind of questions?'

'Oh, you know.'

'No, actually, I don't.'

'Information that will be helpful to the organisation.'

'Yes? And exactly which organisation are you working for, Marcus?'

'Still suspicious, aren't you? That's good. The Swiss-Levant Trading Company is wholly-owned by Bricha, but it is a real business. It uses Swiss money to ship refugees to Palestine.'

'Illegal immigrants?'

'Yes, if you want to be specific. Immigrants the British government are keeping out of Palestine against all the norms of morality.'

Asher stopped and put his hand on the other man's arm. 'Marcus, you don't have to lecture me. I'm on your side, remember. I know what you're thinking, that I got through the war in relative comfort and safety. That's true, I won't deny it. I used my money and my contacts to stay in hiding for most of the time, and I could buy a new identity for the other times, but you know I used that identity to travel here while the war was still going on, to set up the account with Bank Baer. Yes, I was fortunate. My father was less fortunate. He died of a heart attack when the SS came to arrest him. You see, pain is relative. I respect what you went through and I'm sorry if you believe I should have gone through it myself, but there it is. We none of us got to choose the particular torture we had to suffer.'

They walked on in this way, oblivious to the people around them who had not gone through the war and would have no idea what they were talking about, and Asher Spiegel agreed to take Marcus Rosen with him to Bank Dreifuss.

2

'So, Michael Jacobs sent you?'

'Yes, that's right.'

'And what exactly did he send you for, Mr Rosen?'

Maurice Dreifuss didn't expect Marcus Rosen to give him a true answer. He knew the way of things better than that. But he was interested in his lies, because they would tell him just how murky was his business.

'Michael's work involves assisting refugees to travel across Europe. I can tell you within these four walls what their destination is …'

'Yes, Mr Rosen, I think we here know that much.'

'Quite. Well, some of those people have assets here in Switzerland. It would be most helpful to them if we could recover some of those assets, to help them settle in, you know, start a business perhaps, buy land, that sort of thing.'

'Yes, I see. It makes sense.'

It did. It was entirely plausible, even laudable, and it was even possible that it was true. The best lie is one that has at least a grain of truth. Well, his interest in the matter went no further than that. As long as there was at least an element of normal banking business going on here, then his position within the Swiss banking community was secure. He had done a lot of work for his fellow Jews, but if the other bankers discovered what he had been doing he would become persona non grata, and that would render him useless for any further work, and he knew there was a lot of work to do yet. There were a lot of skeletons in cupboards and he was in a unique position to help discover them.

'Yes Mr Rosen, I see no reason why you should not come with us to Bank Baer, if it helps your investigations. You will, and I hope I don't need to spell this out, be discreet?'

'Oh, very.'

'Good, well, let me see', and to the other men's amusement he took out from his waistcoat an old-fashioned pocket watch with no sense that he was about a hundred years out of date, Oh yes, I think we could be leaving now. Well, gentlemen, let's see what we can find out shall we?'

As they walked out of the panelled banking hall Asher Spiegel was reminded that this man, who had done so much good work for them throughout the war, not least in the matter of the gold, was Swiss first and Jewish second. Well, he was on home ground here. He had never experienced what he and Marcus Rosen and so many others had. Did he fully understand what that meant? And anyway, did it matter? Could Asher go on for ever judging people by the amount of suffering they had or had not experienced, giving the highest value to those who had been in the ghettos and the camps, lost their families, somehow survived? Would he always look down upon Jews like Maurice Dreifuss, men who would never know what it was like? He made up his mind that he would not judge him, that it wasn't his fault he was born Swiss, and anyway, he did what he could. No-one could ask for more.

Hans Baer was a little surprised to see three of them. He had been expecting two, and the third one troubled him. He had a lot to be troubled about, and he didn't like surprises. They explained Marcus Rosen away as an auditor doing a check on their work. Auditors were something Hans could understand. He sent his secretary out to an early lunch and locked the door after she went out.

'Well, gentlemen, how can I help you?'

Marcus sat a little to the back, as befitted an auditor, and took no part in the conversation at this point. Asher let Maurice do the talking. He knew his fellow banker.

'As you know, Hans, the little arrangement we had during the recent hostilities was carried out entirely to our satisfaction, and I want to thank you for your help in that matter.'

It was a little unctuous. He knew that and Hans knew it, but it was the normal banking way of talking and Hans nodded slightly in acknowledgement of the compliment. He had been paid very well for his work but even so, a little courtesy is always appreciated.

'So, does this not mean that our business is now, shall we say, concluded?'

'Well, no, not exactly. You see, Hans, there are certain assets we would like to trace, and we feel you might be able to assist us in this matter.'

'Assets? What kind of assets?'

'Oh, you know, cash deposits, obviously, but also stocks and bonds, and also insurance policies.'

'Oh, well I'm afraid beyond the first the bank has no dealing with such things.'

He wriggled very slightly in his chair. Only Marcus noticed it. He was the only one looking for it. Maurice sat back in his chair. He didn't want to put pressure on Hans, yet. He was aware that the simple act of moving his body away from his adversary would have the effect of putting him off his guard, make him feel he wasn't being threatened. He said nothing for a few seconds. They suddenly became conscious of a clock somewhere in the room ticking loudly. He folded his hands together and gave the appearance, for a moment, of a priest about to start a sermon. He was in control of this situation.

'You see, Hans, that gives me a problem. I'm afraid my sources are very insistent on this point. They have, apparently, documents, you know, receipts, that sort of thing, for policies and so on that were deposited with the bank before the war.'

He spread his hands now in a gesture that clearly meant what can I do, I'm just the messenger, help me out here. Hans took a few seconds to come up with a story, and it was a good one.

'Oh, now I know what you mean. Yes, there were perhaps a few deposits made back then. It was a long time ago. Not our normal practice, but they weren't, I suppose you could say, normal times. We may have certain documents in our safes. I can have someone look for them, shall we say in the next week or so, if you would like.'

Maurice opened his mouth to respond to this but at this point Marcus Rosen lost his patience. He wasn't a banker and he saw no point in beating about the bush. He wanted answers.

'Mr Baer, I don't think that will do.'

The other three men looked at him with surprise. It wasn't what you would expect an auditor to say.

'You see we know you have these items, and we want to retrieve them for their rightful owners. Now.'

'Now? But I'm afraid that is quite impossible. You see …'

'No Mr Baer, impossible is not part of my vocabulary. I don't deal in excuses and prevarication. I have a busy schedule. You will oblige me please by getting the key to these safes, now, and escorting us there so we can take what we came for.'

Asher was shocked and embarrassed. He hadn't expected this. It wasn't helpful, not the normal way to get things done among bankers. On the other hand, he was also slightly amused. Whoever this Marcus Rosen really was, he didn't waste anyone's time. Hans Baer was upset. He didn't like this man. He didn't think he was an auditor at all.

'Mr Rosen, I think there has been some misunderstanding. You can't come in here and demand such things ….'

He stopped there though, because now he found himself looking down the barrel of Marcus's pistol. Attached to it was a silencer which somehow managed to make it look even more menacing. Maurice and Asher jumped to their feet but Marcus stayed exactly where he was. He was in charge now. They had got him in to the bank and he was going to take what he came for.

'Mr Baer, I think I have now made my point somewhat more clearly. I am not asking you, I am ordering you.'

Hans Baer was afraid, but he was also angry. He had got all through the war without any nastiness, and he didn't want any now.

'And if I say no?'

'That is your choice. Life or death, you do at least get a choice.'

'But if I refuse, and you shoot me, you will never get what you want.'

'Mr Baer, I can shoot you and still get what I came for. First I will shoot one leg, and then one arm, and then the other leg and so on. You will live long enough to open the safe. Then you can bleed to death for all I care.'

Hans Baer was now very scared, but he was also offended, and that made him defiant. 'And if I still refuse? If I have principles?'

Marcus laughed. 'No, I don't think you have principles, but you might be stupid enough to die before you open the safe, so we have taken certain precautions.'

All three men looked at him. This was a new development. They couldn't imagine what that meant.

'Your wife Lotte and your daughter Gretchen are at this moment entertaining a visitor in that lovely home of yours by the lake.'

He waited for the expected response, and it was precisely as anticipated. Hans Baer was distressed.

'My family. You wouldn't harm them.'

'Really? What an interesting idea. No, I assure you, if I don't call your house in, let me see, the next four and a half minutes, your wife will die, and then your little girl.'

Maurice felt sick. he couldn't believe this was happening. He said nothing though. What could he say?

'So? Shall we make that call?'

Hans Baer looked defeated. He nodded and hung his head. Then he picked up the receiver on his desk and dialled his home number. It was answered by a stranger and he knew this was all true. Then he handed it over to Marcus. Marcus spoke quickly, in Hebrew, and put the receiver down.

'Good, they are safe. Now, before your staff come back from lunch, perhaps we can get down to business? Lead the way, if you please.'

Hans took a bunch of keys from his desk and led them out of his office and down a flight of stairs. There, they faced a large steel door. As if it mattered, he turned his back so they wouldn't see the combination, and after that he turned first one large key and then another. The door swung open to reveal a row of steel boxes on either wall. He knew exactly which ones to go to, and unlocked them in turn. It only took a few minutes.

'Good, now I should like the keys to your car please. Don't worry, you will get it back. We don't take what doesn't belong to us.'

The three of them carried the boxes out in relays, Maurice and Asher working as if this was normal, but they did it without being asked. It was, after all, what they had come for. It was just that they hadn't expected it to happen so easily, so quickly. But then they hadn't come armed.

Finally, Marcus Rosen ushered his colleagues out of the safe and asked them to wait. Pulling the door almost closed behind him, he removed the pistol from his pocket and shot Hans Baer, once, through the head. Then he joined his colleagues and locked the safe door behind him.

'Don't worry, he will be alright. There is an emergency phone in there. After lunch his staff will let him out. Well, I suggest we get moving.'

Maurice Dreifuss had a hard time explaining to the police that he had nothing to do with the murder. He had stayed in the office, he said, while this stranger went down with Herr Baer to the safe. He had no knowledge who the stranger really was and why he had killed the head of the bank. As there was no evidence against him the police finally had to admit they couldn't touch him and let him go.

Maurice was furious. Even if the police couldn't touch him, his position in the banking community was now fatally compromised. These people, whoever they really were, were stupid. It was one thing to extract what was owed, but not murder. He left it a while, to avoid suspicion with the authorities, and then he packed a bag and went to find Michael Jacobs.

3

He found Michael in Vienna and they met in the restaurant that Michael referred to as his office. He travelled so widely that almost every city in Europe had a restaurant that doubled as an office. Vienna was under the control of the Allied occupation forces and so was safer than some of the places he worked.

Maurice told him what he already knew from his own sources, that a Jewish group had murdered a Swiss banker who had laundered money for the Nazis. He didn't like it any more than Maurice did and he sat and listened patiently as the latter told him the details, shaking his head in disbelief like he had when he first heard it. It wasn't the first time either. He told Maurice that this was happening all over Europe, that someone was finding the supposed enemies of the Jews and executing them. Well, he had a certain amount of sympathy when it was SS officers and their like in the SD or the Gestapo, but Swiss bankers and other collaborators, that was stretching things. It was not only one small step removed from how the Germans had behaved but was likely to be counterproductive, witness the difficult position it now placed Maurice in.

He apologised as if he was somehow himself responsible for the murder, and promised to take it up with a higher authority. Maurice thanked him and went home. There was nothing else he could do.

Michael then went to Berlin to see his boss in Bricha, David Schulman. David had recruited Michael from the American Joint Distribution Committee into Bricha and knew what an asset he was. If Michael brought him a complaint, he was inclined to take it seriously. His contacts in US Army Intelligence were of inestimable value to the organisation and he had proved himself highly effective on a number of operations. In addition to all of that, he had brought them Roza's gold.

'So, Michael, what do you want me to do?'

'I want you to stop it.'

'Because?'

'Oh come on David. Because to start with it's alerting the occupation military police in a number of countries to look out for travelling Jews and that's making our job harder. But apart from that, it's not right.'

'You mean you don't think it's right. Personal opinion.'

'What? Do you?'

'Me? Well, let us just say I have a certain amount of sympathy for these people.'

'I see. Anyway, what people? Are they some kind of organisation, you know, a formal group?'

'Well, I don't of course know a lot but I would say yes. I hear rumours, you know, in my position.'

'What kind of rumours?'

'An organisation called Din.'

Michael tried to remember what that might mean, but he didn't even know what language it was.

'As in the Hebrew Beth Din, house of judgment. Din is judgment. The group is acting as police force, prosecutor, judge, jury and executioner, usually skipping from the first bit to the last without wasting much time on the ones in the middle. They consider that the Allies aren't trying hard enough to apprehend war criminals or put them on trial. They know who their targets are so trials are considered a waste of time. Anyway, they would be a luxury they can't afford, as the occupation authorities and various police forces don't quite see eye to eye with their activities.'

'I see. You know quite a lot.'

'Well, I know a little and surmise a lot.'

'And can you speak to them, get them to stop, or at least to act with more circumspection if they won't stop?'

Michael didn't completely disagree with Din. He just didn't want them muddying the waters he swam in.

'I'll try. Look, leave it with me, I may be able to make some contacts. Meanwhile, I want you to take some leave.'

'Why?'

'What kind of question is that? You know, the war is over. People take a break from time to time. It's good for you. Go home to see your parents. Your father isn't so good these days, I hear.'

'You hear a lot.'

'Well, you know, it's the job. I carry a lot of responsibility and everyone is my concern. So will you go?'

'I'll think about it.'

'Good.'

'I said I'll think about it, not that I'll go.'

'I know. That's what I meant.'

They embraced warmly and Michael left for the station. He had a lot of faith in David Schulman, and not a little love for him. He was a good man. But was he also something else? Was he telling Michael the whole truth? He thought back through the conversation they had just had and decided he didn't think so. David was, he suspected, closer to Din than he might be prepared to admit.

Suddenly, though, the idea of a vacation seemed attractive. He made a few international telephone calls from Berlin and, since he always travelled ready for any eventuality, he simply took a train to Hamburg and enquired about the next departure of any ship for New York. The SS Lake Michigan was sailing in two days.

He was tempted to do some more work in that time but instead he gave in to the urgent need for a break and just wandered round the city whiling away the time. Hamburg was devastated. Where the Degussa smelting works used to be was nothing more than a large hole in the ground. People grubbed about among the rubble of apartment blocks looking for God only knew what. If you didn't know why they were in this state, that they were reaping the results of their own militaristic fantasy, you might feel sorry for them. There was precious little food available so he dropped in to the headquarters of British Army Intelligence and reminded a few old friends they owed him a meal or two. He overate and got drunk and generally felt good, and two days later when he arrived at the docks to board the Lake Michigan he had already let go of the problems he was leaving behind in Europe.

The crossing was a rough one and no-one on board felt much like socialising so he kept to his cabin apart from a self-imposed exercise regime round the decks three times a day. The other passengers and the crew thought he was mad to go running in a gale but he loved it. There were times when he had to hold on to a railing or deck fixture to stop himself being thrown about but it was part of the process of reinvigoration.

The only other passenger out on deck in that weather was a girl wrapped up in a cloak up to her chin with a large waterproof hat pulled down over her eyes. As he ran past the first time he didn't notice her but she saw him. Her eyes followed his progress from their hiding place and she decided he was some kind of nutter. When he came round the second time she pushed the brim of her hat up a little to inspect this crazy person and so he noticed her and gave her a cheery smile and ran on. He had planned to do just two laps today, but now he was interested to see this girl so he made himself go round again. When he got to the place where he had seen her, she was gone.

He stood there for a moment and wondered if he had the right spot, or if perhaps he had imagined her, and if it mattered that she had gone, and he thought that yes he did, no he hadn't and well, perhaps. A little company wouldn't go amiss. Still, his chance had gone.

Except that it hadn't, because after a hot shower and change of clothes he found her in the bar nursing a glass of whiskey.

'Hullo, excuse me but are you ....'

'Yes.'

'Yes you are what?'

'The person you ran past twice on deck and then came back to chat up, and now you've had to look all over the ship to find me and here I am.'

'Now look here, I didn't look for you. I was coming here anyway.'

'It's alright, I'm only pulling your leg. Anyway, now you're here, I think you should sit down and have a drink. You must need it after that run. Some kind of fitness fanatic, are you?'

'Yes, well, no, not exactly.'

'Funny, I didn't have you down as the tongue-tied kind. Is this how you always respond to attractive women?'

He wasn't sure how to answer that, so he didn't.

'I'm sorry, you will have to forgive me. I've been on this ship for two days and no-one has spoken to me yet. I was getting desperate.'

'I'm not sure I should take that as any kind of compliment.'

'Well, OK, I'll add that even if I hadn't been desperate I would have said something, although not perhaps as outrageous as that. American, huh?'

'Yes. I'm sorry, let me introduce myself. Michael Jacobs, from Rochester, New York.'

'Miriam Fillon, from here there and everywhere but currently resident in New York City. How do you do.'

'American?'

'Kind of. And kind of French too.'

'Ah, that explains.'

'The accent?'

'The looks. Oh, sorry, that was pretty forward of me. I didn't mean …'

'That's alright Michael. If you think it say it, that's my motto.'

'Oh, mine might be described as just the opposite, but that's my upbringing, I'm afraid.'

He was being a little disingenuous, but how do you explain to a very attractive young woman with whom you suddenly hope to spend the next few days that your job involves never saying what you think? Well, probably on this trip there would be no time to go into such detail.

He didn't know what to say next. It had been a long time since he had talked about anything but the war and refugees and here he was supposed to have a proper conversation with a young woman about normal things.

'So, since you ask, I work for the United Nations Relief and Rehabilitation Agency. You were going to ask weren't you?'

'Yes, well, I mean …'

'You mean you would have asked me if I was a man, but girls don't have jobs.'

'Do I?'

'Don't you?'

He lied. 'No. I just mean I didn't know what I was going to say, and anyway it doesn't matter because a man doesn't get a chance to say anything with you, does he?'

She laughed, the kind of laugh a man would die just to hear once more. 'Sure, like you just did. No, you're right, I talk too much. Sorry, it's my upbringing, the Jewish side.'

He looked at her again. How could have missed it? His radar was usually better than that. He must have been distracted.

For three more days the SS Lake Michigan ploughed through the North Atlantic with, as far as Michael and Miriam were concerned, only two people on board. They talked incessantly. Michael lost his shyness with her and she made him laugh and it was so good he forgot where he had been and what he would have to go back to when he returned to Europe. She was French but she was more American and even more Jewish and he found the combination hard to resist.

By the time the ship docked in New York he had promised to come and visit her in the city once he had been home, perhaps even have her up to Rochester, not to meet his parents as such, which was not at all what he meant when he said it, just to show her the attractions of upstate New York.

He was looking forward to seeing his family and enjoying a well-earned rest. If his father was well enough he would take him up to the Catskills to their favourite lake and do some fishing. He would see then how he felt about Miriam, or if this really had just been a shipboard thing between two bored people. Perhaps she wouldn't be interested when he called, but he knew she would be, he saw it in her face as she listened to him speaking, the way she soaked up everything he said. He saw something else too, a sadness she hadn't spoken about, for all her loquacity. She talked about a lot of things and it's funny but after just three days, even such intense days, you can think you know someone but of course you don't, you just know the bit you have seen, and Michael had enough experience of the war and its aftermath to know that Miriam Fillon had a lot to tell him yet.

4

On the train to Rochester he realised he had forgotten about Europe. He expected to come home full of stories about his war but suddenly it wasn't the most important thing. It was as if Europe was not only on the other side of the Atlantic but it was some other planet and he had travelled through space, and perhaps even time, and landed back in the place he grew up in, a place that had no possible connection with that other place of death and terror and destruction. America had joined the war for her own reasons which were nothing to do with Europe or even Germany come to that, and now Japan was defeated and the boys were mostly home America looked prosperous and content with itself. For Americans the war was over and could be forgotten. His war was still going on over there but how could he explain that?

His mother looked older but was as strangely beautiful and glamorous as he remembered and welcomed him home as if she wasn't quite sure where he had been or why. The war had passed her by almost unnoticed. She drank too much still and she had a house full of people at all times of the day or evening, socially-important people, and they greeted him as if he was slightly amusing or had been brought in to entertain them. They were not people he wanted to talk to. They wouldn't know what he was saying.

His father looked ill. While Michael had been away he had suffered another minor stroke and he tried to hide it but his left arm hung slightly uselessly from his shoulder. Siggy Jacobs was a fighter but he was running out of resource to fight with. While his wife entertained he sat quietly in his study and read, increasingly Torah or

Talmud, books from his childhood that he turned to in his dying days. He didn't share his wife's interests and she didn't share his. She only shared the lovely house he had bought with his hard work and spent his money on things that were of no concern to him. He didn't mind. He understood that wealth mattered to her and why, that it was the only way she had of proving her worth in a country she didn't belong in, among people who judged her by her clothes and her dinner parties because that was all she had to offer them.

The first time one of his mother's friends asked him what he had been doing they responded to his answer with glazed eyes and he knew they had no idea what he was talking about. Many asked him if he had come home to go into practice and were slightly shocked when he said no, and at least one man said he should call when he was ready to join a law firm because he was sure he had a place for Siggy Jacobs' son. Michael made polite noises and decided this wasn't a vacation. Taking his father up to the Catskills in his condition was hopeless. He could have another stroke at any time, Dr Levy said, and he should be close to medical treatment at all times.

By the third day Michael had taken to sitting quietly with him and listening to passages from the Torah. He remembered some of them from his youth in religious classes but they meant little to him now. Still, he enjoyed the sound of his father's sonorous voice and he also enjoyed being there for him because he knew no-one else was. His sisters had both left home while he had been away, Shula to go to university in California and Simone had finally married her man but no-one had written to tell him, or perhaps they had but the letter never arrived. What was he going to do, travel all the way from Poland in the middle of a war? Still, she was only in Boston. He would go and see her.

He knew of course that it would be pointless inviting Miriam. He didn't even tell his parents about her. The only person he told was old Dora. When he went to the kitchen to find her she flung her arms round him like he was her son and cried terribly and now, for the first time, he felt like he had been welcomed home. Each morning he sat in the kitchen and let her make an enormous breakfast for him and they talked about life in the house and why she had stuck it out instead of going off and having some kind of life of her own. Michael flattered her and said some man would be grateful for her hand still and she blushed and said at sixty-seven she didn't think so but even so, she loved him for saying it. Now he was home safely, she said, she was happy. He didn't have the heart to tell her it was only a visit.

What he did tell her was about Miriam, and she threw her arms round him a second time and he said hold on, she's just someone I've met, let's not get carried away but Dora was already carried away. She was so happy he tried to go along with the fiction that this was the one and there was going to be a chupah. Dora had lived in a Jewish household for so many years she used all the Jewish words. Talk of marriage embarrassed Michael, as if he was being presumptuous even allowing Dora to talk about it. It suddenly reminded him that he had once had a fantasy about bringing Roza here. Now he was home he wondered how she could possibly have fitted in. She couldn't. They would have gone up into the mountains where she would have lived with the trees and the deer and been happy. It was hard to think about her now. He wanted to tell Dora but he didn't know how to, but she saw a sadness pass over his face and she knew, better than his mother or father, that he had been through something none of them would ever understand. She had known Michael since before he was born and there was nothing he could ever hide from her. Well, he would talk to his Dora when he was ready.

Michael was grateful to her for understanding him and for caring, for her wonderful meals too, but most of all for her devotion to his father. He was even grateful to her for not being judgmental of his mother. He would take care of Dora in her old age, he knew that and just in case she didn't know it he told her and then she hugged him again and wet his neck with her tears. She knew that Siggy was dying and it hurt her badly. Still, Michael was back now. He would make everything alright.

As soon as was decent, which was very soon because no-one knew where he went or much cared anyway, he took the train down to New York and met Miriam. It was an anxious moment, waiting for her at Grand Central Station, and he was reminded of something he had read about love, that you know you love someone when you see them again. Whatever it is you feel the first time you look at them is how you feel about them for sure. And when she burst through the door in that way she had of making an entrance he knew. He saw too how other men looked at her and his jealousy confirmed his feelings. She gave herself completely to his embrace and he was at that moment the happiest of men. And when she looked up into his eyes he saw it in her face too, the same feeling, and they didn't need to say anything, they just walked hand in hand and from time to time she put her head on his shoulder and it made him feel completely wonderful.

'OK soldier, how was it with your parents?'

'Well …'

'That bad, huh?'

'I guess so. How about you?'

'What about me?'

'Your parents.'

'Michael, we never somehow got around to that, on the ship I mean.'

'To what, parents?'

'Yes. I don't have any.'

He stopped and looked at her. Her expression was different. He had already learned it could change in an instant. She had a very ready smile, but it could be wiped away just like that.

'Hey, come on soldier, it's OK. I had some once so don't worry about it.'

He wanted to ask, he needed to know this about her, but he didn't know what to say.

'Look, it's no big deal. OK, it is. I tell you what, come back to my apartment and I'll cook us both a meal and tell you all about it.'

'Well only if you want to.'

'What, cook or tell?'

'Tell.'

'I do. No, seriously, I do. It's part of me, isn't it? You should know everything there is to know.'

'OK. In that case, let's go shopping and then you can show me how good a cook you are. I warn you though, you've got some stiff competition if you want to win my affections with food.'

'Oh yes? Your mother?'

'Good God no. No, Dora.'

'Dora huh? Is she your other woman?'

'Yes, she's sixty seven and she cooks like an angel.'

'Michael, is this Dora the family cook or something?'

'Yes, of course, what did you think?'

'I mean, well, is your family rich, you know, seeing as how you have a cook.'

He stopped and thought about it. No, not rich. Everyone employed a cook, didn't they? In America, anyway.

'Well, my father was a successful lawyer. He came from Germany with practically nothing but he studied and worked hard and so on, you know, the typical Jewish success story. He got lucky too, built up a specialised practice in commercial law, had some big clients, made a lot of money I guess. He's retired now.'

'Oh, how old is he?'

'Not old, but he's not well either. He's had a series of minor strokes. At first he carried on working but finally he had to recognise he could no longer do it. His brain just doesn't function like it used to.'

'Oh, I'm sorry. And your mother?'

'Don't ask.'

'Oh, OK. And you?'

'Me? What about me?'

'Well, you're a lawyer. Aren't you going to take over your father's practice? Isn't that what sons do?'

'No. He wanted me to of course, like any father, but when he had the first stroke and I was already in the Army it was obvious that wasn't going to happen. He's got a junior partner he's grooming to take over.'

They had by now arrived at a large grocery store and the conversation came to a natural end. They bought more food than was decent for just two people, just for the pleasure of shopping like a married couple, and there was so much they had to get a cab to Miriam's apartment.

'Sorry, it's probably not what you're used to. It was the smallest apartment I could find without my feet sticking out into the hallway when I'm in bed. It's an apartment specially built for small people. That's why when I advertised for someone to rent it while I went to Europe I had to stipulate only midgets accepted.'

'Oh, and where's your tenant now?'

'She's pushed off to her family in Chicago while I take over. Her name's Ginny. As soon as I measured her I knew she was the right one to look after the place. Five feet exactly.'

She talked like that, laughing a lot as she spoke, while she cooked in the tiny kitchen space tucked into a corner of the living room. Michael tried to help but there just wasn't room so she sat him on the sofa with a beer and he listened to her babble from there. He wondered if she talked as a displacement activity, to avoid thinking. From time to time she stopped and that sad look came over her momentarily, and then she would find something else funny or foolish to tell him and off she went again. He was already afraid that if she ever came down to Earth she would land badly.

Apart from trying too hard in an obvious attempt to impress him, her cooking wasn't bad. A mixture, which he kind of expected, of French and American.

They ate on their knees on the sofa and after she had cleared away she came back and they drank their wine thoughtfully. He knew she was building up to telling him.

'OK soldier, you want to know about my family, yes?'

'If you want to tell me.'

'I'm not sure I do, but I'm going to anyhow.'

She took a sip from her glass to avoid having to start but then suddenly she was off and didn't finish until the story was told.

'My mother went over to France as a volunteer nurse in 1916, to serve with the French Army in the first war, before the United States declared war. That was the kind of woman she was. Impulsive, like me I suppose. She served in a hospital in Lyon and then they asked her to go to a front-line dressing station. She came through physically unscathed but I don't think she ever recovered from what she saw. She was always, should I say, delicate.

'She met my father there. He was wounded and you know, it sounds like a cliché but they fell in love and after the war she stayed in France and married him. I was their only child.

'My father didn't know what to do when the war was over so he stayed in uniform, at first in the Army and then he left and joined the police in Lyon and we lived there. He did pretty well and by the time the next war started he was the local assistant police chief. When the Vichy regime did a deal with the Germans his chief refused to carry on in the police. He had principles which my father didn't have, so they took him off and shot him and gave my father his job.

'Only there was one condition. They couldn't have a police chief with a Jewish wife. He was told he would have to divorce her.'

She bit her lip. This wasn't easy.

'Did he?'

'Of course he did. I was over here by then at university and my mother wrote at the beginning of the war and told me to stay, she would try to send me a little money each month to live on. His salary was quite good by then. But after the divorce there was no more money and then after a while there were no more letters either. I made enquiries and it took a bit of persistence but I finally got a reply from the authorities in Lyon. My mother was dead. She had committed suicide.'

She stared down at the floor to avoid looking at him and took a sip of wine. 'Well, I couldn't get over there to see her grave, but as soon as the war was over I got a job with UNRRA. It paid my passage over and gave me a reason to be in Europe. Speaking English and French helped.'

'And did you find your mother's grave?'

'Yes.'

And what about your father? I mean, have you heard anything about him?'

'Yes and no. Senior Vichy police officers are considered as collaborators by the French. There is no doubt my father was responsible for arresting and deporting Jews, Jews from Lyon who were shipped to Poland and murdered, thanks to him. All I have been able to find out is that he went on the run and hasn't been seen since.'

'And what would you do if you found him?'

She looked up now, straight into his eyes, and hers were full of hate. 'I would kill him.'

5

Michael took Miriam up to Boston to see Simone. His sister welcomed him the way a sister should and made a big fuss of Miriam and when she had a chance to speak to her brother quietly she said what a lovely girl she was and was there going to be a chupah and he said no, of course not, we hardly know each other, to which she replied well get to know her and marry her because girls like that don't come along every five minutes. He brushed it off as nothing but banter but even so she sowed a seed in his mind.

She also told him he had to introduce Miriam to their parents. It might be uncomfortable but it was necessary, the done thing. Michael had always done what Simone told him and so he agreed to this as well. He warned Miriam what to expect but in the event it wasn't as bad as he made out, at least she said it wasn't, he must have been exaggerating.

By the second day at the house, though, the two of them gravitated to the kitchen where Miriam and Dora exchanged recipes and competed to cook the choicest food for Michael. He let them do it. It was good for them and he enjoyed what they presented him with. It was friendly competition, and when she got a chance Dora took Michael aside and said he should marry this girl, she was a gem. He said he hardly knew her and she shrugged her shoulders as if she were Jewish and said what's to know?

And then David Schulman rang from Washington. He was over on business and asked Michael to invite him down to Rochester and Michael obliged. The next day he arrived by car and made a big fuss of Miriam and schmoozed Michael's mother and he even sat in the study and discussed Talmud with his father, all in the space of a few hours. There was seemingly no-one who was immune to David's charms, even Dora, who baked a cake.

Finally, he took Michael to one side, but Michael was ahead of him.

'Look, David, I know what you're going to say so I'll save you the trouble.'

'You do?'

'Yes. She's a lovely girl and I should marry her. Well for your information I agree with you, OK?'

'If you say so, but as it happens that's not what I was going to say.'

'No? Oh.'

'Michael, I haven't got long. I hitched a ride on an Air Force plane over here and they've got a place for me going back in the early hours of tomorrow morning, so I'll come to the point. You've only been over here a week but in that time things have changed over in Europe.'

'In what way?'

'Look, Michael, your work in Bricha has been tremendous, really, but you know what we in Bricha are doing is only part of the bigger picture.'

'Uhuh. What picture would that be?'

'We're getting people to Palestine, sure, OK, not a lot and to be honest we're losing more to British prison camps than we're landing but even so, under the circumstances, we're doing OK.'

'Have you got any more information for me about Krystyna and the boys?'

'Well, all we know is they're being held in a camp near Famagusta on Cyprus. It's all completely illegal of course but …'

'Illegal? How?'

'Come on Michael, you're a lawyer, start thinking like one again. A shipload of people, let's call them refugees, sail towards Palestine and the British navy arrests every man woman and child on that ship, in international waters, and incarcerates them without trial when not one of them has even committed a crime on British soil, or come to that a crime at all.'

'Yes, but the British argument is that by sailing towards the

Palestine coast they show intent to land.'

'Sure, and I wouldn't argue with that as far as it goes. But there is no law against wanting to commit a crime. There is no statute book in the world that makes it a crime to think, not yet anyway. So that's the first point. The next point is that no civilised country in the world imprisons people without trial. There are tens of thousand of Jews locked up by the British, on Cyprus and in Germany mainly, without any attempt whatever to bring them to trial for any stated offence. And those people, I need hardly remind you, include children. What exactly are they supposed to have done to justify a prison sentence? And that's the next point. Those people are in prison without even having been sentenced. In other words, they are in prison indefinitely. In fact what they are is hostages. The British want to defeat the Jews of the Yishuv …'

'The what?'

'The Jewish population of Palestine. They want to limit immigration because that suits their relationship with the Arabs. Look, I don't need to tell you all this stuff, do I?'

'No. What you do need to tell me is why we're having this conversation.'

'Because, my friend, I have been asked to find a lawyer who will take on the British Government.'

'Oh, is that all? And have you? Found one, I mean.'

'I have now.'

'I was afraid you were going to say that.'

'Well?'

Michael didn't answer straight away. How could he? It would mean a huge change for him. Still you can't make a decision if you don't know what's on offer.

'OK.'

'You'll do it?'

'No, I mean OK I'll think about it. First of all, where would I be based?'

'Well, you'll need to spend time in London of course, and Germany with the occupation authorities, and it would mean trips to Cyprus too.'

'Cyprus? In that case, David, you have just hired yourself a lawyer.'

David had gone before Michael stopped to consider what it was he had just agreed to. He would have a staff of researchers but the responsibility, for tens of thousands of people, was going to be his. Their freedom would depend on him taking on a government and winning. The more he thought about it the more he thought it was a fool's errand, a complete no-hoper. And anyway, why him? He wasn't experienced in international law, and he hadn't even practised since before the war. It didn't ring true. Maybe it really was a no-hoper and David knew that and whoever he reported to knew it as well and they didn't want it to go too far. That was probably it. He was just being used to satisfy someone's demand that something should be done, and if it couldn't be done they should at least be seen to try. Maybe he was nothing more than their token lawyer. Whoever they were.

He met Miriam in the kitchen. 'Nice guy, that friend of yours.'

'Well, he's not exactly a friend. I work for him. And yes, he's Mr Nice. It's what he does. Even my mother liked him.'

'So, what did he want?'

'Oh, you know.'

'No I don't. It's why I asked.'

'Miriam, did they teach you nothing about discretion wherever it was you were educated?'

'Nope.'

He couldn't help himself laughing. He never could with her. It was one of the things he liked so much about her. He was finding it easy to forgive in her what he might not have done in another person. He hoped the effect wouldn't wear off, either that or she would settle down and be a bit less edgy.

'Well if you insist …'

'And I do.'

'Yes, well, he's offered me an opportunity.'

'An opportunity or asked you for a favour?'

'What on Earth makes you think that?'

'Michael Jacobs, I haven't known you very long, I readily admit, but I have a degree in psychology and if you don't want a girl who is going to analyse everything you say you should chose one with a different major. It's not that hard actually, I could teach it to you in about ten seconds. It goes like this. Someone who has just been given an opportunity looks happy.'

'Miss Fillon, you are truly amazing. I hereby award you a Bachelor of Science in reading my thoughts.'

'Thanks. I'll add it to my collection. Seriously, do you want to tell me about it?'

'Yes. But I can't.'

'Oh right, hush hush huh?'

'Something like that.'

'OK, tell me this if you can. Does it involve going back to Europe and getting shot at?'

'Yes and no.'

'I don't like the sound of that.'

'Yes to the first bit and definitely no to the second. The war's well and truly over. It's legal stuff.'

'Oh, right. That sounds great. I mean, it's what you do, isn't it?'

'Yes and no.'

'Please, let's skip the next bit. Just tell me, do you really want to do it?'

He put his arms round her and looked into her eyes. 'What I really want, Miss Fillon, is you.'

'Oh, you do?'

'Uhuh.'

'In that case, soldier, lead the way.'

Miriam was leaving for France a week later, and they made the most of their time together. Every time they went to the kitchen Dora looked at them knowingly, and before Miriam left Dora took her aside and had a talk.

Michael was curious. 'So, what was that about, you know, you and old Dora?'

'Oh, nothing.'

'Nothing huh. She just took you out into the garden and said nothing.'

'Michael, you can be awkwardly dim sometimes. When a girl says nothing what she means is nothing she wants to discuss.'

'I see. Women's talk, then.'

'Something like that, yes.'

'Now, little Miss Mindreader, let me see if I can tell you what that nothing was about. Would I be right in thinking that our Dora asked you if your intentions towards me were honourable?'

'OK, as it happens, she did. Well, something like.'

'And what did you tell her?'

'I told her my intentions were entirely dishonourable.'

'Oh yes, and what did she say to that?'

'Enjoy.'

Michael roared. 'Good old Dora, the most Jewish person in this household. She's a gem. I told you you would like her. So, tell me, have you enjoyed?'

'Very much.'

'Look, I'll be following you over in a couple of weeks, once I've got the basics sorted out here. I'll try to base myself in France. It's as good as anywhere, Paris probably.'

'I see. That's good for this job that you can't tell me about is it?'

'Yes. Well, it will do, and since I have been told I can work wherever I'm most comfortable I have decided to work there. I'll need to travel to England quite a lot and er, one or two other places, so France is just fine.'

Actually he had already discussed France with David Schulman and David had expressed some doubts about Paris. He said why not London? Michael said alright if you must know because of Miriam and if you don't like it you might want to look for another lawyer and David sighed and said it wasn't for him to get in the way of young love and if Michael didn't mind commuting to London, well, that was up to him.

Three weeks later he was set up in an apartment-cum-office in a back street near the rue de Constantine and Miriam had arranged a transfer to UNRRA's Paris office. She said there was no point her trying to find another apartment, what with the expense and all, and he said that was true, she might as well move into his, and she did.

Their first visitor was David Schulman. He looked around the place and nodded his approval. Miriam was out at work.

'So, got your girl with you, have you?'

'Uhuh.'

'You don't waste much time.'

'No, well, the war taught us that, didn't it?'

'I suppose it did. Does she know what you're doing here?'

'No, I've told her I don't want to talk about it and she respects that. She is Jewish, you know.'

'Half Jewish.'

'So, you've checked up on her.'

"Fraid so, kid, that's another thing the war taught us, isn't it, knowing whose side everyone's on. You know about her father, I suppose.'

'Yes, she's told me everything. What do you know about him?'

'Well, I've seen a dossier on him. I can't tell you why or where, but it's reliable.'

'OK David, I'm going to put it straight and I would appreciate a straight answer. Is he on someone's list?'

'Oh, I can tell you that much. Yes he is. Your little lady's father is a wanted man.'

6

Michael set up a team of researchers in London, Washington, Berlin and Tel Aviv. He wanted to know on what legal basis the British government was able to arrest thousands of refugees who had committed no crime, and detain them indefinitely, with no recourse to legal aid or the courts of any country.

The first issue to understand was on what basis Britain operated in Palestine at all. That was clear. She held a mandate to govern the territory, so he gave his man in Washington the task of assessing which powers that mandate gave the country, and which it didn't. He put his Tel Aviv woman onto researching precisely where the Levant Trader had been detained, because it was imperative they know if the ship was stopped in international waters, which would mean that at least one shipload of passengers was being held illegally, regardless of any other issues. That that shipload included Krystyna and the boys was of particular concern to Michael.

His man in London had the hardest task. Michael instructed him to make friends there. It was all very well being able to prove that the British action was illegal, but that was no use if no-one in England cared. Having the law on your side goes only so far. You have to be able to threaten your opponent with legal action in some kind of court, and the biggest problem so far seemed to be that there might be no court which could hear such a matter. Michael didn't know how independent the English courts were of the British government, and whether they would hear a case against their own government, and if they did, if they would hear it impartially or could be nobbled. He knew how it worked in the States, but that was quite different.

His London man had a second task, but one that might turn out to be equally critical. He was to make yet more friends, this time in the Press. If the legal route turned out to be a no-go, they would try the court of public opinion. The Levant Trader had broadcast from the Mediterranean and papers in a number of countries were now interested in the story, but they would only stay interested if his team could keep the issue live. The US media had little love for the British, whom they saw strutting around the globe as if half of it was still under their imperial rule. Americans had seen British fallibility in the war, a war they perceived as being won by US forces coming to the assistance of their former colonial masters. The relationship was a precarious one, and now that Winston Churchill, loved by Americans and by the British too until they chucked him out as soon as the war was won, could no longer provide the cement that tied the two countries together, Americans were in no mood for British self-aggrandisement. A story about Jewish survivors held in British prison camps, legally or otherwise, could play well in his home country.

London was the key, and a week into the job Michael packed a bag and left Miriam in charge of the apartment. She was emotional. She imagined that wherever he went he was likely to be in danger and he took her on to the balcony of the flat and made her look out at the Paris skyline. This city he said, was recently under the occupation of the German Army, but now Hitler has gone, and so have his troops. It's over. And if it's safe here, how safe do you think London is? She knew he was right but he saw it in her eyes, the fear that for some reason would not go away. For all her joie de vivre, now he knew her a little better he was getting used to her insecurity. He also started to formulate an idea of why.

He was met by his man in London at Victoria Station. George Billingham was unusual on Michael's team, in that he wasn't Jewish. It was felt that the English would talk more freely with someone they perceived as one of their own. He had a range of qualifications that suited him perfectly for the task, a law degree but never practised, a fellowship at a prestigious English university before the war, and then a commission in the Queen's Regiment and service in Italy and

Normandy. His regiment had been involved in the liberation of Bergen-Belsen.

Everything about George was hard, his tough exterior and his uncompromising dedication to the job. He would be able to talk with Civil Servants and politicians, lawyers and the military, and the Press loved him. He had featured on the front page of more than one paper receiving his George Cross from the King at Buckingham Palace. The tabloids even joked that the medal was named after him, a joke the King was said to appreciate.

He shook Michael's hand firmly, a little too firmly in fact.

'Sorry Mike, clumsy of me. You'll get the feeling back in your fingers in a day or two.'

Michael didn't remember suggesting Mike, but from this man he didn't take offence. Perhaps he thought it was the American way.

'OK with you if you kip at my place? It's quite convenient and it'll save you a couple of quid a night B and B.'

Michael looked at him quizzically. It was going to take some time to get used to English the way it was spoken on this side of the Atlantic. 'Sure George, lead the way.'

George took him by what he called the scenic route in a taxi, via the Palace, along the Embankment and finally the cab headed north to Islington. Michael looked out at London in what was supposed to be the summer and thought it was a grim place, for all George tried to impress him with its sights. It looked, he commented, like a bomb had hit it, and George laughed. One or two, he said, with what Michael was going to learn was George Billingham understatement. He had come highly recommended, and Michael himself had interviewed him in Paris, but he hoped they weren't wrong, that this man was more than his easy-going exterior suggested. What he liked about him was the fixed look his face took on when he was being serious, a look that said nothing was going to stop him, the British bulldog look, he supposed.

When they got to his flat George switched off his taxi-ride manner and became deadly earnest.

'OK old chum, throw your bags down somewhere and come and sit down. I'll make you some tea and then I'll give you a thorough briefing.'

George's tea left something to be desired and when Michael enquired about coffee he laughed and said you must be joking, haven't you ever heard of rationing? He also supplied copious quantities of toast and something called Marmite, which he appeared to live on, to go with the tea, and while Michael ate he talked.

After an hour, it was all said, and it didn't sound hopeful. George looked apologetic but said he had to give it to him straight.

'So the long and short of it is we've got a vaguely-worded mandate that the government can take to mean anything it wants, and a Colonial Office that just won't talk about Jews, partly through a policy of doing whatever it takes to keep the Arab countries on our side but also I'm afraid with a certain amount of old-fashioned racism thrown in for good measure. A few of the papers, especially the left-wing ones like the Manchester Guardian, are sympathetic. And then there's the Board of Deputies.'

'You haven't mentioned them. Who are they?'

'Well, ostensibly they're the representatives of the Jewish community in the United Kingdom, so they should be our first point of contact, but I'm afraid it's not that simple.'

'Nothing ever is, but why?'

'I have to say as an outsider I don't really understand where they're coming from. I haven't met them yet, which by the way you will have the pleasure of doing tomorrow, but I've been able to glean quite a lot of info about the set-up. The Board itself is made up of establishment figures who have an obvious interest in not upsetting anyone. Then you've got the split between one lot called the Ashkenazim and another lot called Sephardim, which might mean more to you than it does to me …'

'It does.'

'OK. But then you've got apparently the Orthodox and several other more liberal groups who are looked down upon by the Orthodox but who in turn look down on them. It's all very confusing.'

'I know. Welcome to the Jewish world.'

'And that's not all, because then you've got politics. Not just the normal politics of left and right, which of course I'm used to, but you've got the Zionists and the anti-Zionists.'

Michael looked surprised. He was unfamiliar with the latter, and asked George to explain.

'Sorry, chum, I can't. Maybe it'll become clearer tomorrow. I've arranged a meeting with the President and the Secretary for eleven o'clock. Meanwhile, I suggest you get some rest. You're sleeping in there. I'll come and wake you at six and and I'll take you out for some dinner.'

Dinner in postwar London was without doubt the least edible of Michael's meals in recent memory, not excluding the partisan camps in the Polish forests. Afterwards, George took him to a pub and introduced him to English beer, for reasons that were not apparent to Michael.

George's flat, it turned out, was unheated, something to do with bomb damage to the gas mains in the street. The London blitz had not been part of Michael's war but he was coming to learn about it, and in any case it didn't bother him. From camping in the Catskill Mountains to service in Europe, he knew how to live rough. He could match George's hardiness, and George appreciated that and found a growing respect for his employer. Michael joked about the food but he complained about nothing and George found in him a man after his own heart.

Well, he complained about nothing until after their meeting at the central London office of the British Board of Deputies. At Woburn House they were ushered in to the Boardroom and asked to wait. Ten minutes later they started to mumble to themselves. They were both military men. The time of a meeting, once fixed, was not variable. The Secretary finally came in half an hour late, without apology, and announced that the President was tied up but hoped to join them later. It wasn't a good start.

'Well, gentlemen, how can I help you?'

'Mr Feldman, my colleague Mr Billingham is not familiar with the Jewish community and is here as our representative in London.'

The Secretary raised his eyebrows. He clearly had a problem with a representative of a Jewish organisation who was not Jewish. He decided to address himself exclusively to Michael and pretend George wasn't there.

'So, Mr Jacobs, please, tell me what you think we might be able to do for you. And you say our. Who, may I ask, do you yourself represent? This was not made clear to me'.

Michael didn't like the tone and even George picked up on it.

'Mr Feldman, I am by profession a lawyer and, as long as it remains within these four walls I am at liberty to tell you I am employed by an organisation called Bricha. You may be familiar with it.'

'Yes, Mr Jacobs, we know of Bricha and its activities. They are not activities, I should tell you, that the Board especially approves of.'

Michael took a moment to consider this piece of information. The interview was already taking on an air he hadn't expected. It was threatening to become confrontational.

'Forgive my surprise, Sir, but perhaps you could explain that for me, and for my colleague here.'

'Yes I can. The Zionists believe that Great Britain can be bullied into establishing a Jewish homeland in Palestine. I personally do not agree with that stance.'

'You personally? And what about the Board, the President?'

'I think I speak for the Board in this matter.'

'I see. Perhaps you would explain then what the Board believes these refugees should do, where they should go.'

'I don't know. Where they came from, I suppose.'

Michael distinctly disliked the sound of that and gave an intemperate response. 'Mr Feldman, these people are Jews.'

'Mr Jacobs, I hardly need you to remind me of that. The Board is painfully aware of the catastrophe that has befallen our brethren in Europe and is not insensitive to their needs. As I speak, a large amount of money is being expended to bring relief to the survivors. But challenging the British Government and getting into arguments with the Royal Navy is not productive. There must be a better way.'

'And the thousands in camps, in Cyprus and in Germany?'

'What about them? You ask me as if I am personally responsible for them. We are, please be assured, doing everything we can to help. Money …'

'Yes, Sir, you talk of money, rather a lot it seems to me. It also seems to me that you believe money can solve every problem. Well, those people in the camps are there, we believe, held illegally by your government, and Mr Billingham and I came here this morning to ask for your co-operation in getting them released, by whatever means. Money will not buy their freedom. It will take a commitment of a different kind, and I sit here before you to ask if you have that commitment.'

He sat back in his chair and looked grim. He didn't know what the other man was going to say, and he didn't think it much mattered. The interview was over. The Secretary chose his words carefully.

'Mr Jacobs, I think you were mistaken to come here. I think you should have done some research before you made a lot of assumptions about the Board. I do not believe, therefore, that there is anything to be gained by prolonging this discussion. Good day to you.'

George saw Michael off at Victoria Station on the boat train that evening. He apologised, as if what had happened was somehow his fault, or perhaps he was just apologising for London in general. It had, Michael admitted readily, been a big disappointment, not just the Board of Deputies but a lot else besides. He assured George, though, that he had complete faith in him, and encouraged him to keep at it and report to Paris by letter or telephone regularly. If there was any major development, he promised to come back. They shook hands sincerely and as Michael sat back in his compartment he reflected that it wasn't going well, but that if there was anything that could be done in England George Billingham would find a way. Meanwhile there were other people working on this from different angles, in Tel Aviv and Washington and Berlin, but more importantly right now there was Miriam waiting for him in Paris.

7

It was no good trying to hide his feelings from Miriam. She was one of those people from whom there could simply be no secrets. She cooked a wonderful meal, but then anything would have tasted wonderful after English food, and opened a bottle of wine and let him talk. By the end of the evening he had told her everything, about Roza and the gold, Bricha, and his present assignment.

She sat with a glass in her hand and listened without interruption, which was a measure of how seriously she took this, and when he had definitely finished she gave him his messages. Without knowing what they were about, she had taken calls from Berlin and Washington, as if she were his secretary.

The next day she resigned from UNRRA and joined the staff of Bricha full time as Michael's assistant.

From that moment she was able to encourage him when he was down, share the little triumphs, which were indeed little and few and far between but still she pretended they were more important than they really were, and packed a bag for him before each trip and welcomed him home with good food and her love each time he returned. Michael spoke almost no French so on that score alone she was a huge asset.

This went on for several weeks and before they knew it they had worked through the summer, and autumn started to show in the leaves of the city's trees. The more time Michael spent with Miriam the more he realised he had fallen in love. She had a disposition he found irresistible and she filled his days with light. Those days were still, though, clouded by the sadness he had seen at the beginning, the sense of impending disaster that never quite seemed to leave her. They talked about it in a superficial way, because he knew she didn't want to reveal all her secrets, but in the course of time he came to understand what was behind it, that it was a secret of which she was ashamed. Her father.

As long as Gaspar Fillon was out there somewhere, and until her relationship with him was resolved one way or the other, he knew now that shadow would never pass. For this reason he started to put feelers out among his new contacts in government ministries and the police. He even re-made a couple of contacts in US Army Intelligence, people who remembered him and were kindly disposed.

Gaspar Fillon had done a very successful disappearing act. Officially, no-one was too concerned. The desire to expose collaborators was not strong in government circles. They were an embarrassment, a Pandora's box no-one was eager to open because too many people in high places were tainted, and the Gaullists seemed to have decided to put the past behind them. There was the occasional show trial and even an execution or two, but it was for public consumption. In any case, chasing Nazis and their sympathisers quickly came to be equated with getting revenge for the Jews, and the number of people, certainly in the former Vichy area of France, who wanted to do that was somewhat limited.

Michael brought the subject up with David Schulman when the opportunity arose and David could at least confirm, without any suggestion that he himself was in any way involved with Din, that a file still existed. He also intimated that Din was not the only group looking for Fillon.

Michael was able to give David little in return. It wasn't for want of effort, but none of his people could give him much either. The British government appeared to be in an unassailable position. No-one wanted to upset things in Europe right now. The enemy had morphed from the Germans into the Russians at the end of the war and there were much bigger issues than a few thousand Jews uppermost in the politicians' minds. Germany, which was supposed to remain a single entity under four occupation armies, had disintegrated into two countries. Relations between East and West were strained to the limit. If Great Britain was determined to hold sway over the Mediterranean, no-one was inclined to bother about it. Since the Levant Trader there had been other ships, and the prison camps swelled with their passengers, but those people had, to the rest of the world, become invisible.

Michael tried to get permission to visit the Famagusta camp, but the British weren't interested. He used his contacts in the Red Cross to get an official invitation but even the Red Cross couldn't budge the authorities, who simply said that the refugees, which is what they called them rather than prisoners, were being well looked after and there was no need for any kind of inspection. In fact the British made out the camps were some kind of safe haven for refugees who had nowhere else to go. They didn't explain what would happen if their guests made a request to leave, but then the camps weren't hotels and there was no facility for checking out.

Meanwhile, in Palestine, there was sporadic fighting between Arabs and Jews, and between Jews and British soldiers. Officially, Haganah co-operated with the Mandate Authority but that was Haganah. There were also terrorist groups, the Irgun Zvai Leumi and the Stern Gang. The Stern Gang in particular was completely ruthless and a constant thorn not just in the side of the British but of Haganah and the Jewish Agency as well. The latter hoped to work with the authorities by appeasement but the Stern Gang's policy was that you don't talk to occupiers. To call the British occupiers was stretching things a bit. They held a League of Nations mandate to govern Palestine after all.

As bad as the camps were, even Michael had to admit that they were, perversely, some kind of safe haven. Jews were trickling through from Poland and Hungary and Romania, from all over eastern Europe, with stories of local people killing former neighbours who returned unexpectedly, or at least chasing them out of town. It was as if the Poles in particular resented survivors and wanted them out of Poland once and for all. They might have thought the German's methods a little extreme, but in principle many Poles saw the point. Poland was not a home for surviving Jews. They had to have somewhere else. Ideally, that was Palestine, but failing that if they were caught in the navy's net they were at least safe.

David Schulman called Michael and invited him to a meeting in Vienna.

'What kind of meeting, David? I'm not really a meeting kind of guy you know. In my experience they are a substitute for action.'

'This one, I promise you, will be different.'

'Uhuh, convince me.'

'Well, for a start, it's with Haganah High Command.'

Michael was listening.

'Look, Michael, I don't want to discuss this on the phone. I want you there, OK? Next week, Tuesday. Travel on Monday and stay with me. Bring Miriam if you like.'

'That sounds like an order.'

'Michael, just be here.'

It was an order. David Schulman found Michael hard to control and he didn't like telling him he had to come but he really did, so there was no choice. Michael was working hard but there were no results. They both knew that. Well, the meeting next week might resolve the situation once and for all.

Miriam was listening in on the conversation but waited for him to put the receiver down.

'I got the gist of it. Do you think they're going to wind the operation up?'

'I don't know. There's more. It's not just a Bricha meeting, it's Haganah too, the High Command. For them to leave Palestine at the moment it must be important.'

'So you're going?'

'Of course. And so are you. David invited us both to stay at his place.'

'Oh, that's nice.'

'Well, I wouldn't put it that strongly. I think he has a bit of a soft spot for you.'

'Ooh, jealous?'

'Yes.'

'Good. I like that. Now come here and give me a reason not to look at another man.'

Miriam was an intensely physical woman. She clung to Michael like a limpet, like her life depended on that contact between them.

He had grown up in a family where physical contact was frowned upon, but Miriam touched him constantly and he found it both exhilarating and slightly frightening. He knew enough about these things, or thought he did, to understand why she did it. She was putting her scent on him, marking him as hers. For all his worldliness Michael's experience of women was somewhat limited and he found Miriam a little overpowering at times, but he was also tremendously flattered that she needed him so much. He asked her, once, about her own past love life and she just shrugged her shoulders and said there wasn't one, not really. Well, not really could mean almost anything, but he knew her well enough by now to know that if she wanted to tell him she would and since she wasn't she didn't want to, and he would be satisfied with that. He was a supremely unselfish man. To him, loving a woman was about what he could give her, not what she could give him.

His heart was filled with love for her but his head had room for more practical matters and as an ex-Intelligence officer it would have been surprising if he didn't analyse her the way he would anyone else. Love may be blind but it is not stupid.

There was something about the upcoming meeting that made him believe the operation was going to be stopped, and he couldn't bring himself to put any more effort in that week. He called his agents and got their reports and told them nothing they didn't need to know yet but he did tell them about the meeting even if he missed out the bit about Haganah which they certainly didn't need to know.

Then he and Miriam did what lovers do in Paris and it all went beautifully until they found themselves in a cafe and on the table was a newspaper and as had become their habit they drank coffee and ordered a piece of tarte tatin with two forks and read the news. On page four there was a piece about a collaborator who had been caught and hanged. The police were reported to be looking into the possibility that the crime had been perpetrated by a group of ex-Resistance fighters. The man's name was Roger Dubois.

They both felt a surge of relief mixed with something else. It may not, of course, have been the same something else for both of them. Dubois was apparently a petty thief who had a sideline as an informer for the Milice in Arles during the Vichy years. He was someone nobody would have any sympathy for, easy to despise, a nice neat story for the paper. The bigger people, the ones with a lot more to hide, had successfully gone to ground or changed their identity or were even brazening it out as if they were quite unashamed of their war record. There was a small comment piece about the fortitude of the French Republic to make its readers feel good and that was that.

Michael held Miriam's hand on the table but she pulled it away.

'No, don't do that.'

'Oh, why not?'

'Because you're trying to tell me how you feel for me but you can't, you don't know.'

'Alright, I don't know. Of course I don't, but can't I say I care about you?'

'You mean you care about me despite that fact that I have a father on a wanted list for war crimes.'

'No, that's not what I'm saying.'

'I didn't say it's what you're saying, I said it's what you're thinking.'

'Good God woman, can't I ever say anything straight without you turning it round?'

'Probably not. I warned you.'

'You did? About what?'

'That this wouldn't be simple, you know, you and me. You can back out any time you know, I won't blame you.'

'Now look here Miriam, is that what you think of me, that I am going to let this come between us?'

She didn't know. She hoped not. She did what any woman would do when she didn't know what to say, she started to cry. Michael felt like a bully. Miriam had remarkable powers of recuperation, and just as she went from happy to sad in an instant, it took not too long for her to revert back to happy again. She had some box where she locked up the black mood when it got in the way, and with Michael it was definitely in the way. She was trying hard for it not to infect their relationship.

So they enjoyed the rest of their little holiday pretending this thing was not there and on the Monday they took the train for Vienna and whatever change that was going to bring to their lives.

8

Some newspapers, depending on their political leanings, were starting to talk about Austria as liberated from the Nazis by the Allies, but every time he visited Vienna Michael saw it for what it was, the capital that had welcomed the Anschluss, that offered its soul up to the Nazis for reabsorption into the German Volk, that welcomed home its conquering hero, Adolf Hitler, and encouraged him to believe he could become Lord of the World.

For Michael Jacobs Vienna was not a liberated city, it was an occupied one, like Berlin, and like Berlin he felt uneasy there, as if some evil force existed there under the surface, a force that was suppressed by military defeat but which glowed like the embers of a fire that you think you have extinguished but haven't.

The autumn sun shone on the city though, by way of exoneration and, unlike Berlin, this city was not in ruins but showed its former Imperial glory for all who might come to see it. David Schulman met them at the station and drove them straight to his apartment. He schmoozed Miriam and she let him. He was a handsome man and she loved Michael, completely, so it amused her. She saw the look Michael gave her in response and she looked at him as if to say what can I do about it if I am irresistibly attractive?

At dinner Michael made a point of asking David how his wife and children were and David laughed because he understood perfectly what was the point of the question and didn't mind. It was all a game to him. He had no intention of doing anything about it. Miriam and Michael were a lovely couple, and the price of his happiness for them was to be allowed just a little flirtation. He considered it his droit de seigneur.

In any case, they all wanted an early night. It had been a long journey from Paris, and the meeting was set for nine o'clock sharp the next morning. The Haganah people were taking a risk travelling to a British-occupied city. They all had a price on their heads in Palestine, and it was their habit not to stay in one place for any length of time.

The meeting was in a house outside the city, and David drove them through the morning civilian and military rush hour. He looked constantly in his mirror. It was an old habit and a good one, but no-one followed them. The authorities of course knew he lived in Vienna and they knew he was somehow connected with the Jewish Agency and that meant he was someone to be watched but he never did anything interesting, not that they were ever aware of anyway, so he was way down on their list of priorities. Had they known that two senior members of Haganah High Command were also in town they would have taken a lot more interest.

The house was a nondescript one in a good suburb where bankers and senior civil servants would have lived at one time, and perhaps still did. It was a little run down now but the houses had a certain grandeur even so. David turned the car into a drive and someone closed the big iron gates behind them. The front door of the house was open and the three of them walked straight in. David led them up a grand staircase and on the first floor he took them through several large rooms which led on to smaller rooms and then, somewhere, Michael guessed, at the rear of the house, he knocked on the wood panelling and it turned into a door which opened to let them enter and closed behind them. It was a bright day outside but the curtains were closed and behind them they saw the shutters pulled to as well. It all had a cloak and dagger air that made Michael smile.

'So Mr Jacobs, you find our precautions amusing?'

Michael looked at this man. He didn't know why anyone would start a meeting with a complete stranger in such a prickly fashion, and he decided to diffuse any potential problems.

'No no, not at all. On the contrary, as an Intelligence man I appreciate them. I was admiring your thoroughness. Anyway, it seems I need no introduction, so may I introduce Miriam Fillon? She speaks excellent English and I see you do so perhaps we can use it for this meeting.'

As soon as he said the name he regretted it and he felt sure Miriam did as well. Fillon. Would it mean anything to them? From the look on their faces, no, nothing at all. Why should they know? Neither, on the other hand, did they display any old-world charm when introduced to a beautiful woman. They seemed to know that Miriam was not a main player and they more or less ignored her.

'I am Yossi ben Zvi and this is Nissim Shorat, and in case you are wondering, which I would certainly do in your position, yes, they are our real names. We are here among friends, and it is not our wish to deceive you in any way. Please, shall we sit down? Madame?'

It was a conciliatory little speech. Yossi ben Zvi was sensitive to the slight awkwardness his comment had produced and regretted it. He meant it when he considered himself among friends and wanted them to believe him. David Schulman already knew him, and he knew that Yossi was a professional. If he made a mistake he would admit it, and that was what he had just done.

'So, Mr Jacobs …'

'Michael, please.'

'Yes, of course, that would be better. David here has briefed me on your work with Bricha. You seem to have done a great deal.'

Michael was genuinely surprised. 'Really? I can't say I would agree with you. I consider we have achieved very little, if anything at all. We had a very specific aim, which was to find a way, legal or some other means, to get the British government to release the prisoners they are holding in Germany and on Cyprus …'

'Ah yes, including Mrs Celinska and her charges.'

'I see you are very well informed. Yes, including them, so if you like as well as the commitment you would have expected this has for me been, I mean still is, something very close to my heart.'

'I believe you, really.'

Yossi glanced at Nissim for confirmation of this and Nissim duly nodded in agreement.

'So, I am afraid I fail to see why you would think I have done anything. Those people are still there and the British have barely even noticed us. If I were defending in a murder trial my client would by now have been hanged.'

'A gruesome illustration but an effective one. Yes, I agree with you, the results have been disappointing.'

'Which inevitably begs the question, why are we here?'

Yossi looked at David and some signal passed between them which Michael noticed but couldn't interpret. David Schulman was, he knew, involved with many people and many organisations. He didn't know what this relationship was, but he had a feeling he was about to find out. Yossi proceeded.

'Michael, we have followed your work with considerable interest, as you might imagine we would. We have had a very great concern for those people on whose behalf you have been working, and so have many of our colleagues in Palestine. You may have felt you were on your own but I assure you you were not.'

Michael noticed Yossi was talking in the past tense, but he decided not to challenge it at this point. English was not his mother tongue after all. Perhaps it meant nothing.

'So, it is felt that, after such a good effort on your part, it might be time to, shall we say, draw a line under this matter.'

Michael had difficulty believing he had heard Yossi correctly. He looked at Miriam for confirmation and she was clearly thinking the same thing, so he had.

'Excuse me? What do you mean, draw a line under it?'

'I am sorry, perhaps my English is not so good after all. OK, I will explain, the best way I can, so please be patient with me.'

'Alright.'

'Getting those people released, is, on the surface, the right thing, of course. Why should they be held in prison camps for no crime? The British are no better than the Germans …'

'They're not killing anyone.'

'No, well, excuse my overstatement. Of course they are not. If they were, we would not be sitting here having this conversation. Mr Jacobs, Michael, it comes down to this. If anyone could have found a way to get them released, we firmly believe it would have been you. We have a lot of respect for your skills in this area, believe me. David here has told me a lot about you. I think if you have failed, and excuse me but I must say that, then it is not possible.'

Michael heard this and he turned to David. 'David, does this mean you are closing down the operation? Is this what you brought me to Vienna for?'

'Michael, please, listen to what Yossi has to say.'

'Thank you David. Look, Michael, there are other issues here.'

'There are?'

'Yes. You see, what you have been working on is getting those people freed, but have you thought what would happen to them if the British gave in, where they would go?'

'Well, to Palestine, surely.'

'No, definitely not. The Mandate Authority has a strict quota for immigration. At that rate it will take the next hundred years to get them all there.'

'Alright, where else?'

'That's the point. There is nowhere else. They want to go to one place only, Palestine, and in any case many of them come from eastern European countries where they are no longer welcome. You see, we have been trying to free them without any good idea of what to do with them if we succeed.'

Michael pondered on this. It made sense. He hadn't given it a lot of thought. He had been too busy trying to solve the first part of the problem.

'So, Yossi, what are you saying?'

'That we leave them where they are, which let us face it we seem to have no choice about anyway. It is the considered opinion of Bricha and the Jewish Agency that the priority now is to create an independent Jewish state in Palestine. When we have achieved that, we can bring these people home, and I promise you we will bring them home.'

It was inescapably logical. Michael had no argument against it and he didn't even try. He was looking at defeat, for now at least. David saw the look in his face and wanted to say something to make him feel better.

'Michael, we have got to do what Yossi says. Creating a Jewish homeland is the only way.'

'I know, I know. But what can I do? I suddenly find myself

without a purpose.'

And then for the first time, to the surprise of both Michael and Miriam, Nissim Shorat spoke. He had, to add to the surprise, a distinct New York accent.

'Michael, you asked why we brought you here to Austria. Well, there was a good reason, believe me. You want to know if you are now unemployed. Emphatically not. We have a proposition to put to you, if you would like to hear it.'

Michael looked at Miriam for support. He didn't know the answer to the question, but his instinct told him there was no harm in listening. They had come a long way, and he was, he presumed, about to find out why.

'Michael, I think we are agreed in this room that the people we have been talking about are stuck where they are until they can be brought to Palestine, legally, by a properly-constituted Jewish government. We believe totally that that will happen. We don't know when, but some of us believe it will be sooner rather than later. We say next year in Jerusalem. Well, maybe the year after, eh?'

Michael didn't respond to this little speech, so he continued.

'Excuse me one moment Michael.'

He spoke rapidly to Yossi in Hebrew, glancing meanwhile at Miriam. A short exchange ensued and he addressed Michael again.

'Excuse me, Michael, but I have to ask, excuse me Madame, but what I am going to say is very sensitive. I will need some assurance about your position ....'

'It's alright. I will vouch for Miss Fillon. Anything you say to me will be shared with her in any case, so I advise you now not to say anything to me you do not want her to hear.'

Miriam looked like you would expect her to look as she listened to these men discussing her and not addressing her personally. David Schulman resolved the situation. He said the same as Michael and on his word Nissim continued.

'Very good. Michael, Miss Fillon, Haganah High Command has a very important job that needs to be done and you, Michael, have been chosen for it.'

'Me? Well, I'll let you know when I've heard what it is whether I'm flattered by your confidence in me.'

'When we achieve an independent homeland we have no illusions, the Arab states that surround us will attempt to destroy our new country. We will have one concern only when that happens. Survival. That survival will depend on three things - people to fight, arms to fight with, and money to buy the arms. We cannot know if, even with those three components, it will be enough, but we know that without them our new homeland will be stillborn. People we're not short of, both already in Palestine and, of course, as we have been discussing, waiting to come, from the camps but from many other places too. Money will be an issue, but we have a certain amount already. Roza Levinson's gold will be the seedcorn that generates the funds for arms. Your part in that operation is very well understood by Haganah and I promise you that you have a reputation among people who know.'

'Really? Oh, OK.'

'And that is why you are here now. Anything in this world can be bought if you have the money. Everything is for sale, never more so than now. Europe is awash with surplus weapons. You know your way around Europe, and you know how to deal with the kind of people we're talking about. We want you to take charge of buying some of those weapons for our army for when independence comes. Haganah wants you to become its procurement officer.'

9

Michael and Miriam travelled back to Paris on the train and they talked of many things except what had happened in Vienna. Of course, they couldn't talk on a train anyway, but also neither of them knew what to say. It would mean a significant shift from helping refugees to being a part of the establishment of the Jewish homeland. By the time they got home, Michael had decided to do it.

Actually, he decided that the moment Nissim Shorat said it, but he wanted to think it through on the journey back, to put his instinctive, emotional reaction on hold while he applied his Intelligence officer brain to the series of questions it raised. There were clearly many problems. Unfortunately, when he sat and thought about them, he couldn't think what they were.

It was in fact a wonderful opportunity. He would be doing something hugely constructive for the Jewish people, but there was also in his mind the reason it had become possible, Roza's gold. He didn't know how significant it was. Nissim had said it was worth about five million dollars. It sounded like a lot of money but when he started to present Michael with Haganah's shopping list it started to sound like it would go nowhere. Nissim assured him, though, that a lot more money had been recovered since the war. Some of it had been returned to its rightful owners, where they could be found, but most of it had no owners now and the Jewish Agency had given its approval that in this circumstance it could be used for the Jewish people as a whole.

A lot more money, in cash, but also in paper that was convertible to cash, was locked up in the vaults of banks, in Switzerland, but also in many of the other neutral countries around the world, Sweden, Spain, Portugal, in South America, and there would be people who would chase that money on behalf of its owners and their successors, for as long as it took. The banks and insurance companies that had thought that Jewish money would never have to be returned would be proved wrong, but that was for other people to worry over. Michael's job was practical, and it was immediate. The arms he would procure could not yet be shipped to Palestine but would be bought and paid for, and then stored in each country of origin, or failing that in some other safe place he would be responsible for finding, against the time when the people of Palestine would be ready to use them.

What Michael especially thought about on that train journey was something he once said to Roza and Mordechai, all that time ago in a dark Polish forest, that they would be needed in Palestine when the struggle started, that they should escape to the promised land, and bring as many children with them as they could. Well, neither of them had made it, but their legacy would, and now it was his responsibility to make sure that they hadn't died in vain. The gold would do that, but also there was young Mordechai, and Moise and Adam too. He had, he never doubted, a personal responsibility to bring them to Palestine, and he would do this new thing but he would never forget his promise. One day, one day he would bring those boys home.

Meanwhile, there was work to do. He would need Miriam's help. She spoke French, she was a mistress of organisation and she had seemingly inexhaustible energy. But he would also need another man, and he knew who he wanted. Just two days after their return to Paris, he took the boat to Newhaven, and that evening he was in George Billingham's flat in London.

George's catering hadn't much improved, which wasn't really surprising. Most food was still subject to rationing, and that combined with George's military contempt for the soft life meant he ate whatever came and thought nothing of it. Michael was supposed to do the same. Dinner was, as always, Marmite on toast.

'So, Mike, welcome back to the centre of the British Empire. I got your message. Not looking good eh?'

It took Michael a moment to revert from his current optimism over the new project back to his pessimism over the old one. He had moved on so far he had to take a step back to where George was.

He took George back through the events of recent days and by the time he had finished George was looking grim.

'So, old chap, you're off to pastures new and George is out on his backside by the look of it. Well, all good things come to an end, but to be honest it wasn't all that good, was it? I'm sorry, I really am. I had high hopes, we all did. Even so, look, if I can ever do anything, you know, you only have to ask.'

'Good. You can and I'm asking.'

'Really?'

'Yes. I didn't come here and tell you a lot of highly classified stuff just because I like you, which by the way I do, although I think your cooking needs a bit of work, I came to offer you a job, another job.'

'Not like the old one then?'

'No, forget all that. This one is, shall we say, of a rather more practical nature, and to be honest George I want someone like you watching my back. We're going to be out there dealing with a lot of unsavoury people, arms dealers, ex-partisans, people who regret the end of the war, that sort of thing. We're going into the armaments business for Haganah.'

'I see. A bit more like soldiering then?'

'A bit. Think you can take that on?'

'Let me think about that, yes.'

'Good man. Now, here's the list of goodies they want. The idea, it almost goes without saying, is to buy as much as possible for a little as possible. We also have to do it with no-one knowing who doesn't need to know, which means every transaction will be checked and double-checked to make sure it's watertight. Where we can trust the seller, we will ask them to look after the goods until needed, and where we can't we will take delivery and store in a suitable place until the same. That will of course to some extent depend on the size of the item.'

George whistled through his teeth. 'I see what you mean. Fighter planes. Quite apart from where we might find the odd Hurricane for sale I'm having trouble imagining where we're going to store it, and come to that how we're going to get it to Palestine when the time comes. Come to that, we're going to need at least one pilot to ferry the things out. Have your people got pilots?'

'No idea. There were a few Palestinian flyers serving in the Royal Air Force in the war. We'll need to find out who they were and see if any of them is amenable.'

'And then there's spares and ammunition. Mm, they don't want much, do they?'

'Well, when you consider that the Egyptian air force alone has dozens of modern fighters supplied by the British with not only their own people but experienced pilots too, I would say the few planes we're going to buy is a bit on the light side, wouldn't you? We'll see if we can't do better.'

'Well, if you say so, chief. Now what else is there? Heavy machine guns, LMGs, rifles, SMGs, uhuh, plus ammunition of course, yeh, tons of the stuff knocking around I shouldn't wonder. Shouldn't be difficult. It's all my kind of kit, infantry stuff, so I can certainly help you there. Mortars, possibly, give me time, armoured cars, armoured cars, now that could be tricky but never say die, fast patrol boat, no, no idea but I might know a man who has. Submarine ....'

'Submarine?'

'Only kidding. No, the rest of the stuff's pretty routine, a lot of it will be dead cheap, still lying around by the lorryload somewhere in Europe. Hold on though, that's interesting, there's something missing.'

'There's probably a lot missing, but what particularly?'

'No tanks. They haven't asked for tanks.'

'Tanks? You're kidding. Where the hell are we going to buy one of those?'

'Michael, Michael, have you no imagination? No, this won't do, can't have a decent war without a few tanks.'

'Look, George, I know you think this is all a bit of fun but really, could we have less levity do you think?'

'No way old chum. Good God, didn't get where I am today being serious.'

'Oh yes, and where exactly are you today?'

'Well, now you come to ask, you've got a point. Come on though, let's pencil in tanks, nothing ventured nothing gained, what?'

'OK, tanks. What colour?'

'What? Oh well ....'

'George, only kidding.'

'Do you know, Mike, I think I'm going to enjoy this lark.'

'Lark? What is that English for?'

'Mike, Mike, what did you do during the war? Good grief man, if you can't enjoy a good fight, I mean, what's the point?'

Michael shook his head. George Billingham was incorrigible. He wondered how he would get on with the po-faced men from Haganah who took their fighting very seriously indeed.

Haganah High Command had quite a lot to say about George Billingham as it happened. When Michael told them he had taken him on they ran a series of security checks on account of him being ex-British military. They weren't averse to British servicemen in principle. Some had been very helpful, but there was always the risk of someone returning to old habits and talking to old friends. Michael assured them George wouldn't do that but he knew what he said would count for nothing. He had been in Intelligence long enough to understand that. They insisted on meeting George in Paris and they were shut in a room with him for five hours and when they came out he could see from the look on their faces that George had won. He was quietly rather pleased. He would trust George with his life. He might have to.

While he was in Paris George sampled Miriam's cooking and almost refused to go back to London. Michael never quite knew when to take him seriously. He did go, though, and he wasted no time setting up the infrastructure and the contacts they would need, especially the latter, of which he seemed to have an inexhaustible supply.

Another item he had an inexhaustible supply of was Marmite, and it turned out he had brought a jar to Paris as a gift for Miriam. To Michael's surprise, she took to the stuff and made him promise to bring back another jar every time he went over to London. He shrugged his shoulders and promised. Women, they were a closed book. There was no knowing why with them, and very little point in asking, in Michael's experience. If he ever asked Miriam to explain why she did what she did or thought what she thought he got a long convoluted explanation which left him wondering why he had asked in the first place. Miriam just shook her head as if to say well, men, the poor dears, what's the point? In short, they had a very normal relationship.

So Michael knew when he went away, to London, or on any of the increasingly extended trips he made to the far corners of Europe, that Miriam would be waiting for him, wanting him, loving him, and he knew that as time went by they were becoming dependent on each other, in a way that could lead to only one thing. Well, this wasn't the time for those thoughts and he put them to the back of his mind. He wondered sometimes, the way she looked at him, as if she was willing him to talk about the future, but it was like the war, he didn't know if there was a future, couldn't put his hand on his heart and promise to be here in a year or ten years, because there was work to do and work always had priority over life. He wondered sometimes what he was afraid of and in his odd moments of clarity he knew, he was afraid of her. Until she resolved the issue that dominated her thoughts she would not be ready for him, not the way he wanted. Well, there was little or nothing he could do about Gaspar Fillon. He had put out feelers but nothing had come back. He was a policeman, or had been at least. If he wanted to disappear, and he certainly had reason to, it was unlikely he would ever be found. And, in any case, even if he was found what then? How would Miriam react? Well, that was the future, and the present was complicated enough without worrying about what ifs.

And then a telegram arrived from Rochester. His father had had a stroke. Miriam told him in no uncertain terms he had to go and he argued that his work couldn't be interrupted and she said look he's your father and he might die and what then, how will you square that for the rest of your life not being there for him? He thought about it, understood why his father was so important to her and knew she was right, of course he should be there, but it would mean being away for at least three weeks, and what if he got there and the old man was on the mend and then he came back to Paris and as soon as he arrived there was another telegram to say he's had another stroke come quickly he's asking for you? How many trips could he make to the States, how long could he spend away? Wouldn't he just get into an impossible situation, waiting for his father to die so he could get on with his job? Miriam got angry and said what about the job, what did that matter against seeing his father and of course she was right, but on the other hand so was he, he could see it clearly enough, he couldn't put everything on hold in case his father died.

He sent a telegram to his sister Simone and asked how serious it was and she replied immediately to say he had just passed away. There was no point going now. He had missed the funeral, and go for his mother? Hardly. Simone had her husband and would cope and Shula didn't need him, so no, he would visit the grave next time, but for now he sat shiva for Siggy Jacobs as best he could and made a rare visit to a synagogue to discover how he felt, if his religion had anything to say to him at this time, but of course it didn't, religion is not something that comes to the rescue in moments of need. You either do it or you don't do it, and Michael didn't. He envied his father's return to the holy books in the last years of his life, but he knew he would never do that when his time came, he could never return because he had never really been there.

It reminded him that he had once envied Roza's complete confidence in the futility of religion. He understood that being Jewish wasn't something you simply shrugged off though. The war had made that point very clearly. He talked to Miriam, and she held him close and gave him what she could but what can any of us do? We are all lost, and all there is is other lost souls to cling to. And so they clung to each other.

10

It quickly became apparent that the original proposal to have arms suppliers store weapons until delivery was called for was going to be impractical. The kind of people who traded in war-surplus arms didn't want the goods hanging around once they were paid for, and in any case Michael and George realised pretty quickly that these were not trustworthy people and were as likely to sell the same goods twice and then disappear.

Michael bought a large-scale wall map of the world and pinned it up in George's flat.

'OK, let's look at some givens. We have a number of countries where we're likely to be buying arms, and just one place they will need to be delivered to in due course.'

He took a thick blue pencil and drew a line round the outline of Palestine. It felt strange, like he had a right to do it.

'Now, from our investigations so far, what have we got as likely sources?'

'Well, almost the whole of central and eastern Europe, plus the Iberian peninsula and Italy, some Balkan countries and Greece, even possibly the Maghreb.'

'Alright, let's say, for the moment, anywhere. Now, a storage depot. One place or more?'

'Well, pros and cons. A number of locations spreads the risk in case of discovery, but a single depot gives us better control. So, in short, I don't know.'

'OK, let's say that's open for the moment. I guess we'll just have to see what comes up. In which case the next thing it where? Looking at this map, which country is our prime target for storage?'

'Well, perhaps the first exercise is to eliminate those that are no possible use.'

'Good, hold on, red pencil for this. Right, well I think we can safely say England is out.'

'Uhuh.'

Michael quickly shaded the whole of the British Isles in red.

'Hold on, hold on, that bit's not Britain. It's Ireland.'

'Yeh, but same difference, huh?'

'No, I wouldn't say so. Tended to sympathise with Germany in the war, not because they loved Nazis but on the basis of my enemy's enemy is my friend. There's enough antipathy for Britain in Ireland to possibly mean our enemy's friend might be our friend. On the other hand, it's a long way from anywhere, and ships would always be vulnerable to interference from the Navy, so no, forget what I just said and put a red line through it.'

'But we're talking about shipping this stuff after Britain has ceded Palestine, aren't we? I mean, isn't that the whole point?'

'In theory, yes, but my beloved country letting Palestine go isn't the same as helping the Jews to defend themselves. I'm afraid you must consider the serious possibility that any arms shipments for a Jewish nation in Palestine will be subject to Royal Navy interference.'

'Really? Could they get away with that?'

'Michael, think about those people on Cyprus.'

'You're right. OK, consider it forgotten, well forgotten but not forgiven. Now Spain and Portugal?'

'Neutral, like Ireland, in the war, strong Nazi sympathies, especially in Spain, would only work if there was no discernible Jewish connection. Plus the long overland route through Allied-occupied Europe, or a sea voyage ditto as per Ireland. So, on balance, no to Iberia.'

'Right, red shading for them. I guess any Axis country occupied by Allied forces is out.'

'Yes, too risky.'

Michael shaded in Germany, Austria and Italy.

'I guess we can discount the whole of the Balkans until they've finished slaughtering each other, especially Yugoslavia.'

'And Greece for the same reason.'

'Scandinavia?'

'Nope.'

'No, you're right, too far. What about France?'

'Mm, don't know. Maybe we could find somewhere close to the Alps, a bit remote, you know, what do you think?'

'Well, not bad. But we would still have a route either by sea or across Italy and the Balkans. No, I don't think so.'

'OK, shade it in. So, the Maghreb?'

'No. Heavy Allied presence, especially still in Libya. plus a lot of British troops in Egypt blocking the route. And of course they are Arabs, of a kind, and may sympathise with the Arabs taking over Palestine. No, forget the whole of North Africa.'

They stood back and looked at the map. It was almost all shaded in red. Except for one country.

'Turkey?'

Michael peered at the map. 'Mm, what do we know about the place?'

'Neutral in the war, as you know.'

'Yes, and declared war on Germany in '45 when the result was clear. Attitude to Jews in Palestine?'

George shrugged his shoulders. 'Well, no obvious hostility. Moslem, but secular as well. How much do you know about Turkish politics?'

'What most people know, I guess. A strongly secular state since Kemal Ataturk. Non-aligned. Poor. Corrupt.'

'And therefore open to bribery. Yes, it looks interesting. Come here, look, good overland routes from the whole of eastern Europe, and even possibly an overland route to Palestine.'

'Still, lots of risk factors on the way.'

'Well old chum, I think you probably realise this is not an entirely risk-free business. I mean, look at the map for heaven's sake. You've shaded almost every other country as useless. No, I think Turkey bears some further consideration.'

Which was what they did. Miriam saw them both off at the station in Paris for what was likely to be a long trip. They travelled by train to Istanbul, and there they hired a car and driver, Mehmet, for a tour of Anatolia. It was a strange thing to do, especially in early winter, but Mehmet was reassured that a Briton and an American might be crazy enough for most things. Anyway, business was bad and these people paid in US dollars.

Mehmet drove them round Turkey for a week, with a running commentary in broken English, most of which they couldn't understand and eventually gave up trying, about the sights to be seen which as far they could tell comprised unbroken vistas of boring scrub, interspersed with anecdotes about his family and their equally tedious history.

George reckoned this must be something like Palestine, a country he had never been to but had seen pictures of, and it started Michael thinking. He wasn't sure how to express what it was he was thinking so he kept the idea to himself but on the last day, when he was about to say they should go back to Istanbul because once you've seen one part of Anatolia you've seen it all when Mehmet launched into some garbled story from which they gleaned that while they were in the area of Birecik would they mind making a small detour to see his uncle Oktay? They could think of no good reason why Mehmet's uncle would be of any interest to them but it seemed churlish after they had travelled so far together not to indulge him.

Oktay Yilmaz's farm was one of those out of the way places that you know as soon as you look at it could never possibly turn a profit, or come to that support anyone. The ground was stony and dry. Goats nibbled at what vegetation they could find and the only water supply was a stream that ran from a river somewhere that was itself a tributary of the Euphrates. Oktay's farm was in a land that time had forgotten. He had apparently had a wife once but she had died, either that or she had gone off and left him, it was hard to tell. He spoke no English at all, and Mehmet's interpretation left a lot to the imagination. The old farmer made them coffee and with a toothless grin insisted they eat some kind of sweetmeat with it that Michael had trouble keeping down. George just smiled in appreciation and ate the lot. There was almost nothing he couldn't eat.

While he did that Michael wandered round the farm with mounting curiosity. There were some ramshackle farm buildings and when he peered through the gaps in the wooden planking they all appeared to be empty. Empty was good. He went back to the farmhouse to find George and took him outside.

'George, this is it.'

'What is it, old chum?'

'It, what we're looking for, our storage depot.'

'But there's nothing here.'

'Exactly.'

'And it's in the middle of nowhere.'

'Precisely.'

George thought about it, looked around. It was desolate and tumbledown. It was so far from the rest of the world that the rest of the world was probably unaware of its existence. The old man lived in his own. Yes, all the ingredients were there.

'Look, get the map out of the taxi. OK, now see, we've come all the way across Anatolia, we're practically in Syria here. And there's Palestine. How long do you reckon by road?'

George scratched his head. 'Well, guesswork of course, avoiding towns, assuming we can cross borders where we choose, a week, maybe less. Failing that, if we can get the stuff to the coast and on a small freighter undetected, we might be able to run down the eastern Mediterranean in one night. And there's something else.'

'What?'

'Well, come here. Look, what do you see?'

There was nothing. Just a straight track running into the distance. It was all just straight and flat. That was what Michael replied.

'Exactly. I reckon you could land a plane on that easily.'

'You mean a fighter?'

'Yep. But not just a fighter. A cargo plane, say a Dakota. Yes, now I think about it, a Dakota could land on that road. I've seen them land in worse places.'

'But what do we want a Dakota for?'

'Mike, look, you're doing what you always do, thinking small. Think big. We're talking about trucking stuff around over hundreds of miles, but what it we could fly it around instead, or as well?'

Michael thought about that, and what he thought was why hadn't he thought of it himself.

'OK, sounds good. A Dakota isn't on the shopping list but once we've bought one it could come in very handy. Yes, I like it.'

'OK, Mike, now you're thinking like me. Now all we need to do is swing the old man, what's his name?'

'Oktay.'

'Well, let's go and try.'

When they re-entered the farmhouse Mehmet got the first question in. It was getting late. Would they mind staying there overnight, set off early the next morning? It played straight into their hands. By midnight they had bought the farm.

The next morning Mehmet was instructed to head straight for Ankara, no hanging around, and take them to a lawyer. Michael wanted it signed and sealed before anything could go wrong. He had drafted a power of attorney that gave Mehmet the authority to sign an agreement on behalf of his uncle.

It was a simple document, but he thought a Turkish lawyer, paid enough money, would accept it as bona fide. The sale agreement included a clause that allowed Oktay Yilmaz to stay on at the property. George reckoned he would be useful, make it look like the farm was carrying on as normal, and as he spoke no English, let alone any other language, there was little chance of him ever learning the truth about what they were doing there.

The sale was conducted on behalf of the Levant Trading Company, which also, while its representative was in the capital, bought three second-hand four-ton trucks and rented a large empty warehouse just outside town to store them in temporarily.

From Ankara, Mehmet drove them back to Istanbul and insisted that they come home with him and his wife would make a meal for them before they left. It was impossible not to accept his hospitality under the circumstances, and they went with him and met Ayshe, his wife, and then each of his three sons was solemnly introduced to the men from far away, and when Mehmet told his wife that these men had just bought Uncle Oktay's farm for at least twice as much as it was worth she laughed, which made him angry, but of course neither Michael nor George had any idea what he said or why she laughed.

Finally, he saw them off at the station with warm hand-shakes and tears in his eyes. Allah, he told them, had brought them to him and his uncle and Allah would assuredly be looking after their business venture. Personally he thought they were mad, but he didn't say that. And they thought that the chance of Allah taking an interest in the business of Jews was itself somewhat limited, but neither did they say that.

11

Michael had a facility to draw cash, in any currency, on the account at Bank Dreifuss in Zurich, from banks throughout Europe. He soon learned, though, that there was one method of payment that was favoured by many of the dealers he bought from, and that was, ironically, gold. He had to purchase it at the going rate wherever he went, and that wasn't always favourable, but it couldn't be helped. Miriam dealt with finance and all the administrative bits and pieces from Paris.

They bought small quantities of weapons here and there but the first big breakthrough came in Spain. George got word that someone was selling a cache of British small arms - Lee Enfield .303 rifles, Sterling sub-machine guns and Bren guns, all with a large quantity of ammunition. The seller was ostensibly a dealer called Oswaldo Martinez in Bilbao but unsurprisingly they wanted to know why a Spaniard had British weapons for sale, so Michael put the word out in the Intelligence community to see if anything came back about this Oswaldo Martinez and in due course he learned that his name had not always been Martinez but that until a year ago he was better known as SS Sturmbannfuhrer Heinz Eichel and that since the war he had enjoyed the hospitality of the Franco government in Spain.

The provenance of the weapons started to come out on further investigation. They had been held in Germany since the early part of the war, part of an armoury left behind by the British Expeditionary Force after the evacuation from Dunkirk. Eichel managed to transport the haul through France and across the Pyrenees in the middle of the war without anyone noticing they had gone missing.

He was probably planning, if apprehended, to claim it was for carrying on the war against the Allies in the event of a disaster. It would have been a halfway-plausible explanation and might have saved his neck. In the event, though, it was never used, and now he needed cash rather urgently and was looking for a buyer. He had a suspicion that Michael represented a Jewish organisation but Nazi ideology was of relatively little interest to him now. Now, what he needed was money, and any buyer with gold was a customer.

Michael and George travelled to San Sebastian in the three lorries which now bore the legend Levant Trading Company on their sides, with a licence for the export of scrap metal, and a Spanish interpreter. The next day they arrived in Bilbao and met the man who claimed to be Martinez. Michael carried in his pocket a photograph of Eichel but he didn't need to refer to it. The ex-SS officer had made no attempt to disguise himself. There was no doubt it was him. His Spanish would certainly pass muster as far as they were concerned but the interpreter assured them it was not his mother tongue. It took several hours to load up the lorries, at a disused factory out of town, and cover them with tarpaulins first and then scrap metal in case of a customs inspection. They didn't stop until they were halfway across France, and while the rest of the crew took a meal break Michael made a telephone call to Vienna, to let David Schulman know where Din would find Heinz Eichel. If they were quick, they would be able to recover the gold Michael had just paid him as well.

In the ten days it took to drive from Spain to Turkey, no-one challenged them. Such was the chaos still in Europe that three lorries carrying scrap metal didn't arouse suspicion. When they arrived at the farm Oktay Yilmaz welcomed them like long-lost friends. He had, as instructed, installed a few more creature comforts, like a decent kitchen and bunks for several workers. He had also got a supply of food in and one of their drivers turned out to be a reasonable cook so they didn't have to suffer any more of Oktay's meals this time.

The various farm buildings had also had some basic repairs and these now started to fill up with the merchandise being shipped in. They didn't make them look too smart though. No-one came to the farm, but just in case they wanted no sign that it was now being used for something else. Not attracting attention, especially from local officials with nothing better to do than pry, was the best form of security for the weapons. Even so, they left one man there permanently, someone with at least a smattering of Turkish. Since all the weapons were in crates Oktay didn't concern himself with what they contained, and if ever he got into conversation with the guard they were always referred to as agricultural equipment.

Next on the shopping list was armoured cars. They asked around but it seemed no-one was selling. Perhaps there was simply no such thing available second-hand. Anyway, in the end Michael went straight to the manufacturers, Skoda, in Czechoslovakia. The Czechs were short of work these days. The Soviet Union had enough hardware to start at least one more war and no-one was ordering new kit. Czechoslovakia needed all the hard currency it could get its hands on, and an order for six armoured cars wasn't a lot but it was welcome, no questions asked.

A month later George took the three wagons to the Skoda factory and loaded up the first three cars. By the time they and then the second shipment arrived in Turkey the farm was beginning to fill up. Oktay had never seen an armoured car before so when they rolled off the back of the lorries he either had no idea what they were or he kept his thoughts to himself. Life was a lot better now the foreigners had come and he thought it a bit odd that goods kept arriving but never seemed to be shipped out again but, well, that was their business, and he had never seen agricultural equipment like this but maybe in other countries they did things differently. Oktay had never been abroad, and as far as he was concerned things happened there which a poor uneducated man couldn't hope to understand. He had been too old to enlist in the first war but he had a son who joined up and wrote letters telling him of the strange things he saw, but he never came back and that was when the farm started to go to pieces and then there was the business with his wife.

The lorry drivers employed by the Levant Trading Company were all Haganah members and when they weren't driving across Europe they spent their time in the various farm buildings unpacking and cleaning weapons, then repacking them carefully for when they would be used. They set up a small firing range and took the opportunity to get in some target practice. Oktay thought this was a little odd too, but then he also had a rifle. Everyone in these parts carried one to protect their flocks of goats and sheep against wolves. That the drivers liked to fire off a few rounds wasn't all that surprising. He watched and admired their up-to-date weapons and compared them to his ancient Ottoman-era rifle, so sometimes they let him fire a few rounds with a .303 and eventually they gave him his own rifle to go hunting with and he killed an antelope and they had fresh meat for a few days.

The other job George had the men do was to erect a large area of camouflage netting against the time when the farm might house fighter planes. Ideally he would have liked a hangar but there were no materials available locally and neither did they have the building expertise for a structure of that size and there was no question of employing builders locally because quite apart from the security issue there were no builders locally on account of there being no-one for miles around, which had been the point of taking the farm on in the first place. No, they would have to hope that any planes delivered there would be gone soon enough and for the short while they were there the netting would have to do. Oktay asked what it was for but language can be a great barrier when you want it to be so in the end he just shrugged his shoulders and lost interest.

It got surprisingly cold as the winter wore on and the men took to doing not very much except huddle round the meagre fire in the farmhouse and tell stories and jokes in Hebrew. As winter finally started to turn to spring Michael arrived at the farm with George and Nissim Shorat. Nissim inspected the store of weapons and smiled, which was a first as far as Michael knew. It was better than he had expected, and he slapped Michael on the back. It was a rare compliment.

'So, Michael, show me round the farm if you wouldn't mind.'

'George, you know the place better than I do. You lead the way.'

Nissim looked slightly askance at George. He had a deeply-rooted distrust of anyone who wasn't Jewish that he found difficult to overcome. People did what you wanted for money usually, but George was obviously an enthusiast. And he had done an excellent job so now was not the time to have doubts.

'Thank you Mr Billingham .....'

'George, please. Either that or Major Billingham, but not mister.'

Nissim contemplated this. 'Well, in that case, for reasons I should like to explain in due course, I shall call you Major Billingham. So, lead the way please Major.'

They did a short inspection tour of the rest of the farm and Nissim shook hands with Oktay and then he looked down the long straight road that George had commented on to Michael when they bought the place.

'Yes, I see what you mean. You could land almost any aircraft here.'

'Even a Dakota.'

'Oh yes. It doesn't need a long runway, depending on the payload of course, but this road stretches on for ever, doesn't it?'

'All the way to Syria.'

'Mm.'

Nissim was thinking and Michael and George stood and watched him do it. He would tell them what about when he was ready, if he was ready, but asking him would serve no purpose.

'Major, Michael, would you say your work here has been a success?'

George looked at Michael and let him answer. It was safest.

'I think so. We have most of the items you wanted. There is still some money available and we will just go on buying until it runs out or you tell us to stop.'

'I want you to stop, for now anyway.'

'Oh, I see. Well, actually, no, I don't.'

'I have another job for you, both of you.'

'Yes? OK, we're listening, aren't we George?'

'Uhuh.'

'I want you to set up a training school here.'

'A training school. And what are we going to be teaching?'

Nissim looked at Michael a little tetchily. He was not a patient man and he didn't expect to have to spell everything out.

'Haganah does a certain amount of training in Palestine but the risks are high. We have already had a number of people arrested by the British for carrying arms, which means we lose the weapons and the people.'

George had a question. 'Mr Shorat, you talk about people. Is that a direct translation from the Hebrew or do you mean what I think you mean?'

'Yes Major, I mean women as well as men. In Haganah we don't differentiate. When the time comes, everyone will be fighting for their lives. You are not used to that in the British Army, where your women stay at home and look after the children, but that is not a luxury we will have. This place has many advantages. We can get our people here quite easily and no-one will bother them once they are here. You will of course have to build more accommodation, but for now we will send you tents.'

'Tents?'

'Yes Major, I think you are familiar with them?'

'Well, yes.'

'Good, then may I have your answer? Captain Jacobs?'

'Well, I guess.'

'Good. Major Billingham?'

'OK, count me in.'

'Very good. In the next few weeks we will send you a team of instructors who will all come under your command, Major Billingham. Oh, and by the way, I am sure you will understand that as your rank in the British Army does not apply within Haganah, you will start at the rank of Captain.'

He didn't ask what George thought about that, but unsurprisingly George was not happy. Michael looked at him.

'Look, George, I know what you're thinking, but you know rank is meaningless really.'

'No it's not.'

'No well, that's not quite what I mean.'

'I know what you mean, Mike. That if you're a captain you can't have a major under your command.'

'Yes, that's exactly what I mean. Good. So you'll accept?'

George had a look on his face that was pure British Army officer class. Michael was impressed. It was all he had with which to salvage his pride.

'Yes, I accept.'

Nissim Shorat might have been pleased that this was resolved but if he was he showed nothing.

'Captain Jacobs, if you will accept it I am authorised to offer you a promotion, effective immediately, to Major in Haganah. Do you accept?'

Michael was stunned. He wanted to say no but he knew there was no point, so he tried to make light of it.

'Does it come with a pay rise?'

'No.'

'Oh, OK.'

'So, Major Jacobs, you are now appointed commandant of Camp Joshua. Mazal tov.'

12

Miriam was not pleased. Michael told her he would still be able to spend time in Paris but he had to admit that he would be spending a lot more time at Camp Joshua. She waited for him to suggest she should come with him but he didn't and she wasn't sure if she was pleased or not. She didn't see herself in a pair of khaki shorts in the wastes of Turkey firing a machine gun. Neither did he, which was why he didn't suggest it. She stomped around for a couple of days being angry and rude and he didn't like it because what he really needed was a warm welcome home from his lover but she had her own issues and one of them, he knew, was that he should be with her. Well he wanted to be but he had a commitment now that could not be broken. In time of war millions of men had left their loved ones at home without knowing if they would ever see them again. Well, at least he knew he would see Miriam again. He was not going to war. Not yet.

They had a few days holiday before he had to return and they tried to make the most of it. Miriam seemed to sense that she was getting it wrong, that being angry with him was not the way to keep him, that it was more likely a way to alienate him. She reasoned that unless he had someone to come home to who made him welcome he might decide not to come home at all. And in any case, she needed to be close to him like he needed to be close to her, and they only had a few days and it was idiotic to waste it on anger about something that could not be helped. The net result of that was that when it came to the time when he had to pack his bags and leave he didn't want to, he really didn't want to. Suddenly it seemed like too much to sacrifice, this happiness, but at five-thirty one cold morning George picked him up in the car they now used and Michael kissed Miriam tenderly on the cheek and left her sleeping. He was excited about this new project, but he had a heavy heart too. He would try and get back as soon as possible. He would find reasons to be in Paris. Haganah would just have to understand.

En route they stopped at a sawmill in the south of Bulgaria where two of the Levant Trading Company lorries had just finished loading up with construction timber, and from there the convoy proceeded into Turkey, crossed the Bosporus and drove into Anatolia. Michael let George drive the last part of the journey and as he sat and watched the now-familiar landscape go past the windows he realised that this was starting to feel like home. His centre of gravity had shifted, irrevocably perhaps, to the east. Europe had long since overtaken America as his idea of home, but now even Europe seemed part of his past. Except, of course, for Miriam.

The first plane to land at Camp Joshua brought six instructors. It bumped down the dusty road and lurched to an abrupt halt about half a mile away. Minutes later the passengers, five men and one woman, walked into camp. They looked around them and Michael knew from those looks that no-one had told them there was no camp, that it was nothing more than a pile of timber and if they wanted a camp they were going to have to build one.

Building, it turned out, was also one of their skills, and if it wasn't it soon became one. One of their number, Avrom Halberstam, pointed out that in Poland ordinary people had been forced to build concentration camps and gas chambers, killing factories for their own people. Making a camp for the redemption of Eretz Israel was a whole lot better than that.

Within the first twenty-four hours everyone had rolled up their sleeves and got to work, even Oktay Yilmaz. He still thought of it as his farm in a way, and these kind people were here putting up all sort of new buildings and every day he looked on with happiness as it blossomed. Michael and George's rank meant nothing to the Palestinians. The two officers were expected to do their bit with the people who were nominally their subordinates, not one of whom had any sense of hierarchy.

A month later they had two sizeable buildings up and with roofs, if not windows. Over one they fixed a large sign that said Levant Trading Company and underneath that Agricultural Training School. The first training group arrived, twenty-two men and women, all of them young, most of them refugees from Europe but some sabras, Jews born in Palestine. What they all had in common though was the same look in their faces, a total commitment to doing this, a yearning to absorb the military skills they were going to need soon, well they hoped soon. George Billingham worked as an infantry instructor, a lot of which he could manage without Hebrew, which was, according to a regulation set down by Haganah High Command, the only language to be used in Camp Joshua.

Michael wanted to teach what he could as well, but Intelligence is open only to a few and of the first group there was only one, a girl called Dvorah, a sabra who spoke English but that was no use. He therefore gave her the task of teaching Hebrew, to him first, then George sat in on the lessons, partly because he wanted to learn but also because Dvorah was a quite attractive young woman. Then a few more people joined the classes, a couple of Poles, a Czech and a Belgian.

They were held in the evenings, after the hard physical work was done. The students learned their skills during the day, then after classes they carried out all the housekeeping functions necessary to the smooth running of a training camp, then their Hebrew lesson and finally, for anyone still awake, and amazingly that was most of them, they sang and danced, something George was learning Jews did whenever a group of them got together. They had between them a guitar, a violin and an accordion, and Camp Joshua in the evening was never without music. Even old Oktay sat and tapped his feet. He had no idea what the songs meant but he liked the sound of them, and sometimes a couple of the girls took his hands and insisted that he dance with them, which made him blush with embarrassment but it also pleased him.

Michael noticed that some of the young men and women quickly paired up at night. They didn't have separate sleeping quarters. It wasn't, apparently, necessary. He asked Dvorah if this behaviour was alright and she shrugged her shoulders and said of course, what's wrong with it? She hinted that Michael had an outdated view of morality and he thought that yes, he probably did, but it was a view that had always served him well. Within a few more days he was pretty sure that these arrangements had now extended to Dvorah herself, and George. He said nothing. He was camp commandment but that did not, according to her, include the pastoral welfare of the youngsters in his care.

It was an attitude he had seen before, in the partisan camps. People who didn't know how long they were going to live didn't worry about these things. They just paired up too. And then some of them had died and he himself had felt they had the right attitude, that some human comfort when you can get it is not something you turn your nose up at because the rabbi or your parents wouldn't have liked it. The rabbis were dead, and the parents too. Their morality had suited them in their own time but that was then, before the slaughter, and now nothing was ever going to be the same again. Now, what he was doing here at Camp Joshua was teaching Jews to stand and fight. These youngsters might not survive the coming war, he knew that, but he also knew that with their courage and his training not one of them would give up his or her life cheaply. He watched them working and dancing and loved them all, and wished he didn't have to do this, that there was no reason for these young people, these precious survivors, to learn the art of war, but war would never go out of fashion. These people, unlike many of the millions who had lost their lives in the recent war, would at least be fighting for something worth dying for, their own homeland, not someone else's.

They had only one religious Jew in the first group, a quiet boy called Yitzhak. He laid tefillin every morning and no-one said anything about it. The others knew it was their past but they simply refused to accept it as their present or future. To Yitzhak there was no future without Torah learning and the following of God's commandments. He fully accepted the view of the others and made no attempt to convince them. Michael watched him and could only feel respect for a youngster who had such conviction, even if he couldn't understand why. It was impossible to provide kosher food for Yitzhak, but the lad ate what he considered enabled him to keep the most basic laws and the rest of the time he went hungry. That impressed Michael even more.

George got word of some mortars that might be for sale in Germany and Michael said he shouldn't bother, he would go, George should stay and run things here. George knew why, that Michael would travel on to Paris, and that was fine by him. He didn't want to go anywhere. Dvorah was here in Turkey. She would be gone in a few weeks and those weeks were not to be wasted.

The trail of the mortars went cold as it happened, but Michael drove on to Paris and spent a week with Miriam. This time she had learned her lesson. She made him feel like he was coming home, and he appreciated that. The problem for him was that he was no longer sure where home was. Paris had no attraction for him other than the obvious one and he wondered about asking her to leave France and come with him but he knew she wouldn't do that, that she had unfinished business there. It wasn't business she had any hope of finishing on her own, and he knew he should be helping, looking for her father, but he couldn't do his job and that as well. He was spending most of his time driving endlessly across Europe and he found it hard to concentrate on one thing while he was doing another.

He suggested she come with him to Turkey, just for a holiday, to which she replied she could think of places for a holiday that might be better than a dusty camp in the middle of nowhere and that she was thinking of making a trip to the States. Some old friends had written to invite her and since he spent most of his time away now she couldn't see any reason not to go. They had sent her the fare already and were pushing her to go. Michael shrugged his shoulders and said well she should go then, it would do her good. He realised after he said it that it sounded a little patronising, as if Miriam was somehow unwell and in need of a break, when he was the one doing the work. She was nominally employed by the Jewish Agency and therefore had a small income of her own but the work didn't occupy more than an hour or two each day. The problem was, she was bored. Miriam was not a woman to tolerate inactivity for long. With Michael in Paris there had always been something to do but that was changed now. He saw this and of course it troubled him. This was a time when they should be consolidating their relationship, getting to know each other better, perhaps even making plans for their future together, but with this job how was that going to be possible?

He decided at least he would take a few days off before he returned to Turkey and she travelled to America, and they drove down to the South for a brief holiday. Michael let Miriam drive. He had spent enough hours and days behind the steering wheel to last a lifetime. It was midwinter now and the roads were quiet apart from some military traffic and the occasional horse and cart. They stopped in villages that hadn't seen a tourist since before the war and bars and restaurants opened up for them and as they were the only customers usually it gave them a lot of time to talk and get to know each other again. Miriam even regained some of her former impishness, and Michael knew that was a good sign. She got low when he was away, he knew that, but she also recovered quickly. She needed him, he already understood that, and it flattered him but it also worried him. In one larger town they came across a crowd of American soldiers on leave and Miriam danced with almost all of them while he watched jealously and he saw on her face that she was enjoying his discomfiture and he had the wisdom to let her see that it mattered. It was exactly what she needed. It gave her the security she craved.

The holiday ended all too soon and he felt her mood change as they drove back to Paris. He wished desperately he could make it different but somehow events seemed to be outside his control. He had to do his job, and she would go to America. He hoped that this short time together had made things better for a while, that she would feel secure now. What he also prayed for was that she would come back to him.

13

Camp Joshua was into its second training group now. The first had gone home full of enthusiasm and Michael shook every hand as they boarded their plane on the dusty road that served as a runway. With them had gone Dvorah and he saw now when he talked to George that his friend missed her. George wasn't the kind of man to talk about personal matters but Michael determined that he would try to bring him out and get him to share his feelings a little. When the new group were all asleep after a gruelling run George had put them through, the two of them sat in the canteen and sipped coffee laced with brandy to keep out the cold.

Michael could see what was on George's mind but neither of them knew how to start the conversation. They just weren't men who talked about their feelings. Michael poured them a neat brandy each in the hope that it would help. It took several but in the end George started, the way men do as if this wasn't really a serious conversation at all.

'Bloody cold, wouldn't you say, Mike?'
'Sure.'

Michael knew that Englishmen always start a conversation by discussing the weather. It was some kind of ritual that had to be observed.

'On the other hand, I suppose it's only to be expected, this time of the year.'

'To be honest George I have no idea what the weather should be like at this time of the year in south-eastern Turkey.'

'No, well, even so.'

George was put off by his friend's lack of understanding of the ritual. Americans. They just didn't have the art of conversation.

'Still, that lot seem to have gone off to sleep OK. They were exhausted after their run. Don't mind telling you I found the going a bit tough myself. Not as young as them. Got to push them though. If they're not fit they're no use to anyone. If you can't run without getting out of breath you can't fire a rifle accurately. I hope they'll remember the lesson when they go home to Palestine.'

'Oh I expect they will. They seem to take everything we give them very seriously, don't you think? I mean that last lot did.'

'Uhuh. They were a good bunch of kids.'

'Not all kids, though, were they? I mean, take Dvorah for instance …'

'I did.'

'What? Yes, well, I mean, yes, I know.'

'Lovely girl.'

'Pretty.'

'Not just that. Intelligent. Good English, a good teacher too, I mean for Hebrew. I learned a lot. It's a shame she had to leave, really. We could use her, especially with Dina going back.'

Dina Abramovitch had turned out, to everyone's surprise, including hers, to be pregnant. She would go back on the next plane, which would leave them short of an armourer. Dina was good. She could strip and rebuild a Bren in twenty-two seconds, a skill that every infantry soldier knows can mean the difference between life and death in battle. She put her students through the routine with every weapon they were likely to handle until every one of them could do it blindfold. The girls were better than the boys, some of whom tended to be clumsy, and they would need a female weapons instructor to replace Dina very soon.

Michael could see exactly where this conversation was going. George had made his point. Tomorrow he would get a message on their radio to Haganah Headquarters and ask for Dvorah to come back. George knew he would do that, that he didn't need actually to ask. In fact he wanted to change the subject.

'So, Mike, how's that girl of yours?'

'Oh, you know.'

'No. I don't know how they do this kind of thing in America but where I come from a question like that is usually asked because we don't know.'

'She's good. Yes, we had a good time, you know, a good vacation. Yeh, it's all good.'

'I take it therefore that things are not so good.'

'No.'

'Want to tell me?'

'No. What's to tell?'

George shrugged his shoulders, which was his way of saying he was a patient man.

'It's this job, being stuck out here a million miles from anyone, well, especially her. We're getting to know each other, at least we're trying to, but if it's going to work we really could do with some more time together. There's some stuff she and I need to work through.'

'Oh? Want to tell me about it?'

'No. Really no. Just stuff.'

'Oh.'

They sat quietly for a minute, unsure where to go from here. They didn't get the chance to go anywhere, though, because from somewhere outside the camp they heard the unmistakable sound of gunfire. There was a moment of uncertainty, as if this wasn't really possible. Who was firing at whom, and why? It was only a short burst, from an SMG, and then there was silence. Some of the students came running in, pulling clothes and boots on, their personal weapons at the ready. It was the correct response, but no-one knew what to do next, because plainly the camp was not under attack. They didn't even put sentries out. There had never been a reason to. They looked at each other, but mostly they looked at George and Michael and obviously expected someone to issue an order, so George did the only reasonable thing and told them to fetch torches, they would go and see. He did a quick check to see that everyone was accounted for, and then they were ordered to cock their weapons and be prepared for the worst, but he also said keep your safety catches on and don't fire unless you are absolutely certain you are under threat. This was not a war situation. There had to be a reasonable explanation.

It didn't take long. About a kilometre out from the perimeter of the camp they came across the groaning figure of Oktay Yilmaz. By his side on the ground lay a Sterling sub-machine gun. He was in extreme pain, and they could see the reason why easily enough. As they shone their torches along his leg what they saw was a bloody mess where his left foot used to be.

'The bloody fool. He's gone shooting rabbits with a Sterling. Who the hell let him have it? This is a disciplinary matter ...'

'George, George, could we do all that in the morning do you think? Let's get him back and see if we can at least stop the bleeding. Old Oktay is going to die of shock if you carry on like this.'

They carried him back as gently as they could and laid him on the big table in the canteen. He had fired off at least ten rounds and now bits of flesh hung from the end of his leg and blood pumped out onto the table. George was the only one there who had seen battlefield wounds, and he quickly got them organised into a field dressing station. Half an hour later Oktay was unconscious, which was a blessing, full of morphine, and the leg was bandaged up. It still oozed blood, but much more slowly now. George looked worried.

'I don't know how much of the stuff he's lost. At his age the effect of shock will be all the worse. I would say his chance of living without a transfusion, even if we can control infection, is limited. Sorry, but there it is. Anyway, he's stable for now, and if you will excuse me I want to ask this lot some questions about how the hell our old friend got the weapon in the first place.'

Michael let him go. Discipline was important, he knew that. It just wasn't uppermost in his mind right now. Oktay needed professional medical treatment, and they didn't have that. They had done a good job as far as it went, but it wasn't going to be good enough. The problem was going to be explaining to a doctor how he got his foot shot off with an automatic weapon. Well, they couldn't go driving off with him in the dark and the nearest town was over thirty miles away so it would wait until the morning.

In the morning Oktay was dead.

It solved one problem and gave them another. They could bury him and hope that no-one would ever know because no-one ever came here anyway. On the other hand, there was his nephew in

Istanbul, Mehmet. He was certain to come sooner or later. None of them knew what the procedure was for registering a death with the authorities but they had a feeling that if they didn't it would create more problems.

In the end George and Michael came to the conclusion that a story concocted of half truth and half fabrication was the best answer. Oktay had taken his own gun off rabbit hunting and had an accident. They didn't find him until the next morning and by then he was already dead. They simply buried him and then drove into town to inform the authorities. It had a ring of truth about it, and why would they lie? On the other hand they were foreigners and some official might take it into his head to sniff around, even order the exhumation of the body. Well, their options were limited.

That afternoon, while the students buried Oktay with due ceremony, Michael drove into Birecik to find a police station. Two hours later, having filled in a great number of forms and paid a large quantity of money, most of which he suspected was bribes rather than registration fees, it seemed that everyone was satisfied and he was free to drive back to camp. He worried that it seemed too simple and told George that but George just said there was probably no-one who cared, they just saw it as an opportunity to make some quick cash. After a few days, they heard from no-one and Michael began to relax.

His remaining worry was Mehmet. He felt they should inform him, as Oktay's only, to their knowledge, living relative. George didn't think it was worth worrying about but Michael became more insistent. It just seemed the right thing to do. He could be back in a couple of days.

Mehmet was surprised and pleased to see him and welcomed him into his apartment, where his wife insisted on feeding him. When Michael told them his bad news they seemed upset but not unduly. Oktay was an old man, and an accident with a gun, well, it was unfortunate but these things happened. All in all Michael felt they took it pretty well. As soon as was decent, he shook their hands, patted the children on the head, and left.

Whilst he was in the city he had a contact to follow up, about mortars again, and after that was done he got a few hours sleep in the car and set off east again. By the time he arrived back at Camp Joshua, the police were there.

'Ah Michael, I'm pretty glad you're back, I can tell you. This chap, Inspector Tasar or some such, says he's had a phone call from Istanbul.'

'Istanbul? What about?'

'Well I have a horrible feeling our friend Mehmet has put his two penn'orth in.'

Michael wasn't familiar with the colloquialism but got the gist.

'But why? When I left him he was fine. Well, not happy, but why would he be? No, surely he wouldn't have started something up.'

'Ah Mr Jacobs. I am Inspector Tasar. My English is not so good, please forgive. I am here to investigate the death of Oktay Yilmaz. You should have registered this with the police.'

'What? Inspector, I assure you I did that.'

'You did? Perhaps there has been some mistake. Where did you do this please?'

'At the police station in Birecik, immediately after the accident.'

'Really? Well, Sir, I assure you I have just come from Birecik, and I have not heard this.'

'Well I must say, Inspector, I'm surprised. Look, give me a moment and I'll find the official forms I filled in.'

Inspector Tasar wasn't eager to see the forms though. Instead, he presented Michael with another set of forms and told him that if he would just complete these he was sure he could clear the matter up. Michael duly did so and Inspector Tasar looked through them to his satisfaction and signed them himself with a flourish. There was, though, a matter of the fee for these forms. So, that was it. Mehmet had called the police in Birecik, probably just to see what trouble he could stir up, perhaps see if he could get some compensation for his uncle's death, and the police in Birecik simply saw it as an opportunity to rake in some more cash. There never was a problem, it was just a money-making exercise. Now he knew what was going on, Michael understood what was the correct tone to take as he handed over the money.

'Well, there you are Inspector. I trust everything is now in order?'

'Oh yes, Sir, quite so.'

'Good. So there will be no more forms to complete?'
'Oh no, no more forms.'
'And no more fees.'
'Fees? Oh no, no more of those. I will see to it personally that this matter is closed.'
'Excellent. Well, on that note, Inspector, thank you for coming all the way out here to sort this matter out, and have a safe drive back.'

Inspector Tasar gave him a salute, which presumably came free with the fee, and climbed into his car. His long-suffering driver, who was certainly never going to see a single lira of this money, started up the engine with a look of resignation, as if to say this was all quite in a day's work, and drove off down the road out of camp.

14

Now that the police in Birecik were aware that an agricultural training school belonging to a foreign organisation was situated in their area of responsibility, Michael found it convenient to drive into town from time to time to buy a drink for Inspector Tasar and his senior colleagues. He wasn't happy about the school becoming public knowledge but it seemed there was no choice in the matter. Oktay had seen to that. Still, it was thirty kilometres from the town to Camp Joshua, so it was unlikely anyone was going to come sightseeing. As long as they kept the police happy then they would stay in Birecik.

Then word came from Haganah High Command. They wanted to add a transport plane to their shopping list. It would be expensive, but they would make the money available. George looked at the message.

'A plane? I see, well, that's not asking much. Anything else?'

'Yes. There's been another message since that one. They want a pilot too.'

'A pilot? Right. For the plane, presumably?'

'I think that's the general idea.'

'I see. And even assuming we can find such an item, the plane I mean, and a pilot come to that, and persuade the latter to come to this godforsaken place, what are we supposed to do with him?'

'Or her.'

'No, I don't think so. There may be lots of girlies in Haganah but I think you will find there are very few, let's call it none, in the various air forces of the belligerent nations of the world. Anyway, you haven't answered my question. What does this pilot person do once he, or she, is here?'

'Search me. That's all they said. So first things first. Can you find a plane?'

'As it happens Mike my boy, yes I can. There are so many going spare that people are just leaving them where they stand to rot. A plane will not be a problem, expensive but not a problem.'

'OK George, I may not be a professor of economics but even I know about the law of supply and demand. Explain to me please how come these things are just lying around waiting for takers but they're not cheap.'

'Good question, and here comes a good answer. These planes are old. They have been worked hard during the war. Old planes that have been worked hard all have one thing in common. Bits tend to fall off. Buying a plane without a plentiful supply of spares is, to put it bluntly, a total waste of bloody money. By the end of the war some air forces were cannibalising their Dakotas at the rate of three or even four dead planes to make one good one.'

'I see. Dakotas, you say?'

'Yep, the camel of the skies. If you can persuade it to go, it won't stop, but you have to be nice to it and lavish a lot of love and attention on it, otherwise it just spits in your face. And there the analogy ends, because a reluctant camel is a nuisance but not dangerous, whereas a reluctant Dak might just fall out of the sky, with you in it.'

'Well, not me personally. Never could stand flying, never understood how the damned things stay up.'

'Really? For an educated man, Mike, that is a surprisingly Neanderthal attitude.'

'Uhuh, I'm an Intelligence man. I deal in information, not technology.'

Three days later, Michael was travelling, by ship, to Baltimore. The United States, George assured him, was the place to buy used Dakotas. He drew him a sketch of one, just to make sure he wasn't sold a pup he said, which left Michael wondering if he was being serious, and gave him a list of likely suppliers, all completely kosher, who purchased old kit from the US Army Air Force. Michael asked him how he knew so much to which he replied, somewhat mysteriously, well that's my job.

A week later Michael was in New York, paying a surprise visit to Miriam. Once she got over the shock, she was ecstatic. She made her excuses to her friends and accompanied him by train across a dozen states, culminating in California, where they found what they were looking for, a desert plane park with enough Dakotas to start a small air force. Harvey Scourfield, the proprietor, would happily have stitched Michael up with a duff plane but he took a shine to Miriam and instead sold him a very fair example of the model, with enough cannibalised spares to keep it in the air, he said, until the second coming. Back in their hotel Miriam asked Michael what it was that was coming second, and he tried to explain, from one Jew to another, the significance of the expression.

One condition of the sale was that he be allowed to take Michael and Miriam out to dinner, which he did, no funny business, and at the end of a massive meal Michael reckoned he knew his man well enough to broach the subject of a pilot.

'A pilot, huh? So you're not going to fly it yourself?'

Miriam chortled.

'Only kidding Mike, only kidding. It doesn't take a genius to tell that you know enough about airplanes to fill one side of a postcard and still leave room for the stamp.'

Miriam chortled again. She had drunk quite a lot by this time. Anyway, her appreciation of Harvey's witticisms made him happy and expansive.

'Well now, let me see, there's Hank Bennett, only he's got just one eye. Mind you, they do say it's a good one, but even so, one eye isn't the same as two, is it?'

Miriam was enjoying this, which only encouraged him.

'Then there's old Paddy Maguire, sixty-five if he's a day but wow, that's a lot of experience. No? OK, what about Big Jim Henderson?'

'Alright, I give up. What exactly does Big Jim Henderson have to recommend him?'

'When he was alive he was a damned good flier.'

Harvey fell about laughing, and Miriam joined him. Michael looked at them and shook his head. Well, it was all good fun but …

'No, seriously Mike, really, I have just the man for you.'
'Seriously?'
'Yep, Augustus Nutberry.'

Miriam giggled but apparently it wasn't a joke. Augustus Nutberry, it turned out, was a real person, which they found out for themselves when they met him at Harvey's used plane lot the next day.

'Nutberry, meet my good friends Michael and Miriam Jacobs.'

Michael blushed at the mistake but didn't attempt to correct him.

'Michael, meet Augustus Nutberry, the man who single-handedly won the air war against the Japanese Army, a pilot so amply decorated by a grateful country they had to open a new mint just to strike the medals for that big old chest of his, a flyer of such ....'

'Mr Jacobs, good to meet you. It's all true of course, but a man doesn't like to boast, and doesn't need to when he's got Harvey Scourfield to do it for him. I take it he's sold you one of his wonderful airplanes? Which one?'

'Er, that one, I think.' They all looked the same to Michael.

'Excellent choice, if I may say so. OK so let's take a ride.'

'Excuse me?'

'A ride, Mr Jacobs. I take it you want to see the plane's performance, plus of course you will want to verify my own bona fides as a pilot. So let's go.'

Michael stood there wide-eyed. He didn't know how to back out of this one, but there was no way he was going up in one of these things. It was one thing to spend good money on one but quite another to risk his life in it. And before he knew it Miriam was kitted out and striding across the Tarmac behind Nutberry. He heard her saying by way of explanation something about him having a problem with his ears, couldn't fly just now, and Augustus nodded his head in a way that suggested he didn't much care, any excuse to fly, with or without the customer, a pretty girl to show off to was a bonus.

Harvey tried to comfort him. 'Don't worry Mike, the little lady is in good hands.'

Michael wasn't sure if he was referring to his woman or his aircraft. The Dakota's engines roared into life and the draught from the big blades could be felt from where he stood. He wondered if it was too late to stop it, to tell Miriam she wasn't to go, but he knew he was being ridiculous and it was one thing to be ridiculous but quite another to look ridiculous in front of other people. He also didn't think Miriam would appreciate it. She had a sense of adventure and who was he to clip her wings?

The Dakota growled down the runway and amazed him by lifting off with a grace he would have thought impossible. Nutberry took it high first, in a great sweeping arc, and then with the sun behind him, came in low over the hangar and it was as the aircraft flew in a straight line towards him that Michael caught some of the excitement of flying, started to see what was so amazing about all those tons of metal defying Nature. He also realised that the Dak's ability to do that depended on a good pilot, and he instinctively knew that Nutberry was one of those, a natural. Flying transports in the war couldn't have been a glamorous job compared with the fighter and bomber pilots, but as an Intelligence officer he knew that no war can be fought without the movement of supplies and men, and looking at the great bird as it flew so steadily towards him he knew that if anyone could invest flying transport planes with glamour it was this man. For a moment, in his excitement, he forgot to be worried about Miriam, and when they finally landed and she climbed down the ladder with a high colour in her cheeks he knew she was glad not only that she had done it but that he had made it possible. As the purchaser of this wonderful machine he was as much a hero in her eyes as the man who flew it.

'So, Mr Jacobs, now you know a Nutberry can fly. So, what's the job?'

'Oh, well, I represent the Levant Trading Company. We want to ship goods around Europe and the Middle East.'

'Uhuh, based out of where?'

'Turkey.'

'Turkey, huh. What's that like?'

Michael looked around him at the scrub and desert. 'Well, not altogether unlike this, actually.'

'And what's the pay?'

'A thousand dollars a month.'

He looked doubtful.

'Plus accommodation and food, plus bonus.'

He stopped looking doubtful.

'And how much flying will I get?'

It was a good question, but it was one Michael couldn't answer because no-one had told him. Just get a plane and pilot, they said, but they should have thought a pilot was likely to ask this kind of question. In the absence of any knowledge he extemporised.

'Well, quite a lot, I guess. Every day?'

'OK, when do I start?'

'How about now?'

'Mister, you got yourself a pilot.'

'And you'll need a crew to ferry it over to Turkey. Can you find the right people?'

'Sure. I'll need a navigator and over that distance I'll want to fly with an engineer too, so that'll cost you for their flying time plus shipping back here. Plus refuelling in Canada, Greenland, Iceland, Ireland and I'll have to check a map but one or two more places before we get to Turkey. It's a long way and a DC3 has a range of about a thousand miles. Depending on wind direction and weather, each leg will mean say six or seven hours flying then an overnight stop.'

'So we can rest?'

'Hell no, the Dak will be doing all the work. To give her a break. Anyway, did you say we? Does that mean you'll be flying with us?'

Nutberry looked at Michael and so did Miriam. It was now or never.

'Of course. Why wouldn't I?'

Miriam kissed him on the cheek and he was embarrassed, as if he were a child who had just done a clever trick.

It took a week to put the team together, service the plane and load up the spares. Meanwhile, Nutberry called ahead and made the necessary refuelling arrangements, on Michael's assurance that they would be paying cash, in dollars.

As the Dakota took off from the southern California desert into a cloudless sky and the substantial figure of Harvey Scourfield rapidly diminished into nothing, Michael knew he was sweating. He had done many scary things in his life, and in battle in Poland he had faced death with more equanimity than this, and as he pondered the days ahead he wondered why the hell he was doing this. He turned and smiled at Miriam and saw she was in her element. She was going to love this. He tried talking to her but the inside of a DC3 is a noisy place and he found it hardly worth the effort, so he fell into a reverie while he held her hand.

They say that the sum total of your life is where you are now, that every experience you have ever had, every person, every place, all the pain and pleasure, absolutely everything, is manifested in what you are doing right now. With so much to think and feel, Michael felt there was no future, only the present, a present that needed to be given his full concentration. Quite apart from his own personal feelings about this flight, he knew sensibly that there were many risks and problems ahead, that flying an old transport plane halfway around the world is not something you do with impunity. Well, he was told it was a good plane, and he somehow trusted that judgment, possibly because he wanted to, and he could tell for himself that he had hired a good crew. Nutberry was a bit on the flamboyant side for his taste, but there was no doubting his flying skill. He had, he told them, flown these birds in and out of what he called some very hairy situations in the war. Now, at least, no-one would be shooting at them. This was nothing more than a test of endurance, the plane's and the crew's. He forgot to mention the passengers.

As it turned out, the plane, the crew, and the passengers, came through. En route the Dakota asked for nothing more than some minor repairs in Greenland and the engineer got a nasty toothache which held them up on the west coast of Ireland for a day while they found a dentist to pull the offending molar out. Twelve days after taking off from a parched airstrip in America, they landed safely on a parched airstrip in Turkey.

There was a reception party of instructors and students to welcome them with enthusiastic applause as they climbed down the ladder. Nissim Shorat was there too, and he gave Michael one of his rare smiles and a slight nod of the head in acknowledgement, and that was worth a lot. George was there of course and he shook Michael's hand heartily.

'So, Mike, you did it. Well done, and welcome home. Ah Miriam, lovely as ever.' He gave her a big hug. 'Welcome to Camp Joshua.'

15

Miriam was overwhelmed by the warmth of the welcome. Everyone took to her, not only because she was the commandant's girlfriend but for herself. Michael was immensely pleased at the unexpected way she fitted in. A week later the next group of students arrived and they simply accepted that she was part of the camp's administration. The new intake brought with them Dvorah Halevi, and the two women hit it off instantly.

Nutberry soon figured out that this was not exactly what he had been told, that Camp Joshua was not exactly a transport depot. Nissim briefed him on the runs Haganah wanted him to make, ferrying students back and forth, gun-running to Palestine, things like that. Nutberry looked at the Jew and shook his head in wonder. Nissim was, he could tell, in deadly earnest. He asked him if there was some kind of war brewing and Nissim said yes and so Nutberry said he would do it. He couldn't stand the thought of going back to California and spending the rest of his life crop dusting. Nissim asked the engineer and navigator to stay too. There was enough money to pay them a basic salary. It wasn't great, he said, and he would understand if they would rather leave, but where Nutberry flew they flew with him, and if there was any chance of a war they wanted to be there, so they stayed. Michael had a small building put up where the plane was parked under the camouflage net, and it became the flight office and crew quarters rolled into one.

And so the training courses at Camp Joshua expanded to include aeronautical engineering and navigation. The Dakota wasn't suitable for actual flight training, but they all knew the Americans were doing an invaluable job against the day when there would be some kind of Jewish air force.

Miriam stayed for a while but there came a time when she knew she would have to decide where home was now. In the end she knew the answer. It was wherever Michael was. In a few more weeks, she agreed, once she was quite certain, she should go back to Paris and wind up their apartment.

The camp was in full swing now and Michael looked on with satisfaction. He was quite certain that the work they were doing was of the greatest importance. They were training the young people who would form the backbone, the officers and NCOs, of a nascent Jewish defence force. None of them knew when it would be needed but that it would be needed no-one had the slightest doubt.

The level of anti-British activity taking place in Palestine was growing. Haganah was at odds with the Irgun and the Stern Gang, and Michael had a strong suspicion that while the Haganah leaders publicly condemned the terrorist tactics of the two smaller groups they were quietly happy that they should be doing their dirty work for them. The British had made it clear they would not negotiate a withdrawal from the Mandate but in the end they would come under intolerable pressure from the terrorists. The British public were getting restive about their soldiers dying for a place no-one cared about. The war was over and they had had enough. Palestine was a stone, an albatross round Britain's neck, and the guerilla leaders knew that if they kept pushing they would win. Meanwhile Haganah fighters were dying too, but they were at least fighting with decent weapons in their hands, weapons purchased by Michael's efforts and flown in to a secret desert airstrip in the Negev on Nutberry's DC3.

It had never been part of Michael's understanding that his work would support a campaign against the British Mandate forces and he knew that George, as a former British Army officer, had some misgivings, but George kept his own counsel. He had been there at the liberation of Bergen-Belsen, and if his own country wasn't going to give the Jews a home without a fight, well, he had already made his mind up as to whose side he was on.

Anyway, George had Dvorah, and Dvorah worked her magic on him bit by bit. He learned, with the Hebrew she taught him, some of the history of her people and she helped him to understand that there had to be a Jewish national home, that it had to be in the land of their forefathers, and it also had to be soon. The remains of European Jewry was desperate for somewhere to go and sooner or later their dream would be realised. He knew that Michael never forgot, not for one day, the people in the camps, held illegally he said, but especially he never stopped thinking about Krystyna and Roza's son and the other boys. He had made a promise and he was going to keep it. George wondered to himself how that was ever going to be possible, if Michael was planning to parachute in his trainee soldiers from Nutberry's plane and liberate the camps on Cyprus. He told Michael that once and Michael laughed but then he looked serious and George said, oh no, definitely no, you can count me out of any crazy scheme like that.

It was of course a crazy idea and not one that Michael took seriously, but it wasn't based entirely on fantasy. He took the pilot to one side one afternoon when things were quiet.

'Nutberry, got a moment?'

'You're the commanding officer around here, so yes, I've got time. What is it, Mike?'

'Well, I've been thinking.'

'OK, that's a good start.'

'Yes, about parachuting.'

'Uhuh. And where are you planning to jump from exactly, and why? I'd be interested to see it.'

'No no, not me.'

'I see. Me then?'

'No, I don't think so. I mean if you jump out who's going to fly the plane?'

'Aha, I'm beginning to get you. You want people to jump out of my Dak with parachutes strapped to their backs.'

'Forgive me, Nutberry, for being picky but can I just remind you, as fond as you are of the Dak, that actually it's ours.'

'OK, OK, point taken. But you can't fly it without me, and I've never flown parachutists before.'

'No, but there's always a first time. I mean, wouldn't it be a challenge?'

'No, it would probably be a disaster. Anyway, even if I knew how to do it, you would need a specialist parachute instructor, not to mention some parachutes.'

'Well, naturally. I know that.'

'And I guess your next question is do I know anyone, and failing that anyone who might know anyone?'

'Well, yes.'

'I might.'

'Really?'

'Hell, it could be fun. OK, Mike, you've convinced me.'

Michael wasn't aware he had even tried. Nutberry was, it seemed, not hard to convince if there was fun involved. He promised to contact Nissim to float the idea, and meanwhile it wouldn't hurt for Nutberry to contact his friend. He drove them both into town the next day to make some phone calls.

Three days later Nissim came back on the radio. The idea had found some support, and he could go ahead, on two conditions. It should be cheap, and it should involve no risk to the students. Michael grimaced when he read that. It was a tall order, but he had the bit between his teeth now. Nissim also said he would be coming over, by boat, to see Michael on an important matter, the next week. There were always important matters. In the excitement of the new project he didn't think too much about it.

Nissim arrived and did a quick tour of inspection, to his entire satisfaction. He noted that both Michael and George now had their women with them and he had some thoughts on that but he kept them to himself. He brought some cash with him to pay the wages and in the evening people did what they tended to do, which was gather in the canteen and sing Hebrew songs. Nissim watched them and Michael watched him and he thought he saw a nostalgic look on the man's face and now he knew who Nissim Shorat's lover was, it was Palestine.

The two of them slipped out to talk quietly.

'Michael, you have done an excellent job here. I personally am unconvinced about the parachute idea but many of my colleagues believe it could be useful so I certainly will not stand in the way of it. There is something else, though.'

'Yes?'

'There is an item on our original list that you have not yet obtained, and High Command are really quite concerned that you should make another effort.'

'Yes? What is that?'

'Fighter planes, or one at least. The Arab countries that will attack us have their own air forces. One plane does not make an air force but we have to start somewhere. Can you do it?'

Michael thought hard before answering. 'Nissim, don't think I have forgotten this matter, but it's not easy. Almost the only planes available for sale are ex-Luftwaffe, and I think that would be a bad idea.'

'Correct. We will not buy a German plane.'

'Well, infantry equipment isn't so hard because there's simply so much of the stuff surplus to requirement and the same goes for transports, but fighters, well, unless they are really ancient air forces tend to just keep flying them.'

'Are you saying it can't be done?'

There was an edge to Nissim's voice and Michael knew he dare not admit defeat. He had never much liked Nissim Shorat, but he had a lot of respect for him. The rest of them tended to treat the whole exercise as if it were some kind of game. It was just the people involved, the personalities, and strangely it worked, and the serious work they had to do got done. But Nissim was only ever serious. He was following his own agenda, for his own reasons, and Michael knew enough about the Jews of Europe, and knew too that as an American Jew he had no right to judge them, to give Nissim all the respect he asked for. If he wanted a fighter plane, he would get one.

'OK, we'll find a way.'

'When?'

When you've just sold your soul you expect a little grace, but not from Nissim Shorat. If you gave him anything, he just pushed you for more.

'Three months?'

'Why three?'

'OK, look, I'm not going to commit to a date without consulting my people and working out a realistic plan.'

Nissim gave him what passed for a smile. It was a professional approach. He liked it.

'Alright. Keep me informed.'

The next day, Nutberry flew Nissim out, and when he returned Michael called a staff meeting of himself, George, the flying crew, Miriam and for some reason he wasn't quite sure about, Dvorah.

'Right, now he's gone I can tell you why he came. He wants a fighter plane.'

They looked at each other and shrugged their shoulders. Inevitably, Nutberry had something to say.

'Mike, fighters aren't like transports.'

'I know. We've already got one of those.'

'No no, I mean buying one is going to be whole lot harder than buying a Dakota.'

'I know that already. I've tried, remember. What I want you to do is to come with me to Ankara and start making contact with anyone and everyone you know who might know someone who might know someone. We have to keep doing that until we find one for sale.'

'Or we don't.'

'No, we do.'

Nutberry had never seen him like this, none of them had, except Miriam. She could have told them the party was over, this was for serious.

Ankara was the place to start, if only because it had more reliable international telephone connections than Birecik, and because if they were going to meet anyone shifty Michael didn't want them to do that anywhere near Camp Joshua. The next day he said goodbye to Miriam yet again but promised he would be gone no more than a week, and they climbed into the car and headed north. There would be plenty for the others to do while they were away. The parachute specialist was due any day, bringing a lorry-load of second hand parachutes with him from Italy, no questions asked but guaranteed reliable and also guaranteed cheap.

Eight days later Michael and Nutberry were back, and George knew before they even got out of the car that they had drawn a blank. The instructors had already rigged up a practice tower for the jumpers and the camp was a hive of activity. George left them at it and the men gathered in the canteen.

'I hardly need to ask you how it went.'

'Afraid not. If you want the details ....'

'I don't think so, thank you. Spare me the messy bits. Did you find anything at all?'

'One MiG, in pieces, a P-38 Mustang in good condition only it's currently in the Philippines and a Hurricane without an engine but the owner reckons he knows where he can pick one up.'

'I see. So, what now?'

'Right now, George, a shower, something alcoholic, and then some sleep. If I wake up in the morning, I'll try to think of a clever answer to that question.'

He shuffled off to find Miriam, and George looked at Nutberry and Nutberry looked at George but neither of them had anything to add to that, so they didn't.

16

Michael was already asleep when Miriam slipped into bed next to him. He had been morose over his meal and she had understood that he didn't want to talk. It was strange the way he decided on something and sulked until he got it. It wasn't as if it was his problem really, it was just that he had promised Nissim Shorat and when Michael made a promise he just couldn't let go. She sometimes thought he took the responsibility for all the Jews of Europe on his shoulders, and that included Cyprus. She knew Nissim's type, and she knew he would use Michael without mercy. Nissim was like Michael only worse, he was obsessive. She pitied the woman who tried to squeeze any love out of that man.

All this because of one stupid airplane. Good God, there must be thousands of the things just lying around. Just lying around. Something about that sounded good, and she said it to herself over and over until she fell asleep, and when she woke up when it was still dark she had the germ of an idea, a crazy idea, but she knew that the crazier the better for this man of hers, that no idea was too stupid to be considered. It was, perversely, one of the things she loved about him.

She shook him and he mumbled something that might have been go away leave me alone to die, but it might not have been.'Michael, Michael, wake up.'

'No.'
'Yes.'
'Why?'
'Because, my love, I've got an idea.'

'Not now, I'm tired.'

'No, silly, not that, an airplane.'

He opened one eye and tried to focus on her with it. 'You've got an airplane?'

'Yes, no, not personally. I've got an idea how you can get one.'

'You mean buy one.'

'No. I mean steal one.'

He opened the other eye now. It sounded like Miriam had said steal one but that didn't make any sense.

'Look, Miriam, I don't know what you're talking about. Could we have this conversation in the morning?'

'It is the morning.'

'Nope, dark, you can't kid me.'

'Alright, smart alec, I've got the most wonderful scheme for getting your rotten fighter plane but since you would rather waste the time sleeping let's just forget about it.'

He was sitting up now.

'That's better. Now listen to Miriam, and listen carefully. At this end of the Mediterranean, I am reliably informed by our flying friends, the British air force has planes at fighter bases, not least in Palestine and on Cyprus. I suspect they don't actually need them all, and could probably spare one for us.'

'I see, I think. So you reckon we should steal one from the Brits?'

'Yes.'

'Miriam, you're crazy.'

She put her hand between his legs and squeezed. 'Say that again, soldier, and you're dead meat.'

Before daybreak the management of Camp Joshua was gathered round the table in the canteen drinking coffee and rubbing the sleep from their eyes. Michael was pacing up and down talking to himself, trying to figure it out, then he turned and addressed them.

'Ladies and gentlemen, Miss Fillon here has come up with a scheme that I just know you are going to love.'

They looked sceptical.

'I see you have doubts. Well, just wait until you've heard what it is. We're going to steal a fighter from the British air force.'

The silence reverberated round the canteen. Had anyone had a pin, they could have dropped it in complete confidence. Michael looked at George, who was scratching his head.

'OK, George, comments, first thoughts, anything you like, don't be shy.'

'You're mad.'

'We've done that. Any more original thoughts?'

'You are actually considering pinching a Spitfire from the Royal Air Force.'

'Is that what they're called, Spitfires? Any good?'

'Are you kidding? They're bloody brilliant.'

'Great, then that's what we'll go for.'

'Look, Michael, this isn't a joke. Stealing a Spitfire from an RAF base isn't .... well it isn't …'

'I know. I know all of that, and now you've got that out of your system whatever it was, I want you to head a task force to evaluate and report. I want a list of options and preliminary plans on my desk, as they say, by the end of the day.'

'You're not kidding, are you?'

'Do I look like I'm kidding? All other activities at Camp Joshua are suspended. Take as many people as you like, brainstorm, think the impossible, but figure it out. I want to know where from, what resources we'll need, and timeframe. OK?'

'Yes Sir.'

For the whole of that day groups of people could be seen huddled in corners, talking, arguing, shouting in a number of languages, waving their hands about a lot too. Some pored over maps, others did calculations on scraps of paper. At one time Nutberry could be seen banging his head against the wheel housing of the Dakota in frustration, but by six o'clock they were all sitting in a circle refining their ideas and after dinner Michael joined them and George told him how they were going to do it.

'OK, this is how it works. First, where does the Air Force have Spitfires in the Middle-East? In Palestine and on Cyprus. Security is much tighter in Palestine, for the reasons we all know about, but on Cyprus there is no threat, and anyway it's an island. We British always feel safe on an island. So that's our target. There's a base at RAF Akrotiri with Spits. Next, how do we get in and out with one of their planes unnoticed? Not possible, so the answer is we don't, they bring it to us. I know, I know, you think that's crazy, but listen, we can do crazy just as well as you. They're not going to let us borrow one of their planes and fly it off the island but as it happens they fly the things themselves so we don't need to. All we need to do is have them deliver it to the wrong place. Well, the wrong place for them, the right one for us.'

Michael didn't interrupt George's flow. Questions would come later, plenty of them, but so far there was something about this that he liked.

'Now comes the tricky bit. We need to know a few things, like where their planes make regular flights to, what the range of a Spit is, where we could have them deliver it assuming not here and some more stuff of a technical nature which Nutberry tells me will be important but which I didn't understand the first time he told me or the second one either.'

Michael could no longer resist asking the obvious question. 'George, it's a good plan, as far as it goes. I mean the idea of having them bring the plane to us is, on the surface, a good one. But how?'

'Aha, I had a feeling you would ask that one. OK, it's not going to be easy, but we think it can be done. This, in brief, is how it works. As you know, we've got rather a lot of people on Cyprus, courtesy of the British government, and when I say we I mean you, I mean Jewish people. Haganah has access to some of those people, the ones, shall we say, with interesting qualifications or experience, like forgers and armourers and so on. Well, as far as we know there aren't actually any aircraft mechanics, but Nutberry reckons he can sketch out good enough instructions for any competent electrical or mechanical engineer to follow.'

'To do what?'

'To get into the airbase and start a small leak in the fuel pipe of a Spit. It's a very difficult calculation, but if we get a plane that's going roughly in the right direction, we may be able to siphon off enough fuel so that it has to land at an airstrip of our choice, eh voila, one Spitfire.'

'Right, but OK I don't know a lot about these things but I know enough to guess that any halfway competent pilot checks his fuel gauge before setting off, or taking off, or whatever it is they call it.'

'Correct. That's why the leak has to be done with a timing device to start somewhere over the Med.'

'Phew. Can it be done?'

'Nutberry reckons so. Nutberry?'

'Yeh, it can be done. Whether it can be done by a man with a torch and some instructions written on the back of an envelope is another matter. We've thought about infiltrating our engineer to do the job but it's too risky. We can't afford to lose him. We're going to ask for a volunteer to get arrested by the Brits and interned. He will then sift through the prisoners and find an engineer. Naturally, he will take with him the timing device that we will construct here.'

'I see. And what, I mean assuming all of this works, about the other end? Where can we force them to land?'

'OK, now come over here and take a look at the map. See, there's Cyprus, we're here, and there's Palestine. Until I've got the figures for speed and range of the Spitfire I can't be sure, but somewhere in this arc, which means, if you exclude Palestine itself, Lebanon. It's the best chance we've got of getting me and the engineer to the site overland to pick up the plane once it lands and bring it here.'

'Can you fly a Spitfire?'

'I can fly anything with wings. Well, I'll figure it out, don't you worry about that.'

'And the British pilot? What do we do with him?'

'Well, we took a vote and decided to shoot him. No, only kidding. He could walk home, but it's a long way, so we'll make sure he knows that we will pass on a message to the authorities where to find him. He'll have no idea where we've taken the plane. We'll repair and refuel before taking off again.'

Michael folded his arms and looked at them. They wanted him to be impressed. He was. It was a totally unworkable scheme, but he was impressed. On the other hand there was no single part of it that was wrong, it was just that they needed every part of it to work. He knew a thing or two about complex military plans. The more complex they are, the more likely they are to go wrong. It's a simple mathematical calculation. Factor in the number of components that have an inbuilt risk and you can work out if it's going to come off.

All military planners do it. Where they go wrong is, having calculated that their plan is full of holes, they then say with luck it'll work. His friends were looking at him, and they expected him to say something.

'Brilliant. Just brilliant. OK, folks, let's get to work.'

And they did. At first, Michael thought they were on the wrong track, but it was the only track anyone was talking about and it was after all him who had insisted they were going after a Spitfire and what were they supposed to do in the face of an order from him? But in time he began himself to believe in this insane plan. He was reminded of an operation a long time ago in Poland and he clearly recalled being asked if that was going to work and he had said yes but meant no but it seemed that saying yes was the right answer, if you believe in that kind of thing, because it gave the operation some hope of success. Michael didn't believe in wishful thinking, though, and he pushed his people and watched them closely and at every step of the way he held meetings in which each person responsible for a separate part of the operation had to present his or her work so far to the rest of the team and justify their decisions. It kept everyone on their toes and left nothing to chance, and hopefully it would leave no possibility of nasty surprises. Of course, nasty surprises, by their very nature, tend to be unpredictable and he knew at the end of the day that there would still be a number of unknowns, and they would still depend on luck. But luck had also been an important ingredient in some of the war's biggest battles, not least Operation Overlord. On D-Day the largest invasion fleet in history had put to sea praying for a change in the weather. It could so easily have gone wrong, and so nearly did. The Allies and the Germans each had their fair share of both good and bad luck but what won the battle in the end wasn't luck, it was planning. It was also sheer grit and determination, and he suspected the Allied troops were that bit more determined to liberate France than the German troops were to hold on to it, but that would be for history to judge.

While all of this went on Michael gave the order for some training to be resumed. Not everyone had something to contribute to the operation and they had a job to do regardless of the Spitfire. The new parachute instructor, Francois Girardin, had been a Sergeant Major instructor in the French Foreign Legion and then trained in parachutes during the war and fought with the Free French. It was an impressive CV and he lived up to his record. He absolutely refused to train women to jump and George had no choice but to give in to his chauvinism. He selected his men after rigorous assessment, and those he picked felt honoured and therefore worked especially hard to earn his respect.

While Michael's operation wore on he kept a watching brief on the rest of the camp's activities. One group of trainees flew back to Palestine and Nutberry brought the next batch back with him. The following day George came to him with a worried look on his face.

'Michael, I think we've got a problem.'

'Only one. It's a good day.'

'No, listen. The new group of students, there's a Romanian-French chap called Farhi. He says he knows Girardin.'

'I see. And?'

'And he says our new instructor is not who he says he is.'

'Bring Mr Farhi to see me. And ask Miriam to come as well, would you? We may need an interpreter. And George, do it quietly.'

Jules Farhi turned out to be a small man. Short men, apparently, were better suited for jumping. They tended not to break their legs. He was strong, though, and he had a look of independence on his face. Michael looked at him before he said a word. He wanted to see what kind of man he was before he heard what he had to say, and he found him satisfactory. He knew men, and this one was on the level, and he was reliable. His English was almost non-existent, though, and Miriam translated for them.

'So, Jules, Captain Billingham informs me you have some information regarding Sergeant-Major Girardin.'

'Yes, Sir, if that is his name.'

'Alright, what is it?'

'Well Sir, I recognised him as soon as I saw him. You see, in 1939 I fled with my family to France from Romania. My father had lived there as a boy. He thought we would be safe there. The Vichy administration was harsh but we could manage. Then suddenly the Milice came and arrested us, the whole family, my parents, me and my two brothers, and my sister.'

'What happened to them?'

'I don't know, dead. I don't know for sure.'

'And you, what happened to you?'

'I managed to escape that roundup but I got caught later and they put me in a labour battalion. I worked in many places, wherever they sent us, but always with other Jewish slave labourers. And always with the same guards, under that man.'

'George, if Jules is correct, it seems we have a former Vichy collaborator in our midst. Quite apart from any investigation into how that happened, I want to know why he's here. Either way, we have to confront him now.'

'Yes, I agree.'

'Jules, has he seen you since you arrived, do you think?'

'No Sir, I am pretty sure he hasn't.'

'And you are prepared to identify him for us, now?'

The Frenchman looked determined but Michael saw underlying that an element of fear too.

'Don't worry, you are safe here. There is absolutely nothing he can do. You are not at his mercy, he is at ours. George, if you please.'

They waited in silence. Miriam looked at Michael but he wasn't her man now, he was the commandant of this camp and she could make no contact with him. Jules stared out of the window into the twilight, as if he was remembering. When Girardin entered, he gave a small start.

'Ah Sergeant-Major, thank you for coming to see me. Please, don't stand to attention. We are informal here. In fact, why don't you sit down?'

'No thank you, Sir.'

'That's alright. We want to ask you some questions. Miriam here will translate for me, so it will take a little time, I'm afraid, but if you prefer to stand …'

Girardin gave no reply to that. He was every bit the soldier, and he had no interest in these pleasantries. Michael shuffled some papers on his desk to give him time to gather his thoughts and to give the other man time to sweat, if that was what he was doing.

'OK, in your own time please, I should like to ask you to run through for me your military record.'

'My record? Why?'

'Because I asked you to.'

He proceeded to give the same details Michael had in the file in front of him, with some embellishment. He was, it seemed, proud of his record. Either that, or he was a very good liar. Michael let him finish uninterrupted, while Miriam did her best to slow him down when he became heated.

'I see. It is an impressive record.'

'Thank you Sir.'

'And in addition to that service, have you ever served under the Vichy regime as a guard in a labour battalion?'

Girardin looked shocked, but then that was to be expected either way. He said no, several times, somewhat indignantly, and he sounded convincing, but he made just one small mistake, so small he was almost certainly unaware of it. He had so far ignored Jules Farhi. He had no reason to remember one face out of many. But some instinct, faced with that accusation, made him glance at him, very very briefly, and another man might not have noticed it but Michael did, because Michael was looking for exactly that, and it told him all he needed to know.

'Mr Girardin, I see you have a sidearm. Would you please, very slowly, remove it and hand it to Captain Billingham.'

But Girardin was one step ahead. As he went to remove the pistol all eyes went to it, and so they were unprepared for what happened next. He was a strong athletic man. He punched George hard in the abdomen and George went down. Then just as Michael was rising from his seat he sprang out of the door. There was a great deal of shouting and confusion, and in the half light of dusk it was difficult to see which way he had gone. Students and instructors became involved in the melee but no-one was sure what they were looking for and so when Michael heard the engine of his car start up he knew his quarry was getting away. The car screeched down the dirt track out of camp leaving Michael standing breathless, unable to give chase because the only other vehicles were the lorries and there was no way they could catch the car.

He went back into the office to check on George. Miriam had sat him in a chair and was making him take deep breaths. He would live. He was also indignant and angry at having been jumped like that. He spluttered an apology and Michael put his hand on his shoulder to assure him that no-one blamed him. They had all been taken by surprise.

So no harm had been done for now. There would certainly be an investigation into how Girardin had infiltrated their operation so easily, but more importantly they would urgently have to review the possible reasons for his presence there. If Girardin posed a threat to Camp Joshua, and there was every reason to believe he did, they were facing closing down the entire operation.

17

Camp Joshua was put on a state of readiness to move out at a few hours' notice. Michael went into Birecik and talked casually with the police officers he knew, but if they knew anything they weren't about to tell him. He sent George and a couple of the instructors to Ankara and Istanbul, but they came back with nothing. From Ankara they contacted Haganah Headquarters to warn them, and Haganah agents throughout Europe were put on alert. But there was nothing, not a word of what it was about. Agents had contacts in the British Army Headquarters in Palestine but they drew a blank. It was getting hard to believe there was anything, that Girardin had not simply been looking for a hideaway and found them by mistake. The longer the search went on for clues the more this seemed to be the only answer. No-one planning an action against the camp would leave it for weeks after Girardin had been discovered. They would either strike immediately, or they would simply assume that Haganah had been alerted and would close it down.

Michael stood them down from their alert state and authorised limited training to begin again. Parachuting, though, was out.

The big question now was what to do about the Spitfire. There seemed to be no good reason any longer for holding the operation off. There was a small risk, but there always had been and the recent incident hadn't much affected that. No, it would go ahead. Michael gave the all-clear and after some celebration his people got back to work. A week later Nutberry's engineer was ready with the timing device, plus a complete spare. He didn't want the technology to let them down at the last minute and ruin all that work, and the device was small enough for it not to be a problem carrying two. He assured Michael it would work but Michael wasn't interested in assurances. He insisted on a mock-up of a plane's fuel system and a full demonstration. It went perfectly.

Getting a man onto Cyprus was going to be relatively easy, except that Michael chose not a man but a woman, called Rifka Leibowitz. Rifka came straight to Camp Joshua from Poland and would do anything to get to Palestine, including, because Michael told her it was important, getting locked up on Cyprus. Anyway, to the best of her knowledge her sister was held in Famagusta, and if she was going to wait to get to the promised land she wanted to wait with her. Rifka and her sister, like all of them, had a history, and the past was too painful to put it away and think only of the future. Michael was truthful with her and said that now she had got this far he could send her, after her training, straight to Palestine with the other Haganah people. She thought about this, and he saw the indecision in her eyes, the terrible temptation, but as much as she wanted to go she now knew she was the best hope they had for this part of the mission, and so she would wait a little longer, and she would wait with her sister, if she found her. Michael shook her hand warmly and Miriam went further and hugged her and Rifka went bright red. They told her that since there was no way she could communicate with them once she was in captivity, she had to complete her mission come what may. It would help too if she found her sister, because that would help her to find the right person, an experienced engineer, for the job.

Now they had to find someone on the island, a Cypriot, who would apply for a job at RAF Akrotiri as a cleaner or other menial. It had to be someone local because the British would be sure to carry out a check on them, but one of the Camp Joshua group would have to go to Cyprus to recruit them. That was going to take time, and it was going to be risky, and the only thing they could offer someone to help them was money, so an instructor called Moise, a Salonika Jew, was selected for this job, and as time was short he went straight away, first by boat to Italy, then on another boat to Cyprus with a false passport.

George led a team of three to drive overland through Syria to

Lebanon to look for a suitable landing strip. This part of the plan was wide open to problems. What if Nutberry's calculation was wrong and the plane didn't land where they wanted it to? What if his calculation was right but the pilot's was wrong and landed too soon, or not soon enough and crashed? Michael had to accept this was not an exact science, and for this reason he risked a second team, who would stay in radio contact with the first, about fifty miles apart, in the hope that between them they would spot the landing. Then the engineer had the brilliant idea of monitoring Royal Air Force radio traffic. If the pilot was going to look for somewhere to land he was sure to radio his base and give them a co-ordinate. If the teams in Lebanon could find the right frequency in time, the pilot might lead them in and make their job a lot easier. As a backup Nutberry decided that he would fly the Dakota along the coast to see if he could make visual contact. Once he found them, he would land the DC3 and let his navigator fly it back to Turkey while he flew the Spitfire.

With this belt and braces approach, Michael felt there was more than a chance they would find the plane in time. In time meant before the British sent a rescue mission. By then the Spitfire had to be well away in the opposite direction.

They pored over large-scale maps of Lebanon until they felt like they had all been there, which they hadn't, none of them had. Then they plotted a route for the trucks which reduced the likelihood of meeting any local militia or even worse French troops. Their presence in both Syria and Lebanon would be strictly illegal, but then stealing someone else's plane was also illegal, and George said in for a penny in for a pound, another of his quaint sayings that Michael got the gist of.

Michael knew they should have a contingency plan, but he also knew there wasn't one. The only contingency was how to extract his people in the event of a disaster. Rifka would stay on Cyprus, and she knew that. The man sent to recruit the infiltrator would have every chance of finding a boat out. He might have to wait if it went badly wrong and there was a security sweep of the island, but then that was going to happen anyway once the plane went missing, so all they could say to him was to lie low until his departure wouldn't be noticed.

The teams in Lebanon would make their way back as best they could. If they were intercepted, they were ordered not to get into a firefight unless the odds were clearly on their side and they were quite certain of winning. If they had to face arrest and internment, well, they would do that. The worst result was if it went badly wrong and the camp itself was compromised. But that would only happen if someone talked, and he was pretty sure none of his people would do that, and even if they did they would be unable to give any useful information. The British, he knew, used torture, and for that reason each person in the operation would be kept deliberately ignorant of the other parts. Even if they gave in to torture they would be unable to implicate any other part of the team. And they were all given a story, the same story, to tell in the event of capture, a story that would lead the trail well away from Turkey. Michael himself took charge of that part of the plan.

The training continued for the others, but the tension within the Spitfire team infected everyone and Michael knew he would either have to send them sooner rather than later, or if that were not possible to give the others something to do away from the camp. It was George who came up with the idea of a field exercise. Until the people in Cyprus were in place, and there was nothing anyone could do to speed that up, the Lebanon teams were in limbo. They had their own exercises, and they trained hard every day, looking for the problems they couldn't see, and every day they found something they hadn't thought of, which was good, but on the other hand it confirmed that when they got out there for real there was almost certainly going to be something they hadn't thought of, but how much can you worry about what you don't know?

For the others, those not involved in the Spitfire plan, there was Operation Haifa. On one of the regular long-distance runs George put everyone through to build their fitness they had discovered, to their surprise, a derelict village no-one had noticed before. It was seven or eight kilometres from the camp and it consisted of a few houses, no more than mud walls without roofs really, and a well. They found the skeleton of a goat down the well and surmised that rather than get it out the inhabitants had simply decided to move on.

Perhaps it wasn't just the well. Perhaps, like old Oktay Yilmaz, they had realised there was no way to scratch a living from this useless earth. Perhaps the goat had been the last straw.

It was the closest the young Haganah people of Camp Joshua were going to get to urban warfare training. Michael knew that when the Arabs attacked the Jews were going to have to fight in the desert and the hills but the most critical positions they would have to defend would be the urban centres of Jewish population, Tel Aviv, Hebron, Sfad and of course Jerusalem itself. Jerusalem was the heart of the Jewish nation and would become the capital of their home in Palestine. It would be vital for the Arabs to deny the Jews their capital if they were to deny them their state. The battle for Jerusalem would be bloody. To compound the problem, Michael knew something George did not. Jerusalem's population consisted mostly of large religious families with a lot of children and many old men who would not fight to defend themselves. He discussed this with his instructors and got a brusque response. As far as they were concerned the old Jews of Jerusalem could defend themselves or face the consequences. Michael could see why they felt this way, those who had wrestled the barren land and made it productive, those youngsters without whom there simply could not be a Jewish homeland because by definition that homeland would only exist if it could be defended from annihilation. The religious Jews of Jerusalem, and other ancient Jewish cities like Hebron and Sfad, would pray to God for salvation, but if God was not on the side of Haganah, and who could say if he would be, then they were all going to die.

Michael decided against trying to convince these youngsters to risk their lives for people who would not defend themselves. Instead, he pointed out, in lectures he gave in the evenings after supper, the strategic importance of Jerusalem. They listened and accepted his ideas, largely because of the huge respect everyone had for him. Michael Jacobs, it was well known, had fought with the Jewish Underground in the war. He came from a well-off American family and he could have had a comfortable law practice in New York but he was here with them because he believed as they did, he was truly one of them. And his girlfriend, Miriam, had lost her parents in the war, which gave her the same credentials as many of them. Anyway, the importance of Jerusalem, the place if not the inhabitants, was not something anyone there needed to be reminded of. If they were recent immigrants, they had all their lives said the prayer, next year in Jerusalem. Jerusalem was Zion, it represented the reason they were here. They would fight for it and die for it if God called on them to do so, even those who didn't believe in him.

Operation Haifa would, of necessity, be conducted without weapons. It was too risky to take them out of the camp. The chance of coming across anyone out there was small enough, but the consequences would be too great and in any case they had no blank ammunition to practice with and George vetoed a live-firing exercise as too dangerous, especially in the dark. He had never lost a trainee yet and he didn't want to start now. What they would practise would be infiltrating a town without being seen, at night, using the fieldcraft they had been taught but had had limited opportunity to try out.

Miriam was non-combatant so she volunteered to sit in the tallest house with a pair of binoculars and mark the positions of any soldiers she spotted or heard. Of the twenty attackers, she found seventeen. It was a dismal effort, and George left them in no doubt about how he felt about their performance. They started again, and this time they slowed down because that was, he said, their biggest problem, they took it too fast, and now Miriam found only eight, which was a big improvement but somehow she knew that George would not be content until she failed to find any. It took three more attempts, and even then she saw one soldier, but he was excused on the basis that he found himself face to face with a snake and jumped up in fright. George said that was all very well but in a real battle he would now be dead but Miriam soothed him and pointed out that he was probably right but how many people would have reacted any differently? George hated snakes, and even if no-one knew this it still made him feel a bit guilty about being too harsh on the man and Miriam won him over. The exercise had been long and hard, and everyone concerned was exhausted and fell into bed fully clothed, including Miriam, but in the morning there were may proud faces as George announced it a complete success and told them how proud he was of them all. They weren't part of the Spitfire operation and they felt they weren't at the moment terribly important but Operation Haifa boosted their self esteem and when they finally boarded Nutberry's Dakota for the flight home to Palestine at the end of their training they were filled with confidence and they shook everyone's hand and then they wished the people who were staying for the operation the best of luck.

As they flew off Camp Joshua seemed suddenly quiet. There would be no more trainees until after the Spitfire, and they couldn't be certain even then if training would restart. It might turn out to be an operation too far, and Camp Joshua might have to be moved hastily or disbanded altogether. The next job was for the weapons to be readied for removal if necessary. They had only the three lorries and there was no way they could carry them all, so George proposed they return to the deserted village and bury a lot of them. It was a great deal of work, but while they waited those last two weeks before the operation took off in earnest it would keep everyone busy, so Michael agreed. Every day, the men went out early in the morning and dug and late in the evening they came back tired and filthy and for once the women in the camp, even those who would be soldiers in Palestine, stayed at home and welcomed them back with showers and hot food. And then, suddenly, it was time to go.

18

Early in the morning, the Dakota lifted off from the dirt track that ran out of Camp Joshua and turned south towards the Mediterranean. As it did so the first rays of the sun came over the horizon and they felt the warmth on their backs as they waved, and it felt like a good omen.

Nutberry would stay in communication as long as possible, but when he came within range of the British listening station in Palestine he would shut down his radio and then they would be able to do nothing except wait and worry. Camp Joshua now consisted of Michael and George, Miriam and Dvorah, and a couple of the instructors who had been involved in the planning and preparation but had been left behind. Michael thought he knew now how General Eisenhower must have felt after the Overlord invasion fleet sailed, sending all those men out into the unknown, with nothing left to do but pray. He didn't know if Eisenhower was the praying kind though.

Michael didn't know how to pray and would never have admitted to Miriam or the others that he did so now, but he did, in his own fashion. He knew it was foolish, but still, it made him feel a little better. The war was over and men shouldn't be flying into danger, but one war finishes and another begins and the war between the Jews and their enemies, the first for almost two thousand years, on the very soil where the Romans defeated the Jewish nation, was about to begin. Perhaps what he prayed for was not just the men and women he had sent out but for everyone, all the young people he had helped to train and arm, and the whole Jewish people themselves. Somehow, stealing a fighter plane from the British air force represented something more than it seemed to be, although that was enough, but something more significant than one plane, which he knew was no more than a token against the combined aerial might of the Arab nations. In his mind he had an image of a Spitfire with the roundels painted out and the Star of David on the wings instead. It was an image that filled his heart with an overwhelming sense of destiny.

He sought George out. It was time to talk to someone who wasn't Jewish, someone who didn't share his dreams, someone who would bring him down to Earth. Supper was over and George was outside sitting on an upturned ammunition box.

'Stargazing?'

'As it happens old chum, yes, well, not the stars exactly, the moon. Just look, and tell me what you see.'

'Er, the moon?'

'Yes. And?'

'Well, there's no man on it, so, sorry, I guess I don't see what you're getting at.'

'Michael, Michael, ever the Intelligence officer. Stop looking with your eyes and look with your soul.'

'George, I don't believe I'm hearing this. You, talking about souls? Aren't you getting a bit carried away?'

'Alright, have a laugh. But you know, when I was a boy, about eight I think, my dad bought me a telescope. It wasn't a very big one, but I set it up in my bedroom, on the windowsill, and every night I looked out into space, when there was no cloud, anyway. At first I was obsessed with the stars and tried to draw maps of the constellations, but then I was drawn to the moon. I started to investigate its surface and the more I learned the more I came to love it.'

'Really?'

'Uhuh, yes, I don't think that's too strong a word. Look, even from here with the naked eye she's beautiful.'

'She? George, come on.'

'No, look, OK, now take the binoculars and take another look. Right, now follow me. See those three large depressions? The one on the left is called the Sea of Rains, and right next to it is the Sea of Serenity and then, just go to the right a touch more, you should find the Sea of Crises. Once you start to learn the names of its features the moon takes on a personality, it becomes a real place, not just a light in the sky. It is in any case a thing of extreme beauty, don't you think?'

Michael did. He was beginning to get the point.

'You know, we just take it for granted, but really, the moon is like another planet to me, a sister to the Earth out there in space, running our lives in so many ways we don't completely understand with its gravity. We shouldn't take it for granted. We should come out and look on in wonder. It's not hard to understand why people in the past have worshipped her.'

Michael still had the binoculars trained on the surface and was now fascinated with the detail he could see. He wondered why this simple pleasure had taken so many years to discover.

'And on the other side it's completely unknown and always will be. The dark side of the Moon. It sounds like we're not meant to know what's there.'

Michael put the glasses down. 'Maybe we will one day, you know, go there and find out.'

'I don't think so. Anyway, I almost hope we don't, that we don't disturb her, that she retains her mystery.'

'Captain Billingham, I'm seeing another side of you, a mystery like the far side of the Moon. You're a bit of a romantic.'

'Oh, there's a lot you don't know about me, Mike. Seriously, I mean what do we know about each other outside of this strange world we have inhabited since we met?'

Michael realised it was true. He decided to change that. 'George, have you ever been married?'

'Me? Yes and no.'

'Hold on, I'm not sure that makes sense. Either you have or you haven't.'

'Well, it's a long story, and I'm not sure it would interest you.'

Which usually means I don't want to talk about it, but Michael, unusually for him, blundered in.

'Yes it would.'

'Alright, since you ask. Her name was Jennifer, Jenny. We were engaged, and a month before the wedding she was riding with her father in his car and they hit a patch of ice and crashed. He was killed outright. She lived, but her back was broken. They had her on some kind of machine that kept her breathing, but really, I mean she was gone.'

Michael was absolutely silent. George's voice had gone strangely quiet, and yet equally strangely Michael heard every word he said.

'After her father's funeral her mother lost her sanity. There was no-one who would take responsibility and the hospital asked me what they should do. You know what I mean? I waited and waited, hoping for a miracle, but they said there wasn't going to be one. I didn't believe them, I mean that's the point about miracles, isn't it, that impossible things can happen? But then I got over that belief and I realised they were right. I sat with her and held her hand but really, she was living because I didn't want her to die. She was living for me, not her.

Because we were engaged and there was no-one else the hospital said in the end I would make the decision. Well I did. But before they did what they had to do I got the vicar at the hospital to marry us. At first he didn't want to, said there was some religious objection to it, but I worked on him and he saw what it meant to me and made me promise I wouldn't tell anyone, as if I was likely to, and that night we crept in and did it. The next morning they switched off the machine. To this day I don't know what it means, but in my heart I think I believe we were married. It helps.'

'Well George, if it helps then you surely did the right thing.'

'Thank you for saying that. I've never been totally convinced, and I've never told anyone else.'

'Haven't you told Dvorah?'

'No. Look, she and I, I mean it's just a thing, you know.'

'A thing?'

'Yes. I don't think she thinks of me as, well, husband material, just company while she's here. Anyway ....'

'Anyway? Are you going to tell me you can't marry anyone, Dvorah or any other woman, because of Jenny?'

'Is that stupid?'

Michael sighed. How can you tell a man he's stupid for loving his dead wife? 'No, not stupid. In fact very laudable. But it was a long time ago. It sounds like a cliché but you have a life to live. Wouldn't she have wanted you to have some happiness?'

'Oh I know all that, and actually you're not the first person to say it.'

'A woman?'

'Uhuh. It went so far but I backed out.'

'Well, look, I don't know what Dvorah wants, but she came back didn't she? If she was just looking to pass the time with a man, do you think she couldn't have found that in Palestine? And a Jewish one at that, although I hesitate to mention it. No, I think Dvorah came back for more than just a thing. My advice, in the unlikely event that you will take any notice of it, is to give this a chance.'

'You really think so?'

'Yep.'

'Mm. And what about you?'

'Me?'

'Yes, you and the lovely Miriam? What's stopping you?'

'Well, it's not that simple, you know.'

'No, it never is, I'm proof of that. What's your excuse? Don't tell me you're still secretly in love with Roza Levinson.'

Michael stood up abruptly and the box he was sitting on fell over with a clatter. 'What? What the hell are you talking about? Where on Earth did you get an idea like that?'

'Oh, well, it must have been something you said. Come on old chap, Roza has come into the conversation a number of times since I've known you and I count myself a fairly shrewd judge of men, and I see the look in your face when you talk about her. So, I'm telling you, after all this time she's still on your mind.'

'George, I think you might have got hold of the wrong end of the stick, as you like to say. Roza, don't forget, was married.'

'Uhuh. And then she was widowed.'

'Oh right, and you think that makes all the difference.'

'Well, yes. Look, I'm not saying you would have wanted it that way, but the fact is she was and you could have taken the opportunity but you didn't.'

'It's not that simple.'

'No, it never is, remember.'

'And anyway, if I had, I mean if she had come back to the States with me, think about the consequences, all of this, it might have been very different.'

'Yes, but that's life. If Adolf Hitler had been a better artist millions of people might still be alive. It's all in a box marked we'll never know. So, you and Miriam? She's a lovely girl. If you don't make it permanent, don't be surprised if some other bloke comes along and takes her from you one day.'

Michael looked up again at the moon. She was exceedingly beautiful, heart-achingly beautiful in fact, and he had never noticed her. Well, so was Miriam, and he had noticed her right from the beginning, but as George reminded him nothing was simple, and he would have liked to have been able to say it but he couldn't, that he was ready to marry her but she wasn't, that there was still unfinished business, and now he saw it, that the business had to be finished, he owed that to her and to himself, that they could be happy but they had to go through the fire and come through to the other side. And he had to be the one to do it with her, because that was the key to her heart.

Well, when the operation was over, he would see what other work had to be done. Perhaps they would carry on here but on the other hand maybe Haganah High Command would have different plans. Things were changing in Palestine. Many people thought it was only a matter of time, that they would get their state. He couldn't imagine it, the Jewish National Home, this thing that so many people had talked about for so long. Of course, all of his work came to that, was for that, from the moment he came to Europe really. But George? Why was he here?

'George …'

'Uhuh? Looking for an argument?'

'No, I want to ask you a question.'

'OK, since it's obviously one of those days.'

'Why are you here?'

'Because I'm talking to you.'

'No, idiot, I mean why are you doing this job? You're not Jewish.

You could have done all sorts of things after the war, so why did you choose us?'

'Things such as what?'

'I don't know. You could have stayed in the army for a start.'

'Yes, I thought about it, in fact I was thinking about it when you came along.'

'Oh, I hope I didn't spoil your plans.'

'No, you rescued me.'

'So, answer the question.'

George needed time to think about it. He wasn't entirely sure himself, and he didn't want this to sound foolish.

'Look, I don't have any of the reasons you people have for all this. Britain is my home, well, England specifically, and I always thought of myself as archetypically English, you know, middle class, comfortable with the status quo and so on. It was the war that changed it all, I suppose. I saw too much, couldn't turn the clock back. It was a permanent change. I know a lot of soldiers felt the same, were going to have trouble going back to civvy street. So why not the British Army? No good reason, but after Bergen-Belsen, well, to be honest, look, I probably never met a Jew before the war, didn't really think about them, but then I couldn't stop thinking, and when this came up, well, it just seemed right. Mind you, if you had asked me when we started if I would have condoned stealing a Spit from my own country's air force, I'm pretty sure I would have baulked, but it happened gradually, this business of seeing it from the other side. The bottom line is that now I'm a traitor, and that's not comfortable, but it's a moral decision and it's one that I have made and will stand by. I think Britain is wrong. Look at Palestine. It's tiny, and look at the whole blasted British Empire, even now after the war, and it's huge. The Arabs are getting their homelands. Since the first war the colonial powers have set them up in Lebanon and Saudi Arabia and Iraq, and Egypt come to that. I didn't realise, until I looked at a map, just what we were talking about. People in England speak about it but they don't know, it's just a spit of land, can't be any bigger than Wales, if you know where that is, and ask me if anyone in England would complain if Wales fell into the sea and I don't think so, but they go on about Palestine as if it means so much to them. No, Britain doesn't need it and the Arabs sure as hell don't need it. I'm sorry, I'm rambling, but if you make any sense out of it all I'm saying that no-one else at home might have thought this through but I have and it's the answer to your question. I think.'

'It sure is. One more, though.'

'Go on.'

'What will you do afterwards, you know, when, assuming we do, we get our state. What then?'

'Come on, do you really have to ask?'

'What do you mean?'

'Well, Michael tell me, what is all this for? Is there or is there not going to be a hell of a punch up?'

'Er, I wouldn't put it like that but yes, of course, we're preparing for war.'

'Well, Michael old bean, if there's going to be a war, count me in.'

19

'What do you suppose they're talking about?'

Miriam was watching the men sitting outside. She could tell they were deep in conversation, but she couldn't hear what they were saying. Michael had been so busy recently, she knew she had to let him do it, but now, well, perhaps there would be some time, after this operation. Camp Joshua didn't need him all the time. George could handle the day-to-day working. Michael had talked about letting the apartment go in Paris, but she wanted to talk about that before they made a final decision. This place had got her all caught up but now she wondered if that was right, because she knew there was only one place to go after Turkey and that was Palestine, and Miriam Fillon was probably the only person in Camp Joshua who wasn't hell bent on getting there.

Dvorah came to the window of the canteen and looked out.

'Oh, them, you know, it's always the same, the Spitfire, the camp, Haganah. They are obsessed.'

'Dvorah, you surprise me. I thought everyone here was obsessed.'

'Ah, there's a difference. The ones who have come from Europe, they can think of nothing else, but I've come from Palestine, I was born there, and I tell you, OK, I understand why they think it is the answer to all their problems but actually, it's not an easy place you know.'

'Don't you love it?'

'Miriam, tell me what love means, because I don't know. Yes, I love Palestine, but all my life the sole topic of conversation, at home, in school, was the Jewish Homeland. Yes, of course, it's what I want, but actually I also want some kind of life, just ordinary life, not planning, not fighting, just living.

'When I was four, some Arabs attacked our village. I don't know why, I was too young, but one person was killed and some more were injured. The head man from the Arab village came and apologised and said the people who did it would be punished and they were, but ever since then we distrusted them. There has never been a time when I can remember not having guns in the house. Alright, it's necessary, to defend ourselves, but I just wish it wasn't. It makes me think sometimes that maybe America would be easier, safer, more normal. You've lived there, what do you think?'

'But I've never lived in Palestine. I've never even been there. I have no idea what it's like.'

'Well, I'll tell you. Most of the time it's too hot, and when it's not it's too cold. There are flies everywhere, and it smells. And it's full of Jews, which would be alright but in the cities at least when you get two Jews you've got two synagogues and two synagogue committees. One lot isn't religious enough and the other lot is too religious. One lot follows these rules and the other lot doesn't. We're not a people or a nation, we're an argument in progress. The idea of a Jewish state fills me with fear. If one small town can't live in harmony, what hope do we have for a whole country? And then you've got the Arabs.'

'So, what are they like?'

'Well in a way they are easier to explain than the Jews. Apart from the Bedouin who are the real Arabs ....'

'What do you mean?'

'The people in Palestine who call themselves Arab are really Levantines. But since the start of the campaign for independence in the Middle East the political people who manipulate the masses have promoted the idea of an Arab people, a nation, but they're not a nation. The people in the Maghreb aren't like the Egyptians, and the Egyptians aren't like the Iraqis and so on and so on. We're preparing to defend ourselves against the so-called Arab hordes but the fact is they will never be able to fight together. Yes, they are much bigger than us and they have better weapons, but they will only ever fight for their own reasons. The only ones with any discipline are the Jordanians.'

'Why them?'

'Because they've got British commanders and British arms paid for with British money, even though they're called The Arab Legion. They're the ones we've got to watch.'

'How do you know all this?'

'Miriam, you don't mean how do I, a mere woman, know all this, I hope.'

'No, yes, well, come on, I don't know many American women who could match you.'

'I'll take that as a compliment. I grew up with it. My father is a Haganah commander, and my two brothers are in. Yossi is in the Palmach, the commandos. We're a Haganah family.'

'And your mother? Don't tell me she's a soldier too?'

'My mother was the person in our village who was killed when I was four.'

'Oh God, I'm sorry.'

'That was when my father joined Haganah. What about your parents? Did they die in the war?'

'Er, yes, well, my mother was deported by the SS. My father died in action.'

'In the American Army?'

'No, French, before the fall of France.'

'So you are an orphan.'

'Yes.'

Miriam fidgeted. She had never told that lie before, but she knew now that she would tell it again. It made it a lot easier. Dvorah said she was sorry about that and that made Miriam feel a little guilty about telling a lie but she could hardly go back on it now.

'Still, you've got Michael. He's quite a catch.'

'Yes, I know.'

'Is he good in bed?'

Miriam looked at Dvorah wide-eyed. 'What? Dvorah, is that the kind of question Palestinian girls ask?'

'Yes, sure, why not? Don't American women?'

'No, of course they don't. Well, they might, I wouldn't know. No, actually, I don't think they do, especially Jewish ones.'

'Are you shocked?'

'Do I sound shocked?'

'Yes.'

'Well, there is your answer.'

They were quiet and looked at the moon that Michael and George were watching. It was as if all that was happening at Camp Joshua was happening under its spell.

'So, will you marry Michael?'

'Huh? Oh, I don't know. He hasn't asked me. Maybe he won't.'

'Why wouldn't he? Does he love you?'

'I don't know. Yes, I think so.'

'Well, has he said so?'

'Yes, he says it quite a lot.'

'And do you have reason to think he might be lying?'

'No, of course not.'

'Well in that case the answer to my question, you know, the one about does he love you, isn't I think so, it's yes, he does. Why are you so coy about it?'

'Dvorah, look, it's not that simple.'

'No, it never is. In which case here's a simple question. Do you love him?'

'Yes. Yes, definitely.'

'Why?'

'Good God, how do you answer a question like that? OK, I could say it's because he's good-looking and strong and he looks after me and he has these wonderful moral values and he's fun to be with, sometimes, when he's not being too serious, and ... well lots more.'

She stopped and Dvorah could see she was thinking and she let her.

'Alright, you and I both know that whatever love is it can't be put into words like that. It's a feeling, isn't it, you know when it's there, it makes you want that person against any rational argument. You just know. But there's more, and I've had men before but now, yes, I think there is something I never knew was an essential ingredient of love and now I believe I understand it.'

'Oh, really? Well do tell me, please.'

'I'm not sure how to explain it.'

'Try.'

'Well, when we fall in love we think it's because we need this man or that man. We see it in terms of ourselves, what we want, what we need. But it's not like that with Michael. Yes, it's like that as well, but there is something else, an extra dimension. For the first time in my life I have found a man who needs me. Michael doesn't know it himself, because he spends all his time being the commandant, or running around Europe doing all this important work of his and he thinks he's in control of his life, but I can see it in him, and yes since you asked, I can see it in bed. It's not just a physical need for my body, it's deeper than that. He takes from me without taking. I know that sounds ridiculous, but I don't know how else to explain it. What he takes he gives back twice over, but he does need to take. That's why I allow him to do it, why it's right that he does. OK, you could say that children need us, and sometimes I wonder about that, if we women treat our men like children, and I look at myself and other women I know and I think there is an element of that, but it's a mistake, a mistake to think that because a man needs us it somehow belittles him, that we should put him where we put a child, because it's not the same need, well, it is a bit I suppose. I don't know if this makes any sense.'

'Oh yes, it makes a lot of sense. You know, in Palestine life isn't like anywhere else, I think. I've seen American films and I would say at home it's a bit like the wild west, and it breeds a certain kind of woman, really very different from women elsewhere. I will think about what you've said, really.'

They looked out at the two men, deep in conversation.

'It's strange the way the two of them get on so well. I mean, they're so different. Your George ...'

'My George?'

'Of course. Isn't he?'

'I don't know. He's not ... I mean, he's not, well ...'

'Jewish?'

'OK, no, he's not.'

'Is that a problem?'

'Yes and no. I mean it would have been at one time. My father, after my mother was killed, he became bitter, not just about the Arabs but the British too. To him anyone who isn't Jewish doesn't understand, can't understand, then when we started to realise what was happening in Germany he just got worse.'

'So he wouldn't understand you being with a non-Jewish man, and a British soldier as well?'

'No he wouldn't. But look, George has shown his commitment. He's here, he's helping us to steal a plane from his own country's air force. What more could you ask a man to do?'

'But is it enough? And I don't mean just your father, I mean for you too. Can you see George as a man and forget where he has come from?'

'I think so, but I do worry about my family. It's not only my father, but Yossi, my brother in the Palmach, I'm not sure he will understand.'

'Have you talked to George about it?'

'Well, you know, we talk about it without talking about it, so we get nowhere. He's a good man, and he's not offended, which he has every right to be. He knows we Jews are prickly people and really, he's very patient. I wish he was Jewish but he isn't and I can't change that.'

'He could convert, if he felt strongly enough.'

'He could, but so what? You can go through the ritual of conversion, but you can never become Jewish. You and I have inherited our mutual history and you do have to inherit it, you can't adopt it. He can become Jewish but he can never become a Jew, with all that means. Before the war I would have said this but now, now we know how alone we stand in the world despite all that has been done to us, I'm even more sure.'

Michael and George had gone now and the moon went behind a cloud and cast the camp in darkness.

'Dvorah, do you think this operation is going to work?'

'Personally, I think it's a crazy idea. Even if they get the plane, which they might and they might not, I don't think they have thought through the consequences. The British will get really mad. These men treat it as if it's some kind of joke, especially George, but it's not. If their Military Intelligence people ever learn about of his involvement in it his life won't be worth living. He will spend the rest of it hiding from them.'

'But in fairness it wasn't their idea, was it? It's an order from High

Command, isn't it?'

'Yes. If it wasn't, I would have got George into bed and when he was most vulnerable I would have told him not to be so stupid.'

'It was my idea, you know. Not getting a plane, I mean, stealing one. It's all my crazy idea.'

'Miriam, it might have been your idea, but you know, not everything a woman says is supposed to be taken seriously, so in this case I think we can blame the men for the whole thing.'

Miriam wasn't sure about that. 'Well, in any case, we can't stop it now.'

'No. So, my dear, if you have a god, I suggest this would be a good time to start praying.'

20

Whether Miriam prayed or not, and whether her prayers were heard or not, the operation, to Dvora's huge surprise, succeeded. The day the two planes were expected, they were up early scanning the skies. Much too early of course, but they were in the dark with radio silence being maintained and they couldn't help themselves.

Midday came and went and they ate without much interest. It got warm and they became lethargic. No-one wanted to talk about it. Each person kept their thoughts to themselves. It was too late to say do you think.

Miriam heard it first. She shook her head to make sure it wasn't a fly buzzing, but it was persistent, just a small sound in the pervading silence, and Michael saw the look on her face and interpreted it correctly, and he looked too. They all had binoculars and without a word passing between them, now they scanned the sky in earnest. They could see nothing for a while but then suddenly a shout went up, a strangulated cry from George, and they followed his pointing finger and they saw them, two dots in the sky, indistinguishable from this distance, but two planes could mean only one thing. Michael rubbed his eyes and lifted the glasses again and now he knew it was true. A Spitfire and a Dakota, heading straight for them, at this distance wing tip to wing tip.

The Spitfire came down first, while the transport plane circled overhead like a mother bird watching its fledgling perform its first landing. As the fighter plane's engines cut out and the propellers slowed to a halt, the DC3 touched down and taxied next to it. It was, as George said excitedly, a hell of a sight. He hugged Michael exuberantly, and then suddenly the crews were down on the ground and everyone was shouting and hugging and crying. Nutberry looked tired but triumphant and he did what the others could only assume was some kind of Red Indian war dance, and then he fell over and just lay there on the ground and laughed.

Michael became serious and said they should get the planes under cover, the British might be coming looking, and Nutberry told him to relax, the Brits were hundreds of miles away, looking in completely the wrong direction. He had been monitoring their radio traffic, and they hadn't a clue, not the slightest notion of who had taken their plane or where it was.

That evening they made a fire and barbecued a deer George had shot and opened several bottles of wine. The flames reflected off the Spitfire and from time to time one of them would go up and kiss it or just smack its rump like it was a horse that had just won a race.

Before they fell asleep Michael insisted they get both planes under cover. It would be stupid to lose them now just because of a chance sighting by a plane, any plane, coming over at first light before they were awake. Nutberry was a little unsteady on his feet but was greatly put out by the suggestion that he was unfit to taxi both aircraft under the camouflage net they had specially extended for this event. He told them he had once flown a Dakota after a two-night bender and had only broken one of the wings off and the navigator had to explain to the others that this was air force humour and it wasn't really true and Nutberry said oh yes it is so Michael closed his eyes and when he opened them again both aircraft were safely put to bed wings intact.

It was very warm and they threw bedding down on the ground and slept under the planes. When he woke in the morning Michael rubbed his eyes to make sure he wasn't dreaming. It was still there. They were both there, the Jewish air force. He took a shower with Miriam and they both giggled like schoolchildren and then, over breakfast, he announced to the others that he and Miriam were going to France. They would deal with the apartment and be back in a few weeks. In that time he wanted the Spitfire painted and extra camouflage installed down to ground level so that any chance visitors like the police from Birecik would at least have half a chance of missing it. Meanwhile, he would discuss the present situation with Haganah High Command and bring back their new orders with him. George was in command of the very small establishment and he was not to allow discipline to slacken. George said there was no chance of that.

On the morning of their departure he drove them in one of the lorries to Birecik. While he was tanking up for the drive to Ankara, Michael went into the police station to show his face. If he did that, he calculated, they were far less likely to come to the camp to see him. When he didn't reappear Miriam went to the station to ascertain what had happened. What had happened was that he had been arrested.

Trying not to panic, she found George at the garage and they sat in the cab of the lorry and tried to understand what was going on and what they could do about it. The police captain had told her nothing, and George said that was a good sign, because had they had a definite misdemeanour in mind they would have charged him. No, it was a bluff. They hadn't extracted any cash for some time and clearly this was an opportunistic action. Michael walks in through the door, they slap him in a cell. It wasn't so much an arrest as a kidnap for ransom. He told Miriam to go back and ask to see him. An hour later she was back. He was right, there was no charge, just delaying tactics. Michael also told Miriam he wanted her out of Turkey, that she should get the train from Ankara as planned and go to Paris. It would be one less thing for him to worry about, then he could concentrate on keeping the police away from Camp Joshua and the planes.

She asked George what he thought, should she go or stay, and he admitted Michael was right. He also promised he would have him out of that cell and on a train within two days.

It took four. The fine, as the police called it, was for something George was entirely unable to understand, which was how they wanted it, but he paid up and took Michael straight to the railway station. The next day Michael was in Paris. It was late, and he was tired. He got a taxi to the apartment and it was dark so he could easily have missed it but someone had parked it under a lamppost and he saw it was a bit battered but there was no mistaking it. It was his car. He fumbled in his pocket for his keys and he found the spare for the doors and the ignition. He could only assume that whoever had put it there was now in the apartment and at the present he had to assume that person was the parachute instructor, Girardin. Keeping in the shadow of the wall of the apartment building as much as possible, he opened the boot. It was a mess but when he lifted up the spare wheel it was obvious no-one had been here before him. Why would they? Under the spare wheel was a 9mm pistol with a full magazine. They obviously hadn't searched the car. He was just grateful they hadn't had a flat tyre on the way here. Well, now all he had to do was get into the apartment and face them, Girardin or whoever it was. He prayed for Miriam, and while he was praying he also pleaded for just one opponent, not two.

There was only one, and it wasn't Girardin. Michael had him in the pistol's sight but the man just sat there, at one end of the dining table, and Miriam sat at the other. Michael didn't look at her. He stood in the doorway and looked at this stranger. He had an uncanny feeling he had met this man before, but try as he might he couldn't place him. What he wasn't going to do was take his eyes off him, for a second. He was seemingly unarmed, and he was also strangely relaxed.

'Ah the US cavalry arrives to rescue the damsel in distress. Excellent. Major Jacobs, I have been waiting for you. It may seem presumptuous, as this is your own apartment, but please, do come in. The neighbours, you know. And by the way, I am quite unarmed, so you have the advantage over me.'

As Michael closed the door behind him he tried to compute what he knew so far. French, with passable English, possibly someone from his past, and in possession of his car which was last seen being driven away in a hurry by someone claiming to be a Sergeant-Major parachute instructor. And if he was telling the truth about being unarmed ... no, that Michael couldn't work out.

Miriam said nothing.

'So, Major Jacobs, now that we are more private, permit me to introduce myself. I am Miriam's father, Gaspar Fillon.'

21

Michael fell back against the door. It was too much to take in and his brain desperately tried to work it out but couldn't. Fillon laughed. He could see the effect he had had and was enjoying it. Miriam was still silent. Michael stepped over to her and put his arm round her, his left arm. His right hand still pointed the weapon at her father.

'Really, Major, I assure you, there is no need for that thing.'

'I will be the judge of that.'

'Alright, I would have said the same myself.'

'Why are you here and what do you want? And how did you get my car?'

'Ah, you saw it. I should have supposed you would, the Intelligence officer, always one step ahead of the enemy. Girardin, he was one of us, you know.'

'Us? Who are you?'

'Oh, that does not matter, but I think you know these foolish French Underground, as they love to call themselves, want to kill me.'

'Yes, I know that. I'm tempted to do the job for them, but first I want some answers. First, I want to know why you are not afraid of me.'

'Ah, very good, very good. Many people would have just been pleased and not wondered why. I should have guessed it of you, of course. The answer, Major, is that you cannot afford to kill me.'

'Oh, why not?'

'Well, apart from the obvious nuisance of shooting someone in a Paris apartment and explaining the noise to the neighbours and disposing of the body, you will not shoot me in front of my daughter.'

'Don't let me put you off Michael.'

Michael was surprised to hear her speak, but even more surprised at what she said. Fillon laughed again. Michael would have liked to think it was a nervous laugh but it really wasn't. He was very cool about this.

'Miriam, I am afraid, is a hard-hearted woman. You would do well to remember this if you marry her. Mind you, she has much to be angry about. Her father is not a pleasant man. Anyway, I have not fully answered your question. You will not kill me also because unless I make regular contact with my people your camp in Turkey and its secrets will suddenly become very interesting to the police in Birecik. I think you will not want that to happen. You have already recently experienced how capricious they can be. Yes, you paid them off, but we are paying them more than you. I can make one telephone call and end your game right now.'

'Alright Fillon, but why? What do you want? Money?'

Fillon laughed. 'Oh no, we have no need for money, I assure you. The Germans, they were most generous at the end, in return of course for certain favours. No, what I want, Major, is to employ the services of the Levant Trading Company, to facilitate my departure from France to a more congenial place for my retirement. You see, I am having a little trouble getting across the borders just now.'

'And the deal is we help to smuggle you across and you will leave us alone?'

'Yes, that is it.'

'I don't think so.'

'Oh dear, that is unfortunate.'

'Because I have absolutely no reason to believe that you will keep your side of the bargain. To be honest I think the best thing I could do now is just to kill you.'

He didn't take his eyes off Miriam's father for a instant. Fillon was good, but Michael was better. He dropped his guard for just a fraction of a second, and Michael knew he had at last frightened him. Fillon held most of the cards but not all of them. He wasn't completely sure he had Michael in his grasp. People don't always behave rationally. Sometimes they just get angry and shoot. But Michael showed in his face that he wasn't going to do that, that his adversary did after all have him hooked. The stakes were too high for Michael to keep playing.

'So, Major, I think we can come to an arrangement, don't you?'

'Alright. I imagine you have thought this through, and that you have a precise list of demands.'

'That is correct. If those demands are met, you can go and have your little war. If not, well, you will find that rather more difficult.'

'Yes, I heard you the first time. What exactly do you want from me?'

'A ride out of France to Turkey.'

'That's all? What about after that?'

'No no, that is all. After that is not your problem. One of your Levant Trading Company lorries will take me there, hidden in a cargo, whatever cargo you choose. Preferably not weapons. It would be a pity if I were to get caught because you were smuggling. So, if you will work out the details please.'

'Timescale?'

'Immediate. I have been hanging around this country longer than is beneficial for my health. Realistically, can you have a lorry in Paris, say, in one week's time?'

'Possibly, perhaps a little more. How do I contact you?'

'I am sorry to sound melodramatic, Major, but you don't. I will be back here in your apartment in one week from now, at six o'clock in the evening, to hear your plans. Do we understand each other?'

Michael looked at Miriam, which he had not done yet, and what he read in her face was do it, do whatever it takes to get him out of here and out of France. Michael put the pistol in his pocket.

'Yes. Now get out before I change my mind and blow your brains out.'

22

Michael held Miriam close and she sobbed deeply into his chest. He couldn't begin to imagine the emotions she was going through. All he could do was to be there for her. She cried for a long time and then he gently sat her down and poured her a drink. She wiped her face and sipped the wine and still he didn't push her. She would speak when she was ready. Any question from him, any attempt to start a conversation, would almost certainly hit the wrong note. It would take very little for her to decide not to trust in him, to withdraw into herself. If they were to have a future this had to be gone through together, and right now Michael wanted them to have a future. He wanted that more than almost anything, for her, but now he knew it was for him too, he knew that he needed Miriam because he had love to give, he had a need to do that, and he would give it to her if she would let him.

In the end he put her to bed and she went to sleep immediately. Then he slipped in beside her and sleep eluded him. He had a lot to think about, and as he listened to Miriam's gentle breathing he let go of his anxiety for her and became Michael Jacobs, Intelligence officer, and he applied his wakeful time to trying to figure out Gaspar Fillon. There was something about this seemingly simple demand that didn't work for him and it took an hour staring at the ceiling but then it came to him.

Fillon could find any one of a hundred ways out of France. It was highly unlikely anyone else was looking for him. He wasn't high up on the list of wanted war criminals for the Allies, so why all this fuss, why all the effort? To send a man to Camp Joshua posing as an instructor, to pay off the police in Birecik, it was all way over the top. No, this wasn't about one man escaping justice. There had to be more, much more. It was as he was falling asleep that the germ of the answer came into his head, and it sat there all night waiting for him to wake in the morning and process it into usable facts. Gaspar Fillon was taking something else out of France. He would not be travelling empty-handed, he would be smuggling, like them.

Well, that didn't particularly concern Michael. All he cared about was saving his own operation, Camp Joshua, and Fillon had demonstrated to his satisfaction that he had the power to destroy it. The man could take anything he liked with him, as long as Michael could be satisfied that it would get him out of their hair. But that niggled at him as well. Maybe Fillon would end it there, but how could they know, how could they ever be sure he wouldn't just call the police anyway? The man was a committed Nazi, if not before the war then for some reason now, and Michael tried to imagine how he would feel in the same shoes, about a Jewish army training and equipping for war.

In the morning Miriam woke late and Michael watched over her like a mother hen but she was behaving as if it hadn't happened. She had somehow decided that Michael would deal with this and present her with the result. She didn't want to talk about it. Well, as it happened he didn't particularly want to discuss her father with her. There were many things he was beginning to understand and they didn't concern Miriam. She had enough issues to deal with.

They spent the week quietly, preparing to vacate the flat, seeing the notary about the lease, visiting the bank, mundane things. And while Miriam did some shopping or sunbathed in the park, Michael made telephone calls and met people in quiet bars and by the time Fillon returned to the apartment he had made the arrangements he had to make but he had also put in train the things that would stop this business once and for all.

It was agreed that Miriam would stay in Paris with friends. Michael convinced her she could be useful there, without being specific about in what way. When her father returned, she wasn't there.

'Ah, I see the bird has flown. Tell me, Major, will you marry my daughter and make her happy?'

'Fillon, I don't think your daughter's happiness is of any concern to you. Let's just get on with the business in hand and forget about Miriam.'

'Hm, as you wish. But you know, you shouldn't believe everything she tells you about me.'

'Well, since you are wanted as a war criminal and she isn't, nice try, but I think I know what to believe. Anyway, it will hardly surprise you to learn that I have seen a file on your wartime activities, and about the business with your wife, Miriam's mother.'

'Ah yes, her mother. A fine woman, but, well, it was necessary.'

'No, it wasn't. For a man with morals it wasn't.'

'True, but then, as you now know, I have no morals.'

Michael couldn't help wondering how Miriam's mother had ever come to marry this man, whether it had been some gross error of judgment from the beginning or he had changed dramatically and become someone different. He decided to believe the latter theory.

'The plan, Fillon, just tell me what we have to do.'

'Very well. Is your lorry here?'

'It will be, the day after tomorrow.'

'Alright. That evening, at eight-thirty, you will take it to this address.'

He handed Michael a piece of paper. 'You know where it is?'

'I'll find it.'

'Good. It is in a poor part of the city, quiet at night, an industrial area. At this address you will find a disused factory. At the back there are three loading bays. Use the door to the middle one. This is the key. Drive the lorry in. You will find inside a van. Load up the contents of the van and stay until the morning. At seven o'clock, drive to the second address on the paper, where I will be waiting. Those are all my instructions. I will leave to you the route out of the country.'

'We have to go to Lyon, to pick up scrap metal. It's our cover.'

'Very good. Can we load that and be over the border into Italy by nightfall?'

'That's the plan.'

'Excellent. Well, Major, you have done well, so far. Until then, I wish you goodnight.'

Michael found it hard to resist the urge to smash his fist into the man's face. He wanted to do that even more than he wanted to shoot him. Shooting was too easy, it wouldn't allow him to vent his hatred and his anger. In any case, Fillon was gone.

Two days later he rode with the driver of the Levant Trading Company lorry to the address on the paper. It was all exactly as described. The two of them loaded up a number of crates and boxes from the van onto the truck. Michael itched to know what was in them but they were all well sealed. There was no possibility of opening them without it being discovered.

An hour later they picked up Fillon. He climbed into the back of the lorry and counted the trunks and checked each seal in turn. Then he settled next to Michael in the cab and they drove south out of Paris. Not a word was spoken until they got to Lyon, and there Fillon helped load up the scrap metal, not Michael supposed because he was a helpful sort but obviously because he was now in a hurry. While he was doing that Michael made a discreet telephone call.

They stopped to eat a couple of times en route and each time Fillon took himself off and ate from a supply of food he had brought with him. Michael and the driver talked quietly among themselves but they said nothing that might give the impression they were conspiring against him. Michael didn't want him spooked. At the border he was especially thankful that the man on duty was one of those who saw the Levant Trading Company lorries through regularly. He scanned the paperwork and checked passports cursorily, put his head under the rear tarpaulin and shone his torch inside for a few seconds to show willing, and then he waved them through. Michael didn't ask Fillon about his passport. That was his problem. In any case it passed muster, which he knew it would. The fugitive was hardly likely to have a poor-quality one and foul everything up at this stage.

They drove the normal route for company lorries across the Alps, the route that Krystyna had once taken on a motorcycle combination with three orphan boys, and soon they were in Milan. From there they drove across the north of Italy heading for Yugoslavia, always, because of the sporadic fighting still going on there, the most dangerous part of the journey.

And it was in Yugoslavia, on the narrow road between Trieste and Rijeka, that for the first time ever a Levant Trading Company truck was ambushed. Half a dozen men in police uniform manned a barrier across the road and the driver had no choice but to stop. It was getting dark and the policemen waved lanterns in the direction of a track off the road to direct him to pull off. That, he thought, was not normal for the police, and also why were there no other vehicles waiting to get through? It suggested the roadblock had been erected hastily just for them. As soon as he pulled onto the track he saw in his mirror that they rapidly dismantled the road block again. They were not the police. He looked at Michael but Michael was looking at Fillon, to see how he reacted. It was hard to tell in the dark, but he imagined he was sweating.

The driver obeyed an instruction to get down and Michael followed him, closing the door of the cab behind him. Only Fillon didn't move.

'Michael, good to see you.'

'George, the feeling is mutual. And David, glad you could make it.'

He shook David Schulman's hand heartily. Fillon watched with a growing realisation of what was happening here. Michael opened the door on his side and spoke roughly. He had his pistol in his hand to emphasise that he was in command here.

'Alright, Fillon, this is where you get out. All of these men are armed and I assure you they will shoot to kill, so just step down and behave.'

Fillon climbed down slowly. He was trying to buy time, trying to figure this out, but he couldn't. His heart was racing and his brain simply refused to co-operate.

'Jacobs, I think you are making a big mistake. Unless I telephone my man in Istanbul to say I have arrived safely in Turkey your operation is finished. This is stupid.'

'Well, you may have underestimated me. Your man in Istanbul is as I speak floating belly up in the Bosporus.'

'But ... but how...?'

'Fillon, allow me to introduce David Schulman. David belongs to an organisation you will not have heard of. We call it Din. That is the Hebrew word for judgment. Din is responsible for finding and executing criminals who murdered Jews during the war. It has agents throughout Europe. You never had a chance of getting through. It was only a question of time before they located your man and despatched him. Now it is your turn.'

'But ... but that would be murder.'

'You could be right. I'm a lawyer and to be honest I'm not sure I could refute that. Still, it's only a word.'

A car sped past on the nearby road and in the moonlight Michael saw Fillon glance in that direction, as if it represented a ray of hope but of course it didn't. Three of the men grabbed him and tied his hands together, then they dragged him to a nearby tree and threw the rope over a convenient branch. Someone produced a crate and they got him up on it and, backing the lorry up slowly, they tied the other end of the rope to the tailgate, then the lorry drove forward slowly to take up the slack.

'Gaspar Fillon, on behalf of the Jewish Nation, the Republic of France and Miriam Fillon and her mother, I hereby sentence you to death for your crimes. If you have anything to say, I enjoin you to keep it to yourself because I assure you no-one here is interested. Now, there are two ways you can die. I can kick this crate away and you will hang relatively quickly, or my colleague in the truck can let the clutch out and hang you very very slowly. Which we decide on is a function of what we find in those crates you loaded up.

It took half an hour to dig them out from under the scrap metal and then they got them down on the ground and George took a bayonet and forced the seal on the first one. It was full of paper, mostly in files and folders, some of it tied up in bundles, all of it in German. George picked up a file and scratched his head, then he handed it to Michael.

'Here you are Mike, you speak German.'

Michael took it and shone a torch onto the sheets of paper. He looked puzzled. He put his hands into the crate and pulled out more files and that made him no less puzzled.

'George, the rest of you, get the other boxes down. I want to see what they've got in them. David, look at this. Is it what I'm thinking it is?'

David Schulman read German well enough. He looked up at

Michael. 'Well, let's check the rest, then we'll know for sure. I'm no scientist but even so, yes, I think we have stumbled on something very important. Let's not hang our man just yet. He might still be useful.'

Thirty minutes later all the crates lay on the ground with their lids off and they knew for sure. Michael strode up to Fillon, still standing on his box sweating. He shone the torch full into his eyes.

'Right, now we know what it's all about. We had some idea in Intelligence that the Germans were making progress with an atomic bomb and now we know for sure. The question is, Fillon, why have you got these files?'

Fillon was ready to talk. He wanted to talk. 'These boxes, Major, contain everything you would need to know to build a bomb. The Reich was more advanced than you people thought. If they had been able to hold out just another year the war would have ended very differently and you would all be dead.'

'But why you? How did you get them?'

'Well, that was just my good fortune. They were smuggled out of Germany ahead of the Russians invading from the east. They have been waiting in France for a suitable way to be found to get them out. I was it, the right man at the right time.'

'But out to where? Who would want this information?'

Before his question could be answered, if it was ever going to be, David spoke up.

'Michael, look at this. I think I've found the answer to that question. Here, see this? '

Michael took from him a letter. He read no Arabic, but pinned to the letter was another in German. It was addressed to Damascus. He shone the torch again in Fillon's face.

'These files were going to Syria? But why?'

'Really, Major, for an Intelligence officer you are not very intelligent. You people are soon going to be at war with the Arabs. The Arabs are friends and allies of the German Reich. It was the least Germany could do before it died, a parting gift. The gift of death for every Jew in Palestine.'

He had a strange smile on his lips as he said it. Michael stared in horror and didn't know what to say. Well there was nothing more that needed to be said. In complete silence he turned to the lorry driver and with a flick of his hand indicated what he wanted him to do. The engine started up, the gears crunched and the rope tightened. Gaspar Fillon screamed, and he screamed, and then he stopped screaming and dangled helplessly, praying wordlessly for death.

EPILOGUE

1973

The Roza and Motti Levinson Retirement Home reflected the late summer sun from its brightly-tiled roof as Michael Jacobs' car pulled up into the drive. The walls of Jerusalem stone shone white. It seemed to him that every new building in Israel was constructed of white stone, and he was reminded of the biblical saying, *ein kol chadash tachat hashamayim*, there is nothing new under the heavens. Well, here everything seemed new. It was something he never stopped marvelling at.

He instructed his driver to wait for him and went inside. A nurse had seen his car arrive and was waiting to greet him.

'Ah, Colonel Jacobs, more handsome than ever, what a pleasure to see you again. Have you come to cheer us up?'

'Sister Emanuel, in all the years I have been visiting you here I have never seen you in need of cheering up. Now where is she and how is she?'

Sister Emanuel's customary smile disappeared for a moment. 'Not good, I'm afraid. We have been so used to her bustling about this place as if she was only seventy or eighty, we forget she has aged with the rest of us. Her next birthday will be her ninety-sixth. Still, she will be delighted you have come. Don't be surprised, though, if she lapses into Polish. She does it more and more these days.'

Krystyna Celinska had finally retired from running the home and was now its star resident, although she still liked to be wheeled into the kitchen to criticise the cook sometimes. She had long since lost the sight in her left eye and only recently her right eye had finally clouded over, consigning her to permanent darkness. She had changed, they all saw that, and would never be the same again. There was not a person there, staff or resident, who did not love her, and it was that love that Krystyna was living on now, because she was surely living on borrowed time.

Sister Emanuel directed Michael out to the garden, as if he didn't know that was where Krystyna would be. She had never been an indoor person. He often thought it came from her time in the Polish forests, but that could have been fanciful. Even at her age, she insisted on being wheeled out every morning to take the sun and smell the Mediterranean nearby.

Michael got over to Netanya whenever he could, but his work kept him busy. As the head of Military Intelligence, he was fed constant reports about the build-up of the Arab armies. The politicians were turning a blind eye, but his instincts told him there was another war coming, and soon. As he strode across the grass he worried. He always worried, but he looked at these frail old people, survivors mostly from Europe, and he wondered when the promised land would ever fulfil its promise of peace for them. It had been good, but they had worked and fought for it and they loved it more than life itself, but sometimes Michael and his generation wondered if they would ever be able to retire, ever be able to stop worrying. He smiled to himself and tried to imagine living somewhere like this and knew it wasn't after all what he wanted. He didn't see himself looking forward to canasta as the highlight of his day. No, perhaps he would die, after all, with a gun in his hand.

Krystyna spoke in her usual heavily-accented Hebrew. 'Ah Michael, I thought I heard you talking to Sister Manny. So you haven't deserted me, have you?'

'Madame Celinska.'

He kissed her hand, but not the hand with the missing finger. Krystyna had, over the years, retained a coyness about that hand, and she kept it hidden even from her old friend. It had long been a joke between them, Madame Celinska and a kiss on the hand. Neither of them could remember why he had started it.

'Now stop flirting, do you hear? And you a respectable married man. Does Miriam know about this other woman?'

'Yes, and she sends all her love, and so do the girls. Is Motti coming?'

'Well, he promised but you know how it is with these young officers, always busy, trying to impress their superiors.'

Michael didn't want to tell her why young IDF officers were so busy. She had lived through two wars with the Arabs. He felt bad about it but he hoped she might not live to see the next one. If Motti were killed, well, she would not survive that.

And on cue he appeared at the door to the garden. On his arm was a girl, in uniform, of course, a girl Michael hadn't seen before. Mind you, he thought, it's a new girl almost every time. Motti stepped up smartly and both he and the girl threw him a salute.

Michael looked at Motti, as he did every time they met, and wondered, wondered what he saw in his face. Some-times he fancied he saw the boy's mother in that self-confident way he had most of the time, but only most of the time, because in moments of self-doubt he showed his other inheritance, the shtetl Jew. Well, the country was full of young men like Motti, confident in their new land and carrying the pain of a recent past that by some miracle had brought them here. He wondered what the future held for these young people, and this young country, and he sighed.

'Stand easy Lieutenant, Sergeant, you don't have to impress anyone here, unless it's Krystyna.'

Krystyna snorted. 'Come here you great lump and give your grandmother a big hug.'

Motti did as he was told, willingly. She still called herself his grandmother, and he had to explain to every girl he brought to see her who she really was. Motti wouldn't go out with anyone Krystyna didn't approve of.

'So Bobba, meet Yehudit Amiel. Yehudit, the Colonel and I are now going to take a walk around the gardens while Madame Celinska questions you impertinently about your intentions towards me. We will be only ten minutes. Believe me, in that time there is nothing about you she won't know.'

Yehudit smiled and laid her rifle on the grass while she sat down at Krystyna's feet. Michael saw the way she looked at Motti and he knew straight away that this was the one. No girl looks at a boy like that and then lets him go. He hoped Krystyna would approve of her. OK, she was in uniform, but she looked like a nice girl. He steered Motti away to leave the women in peace.

'So, Motti, have you given any consideration to my proposal?'

'Yes, and I'm afraid the answer is no. It would easy to join the Intelligence Corps and stay out of the firing line but you know, I've got nicely bedded in with my men now and I won't leave them. If there is war, well, they expect me to go through it with them. You understand?'

'My boy, I understand perfectly well, and to be honest while I would have liked to keep you safe I was only doing it because Krystyna asked me to. It's not that I want to see you come to any harm, but I'm proud that you decided against. You know, your parents would be proud of you too.'

He was going to say more but somehow he couldn't. He never forgot Roza, or Mordechai Levinson. It had been his idea to name the home after them, the one Krystyna built with the diamonds she brought to Palestine. They walked on and on now, basking in the sun, while Michael told Motti the final chapter in his story, the story he had been telling him for years, always remembering something new to add, some-thing that had slipped his memory. There was only one part he couldn't tell him, or anyone, about how Israel came to have a head-start in nuclear weapons research courtesy of the Third Reich.

Motti needn't have worried about Krystyna's approval. She and Yehudit were getting on like a house on fire.

'You know, you young scamp, this girl is too good for you. I've told her so but she insists she doesn't mind. Well, young lady, don't say I didn't warn you. Now, she's been itching to tell me something but says I have to wait until you get back. So, tell me.'

'Alright. Bobba, Michael, you are the first to know, of course, apart from Yehudit's parents. I have asked her to marry me and she has said yes.'

He was watching Krystyna's face closely when he said this and even though she had expected it she couldn't help herself and a tear ran down her cheek. She tried to wipe it away but they kept coming and finally she buried her face in her handkerchief and gave in to her happiness. Michael could have cried himself. It was like a dream coming true. He told them to wait a minute, he wanted to return to the car for something. He was back with a small package in his hand wrapped in cloth.

'Motti, Yehudit, I have been carrying this in my pack everywhere I go since 1948. It has been with me through two wars and I believe it has somehow watched over me. But really, it is yours Motti, and I have always known that one day I would return it to you. I think that day has come. Krystyna, you take it. I want you to give it to him.'

Krystyna was perplexed but she held out her hand. As she took it, she had a premonition, but no, surely, she must be wrong. Carefully, afraid that she might be, she unwrapped the cloth, and there, catching the sunlight she couldn't see but now she knew she was right all the same, was the mezuzah from the inn in Poland that Mordechai Levinson had saved.

Michael sat on the grass while Krystyna turned it over in her hand and remembered, and he told them all a chapter none of them knew, how an American army Captain had found a burned-out motorcycle in the Alps and as luck would have it he was a Jew and understood that this meant a lot to someone. He carried it himself, not knowing how he could possibly find its rightful owner, until he too made aliyah and came to make his life in Israel. If he hadn't been called up for military service, if he hadn't met an officer who introduced him to Miriam Jacobs at a party, if Miriam hadn't told her husband that night about the conversation and the mezuzah she had been shown, well, all these things did happen, against all the odds, and now Krystyna held Motti's precious inheritance in her hands. Finally, with love and happiness, she took Motti's hand and placed it reverentially there and then she searched for Yehudit's and placed that on top.

'You two young people, this is our wedding gift to you. I want you to promise me, whatever else of your Jewish inheritance you follow or don't follow, that when you have a home of your own you will nail this to the doorpost in memory.'

It was certain that they would do that. Motti wrapped it up again carefully and put it in his uniform pocket. There was really nothing more to say. Except for a question he had to ask.

'Michael, you have told me a lot about my parents over the years, and what my mother did is in the history books, but there is one thing you have never told me. What kind of woman was she?'

It was a simple question that was of course impossible to answer, for anyone, but perhaps especially so for Roza Levinson, and it was all a long time ago, but perhaps there was an answer, the only answer really. Michael Jacobs looked up at the bright blue sky and as he did so a small wisp of cloud scudded into view.

'Your mother? Well, Motti, I would say she was an angel.'

And at that precise moment an Israel Air Force jet streaked across the sky above them, and as they looked up they caught on its wings the Star of David, the symbol of their promised land, and they knew that no story is ever finished.

ABOUT THE AUTHOR & PUBLISHER

R S Brynin is the Director of The Doctor Richard Mackarness Foundation, a non-profit public health promotion service in the UK. His book, *Our National Health, Are We Taking the Right Medicine?* was published by the Foundation in 2020.

Growing up in a family that did not identify as Jewish, his Zionism was awakened in his youth by Leon Uris' book, *Exodus*. It is hoped the present book may do the same for those Jews who have become alienated from Israel by the pressures of modern anti-Zionism. For this reason, the book is sent, at the author's own expense, to Jewish organisations worldwide.

He spends time, when possible, with his sons in Jerusalem, but lives for the most part, quietly, on a farm in rural Herefordshire.

He can be contacted at robert@brynin.com.

ADDITIONAL NOTE

An extract from *An Angel from Auschwitz* was selected for publication, under the title *Hannah Bauman*, in the Chanukah 2021 edition of the Canadian literary website jewishfiction.net.

Made in the USA
Middletown, DE
03 February 2022